About the author

Chris Manby is the author of seven romantic comedy novels published by Hodder & Stoughton. She is also editor/contributor to the *Girls' Night In* and *Girls' Night Out/Boys' Night In* anthologies, which have so far raised more than £600,000 for children's charity War Child, and topped book charts all over the world. Chris grew up in Gloucester but now lives in London. She is working on her second screenplay.

Deep Heat Flatmates

Chris Manby

CORONET BOOKS

Hodder & Stoughton

Deep Heat

To Kathryn Arnold

ACKNOWLEDGEMENTS

To the lovely Paul Drummond, for advice and inspiration and feigning interest in stupid questions. To my editor Kate, and to Ant and Natasha for their continued dedication to this cause. To the Lavender Hill Mob: Jane, Wendy, Mark and Jacqui but especially Ripley, for tea and other distractions during the 'fat book days'. To Peter Hamilton, the Delia Smith of science fiction, for friendship, advice and superb roast potatoes. To David Garnett for bringing up the 'L' word whenever I get complacent. To Guy Hazel for being my best friend from Battersea to Bombay. To Mum and Dad for their continued support and patience (I will get a mortgage next year, I promise). And to the rest of my family for the grass roots publicity (room for this one in Hucclecote Library, Uncle Roger?).

This book is dedicated to my sister Kate, who is far nicer than any of the sisters herein!!!

CHAPTER ONE

The week before Christmas just wasn't my week. It started like this. Two days before Christmas Eve, I was meandering down the fruit and veg aisle of Safeway, vaguely thinking that I ought to eat less spicy food, when my appendix burst on me. Pop! Just like a soap bubble. I can't begin to describe the pain. I fell to the floor like a blade of grass before a mower and lay writhing on the obligatory unidentifiable sticky patch you get on supermarket floors for a good ten minutes before someone asked me if anything was wrong. And then only because I was obstructing the avocados.

On the way to hospital I drifted in and out of consciousness. My name escaped me. My address escaped me. My date of birth escaped me. In fact everything escaped me but the fact that I was wearing uncoordinated underwear. (My mother had warned me about that more than once.)

Next thing I knew, I was propped up in a hospital bed, with a new scar on my abdomen and a bunch of yellow chrysanthemums on the bedside table. My mother, my father, my two kid sisters and my gorgeous fiancé David regarded me gravely from behind the white metal grill designed to stop me from falling out onto the floor in my stupor. As they swam into focus before my eyes, they said all the proper things that hospital visitors in television dramas say.

'She's coming round,' said my mother.

'Can you hear us, Ali-baby?'

'It's your father here, Alison. Do you remember me?'

'She's had her appendix out. She hasn't got amnesia,' said my youngest sister, Jo.

'Where am I?' I asked for effect.

'You're in the Brindlesham General Hospital,' said my father. 'You've just had your appendix out.'

I thought that was what Jo had just said.

'The nurse said you can have it in a jar if you like,' Jo added gleefully.

'My appendix? Whaaaa?' I felt a vague aching sensation as I hooked up my nightdress, much to my mother's disgust, and inspected the wound. Well, I inspected the fat wad of cotton wool and surgical tape that was covering it.

'What did they do that for?' I asked. 'And how big is the scar?'

A girl knows her priorities.

'It's all right, darling. The scar will be barely noticeable.'

I recognised that big strong hand on my arm. David, my fiancé, leant in to kiss me on the cheek. 'You had us all very very worried,' he continued. 'For a minute back there I thought I was going to have to get a refund on the engagement ring.'

I laughed. Painfully.

'But you're getting better now,' said my mother,

rearranging my nightdress so that it covered my belly-button once more. 'The doctor says you should be out of here by Christmas Eve. Thank goodness. Not that they don't do their best to make things festive in this hospital, God bless them, but the Christmas decorations in here are terrible.' My mother had recently thrown out a box full of family heirlooms in favour of a tremendously naff fully coordinated tree ensemble in silver and navy blue glitter.

'I brought you these,' said my sister Jane, thrusting a box of Ferrero Rocher in my direction. David looked at them accusingly. I had promised to give up all chocolate (and pretty much everything else that makes life worth living) until I was a comfortable size twelve again. For the wedding, you understand. Still, I figured I must have lost at least a box of chocolates' worth of weight in the shape of my appendix so I accepted the gift with more than good grace.

'Thanks. Can I eat these yet?' I asked the first nurse to pass by.

'I see she's getting better already,' the nurse commented before she added: 'Only two visitors per bed.'

Because they couldn't make their minds up about which two should stay, all my visitors suddenly departed at once. It only really dawned on me then that I was sitting in a hospital. I tried to piece together my journey to this shining white ward in which I found myself. I remembered squeezing a Galia melon. I remembered a feeling deep in my insides like excruciatingly bad wind. The sticky patch. The uncoordinated undies nightmare. No more.

I was wearing one of my own nighties now at least.

* * *

But so much for Mum's promise that I would be out for Christmas Eve. On the afternoon of the twenty-third, my surgeon, the painfully handsome Mr Hedley, decided that he wasn't happy with the way I was healing and prescribed another couple of days in bed, just in case. As the Christmas holiday approached, anyone fit enough to stagger to the hospital door was pointed in that direction, leaving only me and a yellow-haired woman called Marina, who had just had a hysterectomy, in Daffodil Ward for the duration.

Marina's husband visited up to four times a day with their toddling children, Tim and Milly. He looked harassed. The children looked hyperactively delighted in the way that children who are being looked after by their father and have been given free access to additives do. When they had departed for what seemed like the third time in an hour, Marina staggered across to my bed, with her saline drip in tow.

'Bless him,' she began. 'He's only gone and brought me all the same magazines he brought me last week. Do you want them?' She dropped a pile onto my legs and I winced in anticipation, even though she had just about managed to miss my scar.

'Thanks,' I said, flipping through the pages of the top one.

It was called *Complete Woman*. It had a carefully air-brushed thirty-something model on the cover, flinging back her head and laughing to reveal zero fillings (though she probably just had lots of those white ones). The pages inside were packed with ideas for the holiday period ahead. Extra special mince pies (add a couple of cashew nuts and some extra jellied peel). Make your own Christmas crackers (but make sure you buy specially manufactured toilet roll innards for the purpose because you don't want to give your children e-coli). Decorate your tree in this year's most fashionable colours (silver and navy blue – so that's where Mum got it from).

'I've got *Cosmo* over there too,' Marina told me. 'I'd lend you that now but the sex quiz might split your stitches.'

'Thanks,' I said. 'I think *Complete Woman*'s my limit.'

Between lunch and tea-time I learned about rag-rolling and appliqué. Though my usual approach to magazines was to flick through them backwards quickly and read the problem pages first, I was aware that I was surviving on limited resources and so I read every single boring word. Even the whole index. My family wouldn't be visiting that night, since they would all be at Auntie Katherine's Christmas Eve jamboree. David wouldn't be popping in either. He had been in that morning, with a poinsettia for my bedside table. (You know, I really hate those things.)

'I feel terrible about you being stuck in here over Christmas,' David told me as he cleared a space on my bedside table for the miserable-looking pot-plant.

'It's OK,' I said bravely. 'The nurses have been wearing Father Christmas hats today. I'm sure we'll have a wonderful time.'

'Well, if it's any consolation I won't be going to

the party at The Rotunda tonight,' he said gravely.
'I couldn't possibly go along without you.'

The Rotunda was one of our favourite haunts. It
was one of those newly refurbished pub/club/sizzling
platter-type places with oars, brooms and bicycle
wheels, in fact with everything but the kitchen sink,
hanging off the walls. (The kitchen sink was hanging
from the wall in the ladies.) Anyway, in the absence of
anything better to do, The Rotunda was Brindlesham's
hottest night-spot and it had sold out of tickets for its
extravagant Christmas Eve bash in late September.

'Don't be silly,' I told David. 'You've got to go to
The Rotunda. You've been looking forward to tonight
for months.'

'I know. But I couldn't possibly enjoy myself. Not
with you in hospital. It wouldn't be right.'

'I don't mind,' I said in frustration, hating to seem
the party-pooper. 'You go.'

'How can I enjoy myself, thinking of you all alone
in this sterile ward?'

'The tickets cost ten pounds each,' I said. 'You go.'

'You're right,' he said suddenly. 'They did cost ten
pounds. No point wasting all that money. Perhaps I
should go after all.'

My mouth dropped open in surprise. That was
wrong. He was meant to hold out until I suggested
that he might like to sit in the ward all night with me
instead.

'You don't mind, do you?' he checked one last time.

What could I say now? Actually, I do.

'No, I don't mind,' I said wearily, as I picked a
dead leaf off the fading Christmas rose. 'You have a
good time.'

'I'll sell your ticket to someone else and bring you the money tomorrow. How about that?'

'Thanks.'

What a consolation!

David left with obscene haste.

That night, as it drew close to seven o'clock, the moment when The Rotunda would open its doors for the bacchanalian festivities to begin, I started to find it difficult to concentrate on *Complete Woman*'s suggestions for the best way to serve your Christmas pudding. On the other side of the ward, Marina was already asleep and snoring lightly. I could hear the nightnurses in the corridor, laughing about something or other. Probably my cellulite.

Up until that particular Christmas Eve I had been one of those lucky people who viewed the impending holiday as a happy time, a time for families to be together, a time for loved ones to show each other how much they care with cards and great big presents. Right then, I felt about as happy at the approach of Christmas as the people who lived in the cardboard city underneath the motorway bridge. No, make that slightly less happy. They probably had some booze to hand.

I slipped the hospital radio headphones over my ears and listened to the last of the Christmas dedications. Perhaps David had asked them to play something special for me? But the DJ soon signed off for the evening with that terrible Slade Christmas classic that even your granny headbangs along to. No message from David. No last-minute visit on his way out to the pub. The nightnurse brought me my tablets and switched off the main ward lights.

I couldn't sleep of course. Not while I knew that the world and his whippet were out there having such a good time. I turned on the little light above my bed and buried myself in *Complete Woman*'s five minute fiction slot. I finished that in three minutes. There were only the puzzles left. The puzzles and the 'fantastic annual competition' (their words, not mine).

Are you the United Kingdom's Most Romantic Couple? the headline asked. *If you think that you and your partner are the most romantic couple in Britain, then why not let* Complete Woman *Magazine and Super Sunshine Tours celebrate your wonderful relationship by taking you both on the holiday of a lifetime? The fabulous all-inclusive resort of Santa Bonita on the beautiful island of Antigua awaits your arrival. Seal your love with a kiss on the golden sands of the hotel's own private beach, Royale Bay. Whisper those sweet nothings beneath a fabulous Caribbean sunset. All you have to do is tell us what makes your relationship so special (in less than 500 words).*

I looked at the photograph of the fabulous Santa Bonita resort. I looked wistfully at the glittering white-gold sand and the sparkling blue sea of Royale Bay. I gazed longingly at the charming little wooden huts that nestled right on the beach (each with its own *en suite* bathroom and coffee-making facilities). I thought I could use some of that.

At the bottom of the page was a small photograph of two people locked in a close embrace. *Shandy Evans and her fiancé Tom Devonshire were last year's winners of the* Complete Woman *Most Romantic Couple competition,* read the caption. *They enjoyed a wonderful, two week long, all-inclusive holiday courtesy of Lion King Tours in South Africa. Shandy and Tom were married in Shandy's local parish church in June of this year.*

There followed an extract of the winning entry which had convinced the judges that Shandy and Tom had such a beautiful thing together. 'He makes me a cup of tea every morning without even being asked,' Shandy wrote. 'He fixes my car and puts up shelves and things while I'm stuck doing the ironing. He makes me feel like I am the only woman in the world.'

'Aw, come on, Shandy,' I murmured to myself. 'That's not a good enough reason. He must have a ginormous cock or something as well.'

On the other side of the ward, Marina stirred in her sleep. I continued to read Shandy's testimony but resisted any further urge to comment out loud. But Shandy made no mention of Tom's physical attributes at all if he had any. It seemed that the secret of his romantic success really did lie in his ability to pull his weight in the kitchen. When I had finished reading, I put the article down for a moment and waited until I was sure that I was no longer in danger of gagging on Shandy's sickly sweet words before I dare read the competition rules.

And to think she had won a holiday in South Africa for that piece of unadulterated slush! I could do far better, I thought. Yeah, I could do far far better than that.

Outside, a few icy raindrops pattered against the window. There was no doubt that we were right in the middle of a long hard winter but, ignoring the wind and the freezing rain, I fixed my mind on the idea of two sunny weeks in Antigua, 'the island with a beach for every day of the year', and started to write on the back of a paper bag.

If I couldn't be with David that night, I could at least still think of him. Of his soft brown eyes and his fluffy, curly hair . . . Of his handsome smile and his infectious laugh . . . I could even think of his strong manly arms flexing as he deftly unscrewed the u-bend or nailed up a brand-new shelf for my cuddly toy collection if that was what it would take to win that holiday in the sun. Five hundred words to sing his praises? I needed five thousand! But I would give an edited version my best shot.

'I always thought that love was just something other people sang about, until I met David,' I began.

I made three rough drafts before I dared write out my final version on the official coupon in the magazine. Then, tearing the page out as neatly as I could, I slipped myself painfully out of bed and staggered towards the nightnurse's desk. She had a good supply of envelopes and, amazingly, she also had a single first class stamp in her handbag. I asked her if it was unusual for patients to ask for a stamp in the middle of the night. She told me that a man on the genito-urinary ward had once asked her for a blow-job.

The nurse promised to post the entry for me as soon as she clocked off her shift that night. I climbed back into bed with a couple of sleeping pills and soon forgot all about it.

Next day, Mum and Dad arrived to see me as soon as the hospital was open for business. Apparently Jo and Jane were still sleeping off the Christmas Eve jamboree. Jo had made an idiot of herself at Midnight Mass. Again.

Mum and Dad watched me eagerly as I unwrapped my presents. Three satsumas, slightly squashed. A large box of bath salts in English lavender (good for disguising the smell of kitty litter – but I didn't tell them that). A new nightie (black watch tartan with a black velvet collar and ribbon trim, Mary Queen of Scots might have worn one the night before she lost her head).

'Thought that one you were wearing the other day looked a wee bit see-through,' Mum explained.

And a matching wash-bag.

'How thoughtful!' I exclaimed.

'Now you need never be unprepared when you have to go into hospital again,' said Mum triumphantly, as she plumped up my pillows.

I wasn't exactly planning a return trip anytime soon. But parents always buy you those boring useful presents, don't they? Christmas for me was about the gift that David would bring. (Oh, and the little baby Jesus, naturally.) What would David have bought me, I wondered as I unwrapped three more chocolate oranges from Dad. Jewellery, perfume, a couple of CDs? A totally see-through nightdress perhaps?

On the other side of the ward, Marina was holding up, and actually cooing over, another tartan nightie, identical to mine. It was from her husband. Still, it wasn't as if she was planning to have another kid . . .

'Did David call at all?' I asked, when I had heard

about Jo's drunken Midnight Mass misdemeanours at least four times. (Loud hiccups during the prayers. Falling flat on her face when she went to take communion. The kind of behaviour you'd expect from a teenager who'd been on the Baileys all night.)

'David?' asked Mum. 'Why should he have called us?'

'Well, I thought he might have done. To find out how I'm getting on. He hasn't called me here.'

'I'm sure he'll be in to see you later on,' said Mum. 'He's probably planning a great big surprise.'

But lunchtime soon passed and he still hadn't turned up. I ate just two mouthfuls of the hospital's abridged version of Christmas dinner. The turkey stuffing had obviously been made from shredded medical records.

My hopes were raised briefly at two in the afternoon when Sister Martin drew back the curtain around my bed (I was protecting myself from Marina's kids' new table-tennis-ball guns) and announced that I had a visitor. But it wasn't David. It was my flatmate Emma. My face fell in disappointment.

'What are you doing here?' I asked.

'Well, don't look so pleased to see me,' she said as she arranged herself at the foot of my bed.

'Aren't you supposed to be having lunch with your folks?'

'Do you think I would miss an opportunity to get out of having to stand up for the whole of the Queen's speech?' Emma replied.

'Oh, so your Auntie Mavis made it then?'

'Yep. The orderlies from her funeral home wheeled her through the door as soon as dawn broke this morning. It's all right for her, insisting we stand up for the Queen. She doesn't have to. She sends her love, by the way. And this present. Seeing as how you're an invalid.'

Emma flicked a little square parcel onto the bed. I opened it without any real enthusiasm, knowing it would be monogrammed handkerchiefs. Emma's Auntie Mavis must have had a franchise in the things.

'Aw. What's up?' Emma joked. 'Wrong colour? Never mind. I've got you something much more exciting in here.' She reached into her bag again and this time came out with a long thin parcel that looked altogether much more interesting. I snatched it from her and felt all the way up and down the wrapping paper, trying to guess what it might be.

'Hmm,' I said. 'It's not by any chance that beautiful single rose vase I saw in Liberty is it?'

'Get real,' said Emma. 'Unwrap it for heaven's sake.'

I ripped off the paper and soon wished I hadn't. Marina's youngest, Timmy aged five, had joined us to see me open my presents.

'What is it?' he asked as my mouth dropped open in horror. 'Does it need batteries or can you play with it straightaway?'

Why did I have to have the most embarrassing flatmate in the world?

'What is it for?' he asked again, all innocence, as I tried to rewrap the 'Black Beauty stimulator' in the scraps of paper I had unfortunately torn beyond usefulness. 'Show me what it is,' he pleaded. 'And I'll show you mine.'

'It's for gardening,' said Emma quickly. 'Digging holes. Can I have a look at your gun instead?'

He solemnly handed over the table-tennis-ball firer

while I secreted the big black vibrator beneath my pillow.

'You're dead, Emma Wilson,' I told her.

'Yeah. You're dead!!' mimicked Timmy, snatching back the gun and popping Emma in the eye with a ping pong ball before returning to his mother for a slap.

'What on earth did you buy me that horrible thing for?' I asked her testily as she checked the damage to her contact lens.

'Every girl should have one,' Emma explained.

'But I've got a fiancé.'

'So. Use it to spice things up a little.'

'Things between us are quite spicy enough,' I said, just a little too smugly.

'Well, save it for a rainy day then. What did you get me?'

'I got you what you asked for,' I replied tartly. 'That silver glitter clutch bag you wanted so much is at the bottom of my wardrobe. Didn't have time to wrap it, I'm afraid.'

'Wow, Ali,' said Emma. 'I'll go straight home and get it now. Thanks a million. That's a fantastic present.'

'Yeah. Good job I don't give to receive.'

Emma soon left to retrieve her proper pressie and feed our shared cat, Fattypuss. At four o'clock the nurses brought round Christmas cake. My sisters Jo and Jane, just about recovered from their traditional seasonal hangovers, had smuggled in a piece of Mum's own cake which I ate instead, since I suspected that the hospital cook had his own unorthodox plans for reducing the hospital waiting list.

'What did David get you?' Jo asked excitedly, as she stuffed two chocolate fondant penguins into her mouth at once.

'He hasn't been to see me yet,' I told them, feeling strangely embarrassed by the admission.

'What? The selfish pig. Leaving you all on your own in hospital on Christmas Day. I expect he got totally rat-arsed at The Rotunda last night and he still hasn't woken up. It was a good night by all accounts. The police had to come out three times. And I'll be old enough to go next year,' Jo added proudly.

'I'm sure he's just got family obligations,' said Jane more reasonably.

'Yeah. You're right. The fact that it's Christmas and I'm in hospital isn't going to stop his mother being an old dragon,' I said, forcing a laugh. 'She's probably making him sit at the dinner table until he's finished his cold Brussels sprouts or something equally hideous.'

'OK. So what do you think he's bought you?' Jo persisted. 'You must have some idea.'

'Jewellery, I hope,' I told them. 'Though perfume would be acceptable, since he's so recently splashed out on a ring.' I gave my sparkler an affectionate little polish on the bedspread. 'As long as it's not that new CK stuff though. I hate that. Smells like Jif.'

In actual fact, he bought me a battered box of Milk Tray chocolates from the little 'Friends of Brindlesham General Hospital' shop in the lobby downstairs.

It was half-past-eight when David finally arrived and I had been fighting back tears since my sisters departed

at six. As he walked into the ward, I noticed straightaway that he looked different somehow; as if someone
had taken my David, sucked out his shining soul and
replaced it with something altogether shiftier overnight. He sat down carefully on the edge of my bed,
put the chocolates on the table and didn't even look
me in the eye.

'Merry Christmas,' I said, pulling myself up painfully so that I could kiss him.

'Merry Christmas,' he replied, as if it was some kind
of Resistance password.

'I thought you'd forgotten me,' I said light-heartedly,
trying not to show my disappointment at the dreadful
gift. 'I'm afraid I haven't got a present to give you,
darling. What with the operation and all that, I haven't
really had time to do much Christmas shopping.'

'That's OK.' He looked strangely relieved.

'Thanks for the chocolates,' I told him. 'Though I
thought I wasn't allowed to eat them, because of . . .
you know,' I patted my tummy.

'You can eat whatever you like,' he said.

There was definitely something wrong.

'Did you have a nice time at The Rotunda?' I persisted. 'Did you manage to sell my ticket?'

'Oh. Yeah.' He fumbled in his jacket pocket for his
wallet and pulled out a crumpled tenner.

'Thanks. Did you sell it to anyone I know?' I asked.

'Actually,' said David sheepishly. 'I sold it to Lisa
Brown.'

'Lisa Brown?'

You know that point in hospital movies where the
patient gets a terrible shock and goes reaching for the
emergency button? Well, this was one of those.

'Lisa Brown?' I shrieked again.

'Lisa Brown,' he said flatly.

What's the problem with Lisa Brown, you ask?

'Lisa Brown, your ex-fiancée?' I asked.

'Yes,' he said.

'Well,' I tried to take this bad news reasonably. 'At least you're on speaking terms with her again.'

'Yes,' he said.

'Must be very hard for her,' I continued. 'Seeing you again after all these years. After all the heartbreak and embarrassment that must have followed your broken engagement. I'm surprised she didn't just thump you on the nose with her handbag.'

'Yes,' he said. He had dumped Lisa Brown for me.

'Was she with anybody?' I asked, longing to hear that she was with a strapping six-foot-five rugby player and that she was heavily pregnant with their first child.

'No. At least, she wasn't with anybody when she arrived,' said David.

'What do you mean by that?' I asked suspiciously.

'I'm afraid that she came home with me.'

Push the panic button. Push the panic button!

'You gave her a lift?' I asked. Best case scenario.

'Sort of.'

'To her place?'

'To my place.'

'To your place?' It was like a conversation between two people who didn't really understand English.

'Alison,' said David, taking a deep breath. 'I'm afraid I've got to tell you that she stayed the night with me.'

'What?!' I did press the panic button that time.

'She stayed the night?' I shouted. 'With you?! Lisa Brown slept with you in your flat? In your bed? Please,

no.' Marina got her husband to prop her up in bed so
that she could get a better view of the fight. 'What on
earth were you thinking of, David? What on earth will
people say?'

'I'm sorry. I don't know what I was thinking of. In
fact I still don't know what I am thinking of now.
Alison, I think perhaps we need to spend some time
apart for a while,' he blurted the ugly words out.

'Spend some time apart? What do you mean? We
haven't got time to spend time apart. We're supposed
to be getting married in April.'

'Alison, I don't think I can . . .'

The nurse had arrived at the foot of my bed.

'What's the matter?' she asked briskly. 'Are you in
pain, Alison? Where does it hurt?'

'Here?' I said, pointing to my head. 'And here.' My
heart. 'And here.' My appendix for good measure. As
the nurse bustled in to rearrange my pillows, David
stood up and started to leave.

'David,' I called after him. 'David, where do you
think you're going? You can't just walk away from
me like this. Not having said those horrible things.
Not while I'm still stuck here in this bed. And it's
Christmas. What about that?'

'I'm sorry, Ali. I've got to go,' he told me sadly. 'I
left Lisa sitting outside in the car.'

CHAPTER TWO

What a difference a day makes. One day I was a girl with an appendix and a fiancé, the next I was merely a girl without an appendix.

When it finally became clear that David really hadn't been playing some twisted practical joke on me, I got the nurse to call my mother and had her abandon the turkey to come in and sit beside her eldest daughter's bed all night long. I was in far worse shape than I had been when my faulty appendix was actually leaking poison into my body. I cried so much that I was threatened with another saline drip.

'How could he do this to me?' was a pretty much constant refrain of mine over the next two days in that bed.

'I always knew this would happen,' replied Mum wisely. 'Because,' (pick and mix your reasons from the following extensive list) 'he wasn't mature enough for the commitment of marriage, his mother still has too much control over him, he thinks he's too good to be part of the Harris family, he's just like his arrogant father and his eyes are too close together.' I had to take issue on the last part.

Jo, sitting at the bottom of my bed and eating the grapes bought for my convalescence, agreed with Mum.

'No, it's true, Ali. His eyes are way too close together,' she told me. 'And the Chinese physiognomy book I got out of the library last week says that squinty eyes are a tell-tale sign of a selfish mind.'

'Well, thank goodness for that,' I said sarcastically. 'Sounds like I've had a lucky escape.'

How long before it started to feel that way too?

I wasn't feeling too much better when, a week after Christmas, the doctor announced that it was time for me to leave Brindlesham General. Someone much much sicker than I was already on a trolley in the corridor waiting for my bed to become vacant.

When I returned to my little flat, Emma had thoughtfully turned all my framed photographs of David face down on the dressing table so that I wouldn't have to look at him. It wasn't until I dared turn one the right way up three weeks later that I discovered she had also given him devil's horns and a Hitler moustache with thick black felt-tip pen.

My boss, Mr Chivers, very kindly allowed me an extended period of convalescence. I went into self-inflicted purdah for a fortnight, never stepping out of the house or even drawing open my curtains. Luckily all I needed to survive was chocolate, biscuits and fags and Emma was only too happy to oblige. It made her feel as though she was helping my recovery, without meaning that she had to go out of her way to buy vegetables or heavy healthy stuff like that.

I got to know the Teletubbies intimately in that time and, towards the end of the fortnight, even the complicated relationships in *Home and Away* started to make some sense. When I looked in the mirror and saw my sunken cheeks, I started to imagine romantically that I was the Lady of Shallot, doomed to pine until I died. (But no, I didn't turn to Black Beauty, Christmas present from hell.) Every time the telephone or doorbell rang, I would be shot through with a glimmer of hopeless hope that made my desertion all the more difficult to take when the caller turned out to be Mum with an emergency steak and kidney pie to stop me from 'fading away'.

But even a mother's love can only be stretched so far. Just four weeks after the op, and David's terrible announcement that his mother had been right all along – Lisa Brown was better than me – my family and friends adopted a policy of zero tolerance towards tears and self-pity. I was sent back to work. OK, I had been hurt, everyone agreed. And things still looked terrible from where I was sitting. But bills needed to be paid, and I was not an invalid. Physically, at least.

Some people, including my mother, even thought that going back to work might take my mind off the terrible disasters that had befallen me since that fateful trip to Safeway. Easy enough to say, if you've never had the misfortune to work as a floating secretarial assistant at the Hudderston Heavy Engineering Co. (purveyors of fine bits of metal covered in grease). Frankly, I would have given dear old Fattypuss to a fur coat factory if someone could have found me something different to do with my nine-to-five. Unfortunately, interesting jobs in Brindlesham were as rare as hen's teeth.

On the morning of my return to the office, I woke up at four a.m. in a cold sweat and couldn't get back to sleep no matter how much calming camomile I chucked down my neck. It was not unlike the feeling I got the morning I started secondary school. Only this time, my colleagues were a known quantity. Back when I was eleven I at least had the excuse of being justifiably scared by the burly fifth formers I had seen smoking behind the bus station.

'It's OK,' said Emma, over breakfast. 'It will be fine. Everyone will be understanding.' My mother had already taken the rather unwelcome step of calling the Managing Director's secretary, Julie Adams, to explain to her just how badly I had been hit by the whole David affair. And my appendectomy.

'Julie was very sympathetic,' my mother assured me.

I'll bet she was! Had my mother never heard the term 'crocodile tears'? There was no love lost between me and Julie Adams. Though as children, we had almost been best friends.

Julie Adams and I had lived on same road and been in the same year at junior school but at the age of eleven, when some horrific fluke sent me to the local girls' grammar while she went to the secondary modern, our friendship seemed to wane.

Julie quickly acquired the sophisticated patina of a life ill-spent. She would hang about with her new friends in the alley by the corner shop, while I rushed home to do my geography homework. They didn't set much homework at Julie's school after the father of one of the boys brought his Rottweiler in to explain how difficult bloody algebra was for his poor child.

Mum quickly decided that Julie was in with the wrong crowd and that I wasn't to have anything more to do with her. Her opinion was vindicated weekly by tales of smoking and shoplifting from the woman who ran the corner shop.

'She came from such a good family,' my mother would gloatingly lament. Until that dreadful week in my third year when I decided that the wrath of my mother would be infinitely preferable to the sneers and goadings of the Brindlesham Comp schoolgirls when I got off the bus in my shiny-elbowed St Olive's blazer.

Tired of being called a scaredy-cat snob, I rashly told Julie that I wasn't afraid to go shoplifting with her. (In fact I was terrified.) She called my bluff, of course, and, that very afternoon, we went to the notoriously insecure changing rooms in Brindlesham's Top Shop and slipped on bright yellow tube skirts beneath our school skirts (this was the early eighties) with the intention of walking out without paying for them. Julie had done it a dozen times before, she told me. And Top Shop was great for beginners. The bored-looking assistants never counted how many garments you took into the changing rooms and they certainly wouldn't lift your skirt to see how many you were taking out again.

With the tube skirt safely stashed beneath my regulation navy A-line pleated number, I stood alone in my cubicle taking deep, deep breaths. I shouldn't do it, I told myself. If I got caught the agony would be endless. But I had to do it. If I didn't do it, Julie's mates would

probably nick my school tie and drape it around the
highest point in the bus shelter. With me in it, if I was
very unlucky. At the very least I would be going home
without my bus money.

'Aren't you ready yet?' hissed Julie through the
curtain. 'If you come out now we might make it to the
door without seeing any assistants. The manageress is
on the phone. Let's leg it.'

It was so carefully planned out. Julie had done it so
many times before. Nothing could possibly go wrong.
So I picked up my neat little satchel and followed Julie
out into the main body of the store. We chucked the
things that we weren't going to nick onto the rail by
the changing room door and started our escape.

'Nonchalant!' Julie whispered loudly. 'Look nonchalant, Ali. And take your time. Have a gander at the
jewellery on your way out or something.'

I took a quick, anguished peek at the price tag on
a set of fluorescent plastic bangles. Then a doubly
anguished glance in the direction of the till told me
that the manageress had put down the phone and was
walking towards me. She knew I was nicking something. In actual fact, she probably didn't, but wanted to
make sure that I didn't purloin any bangles. I dropped
the bangles immediately and scuttled after Julie, who
had already made it into the sunshine and was poised
to do a Linford Christie all the way home.

'Leg it!' she shouted. Giving the game away immediately. If it hadn't already been blown by the fact that
the tube skirt I had chosen was three sizes too large
and had suddenly decided to make its way down to
my ankles. Tripped by my bounty in quite spectacular
style, I ended up crashing down, to land with my chin

on an artfully arranged display of cerise kitten-heel slingbacks, right in the middle of the shop's picture window.

Julie and her tough-girl friends looked on in horror from the safety of the record shop on the other side of the road, as I was bodily lifted to my feet and taken to the back of the shop for interrogation. It must have been obvious that I was a first timer, as I cried for my mummy, and then had to beg with the manageress not to call her. She would be so disappointed. I was the first person in our family to get grade three piano.

'And you from the grammar school,' said the manageress, as if that might have made me immune to the two evil forces of fashion and peer pressure.

Unfortunately, my tearful display didn't manage to dissuade her from calling the police. It may well have been my first time, she said, but I had to be made an example of. I sat stiffly on that stool at the back of the shop for a full hour before the local bobby arrived to take me home. As he marched me to his liveried Mini Metro, I hung my head in shame. The entire town seemed to have gathered on the pavement outside Top Shop to watch me being taken away. At the very least, the policeman might have offered me a blanket to cover up my head.

By the time the police car drew up outside our house, Mum was already in hysterics because I had promised to be home by four thirty and it was now getting on for half-past six. She was mortified when the policeman asked if he might have a word about her daughter's delinquent tendencies.

I wasn't charged. I got off with a warning. But in Mum and Dad's eyes I had called down shame upon

the Harris name and they wanted to mete out their
own punishment. They cancelled my subscription to
Just Seventeen and took away all my pocket money.
Added to that, I wasn't allowed out of the house for
six weeks, except to go to school and Mum escorted me
both ways to make sure I couldn't get up to anything
on that short trip either.

By the time I was allowed out on parole, all my
chances of getting in with Julie's hard-nut gang had
been blown. They had decided that I had nearly sent
them all to Holloway with my pathetic first shoplifting
attempt and now called me 'stool pigeon', a reference
to the stool at the back of the shop and the Kid Creole
song rather than anything clever, amongst the usual
barrage of accusations that my navy blue uniform
made me a snob. Oh, and a lesbian.

Anyway, Julie left school at sixteen to join the youth
training scheme at the Hudderston Heavy Engineering Co. I rather smugly thought myself doing better
than her when I left Brindlesham to go to university
in Sussex. But six months after graduating with a
degree in photography and catering management and
with no real prospect of graduate employment on the
horizon, I had to go cap in hand to Hudderston Heavy
Engineering for a temp job in their typing pool. In the
meantime, Julie had worked her way up to the heady
heights of secretary to the MD. A position that was
accompanied by a decent typing chair, a colour screen
on her computer, and all the Karen Millen suits she
could wear.

She was wearing her red brocade one when I arrived
at work that first morning after my operation. She had
done her nails and lipstick to match, of course.

'All right, Ali?' she cooed, slinging a protective arm around my shoulders as she led me to my desk, though I hadn't actually forgotten where it was in the four short weeks I had been away.

'You just take it easy today, darling,' she said, pointing towards my in-tray, which looked as though it was going for the *Guinness Book of Records* biggest pile of crap in an in-tray entry. 'And let me know if it all starts getting too much for you. There's always a friendly ear for you in my office,' she added.

I sat down and flicked aimlessly through the top quarter of my typing pile. Julie had stopped en route to her office to gossip with Irene from accounts.

'Yeah. Well, she'll be better now that she's surrounded by her friends,' I heard her say.

Friends? What friends? I hadn't had any that I knew of at Hudderston Heavy Engineering when it came to the whip-round for my birthday. Two Walnut Whips and a card from the corner shop. Pathetic.

'All right?' said Irene as she too passed me by. Maybe they were just being concerned, I told myself. But I had a sneaky suspicion that a jilted fiancée recovering from a complicated appendectomy was up there with a serious road traffic accident in the entertainment stakes. People like to be reminded that other people are having an even shittier time than themselves, I suppose.

Emma called me halfway through the morning.

'All right?' she asked.

'Please don't ask me if I am all right,' I snapped. 'Because if one more person asks me if I'm all right . . . I shall have to . . . I shall have to . . .' I sniffed loudly. 'Cry!'

Julie was upon me like a vulture, tissue in one hand and big ears at the ready.

'Tell me all about it,' she insisted. 'I might be able to help.'

'Not unless you can hypnotise David Whitworth and convince him to come back to me.'

'Maybe it's for the best. I always say, if it isn't meant to be, it isn't meant to be. There's no point pushing it. David was too good for you,' she said, adding quickly, 'I mean you're far too good for him, Ali.'

I suspected that the former was more than a slip of the tongue. Julie had been on David's case for years, ever since his family moved into the area, bringing David, aged fifteen, and already with a fluffy little moustache staining his top lip, to become the heart-throb of pretty much all the teenage girls in our neighbourhood. The bus stop near our house had been plastered with hastily scrawled notices to the fact that Julie loved him, that they were '4 ever'. As far as I knew, it had never actually happened.

'Time is a great healer,' Julie continued. 'And there are plenty more fish in the sea. A watched pot never boils,' she also added incongruously. 'Perhaps you should come out for a drink with us, after work,' she said. 'It's all too easy to lose touch with your friends when you're in a relationship and then find yourself all alone, but we'll forgive you for that,' smiled Julie. Irene nodded. 'We'll let you back into our gang. Let's go somewhere tonight. There's a new bar opened up by the bus station. It's one of them places with all the pine furniture. Classy. You can get wine if you want it. Chardonnay and everything. What do you say, Ali? We can talk about old times.'

I had a terrible feeling that it was going to be the shoplifting thing all over again.

CHAPTER THREE

I didn't want to go but I figured that I had to. If I didn't, I would continue to be labelled as stand-offish and snobby. And perhaps it wouldn't be so bad, I tried to convince myself. I could have a couple of glasses of wine and race home in time for *EastEnders*. But no such luck. When work finished, Julie announced that we weren't going to be going to the classy winebar after all. We were going to go to 'Top Hat's Discotheque', the one and only discotheque in the area that got passed over in the 1980s flurry of refurbishment that turned most other clubs into half-decent establishments.

I dragged myself along behind Irene and Julie like a toddler being marched around British Home Stores. Once we had struggled through the door and the unnecessarily frisky security men, Julie hustled me straight into the loos. I only just got out of having to have bright silver lips by claiming that I was allergic to the whale fat contained in most lipsticks.

'But it hasn't been tested on animals,' she tried. I shook my head again. 'Pity. 'Cos it's all the rage,' she said, applying a thick layer to her own lips so that she looked as though she had spent a week lying at the bottom of a reservoir. 'You ready for this then, girl?' she asked, fluffing up my hair. 'We'll find you a new man before closing time.'

'I'm not sure that I want one, I mean, not yet.'

'Don't be ridiculous. Every girl needs a man. I know I'm not complete without that warm feeling they give you inside,' she laughed raucously. 'I've got condoms in my bag if you get lucky. Help yourself.'

I blanched at the thought. I hadn't slept with anyone other than David for years. And the boyfriend before him hardly counted, since in his youthful enthusiasm Fred Spencer never really kept at it long enough to make a lasting impression. It struck me then, that one day, and in the not too distant future, I hoped, I might have to take the plunge and sleep with someone else. Oh the agony of finding those incredible positions that disguised my pot belly all over again. Not until I had had time to use up a couple of bottles of Christian Dior's Svelte, I decided. And certainly not that night.

'You looked shocked,' said Julie, misreading the panic signs. 'Listen, I know that carrying condoms makes you look like a bit of a slag, but you've got to be responsible these days. And men, they're so unreliable. But I'm sure you know that.'

Didn't I just.

Irene emerged from the loo then. She had changed out of the tidy little suit she normally wore for work into a black lycra number. 'What do you think?' she asked, twirling for our benefit.

'Sexy,' said Julie.

'You've got a bit of loo paper stuck to your heel,' I said, figuring it was best to be diplomatic.

Irene ripped the trailer off. 'Ready.'

'But you're not,' said Julie, turning her attention to me again. 'At least undo some of the buttons on that shirt of yours.' She yanked the top two open to reveal my grey cotton bra. Well, it was more of a vest really.

'Wonderbras really passed you by, didn't they?' Julie observed. 'Better keep the buttons done up.'

I had downed just two Bacardis for Dutch courage when Julie dragged me out onto the dance floor. Once we had made ourselves a space with our handbags, Irene started a shimmy that had to be interrupted every two minutes so that she could readjust her skirt.

I jigged about unenthusiastically, unable to find the beat with any muscle in my body. Julie waved her arms and pouted her lips. Irene shook her bottom. Halfway through one song, Julie grabbed my hands and made me wave them about a bit.

'Having fun?' she mouthed over the music.

I nodded, gritting my teeth hard together. Beside me, another girl involved in a complicated grinding movement, bashed into me and then gave me a look that suggested she had a shotgun in her handbag, not tampax.

Pretty soon, I had remembered all the reasons why I no longer went to nightclubs. The noise, the heat, the competition. Stick a bunch of women in a nightclub and they are suddenly transformed from allies in the great sisterhood into bitter enemies in a gladiatorial vogueing battle to attract the attention of a bunch of men you wouldn't look at twice in a super-market.

I had to go. While Julie and Irene were getting down to some fascinating rhythm, I slipped away unnoticed. I hid myself in a toilet cubicle and had a sneaky fag while I pondered making a more permanent escape (I told Julie that I didn't smoke because she never buys her own, know what I mean?). Unfortunately the club the girls had dragged me to was five or six miles from home. I didn't have enough money to get a cab on my own. I would just have to sit the night out until Julie and Irene decided that they were ready to go too.

I sat on the closed loo seat for about half an hour, listening to the comings and goings outside. Every five minutes or so, someone would come in and have a fit of the giggles/burst into tears because so-and-so had just asked them out/chucked them for someone else. Then I heard the familiar dulcet tones of Julie and Irene.

'Well, of course, it was bound to happen. She hardly makes an effort, does she? If I was a man I wouldn't want to marry her.'

'Mmm,' Irene grunted.

'I mean, she never wears any make-up. And the way she dresses? I've seen a sack of potatoes with more sex appeal. Look at that dress she's got on tonight. What is it? A-line? Hardly going to raise any man's temperature in an A-line, are you? Well, I've offered to help her. I said I would help her choose what she wanted to wear tonight but she wouldn't hear of it. Says she's got her "own particular style". What style, I say. Can't imagine she's ever been anywhere near Karen Millen. And her hair?

All those wonderful styling products on the market and she's still going for the natural look. No, you know what her problem is, Irene, she's a snob . . . and it wouldn't surprise me if she was a secret lesbian.'

Oh, how the years fell away when I heard those damning words. I was suddenly back at the bus stop. They could only be talking about me. I didn't know what to do then. Should I walk out of the cubicle, all nonchalant, and pretend I hadn't heard a thing? Or should I stay locked away in there until I died? I opted for the latter. Hidden until death, or at least until I was sure that they were safely out of the way again.

But they were determined to take ages. Julie's shrill voice continued to pierce its way to my ears.

'Went off to do that fancy degree, and then comes back to work with us. Well, she doesn't even know how to use a computer properly. And did I ever tell you about the time she got done for shoplifting?'

By which time I was wondering why she had ever pretended to be my friend.

God, how a minute can feel like a lifetime. I covered my ears and focused on the snag in my tights. Then my attempts at isolation were interrupted by a banging on the door. A fierce hammering, a sign that someone wasn't about to cut their losses and go away.

'Come on, you've been in there for bloody ages. What's the matter? Got diarrhoea or something?' It was Julie.

I tried to disguise my voice.

'I think I need to be in here for a bit longer yet,' I squeaked. 'Can't you use one of the other cubicles?'

'No I can't. One of them's got no seat and the other one's bunged up with loo roll. Get a move on.'

She started up a chorus of 'why are we waiting?' It sounded as though there were fifty girls in the queue for my cubicle. Fifty drunken girls who might just take the measure of kicking the door down if I didn't come out of my own accord soon.

'Alright. I'm coming.' I stood up and flushed the chain. I would walk out there with my head held high. I would look her in the eye and see her blush crimson red at the thought that I had heard all her nasty gossip about me . . .

As it happened, I came out looking at the ground.

'Oh, hiya, Alison. You should have said it was you. She's had an operation,' Julie explained for the benefit of the other waiters. 'I'll just have a slash and then we'll get another drink, yeah? Oh,' she added with a fake coy giggle. 'You didn't hear all that nasty stuff I was saying about Bridget just now, did you?'

Bridget was the other temporary secretary at Hudderston Heavy Engineering. She had never fitted in. She said she liked Vivaldi.

'I won't tell her,' I squeaked. I knew it was a lie, but at that moment, it was a lie that I had to believe in order to be able to walk out of that cubicle on my own two feet.

I should have got a taxi then. It wasn't too late. And I could have got him to wait outside the flat while I begged Emma to put up the fare. But instead, somehow rooted to that club with fear, I found myself back at the bar between Julie and Irene, listening to them adjust my life story so that it appeared to be the story of Bridget. I tried to believe them but as far as I knew, Bridget had never even talked to a man without the supervision of her mother, let alone been engaged to one and lost him because of her penchant for A-line skirts and jersey underwear.

'What about him?' Julie asked later at the bar, nudging me excitedly so that most of the ice-cubes jumped out of my Bacardi and coke.

'Who?' I asked. Squinting in the direction of her pointing and seeing only a man who looked as though he had recently been released from a prison where daily face-bashing with a frying-pan was an integral part of the regime.

'Him,' she said, confirming my worst fears. 'Him in the nice Dolce and Gabbana T-shirt. Do you like them, Ali? They're some of my favourite designers. Do some lovely jeans. Do you want me to call him over for you?' she added seamlessly.

'Er . . .'

But it was a *fait accompli*. Soon Barry had joined us, and was telling Julie, in a peculiar kind of gangsta patois, about his mobile phone.

'He's got a mobile,' she told me excitedly, as if I hadn't heard. I resisted the temptation to respond that even my Dad has a mobile these days, so that Mum can harangue him when he's walking the dog.

'And he's got a car,' she whispered loudly, as one does in a club, while he got in the drinks.

'What kind of car?'

'Mark II Golf. And he says the stereo cost more than the wheels.'

Somehow this only confirmed that he wasn't going to be my kind of man.

'I think he's alright,' Julie continued. 'Do you think he's alright? He's got a nice pair of arms on him.'

True. Though they didn't exactly match up with his legs. Think chimpanzee effect. With a naked lady stencilled on in biro.

'And his hair. I like that.'

True. It was very nice hair. Unfortunately I have a rule of thumb that prevents me from dating men who look as though they spend more on conditioner than I do.

'Ask him for a dance. You can tell what a man will be like in bed from the way he dances.'

David had the disco style of a three-legged llama, I recalled with a faint 'harumph'.

'Go on,' Julie prodded me in Barry's direction. 'Dance with him. Dance with him or I'll tell everyone at work that you're a lesbian,' she added with a cackle.

'That's fair,' I thought. I was about the enter the outer circle of hell.

'Wanna dance?' Barry asked. Julie nodded enthusiastically on my behalf.

'I'll hold your drinks,' she said helpfully. And Barry guided me onto the dance floor by equally helpfully man-handling the cheeks of my bum.

We hadn't exactly chosen the best tune to start dancing to. It was some jungle track that alternated between slow and painful bass beats and frantic riffs that required the dancing skills of a Mexican jumping bean. Barry convulsed before me, his pelvis twitching backwards and forwards within dangerous range of my own. I subtly backed away from him, again and again and again, until I was dancing with my back right against the mirrored wall. The only option then was to sidle along the glass, hoping that Barry would maintain a decent three-inch distance between us.

'All right,' he asked, flooding my face with beery breath.

I nodded, eyes wide like a panicked deer as he leaned forward, lips puckering almost imperceptibly. I couldn't believe his cheek. Trying to grope me when I didn't even know his surname.

Then the music changed. Faster than ever. And this time the lights began to strobe and flash, making everything move in slow motion, like the frames of a film being run too slow through the projector. Barry stumbled backwards a little, his eyes open again. Good, I thought, he's given up on the kissing idea. You can only imagine my horror when he suddenly slumped forward into my arms and began twitching against me with a vengeance.

I was about to make a grab for his balls and twist them from his body when the incredible weight of his body against mine made me realise that he had actually lost consciousness. His grip on my shoulders relaxed as he slid slowly to the floor and lay there in a heap, lips a-quiver and big eyes bulging red.

'Help,' I squeaked. Around us, the crowd continued to dance. It was just like my accident in Safeway. No-one wanted to get involved. Just the occasional snarl when a dancing girl got her stiletto heel caught in Barry's flapping T-shirt.

'Help.'

Barry's face was rapidly turning blue.

With a strength that I could probably never find again even if I wanted to, I managed to haul Barry's inert body to the side of the dance floor and finally,

with a sense of perception lacked by the majority of
DJs, Mixmaster Mickey Mouse, noticed that something
was wrong.

The music came to an ugly halt and all eyes turned
on me.

'Help?' I said pathetically. 'Is there a doctor in the
house?'

No answer.

'A nurse?'

'Stand back, I'm a vet,' said someone suddenly.

A vet? Well, I know that I had thought Barry a bit
of a gorilla, but I couldn't really see how much help a
vet would be at that moment.

The vet however, thought otherwise. He got down
on his hands and knees next to Barry and quickly
started to administer first aid. He rolled him, with
some difficulty, into the recovery position, opened
his mouth and checked for obstructions. All the time,
Barry seemed to be calming down, his body relaxing.
Perhaps he wasn't going to die after all.

'Epilepsy,' said the vet decisively, when he was
happy with his patient's condition. 'Brought on by
the strobe lights, I expect. Didn't you know your
boyfriend was an epileptic?' He was directing that
question at me.

'He's not my boyfriend,' I said quietly. 'I just met
him tonight. I don't really know who he is.'

'Who's he here with then?' The vet scanned the
crowd.

'I don't know.'

'He's my brother,' said a girl, with similarly long
arms. 'Let me see him.' As she pushed her way to the
front of the crowd that had gathered around the little

scene, I allowed myself to slip slowly backwards into
the sea of faces.

I couldn't see where Julie or Irene had got to. I didn't
really want to know. I just wanted to get out of there
again. I took one last glance back at Barry where he lay
on the floor and caught the vet's eye. I copped a full-on
gaze right into his baby blues. He actually seemed to
be looking into the crowd after me, concerned perhaps.
Disgusted, more likely. But for a moment, I had that
delicious shudder you get when you lock eyes with
someone that you hope you might one day be locking
more with.

Typical for me to encounter him in such a ridiculous
circumstance though. He probably thought I was a
bitch to run off like that and leave a man while
he's down.

I walked home. It was a long way, not helped by
the fact that I went the first half mile in completely
the wrong direction. Then the rain started. Just spitty
spots at first, but soon it was bucketing it down with
a vengeance. I didn't care that I was wearing only
my deeply unsexy A-line dress and a denim jacket. I
wanted to catch pneumonia. I wanted to die there and
then. I wanted everyone to be really sorry for me. But
then I had a vision of my own funeral. Of Julie weeping
at my graveside, telling everyone what a good friend I
had been so that they would heap hugs and sympathy
on her, and decided that it would be more spiteful to
live and exact my revenge at leisure.

'What on earth happened to you?' Emma asked
when I staggered into the house. 'Been in a wet T-shirt
competition? Julie phoned. She said she was worried
about where you had got to. Said you were involved in

some kind of medical emergency in a nightclub? You
didn't hurt your scar, did you?'

'No, it's fine,' I assured her. 'I went dancing with the
girls from work. I guess I just wasn't up to it. Oh, and
then this bloke who was chatting me up went and had
an epileptic fit on me.'

'How grim,' Emma said, reaching for the restorative
kettle. 'Was he good-looking?'

'No.'

'Ah well.'

'The vet who did first aid on him looked alright
though.'

'A vet? Oh well, I guess if you can deal with an
elephant you can deal with most of the men in
Brindlesham. So the vet was gorgeous? Did you ask
what his name was?'

'Of course I didn't. It was hardly the right time. But
it's no good anyway, Emma. I just can't do it. I just
can't go out there and meet people yet. David is too
much on my mind. No-one can ever match up to him.
I'm doomed to be single forever.'

'Give yourself some time,' said Emma sensibly, as
she gave me a consolatory hug. 'And don't leave the
match-making up to Julie Adams. Unless you're into
primates, of course. But believe me, things will get
better.'

Perhaps she was right. Certainly, my operation scar
was no longer wrapped up with a duvet's worth of
wadding. It was just a bit pink. If I didn't poke it, I
couldn't even feel that it was there.

I decided that I'd just have to apply the same theory
to David.

CHAPTER FOUR

January the 30th. David had been gone from my life for a whole calendar month and five days. I was just congratulating myself for not having thought about him for at least twenty-four hours (telling myself that I wasn't thinking about him didn't count as thinking of him, you understand) when the postman arrived. Three envelopes tumbled onto the mat. Two were brown and addressed to Emma. The third was white and addressed, in neat typescript, to me.

Now this was unusual. I didn't get letters. I got credit card bills and final demands for the council tax. Maybe it was *Reader's Digest* writing to let me know that I really had won something in one of their fantastic prize draws. A cheque for a whole pound perhaps? One of those infinitesimally small cheques that I must be the only person in Britain sad enough to actually cash in.

But it wasn't from *Reader's Digest*.

It was from *Complete Woman* magazine. The modern woman's Bible. Otherwise known as the magazine for girls who like to pretend they are really doing something rather interesting with their lives other than simply waiting for Mr Right to come along and take them away from it all. Looking at the address at the top of that letter, for a moment I couldn't even remember ever having picked the magazine up.

Dear Miss Harris, the letter began. *We are delighted to inform you that you have won a holiday for two at the fabulous Santa Bonita all-inclusive resort in Antigua.*

Oh my God! A holiday! My heart leapt for joy at the word. I'd won a holiday in the sunshine and, believe me, a holiday was exactly what I needed after that miserable month without David Whitworth. I started to shake with excitement.

But the letter continued . . . *The whole* Complete Woman *office was touched by your heart-rending account of your fiancé's devotion to you throughout your terrible illness. There can be no doubt in our minds that you and David Whitworth are the* United Kingdom's Most Romantic Couple! *A member of staff will be contacting you shortly to arrange a convenient time for a photo shoot of you and your fiancé to accompany an article about your successful relationship for our magazine.*

'Pah!' I spat. Now I remembered *Complete Woman* magazine only too well.

May we congratulate you once again on being the United Kingdom's Most Romantic Couple 1998, the letter ended.

'Ha!'

I tore the letter in two and threw it onto the carpet.

I had won a holiday in the Caribbean and, thanks to that scumbag ex-boyfriend of mine running out on me, I couldn't even take it.

Emma sauntered downstairs just then to catch me in the throes of my impression of a soloist in *Riverdance*.

'Telephone bill?' she guessed insightfully as she rubbed the sleep from her eyes.

'No. Holiday for two in Antigua,' I replied.

'Bloody hell,' she was suddenly very much awake again. 'What are you doing then?' Emma made a dangerous dive to retrieve the now tatty scrap of paper from beneath my feet.

'What are you doing?' she asked again, as she smoothed out the paper until it was almost readable.

'I've won a holiday for two in Antigua. First prize in *Complete Woman*'s Most Romantic Couple competition.'

'You're kidding?' Emma quickly read the letter and confirmed that I was not having one of my sarcastic moments and merely pretending that I was not stomping on the telephone bill.

'You're not kidding. Most Romantic Couple? Fuck me, Ali. You're right,' she said.

'I wish I was fucking you,' I said blithely. 'Then we could go together.'

'They want to do a photo shoot of you and your fiancé,' Emma read.

'That's right.'

'Oh, Ali,' said Emma. 'Bad luck.'

So much for not thinking about David. The news that I had won the *Complete Woman* romance competition brought it all flooding back. Spending Christmas Eve alone in the hospital, writing out a thousand reasons why I loved David Whitworth more than anyone or anything else in the world, while he was out giving my Christmas Eve dance ticket and his wicked fickle heart to the girl he had promised he would never see again.

How could she have done it? How could Lisa Brown have taken advantage of the fact that I was languishing in hospital? Never mind that I had spirited David out of his commitment to her while she was on a mercy mission to Bosnia as part of her employer's personnel personal improvement course.

I hadn't seen David since Christmas Day but my sister Jo had gleefully reported that David and Lisa had been seen hovering with intent outside Ratners. When I asked her why she had to be so spiteful, Jo claimed that she was only trying to do me a favour by reminding me what a rat he was.

I still had my own engagement ring, though it no longer lived on my finger. Now the tasteful little diamond solitaire sat forlornly on my dressing table in a ceramic heart-shaped box with flowers on the lid that David had bought me on our first Valentine's Day together. I had thought about marching round to his flat and hurling the ring at him, or down a drain in front of him, but Emma said that would be undignified. Why didn't I just take it to a pawn shop instead? I could buy a flight to Rio with the proceeds. And take her too, of course. Have a good time. That would be true revenge. But perhaps I didn't take her advice because, even after hearing that David had been window-shopping at the jeweller's with Lisa, I was still harbouring the foolish notion that this was a nightmare from which I would soon wake up. (In any case, if I did try to pawn the ring, I had a terrible feeling that it would turn out to be cubic zirconia anyway.)

'What are you going to do about this holiday?'

Emma interrupted my downward spiral of thought as I moped over toast and marmalade.

'I suppose I'll just have to ring the people at *Complete Woman* and tell them that they picked the wrong couple.'

'Perhaps they'll feel sorry for you and say that you can still have the holiday regardless. You could take me with you instead,' she said optimistically.

'I can't see that happening,' I moaned. 'They're planning to make a big feature of their most romantic couple. They don't want to have to tell their readers that the winners of their Most Romantic Couple competition have sadly separated but "here are some pictures of Ali Harris and her flatmate in their spinster pad with a cat instead".' I mimicked a *Complete Woman*-type voice.

'Try it,' Emma insisted. 'You never know. Like I said, they might feel sorry for you.'

'I don't want people to feel sorry for me,' I snarled in frustration. 'No, Emma, I'm going to come clean and suggest that they award my prize to the people who came second instead.'

'Your altruism makes me puke,' said Emma as she left for work.

By the time I got into the office, the news that I had left some poor bloke dying on the dance floor had already been distributed on the ultra-efficient Hudderston grapevine. Julie and Irene regarded me judgementally as I slunk to my desk.

'I wonder if he's alright,' said Julie loudly, then she came across and leaned on my desk. 'We were worried about you,' she said, full of *faux* concern for me all of a sudden. 'Going off like that without saying goodbye. What were we supposed to think?'

'I had to get some air.'

'We could have looked after you. That guy that saved Barry wanted to know where you'd gone as well. He said he thought from the look of you that you might have gone into shock.'

'Really?'

'Yeah. Said he would have given you a lift to the accident unit to get checked out. As it was, he gave us a lift home instead. He was really nice. A vet. I've never been out with a vet myself,' she mused. 'But I suppose it must be like going out with a doctor without having to worry that he spends all day ogling other women's tits. Anyway, I told him you'd just split up with your fiancé and had your appendix out, so that was probably the real reason why you looked so pale.'

'Thanks.'

'You look awful this morning too,' she added. Just to really cheer me up.

Later that day, I must have looked even paler as I dialled the number of *Complete Woman* with shaking fingers and asked for Amanda the editorial assistant.

'Speaking,' she said, taking me by surprise.

'I, er . . . I . . .' I whispered, wanting to get this thing over with without attracting Julie's attention.

'Yes?'

'I, er . . . I won the competition.'

'Which competition, darling? We've got lots of competitions going on here at *Complete Woman*,' she told me chirpily.

'Er, Most Romantic Couple.'

'Most Romantic Couple! Fantastic. Then you must be Ali Harris. My goodness, how lovely to hear from you!' I could almost hear her beaming. 'Oh, Ali. We were all so moved by your story. It was absolutely heart-rending. I swear I was nearly in tears by the time I finished reading it. Are you completely better now, my love?'

'Yes,' I said guiltily. 'I'm much better now.'

'I bet you're really looking forward to your holiday then. It'll help you recuperate from your operation and be such a nice rest for David after the way he single-handedly nursed you through your pain.'

'Mmm,' I said. (I suppose I ought to warn you at this point that I had exaggerated my appendicitis into something a little more long-term and life-threatening. Artistic licence, I thought at the time. I guess that what I had experienced since then might well have been divine retribution.)

'Have you decided when you're going to take the trip?' Amanda continued. 'February is simply gorgeous in the Caribbean. With a bit of luck you might even be able to be on the island for Valentine's Day. Wouldn't that be great?'

'Er . . .'

'But listen to me waffling on. You go when you want to of course, Ali. It's your special holiday after all. All we at *Complete Woman* ask is that we get to see the holiday snaps when you return. Naughty ones edited out of course. Ha ha!!'

'Amanda, I . . . I . . .' I had to tell her that I wouldn't be going before she exploded with enthusiasm.

'Yes, Ali. What is it? Do you want to arrange a date for the preliminary photo shoot now? I know that the fashion department are just itching to get their hands on you for a reader makeover. You know – how to look good in a bikini without being embarrassed about nasty operation scars – that kind of thing. And the features department will definitely want a few juicy quotes for a piece they're putting together on the secrets of maintaining that perfect love affair. Do you have your diary open in front of you now?'

'Actually, Amanda . . . I . . .'

'You can come in to the studio, or we can send someone round to your home, if you prefer. I quite understand if you don't want to travel long distances in your fragile condition.'

Rubbish, I would happily have travelled a very very long way away right then. I had to put her straight. Or at the very least put her off before she booked me in with Lord Lichfield.

'Amanda,' I said in the most measured tone I could muster. 'As you can probably imagine, all this has come as rather a surprise to me. I mean to us, to David and I. I'm not looking my best after the operation. I wonder if you could be kind enough to postpone the photo shoot for a week or so? Until I'm feeling more in the pink, as it were.'

'Ali,' said Amanda smoothly. 'It really is no problem at all. Though the make-up girl we've got here at *Complete Woman* can make anyone look in the full flush of health. She trained as a mortuary assistant. Ha ha ha. Only joking. Can't I persuade you, darling?

You won't believe the difference some of those new mascaras can make.'

'Amanda, I'll call you tomorrow,' I told her. Julie was striding across the office in my direction.

'OK. Think it over for as long as you like. As long as you can give me a decision within twenty-four hours that is! Ha ha! Mwah, mwah. Please give our regards to that darling little man of yours. We're all simply dying to meet him.'

I put down the phone and felt a hot and cold flush race over my body leaving me covered in freezing sweat.

'Are you sure you're OK, Ali?' Julie asked, as she plopped a pile of typing into my in-tray. 'You were looking rather stressed out on the phone just now. It wasn't you-know-who by any chance?'

'Who?' I asked in genuine confusion.

'The D-word?' Julie mouthed. 'I know it's hard, Ali, but it really is best not to call him, you know. The harder you chase him, the faster he'll run away.'

'It wasn't David,' I put her straight. 'Whatever you think of me, Julie, I'm big and brave enough not to have to phone my ex-fiancé begging him to come back,' I added snappily.

'Fine,' said Julie. 'But in my capacity as secretary to the MD, I suppose I ought to remind you that personal phone calls are strictly forbidden in any case. Except emergencies.'

Then she left me to have an emergency telephone conversation with her friend Stella about the outfits they were going to wear when they hit the town that night.

My own emergency telephone conversation with

Amanda at *Complete Woman* had not been what I could have described as a success and now I felt doubly bad because I had accepted Amanda's praise for the fantastic state of my currently non-existent love life. This was going to be far harder than I thought. But by the time I called her again the next day, I resolved, I would be a big enough person to come clean.

I'd get some moral support from my friends. Marvin Naylor, my best friend but one, was having a dinner party that night.

CHAPTER FIVE

The only reason why Marvin actually invited women to his dinner parties at all was so that they could cook all the food for him. I swear that he used to tell us girls to arrive an hour earlier than the men, and then, when we arrived, we would find Marvin sobbing in the kitchen, with flour all over his forehead and every pan in his usually pristine kitchen, dirty and piled up in the sink.

'Ali, I just don't know what to do,' he would whimper pathetically. 'I wanted so much to impress you all tonight. I thought I'd make a soufflé. No one told me it would be this hard.'

Upon which, we girls, granting him major brownie points for having even decided to attempt something more complicated and glamorous than spag bol in the first place, would step in and cook the whole bloody lot for him. We did this several times, until one day Emma pointed out that all the dishes in Marvin's sink bore the remains of cornflakes and baked beans, and that there was no evidence of soufflé-making whatsoever, however abortive. We decided that sneaky old Marvin might just have rubbed flour into his hairline for effect as we arrived and resolved never to help him out by turning up early again.

Besides, this particular evening, I didn't have time to turn up early and help out in the kitchen. My embryonic friendship with Julie had obviously hit the skids already and she spitefully had me stay behind in the office till seven typing out some awful report.

By the time I had finished at work, I just wanted to go home and flop out on the sofa until retirement age. Marvin only enticed me away from my regime of biscuits and soap operas at all by guaranteeing me at least one single and attentive young man if I went to his party. A single and attentive young man without tattoos, a mobile phone or a tendency to pass out in my arms at inopportune moments. Oh, and not a gay one either.

With Marvin's promise in mind, I needed to dress to impress. Incredibly, despite my haphazard chocolate digestive, Wagon Wheel and Camel lights diet, I had actually lost a little weight since Christmas. How this happened, I wasn't sure, though my mother had a theory that you could cry out fat with tears. Anyway, as a result, none of my dresses fitted me properly any more. Emma walked in on me as I was gathering in the waist of my all-time favourite dress with the bit of fancy rope that normally tied back the curtains in my bedroom.

'Are you really wearing that?' she asked in the voice that she also used for saying 'Are you really eating that?' when I ordered a tuna pizza with extra anchovies.

I nodded. 'Think I need a belt with it though.'

'It always looked like it needed a belt,' she told me. 'That dress is horrible, Ali. It looks like a flippin' sack.'

'It was David's favourite,' I whined.

'Exactly. Don't you know he only made you wear it so that no other man would look at you twice?'

'Really?'

That came as news to me.

'Really. And these days you need a man to look at you twice. You're not going out like that. Try this.' She threw in my direction a little red dress that looked as though it had a day job as a tubi-grip.

'I'll look like a slapper,' I protested.

'Perfect,' said Emma. 'Because Marvin tells me that a slapper is exactly what the spare man at his dinner party wants in his life.'

'And that's supposed to encourage me? Great. I don't want to be somebody else's consolation prize.'

'Oh, live a little,' said Emma as she started to vigorously back-comb my hair, giving me a painful flashback to the nightclub ladies' toilets. 'One night stands are good for the soul. There,' she said, when my hitherto sleek and sensible hair had started to resemble candyfloss. 'You look better already.'

I sat down at the dressing table and surveyed my new look critically. Fattypuss, our ageing tabby, leapt onto my lap to offer some encouragement and put a big hole in my tights.

But a constant stream of encouraging words from Emma just about helped me make it to Marvin's house. When he opened the door, he was covered from head to foot in flour.

'Where on earth have you bad girls been?' he asked

distractedly with one eye still on something that was boiling over in the kitchen. 'It's half-past-eight. I thought I said six thirty.'

'Yes,' said Emma sweetly. 'You did. But we always seem to arrive while you're still up to your elbows in the kitchen. We didn't want to get under your feet again. What are we having tonight, Marvin?'

'Spaghetti bolognese,' he snarled.

'Who's here?' asked Emma cheerfully as we wound our way down the dark corridor towards the dining room.

'Fred, Tiffany, Andrew and Peta.'

'Is Peter the mystery man?' Emma asked.

'No, Peta's a girl. The mystery man has yet to arrive,' he smiled.

We emerged into the light of the dining room. Marvin looked me up and down. 'Oh, Ali,' he said, taking in my red tube dress properly. 'You look nice. Different. Though you should maybe try some finer tights with that dress.'

Thanks, Fattypuss, I thought.

'Sexy.' Andrew gave a low wolf whistle that boosted my self-esteem stock by twelve points. Marvin kissed the tips of his fingers before returning to the nightmare in the kitchen.

'Guess what Marvin's making,' Tiffany whispered.

'I know,' said Emma. 'Spaghetti bolognese. Did you turn up late too?'

'You bet I did. Those deep fried zucchini he took so much praise for last time we ate here made an absolute disaster zone of my Nicole Farhi shift dress. He didn't even provide me with an apron.'

'I just got so sick of him shouting at me,' said Peta.

'Last time I was here he had me dicing up onions the second I stepped through the door and then he had the bloody cheek to shout at me for not doing it thinly enough. I felt like one of those underlings in a Marco Pierre White restaurant. And my mascara was all over the place. I don't know why he insists on such complicated menus. Hasn't he heard of Marks and Spencer? I noticed they've increased their range of vol-au-vents the other day.'

'Marvin's dinner parties are legendary,' Andrew piped up.

'Yes. But not because of the food,' said Peta. 'It doesn't matter what's served up as long as the wine keeps flowing and you're surrounded by good company. He should know that.'

'Hope you still feel the same when you taste his spag bol,' said Emma into her glass.

'Is everybody here now?' asked Tiffany.

'Just one more to come,' said Emma. 'A mystery man for Ali here.'

All eyes turned to me and I coloured to match my dress. 'Don't say that kind of thing, Emma,' I protested. 'You make me sound like some Indian spinster that's got to be married off tonight or else burned to a crisp on my father's funeral pyre. Besides, I'm not the only single girl in this room.'

'That's true enough.' Emma was single too, but as far as social gatherings went, she and Marvin were almost what you could call an item. They had met each other on an art foundation course at the local sixth form college. Emma had developed an immediate and intensely deep crush on Marvin, who had seemed so creative and different from the other boys in his purple velvet tail coat and his Cuban-heeled suede boots. Sadly, it soon turned out that he was different from the other boys in more than just his attire.

The crush came to a climax one terrible evening when Emma tried to seduce Marvin at one of those 'two items of clothing parties' thrown by the students' union, where you get free drink all night if one of the items you're wearing is a hat. Faced by Emma in a leopard-print negligee Marvin had broken down and flung himself headlong out of the closet. Emma didn't speak to him for three days. After that, they made it up and strangely seemed closer than ever. They declared themselves to be 'platonically in love' and Emma took on the honorary mantle of Marvin's 'stunt girlfriend' for those tricky formal occasions when a boyfriend dressed like Carmen Miranda just won't do.

Emma swore that her crush on Marvin had ended on that terrible night, but I wasn't so sure. She had had boyfriends since then. Lots of them. Handsome but thick ones. Ugly but artistic types. Rich bastards. Poor diamond geezers. None of them stayed around for long, though some of them continued to phone up and cry on my shoulder for years after Emma lost interest. For a while I tried dressing and wearing my hair like Emma in the hope that some of her cast-offs might find a bit more physical solace with me than just blubbing. But I grew so used to rejection that it took me six months to notice when someone was taking a real interest in me, not just using me as a medium to get a message of love across to Emma.

'David Whitworth really fancies you.'

I can remember so clearly the time that Emma first said it. We were standing at the bar of The Rotunda –

The Rotunda as it was before the trendy, new brewery image bods got hold of it. This was back in the days when you could stand at the bar without risking having your eye poked out by a combine harvester hanging artistically from the shelf where they used to keep the pint glasses. In fact, I was peeling a big piece of that lovely fleecy red wallpaper off the wall when Emma dropped the bombshell.

'David Whitworth,' I said in surprise. 'But he's got a fiancée, hasn't he?'

'So?'

So indeed. Emma beckoned David over and started the chat off by asking him about his souped-up Escort GTI. Then she said something truly awful like, 'Ooh, this cystitis of mine is killing me. I've got to go to the bogs,' and left me alone with him.

'How's your fiancée?' I asked straightaway, glad that Emma wasn't around to kick me for opening up with such a conversation-stopper.

David then told me, 'She's not my fiancée any more.'

That wasn't strictly true. In fact Lisa Brown was still his fiancée until David and I had our first passionate encounter on the grey velvet sofa in the flat he actually shared with her. She was a police switchboard operator. Her shift wasn't meant to finish until eleven. Unfortunately she got off early because a punter who rang up shouting rude things about 'Pigs' had put her under 'unnecessary stress'. Not as much stress as she was about to be put under at home.

Lisa Brown really did cease to be David's fiancée that night and I must admit that I didn't think about the horrors I had put her through very much at all.

Emma was actually impressed by my wicked achievement and insisted on calling me Homewrecker-Harris for about a month. But I was almost sorry now that I knew what it was like to have your intended whipped away from under your nose, which was why I was at Marvin's dinner party, eagerly, but not without trepidation, awaiting the arrival of a single man.

'Ali, are you listening to me?' Emma dragged me back into the conversation. 'I was just saying to Tiffany that our landlord has refused point blank to mend the leaky ceiling in our bathroom. I've phoned the letting agents but they're completely bloody useless. What do they think their job is, eh? They're more than happy to take a share of the tenants' money but they act like you're the scum of the earth when you ring up and ask if it would be possible to have a roof over your head for the money you're paying.'

With a sigh I thought of the week before Christmas, the calm before the storm, when the bathroom leak saga had begun. I hadn't taken much notice of the problem then, figuring that I would be moving into a brand new place with David after our wedding in April anyway. Now, however, Emma and I had just signed a lease on our grotty little flat above the kebab shop for another six months. It was a symbolic act for me, underlining my status as a girl without a man and no hope of biblical style co-habitation in the immediate future.

'Renting is a nightmare,' Tiffany agreed. 'But you can't possibly hope to buy a place on your own these days. Andrew and I couldn't have managed without each other.' She gave Andrew a smug little smile with that. It made me feel quite sick.

'Perhaps Ali and I will have to go in on a place together one day,' said Emma. 'What do you think Ali? A spinster pad of our very own. We could get another cat.'

Marvin emerged from the kitchen just then. 'Ladies and gentlemen,' he sighed, rubbing a flour-covered arm across his forehead. 'Dinner will be ready in just a short while. In the meantime, to whet your appetite for the main course, I've made some delicious canapés.'

He dumped a plate in front of us. The canapés looked suspiciously like little triangles of toast covered in fish paste and Marmite to me.

'Thank you, Marvin,' said Emma as he retreated to finish stirring the spag bol. 'Do you need a hand out there?' she teased. 'No? Of course you don't. I'm sure you've got it all under control, you clever lad.'

Andrew gingerly tried one of the canapés. I guessed then that I had been right about the ingredients since he quickly replaced the bitten triangle at the bottom of the pile and refilled his glass with something to wash the taste away.

'Andrew, take it easy on the booze,' whined Tiffany. 'You've already had far too much to drive me home. Now I shall have to be on water for the rest of the night, you selfish little man.'

'Makes you glad to be single, doesn't it?' whispered Emma to me.

Almost, I thought. But I'd make my mind up about that when I finally met the mystery guest. Meanwhile, I was matching Andrew on the booze front, glass for glass. Dutch courage. I had enough for a football team.

The doorbell rang three times in quick succession,

interrupting an intense discussion about the real meaning of *Captain Pugwash*.

'That'll be Marvin's mysterious friend,' said Tiffany.
'I don't have any idea who it is? Do you?'

'Marvin's been acting like we're awaiting the appearance of Mick Jagger. It's probably one of his terrible
drug-dealer friends,' said Peta.

I felt the butterflies rise in my stomach and hit their
heads against the walls. Sod butterflies. There were
bats in there too. I hoped the stranger would like
me. I hoped that I would like him. I decided that I
would like him, even if he was short with a beard
and thick glasses. Even if he wore grey slip-on shoes
and white socks. Even if he had a speech impediment
that made him pronounce my surname 'Hawwis'. Sad
to say, in case you hadn't guessed, I was desperate for
even a scrap of male attention from someone with a
measurable IQ.

'Hello!! How are you!!!' we heard Marvin trill.
'You're just in time. I've been slaving away in the
kitchen since lunchtime. Everyone else is just lazing
about in the dining room. As per usual.'

The mystery guest muffled something in reply. Still
no clues as to who he was. The assembled group in the
dining room went silent in anticipation. I knew that
if I opened my mouth the nerve bats would escape
so I just sat there too and gulped down my fear in
huge mouthfuls. We could hear Marvin bringing the
guest up the long dark corridor towards us. He was
chattering away about the burnt sienna paint he was
going to use on the walls when the plastering had been
done. How long could it possibly take them to walk up
that bloody hall, I wondered?

The door opened. I sucked in my stomach automatically.

Marvin entered, followed by . . .

'Oh my god, Marvin. How could you?' Emma started shrieking. 'How could you do this to us? You utter, utter creep.'

To us? Do this to us? As Emma quickly shuffled me from the dining room into the bathroom and locked the door behind us, I got the vague impression that Marvin's mystery guest was in fact my ex-fiancé.

CHAPTER SIX

'There, there,' said Emma, dabbing at my eyes with a piece of rolled up loo paper before I had even got around to crying. 'We don't have to stay here a moment longer if you don't want to, Ali. I can't think what Marvin was playing at, inviting that stupid bastard along.'

'It was David, wasn't it?' I asked. I wasn't quite sure. Emma had whisked me out of the way so quickly my head was still spinning.

'Yes, it was David. The smug bastard. If he had even a hint of decency about him, he wouldn't have agreed to come here at all.'

'Perhaps he didn't know that I was going to be here?' I reasoned.

'But he knows that we're always here whenever Marvin has a dinner party. Who else does he think would do the washing up? We're practically Marvin's live-in geisha girls.'

That much was true.

'I'm going to go out there and give Marvin a piece of my mind. He did it deliberately, the spiteful little worm. How could he do such a thing to his friends? We've stood by him all these years . . . I practically wiped his bum for him when he had that bad turn after splitting up with Marco.' (Marco had been a holiday romance.)

'Emma,' I restrained her first with a hand on her shoulder, but later more bodily when it was clear that a hand wasn't going to be enough. 'Emma, perhaps Marvin meant well. Perhaps he thought he could hurl me and David back together tonight. Men don't understand about relationships and the etiquette of keeping exes apart for a given time like women do.'

'Of course Marvin understands about relationships,' Emma protested. 'He's gay. And right now I'm going to kill him.'

'Emma,' I held her tight against my chest so that she couldn't possibly escape. 'Please don't make a scene about this. I'm begging you. For my sake.'

'Scene? Scene?' she shrieked. 'I'm going to make a whole bloody opera out of this.'

'But don't you see, that's exactly what everyone wants. Supposing, just supposing, that Marvin really is nasty enough to want to see me squirm in the face of my ex-intended, if you go out there shouting the odds, he will have got exactly what he wanted, won't he? If, however, we carry on as if nothing has happened, as if David and I are just two old friends who simply haven't seen each other in a while, Marvin will be robbed of his drama and I might just about make it home with my self-esteem intact.'

'You don't understand,' Emma shrieked, as she wriggled to be free.

'No. You don't understand,' I told her fiercely. 'It's

my relationship, Emma. Rather, it was my relationship and as such, I think it is my right to choose how we're going to handle this little scenario.'

Emma's struggling grew a little less frantic. I released her to sit on the loo seat with her head in her hands while she calmed down.

'It's so embarrassing,' she whined. 'He doesn't know how much this hurts.'

'Emma,' I reminded her, a little less patiently this time. 'Which one of us was actually dumped by that bastard out there? You or me?' Emma looked at me and I could have sworn her eyes were blinking back tears. 'It was me, right? And I'm still standing even though David Whitworth is just on the other side of that wall. What do you say we go back out there, with our heads held high, and watch the bastard choke on Marvin's bolognese?'

Emma sniffed up a little smile.

'You're right,' she told me. 'You're so right.'

I hustled her back into the dining room before I stopped feeling it.

'Everything OK?' asked Marvin ingenuously when we emerged.

'Yes, thanks,' I said, as nicely as I could. 'Hope we're not holding dinner up. Emma got something stuck in her eye.'

I sat back down in my seat and noticed to my horror that I had been seated right opposite my ex-fiancé. David smiled an unsure smile.

'Oh. Hello, David,' I said shakily. 'Long time, no see.'

'How's your appendix?' he asked.

'Don't know. I haven't got it anymore,' I replied.

I sensed that the eyes of the whole table were upon us as we made our first faltering attempt to have a civil conversation.

'That's a lovely dress,' he said suddenly.

I looked down at my cleavage involuntarily. 'Thanks,' I replied. 'It's Emma's.'

'Right,' said Marvin, breaking the tension at last. Everyone in the room seemed to breathe a sigh of relief. 'Dinner is served. Everyone for spaghetti? You'll have to serve yourselves. I'm exhausted.' He plonked two saucepans down in the middle of the table. One was full of spaghetti. Not drained. The other was full of red stuff with floaty black bits in it. The black bits later turned out to be burnt scrapings from the bottom of the pan.

'Can I get you some of this sauce stuff?' David asked me, when I had managed to pull three strands of spaghetti safely from the knot Marvin had presented us with. I passed my plate across the centre of the table and for a second, I had one of those big budget movie moments, when the conversation around the heroine is faded out and all you can hear is her heartbeat as the hero uses the excuse of taking her plate to touch her hand.

Dream moment was rudely interrupted however when Tiffany bumped David as she reached for some burnt garlic bread, and my hard-won spaghetti ended up on the floor. I came round to notice Emma staring daggers at me. 'He was touching your hand,' she hissed.

'I know,' I mouthed back.

Fortunately, I didn't want to eat much anyway.

Seeing David again for the first time was not at all as I had imagined it. I had imagined a sordid rendezvous in the supermarket car park where we would swap back the items of each other's property we had gathered over the years. There would be an argument over who owned the programme from that matinee performance of *Grease* we saw on our first proper date. It was signed by all the cast. He would let me have it, of course, because when it came down to it, he didn't have such a big thing about Shane Ritchie as I did. But then David would drive off to meet Lisa from her late shift and I would tear the programme up anyway and let the pieces scatter across the wet ground. Symbolically.

Instead, David and I were sitting across a table at Marvin's house, of all places. There were no bitter recriminations. He wasn't even paying too much attention to me in the way that people do when they know they've done you wrong. He was discussing engine sizes with Andrew. Just like old times. Then, suddenly, David turned and looked at me. He actually smiled at me in the special way he had smiled at me during dozens of these dinner parties over the time that we were together. It was a smile that said, this guy is boring me rigid, can't wait to rip these morons apart with you on the journey home. Can't wait to rip your clothes off when we get home, was what it usually also meant.

I blushed and pretended that I was really interested in the pattern on my plate. Only the plate was actually plain white. When I looked up again, David was still looking at me. When I looked down again, his left foot, minus a shoe, was in my lap.

My mouth dropped open. What did this mean? It was what he always used to do at parties. He would wriggle his toes in my crotch until I was barely able to speak for excitement. But that was back then. In the good old days. Now, in the context of our new status as ex-lovers, it was surely a wholly inappropriate thing to do. I gave him a 'what do you think you're doing?' kind of look.

He gave me an innocent 'am I doing something wrong?' kind of look back.

Emma leaned across to ask me to pass the salt. I quickly covered David's foot with my napkin before she could see what was going on.

'Are you OK?' she asked, seeing the surprised and perturbed look that I just couldn't keep off my face. 'You look a bit weird, Al.'

'It's hot in here,' I said hurriedly. 'Aren't you hot too?'

'No.' Emma put some salt on her inedible pasta and thankfully returned to that interminable conversation about the benefits of a mortgage over renting with Tiffany.

As I tried to force down a piece of rock-hard garlic bread, David's toes began to move. It was almost imperceptible at first, but pretty soon, I was sure that everyone in the room must have been able to see the napkin jumping up and down in my lap. I forced myself further back in my chair in an attempt to make myself out of his range. David, while continuing to talk house prices with Andrew, abandoned his food altogether and slid lower in his chair to better help him get to me. I gestured at him to stop, wildly flashing my eyes, but David wasn't even looking at me so that he could get the signs.

Finally, I had no choice. This had to stop. David Whitworth no longer had the right to try to turn me on.

So I stabbed him with a fork.

'Fuck!'

Andrew fell off his chair and began to roll about on the floor, clutching desperately at his newly perforated ankle.

CHAPTER SEVEN

'Fuck! Fuck! Fuck!'

'Andrew, what's wrong?'

Tiffany leapt up from her seat and went to his rescue.

'What's wrong, darling? What's wrong? What on earth has happened to you?'

'Must have been stung by a bloody wasp or something,' Andrew muttered. 'Underneath the table.'

Everyone peered beneath the tablecloth in horror.

A wasp? In January? That was a good one. I made a swift beeline myself for the bathroom. Safely locked inside, I listened to the commotion continuing downstairs. Tiffany was getting hysterical.

'But I can't find the sting!' she shouted. 'It must have gone in really deep. We'll have to get him to hospital. He's bleeding so much. Might be an allergic reaction. Call an ambulance. Help me somebody. Quick!'

Poor Andrew, I thought as I made myself comfortable on the loo seat and lit up a fag. If I had known it was him, I wouldn't have been quite so vicious. Just a little pinch would have been enough for him. But hell,

I told myself, men who go around putting their toes in ladies' private places deserve to be stung by the occasional wasp. No wonder David had been looking at me as if I had gone mad when I thought that it was him who was toying with my affections.

I was just stubbing my fag out in Marvin's soapdish when I heard a knock at the bathroom door.

'Nearly finished,' I said out of habit.

'Ali, it's David. Can I come in?'

I opened the door just a crack.

'David? I don't think you can pee in front of me now that we're no longer engaged,' I warned him.

'I don't want to pee. I just want to talk.'

Beyond David, the house was suspiciously quiet.

'What's everybody else doing?' I asked.

'They've all gone to the hospital, of course.'

'What? All of them?'

'Yes. Andrew because he was "stung" (heavy sarcasm on that word). Fred because he had to drive. Tiffany was too shocked to drive but she had to go to give Andrew moral support and Peta won't go anywhere without Fred or let him go anywhere without her. Emma and Marvin just went along to ogle young doctors in the Accident Unit.'

'Incorrigible pair,' I laughed.

'So we're all alone,' David concluded. 'You can even come out of the bathroom now if you like.'

'I'm not sure how much I like the idea of being alone with you anymore,' I told him as I emerged, lighting up another precautionary fag to help him keep his distance. David had always hated me smoking.

'I see you're smoking again,' he said.

'Yes, I know. Does it annoy you?' I asked innocently.

'You know it does. It annoys me when anyone smokes in my presence. But I don't suppose I have much right to complain about your disgusting habits anymore, do I?'

'No. I don't suppose you do.'

We sat down together on the top stair.

'You really do look fantastic in that dress by the way,' he told me.

I flicked my hair backwards over my shoulder seductively. 'Really?'

'Wonderful. Red suits you. Don't know why you don't wear it more often. It brings out the highlights in your hair.' He wrapped a strand of the said hair around his fingers. I pulled my head away.

'You can stop buttering me up now, David,' I warned. 'I thought you wanted to talk seriously with me, not be a creep about my hairdo.'

'I do want to talk seriously. Listen, Ali,' David began. 'I suppose that the first thing I should do is apologise to you for the way I've behaved.'

'It's certainly a start.'

'I know I've been really out of order over this whole thing. It was really shitty of me to tell you that it was all over between us on Christmas Day, while you were still in hospital recovering from your operation and everything.'

I nodded. But there had to be more or I would push him down the stairs.

'We always had a great time together and we were more than just lovers . . . You and I were best friends, Ali. I owed you a decent ending because of that more

than anything else. But I ran off like a real coward. I
didn't know what to do. My emotions were whirling
like a maelstrom.'

'Nice choice of word,' I said flippantly.

'Seriously,' said David, annoyed that I was interrupting the deep bit. 'They were. My mind was all over
the place. I didn't know where to turn. I was like a ship
adrift on the ocean. I suppose I should have just kept
it all inside until you were better. Thought about the
consequences more instead of steaming ahead. That
would have been the decent thing to do.'

I stubbed out my cigarette on the carpet. Then I
remembered that though I was talking to David I
wasn't actually at his place and I had to make a
desperate attempt to cover up the burn hole I had
made so symbolically.

'I've been meaning to call you for a long time, Ali,'
he said.

I nodded in the cynical way we girls reserve for such
statements as that.

'I have. I really have,' David protested. 'But it's so
hard to know where to start. I don't think you know
how difficult all of this is for me.'

Talk about red rag to a bull. I think I may actually
have snorted with disgust.

'What? Is it as difficult as taking a wedding dress
back to the shop and asking for a refund?' I asked. 'Is
it as difficult as uninviting 150 guests to a reception
you've just lost a thousand pound deposit on, perhaps?
Is it as difficult as cancelling a five-star honeymoon in
Barbados?'

David looked downcast. 'I'm saving up to pay you
back for all that, Ali. Really, I am.'

'It doesn't matter,' I told him quietly. 'I'd hate to think that all this boils down to is how far I am out of pocket. The money's inconsequential.'

David suddenly reached into my lap and took hold of both my hands.

'You know, I knew that you would take it like this. You're so composed, Ali. A lot of women wouldn't be in this situation. Lisa certainly wasn't when I ended things with her.'

'There's no need to use the L-word with me,' I said.

'When I see you being this brave, this big and forgiving, it makes me think what a fool I must have been to ever let you go.'

I squeezed his hands then let them fall back into his lap. So much for my bloody composure, it was slipping away by the minute. 'Don't say things like that,' I told him. 'It only makes it worse.'

'Ali,' said David, taking my chin in his hand and twisting my face towards his. 'You know that you will always be very special to me, don't you? That deep down, whatever happens, I will always have loved you. Do still love you, in fact. Even now. Even though we're apart.'

'David,' I whined. 'How can you say that to me now?' At which point my composure fell to the ground and was swiftly trodden underfoot by a dozen other things fleeing my body, like common sense, and dignity, and that last little bit of self-esteem. 'How can you leave me this way?'

He answered me with a kiss. A kiss that sucked out the last vestiges of the big, brave woman I thought I had become since he called off the engagement. Before

I could remind myself that this was the man I was going to spit on if I ever saw him again, we were rolling around like a pair of teenagers on Marvin's landing. David's hand was beneath the hem of the little red dress that Emma had loaned me so that I could look marvellous for the mystery man and I was doomed, suckered like a chocaholic faced with the world's last remaining Twix.

We broke off from rolling about for just long enough to call a cab to take us back to David's place. Then we snogged in the hallway until the mini-cab driver rang the door bell. As we canoodled in the back of the taxi, I swear he took us four times around the city walls and bumped our fare up by a tenner.

'David, we shouldn't,' I protested half-heartedly as he struggled to get his key into the door without taking his lips from my face.

'But it feels so natural, Ali. So right.'

So it should have done. We had had enough practice at the business over the last three years.

Reason made one last stab at saving my dignity as I popped into the bathroom to empty my bladder. I couldn't have missed the gaudy pair of gold earrings that sat on the shelf by the sink. A pair of earrings that certainly hadn't been left behind when I last cleaned my teeth in that bathroom.

'He's with Lisa now, you idiot,' screamed Ms Reason from deep inside me. 'There's the solid evidence. What more do you need? Get out, get out, get out!!!'

But then David appeared at the bathroom door, wearing nothing but his silky boxer shorts and smiling that disarming smile. 'What's taking you so long?' he asked. 'I'm getting cold out here without you.'

I quickly took out my own earrings and flipped the mystery pair haphazardly into the bin. With my cubic zirconia sparklers in their place, I felt triumphant. Lisa, Schmisa, I thought as I trotted eagerly into the bedroom. Lisa Brown was just a blip in the smooth history of our relationship. I had wrestled David Whitworth from her terrible clutches once before and I was about to do it all over again.

Waking up the next morning was a surreal experience. Everything looked strangely normal. Exactly the same as it had done every other morning for the past two years. And yet it was not normal. I was in David's bed, but we were no longer engaged to be married. As far as I knew he was still, strictly speaking, another woman's man and thus together we had committed an infidelity.

David wasn't awake. He was snoring. Something which he had always done while we were together and something which told me that he was going to be asleep for a fair while yet.

Gingerly I put a toe out onto the carpet. When David and I were engaged and spending every other night together at his house, I had kept a spare pair of slippers in his room. Not slippers exactly, but some tatty blue cotton espadrilles that were no longer smart enough to be taken on holiday. Instinctively, I looked under the bed to see if they were still there.

They weren't.

And neither was my special Snoopy toothbrush, I discovered to my horror when I made a proper foray around the bathroom. My heart sank fifty feet as

I surveyed the new contents of David's bathroom cabinet. Lady's razors for sensitive skin in germoline pink, and a tube of contraceptive jelly.

As if I was hoping that it would morph into a tube of Savlon, I picked the contraceptive jelly up and looked at it. Who did that belong to? As if I didn't know. But, against all rationality, I told myself that at least the cupboard was bereft of evidence to suggest that she had really moved herself in. No mascara, no foundation, no lipstick, and I knew that Lisa Brown was the kind of major shareholder in Max Factor who couldn't let the cat out unless she was wearing her 'face'.

Added to this was the fact that David had brought me back there at all, which he wouldn't have done if he was actually living with her, surely. Hang on a minute, cried a deep buried memory, what about the time that he . . .

OK, OK, I acknowledged that particle of brain. So he had taken me back to the flat that he shared with Lisa before they split up for the first time. But the majority of my grey cells were still bathed in a dangerous soup of optimism and denial as I dressed myself that morning. She doesn't seem to have taken root, they said. No problem to get rid of every last trace of her if she hasn't really taken root yet.

I scrubbed at my teeth triumphantly with David's toothbrush. Forget rampant shagging and the swapping of bodily fluids, everyone knows that sharing a toothbrush is the ultimate gesture of intimacy. Then I squirted beneath my arms with his manly deodorant. I had often done that while we were together, then later on, while I was at work, every time I lifted my arms up to do something like fetch down a file or draw a blind, a waft of the stuff would remind me of David and my luck in being with him.

Returning to the bedroom, I shook David gently by the arm.

He woke up and gave a little start, which disappointed me, until the surprise on his face was replaced by a contented smile.

'Ali,' he murmured softly.

'That's me. Listen, David, I've got to go to work. Will I see you later on?' I asked.

In answer David wrapped his big arms around my waist and tried to pull me back under the covers.

'No. Don't start that,' I said, happily wriggling free from his embrace. 'We can do it all again later on.'

'Yes, later on,' he murmured.

'What time?' I asked. I had to pin him down again. 'What time? When are you working today?' The employees in his insurance company office did shifts for customer convenience.

'I'm not working at all today,' he told me. 'I've got a day due in flexi-time. I'm taking it off.'

'Oh.' I hovered between getting up and sitting back down again. Maybe I should take the day off as well. We could spend the whole of it together. In bed. Cementing things. Putting our relationship back together for good. I could tell Julie that my appendix was giving me pain again. But I decided against it. One thing I had promised myself in the long month since we were last together is that, if David ever did come crawling back to me, he would find me slightly changed. More independent. Much less likely to drop everything for him when he gave the nod.

'Have the day off too,' he said.

The fact that he wanted me to was all that I needed right then.

'No,' I said, firmly but affectionately. 'I have a job to go to. I had to have a long time off work because of my appendix, remember?'

'Your appendix.' He traced the place where I had a scar. 'It doesn't hurt you anymore, does it, Ali?'

'No, it doesn't hurt,' I said, pushing him back down into the pillows. 'Listen, you just behave yourself today and I'll see you later on.'

'Come round as soon as you've finished work,' he told me.

'I'll see what I can do,' I said as nonchalantly as I could manage.

I knew I'd be there like a shot.

CHAPTER EIGHT

In the excitement of my reunion with David, I had almost forgotten about the terrible dilemma that was the *Complete Woman* Most Romantic Couple competition. But just as I was about to leave the office at five on the dot to rejoin David in bed, the telephone on my desk rang out accusingly.

I could tell it was an external call because of the ringing tone. I didn't normally get external calls. All my calls were from my boss, Mr Chivers, asking why I was still such an appalling typist after three years of promising to change and a fortune spent on computer courses.

'Ali Harris's desk,' I said officially.

'Is Ali there?'

'Speaking,' I said, wondering briefly why I had referred to myself as a desk.

'Hi, Ali. It's Amanda here. You said you were going to call me today, you naughty girl. Remember? About the photo shoot? For *Complete Woman*?'

'Ah, Amanda, yes,' I said, sitting down again so that my thinking muscles wouldn't be overstretched

by having to keep me upright as well as sensible. 'I
did promise to call you, didn't I? I'm sorry. I've been
ever so busy at the office today. I'm sure you know
how it is.' In fact I had spent most of the day in the
seedy little smoking room, mulling over the details of
my sudden reunion with David with Kim from the
reprographics department. Julie, surprisingly, hadn't
wanted to know apart from telling me that it would
all end in disaster.

'Well?' asked Amanda.

'What?' said I.

'Well, have you decided when we're going to do
these blasted photos? I know it's a bit of a bore darling,
but frankly it's a small price to pay for a fortnight at
Santa Bonita, don't you think? All inclusive. I went
there myself last year. It's fabulous. Really luxurious.
You will love it, love it, love it.'

A vision of the hot sand and the blue sea wafted
briefly through my imagination. I would love it. Yes
please. But how on earth could I take the Most Romantic prize up now that I no longer had a fiancé?

'Have you spoken to your other half about days
which would be suitable for him?'

'Er . . . er?' I fumbled. Then suddenly it hit me. I almost
had an other half again, didn't I? And I was supposed to
be on my way to see him at that very moment. Surely
it was just a matter of time before that ring was back
on my finger. I didn't have to turn the holiday down
anymore. I just had to ask David to come with me.

'Amanda,' I said happily. 'You know what? I'm
supposed to be meeting David in just ten minutes
time. I'll run some dates past him tonight and call
you first thing tomorrow morning. OK?'

'Promise me, Ali,' said Amanda gravely. 'I'm on a tight deadline, you know. Will you really call tomorrow?'

'I will,' I promised.

I put the phone down and allowed myself a moment of smug reflection on my luck before heading over to David's. However, just as I was about to close the office door behind me, the phone rang again. External.

I bit my lip. Should I answer it, or should I just leave it ringing? It was probably just a pesky customer. But what if it was David, frantic with worry that I hadn't arrived home yet? Or calling to ask if I wanted to be picked up in his nice new car? I picked up the phone to talk to him.

'I hate you,' said the caller.

'Oh,' I said. Fear spread through my body like ice forming on the surface of a puddle. Was it Lisa Brown? Did she know about last night already?

'What happened to you last night, you whore?'

No. I sighed with relief. It was only Emma.

'When we got back from the hospital you were gone. I was really worried about you, Ali Harris. Until Marvin pointed out that David had left a note on the kitchen table to say that he had "scored".'

'He did what?' I asked. The scumbag, I thought. Must have been while I was fetching my coat.

'He said that he had "scored". Am I right to assume that the unlucky woman was you? No, don't tell me . . . The real story is, you didn't get off with David. You called for a taxi home and ended up spending the night in the back of a Ford sierra with a delicious mini-cab driver instead? Since we both know there's no such thing as a delicious mini-cab driver, as I said when I first called up – I hate you, Alison Harris.'

'Why?'

'For letting me down again.'

'Letting you down?' I repeated incredulously.

'Yes. How long did you make him grovel for this time, Ali? Ten minutes? Five minutes? Two minutes? Or did you grovel to him perchance while we were all down at the hospital tending to poor sick Andrew?'

'I did not grovel to David.'

'You do know what he's after, don't you?' she asked.

'He said that he's missed me since we split up. He thinks he wants us to get back together.'

'Pah!' Emma spat. 'He just wants to go to Antigua.'

The words seemed to sting.

'How can he?' I protested. 'He doesn't even know about that! I only told you.'

'Yeah. And I told Marvin. And Marvin, as you must have guessed, told everybody else at the party while we were having that panic in the loo. It's obvious, Ali. David simply thinks that if he gets in with you now, he's got a chance of a two week all-inclusive holiday in the sun. Gratis.'

'It's not like that. Don't be so cynical. He's asked me to go straight round to his place after work. Why would he do that if he wasn't serious about getting back together with me? Lisa might come round at any minute.'

'Unlikely. Lisa Brown is on a three week self-assertiveness course in Hastings,' said Emma smugly. 'Marvin told me. He knows her sister.'

'Well, she won't walk in on us then,' I replied frostily.

'But I'm not stupid, Emma. I know when someone's just taking advantage of me for sex. And David isn't. David's serious about getting back together. I could tell it from the way he kissed me last night.'

'Oh please. David's a schmuck.'

'We'll see about that. I'll ask him straight out about him and Lisa and about whether he's only interested in me for the holiday. How about that? I know what he'll say to me, Emma. I'll tell you the good news later on.'

'If you come home,' Emma snorted.

'Well, you could try to be optimistic for me. You're supposed to be my best friend.'

'If I wasn't your best friend I'd be delighted that you're getting your oats. As it is, I don't want you to get hurt all over again. Look, just don't do anything I wouldn't do tonight, OK? And by that I mean don't go inviting any slimy ex-boyfriends of yours to Antigua . . .'

CHAPTER NINE

'**D**avid,' I said, almost as soon as he opened the door to me. 'Do you want to come to Antigua?'

'Antigua?' he asked disingenuously. 'Where's that then, Ali? What's happening there?'

'It's in the West Indies, silly,' I told him. 'I've won this fantastic fortnight-long holiday for two in a magazine competition. It's going to be all-inclusive. Do you want to come?'

'Does the Pope have a smoking handbag?' David replied excitedly. 'When do we go?'

'Well, two weeks next Thursday provisionally. But I can change the dates if you'd prefer.'

David made a mental calculation and nodded. 'No. Two weeks next Thursday sounds perfect to me. How did you win this trip, you clever girl?'

'Oh, I just had to answer a couple of questions and finish a tie-breaker,' I lied. 'You know the kind of thing.' No point in telling him the truth just yet, I figured. I didn't want to frighten him off again by putting him under the pressure of being one half of the alleged happiest couple in the world.

'I had no idea you could do that kind of thing,' David marvelled.

'I had a lot of spare time while my appendix scar was healing up.'

'But are you sure you want to take me?' David asked suddenly. 'I mean, I haven't exactly been the best of friends to you since then.' He stroked the base of my neck, fishing for forgiveness. 'You could take Emma instead.'

'I know. But I want to take you,' I assured him. 'I don't want to have to share two weeks on a paradise isle with Emma. She snores. And I can't say I really fancy her all that much.'

'A paradise isle,' David mused. 'This is just what we need, Ali. To put our relationship back on the right track. Two weeks away from all the trials and pressures of everyday life.'

We both lay back on the sofa and dreamed about feeling the sun beating down on our hot bodies as we lay on the golden sand.

'All-inclusive, you said?' David asked suddenly. 'Does that mean booze as well?'

'Local drinks, it said in the brochure they sent me. I think that just means rum. But I'm sure you can buy lager there, if you want it.'

'It's a small price to pay, I guess, for two weeks in the sun with my dream woman.' He pulled me close to him and kissed me on the top of my head. 'You're such a clever girl, Ali. What did you say the tie-breaker was?'

'I didn't. But it was to do with suntan lotion, I think,' I added quickly for authenticity.

'Aw, come on, Ali. Stop trying to pretend you can't remember what you wrote. You must do. Tell me. You should be proud of your slogan. It's taking us away on holiday after all. Tell me, Ali. Please.'

'No, it's really very silly,' I protested.

'Tell me, Ali.' He grabbed my left ankle and I knew he meant business. If I didn't tell him a slogan, he would tickle me to within an inch of my life.

'Er. It was "Make sure you slap me on, before you go and sit in the sun",' I blurted before he could start tickling. 'Do you get it?'

'I think so. And that was it? Doesn't even rhyme properly,' David commented as he dropped my foot.

'Guess the others must have been even worse,' I said.

'Guess they must have been. Ah well, who cares? We won!'

He started to sing 'Viva Espana!'

'We're going to the Caribbean,' I reminded him. 'Not Spain.'

'Don't know any songs for that,' he replied. 'Now, are you sure I don't owe you anything for this trip?'

'Well,' I said as I wriggled into a prone position on the sofa. 'Perhaps you could give me something in kind.'

I was happier than a pig in shit as I fell asleep that night. David was curled up like a puppy dog beside me, his big hand resting gently on my waist, just near my scar. I looked across at him, at that familiar handsome profile, and suddenly it was as if the sun had started to shine on my life again. The terrible revelations of Christmas Day seemed like something I had just imagined in the aftermath of my operation. We were back together again. And stronger for the time we had spent apart.

'I'll never let you go again, David Whitworth,' I whispered into his sweet-smelling hair. 'You mean more to me than anyone in the whole wide world and I really, really love you.'

'I love you too, Lisa,' he said.

I sprang upright against the pillows and stared at him. But he was still fast asleep, oblivious to his little cock-up. It was an easy mistake to make, I decided. He had spent a lot of time with her recently. But by the time we got back from Antigua, Lisa Brown would be totally forgotten. If he said her name then, though, I'd throttle him with my bare hands.

'Can I use your phone?' David asked the next morning.

I had insisted that we go back to my place because I wanted to parade David in front of Emma at the breakfast table to show her how wrong she had been about our reunion. As it was, Emma didn't have the decency to be home when I wanted to gloat. She later let me know that she had decided to stay with Marvin to give me some privacy while I came to the right decision. Instead, the only member of the flat team to witness the historic moment was Fattypuss. She was unimpressed, since she had been sleeping on my bed since David's departure and felt usurped by his sudden return.

'Who do you want to call?' I asked him innocently.

'Well, I've got to call my boss as soon as possible.'

'It's Saturday morning.'

'He'll be in the office. Almost lives there. I've got to call him right away because I need to get two weeks worth of holiday all of a sudden. Remember?'

'Of course,' I smiled coyly. I gestured to the Mickey Mouse phone which stood on my bedside table.

'Er, haven't you got another phone?' David asked.

'It works,' I reassured him. 'You just dial the numbers on the back of Mickey's ear.'

'I don't think I can talk to my boss on that phone,' David said firmly.

'You've done it before,' I protested.

'Yes, but not when I have had to think this hard and this seriously about something. I've got to come up with a really good reason why I want to take two weeks off in the middle of the busiest period of the business year, Ali. February's a boom time for burst pipes and floods. I need to be able to think straight. Come up with a foolproof excuse.'

He looked stern.

'You can use the one in the living room,' I conceded.

He jumped up and headed for the door, closing it carefully behind him. I lay back in bed for thirty seconds, revelling in the smell of his aftershave on my pillow before the curiosity bug bit me. I wondered what kind of tale of woe he was making up to convince his boss that he should have two weeks off work. I hoped he wasn't using the old 'got to go to a funeral' trick. That always seemed too much like tempting fate to me.

Mickey the phone smiled at me vacantly from the side of my bed. If I picked the receiver up I would be able to hear exactly what David was saying downstairs.

No, that would be underhand, I chided myself. He would tell me what he had said himself when he came back to bed.

But then again, I wanted to hear his boss's voice, to see

if he was really convinced by the excuse. David would never know that I had listened in. I had practised the art of picking the receiver up noiselessly during the brief paranoid period when I had thought that Emma might be flirting with my man. She hadn't been, of course. But it's hard to believe that your Mars Bar of a man could be someone else's fish paste sandwich. Emma only had eyes for her hopeless case Marvin.

'Fattypuss, don't you tell a soul what I am about to do,' I warned the rotund tabby peril as I picked the receiver up. She merely continued to clean her paws haughtily. My secret would be safe with her.

'. . . so you see, I'm going to be away for two whole weeks. You'll be able to manage without me for that long won't you?' said David on the other line.

Wow, perhaps he was simply telling his boss the truth, I thought. Now that would be a novelty.

'Oh, David. I don't know if I can,' said his boss.

Hang on a minute, I said to myself. I thought David's boss was a man.

'But it's my big chance for promotion,' David continued. 'You always knew that to get ahead with my work I would have to travel abroad. It's just two weeks, honey-pie. Two liccle-iccle weeks. I'm doing it for us, honestly, my sweet.'

'Do you mean that, Twinky-winky?'

Twinky-winky? It suddenly hit me right between the eyes that David wasn't talking to his boss at all.

'I really mean that, my little angel,' David continued. 'And I'll bring you back a lovely present.'

I put the Mickey receiver back noiselessly and surprised myself by managing not to scream out in pain. It was another three minutes before David came back to bed. I guess he must have called his boss for real after hanging up on Lisa bloody bitch-face Brown.

'Hello again,' I said, aware that my voice was shaking. 'Do you think you got away with it?'

'Scot-free,' said David proudly as he slid beneath the duvet and put his hand straight up my tartan nightie. 'No-one knows anything. I could do with a cup of tea to calm my nerves down again though. You going anywhere near the kitchen, Twinky-winky?'

'Twinky-winky?' I repeated accusingly.

'That's my new name for you,' he said hurriedly. 'Suits you, don't you think?'

'I'm not sure,' I replied. I got to my feet unsteadily. David had never used a pet-name for me before. In fact, he had once actually said that people only used pet-names when they were frightened of being caught out by saying the wrong real one at an inconvenient moment.

'I'll make that cup of tea,' I said, knowing that if I didn't get out of that bedroom pretty damn quickly there was going to be blood on the duvet and it wouldn't be mine.

'Tea. Milk. Two sugars, my Caribbean Queen,' David murmured, holding me back for a moment and kissing each of my fingers in turn before letting go of my hands. 'Though I'm sure you haven't forgotten how I like my cuppa.'

'Tea, milk, two sugars,' I murmured in reply as I stood at the door to my bedroom and looked back at David settling himself back under the sheets. I walked to the kitchen about as steadily as someone who had just received a hard blow to the head.

*   *   *

I put the kettle on and felt the steam rising in me as the water in the kettle boiled. This was not working out as I had intended. The evidence presented to me by my sneaky snooping suggested unequivocally that David had no intention of telling Lisa that things were over between them yet. In fact, it seemed he was planning to go straight to see her as soon as our plane touched the ground.

I should tell him where to go, I thought.

On the other hand, I could hardly have expected him to break the news of our reunion to Lisa over the phone, could I? Not while she was on her self-assertiveness course in Hastings. He was probably intending to tell her the truth when we got back. Or perhaps he was going to write her a 'Dear John' letter to read while we were away in the sun.

I should go ahead with the trip as planned, I thought.

But why on earth would David Whitworth be bothering to be so bloody tactful? So, Lisa Brown was on a self-assertiveness course? I had been recovering from a serious operation on Christmas Day when he pulled the plug on me!!!

I should tell David exactly where to stick his bucket and spade.

He was obviously intending to use this period while Lisa was out of town and I had two tickets to the sun to help him choose between us. But I didn't want him to have to make his mind up. I wanted him to know that he wanted me right now. I couldn't go to Antigua with David while there was still the vague chance that he would run straight into Lisa's longing arms upon our return. It would turn the whole dream holiday into a nightmare. I didn't want to feel like I had to perform all the time in order to hang on to him. Worse still was the nagging doubt that he had already chosen and the winner was Lisa. I was getting the booby prize. Two weeks of togetherness in lieu of forever.

The kettle finished boiling and I slopped the hot water onto two tea bags in the mugs. David had a thing about his tea. No mugs and definitely no tea bags. Strictly bone china and leaves for him. But right then I wasn't sure he deserved such close attention to his whims.

Maybe I hadn't made my mind up about him either, I told myself as I slopped in the milk (slightly curdled). Maybe I should look upon this two weeks in Antigua as an opportunity for unbridled sex that I could leave behind with my flip-flops at the end of the fortnight. Maybe I could use him too.

No way, I was telling myself by the time I stirred in two sugars. I was way too emotionally involved to use someone. I had never had a one night stand and walked away in the morning leaving the wrong phone number on the poor sucker's pillow as Emma seemed to do on a weekly basis. And I had read far too many magazine articles about the dangers of trying to have unbridled passion with an ex. It is never unbridled. Never. Never. Never.

I slumped onto a stool and sat staring at the tube of Hot Stuff Heat Rub Emma had bought for her dodgy stiff knee while I waited for sanity to return in full.

'That tea ready yet?' David shouted from the bedroom.

'Nearly,' I called like the girl I used to be, before Lisa Brown and before the loss of my appendix, while squashing the tube of Hot Stuff Heat Rub hard in the middle to keep the anger out of my voice.

'Bring it up here then, will you? I'm gasping.'

Dutifully, I loaded a tray with the two mugs of tea and a packet of chocolate biscuits and began the climb up the stairs. As I handed him his mug, David's nose wrinkled in just the slightest hint of disdain at the presentation.

'Lovely,' he said. 'You always did make a good cup of tea.'

'Thank you.'

'Now,' he said. 'Hop in here next to me. I've been getting cold in bed without you.'

David turfed Fattypuss off the bed unceremoniously to make a space for me. I slipped in under the covers with him and let my dressing gown fall open seductively. David's eyes slipped involuntarily to my breasts.

'How about some unbridled passion and rampant sex?' I asked him shakily. Maybe I could do it. Detach the physical from the emotional. Maybe I was strong enough to separate love and lust and play him at his own game.

I kissed him before he could answer, pushing him back into the pillows and sliding my hand into his boxer shorts with the kind of all-in-one manoeuvre that I had only ever seen on TV.

'Wow!!' said David when I let him up for air.

'Thought I would give you a little help in choosing between me and Lisa Brown, since I know that's what you're doing, David Whitworth,' I told him ominously as I reached for his cock. 'Hmmm, maybe my hands are a little rough,' I said. 'Perhaps I ought to use some lubrication.'

'Lubrication!' sighed David, like it was a new word for fellatio.

I reached into the pocket of my dressing gown.

'Close your eyes,' I murmured seductively.

He obliged quite willingly.

I squirted a big dollop of Hot Stuff Heat Rub into my palm and made a grab for his willy. It took just two firm strokes up and down before he opened his baby blue eyes with a hideous look of recognition that there is a very fine line between pleasure and pain.

'Hells-fucking-bells.' He slapped my hands away and leapt to his feet. 'What the fuck, Ali? My balls, my balls! What have you done to me? I'm burning up! I'm dying.'

He raced to the bathroom and I soon heard the cold tap being turned on full.

'Bugger! Fuck!' he shouted.

I guess it must have been stinging pretty badly.

'Call an ambulance for crying out loud, Ali. Fuck! You've finished me!'

I meandered to the bathroom door and leaned nonchalantly against the door frame.

'What's wrong? Are you hurt, my dear?'

'What the fuck did you put on me, you bitch?'

'Nothing. I mean, just something I thought would make things a little more exciting for you.' I brought the tube of Hot Stuff out of my pocket again and looked at it as if I didn't know what it really was supposed to be used for.

'You put Heat Rub on me!' he screamed. 'You're a bloody psycho!'

'What did I do wrong?'

David turned away from the sink then and ran back to the bedroom still clutching his balls. He then redressed with obscene haste.

'What's wrong with you, you nutter? What do you think? Were you trying to hurt me deliberately?'

'Were you trying to hurt me deliberately?' I countered. 'I just listened to you telling Lisa Brown that you're going to be away from town on business for two weeks. You weren't going to tell her about me and the holiday at all, were you, you scumbag?'

'Eh?'

'I used Mickey Mouse while you were on the phone downstairs,' I explained. 'I can't do it, David. I can't go to Antigua with you knowing that you're going to go straight back to her when we get home. You have to choose between us right now. Me or Lisa Brown? Make your choice.'

'Oh, I've bloody chosen all right,' said David, still cupping his balls like they were made of solid gold. 'I don't need a holiday this much. You can go on your own for all I care. You're a nutter, Ali Harris. A nutter and a psycho. You ought to be locked up for good!'

'And you're scum, David Whitworth,' I screamed from my bedroom window as he ran quickly from the flat to his car like a Bosnian escaping sniper fire. 'You're two steps down from plankton. No, make that three steps! And one day Lisa Brown will realise that too.' He fired up his engine. 'Why would I have wanted to lie on a beach next to you anyway, you big fat lump of lard?' Unfortunately I don't think he heard that particularly inspired remark.

David's car disappeared around the corner. I closed the window when I noticed that the man across the road was looking in at me in my untied dressing gown.

Bugger, bugger, bugger.

David had gone again.

Why did Emma always have to be right?

CHAPTER TEN

As if to rub my nose in it, the day that David chose to exit from my life again was the day that my parents celebrated their thirtieth wedding anniversary. When I called Mum to say that the bottom had fallen out of my life again and what possible choice did I have but to fling myself headlong from a high window onto a spiky wrought iron fence, she was too stressed out by her vol-au-vents to care.

'I'm sure they're supposed to have puffed up by now, but they're not even slightly bigger,' she wailed. 'This is going to be a disaster. We should have got a professional caterer in, but oh no, your father said that it was too expensive. Said that they would only charge us a fortune to put some Marks and Spencers titbits in the microwave. We could do that ourselves and save loads of money, he said. He's always been the same. Ever since I met him. Tight as a tick, he is. Always coming up with some money-saving plan that turns out to be a disaster that costs us twice as much as getting a professional in would have cost in the first place. Thirty years we've been together. It's a wonder we lasted thirty minutes.'

'Mum,' I said, attempting to interrupt while she drew breath. 'Mum, I don't think I can come to your party tonight.'

'Whaaattt!?!'

'I said, I don't think I can come to your party tonight. You know, David suddenly calling things off again has laid me pretty low. If I come to your party I'll only spoil things by standing around looking miserable all night.'

'John! You'll never believe what your eldest daughter is saying to me now,' she shrieked to my father. Strange how I was always his daughter when I was pissing her off. 'John, come in here and talk to her at once.'

With that, my mother put the receiver down. Not down so that I got cut off. Just down on the hall table while she went to fetch my Dad. I could hear her shrieking even when she was out in the garage, where Dad would probably be hiding on the pretence of tidying up some old deckchairs so that they could be brought into the house for the anniversary bash. I knew my family so well.

When my mother really started to raise her voice, Berkeley the family dog would always join in too. I could hear him barking now. It was five minutes before the receiver was picked up again. It wasn't Dad though. It was my sister Jo.

'Listen Ali, you'll be in deep shit for the rest of your life if you don't come to this party tonight,' she warned me. 'How could you even suggest that you're not going to come? Dad is getting it in the neck something chronic because of you.'

'Put him on,' I begged her, thinking that he, of all the people in that house of insensitive ball-breakers, might understand the plight of the recently broken-hearted.

'I can't. Mum hasn't finished with him yet. And I'm going to have to put the phone down on you now anyway. I'm waiting for a call.'

'A man?' I asked.

'Of course,' she said. 'I'll see you later. Don't be late.'

My little sister put the phone down on me. I stared at the receiver for a while. Then I picked it up and tried to call home again. I thought I would disguise my voice and make sure that I got Dad by pretending to be calling from a garage or something. But when I called back the phone was engaged. I imagined Jo sitting at the bottom of the stairs, twisting the phone cable round and round her elegant fingers as she listened to some poor sap telling her how beautiful and talented she was. Pretty much the entire upper sixth form of the local boys' grammar school had failed their mock A-levels because of our Jo.

Then I thought of Dad in the garage, faced by Mum and the dog, and with nothing to look forward to but a night with his mother-in-law and her cronies, and suddenly there was no doubt that I would be at that anniversary party after all.

I went upstairs to my bedroom and studied my bedraggled-looking face in the dressing-table mirror. My hair hung about my cheeks like two lank curtains of seaweed. My eyes were barely visible for the big puffy bags that surrounded them. I looked like the kind of hideous mess that not even Clarins Beauty Flash could deal with. And what on earth was I going to wear? What did one wear to one's parents' anniversary party? Most of my wardrobe sent my mother running for her old Doctor Spock manual to see where she had gone wrong.

Emma would know. But of course she wasn't in. Where was she when I needed her?

You know how it is at these moments in your life. Things seem interminably black. You can feel your canoe scraping along the bottom of life's river. You've got a hole in your boat and you can't bail out fast enough. You're rapidly sinking, but from somewhere deep inside you a little voice calls out: 'We've done this all before, remember? When the canoe hits the bottom, you can let it sink and swim for it instead!!' And then you start the long hard metaphorical swim back to happiness. Well, I was having exactly that thought when the phone rang and my canoe went over a waterfall, with me still pathetically trapped inside.

'Ali!' trilled a voice which had become all too familiar to me. 'Ali darling, it's Amanda from *Complete Woman*. We've still got to sort out that photo shoot haven't we, you naughty little Miss Camera-shy you. Listen, I know it's Saturday, and you're probably up to your eyeballs in the ironing, but I've got a photographer in your part of town right now. Is your better half available to do the photographs at your place tonight?'

'Tonight?' Suddenly what to wear to the anniversary party was the least of my worries. 'Tonight, tonight?'

'Yes. Tonight. Well, about six o'clock to be precise. That's not too late is it? Doesn't interfere with any plans you might have?'

'Well, actually,' I began, thanking heaven for my latest excuse. 'It might do. You see, tonight is my Mum and Dad's thirtieth wedding anniversary party. I promised to help. You know how it is. I've got to be there at five to help cook the vol-au-vents.'

'Mmm, interesting,' said Amanda. 'Where do they live?'

'Brindlesham,' I said. But probably nowhere near me or Amanda's convenient photographer, I added hastily.

'Farehurst Street? Why, fabulous. That's just round the corner from the photographer's first call. Did you know there's a woman who does really accurate horoscopes for pets in your town centre?'

I certainly didn't.

'Listen, Ali,' Amanda persisted. 'I've just had the most fantastic idea. Why don't we take the photos of you and David at your parents' anniversary party? It'll make a great feature. Really interesting. I can see the headline now: *Britain's most romantic couple celebrate their everlasting love with the older generation.* I love it.'

'Er, er. I don't know how Mum and Dad will feel about that,' I blustered. 'I mean, it is their party and I wouldn't want to upstage them.'

'Nonsense. They'll be delighted,' said Amanda with unshakeable certainty. 'Believe me. Think of what a fabulous souvenir it will be for them. Their thirtieth wedding anniversary celebrated in the glossy pages of *Complete Woman*. There aren't many couples who can say they've had such an honour.'

I collapsed onto the stool beside the telephone table and clutched up a handful of my hair, ready to pull it out.

'OK,' Amanda continued regardless of my reservations. 'What time will things kick off in earnest? When will David arrive at their house?'

'Actually, that's the problem.'

Was I about to tell her the truth?

'What's the problem, Ali?'

'David won't be there,' I said very slowly.

Peculiar silence on the other end of the line.

'David won't be there?' Amanda asked eventually. 'But it's your parents' thirtieth anniversary party. How could he possibly not be there for you? What are you talking about, sweetheart?'

'David and I,' I began. 'David and I have decided that it's for the best.'

'Ali, what are you trying to tell me?'

'It's for the best that he isn't there.'

The longer this took, the further away from me my courage was running. It was at the front door already, taking off the chain and fiddling at the latch.

'It's for the best that he isn't there because some of the old ladies present at the party might be susceptible to shingles.'

What? I thought even as I said it.

'What?' said Amanda.

I took a deep breath. 'You see, David has just come down with chickenpox. He missed it as a child, but he has it now and, as you must know, chickenpox can have terrible complications in the elderly. We thought that it wouldn't be fair to expose them to that risk. Not while he's still contagious. And of course, the spots are another reason why David isn't terribly keen to have his photograph taken just yet. I don't know why I didn't tell you earlier, Amanda. I suppose I just thought that you wouldn't believe me.'

'Oh, Ali.' I could tell immediately that I had her hook, line and sinker. 'How could you have thought that of little old me? Of course I believe you. Of course I understand. Chickenpox is such a nightmare! I didn't

have it until my teens, you know. I tried ever so hard not
to pick at the spots but I still managed to end up with
some terrible scars. Have you had it yourself?'

'Fortunately yes.'

'Oh, thank goodness for that. Because the last thing
a bride needs on her big day is to have to cover up
chickenpox scars. Well, I suppose we're just going to
have to put that photo shoot on hold till he's better.
I'm so terribly sorry to hear he's unwell. I wouldn't
have hassled you half so much if I had known the
truth. I thought you were just being shy. Anyway, I'm
sure you've got calamine lotion to dab. Please pass on
the very best wishes of *Complete Woman* to your poor
dear man.'

'I will,' I said. 'And I'm sure he'll appreciate it. Better
go. I think I can see David scratching right now.' I
looked in the direction of my empty bedroom. 'Oh,
hang on. There's something I've been meaning to ask
you. Amanda, I was wondering, what would you wear
to an anniversary party?'

'Oooh, now there's a conundrum,' she muttered.
'How about a little white trouser suit with flat gold
loafers and a pistachio silk blouse?'

Yeah, how about that, I thought. 'Thanks, Amanda.
I'll call you as soon as the spots have gone.' I put down
the phone and clutched my head in my hands.

CHAPTER ELEVEN

I n the end I went to Mum and Dad's anniversary party dressed in the navy blue suit I kept for job interviews and a mustard coloured blouse that I pinched from Emma's extensive wardrobe. When I arrived, Mum seemed to have forgiven me for the shock I had given her that morning, but she still disapproved of the outfit.

She herself was dressed from head to toe in baby pink Frank Usher with enough sequins on the bodice for a whole episode of *Come Dancing*. My sisters were in matching stretchy velvet mini-dresses of the kind that I would have thought were vetoed in front of my miserable old Auntie Eileen.

'This is supposed to be a party, Ali,' Mum told me when she saw what I was wearing. 'You look like you've come to do an audit.'

Feeling thoroughly dowdy, I was summoned straight into the kitchen where a veritable production line of vol-au-vents and sausage-on-stick-type things was in operation. Jane was laying the vol-au-vents out on baking trays and Jo was slopping milk from a jug onto the little pastry cases to make them shine. There were already enough completed canapés to feed the five thousand balancing precariously on top of the microwave.

'Who is coming tonight?' I asked, as I filched some cheese and pineapple. 'Billy Bunter and his family?'

'We've had fifty-seven RSVPs,' said my mother proudly.

'Wow. I didn't think we knew that many people. Who?'

'Auntie Eileen, Auntie Maureen, Auntie Gwendoline, Auntie . . .'

'OK. Stop right there,' I said. 'All the maiden aunts, of course. They'll go anywhere for a free sausage. But who else?'

'The people who used to live next door,' said Jo with a wicked smile on her face. 'The Baxters. Do you remember them from when we lived in Saintbridge Road?'

'The Baxters?'

'Yes,' said Jo. 'And Jeremy.'

'Jeremy Baxter?'

'Jeremy Baxter,' said Jo.

'But . . .'

'Mum invited him for you,' my little sister said, exploding with laughter at the thought.

'Mum!!!' I whined. 'How could you?'

You see, Jeremy Baxter was the first boy I ever kissed. As you've probably gathered, he and his family lived next door to my family in the house where I spent my early and most formative years. Jeremy Baxter was a year older than me, which made him a good catch in those days of skipping ropes and Bubblicious. And because my sisters and I weren't allowed to play any further away from our house than the end of the road, I didn't really have much to compare him with. But when I got to junior school and heard him referred to as a dweeb, I quickly stopped trying to make him kiss me behind the greenhouse. By the time I was twelve and he was thirteen, Jeremy had been struck by acne and I never really spoke to him again. The fact that Mum had invited him to this party was obviously divine retribution for the time that I had refused to invite him to my thirteenth birthday party because he had big red pustules on his neck.

'Wonder what he looks like now?' said Jane wistfully.

'I know! I know!' shrieked Jo. 'He's probably spent the past ten years glued to a computer screen. He will be wearing glasses this thick,' she picked up a couple of whisky tumblers to demonstrate. 'And his skin will be like the skin of one of those translucent fishy things that lives at the bottom of the sea and never sees the light of day. He will either be a pathetic weed or he will make Jabba the Hutt look like the latest winner of Weightwatcher of the Year.'

'Don't be so cruel,' warned my mother.

'But I'm probably right, Mum! You know I am,' Jo protested. 'I bet he's still got those disgusting boils on the back of his neck as well.'

'I wonder if he's hairy,' asked Jane. 'His dad was horribly hairy. He had to shave right down to the top of his T-shirt.'

Both my sisters gave an involuntary shudder at the thought.

'Ah well,' said Jo. 'Who cares? It's Ali that's got to look after him if he is a wart hog. Not us.'

'I have not got to look after Jeremy Baxter. I'm not going anywhere near him,' I protested. 'Tell them, Mum.'

'You will not ignore any of my guests,' Mum suddenly exploded. 'You girls may all be almost adults now, but under my roof, you will abide by my rules. And my rules say that you will all be nice to Jeremy Baxter, no matter what he looks like. And you won't make fun of his stutter.'

Oh yes. His stutter. I had forgotten about that.

'I would never m-m-make f-f-fun of s-someone with a st-st-stutter,' said Jo.

Mum twatted her around the head with a tea towel.

Fortunately any further violence was curtailed by the return of our Dad from his first taxi trip to the OAP's home to fetch the pensioners who had been slightly spritlier guests at their wedding thirty years before. My own maternal grandmother was among the first load from The Daisy Lawns Senior Citizens Complex, otherwise known as God's waiting room. When I went outside to help Dad wheel Gran up the garden path in her souped up turbo wheelchair, I noticed to my horror that she was wearing exactly the same dress as Mum beneath her tartan travel blanket. Only Gran had accessorised the chiffon ensemble with a hat. A hat that looked as though it had been made from the tissue paper the dress had been wrapped up in.

'Dad,' I hissed, as we positioned Gran by the fire, but not too close in case the synthetic extravaganza on her head went up in flames. 'She's wearing the same dress as Mum.'

'So?' he said.

Men never understand these things do they?

'So, Mum will be really upset,' I explained. 'She wants to be the belle of the ball. It's her special party. She can't stand out from the crowd if her mother is dressed in exactly the same outfit as her.'

'What are you whispering about?' Grandma asked.

I know you're supposed to love your Granny and all that, but our Grandma Wilson was a cantankerous old bat with ears to match. She could hone in on gossip from 150 yards. And grab the wrong end of any stick you were offering at the same time.

'We were just saying how lovely you look in that dress, Grandma,' I lied. She fluffed out her skirt like a strutting pea-hen. 'Dad,' I whispered even more quietly then. 'Who's going to tell Mum?'

'Where's Josephine?' asked Grandma. 'Where's my daughter? Why isn't she here to greet me like a proper hostess?'

'She's in the kitchen, Gran,' I said loudly. 'She's putting finishing touches to the food.'

'Well, tell her to come out here and make her guests feel at home. I'll have a gin and tonic for a start.'

I could hear Mum coming through to the lounge already. I raced towards the kitchen and blocked her path.

'What's the matter with you?' she asked, as I ushered her backwards down the hall.

'Mum, I don't know how to say this,' I began. Then I decided on the direct approach that would probably get me, the messenger, shot. 'It's Gran,' I blurted. 'It's her dress. She's wearing the same dress as you.'

'What!'

'The exact same dress, Mum. With the matching chiffon scarf and everything.'

'In pink? Or in the blue? They had it in blue too,' my mother said desperately.

'In pink,' I admitted.

'Oh, how could she?'

'She looks just like Barbara Cartland if it's any consolation.'

It was no consolation whatsoever. Mum slumped against the refrigerator with her head in her hands.

Jo burst in. 'Shit, everybody. Have you see what Grandma's wearing . . . It's exactly the same as . . .'

'We've all heard, thank you very much,' said Mum, straightening up and setting her face to 'hard'. 'Well, she'll just have to go home and change into something else, won't she?'

'Mum,' I protested. 'She can't. That means that Dad will have to drive her all the way back to the home. Then one of the nurses there will have to dress her again. You know how long that will take. If she agrees to change at all. You know what she's like. She'll probably take offence and won't come back again after that.'

'You're right,' said Mum sadly. 'Oh, I can't believe it. How could she even afford a dress like this on her pension?'

'She sold that shepherdess figurine you liked so much,' said Jo helpfully. 'She just told me.'

'I don't know why you think that's so funny,' Mum replied. 'She's frittering away your inheritance too.'

Jo clamped a hand across her mouth to muffle the sound of her giggles. Jane had wandered back into the kitchen too.

'The blancmange wants a gin and tonic,' Jane said.

'Ooh, I'll give her bloody gin and tonic,' spat Mum. 'Does she want arsenic in that too?'

'Mum,' I said, in a voice intended to be calming. 'Perhaps it doesn't really matter. Perhaps you can get away with wearing the same dress.'

'What? And have her pretending that we're twin sisters all night? No thank you. She's done this to me one too many times. When I was first seeing your father, she turned up at a dance we were at wearing exactly the same Biba dress as me. I was eighteen. She was forty-two. She kept fishing for compliments about her legs all night long and for about six months afterwards people kept asking me when I was going to bring my big sister out again.'

'Go Gran,' said Jo. I shot her a 'shut-up' look.

'Come on, Ali,' said Mum despondently. 'I suppose you'll have to help me choose something different to wear. I'll just have to take that dress back to the shop on Monday morning and use the money to buy a new Hoover.'

'Never mind, Mum. You'll have a good twenty years to wear whatever you like after she's dead,' said Jo.

'Jo-anna,' said my mother sharply. 'Go and make sure your Gran doesn't choke on the peanuts.'

So my mother's Frank Usher fantasy was consigned to a plastic hanging bag and half an hour later, Mum re-emerged wearing her best navy blue suit. To be honest, I thought she looked much much better. Pink frills had never appeared in *Complete Woman*'s list of fashion musts for the fuller figure.

Mum kissed Gran hello, then returned to the kitchen to fume while my sisters and I were subjected to the usual round of grandparental inquisition.

'Got a new boyfriend yet?' Gran asked me predictably once we had established that Jo's new shoes would probably give her corns.

'Not yet, Gran,' I replied.

'Hardly surprising,' she said, momentarily dislodging her false teeth and pushing them forward so that she looked just like the dog. 'Wearing that horrible outfit. You look just like your mother. If only you'd both inherited my sartorial good taste.'

'If only,' I replied.

CHAPTER TWELVE

The Baxters arrived shortly after the last bus load of toxic grannies from God's waiting room. That is the Baxters minus their youngest son Jeremy. Their older daughter, Jennifer, who had seemed so cool during the early eighties in her ankle length pink tube skirt with her spiked up hair, was very much toned down. Turned out that the teenage rebel had gotten herself mixed up in Marks and Spencer management traineeism and it was all downhill from there. Now she looked like the kind of daughter my Mum had always wished for. Albeit unmarried. Which was a surprise that cheered me up immensely in my sorry position.

'Where's Jeremy?' asked my sister Jo, before even saying hello to the rest of the Baxter family. Seeing Jennifer Baxter looking like a Stepford creation was pretty gratifying but not half as interesting as seeing how the real geek in the family had turned out would be.

'Jeremy will be along later,' said his father. 'He didn't get up terribly early this morning. Looks like he's got a bit of a hangover.'

Hangover? Jo and I exchanged a look of surprise. Later in the kitchen she said, 'Cider. That'll be it. It's what all those computer geeks drink.'

'Still living at home though,' I said smugly.

'Actually,' interrupted Jane, the only one of we three sisters who was actually polite enough to listen long enough to catch the real truth behind the gossip. 'Actually he isn't living at home anymore at all. He's been living in Poland for the past twelve months.'

'Poland? What's he want to live there for?' asked Jo. 'It's cold the whole time.'

'Something to do with his computer job.'

'Oh,' said Jo. 'For a minute I thought he was about to get all exciting. Like turn out to be a spy or something.'

'Ex-pats get a lot of leave apparently,' Jane continued. 'He's back in England for a whole month. Staying with his family.'

'At least now the skinny geek stroke fatty lard bucket question is solved,' Jo interrupted. 'He'll be a fatty lard bucket for sure. This girl from the year above me at school had to go to Poland as part of her language degree. She said there was nothing to eat but potatoes and pork scratchings – or whatever their Polish equivalent is. She came back weighing fifteen stone.'

'If you're talking about Samantha Leeson, she went out there weighing fourteen and a half stone,' said Jane. 'The fact that Jeremy has been living in Poland for a year proves nothing.'

'OK. Let's take bets,' said Jo. 'I'll put a fiver on him being Mr Wobble-bottom.'

'And I'll put a fiver on him still looking thin as a string bean,' retorted Jane.

'What about you, Ali?' asked Jo.

'There isn't an option left for me to bet on, is there?'

'Yes there is,' said Jane, thinking quickly. 'You can bet on him being completely normal.'

'But the odds on that are ridiculous! Do we mean normal, normal? Or do we mean "normal" in the weird sense of the word?' I asked.

'Normal as in you wouldn't kick him out of bed for farting. If he had just paid your credit card bills,' Jo added as a proviso.

'I wouldn't kick a man out of bed for being an axe-murderer if he had just paid my credit card bills,' I told Jo. 'OK. You've got my fiver.'

Jo pocketed all three bills. 'Right, the winner gets all fifteen pounds. Which is just enough to cover the cost of that new *Squeaking Fieldmice* album I've been after.'

'Dream on,' said Jane. 'It's going towards my new Birkenstocks.'

The doorbell rang out again.

'The moment of reckoning is nigh, methinks,' said Jo with a smug smile.

We practically fought each other for the opportunity to open the door then, not to Jeremy, but to the man who lives next door to my parents now. He stepped back in delighted surprise at the sight of three young girls fighting to get a look at him.

'Well, well, well,' he said, smoothing back the three strands of hair that still clung grimly to his shiny head and grinning widely. 'This is quite a welcoming committee. Three lovely young ladies just for me.'

Jo and Jane disappeared instantly, leaving me to deal with old Mr Griffiths' coat and his absurdly continental way of kissing me hello. While his chilly lips were locked to my cheek, I caught sight of another guest meandering up the garden path. Though at first sight, I thought that he couldn't possibly be a guest at my parents' anniversary party. Perhaps something else, something far more hip and happening, was going on further down the street.

The handsome young man was carrying a vast bouquet of roses that by rights only ought to go to the kind of girl who wears Impulse and nothing else. He was dressed in a beautifully cut blue suit, that had a Nehru collar, with a white collarless shirt beneath. No tie. No ridiculous witty cartoon-character printed waistcoat to mark him out as someone who didn't normally dress up for any occasion but snooker tournaments like most of the men in our little town. He was tall, but not gawky. He looked comfortable with his height. He had sun-kissed blond hair that fell into his eyes, just asking to be brushed gently out of the way by a loving hand . . . In short, he was gorgeous.

And he was coming up our garden path!

'Yes?' I asked the stranger, simultaneously pushing Mr Griffiths away politely but firmly and directing him in the direction of the other geriatrics. 'Can I help you? Are you lost?'

'I don't think so,' said Mr Unfeasibly Gorgeous. 'I spotted my Mum and Dad's car parked just down the road there. This is the Harris family's house, right?'

'Right?' I said. I wondered who of the guests already assembled he could possibly belong to.

'Then can I come in? I've brought these roses for Josephine.'

'For Josephine. You mean, for my mother?'

'She's your mother?' he asked in surprise.

I didn't know whether to be offended or relieved that he didn't make an immediate connection.

'Yes, she is.'

'Then that must make you Jo, the little one.'

'Oh no,' I laughed. 'I'm not the little one. I'm Ali. The big one, in fact. In age, I mean.'

'Ali?' Did I see his eyes narrow at my name? 'Ali Harris? My God, you've changed.'

'So have you,' I told him. 'I mean, I don't wish to be rude or anything, but who exactly are you? Are you my mother's toy-boy, come to break the party up by declaring your love for her in front of my father?'

'You don't recognise me?' he laughed. 'I don't believe it. I haven't changed so much surely.'

He certainly had. Whoever he was. I had never known anybody so gorgeous, or with even the seeds of such rampant gorgeousness waiting to sprout after puberty.

'You really don't recognise me, do you, Ali?'

''Fraid not.'

'Well, I'll put you out of your misery. It's Jeremy, Jeremy Baxter.' He thrust out his hand.

OK, OK, I thought as we shook. And the next person to walk up the garden path would be Jeremy Beadle . . .

'But you can't be,' I said. I looked back up the hallway to see if Jo and Jane were sniggering at the top of the stairs, having summoned one of their good-looking mates to pop round and make me think that I had won the Jeremy Baxter bet.

'Do you need to see some ID? Or can I come in anyway? It's not exactly hot out here in the street, you know.'

I stood aside to let him pass.

'Wow,' I said banally. 'You've really changed.'

'You're not exactly the Ali Harris I remember, yourself. What happened to the pigtails?'

'Disastrous perm at the beginning of my third year in senior school. What happened to your glasses?'

'Never heard of contact lenses?'

'What happened to your hair?'

'The miracle of Sun-in. Hey, you used that once, didn't you, and it made your fringe go orange. That was hilarious.'

'Huh. For everyone else,' I laughed. 'What about the time you tried gluing back your ears?'

'Three days in hospital. Thanks for reminding me. And they still stick out, look.' He lifted up a flap of hair.

'My God,' I said, realising how rude I had been. 'I didn't mean to say that. I mean, about your ears . . . It was like we were twelve again for a moment there. I can't believe it. It really is you.'

Jo and Jane had appeared now, and were hovering a couple of feet behind us waiting to be introduced.

'Who is this?' asked Jo worriedly. 'Is he here to deliver those flowers?'

'Don't be so rude,' I said triumphantly. 'Jo and Jane, this is Jeremy Baxter.'

'Ohmigod. It can't be,' said Jo.

But before Jeremy could show her his passport, my mother appeared to rescue him. She took the flowers with a beam.

'Oh, Jeremy, so glad you could make it at last,' she simpered.

'That's a lovely outfit, Josephine,' Jeremy said as she led him through into the sitting room.

'Thank you,' she said. 'One tries so hard not to be mutton dressed as lamb,' she added, shooting a look at her own mother.

'What's wrong with her?' said Jo, as we followed Mum and Jeremy through into the party. 'She's batting her eyelashes at him for heaven's sake.'

'Well, wouldn't you bat your eyelashes at him,' said Jane. 'He's gorgeous.'

'That's a bit of an exaggeration, surely,' Jo protested. 'What do you think of him, Ali?'

I shrugged my shoulders in a non-committal way. 'Well, he's definitely normal. In the normal sense of the word. Where's my money, Jo?'

'Hang on. We don't know that he's completely normal,' Jo protested. 'I haven't heard him speak yet.'

'I thought we were going on physical appearance alone,' I reminded her. 'Anyway, I have heard him speak. And he didn't stutter once.'

'Unbelievable,' said Jane. 'Do you think he's been having some kind of speech therapy?'

'Can't be him,' insisted Jo. 'You must be mistaken.'

'Pay up, Joanna.'

Jo pulled the crumpled fivers out of her pocket reluctantly.

'Great,' I said, folding them into my own purse. 'I might just treat myself to some new underwear.'

'New underwear? What do you need that for?' Jo asked me.

'Perhaps she fancies her chances with Jeremy,' said Jane.

'Jeremy? You've got to be joking. Besides, looking like that, he's probably got a girlfriend already.'

'Or a boyfriend,' said Jo. 'I mean, have you seen what he's wearing. He's definitely gay.'

At that point Jeremy briefly looked up from the conversation he was having with Grandma and shot we three witches by the kitchen a dazzling smile.

'He must have heard that,' said Jane.

'Well,' I found myself saying. 'I hope Jo is wrong.'

With all the guests finally present, the party really started to kick off. If you can imagine a room full of people over the age of fifty doing such a thing as 'kicking off'. Dad had brought the record player out of the attic, to where it had been consigned just six months before, when he finally went CD-crazy, and the old biddies went gaga over his collection of 45s from the fifties and sixties (and 78s too. Have you ever even seen one of those?).

Despite his colostomy bag, Uncle Harry led the dancing as usual. The maiden aunts lined up in a row behind him to do can-can style high kicks, with Jo and Jeremy on one end and Jane and I on the other end of the line to provide some stability. Why is it that the older women get, the higher they seem to want to throw their legs, eh? The room was soon a flurry of beige pop-socks and waist-high knickers. Then one of the biddies fell over of course and the festivities were toned down to a nice game of charades, while Mum busied herself with picking vol-au-vents out of the carpet.

'*Upstairs, Downstairs*?' asked my sister Jo, when Auntie Alice had finally finished a protracted mime that was very nearly the death of her. 'What on earth was that about?'

'Beats me,' said Jane. 'Must have been on at the same time as that "Z-*cars*" thing Uncle Harry was trying to do.'

'Well, I can't guess any of these,' Jo complained. Then Uncle Harry announced that it was her turn to mime and the rest of the room spent three quarters of an hour struggling with a lesser known track by Oasis.

By this time the excitement was way too much for me, so I elected to start tidying up the remains of the buffet. It was a great trick that I had learned over many a family Christmas. When the going gets excruciating, get going into the kitchen. That way, I got out of having to make a complete idiot of myself with a mime of *One Flew Over the Cuckoo's Nest* or, worse still, *The Poseidon Adventure*, while simultaneously winning hundreds of 'good daughter' brownie points because people actually thought that I was sacrificing my own enjoyment to do the hard work. Jo and Jane had never cottoned on, not quite believing that washing-up could ever be preferable to Harris family party games. But that evening I discovered that someone had beaten me to it. Someone was already donning the Marigolds. It was Jeremy Baxter.

'You don't have to do that,' I told him. 'It's my parents' party. Get out there and enjoy yourself with the other guests.'

'What?' he looked horrified. 'No, please, Ali. Let me help you out here. They're still playing charades and I hate that game. I can never think of anything to act out.'

'Ah, so the truth will out,' I said. 'In that case, I don't know if I should excuse you.'

Jeremy got down on his knees with the tea towel clasped between his hands.

'Oh, OK then,' I conceded. 'Just this once. Especially

as I feel exactly the same way. It's the worst game ever, isn't it?'

'I thought that old lady doing *Upstairs, Downstairs* was going to have a heart attack.'

'Don't joke,' I warned him. 'She had a funny turn at the Church barbecue last year. They were playing Pass the Parcel at the time.'

'Pass the Parcel?'

'The stakes were high,' I explained to him. 'The prize was a packet of Maltesers.'

'Now I have heard everything. Listen, do you have any idea how much longer this party is going to go on for? I mean, don't the old dears have to be back in their retirement homes before a certain curfew?'

'Unfortunately, I think they all have late passes tonight. But surely you don't mean to say you're getting bored by all this?'

'It's not that, Ali. It's just that I've been out of the country for a while. I've only got a month here in Brindlesham and there are lots of people I'd really like to catch up with before I go back. Places I'd like to visit. I'd kill for a pint at The Rotunda . . .'

The Rotunda. I winced. After David's fatal infidelity had been revealed I hadn't been able to bring myself to go back to the place where the end of my engagement started. In fact, I couldn't even walk past it these days without needing to burst into tears.

'Is it still the same old place?' Jeremy asked me.

'I'm not sure,' I told him, hoping we could quickly change the subject. 'Last time I went there they had a variety of farming instruments for decoration but now I hear they might be turning it into an underwater-themed bar with topless mermaid barmaids.'

'No kidding.'

'No. I was kidding. I'm sure it hasn't changed at all since you were last there. It's just that I haven't been near the place since December.'

'Oh, found a better place to go?'

'I wish.'

'I take it that Fifth Avenue is still the only club round here then?'

'Not since someone was fatally wounded with a flick-knife there last weekend.'

'Then this party is probably as good as the local nightlife is going to get?'

'Oh, it'll get better. Can you hear that?' I cupped my ear, as if listening for the sound of distant drums. 'They're striking up the conga!'

'Well, what do you say to you and I escaping all this hilarity and going for a coffee somewhere?'

'Me and you?'

I thought that he then smiled a twinkly, flirtatious kind of smile. But I shrugged it off. I had been at the Bacardi and coke all evening, so it was far more likely that he was giving me a simple friendly smile, transformed in my mind into something more by some serious wishful thinking.

'Where could we go?' I asked, ready to bring out the dampeners. 'It's already half-past ten. The only place you can get coffee at this time of night is at Keith's Korn-Fried Chicken, which serves the only cup of coffee I've ever seen that actually has grease swimming on top of it. Besides, I can't leave my mother to deal with all this cleaning up. She'll go spare.'

'You've got to get back home at some point though, haven't you?' Jeremy persisted.

'I was planning to stay overnight.' I continued to shoot myself in the foot.

'Say you've changed your mind. Say I've offered to give you a lift home, but we have to leave immediately.'

I chewed my lip. 'To do what?'

'We'll go to Keith's FC. I can stand the grease and you can fill me in on all the gossip.'

'I'm not sure that Mum will appreciate that. I've got to stay.'

Jeremy shrugged. 'Well, if I really can't persuade you . . . I'm not the kind of guy who asks twice. I'll see you around, yeah?'

With that, Jeremy folded up the tea towel and went to take his leave of my mother. He kissed me lightly on the cheek, making sure that his aftershave would stay in my mind to make me regret being such a chicken for at least the next hour. There was much kissing in the sitting room too. A result of far too much sherry on my Mum's part.

'Ooh, I always knew you'd grow up to be a handsome bugger,' my mother shouted as Jeremy tried to make his way through the groping grannies to the door with his dignity still intact.

'I wish she'd told us that,' said my sister Jane as she joined me at the kitchen window to watch his car drive by. 'He's a dreamboat.'

'Ugh. He's such a creep,' said Jo. 'It was disgusting in there. All those crusty old grannies slobbering over a piece of young flesh. He's only after a spot in their last will and testaments.'

'He seemed genuinely nice to me,' I mused.

'Handsome,' murmured Jane once more.

'Oh, cut it out, you two,' Jo interrupted. 'Mum says she wants one of us to make sure Mr Griffiths gets home in one piece. He's been hoovering up the Babycham all evening. Either of you two girls want to volunteer or shall we just say that the loser is the girl with the most fivers in her possession tonight?'

That was me of course.

'Oh, this takes me back,' said Mr Griffiths as I used every last ounce of strength in my body to heave him over his front step and into his hallway. 'Are you going to help me get into bed now too?'

I settled him on the bottom step of his staircase and found a rather hairy blanket from his grumpy Jack Russell's basket with which to cover him up.

'No, I'm not going to help you get into bed,' I told Mr Griffiths firmly as he grasped hold of my ankle when I made to leave. 'You'll be perfectly fine there.' I'd get Dad to check that he wasn't dead in the morning.

As I walked back up Mum and Dad's garden path to see Grandma flashing her knickers with an impromptu impression of the Follies Bergères, I began to wonder exactly where it was written that the elderly deserve our respect. If only I hadn't been such a good daughter, I mused. Right then, I might have been gazing at a handsome man over coffee at Keith's FC. Though maybe I wouldn't have had the guts. Something about Jeremy Baxter made me feel quite shy.

I rejoined my sisters in the kitchen and we set about washing up. Rather Jane and I set about washing up. Jo just flicked washing-up bubbles at the dog, while she regaled us with an improbable tale about a boy at the local grammar school who had tattooed her name on his arm with a compass and a biro. (She still wouldn't snog him, poor fool.) Then Jane twisted up a tea towel into a painful looking knot as she told us hopefully about the new guy who had just started at her office.

At the bottom of the garden, just about visible from the kitchen window, Dad lit up a well-earned cigar. Mum soon stalked down the path after him, but, for once, instead of berating him, she simply wrapped her arms around him and gave him a kiss. Quite a passionate one for a pair of oldies.

'There's someone for everyone,' said Jane wistfully, as she drew down the blind on this happy little scene.

And then I was hit with a crippling vision of my special someone with someone else.

CHAPTER THIRTEEN

'You need to get out more often,' said Emma later that week, as she cleared a space for herself on the sofa amongst the detritus of too many TV dinners.

'I get out every day,' I assured her.

'You drag yourself into work looking like someone who should be en route to the out-patients department,' she corrected.

'I went to my parents' anniversary party on Saturday.'

'Family occasions do not count as "getting out". When I say "getting out" I mean, you need to start rebuilding your social life. Your single social life. As a single woman.'

'I'll do it in my own time.'

'That really isn't good enough, Ali. If you wait until you think you're ready to get out on the town again, my grandchildren will be coming round to help you get into your wheelchair. Why don't you come out with me tonight?'

'What? To The Rotunda? To face the humiliation of everyone in that place knowing that David has gone back to Lisa Brown again? Or to watch you getting chatted up by life-forms slightly further down the evolutionary scale than amoebas? I'd rather stay in and watch *You've Been Framed* thanks all the same.'

'Has it never occurred to you that there might be more to my life than the eternal search for Mr Right?' she reprimanded.

I had to admit that it hadn't. Men were Emma's *raison d'être*, surely. Just as they were the *raison d'être* of every woman I knew. Except for the two lesbians I had encountered in my media class at college, and they were just as sad about the search for eternal companionship in their own special way.

'I've got myself a hobby,' Emma said proudly. 'So that when the time comes, I can at least say to myself that whatever else happens I got something out of my life other than a lifetime's worth of tips about man-catching mascara that only works for girls who are supermodels already.'

'A hobby?' What was one of those? I seemed to vaguely remember having one at school. For the purposes of French conversation class, at least.

'What is your hobby?' I asked sarcastically. 'Stamp collecting? Train-spotting? Or best-friend baiting?'

'It's first aid, actually.'

'First aid? That's not a hobby, Emma. That's something you have to do to get a senior job at McDonalds.'

'Actually, it is a hobby. Probably the most noble hobby at all, since one day, it might actually come in useful. You'll be laughing on the other side of your face when I save you from choking to death,' Emma added.

'What? On my own disbelief?'

'OK. You just lie there and scoff, Ali Harris. And

scoff,' she added, referring to the bag of tortillas I had just opened. (My second that afternoon.) 'Believe me, the feeling of satisfaction I get from tonight will last far longer than the feeling you get from that junk food. Though your waistline might taunt you with the memory of your choice of pastime for years to come.'

That was it. Emma knew that the best way to scare me into action was the 'lingering evidence' threat. I folded over the top of the tortilla bag to keep them fresh and then put them out of reach on the coffee table.

'So are you coming?' she asked.

'Well, first aid doesn't exactly burn calories, does it?' I reasoned. 'I'll be all right if I just watch soaps and don't touch the tortillas.'

'But you'll be better than all right if you walk to and from the health centre and spend half an hour or so puffing into a pair of plastic lungs.'

'Yuk,' I said, remembering the horrible wax-faced doll we had been forced to practise artificial resuscitation on at Brownies. I always seemed to have to go after the girl with a cold sore.

'The male to female ratio is going to be two to one,' Emma continued. 'Since tonight is training night for the sea-scouts.'

The sea-scouts? What a temptation! Little did Emma know that she was making it much easier for me to resist. A pair of plastic lips to kiss in front of a bunch of spotty sea-scouts? It was bad enough that she was expecting me to get up from the chair I was sitting in, let alone put make-up on. Because I would have to put make-up on if there were going to be members of the opposite sex present.

'It's too much effort!' I wailed.

'Anything worth anything in this life requires a certain amount of effort!' Emma replied. 'Please come with me.'

'You'll have more fun on your own.'

'I won't,' she whined, and I had a sense that the truth was about to be outed. 'I need you there. I can't go on my own, please come with me.'

'Take Marvin.'

'I can't. I have to take a girlfriend. If I take Marvin, the situation will be too . . . too ambiguous.'

'And why should that matter?'

'I need to make it clear that I'm single.'

'To do first aid?'

'No,' Emma finally cracked and owned up to it. 'If I'm going to get off with the instructor.'

Turned out that Emma had taken a fancy to one of the doctors at the accident unit on the night of Marvin's dinner party and had recently discovered that he also gave first aid classes. She'd heard him discussing the fact with another doctor and then used all her powers of research and deduction to find out the 'when' and the 'where'. After that, it was easy to join up. But then her courage deserted her, which was where I came in. As moral support stroke straight man to her glittering wit. (She'd just been reading an article about men who like funny women.) There was also the fact that, in my post-David state, I would make her look like Cameron Diaz even if I dressed up in Gucci stilettos and a ballgown to her jeans.

Emma was pathetically grateful when I agreed to accompany her after just another hour of haranguing.

So grateful in fact that I managed to secure a promise that if I ever had a date again in my life, it would be while wearing her favourite silk Armani jacket.

Before we left the house, Emma slapped up. Lipstick, eye-liner, foundation, the works. I just combed my hair, figuring that if, by some fluky chance, I met the sea-scout of my life, he would probably appreciate my fresh-faceness as a sign that I would be happy to get wet in a catamaran with him.

'Jeans or leather skirt?' Emma asked for a fourth time as I waited for her in the hallway.

'Whichever you feel most comfortable in,' I said, again for the fourth time. I was wearing my jeans.

'I'll wear the leather,' she said. Hardly the most comfortable garment in her wardrobe. It took two of us to zip the thing up.

When we finally got to the hall where the class was being held, with Emma changed once more into some sensible trousers, Emma then stopped me from charging inside while she said her mantra. Not a high-brow Buddhist mantra, you understand, but 'You are irresistible', for what seemed like three hundred times.

'Am I glowing yet?' she asked when she had finished.

'No. But you are going mad. Do you think that chanting business really works?'

'Well, I did it before I went into the corner shop last Friday and the assistant winked at me when he gave me my change,' she told me.

'He always winks,' I said, hoping I wouldn't disappoint her too much. 'He's got a lazy eye.'

'Christ! Just blow my confidence to pieces why don't you?' she snapped. 'Now I'll have to do the other chant to compose myself again.' Cue, 'I am a warm and wonderful human being, ad infinitum'. In the old days she would simply have had a fag.

'Are we ready yet?' I asked while she finished off her chanting with a nice long 'ohm'. It wasn't exactly warm standing where we were in the car park. The sea-scouts had already arrived in a minibus and filed inside with regimental precision. Then the instructor arrived, in his dashing little blue Metro, and started to unload huge crates of equipment from the tiny boot.

'There he is! It's Doctor Martin!' Emma swooned.

'Like the boot?' I asked.

'Don't you dare make that joke.'

'Well, do you think we should help him?' I asked, seeing him buckle beneath the weight of a box of bandages. 'That'd earn you some brownie points.'

'Good idea,' Emma agreed. And we were about to offer our services when someone beat us to it. Someone who looked incongruously, for our little town, like an extra from *Baywatch*.

'Who's that?' asked Emma as she pulled me into hiding behind a wall.

'I don't know.'

'God. I knew it. I bet it's his girlfriend. I knew he had to have a girlfriend. It just wasn't possible that someone as gorgeous and wonderful as he is could be single and just waiting for me to come along. Let's go home.'

'Now hang on a minute,' I said. I had come round to the idea of learning how to do bandages again and was quite looking forward to it. 'Let's not jump to conclusions. She didn't arrive in the same car as him.'

'You're right,' said Emma, face brightening.

'So she obviously doesn't live with him. And if she was his girlfriend, don't you think she would have thrown her arms around him dramatically as soon as she saw him?'

'She kissed him,' said Emma gloomily.

'On the cheek. That means nothing. It was a social kiss. Marvin kisses everyone.'

'You're right. She's probably a lesbian.'

'Well, I wouldn't have gone that far, but I think it's pretty safe to say that all is not lost at this stage. Let's get in there.'

As if on cue, the *Baywatch* babe, bid the doctor farewell and headed off in the opposite direction. The change in Emma's facial expression was like the sun coming out after a weekend of rain.

'He's dreamy, isn't he?' Emma sighed as we watched the brave doctor carry the artificial resuscitation dummy inside alone. 'I just wish I was that doll.' We walked into the hall behind him and settled ourselves at the back of the class.

'OK, everybody,' said Dr Martin in his loud instructor's voice. 'It's time for you to partner up and practise your bandaging skills on each other. If there's anyone left without a partner, they can come up here and practise on me.'

Emma made a lighting fast calculation of the number of people in the room. There was an odd number of sea-scouts and before I knew it, she was pushing me in the direction of a gangling looking lad with a spot of germoline hovering like a jellyfish over his top lip.

'I think it's a good idea to mix with people you don't know at these things, don't you?' she said by way of an explanation, then she proceeded to battle off all-comers who wanted to partner her, until she was left standing alone, and looking faintly forlorn, in the middle of the room.

'I seem to have missed out in the rush for partners,' she said sweetly.

Dr Martin waved her towards him and bade her take a chair on the platform. She wiggled her way up to it and gave me a wink.

'Now, I'm going to demonstrate the sling just one more time,' he told the class. Emma looked ecstatic as he bound her arm to her chest. Then Spotty Lip started on me and managed to stick a safety pin right into my funny bone.

'Want me to kiss it better?' he asked.

'I wouldn't bother if I were you,' I said primly. 'I've got impetigo.'

'Last new trick of the day,' Dr Martin announced when I had managed to bind Spotty Lips roving hands safely behind his back in the strangest sling I've ever come across. 'Now the thing that most people are most interested in when they come to a first aid class is arguably artificial resuscitation. Otherwise known as "the kiss of life",' he added, raising a ripple of titters from the sea-scouts.

'Do we need to stay with our partners for this?' Emma asked hopefully.

'No, because if you practise on a normally breathing human being, you might do them an injury.'

'Can't you just pretend to blow?'

'That wouldn't be very good practice, would it? Now, ladies and gentlemen, if you'd like to form a circle around me and Dolly here, I'll show you how it's done.'

Emma was sidelined for the wax-faced doll and joined me at the back of the group.

'Lucky bloody dummy,' she muttered. 'Did you see me up there, Ali? How do you think I did? And how did he look when he was bandaging up my ankle? I knew I should have worn a skirt instead of these stupid trousers.'

'If everyone would be quiet, perhaps I'll only need to explain this once,' said Dr Martin suddenly. Emma snapped to attention.

'Perhaps I should feign a faint,' she said a moment later, when the authority of his command had worn off. 'Then he'd have to give me the kiss of life, wouldn't he?'

'He might make one of the sea-scouts do it instead,' I warned.

'I suppose you're right. And it could be that one with the cold sore.'

'You mean the one you left me in the capable hands of just now? I tell you what, I'm getting in front of him in the queue for the blow-up doll,' I told her.

'Me too. Yuck. Think I'll just put on a protective layer of lipstick to fight off the nasties.' She began to apply a carmine coating to her pout. In the meantime, we had missed all of Dr Martin's instructions and Emma didn't have a clue what she was supposed to be doing when Dr Martin said: 'Emma, perhaps you'd like to come up here and have first go?'

The sea-scouts parted to let her through, and suddenly Emma was face to face with Dolly.

'Haven't you got a male one?' she joked.

'I'm afraid that first aid situations aren't exactly gender specific,' Dr Martin said humourlessly. 'Off you go.'

'OK,' said Emma. 'As long as she doesn't use her tongue.' Then Emma went straight to it. She put her lips, tightly closed together, against the dummy's lips and stayed there, locked in a chilly embrace, for what seemed like a couple of minutes. When she pulled away, smiling broadly, the room exploded into laughter.

'Now that was a great demonstration of a real lip smacker,' said Doctor Martin, as he wiped Emma's bright red lipstick off the dummy with just the faintest hint of disdain, 'but rather than the kiss of life, that would have been a kiss goodbye. Why?' He pointed to a sea-scout for an answer.

'Because she didn't tilt the dummy's head back,' said the first.

'Because she didn't check that the dummy's airways were clear,' said the next.

'And because she didn't actually blow,' said Dr Martin. 'Remind me not to drown in your garden fishpond,' he added as she tried to fade back into the ranks.

'Why didn't you tell me what to do?' Emma snarled at me.

'I didn't know either. I couldn't hear what he was saying because you were so busy yacking.'

'Quiet at the back,' said the sea-scout master, obviously thinking that the muttering was coming from two of his charges. 'The harder you concentrate, the more quickly we can be out of here and back to the hut.'

'Well, I'm going now,' said Emma.

'You can't,' I protested. 'Everyone will notice.'

'So? I'm never coming back here again. I've never been more humiliated in my life.'

'But this is your hobby, Emma.'

'Was my hobby.'

'Just hang on till the end,' I persuaded her. 'When he was bandaging your ankle, I really did think I noticed a flicker of interest.'

'You did?'

'Yeah.'

'Really? Well, maybe I should stay until this bit is over.'

In fact, we stayed for an hour after class. Emma used the excuse of her poor technique to have Dr Martin explain the finer points of artificial resuscitation at least eleven times. But when I thought I'd try to help her out by reminding her that we had an appointment at the pub – thereby giving her the perfect excuse to ask him to join us, I thought – Dr Martin made his excuses. He was going to be on call, he said, all night long.

'He's so selfless,' Emma swooned as we waited for the bus to take us home. 'Making sick people well all day, then teaching us first aid in the evenings and helping the sick again all night long. I would never have believed that anyone could be so altruistic.'

I nodded.

But then her face fell. 'Because nobody could possibly be that altruistic, could they? Do you think he was just fobbing me off with that "on call" business?'

I shrugged.

'Oh, God. I'm going to die,' she whined. 'Why does this always happen to me? Why do I always throw myself headlong at men who aren't interested in me? Why, Ali? Why?'

'I don't know. I mean, if I knew, I probably wouldn't keep doing exactly the same thing myself. Look, he probably was on call. I just shrugged because my own love life has made me feel so pessimistic about romance.'

Emma hugged me. 'I'm sorry. I was forgetting all about what you've had to go through these past few weeks. How are you feeling right now?'

'Much better actually,' I had to admit. 'You know, it was a really good idea of yours to drag me out. I was almost enjoying myself when I got that ankle bandage right.'

'Good. Then we'll go to the class again next week.'

'I don't know about that,' I said warily.

'But you said you enjoyed yourself.'

'I did. It's just that there's not much opportunity to pull at a first aid class, is there? I mean, you've got the instructor to work on, but I've just got the sea-scouts. I was thinking we might have a proper girls' night out instead. No bandages. No plastic dummies. Just lots of margaritas and a place where we can find men over the age of consent.'

Emma grinned. 'I know just the place.'

'Great. Because I think it's about time that Ali Harris faced the world again. Properly.' I got to my feet dramatically and waved my arms about in the air in an approximation of a dance. 'Lock up your sons, Ali Harris is back!!'

But before Emma had time to give me three cheers, someone opened that trapdoor beneath me again and I was plunged back into misery. Crossing the road and scuttling to get out of my sight as quickly as they could, was a painfully familiar couple. My arms dropped weakly to my sides as I recognised David's car and watched him open the passenger door for her. My successor. Lisa Brown.

'Don't look,' said Emma, covering my eyes with her hands.

'It's too late. I've already seen them,' I squeaked.

Where had they been? I wondered. The only place around there worth visiting, if you didn't have to go to the hospital, was the wonderful Chinese restaurant that David and I had discovered after I picked him up from the accident unit on the day when he nearly killed himself by attempting to mend the photocopier with wet hands. Unless Lisa Brown had had a terrible accident (and I promise that I tried to stop myself from wishing it) David must have been taking her to our special restaurant. The restaurant where the proprietor knew me by name and had taught me how not to use my chopsticks like a peasant. (I had to hold them right at the ends apparently, preventing me from picking up even the smallest mouthful – no wonder Chinese women are so short.)

'He's been taking her to our special places,' I sobbed.

Emma, in her inimitably tactless way told me, 'They were probably her special places too before you came along.'

I stared after David's brakelights until his car disappeared round the corner. It was too late. I was filled with melancholy once more. The good work that Emma had done by taking me out was all but negated by the terrible reminder that my fiancé was not mine anymore. He was getting on with his life with someone else. The pinnacle of my recent social life had been an evening practising life-saving snogs on a dummy.

When we got home, I crawled beneath my duvet on the sofa and had Emma bring me cups of tea and listen

to my rantings about David until the Open University
came on.

'We will both find true love yet,' Emma insisted.
'We're young.'

'I'm twenty-six.'

'We're attractive.'

'That's a matter for debate.'

'We are positive-thinking women.'

'I'll let you know in the morning,' I said.

And so another week crawled by in an agony of trying not to think about David and avoiding calls from
Amanda at *Complete Woman* who was eager to know
whether his spots had cleared up. On the Thursday
evening, I was summoned to supper at the family
home so that my mother could convince herself that
I wasn't starving/drinking/working myself to death
in my misery. Jo, having unravelled herself from the
clutches of someone who looked not unlike my dreaded
sea-scout at the bottom of the driveway, came into the
house full of news.

'I just saw Jeremy Baxter,' she said.

'So he's still in town,' Jane sighed.

'For another four weeks. He said he's decided that
he's missing England so much that he got an extension
on his leave.'

'He's probably got a girlfriend over here,' said Jane
wistfully.

'He wasn't out with her, if he has,' Jo explained.
'He was in The Rotunda with a couple of other lads.
No girls.'

'In the where?' called my mother from the kitchen.

'The Rotunda,' said Jo innocently before she could stop herself. Realising too late what she had just let slip, her face had all but drained of blood when Mum stormed into the sitting room to shout, 'I thought I told you never to go near that place again. You're not eighteen years old yet, Joanna Harris. Do you want to bring the police round here to have you up for underage drinking? And it's a school night. You're out of control, you are. You all were. I don't know where I went wrong with you girls. I'll never forget the shame of the Top Shop incident.'

I groaned at the memory.

'But I was never in trouble with the police,' said goody-goody Jane.

'Only because they didn't catch you,' replied our mother. 'You look like you're on drugs, wearing those horrible black clothes all the time. Come here,' she said to Jo. 'Open your mouth. Let me see if you've been drinking.'

CHAPTER FOURTEEN

I left my mother smelling my sister's breath and went home to the flat, where Emma was reading a first aid manual.

'Got to get to the head of the class,' she explained.

When I had tested Emma on the ABCs of artificial resuscitation (don't quote me on that), we set the next Saturday evening as the date for our girls' night out. It was going to be a big one, we decided. Epic. Lock up your sons and all that. So naturally we would have to go shopping that Saturday afternoon for the kind of dresses that would make us feel like man-eaters and look like supermodels. As opposed to feeling like men and looking like super-noodles, which was the usual scenario.

Three o'clock, Saturday afternoon. We were just walking out of Miss Selfridge with our bags of swag when Emma spotted him.

'There he is,' she shrieked, digging her fingers into my sleeve.

'Who?' I asked, squinting into the crowd. I really needed to get my eyes tested.

'Doctor Martin. He's over there. Just coming out of Marks and Spencers. Is he on his own, Ali? My God, please tell me he is on his own. I can't bear to look.' She covered her eyes with her fingers.

I hadn't even managed to locate Dr Martin yet.

'He's in the navy blue puffa jacket,' said Emma impatiently. 'He's got aviator-frame sunglasses on and he's carrying three shopping bags. Two from M & S and one La Senza.'

I was just taking in the fact that Emma had managed to memorise such a lot about her hero's appearance in such a short space of time when the gravity of her words hit her like a skip full of bricks. 'La Senza!' she groaned. 'That's an underwear shop. Who's he buying underwear for?'

'Himself?' I said helpfully.

'From La Senza? Not likely.'

'They do boxer shorts.'

'Yeah. But they wrap them up in all that smelly tissue-paper stuff. No man in his right mind would go in that shop unless he had to. Unless he had to buy a present for his girlfriend,' she intoned ominously.

'Now we don't know that,' I began.

'We do. We do know that. It was that girl in the car park after all. They are an item. Oh, God. He's crossing the road now. He's coming this way. What shall I do?'

'How about saying hello to him?' I suggested.

'No way,' she said, looking at me as if I were the mad one. 'Let's hide.'

With that, she dragged me backwards by my shirt collar into Dixons and had me duck down behind the stereo equipment. It was probably not the best place in town to hide out from a man, I thought, and sure enough pounds worth of stereo equipment flying. Straight off the shelf and into Dr Martin.

'My God! What are you doing here?' Emma squeaked as the poor man tried to defend himself from falling hi-fi pieces.

'Shopping,' he said flatly. 'What are you doing here? Trying to create a first aid emergency?'

Emma gave a single hysterical snort of laughter, then the three of us smiled stiffly. Meanwhile, assistants scuttled around us, picking up their stock and trying to assess the damage.

'Are you hurt?' asked Emma hopefully. 'I know how to do bandages.'

'No. I'm not hurt. But . . . er . . . I've got to go now or I'll be late for work. Will I see you girls on Thursday night?'

Emma gave the thumbs-up sign. 'You bet. Wouldn't miss it for the world.'

Then Dr Martin nodded, in a worried way, I thought, and scurried out of the shop like a cockroach out of the kitchen when you turn on the lights.

'In a hurry to get to the hospital,' Emma explained to the shop assistant, whose face had gone from helpful to thunderous in the space of her blunder. 'He's a doctor, you know. Everything OK?'

'Actually, no,' said the assistant. 'And I'm afraid you'll have to pay for the damage.'

So, we ended up going home without the drop-dead outfits we had searched so long for to pay instead for a brand new stereo. Albeit a brand new stereo without a door on the tape deck, and whose CD player would only work properly if the whole thing was set on a slope. But Emma didn't seem to mind that she had just inflicted four hundred pounds worth of damage on her already heaving credit cards.

'He asked if he'd be seeing us on Thursday,' she muttered again and again like a mantra. 'That must mean he wants to see me.'

I wasn't going to burst her bubble.

But so much for our girls' night out. Emma tried to cry off a big session for financial reasons, then we got home to a message on the answer-machine from Marvin, saying that he had been stood up by a dishy German bloke he met at the local Turkish Baths and so we had agreed to let him join us for dinner. When he finally turned up, an hour later (owing to a problem with getting his highlights to take or something), there followed a bitter squabble about whether it should be Indian or Italian. Garlic in both, which would not be good for our pulling power on a Saturday night, but Marvin insisted that the garlic in Indian food seems to linger longer. So Italian it was. You never can tell when your ship is going to come in, said Marvin, flicking his fringe.

Between us, we polished off two bottles of red wine while we picked at our pasta (Emma in love, Marvin on a diet, me simply too depressed to stuff myself that night), but we didn't feel the effects of our overindulgence while we sat around the checker-clothed table. We were too serious to get giggly anymore, having got to that stage in our lives where conversations about who we fancied quickly became heart to hearts about whether we should start going for older men who, due to the dual forces of receding hair and expanding waistlines, might be inclined to settle down before we girls started to need HRT.

'He's a doctor. And they tend to settle down more quickly than, say, lawyers or men who work in the City,' theorised Marvin on Emma's Dr Martin. 'It's all that death and disease they encounter. Makes them realise that life is short and you need to seize the moment with both hands. If you catch him, Emma, I reckon you could be engaged by Christmas.'

'Do you really think so?' she purred delightedly.

'I'd place a bet on it. So when are you seeing him next?'

'Thursday night. At the first aid class.'

'Then you need to formulate an action plan right now. What are you going to be wearing?'

'My black jeans, I thought. With that stretchy lace top. The red one.'

'Jeans?' said Marvin, pulling a face. 'What about that leather mini-skirt you bought? Much sexier.'

'I know. But we have to spend a lot of time on our knees, dealing with that stupid artificial resuscitation dummy,' she explained. 'I'd have a load of sea-scouts looking at my bum.'

'What a delightful thought,' sighed Marvin. 'But where's your problem with that anyway? You go out in a short skirt to a club don't you.'

'That's different. I don't have to bend down and look proficient in a club.'

'Perhaps you should. You might get more offers.'

And so it went on. Marvin and Emma bickering about the best way to catch a man, with me staring wistfully through the steamed-up window onto the rain-swept street outside. I was having one of those 'this time last year' moments that are particularly dangerous in the newly single.

This time last year, I thought, David and I had been on a ski-ing trip to Andorra. Neither of us had ever skied before, but David had been invited on the trip by his boss and was keen to ingratiate himself by going along. Unfortunately (or fortunately in my case), he had sprained his wrist first time out on the slope and we didn't have to reveal the extent of our ski-ing ignorance. David and I spent the rest of the week sight-seeing. And it was on that trip that we decided that our next big holiday, our honeymoon, would be somewhere fabulously hot. Barbados was the first choice. We were neither of us snow bunnies.

Of course, that particular train of thought brought me crashing back to earth with the reminder that I was currently the holder of a ridiculous title and a fabulous prize holiday in the blazing sun. Amanda still needed to know the truth. A week after the Hot Stuff Heat Rub incident, David had only called to leave a message on my answer-machine requesting the swift and safe return of his Fun Lovin' Criminals CD. We weren't about to get back together any time soon.

'Ali,' Marvin said, bringing me back from the land of the loveless. 'How much was your starter?'

We split the bill precisely. As we always did. We used to do the straight three-way thing but Marvin and Emma would always end up rowing over who had drunk the most expensive brandy. With the bill paid, the waiter helped Emma and me on with our coats and Marvin looked extremely disappointed when the waiter merely handed him his.

'I thought I was in there,' Marvin explained as he sneakily took back one of the four pound coins we had left as a tip.

'He wasn't gay,' said Emma flatly.

'What? With that haircut? Darling, the boy was as camp as a row of tents.'

'That haircut was camp? Looked perfectly normal to me.'

'No no no. It was parted in a special way,' Marvin explained as we meandered to the bus stop. 'It's something we gay men are attuned to. One of those little signals that lets you know when you're of a similar mind. Now, you see that tall guy getting out of the blue car over there?' He pointed to a man locking up a smart Mini metro.

'If you tell me he's gay, I will kill you,' said Emma suddenly. Then she grabbed my arm as she started swooning. 'It's him. It's Dr Martin. He's the one I've just been telling you about.'

We froze on the pavement to watch Dr Martin checking that he had locked up his boot.

'Oh my God. He's gorgeous,' said Marvin.

'But is he gay?' asked Emma.

'One can only hope.'

Emma swiped at him with her handbag. 'Marvin. Stop messing me about. Is he gay or not? Bear in mind it could be the end of me if he is.'

'OK,' Marvin sighed. 'I don't think he is. Though his hair is a bit on the tidy side for a straight guy.'

'Has to be tidy for work,' I said, hoping to avoid a fatal argument between my two favourite people.

'So, aren't you going to introduce us?' Marvin asked Emma. Dr Martin had finished checking his car security and was starting to walk away. He hadn't even spotted us, I hoped.

'I can't introduce you,' Emma wailed. 'It'll be too embarrassing. My mouth goes dry. I get all tongue-tied. I just can't talk to him like I would to any other normal person. He's like a demi-god or something. I need an excuse to go up to him.'

'An excuse? Right, let's sort this out once and for all,' said Marvin firmly. 'Emma Wilson, prepare to be a heroine.'

Emma and I shared a split-second worried glance before Marvin went into his world-beating impression of a man in terrible pain.

'Aaagh! Aaaagh! My ankle!' he shrieked. 'These high heels! I should never have worn them. My ankle! I think I've just broken my ankle! Can anybody help?'

Marvin staggered realistically from one side of the pavement to the other, then, as if some terrible fate had been tempted, he staggered straight off the pavement and into the path of an oncoming car.

'Screeech! Crash!!! Aaaagh!!'

Only this time it was for real. Dr Martin was on the spot in a second. I half expected him to strip off his anorak to reveal a white coat beneath. Emma meanwhile was frozen where she stood in shock. Marvin had always claimed that he would do anything for her, but this . . . This was truly ridiculous.

'Is he dead? Is he dead?' was all Emma could ask as she peeped at me through her hands.

'He's not dead,' said Dr Martin reassuringly. Marvin swooned on the pavement beneath the doctor's healing hands. 'But he does need to go to the hospital for a check-up and so, by the looks of it, do you. I think you might be suffering from shock.' He put his arm around Emma's shoulders in a gesture of concern and she nodded in a distant kind of way. She was so shocked in fact, that she had completely forgotten how to simper.

'How's the driver of the car?' I asked. 'Is he all right too?' I couldn't bear the thought that our stupidity might have been the cause of an innocent stranger's injury. The driver of the bright yellow Megane had been sitting behind his wheel all along. Too afraid to move, I supposed.

'He's fine,' said Dr Martin, after administering a quick health check through the driver's window. 'He's a little shocked, understandably. But thankfully, he was just reversing his car into a parking space, so he was going pretty slowly and hasn't suffered any whiplash. What was it that made your friend stumble into the road anyway?'

Emma declined to answer. Instead, she limped in the direction of the newly arrived ambulance (her own 'fuck-me' boots were killing her) and I followed. Then, while I was sitting on the tailgate of the ambulance, watching Marvin being loaded onto a stretcher, the driver finally got out of his car and suddenly Emma wasn't the only one suffering from shock.

'Alison Harris, we meet again,' he said. 'Didn't think it would be because I knocked one of your pals over, though! Sorry!'

'Who's this?' asked Emma brusquely.

'Emma, this is Jeremy Baxter.'

So, that night at the accident unit was a bit of a result

for both of us. Emma got to be bandaged lovingly by her hero. (The boots had rubbed her heel quite raw.) And I got to meet Jeremy Baxter again, without having to contrive some terrible reason to get his phone number from my mother. Fortunately, Dr Martin had been right and Jeremy had come away from the catastrophe without a scratch. Marvin hadn't been quite so lucky. He really had hurt his ankle, having managed to get his big fat foot stuck firm beneath the back wheel of Jeremy's car. And as for his new suede boots? Well, they were a total write-off.

'One hundred and twenty quid, he says they cost,' moaned Emma later. 'And he expects me to pay for them.'

'Why?' Jeremy asked innocently.

'Emma spilt spaghetti sauce on them in the restaurant,' I said quickly, thinking it was probably best not to go into the real details of that evening's events.

'Yeah, well. I suppose it was worth it,' Emma conceded. 'Since he's agreed to go for a coffee with me.' She grabbed my arm excitedly. 'Dr Martin. Tonight. When he finishes his shift. God, I hope no one else has a car accident tonight.'

Lovely Emma. Always so concerned about others.

'I guess I'm going home on my own then,' I said, since Marvin was being kept in overnight for observation. He didn't mind too much, since he rather fancied the hunky male staff nurse who would be giving him a sponge bath in the morning. 'Hope the buses are still running.' I added.

'I could give you a lift,' Jeremy said suddenly.

'But your car . . .'

'Is fine. Only evidence that anything happened to it

at all is a bit of leopard-print suede snagged on one of the wheelnuts.'

'Go for it!' Emma mouthed to me from behind his back.

'Is it on your way?' I asked him.

'I think I can make a little detour for you.'

Emma gave me a wild thumbs-up sign.

'Come on.'

I gathered up my bag. 'I'll see you later,' I told Emma.

'Not if I can help it,' she replied.

So I left Emma flicking through the pages of *Woman's Own* and followed Jeremy Baxter out to his car. It was a spotless, brand new Renault Megane in bright yellow with body-coloured bumpers.

'Everyone's got to have one little indulgence,' Jeremy told me as he pulled on his leather driving gloves. 'Where will it be, Cinderella?'

'Nowhere much to go at this time of night,' I shrugged. 'How about The Trout? That sometimes has a late licence.'

'Sounds perfect,' said Jeremy. And we sped off into the night. Carefully observing the highway code as we went, I noticed.

CHAPTER FIFTEEN

So it was that I found myself in The Trout on a Saturday night.

The Trout was what we girls called an old man's pub, full of regulars who had their own tankards hanging from the shelves behind the bar and their own special chairs that only the truly stupid would dare to sit in uninvited. Having said that, The Trout had once been quite a hot spot for Brindlesham youth. That was for all of two weeks in 1989, when our regular den of iniquity was under serious surveillance from the police for suspected underage drinking. It was easy to convince the one-eyed barman at The Trout that our sixth-form college library cards were in fact the official over-eighteen ID cards that the local Council had tried so hard to push.

'I used to come in here quite often,' said Jeremy, as we settled ourselves in a seat by the fire that had recently become vacant through the sudden death of some old git. 'I never quite felt at home in The Rotunda,' Jeremy continued. 'Never quite fitted in with the cool crowd. All the misfits came in here.'

'Well,' I told him. 'We girls from the "cool crowd"

didn't dare come in here because of all the Goths and Heavy Metal freaks. They looked so hard. Especially the girls.'

'That's the irony, you see,' Jeremy laughed. 'You can pretty much guarantee that someone who has a penchant for black leather and skull and crossbones earrings is a vegetarian, or a librarian, or both. It's camouflage. Self-defence. So many people are not quite what they appear to be.'

'That's deep,' I sighed.

'I remember seeing you in here once though,' Jeremy continued. 'You were wearing a short green dress, with some kind of scoop neck.'

'I remember that dress,' I laughed. 'I kept having to pull it down to cover my knickers. I can't believe you remember me in it though.'

'How could I forget? You looked fantastic that night. I thought about walking up to you and introducing myself. But I was afraid that you wouldn't remember who I was, let alone actually want to talk to me. Besides, you were with that ugly bloke you used to go out with.'

'Ugly? Oh, you must mean Stu Chivers.'

'That's the one. Whatever did you see in him?'

It was hard to remember. But I tried to find an explanation. 'I'm not sure really. I suppose it just seemed glamorous at the time. He was older. He had a Vauxhall Chevette when every other bloke I knew had a BMX bicycle. And he was always saying that he was going to get a tattoo.'

'Did he?'

'You've got to be kidding. He cried whenever he had to pull a sticking plaster off.'

'I've got a tattoo,' Jeremy whispered, leaning in close.

'Now that I find very hard to believe.' I murmured, as I wondered if he could feel the heat from my burning cheeks as he crossed that strange interpersonal space line from friendly to 'with intent'.

'You'll just have to ask me if you can see it later on. Shall we go?'

'Go?' I looked at my watch reflexively. 'Where to?' I felt a nervous rumble deep in my stomach. Was Jeremy Baxter propositioning me?

'Your carriage awaits, madam. It's not quite a Vauxhall Chevette but how about we just get in my Renault and go where the mood takes us?'

As it was, the mood, and the late hour, took us to Keith's Korn-Fried Chicken.

'I'm so sorry about the way we acted when you first showed up at my parents' party the other evening. We were so rude,' I said between picking the last of a chicken supreme out of my back teeth.

'It doesn't matter,' said Jeremy. 'In some ways, it's comforting to know just how much I have changed. I was a total geek when we last met. There's no denying that. The way people react when they see me is recognition of a long time in surgery.'

'Plastic surgery?' I squeaked.

'No, not really. Just a long time in the gym.'

'Must have been a very long time,' I said before I could stop myself. 'I mean, I wish I had your dedication.'

'By the look of you, I thought you already did.'

I felt a blush spread across my cheeks. 'You don't mean that.'

'I do. You've changed a great deal too, Ali. I never

imagined that the skinny little tomboy who lived next door would grow up to be such a fabulous, beautiful woman. So, er . . . curvy.' He made a little demonstration of my figure with his hands that had me going magenta.

'Oh, Jeremy,' I squeaked.

'I like a curvy girl. Women these days are so concerned with being thin they diet away all the bits that men are actually interested in. But not you. You're perfect.'

Boy, was I glad it was dark in that car. I fanned my neck with my collar.

'Jeremy,' I said. 'If I hadn't known you since we both started primary school, I might think that you've been flirting with me all night.'

'Thank God, I thought you'd never notice.'

'You mean, you have been flirting with me?' I said in astonishment.

'I've been flirting with you since we met on the doorstep of your parents' house last Saturday evening. I prayed that fate would hurl us back together before I had to leave England for Warsaw again.'

'Jeremy . . . I . . .'

'What is it, Ali? Listen, before you start to get all heavy-hearted and introspective about things, I know you've just split up from your fiancé and I know that you're probably still feeling a little raw about that, but if it's OK with you, I'd really like to see you again before I go back to Poland.'

I didn't know what to say. I was still trying to digest the fact that someone had already briefed him on my sex life. (Rather my non-existent sex life.) The culprit was my mother undoubtedly. Then I started to wonder whether she had offered up the information unsolicited or whether he had actually been interested enough to ask.

'Just for a coffee or something?' Jeremy persisted.

Was he really asking me out? On a proper date? Or a sympathy one?

'In fact, if you don't think I'm being too forward, I could use a coffee right now.'

'But we've just had one,' I said.

'Bit small weren't they? Why don't you make me a bigger one at your place? You can ask me to go whenever you like.'

Go? I didn't want him to go. Ever. Instinctively, I looked up at the windows of my flat in an attempt to guess whether Emma was in and up. The flat was dark. She was still at the accident unit.

'OK,' I said. 'Come in.'

'This is a beautiful flat,' said Jeremy as I guided him into the sitting room, which was frankly rather tatty.

'Don't say that,' I warned him. 'It might make me think that everything you've said so far has been a lie. Tea or coffee?'

'Coffee. Tea is for grandmas.'

'Well, I'm having tea. Camomile tea in fact.'

'Why? It'll make you go to sleep.'

'Which is what I need to do. I've got to go to Mum and Dad's for lunch tomorrow.'

'Your parents won't mind if they think you're late for a good reason.'

'Such as . . .'

'Such as catching up with your childhood sweet-heart.'

'Childhood sweetheart?' I exclaimed. 'Since when were we childhood sweethearts, Jeremy Baxter?'

'Since you promised yourself to me, Valentine's Day 1979. Don't you remember? At the time I think I may have churlishly turned the generous offer down, but since then I've definitely changed my mind.'

I remembered now the Valentine's card that I had slipped under the garden fence at the point where Jeremy and I would sometimes sneakily exchange pieces of chewing gum. This was long before the days when smoking was the worst thing I could do in my parents' eyes. I had never been allowed chewing or bubble gum as a child for fear that I would swallow it and clog up my lungs with the goo. Jeremy's lax parents actually bought him cola flavoured Bubblicious.

'You broke my heart then,' I told him jokily. 'I don't know if you get a second chance.'

'But I was young,' he protested. 'Besides, when we went to secondary school, I seem to remember that it was you who broke off all channels of communication because I just wasn't cool enough for your new found friends, like Stacey Mitchell and Darren Applefield. By the way, what happened to them?'

'Darren's warehouse manager at Safeway and Stacey is married with two point three kids and a labrador. At least she was married when I last saw her. Apparently since then she's been passed over for the barmaid in her husband's local.'

Jeremy tried to suppress a smug smile. He didn't manage it.

'Still think Darren's cooler than I am?' he asked me.

'That's not fair,' I replied. 'I haven't seen him for years. Besides, you are a computer geek.'

'I'm a computer geek with the whole of Eastern Europe in the palm of my hand,' he corrected. 'Don't knock it.'

He took hold of my hand then and pulled me down onto the sofa beside him.

'I claim my prize,' he murmured. 'February 14th 1979.'

'Jeremy!!!'

Before I could protest, he had fastened his mouth onto mine and was fast working his tongue in between my teeth. As his hand crept up the back of that disgusting mustard shirt of Emma's, I finally managed to forget the Jeremy Baxter who had once shown me his collection of worms and let myself relax into his embrace.

Soon, his feet were no longer proprietorially on the floor and we were both fully prone on the sofa. He had my skirt up round my waist and my knickers halfway down my thighs. My bra was undone and he was tweaking my nipples into erection. All this without taking his mouth away from mine for even one breath. He was amazing.

'Wow.' In the end it was me who pushed him away before I suffocated. 'Wow! Jeremy!'

But I was looking into the eyes of someone different. No longer Jeremy Baxter, but Jezzie B. The intelligent, charismatic, if somewhat arrogant, computer genius stroke businessman with the whole of Eastern Europe at his feet. And he wanted me. I could tell. He was drooling.

'I want you so much,' he said, confirming my suspicions. 'I want to sink my teeth into the firm white flesh of your glorious breasts.'

It sounded painful but I guessed that it was meant to be romantic so I nodded.

'I want to drink deeply from the cup of your hidden desire.'

Was that something to do with oral sex, I wondered? I wasn't overly familiar with the concept, let alone the metaphors. I nodded again.

'I want to give you a night of passion that neither of us will ever forget, when you are alone again here in Brindlesham, and I am in my lonely cell in the never-ending winter of Warsaw.'

'Oh, Jeremy.' I was just too flustered to be poetic back.

'Let me take you, Alison. Let me take you to places where you have never been. Let me awaken parts of your body that didn't even know they were still alive. Let me take you to the doors of passion and lead you further inside the dark warm corridor of love.'

Oooh, sounded good to me. And all the time he was keeping up the physical persuasion. I hate to say it, but I was starting to feel like the heroine in the trashy novel that Emma kept under her bed for fallow periods in her love life. My breasts were growing rosy with the first flush of desire. I was wetter than a haddock's bathing costume. (OK, so the author of Musical Affairs might have put it better than that.)

'Er, Jeremy,' I said, when he flung my purple knickers across the room to hang rakishly from a standard lamp. 'Do you think we might go into the bedroom before we start?' I was convinced that someone would walk in on us.

'I will go with you to the ends of the earth, my princess,' he replied smoothly. And with that, he scooped me up and carried me through to the bedroom as though I was light as a feather and not nudging ten and a half stone. He carried me all the way to the bed that I had last shared with David Whitworth. And somehow, slipping between the covers that I had not even changed since David left in such a hurry was the biggest thrill of all.

CHAPTER SIXTEEN

Well, they say that the best sex is the kind you can laugh about afterwards. No sooner had Jeremy jumped into my bed than he jumped straight back out again.

'Aaa-choo!!!' He sneezed so hard that he had to check his contact lenses hadn't flown out. 'Aaa-choo! Aaachoo! Aaa-choo!'

He staggered backwards against the dressing table and rubbed violently at his eyes.

'What's wrong?' I cried clutching the duvet protectively to my chest.

'You've got a cat, haven't you?' he said accusingly.

'Yes,' I told him. 'Fattypuss. Are you allergic to them or something?'

'If I get into contact with the hair it brings me out in blotches,' he confirmed.

'Oh.'

'It must have been on your bed,' he said, looking at the duvet as though it was covered in fleas.

'Well, yes,' I said. 'She always sleeps in here during the day. I'll shake the duvet out, if you like.'

'That won't make a difference, Ali. I can't get in there with you again. My throat might swell up and suffocate me in the night. It's happening already.'

'You're suffocating? But that's terrible! What can we do?'

Jeremy opened the window and hung his head outside to get some air.

'Well, we can't go back to my place,' he said. 'I don't think Mum would approve of me bringing a girl home, even now I am twenty-six and a half.'

I clutched the duvet more tightly around my body. With Jeremy standing on the other side of the room, I was rapidly going cold again. Just my luck to find a man with an allergy to girl's best friend.

'The cat isn't in the room now,' I tried. 'Won't you start to get used to it in a minute?'

'Get used to it? No,' he wheezed. 'I'll be dead first. I've got to get out of here, Ali. I'm sorry. I've got to go.'

'You were OK in the other room,' I reasoned. This was not going as planned.

'I did feel a bit sniffly even then. Isn't there a room in the house where the damn cat hasn't been?'

'Well, she won't go in the bathroom after Emma got her with the shower hose one morning,' I tried.

'We can't do it in the bathroom. What if one of us slips on the tiles?' he said sensibly.

'Oh,' I said, disappointed. I'd always wanted to try it in the shower. But then I had a sudden flash of inspiration. 'Hey. She doesn't go in Emma's room at all,' I told him. 'Fattypuss and Emma don't get on that well, you see.'

'Great. Let's go into Emma's room.'

'But . . . but what if she comes home?' I asked, suddenly thinking better of the whole idea.

'I don't care. Emma can sleep in here. We'll leave her a note. Nothing is going to stand in the way of my desire tonight. I have to have you, wherever we are.'

'Oh, Jeremy,' I sighed.

He risked asphyxiation to pick me up from the bed – a little less manfully this time – and as he carried me through the door he sneezed and knocked my head against the doorframe. But I was so excited I barely felt the bump.

Next hurdle was finding a pen that worked to leave a note for Emma. The last thing we wanted was for her to burst in on us when we finally got going. The three ancient biros in the pot on the window-ledge had long since run out. In the end, I resorted to using my electric blue eye-liner pencil, snapping it in half as I scrawled, 'In your room. Use mine.'

'Fantastic, fantastic,' Jeremy muttered as he shuffled me quickly into Emma's bedroom. I tactfully flicked her fancy frilly knickers off the bed into a dingy corner and closed the door behind us, much to the disgust of a doleful Fattypuss who had thought she might try to follow.

'Sorry, Fattypuss,' I told her in my head. 'But there are some nights in a girl's life when she needs more than a flatulent old tabby.'

And so, at last, I was about to do it. I was about to do it with a man who wasn't David. I was momentarily exhilarated by the thought. Then it hit me that I was about to do it with a man who didn't know and love my lumps and bumps. (Actually, there was little evidence that David had loved my lumps and bumps either.)

And I was terrified. Perhaps I should try to put it off, I thought, wrapping the duvet more tightly around me. Until I could afford that Dior Svelte. I could fob Jeremy off with a tale about not being ready to dive into a sexual relationship again, the usual thing. The wait would probably drive him wild. Only problem was, the wait was driving me wild too. Without wishing to be too descriptive, I had started to feel stirrings deep inside even during that disgusting meal at the chicken shack. I couldn't wait until my thighs were in shape before we did it. That could mean waiting forever.

Instead, I did the next best thing to exercising for six months before embarking upon a new affair, I casually rolled over Jeremy and made a grab for the bedside light switch, intending to black the room out. But instead of pulling the light-switch, I managed to pull the whole thing off the table, and Emma's beautiful antique tiffany lamp-stand was soon a mess of smashed ceramic on the floor.

'Shit,' I said, jumping up to clear away the mess.

'Forget it,' Jeremy thundered, hauling me back onto the bed. 'We'll buy her another one.'

'There isn't another one, that lamp was unique.'

'And so am I,' said Jeremy testily. 'So have me now, or you won't have me at all.'

As it was, it all happened rather quickly after that. At least we were in the dark.

'What's this?' Jeremy asked me afterwards as he ran a gentle finger over my bright pink scar.

'I had my appendix out for Christmas. Didn't sew me up again very tidily, did they?' I added, trying to defuse the situation with a joke.

'I think it's beautiful,' he murmured, as he planted a row of kisses along its length.

'You don't really mean that,' I said, pushing his head away and rearranging the duvet so that I was covered right up to my neck.

'I do mean it. Every inch of you is beautiful, Ali. Even the bits that are damaged,' he pulled the duvet down again.

'It's a scar,' I said flatly.

'Yes. But it's our scars that make us interesting, don't you think?'

'I've never thought about it like that before.'

'Well, you must, Ali,' said Jeremy, kissing his way up to my belly button. 'A scar shows that you're a woman of experience. I could see that in your face too. In the way your eyes are slightly crinkled at the corners. Laughter lines.'

My hands flew up to check automatically. Crows' feet. Damn. I was only twenty-six.

'You've lived life to the full,' Jeremy continued. 'You've known happiness, but you've also known tears.'

You can say that again, I thought, making a mental note to buy some more miracle-working eye gel.

'Physical perfection betrays a lack of those emotions that make a human being wonderful.'

'Do you really think so?' Funny how physical perfection was still what most of us went after.

'I really do,' he promised.

CHAPTER SEVENTEEN

But when I woke up the next morning the bed was empty. I should have known that all that stuff about scars and personality was just so much flannel, I berated myself. It was just a wicked way to get into my pants. One that I hadn't met before, granted, having hitherto only been out with the kind of seductive Neanderthals who relied on the pulling power of their souped-up cars. I was just about to call the Samaritans and ask whether being deserted twice in just over a week was some kind of miserable record when the bedroom door creaked open and there stood Jeremy, with breakfast laid out on a tray. And not just breakfast. He had used an empty Perrier bottle to make a vase for a single red rose. Albeit a plastic one, nicked from the naff bouquet on the bathroom windowsill.

'Good morning, Sleeping Beauty,' he said. 'Hope these are your cornflakes.'

'Jeremy, you're still here,' I exclaimed.

'Of course I'm still here.'

'I know but . . .' Get a grip on yourself Ali, said a voice deep inside me. Acting like you're always being deserted is a sure way to put the idea of running away into a man's mind. 'But I thought you might have rushed home to be with your parents today,' I continued. 'What with you only having a month left in the country and all that.'

'I still feel like I have a lot more catching up to do with you.' He set the tray down on the floor beside the bed and slid his hands beneath the covers to caress my thighs. I wriggled in a mixture of excitement and discomfort. The night before it had been pretty dark and I had been quite pissed. Now, in the cold light of day, things might suddenly be quite different. I figured that Jeremy Baxter wasn't one of those rare men who hadn't heard about cellulite and didn't recognise it when they jiggled it.

Jeremy slipped off his shoes and slid under the covers beside me.

'Well,' he asked. 'Aren't you going to help me take my clothes back off?'

I didn't get a chance. Before I even had Jeremy's belt buckle undone, we were rudely interrupted. Emma had obviously come straight from the front door to her room without reading my note. She hadn't been home all night.

She was halfway through taking her dress off when she noticed that she wasn't alone.

'Ali! What are you doing in here?'

'I needed to borrow your room.'

'Well, you can get right out again. I didn't get a wink of sleep last night. I had to wait in the accident unit until half past two for Ashley to finish work. That's his name, Doctor Ashley Martin. Wonderful isn't it? Anyway, he got tied up in stitching up some idiot guy who'd been in a pub brawl. If they're going to fight, let them bleed, I say. But when Ashley finally got free he more than made up for it. He took me to this special doctor's cafe place. It's open all night long . . . So they can get pissed whatever time their shift finishes.'

She obviously hadn't noticed that Jeremy was sticking out from both ends of the duvet.

'So we got completely trolleyed,' Emma continued, as she turned her back on me and unhooked her bra. 'Then we went back to his room in the medic's quarters and he spent the rest of the night explaining the finer points of female anatomy to me. I tell you, it was fantastic.'

'Emma,' I squeaked. 'Keep your knickers on.'

'What do you mean, keep your knickers on? I'm only telling you what happened with Ashley. I'm not in a bad mood even if you are hogging my bed.'

'No, Emma,' I said more slowly. 'I mean, keep your knickers on. Literally. And your dressing gown. I can't wait to hear the rest of the gory details of your night with the doctor, but do you remember how I didn't go home alone last night? How I met up with an old friend who offered to give me a lift?'

'Oh yeah,' said Emma with a disgraceful leer. 'What happened there? You're a bit of a dark horse aren't you, Ali Harris? Where did he take you? Was it worth a ride in a Renault Megane? I saw you getting into it from the accident unit window. Did he choose it himself? Or is he some kind of travelling salesman?' She pulled a face of thinly veiled disgust. 'Weird dress sense too,' she added.

At which point Jeremy poked his head cautiously out of the duvet and said, 'Hello.'

Emma shrieked and clutched her dressing gown to her chest.

'You've got a man in there!'

'Yes, I've got a man in here. That's what I've been trying to tell you since you walked in. I left you a note on the kitchen table.'

'Well, that's a great place to leave me a note. How was I supposed to find that?'

'You usually go into the kitchen when you come home,' I protested.

'Yeah. But this time, I didn't. God, how embarrassing.' She snatched up her sweatshirt. 'What are you doing in my bed with a man anyway? Do you get some kind of weird kick out of doing it under other people's duvets?'

I made a throat cutting gesture at her then, as I saw Jeremy's hand appear from beneath the duvet and grope about on the floor for his socks. While I argued with Emma, I could tell that he was pulling them on.

'Uh-hm,' he coughed politely while Emma spouted on about the best place to leave a note for her if I ever needed to take liberties with her property again. And would I mind washing the sheets when I'd finished? And what on earth had happened to her lamp?

'I think I should go,' said Jeremy, slipping from my side, gathering his remaining clothes and fleeing before I could protest.

'I'll call you later, Ali!' he shouted as he slammed the front door behind him.

Emma shut up for long enough to look surprised.

'What's up with him?' she asked innocently.

'Perhaps he didn't feel welcome,' I snorted. 'Look,

Emma, I'm sorry I used your bed without asking, but you did the same the night that you got hideously drunk and wet yours. We couldn't stay in my bed because Jeremy is allergic to cats and Fattypuss had been sleeping all over my duvet again. And I'm really sorry about your lamp. But couldn't you have made yourself scarce for half an hour? Couldn't you see that I was in the middle of something?'

'I don't want to think about that,' she quipped.

'Emma!' I flew at her like an angry cat, claws out. 'You scared him away with your horrible comments about his car.'

'I did not. You heard him. He said he'd call you.'

But suddenly, a wave of doubt washed me out into an ocean of despair. 'He can't call,' I told her pitifully. 'He doesn't have my number.'

'Idiot! I didn't know that.' We both flew to the bedroom window to see if we could catch his attention.

Emma shouted after him, 'I didn't mean to be rude about the Megane. I was just jealous. I've never been out with a man who had anything more than a bicycle. And I'm not really angry about the lamp.' But Jeremy either didn't hear her, or he had chosen to ignore us, and moments later, his beautiful yellow Renault was sailing around the corner and out of my life. I was desperate. 'How could you do this to me?' I asked my former best friend.

'It's not the end of the world,' she promised me. 'He does know where you live, after all.'

'Yeah, but . . . But he can't just come round, can he? That's like, way too formal. He'll never do it.'

'He will if he wants you. You know he will.'

'Perhaps he doesn't want me. If he did, he would

have made sure he had my number before he left, right? Oh, Emma. Why did you have to be so rude about him?'

'If his skin's that thin, I've probably done you a favour,' she said, as she ran an inspecting eye over her duvet cover and started to pick up the remains of her lamp.

'This is so unfair,' I whined, then I flopped down onto her bed again and began to plough my way through a rainforest's worth of tissues.

'Honestly, Ali. By the time he gets home he'll have forgotten about my snide remarks. Philip Allard went out with me for two years after I called him "Radar" because of his ears.'

'You were only twelve at the time. And he's since committed suicide.'

'OK. So I've really cocked up again, haven't I?' Emma asked. 'Still, look on the bright side. At least my intervention has forced you to ration yourself. It's given him something to look forward to. To make him come back.'

'If you think that really works, then you should have been around last night,' I told her miserably.

'You mean, you've already done it with him?'

I nodded

'Bloody hell, Ali. That was a bit quick, wasn't it?'

'He is an old friend.'

Emma's eyes narrowed. 'Hang on a minute. That Jeremy, wasn't *the* Jeremy we were talking about last night? At the restaurant.'

'Jeremy Baxter? Yeah. It was him.'

Suddenly Emma exploded with laughter. 'Oh my God, Ali. Talk about scraping the barrel. Jeremy Baxter!

I didn't even recognise him. Did he have those awful boils of his on his you-know-what?'

'No,' I said flatly. 'He didn't.'

'I can't believe it. Old Boily Baxter. Just wait till I tell Shona about this.'

'What is there to tell her? He's changed. You saw him.'

'Yes, but not without his clothes on. They could be hiding a multitude of sins. You'd never let on, would you?'

'I assure you they weren't. Anyway, what does it matter. You've ruined everything, Emma. You've finished it all before it even started. I'll probably never see him again.'

She pulled a comically guilty face. 'I've probably done you a favour.'

'Well,' I said, getting out of bed and wrapping myself in my tatty towelling dressing gown. 'I wish you hadn't. I'm having a bath now.'

I locked myself in the bathroom and tried to steam out my rage. But I was just sinking into the warm soup of bubbles and bath oils when the telephone rang. Instinctively, I tried to struggle out again, just in case, by some fluke of flukes, it was for me. I twisted my ankle on the bathmat in my hurry.

'Oh hello, how are you?' Emma trilled in her flirtatious voice. Might have known it would be for her, I thought miserably. I had one foot back in the delicious bath when she called out mischievously, 'Ali, it's a man for you!!'

My heart beat a path to my mouth. He had got my number. Already. Somehow Jeremy Baxter had tracked me down. It wouldn't have been that hard, of course,

since there was such a thing as directory inquiries and I
had taken the precaution of being listed therein for just
such an incredible occasion.

'Hello,' I said breathlessly into the receiver. Keen but
cool, I hoped.

'Oh, hello, love,' said my Dad, sounding a little
surprised at my keenness. My heart plummeted back
into my boots. 'Your mother told me to call. Wants me to
remind you that you're expected over here for Sunday
dinner.'

'What?' I said, unnecessarily snappily. 'Did I really
say I'd be over today?' I knew I had, but I still was
hoping that I could get out of death by lunch by pleading
ignorance.

'I think so. At least that's what your mother says, and
she usually knows. Your grandmother's coming too.
Shall I pick you up on the way back from fetching her
from the home? That'll give you another hour to get
ready.'

My shoulders sank. My heart sank. My so recently
hopeful spirit suddenly resembled the *Titanic*. That
day had started off with the promise of a romantic
twenty-four-hour bedathon, now it was rapidly turning
into the kind of Sunday that Morrisey used to write
miserable songs about. Sunday lunch with Gran. Hang
out the flags.

'I'll be ready in an hour, Dad,' I told him.

At least I wouldn't be able to sit and stare at the phone
if I wasn't at home. But by the time I had hung up on
Dad, Emma was already in my bath-water.

'Thought you would be ages on the phone,' she
explained as she rinsed my new deep conditioner out
of her hair. 'You don't mind, do you, Ali. Only Ashley

doesn't have to work this afternoon and he's taking me out to lunch.'

He would be. Funny how there's such a thin line between your best friend and the person you hate most of all in the world sometimes.

'I'm having lunch with my Grandma,' I said, despondently.

'Ah well, chin up,' said Emma. 'Can't be too much longer until you see the will now.'

'That's no consolation,' I told her. 'As far as I can tell, the front-runner for her fast-dwindling fortune is still the family dog.'

CHAPTER EIGHTEEN

In fact, the dog was sitting in the front passenger seat of Dad's car when he arrived to pick me up (Fattypuss spat her disdain from the safety of my bedroom window). Gran was in the back of the car, wearing another Barbara Cartland rip-off with matching hat and handbag.

'Couldn't resist it,' she explained to me, as she ran a shaking hand over the beaded bodice. 'Pink goes so well with my colouring. So I thought, what the hell. I've always hated that bloody shepherd boy ornament your grandfather bought me. May as well flog it and wear the proceeds instead.'

'Which shepherd boy?' I mouthed to Dad.

'The Meissen,' said Dad, somewhat desperately.

'And there was just enough money left over for me to buy a lovely present for my favourite grandchild.'

Which one of us was that, I wondered for a foolish second. Jane, Jo or Ali? The answer was, of course, the dog.

'Don't you think it looks wonderful with Berkeley's fur?' Gran continued. Berkeley obliged me with a

closer look at his new collar as he slobbered half my
foundation off with his big pink tongue. The tag was
engraved. And it was silver. Tiffany silver. I quickly
estimated that that stinking mongrel was wearing a
choke chain that had probably cost more than my old
engagement ring.

'It's lovely, Gran,' I said with all the good grace I could
muster. I could tell that Dad was already plotting to
pawn it as soon as he had taken her home again.
We could say that it had slipped off over Berkeley's
pea-brained head while he was out on an extra long
walk.

So, as you can imagine, from the very start I knew
that Sunday lunch was going to be a nightmare. Mum's
tight-lipped smile when Gran pointed out Berkeley's
new collar reached new heights in the 'barely containing
a scream' stakes. Jo was in a sulk because Dad was
refusing to lend her the money to buy a motorbike.
Jane was in a panic because her insurance company
exams were less than a week away.

Only Berkeley seemed truly at ease that Sunday
lunchtime. He sat at Grandma's feet, occasionally
poking his nose out from beneath the table for a scrap.
Berkeley would even eat Brussels sprouts if Gran was
offering them. Such a fickle dog that one.

'Gran, you will lend me the money to buy a motorbike, won't you?' Jo said when the conversation found
another one of those natural pauses that never seem
to end.

'What's that, dear?'

Gran was selectively deaf and, right then, she
wanted Jo to repeat her request to better enrage my
mother.

'A motorbike, Gran,' Jo obliged.

'Don't be ridiculous, Jo,' interrupted my mother. 'You know what your father and I think about that.'

'I'm not asking you and Dad,' said Jo. 'I'm asking my Gran.'

'Well, your gran doesn't want to be bothered with things like that. She hasn't got money to burn, you know. Not living on her pension.'

'Who's she?' said Gran. 'The cat's mother? I may have entered the third age, Josephine, but I am not finished yet. I can hear perfectly well. And I've got plenty of things left to sell to raise money. What kind of motorbike do you want, my darling?'

Jo grinned in triumph. 'Just a small one. To start with. I only need about five hundred pounds.'

'That's not fair,' Jane piped up suddenly. 'I needed five hundred pounds to retake my insurance exams. No one would lend any money to me then.'

'Let's stop all this talk about money,' said Dad bravely. 'It's Sunday. God's day. There's no place for money talk today.'

'What's he on about?' Gran asked my mother loudly. 'God's day? He's a religious bloody nutter, he is. I always knew you should have married that other one. You know, what was he called?'

Mum went slightly red and a little vein began to pulse on Dad's temple.

'Marvin Shinshanker,' Jo obliged. 'The man from America.'

'Yes, the one from America. Now he was always going to make something of himself. You wouldn't be stuck here today if you'd married that Marvin Shinshanker. Your poor old mother wouldn't have to worry about giving her granddaughter five hundred pounds if you'd married Marvin Shinshanker.'

'You wouldn't have any granddaughters at all if I'd married Marvin Shinshanker,' Mum pointed out. 'He was as queer as a nine-bob note.'

Jane and Dad both smirked.

But Gran hadn't finished.

'Didn't seem all that queer when he came to see me.'

'Mother, you didn't.'

'Well, someone had to console him after you decided to throw away your life on this bloody loser. What have you done to these sprouts, Josephine?' she added seamlessly. 'Taste like bullets.'

'If only they were,' said Dad.

Gran fixed him with her good eye. 'I beg your pardon, young man?' And we waited for all hell to break loose.

Then the phone rang. You should have seen us. We were like five greyhounds. Me, my sisters, my Mum and Dad all raced to answer the phone, praying that we would be the lucky one. Praying that the caller would give us an excuse to escape the wrath of Gran.

Jo got it. She had the youngest legs after all.

'Hello?' she said breathlessly. Then, with a look of disbelief on her face she exclaimed, 'My God, Ali. It's for you. And it's a man.'

I took the receiver from her hand and the world seemed to go into slow motion as my family drifted back to face their fate in the dining room. I held my hand over the receiver as Gran squawked 'What are we having for dessert?' and thanked God for the gradual decline of short-term memory with age. A disaster had been averted by senility.

Who would it be? David? Marvin calling from the

hospital to say that he needed picking up since he couldn't walk on his jippy foot?

'Hello?' squeaked the receiver.

I had almost forgotten that there was actually someone waiting for me on the other end of the line.

'Oh, hello. Who is it?'

'You don't recognise me, Ali? Crikey, it's only been half a day since we were in bed together.'

'Jeremy?'

He must have called as soon as the last mouthful of his mother's torturous Sunday lunch passed his lips.

'Jeremy, I didn't expect it to be you. How did you know where to find me?'

'It didn't take that much detective work, Ali. Though I didn't actually expect to find you on this number. I thought I'd get your home number off your mum. You didn't let me have it, did you? And if the truth be known I feel a bit of an idiot now. I suppose you didn't give me your number because you didn't really want me to ring you.'

'Oh, no, no, no,' I protested, a little too keenly in all probability. 'I . . . er . . . (I wanted to tell him I'd been thinking of nothing else since he left but that would have been sad . . . and my family were listening). I'm glad you caught me here,' I said instead. 'I was going to track you down myself.'

'Good. Because I am missing you so much already,' he said seductively. 'I thought about you all through lunch. Every time I lifted a glass to my lips, I could smell the rich warm smell of your body on my hands.'

I squirmed very slightly at the thought.

'When Mum brought out her famous raspberry pavlova, all I could think about was that pavlova, your beautiful flat stomach and not having to use a spoon. I want you, Ali. I've been wanting you all day and I don't know how much longer I can stand to be without you. It makes me hard just thinking about seeing you again.'

'Jeremy,' I murmured, fanning my neck with my collar. 'I'm at my parents' house.' And the dining room had gone silent while my family strained to hear my private conversation.

'I know. I'm sorry. I'm being a naughty boy. But it's just so difficult for me to keep these feelings under control. I've never met anyone quite like you, Ali Harris. You stir me deep inside. You really do. I just think of your beautiful body and I need to explode.'

'Oh.' I put my hand up to my burning cheek instinctively. This was getting a bit embarrassing.

'Don't keep me in suspense, my darling,' Jeremy continued. 'Can we meet again tonight?'

I glanced across at my family. Five interested faces peered out from behind the slightly open dining room door.

'Yes,' I said. 'Yes. I guess we can.'

'How about we go out for dinner?' he asked. 'Most of what I had at lunchtime ended up in the dog. I couldn't eat for thinking about you.'

'Where can we go? It isn't exactly Egon Ronay central round here.'

'How about The Aspidistra?' he asked. 'I hear that's pretty good.'

'So do I,' I gasped. 'If you're a Rockerfeller. It's so expensive, Jeremy. I don't know . . .' The Aspidistra was so posh it had even been visited by Michael Winner! Not so posh that it had turned him away again, though.

'Stop right there. Forget the money. I'm the man in

charge of Eastern Europe, remember? And before you say it, Ali, we're not going halves. After what you gave me last night, I think I'm going to be owing you dinner for the rest of your life.'

'Really?'

'Really. Alison, you were like a tigress. A tigress that hasn't been fed in weeks.'

'Make that years,' I said, suddenly viewing the whole of my relationship with David as an emotional famine compared to that one night of bounty with Jeremy.

'Well, I'll be round to fetch you from your place at eight-thirty. Make yourself look special, my darling. Shouldn't take you more than thirty seconds.'

I put the phone down and floated across to the dining room.

'Who was that?' my sisters asked.

'I'm going out for dinner with Jeremy,' I told them.

'What? Jeremy? Jeremy Boil-face Baxter?' Jo asked.

'The very same.'

'Urgh. I don't believe it! He's disgusting. He's got warts and boils all over him.'

'Not anymore, he hasn't.'

'Ooh,' said my mother. 'This is a nice surprise. He's a lovely young man, Ali. Very eligible. You go and have a good time.'

'Just make sure you don't blow it by dressing like a bloody nun again,' said Gran.

Emma was in again when I went home to change. Her lunch with Ashley had been cut short by some inconsiderate buggers staging a motorway pile-up that had him bleeped into ER halfway through dessert.

'I'm sorry about this morning,' she said, looking sheepish.

'You're forgiven,' I breezed. 'He called me.'

'He called you? Where?'

'At Mum and Dad's house. We're going out tonight. To The Aspidistra.'

'My God. Better make yourself beautiful then,' Emma said. 'You look like you've been sleeping on a bed of nails.'

'Do I?' I sat down on the sofa and ran my fingers through my hair distractedly. 'I feel fabulous. He's so romantic, Emma. He already calls me "darling". Isn't that just fantastic?'

Emma put the tub of ice-cream she had been eating from straight down on the newly polished coffee-table.

'He calls you "darling"?' she repeated.

'Yes. And Sugar-lump and Sweetie-pie.'

'Well, just make sure that he's not calling you those names so that he doesn't have to remember your real one before you invite him to Antigua.'

I'd almost forgotten about that.

CHAPTER NINETEEN

'I'd like you to come to Antigua with me.'

Jeremy's eyes grew to the size of saucers in seconds.

'Antigua?' he repeated incredulously. 'You mean the Antigua? In the West Indies?'

'Yes. The very same. I've won a two week holiday there. All-inclusive,' I gabbled. 'It was first prize in a writing competition held by a women's magazine called *Complete Woman*. I'm meant to be leaving on Thursday morning, but the person I was supposed to be going with has dropped out.' That was putting it nicely.

'Dropped out? Of two weeks all expenses paid in Antigua? That other person must be completely mad,' said Jeremy.

'Yes, well. He had his reasons,' I said, thinking it best that they were glossed over right then. 'Would you like to come instead?'

'Like to come? I'd love to come. I can't believe you're really asking me. But shouldn't you be taking Emma? She is your best friend, after all.'

'I know,' I sighed. 'But the person I take has to be

a man. You see, there are a couple of complications, Jeremy. To do with the competition. If you want to come with me, I'm afraid that I'll have to ask you to do me a little bit of a favour first.'

'Fire away,' he said, settling back into the armchair as if I couldn't really ask him for too much right then. We had had a wonderful meal at The Aspidistra (which went on his company credit card) and had talked like friends who had known each other forever. We had, of course, known each other for almost ever, but what I really mean is that it was as though we had liked each other for all that time too. Now he probably thought I was going to ask him if he could find somebody to look after my cat Fattypuss while we were away.

'You'll have to do a photo shoot with me,' I told him. 'A kind of makeover thingy, for the magazine.'

'A makeover? You mean with stylists and stuff? No problem,' he said, laughing and smoothing down an eyebrow. 'In fact, I've always fancied myself as a bit of a model. Is that it? Is that the favour?'

I smiled nervously. 'I'm afraid it's not. The difficult bit comes next.' I sat on the arm of the chair he had chosen and twisted a lock of his hair in my fingers in an attempt to be especially appealing. 'Jeremy, if you want to come on this holiday with me, you're going to have to pretend to be my fiancé.'

There, I'd said it. Now for the fireworks. And the point blank refusal to cooperate with my hairbrain scheme.

'Your fiancé?' he repeated slowly and his face grew slightly pale. 'Alison, we've only really known each other for a couple of days. I mean properly known each other, not counting when we were kids, of course.'

'I know, Jeremy. But I'm not asking you to actually be my fiancé,' I elaborated. 'I'm just asking you to pretend you are until we get to Antigua. You see, the competition I won was to find Britain's Most Romantic Couple. I entered it while I still thought that David and I fitted the bill. The prize was intended for me and him. If the people at *Complete Woman* find out that David and I are no longer together, I'm pretty sure I won't be allowed to take the prize up on my own.'

'But I'm not David, Ali. What if they don't let you take me instead?'

'But they won't have to know that you're not David, don't you see? They've never met him. They don't have a clue what he looks like. Oh, except that I think I did mention he had brown hair in my winning piece about our doomed relationship,' I sighed. 'Never mind. We can always say that you've dyed your hair since then. I just need a male body for the photo shoot.' I clapped my hand to my mouth. 'Shit, I didn't mean to say that. I don't mean to imply that just any male body would do, you understand. I need you, you specifically. Can you imagine anything better than two weeks in the Caribbean?'

'I have to say that the idea of two weeks in the sunshine before I have to go back to Warsaw sounds very, very tempting indeed.'

'It's only a teensy-weensy little white lie I'm asking you for.'

'You're asking me to pretend we're getting married, Ali! What if my Mum finds out?'

'How? I can't imagine that she'd be the type to read *Complete Woman*,' I lied. In fact, she was exactly the type of woman who would be attracted to its unique blend of expert gardening advice and healthy relationship tips.

'I'll do it,' Jeremy said suddenly, throwing his hands up in the air in a gesture of playful defeat. 'I'll do it. Of course I will. What possible harm can it do? I would lie about anything to spend two weeks in the sun with you.'

'Would you really?'

'Anything. Take me to the photographic studio at once.'

'Oh, Jez,' I squealed, jumping up from my seat and flinging my arms around his neck. 'You can't begin to know how much this means to me. You're so kind to do this.'

'Kind? Pah! It's not difficult to be kind when you're faced with the reward I've just landed. Two whole weeks in the Caribbean. Can you show me a picture of the place we're going to?'

I delved eagerly into the wastepaper basket to retrieve the Santa Bonita brochure which had been consigned there after David's last departure. I squeezed into Jeremy's armchair beside him and pointed out all the beautiful details. The air-conditioned cabanas with front doors that opened straight onto the pure white sand. The glittering blue sea. The watersports. The twenty-four-hour seafood buffet. The swim-up poolside bar. I nearly wet myself with excitement.

'Wow,' said Jeremy. 'I would even pretend to be married to you if I had to for two weeks of this. You've got no idea how much I love water-skiing, Ali. Don't get much opportunity to practise in Warsaw.'

'It's going to be fantastic,' I murmured into his ear, while simultaneously nibbling at his lobe.

'Mmmm.' Jeremy grasped my hand and pressed it to the front of his trousers where a hard-on was already beginning to bulge. 'I can't wait. I'm going to have you in one of those cabanas, then on the white sand, then in the glittering blue sea, and then on top of the sea-food buffet. If I've still got the energy.'

'I've got to phone Amanda and arrange the photo shoot first,' I protested as Jeremy slipped his hand under my blouse.

'Later,' he murmured. 'Call her later on.'

Next time I saw the outside of my bedroom (I had exiled Fattypuss for the time being and changed the sheets), it was tomorrow.

CHAPTER TWENTY

'At last! Thank goodness you've called,' said Amanda in a most disgruntled tone of voice when I called her first thing the next morning. 'I have left about a hundred messages on your answerphone, Alison Harris,' she spat. 'The deadline for copy for next month's issue is this afternoon, you know. You've given me a very, very big headache about all this indeed.'

'Well, I'm calling with good news,' I told her reassuringly. 'David's chickenpox finally seems to have cleared up. He thinks that he's spot-free enough to do the photos now. In fact, we're both free to do the photo shoot this morning if you like.'

'This morning? Hmmm.' I could hear Amanda flicking through her diary. 'Can you get into London for eleven o'clock? Don't you dare try to cancel this time.'

'Eleven o'clock sounds fine. Where?' She reeled off the name and address of a photographic studio which I quickly scribbled down.

Jeremy and I were at that central London address at

eleven on the dot. I had to take another sickie from work to do it. Complications with my appendectomy scar was the reason I gave Julie. She didn't question it for a minute, she was too keen to tell me the latest gossip about Bridget and the new assistant in accounts. Naughty goings on in the stationery cupboard. I listened for ten minutes then faked a spasm of pain. We'd never have got out of the house and to London otherwise.

Upstairs in the photographer's studio, which was basically a dusty attic room in a draughty old warehouse, Amanda was already knee deep in the bright and beautiful clothes that she and the fashion editor had chosen for the shoot. Amanda wasn't at all as I had expected. I had imagined her to be all Lycra and highlights. Instead, she looked not unlike a home counties mum in her neat jumper and knee length skirt and when she saw us, her eyes lit up to match her gap-toothed smile.

'Deedee, I told you,' she said to the fashion ed, who really was all lycra and highlights. 'Perfect size twelve.'

'Bordering a fourteen,' said the fashion ed, without even saying hello.

Amanda got up from the little nest she had made out of party dresses and slingbacks to welcome us to the world of *Complete Woman*. She shook my hand warmly enough but I noticed that she lingered a little longer over her handshake with Jeremy.

'You must be David,' she purred. Inappropriately seductively I thought, considering he and I were meant to be engaged to be married. 'David?' she repeated when he looked at her somewhat blankly. I pulled a desperate look at Jeremy until he remembered that he was indeed that man.

'That's right,' he said smoothly, pulling Amanda into an unexpected continental kiss situation which I hoped would take her mind off the unnatural pause while Jeremy remembered his name. 'And you must be Amanda. Ali has been telling me all about you. I'm sorry it's taken so long for us to get around to doing this photo thing. You know how it is with such a high-pressured job as mine.'

'And your chickenpox, of course,' added Amanda kindly, as she fiddled with the single string of glossy pearls around her ecru cashmere polo neck. Jeremy looked confused. As Amanda conferred with the photographer on the subject of backdrops, I had to fill Jeremy in on the situation using sign language.

'What on earth's the matter with you?' Jeremy hissed as I mimed out the scratching. 'Have you been bitten by another cat flea or something? Bloody unhygienic animals, cats. You should have it neutered.'

Before I could protest that Fattypuss was a girl anyway, or explain about the chickenpox, Amanda returned to whisk Jeremy away to the changing room where he was transformed from gorgeous to bloody gorgeous in the poof of a powder puff.

'No scars,' the make-up artist commented, referring of course to the chickenpox. 'You must have been really lucky, David. I had loads of scars and I swear I didn't pick a single one.'

'Me too,' sighed Amanda. 'I've got a really big one just here,' she added, giving him a flash of her midriff, which, as far as I could see, was pretty damn flawless. 'Would you mind trying some of these bits and bobs on for me,' she added, passing him a couple of beautifully cut suits. I noticed that she didn't bother to offer to leave the changing room as he did.

'Perfect,' she murmured, before Jeremy even had the silky Armani trousers past his knees. 'What do you think, Ali? The green or the blue? You know him best. Perhaps he should try the blue again.'

Another excuse to see his pants, I thought. Though I couldn't really blame her. He was gorgeous in his stretchy cotton Calvins.

Next, it was my turn. I had been dreading the makeover moment, thinking that Amanda would have me made up like all the other women I had seen in her mag – or worse, like her – that is, looking like I was going to ladies' night at the local golf club. But my fears were unfounded. To my eternal relief Amanda picked out a beautiful little blue shift dress that perfectly complemented the suit she had finally chosen for Jeremy after making him dress and undress at least five times. With my hair bouffed out by the hairdresser to give it the kind of body that no shampoo on earth could achieve, no matter how much I spent on it, and all my facial flaws covered in slap, I took my place beside Jeremy in front of the camera.

'Gorgeous,' Amanda murmured. I guessed she was referring to Jeremy again. Then she added. 'You two look as though you were made for each other. Lovely. Really lovely.'

I couldn't help grinning like a fool at the thought. Made for each other. Oh, how I hoped we were. I gazed at Jeremy through rose-tinted contacts. Jeremy however, had gone straight into supermodel mode and wasn't looking at me at all. He stared directly into the long lens of the camera and licked his plump, smooth lips. If he had had long hair, he probably would have flicked it back.

'Fantastic,' said the photographer, another woman, called Running Star or something like that. I just remember that she had a Red Indian name though her accent was pure scouse. 'That's great, David. Just keep giving me that face. Ali, could you turn to the left a little,' she said to me. 'Full face really isn't your best angle.'

'Oh. OK. Thanks,' I said. What else could I say to that? I angled myself so that I wouldn't crack the lens.

'Right. That's brilliant,' the photographer continued. 'Wow, David. You're really smouldering over there. Have you ever thought about being a model? You know, professionally?'

Jeremy placed a hand on his chest in a gesture that reminded me of being in the chorus line of a junior school production of Hans Christian Andersen's *Ugly Duckling*. It came at the point when the duckling said, 'Me? A swan?' Anyway, I'm sure you know what I mean.

'She's right,' I simpered, while the stylist adjusted the bulldog clips at the back of my dress so that they wouldn't be in shot. I had just ruined half a film by turning so that they were in view. 'You're really good at this modelling thing.'

'I have to say I'm quite enjoying myself,' he replied. 'Thanks to you.'

'Ali, keep your chin up, darling. I keep thinking I've got double vision,' said the photographer, crushing our intimate moment beneath the hot studio lights. Not to mention my self-esteem.

Amanda and her assistant pored over a Polaroid at the back of the room. 'David, you look fab,' Amanda announced with a thumbs up. 'But Ali, you just look worried.'

'Yeah,' said the photographer. 'Unclench your jaw, sweetheart. You look like you're doing pelvic floor exercises.'

The magazine crew fell about laughing.

'Either that or holding back a fart,' added Amanda.

I almost began to regret all those times I had scoffed when supermodels said in interviews that having your photo taken for a living is really hard work. Then, as if I couldn't feel any worse, the photographer's assistant, a girl called Jo who didn't smile – ever, since it might just give her wrinkles – opened the studio window and I was hit by a blast of cold air. It was alright for Jeremy. He was wearing a jacket. I asked if I might have one too.

'Not now we've got the line right, Ali,' sighed Amanda. 'Only another roll and a half to go. Stiff upper lip!'

I gritted my teeth (but not too hard), tried to contain one of my chins and to think myself warm. But by the end of the shoot I felt as though they had been testing my face in a Rover car factory wind-tunnel. I could barely move. That last smile was more of a rictus.

With the shoot over and the photographer busy dismantling the set they had built around us, Amanda helped Jeremy to undress. It was necessary, she assured me, to make sure that the delicate Paul Smith suit she had chosen didn't end up in a crumpled heap on the floor. It seemed that I, on the other hand, could fling my Armani about exactly as I wished.

'What a gorgeous man,' Amanda sighed as the make-up artist helped Jeremy take his war-paint off. 'You're ever so lucky, Ali. When we read your competition entry we all knew that David was going to be a gem, but we really had no idea that he was going to be so . . . well, so bloody good-looking. Makes a single girl quite sick.'

I beamed with pride, as if she were complimenting me.

'If I didn't think you'd been through such a lot together,' Amanda confided with a smirk. 'I might have tried to steal him for myself.'

'Well, thanks for being so restrained,' I told her.

Jeremy had finished cleaning up now. He walked across the studio with a lollop carefully designed to put magazine editors in mind of a catwalk king. He kissed Amanda on both cheeks.

'Thank you so much, Amanda. We've had a wonderful day,' he said.

I nodded. The feeling was just about returning to my wind-frozen arms.

'Oh,' Amanda sighed theatrically. 'You lovely man. Take him away before I faint, Ali. But wait, before you go, I've got something for you. David, take this.' She handed him her card. 'Just in case you ever decide to give up that boring old insurance job of yours.'

'Insurance?' Jeremy asked. For a moment, Jeremy had completely forgotten who he was supposed to be.

'Ha. Isn't he funny?' I covered. 'Pretending that a day being a model has made him forget what he really does for a living. Let's go.' I dragged him down the stairs before things could get any worse.

'Don't go signing up with any model agency without

speaking to me first,' Amanda called after us. 'Mwah! Mwah! Safe journey, darlings!'

'What was she on about? Insurance?' Jeremy asked me when we were out on the street again.

'It's what David does, stupid. You nearly dropped us in it. Come on, let's get out of here. I need a drink. My hands are shaking.'

'You should have filled me in properly before we came out,' Jeremy complained.

'I did. You must have forgotten everything I told you while you were busy being the male equivalent of Cindy Crawford. Still, it doesn't matter now. I think we pulled it off, don't you?'

'Hold on a minute!'

We were halfway up the street and almost out of sight of the studio's dusty windows when Amanda caught up with us. 'You thought you could get away with it, didn't you?' she shouted.

I felt my blood temperature drop ten degrees. What had happened? How had she found out? Had Jeremy dropped his credit cards, plastered all over with his real name, on the way out of the studio? Or had she heard our revealing conversation on the stairs? We stood guiltily still as Amanda drew up alongside us. But when she did, she was grinning.

'Well, we've done the pictures,' she said breathlessly. 'But you naughty children haven't given me any decent quotes for the accompanying article. I was so caught up in the excitement of our session that I didn't write down a word either of you said.'

She brought a Dictaphone out of her handbag and held it in front of our noses.

'OK. Let's have some sound-bites from you two

young lovers,' she giggled. 'David, can you tell me in just one short sentence, what you believe to be the secret of your romantic success?'

Jeremy looked at me and bit his lip, thinking hard. Then he turned back to Amanda with a beam. 'Let's just say, the secret of my romantic success is that I happened to meet and fall in love with the most wonderful woman in the world.'

Amanda recorded the platitude, then turned her Dictaphone off and sighed.

'Oh, David, that's perfect. You are such an angel. Ali, I may have to kill you and steal your man after all,' she added with a disarming smile. 'I know you've been through a lot together, but all's fair . . .'

'Wonderful,' I replied.

'Only joking. And you, Ali?' she continued. 'What do you think your secret has been?'

'Oh, there's no secret,' I told her. 'It's easy to be romantic when you wake up every morning next to the most beautiful man in the world.'

Jeremy and I locked eyes and smiled beatifically.

'Lovely,' said Amanda. 'Well, that should just about do it. I'll make the rest up, if you don't mind.'

'Not at all,' Jeremy and I assured her. I had heard that's the professional way after all.

'Ah,' Amanda sighed again, hugging her Dictaphone to her chest. 'Seeing you two looking so happy together in that studio reaffirms my faith in romance. There really is someone for everyone, isn't there?'

We nodded. Amanda put her Dictaphone back in her handbag and kissed us both goodbye. Mwah! Mwah! Mwah! Jeremy got two.

'Now, you two make sure that you have the best

holiday of your lives. I'll be thinking of you both. Jealously!'

Then she re-adjusted her velvet Alice band, turned and went back to the studio, leaving Jeremy and me just about ready to crack up with the tension of it all.

'My God, they take their romance seriously at *Complete Woman*,' said Jeremy as we got back into his car for the drive home to Brindlesham.

'Yeah, makes me feel a bit guilty to tell you the truth, telling her all those lies.'

'Rubbish. People like her deserve to have the wool pulled over their eyes from time to time. Someone for everyone? She'll be lucky. I'd run a mile if a girl like her came over to me and started gushing all that crap about true romance.'

I made a mental note: 'I must remember not to gush crap.'

CHAPTER TWENTY-ONE

So at last I had my escort for the holiday of a lifetime and the photos had been taken to prove it. The only hurdles remaining were how on earth I would manage to get yet another two weeks off work without losing my job altogether and how to tell my mother what was going on. Work was relatively easy. I simply put a handkerchief over the receiver and called Julie.

'Feeling worse,' I croaked. 'Septicaemia probably. Seeing the doctor this afternoon.'

'Well, you just stay home until you start to feel better again,' she said, all mother hen (though I had been at Hudderston's for long enough to know that the second she was off the phone she would be taking my name in vain around the office). I remembered when Bridget the other temp had a throat infection so bad that they thought they might have to amputate her head. A temperature of 104 degrees, yet as soon as Julie let Bridget go home, Julie was on the edge of my desk complaining about skivers. (The same rules didn't apply when she had to get her ingrowing toenail seen to during office hours, of course.)

'Call me this afternoon to let me know what the doctor says though,' she said, just when I thought I was in the clear.

Mum was going to be altogether more difficult. I had yet to even tell her about winning the competition because I hadn't wanted to go through another round of 'told you sos' about the end of my relationship with David, but now I had no choice. Not least because I was going to be out of the country on February the 14th.

February the 14th? Valentine's Day? So what, you ask. So February the 14th is my maternal grand-mother's birthday and nobody in our family has ever got out of the torturous celebratory tea-party that usually marks the occasion. At least not for as long as I can remember. In fact, attendance had been made far stricter over the past couple of years, since every time dear old Granny sneezed over the pepper she would try to convince us that it was a herald of the beginning of the end, and we had all better be a lot nicer to her in future if we wanted to see any of her vast collection of figurines when she was gone. (Only Saddam Hussein could have commanded more obedience from his family.)

'It only takes one of you not to be there and that's the whole lot of us out of the will,' my mother had told Jo only last year, when Jo tried to get a special dispensation by pleading that she had a starring role in the school play. School plays happen every year, said Mum adamantly. But so did Gran's birthday, and I was pretty sure that Gran's birthday would still be an annual event long after Jo had finished her A-levels and had kids of her own. My previous attempts to get Valentine's Night off for a romantic dinner with David had been met with the emotional equivalent of a United Nations air-strike.

Anyway, I drove round to Mum and Dad's and started to improve the chances that I would not be disinherited by helping Mum to clear out the kitchen cupboards. She was having one of her spring clean binges. Complicated this year by the fact that she had been watching some programme about Feng Shui and wanted all her tin labels facing east. God, was it dusty in those cupboards. There were packets of blancmange in there for heaven's sake and I'm pretty certain that no-one under the age of twenty-three has even heard of the stuff.

'What are you being so helpful for?'

With her powers of maternal deduction, my mum had me sussed as soon as I donned an apron.

'Er, nothing,' I began. I would keep up the 'nothing' line until I really had to cave in and confess. That was my usual modus operandi.

'Rubbish. I can tell when you're up to something, Alison Harris. I'm not your mother for nothing, you know.'

'Well, I might as well tell you the truth . . .' I sighed, straightening up from scrubbing at a particularly persistent puddle of molasses.

'You're pregnant, aren't you?' she sighed dramatically. 'Good God, whatever will the neighbours think? Me, a grandmother at forty-three?'

(And the rest.) She seemed to have forgotten that she'd just celebrated her thirtieth wedding anniversary. Was I suddenly supposed to believe that she had married at thirteen?

'No,' I protested. 'No, Mum, I'm not pregnant.'

'Oh. You need a bigger pair of trousers then.'

'Thanks a lot.' After that morning's photo shoot my self-esteem was already at an all-time low.

'Do you need a loan?'

'No.'

'You scratched your father's car on the way into the driveway?'

'No.'

'You're off to join the Moonies?'

'No.'

'Then what is it? I've been through all the obvious things.'

Moonies? Obvious? Perhaps if she had been talking to my hippie sister Jane.

I decided to take my life in my hands. 'I'm going to be away for Grandma's birthday.'

'You what?' My mother let the dishcloth plop into the washing-up bowl, splashing bubbles all over her newly cleaned work surfaces.

'I'm not going to be at Grandma's birthday party.'

'Why not?'

'I'm going to be in Antigua.'

My mother leaned against the sink and looked at me cleaning out the cupboards through narrowed eyes.

'And what's that? Some posh new club opened up in town, I'll bet. You mean to tell me that you're going to go out with your friends to some gin palace on your grandmother's birthday? Which, incidentally, could be her last.'

'Mum, you know as well as I do that Gran will outlive the Queen Mother and the Queen Mother will outlive just about everyone else on this planet. So I'm going to miss her birthday tea on this one solitary occasion to go to Antigua the country,' I tried to explain. 'It's in the Caribbean. I've won a competition, Mum. I won a holiday. I'm flying out tomorrow.'

'Tomorrow? That's a bit bloody sudden. And when exactly did you win this competition?'

'About two weeks ago.'

'Two weeks ago! And you didn't warn me that you were thinking of going away as soon as you heard?'

'I didn't bother telling you because I didn't think I would be going. And I didn't plan to go over Grandma's birthday either, it just sort of happened like that.'

'Well, can't you change it to some other week?'

'No. I can't.'

'And who are you taking on this jolly jamboree?'

'No-one. Just me.'

'Rubbish. The prizes in those competitions are always for two.'

'Not this one,' I lied. 'It's just me. On a beach. On my own. Recovering from my annus horribilis.'

Mum pursed her lips cynically. 'You can cut out the Latin when you're talking to me. I bet you're taking that floosy Emma. It's your Grandma's birthday and you're jetting off to the sun with that no-good flatmate of yours. She's a bad influence on you, she is. Hardly ever sees her family.'

'She's not coming with me.'

'Then you can take your Gran.'

'What?'

'If you're not going to be in England on her birthday, then she can bloody well be in the Caribbean with you. Might take her mind off selling any more of the family silver. She flogged the little violet seller figurine on

Thursday night and bought herself a Sega Megadrive with the proceeds.'

'Good for her,' said Jo, who had wandered in for a biscuit.

'She hasn't got a flippin' television to watch it on,' said Mum. 'No, Alison, you've got to take her with you to try and stop this madness. If she sells the Staffordshire Pottery King Charles Spaniels I don't know what I'll do.'

'Mum!'

'What about the family, Ali? This could be your grandmother's last chance to see some of the world. She never gets to go on holiday.'

'She went to Scarborough in November,' Jo pointed out.

'Oh, that hardly counts. If you take her to the Caribbean, she might finally stop going on about how your Auntie June's family has always loved her more than us. Auntie June can afford to take your Gran on fancy trips because she lives two hundred miles away and doesn't have to put up with her every bloody weekend. I should have followed her out of Brindlesham when I still had the chance. Brains, that's what my sister's got. Great big bloody brains.' Mum was almost sobbing.

'I can't take Gran, Mum,' I said in desperation. 'I'm taking someone else.'

'Who?' asked Jo. 'You haven't got any friends except Emma and David's still going out with that Lisa Brown girl.'

'You don't need to remind me of that,' I warned her, riding the stab to my heart with considerable poise, I thought. 'I'm taking Jeremy Baxter.'

The room fell silent. Even Jo stopped chewing on her Wagon Wheel to stare at me in wonder.

'What did you say?' said my mother finally.

'I said, I'm taking Jeremy Baxter to Antigua.'

Another minute's silence.

'But you hardly know him,' Mum protested.

'I've known him all my life,' I said.

'You'd have slapped me if I said that,' said Jo.

'Shut up you,' Mum told my little sister. 'Shouldn't you be doing some revision?'

'Oh, I've finished for today. It's only Further Maths mock tomorrow and I'm not expecting to pass that anyway.'

'Jo-anna,' thundered Mum, pointing her towards the door.

Jo shrugged. 'OK. But Alison might want a witness here if you're about to kill her.'

Mum turned her ocular destruction lasers on Jo and sent her scurrying up the stairs. I put my coat on, ready for a quick escape.

'There's a name for girls like you, going off on holiday with men they've only just met,' she began.

'Young women on the verge of the twenty-first century?' I tried.

'Don't get saucy with me. You'll just have to tell him that the holiday's off. You've got family obligations.'

'It's too late. His name's on the ticket. In any case, I've got to take a man.'

'Then take your father,' Mum said. 'I could do without him under my feet for a fortnight. Your Grandma won't miss him. She'll probably be pleased he's gone.'

'I can't take Dad. I've got to take a young man. I've got to take a man who's supposed to be my fiancé.'

'You've got engaged?' Mum shrieked then, hearing half of the message. 'You've gone and got engaged again without telling us. Haven't you learnt your lesson after that David Whitworth? You needn't think your aunts are going to be happy to go buying you engagement presents again. Auntie Eileen has already asked for her British Home Stores saucepan set back.'

'Don't panic. I'm not engaged, Mum. I'm just pretending to be. Jeremy is pretending to be David.'

'Why?'

'For the competition. I won it for me and David, but I can't take him now, can I? Not now that he's gone back to her.'

'You should have tried harder to keep your hands on him when he started messing around with that Lisa.'

'Perhaps he should have tried harder to keep his hands off her. Look, Mum. The bottom line is, I'm going away tomorrow and I'm going with Jeremy Baxter. I don't care if I am telling a big porky to get this holiday. There's going to be no more Miss Nice Guy from me. I'm always getting walked on but I'm going to go out and get what I want from now on.'

'Well, my dear. You go ahead and do exactly as you want,' my mother sighed as though her heart was breaking. 'Heaven knows you always have done before. But mark my words, Alison Harris. No good ever came of telling lies.'

'This time it will,' I assured her.

'And even less good ever came from answering back.'

Terrific. A chance for real happiness in my life at last and my mother refused to give me her blessing. I couldn't see Jeremy that afternoon, since he was under obligation to visit some relatives in the country before he disappeared again, so I decided on a spot of retail therapy to cheer myself up. I had a lot of pre-holiday shopping to do. First stop was Brindlesham's solitary big department store for a bikini. I knew that Hays and Sons had an all-year-round 'cruise-wear' collection and rather fancied myself in a gold lamé two-piece. Credit card in hand, I was ready to spend whatever it would take to turn me into Bridget Bardot. Bridget Bardot in the sixties, that is. I could already do a pretty good impression of Bridget Bardot the dotty animal lover. Unfortunately, the swimwear buyers at Hays and Sons obviously assumed that no-one under the age of fifty ever went on holiday outside August and I came away empty handed after trying on a ruched bottle-green one-piece that reached down to my knees.

Toiletries next. One of the most important things on my list was sun-screen. I had a bottle of it at home, but it had been bought eight years earlier for my post-A-levels trip to Majorca and if it was still any use at all, I couldn't get it out of the bottle.

'Going on holiday at this time of year?' asked the cashier in Boots as she swiped my Ambre Solaire and a packet of bikini line wax through her EPOS. The cashier's name was Lorna. I knew her vaguely. She had been going out with David's best friend's brother or some spurious connection like that and we'd swapped platitudes a couple of times over rum and coke in The Rotunda.

'I am actually,' I told her smugly.

'Anywhere nice?'

'Antigua. It's in the Caribbean.'

'You're kidding me? The Caribbean,' she sighed. 'I've always wanted to go there. Fred says we might make it out there for our honeymoon but only if he has a really really good year with his carpet cleaning business. Who are you going with, if you don't mind me asking? I mean, I know that you and David Whitworth aren't together any more. Heard it on the grapevine,' she said with a sympathetic smile. 'Very sorry to hear that news. I never did much like Lisa.'

'It's OK. You don't have to say that.' I knew damn well that she and Lisa were as thick as thieves. 'Besides I've got a new man now,' I told her triumphantly, secretly hoping that it would get straight back to David's ears. 'His name is Jeremy Baxter and he's in charge of the whole of the Eastern European market for this huge computer company. You probably won't have heard of them.'

'Wow,' said Lorna. 'Head of Eastern Europe. He must have a bob or two to take you to the Caribbean and so quickly after getting together. And over Valentine's Day. He must be a romantic.'

'Actually,' I said, slipping the suntan lotion and wax into my bag, 'I'm taking him.' Lorna's mouth dropped open.

'I'll pop round when I'm back and show you my tan.'

Then back home to call in to Hudderston's one more time before the great escape. I did my bikini line simultaneously for that authentic hint of anguish to my voice. I got through to Irene first but Julie insisted on taking the call herself.

'Feeling any better?' she asked. 'I don't mean to put the pressure on you, Ali, but your in-tray isn't looking terribly tidy.'

I coughed into the receiver, then pulled a sticky, warm wax strip from my pubic bone and the tears flooded into my eyes. 'Well, if you're really really pushed, I'll drag myself in. But the doctor said that because my scar's gone septic again, I really shouldn't try to move out of bed at all. In case it bursts and I get blood poisoning. Which can be fatal, you understand,' I added with another rattling breath.

'Oh, is it catching?' Julie asked.

'Septicaemia? Certainly sounds it,' I replied, ripping off another strip. I sucked in a breath in genuine agony.

'Alison, you sound terrible.'

'I'm fine,' I said bravely, pressing down on my freshly plucked skin in an attempt to dull the painful stinging. 'I mean, I'm not fine, but I will get through this. I just need some more time. About another two weeks, the doctor says.'

We decided that I should probably stay off work for as long as I needed to for the sake of the rest of the workforce who had children and wives.

Emma had listened to me make the call.

'Was I convincing?'

'Terrifying. I was scared to sit too close to you,' she muttered as she peeled one of the discarded wax strips from where it had landed on the wall beside the telephone.

CHAPTER TWENTY-TWO

Before I knew it it was two o'clock in the morning. In less than twelve hours I would be in the air. I had just finished packing and was preparing myself for some serious beauty sleep, complete with a pair of soggy tea bags taped to my eyes, when Emma appeared at my bedroom door with a very weary look upon her face.

'Ali,' she said. 'It's David. He says he wants to talk to you. Desperately.'

'Well, tell him I'll call him when I get back from my holiday,' I told her, without even bothering to uncover my eyes.

'He's not on the phone,' she sighed. 'He's here. In the house.' And before I could make myself look presentable she had let him into my bedroom. David Whitworth stood at the bottom of my bed like an apparition of Valentine's Eve past, pale-faced and with a huge bouquet of white roses held tight in his clammy little hands. Emma slipped out as he came in.

'Ali,' he said. 'Ali, are you awake?'

'I am now, you idiot,' I snarled, taking off my tea bags

and putting them into the ashtray on my bedside table. 'What do you want?'

'I want to talk to you,' he told me feebly.

'About what?'

'About us.'

'There is no "us" anymore, David,' I spat at him, as I pulled my pyjama top tighter around my neck. 'There's only you and Lisa Brown and me and my new man.'

'Your new man. I heard all about him. Fred's girl-friend Lorna said you were in Boots today crowing your head off about him.'

'Hardly crowing. I was just answering her nosy questions.'

'She said he was some Eastern European diplomat or something. Where the hell did you meet someone like him, Ali?'

'Not down The Rotunda, that's for sure.'

'And how long has it been going on?' he asked accusingly.

'Well, if that cloth-eared bimbo had listened properly she would have been able to tell you that my new man is not actually a diplomat, he's the head of the Eastern European branch of a multi-national computer conglomerate, and it's been going on since about twelve hours after I found out that you were seeing Lisa Brown again. It is allowed, you know. I am single again, remember? Or do I have to go into a convent until you decide that you want me back once more?'

'Who is he?' asked David with an anguished look upon his creepy mug.

'No-one you know. At least, I don't think you know him.'

'Just tell me his name,' said David passionately.

'His name's Jeremy Baxter. He used to live in Saintbridge Road.'

'Not the Jeremy Baxter,' David asked, a sudden glimmer of joy crossing his deliberately downcast eyes. 'Jeremy Baxter with the boils? You're joking?'

Why would no-one let that single unhappy incident lie? The boils had only lasted for two weeks.

'That's the one,' I said coolly. 'But he doesn't have boils any more, thank you very much. He's grown up a great deal since junior school. Changed. Matured. Become a real man. You know, like people are supposed to do as they get older?'

'But I've changed too,' David protested.

'What? Since the Saturday before last? Now come on,' I warned him. 'I seem to remember hearing this little speech back then too. Evolution happens over millennia, David, not weekends. It'll be a long time before I even consider your species to be part of the human race again.'

'Ali, will you just cut the wisecracks and listen to me?' He flung the roses down upon my bed to underline his frustration. 'It's no wonder that things have got so bad between us lately. Every single time I try to apologise to you for the way I've been behaving, you just start making stupid digs at me and before I know it, I'm storming out on you again.'

'You limped out last time,' I reminded him.

'Yeah. And if I wasn't such a nice guy, you could be talking to my solicitor right now, not me. You did me some damage with that stuff.'

'Huh. I could get my solicitor to talk to you about forcing your way into people's houses in the middle of the night.'

'Emma let me in. I didn't force anything. But I'd appreciate a little bit more respect from you, Alison Harris. Because I could still be tempted to press charges for grievous bodily harm, you know.'

'Is there permanent scarring to poor Mister Stiffy then?' I asked hopefully.

'No.'

'Shame.'

'But it still hurts when I pee,' he said pathetically. 'I might never be able to have children, you realise.'

'Oh, don't be ridiculous. It won't come to that. I'm sure I read in one of your lad's magazines that Hot Stuff Heat Rub is a great aid to foreplay.'

'You're thinking of Vaseline,' said David dryly. 'Whatever, I don't want to talk about that right now. Just thinking about that Saturday morning brings tears to my eyes. I haven't been able to get an erection since I left this house.'

'So? Hasn't affected me much,' I shrugged. Then it clicked. 'Oh, are you using this as an obscure way to tell me that you haven't been porking Lisa since you left me in the lurch? That you've been almost faithful to me by default? No, I forgot. Lisa hasn't been in town. Are you telling me you've been trying to get a hard-on with some other old slag instead?'

'Ali. Why do you have to talk like a fishwife all of a sudden?'

'If I was still going to be your wife I might take some notice of that comment.'

'OK. Point taken.' He sat down on the end of the bed then and put his hand on my knee beneath the sheets.

'Out of bounds,' I told him, not least because it was

still stinging from the leg wax I had given myself that afternoon.

He took his hand away.

'Look, Ali,' he whined. 'This is all going wrong. Let me start again. I've come here tonight to tell you that I've been thinking about you non-stop all week. I can't help myself. I miss you. Really miss you. I miss the things we used to do together. I think I'm going to miss them for the rest of my life. Unless you can do something about that now.'

'You miss things like what?' I probed.

'Like the way you used to laugh at my jokes. The way you smile. The dimples in your cheeks when you giggle. That funny squinty look you get when you're reading your stars on Teletext.'

'Do I squint?' I asked in horror.

'Only a bit. But I miss it. Like I miss the way you push your hair back from your face.'

'I thought you said that irritated you?'

'It used to but . . . oh, just shut up for a minute will you, Ali? I'm trying to tell you something really important here.'

'Oh, my lips are sealed if it's something really important,' I said sarcastically.

'It is. It is. I'm trying to tell you that I've been a fool. Again. I'm trying to tell you that I can't live without you, Ali. And I just can't bear to think of a future without you beside me. I don't want to be with anyone else. Not even Lisa Brown. And I'm prepared to forget all about the Hot Stuff Heat Rub incident if you tell me that you'll be my wife.'

'This isn't happening,' I murmured to myself. 'I'm supposed to be getting my beauty sleep, ready for a fortnight in Antigua with my handsome new lover, but instead I'm listening to an apparition in the shape of David Whitworth muttering on about my charming dimples. I know he must be an apparition because he's just asked me to be his wife.'

David moved up the bed to grasp my hands in a pleading kind of way.

'Stop messing around. I'm serious, Ali,' he told me. 'Deadly serious.'

'Well, I'm glad. Because I wouldn't want to be woken up in the middle of the night by someone who wasn't deadly serious.'

'What do you say, Ali? Marry me. I'll forget all about that Saturday morning. I'll wipe the slate clean. You'll call off going to Antigua with that boil-faced boyfriend of yours and we'll go out there together in a week or so and be a proper couple again instead. Like we used to be. It could even be our honeymoon. I'm sure we could fit in a quickie ceremony at the registry office. Ali and David Whitworth, we'd be. Together forever.' He puckered up his lips and started to move in for a kiss.

'Now hang on,' I said, darting out of range. 'I think you'll find that the dirt on your side of the slate goes back way beyond last Saturday.'

He looked confused.

'Lisa?' I reminded him.

'That's over. I've told you.'

'But have you told her?'

David squirmed. 'Er . . . Not yet. She's at the training group in Hastings again. Some course or other. Information technology, I think. I didn't like to upset her before she went.'

'Ha!' I spat. 'So when exactly were you proposing to do the deed?'

'When she gets back. On Saturday night. I'll call her from Antigua if you want me to.'

I shook my head and laughed bitterly. 'Too late, David. I can't give up a fantastic holiday that starts tomorrow on the off-chance that you'll get round to chucking Lisa Brown in four days time. Tell you what, why don't I go to Antigua with Jeremy as I've planned and we can discuss all this again when I return? In the day-time perhaps next time. It's only two weeks. You can wait that long, can't you?'

'No way!' David exploded. 'If you go away with him tomorrow you can kiss goodbye to me forever, Alison Harris. Forever. I really mean that.'

I blew him a kiss and rolled over to hide my face in the pillow so that he couldn't see me sniggering. 'Bye-bye then, David. You know your way to the door.'

David stood shaking in the middle of my bedroom floor for a minute longer, as if he didn't know the way to the door at all. Then he picked up the roses and shook them at me in a vaguely threatening fashion.

'You'll be sorry.'

'I'll let you know,' I told him. 'Now if you don't mind, I really must get some beauty sleep.'

David stood there for a moment longer, opening and closing his mouth like a grounded fish as he struggled to find a reply. Then, giving up as suddenly as he had arrived, he turned on his heels and began his grand exit. As David made a grab for the handle and yanked the door open however, Emma tumbled onto her back on the landing and nearly tripped him up. She had been listening at the keyhole, quite unprepared for the discussion's sudden end.

'You've had it now,' David warned me from the doorway. 'I'm going to sue you. I swear. You could go down for a long long time you know.'

'Just because I didn't?' I laughed, surprised by the cleverness of my own impromptu joke.

'I'm serious, Alison Harris. It's no laughing matter. When the men of this town find out what a psycho bitch you are, you won't ever see the inside of a man's bedroom again.'

'Promises, promises.'

'You're finished. You wait. When you get back from your wonderful romantic holiday in Antigua, you'll find a letter from my lawyer waiting on your door-mat.'

'I'm shaking in my boots,' I said.

Then he raced down the hallway shouting obscenities to do with my thighs in a bikini and slammed the front door shut behind him. Emma and I waited until we heard the engine of his little Fiat Uno firing up before we burst out laughing.

'Jesus Christ, Ali,' Emma exclaimed. 'Did you really Hot Stuff Heat Rub him on the you know what?'

'Only a little bit.'

'Excellent. That must have hurt like hell. Not that he didn't deserve it after all he's done to you. But you could have really done him some serious damage, couldn't you?'

'Absolutely not. He's pretending.'

'He was limping a bit when he left just now.'

'That's because of his ingrowing toenail,' I assured her.

'Yuk. There is no bigger passion killer than an ingrowing toenail. Hot Stuff Heat Rub, eh?' she mused again. 'You're my heroine, Ali. So clever. I would never have thought of that.'

'It was your Hot Stuff Heat Rub,' I told her.

'Wow! Thanks,' she said sincerely. 'I feel like I was part of it now. When I get into college tomorrow morning I think I'm going to set up a new Web-site in your honour – Alison Harris is The New Lorena Bobbitt. Women can write in for handy revenge tips. Got any more up your sleeve?'

'How about taking a studmuffin to Antigua for two whole weeks?'

CHAPTER TWENTY-THREE

But so much for beauty sleep. I could barely sleep at all for the rest of that night. If the truth be told, I think I might even have been feeling just a little bit guilty about David. The ugly thought nagged at the back of my mind that he might have been genuine when he asked if we could get back together and I had well and truly slammed the proverbial door in his face. Did I care? I wasn't sure.

By going away with Jeremy I would be sealing that part of my life I had once shared with David into a tomb. We girls may be soft enough to have men back time and time again when they've been dip-sticking all over the neighbourhood, but I know how different it is for men. They prize their pride well above their emotional well-being and I knew that David would never have me back if he thought I had slept with Jeremy. As I was obviously going to do on this trip. Several times if I was lucky.

Anyway, I was up at seven, checking and re-checking my baggage, moving my passport from one pocket of my jacket to the next until I had decided which of them would be simultaneously easily accessible to me and utterly inaccessible to passport snatchers.

The plane tickets lay in a prominent position on the kitchen table. Hard to believe that those little pieces of paper would soon be transformed into two weeks of utter joy. Jeremy was due to arrive at my house at ten past ten so that we could catch a taxi to the airport together. (I had suggested that we took the Megane but he told me there was no way he was leaving his precious baby in an airport car park.) By five past ten, I was getting twitchy. At eleven minutes past ten, I was almost in tears.

'He'll be here,' Emma comforted me. 'He's not going to drop out of this trip is he?'

'Why not?' I said tragically. 'David did. And what if Jeremy hasn't dropped out? What if he's had an accident?'

Emma swiped me around the head with my passport. She had slipped it out of my ultra-safe pocket while I was blubbing on her shoulder.

'If he turns up at the accident unit, Ashley will call to let you know. Look Ali, I'll sympathise with you when he still hasn't rolled up at half-past eleven. Right now it is ten past ten and fifty seconds. He isn't even a minute late, which in my opinion isn't late at all.'

'He is two whole minutes late,' I wailed, pointing at the dial on my ancient Sekonda. 'Besides, I only said ten past ten as an approximate time. I expected him to get here a bit early, just in case. Surely he would have been here early if he was as excited as I am.'

'He will be here,' said Emma impatiently, as she walked to the window to scan the streets with me again. 'Look, there he is.' She grabbed my head by the ears and turned it in the direction of a very distant figure.

'How do you know it's him? I can't see him properly from here.'

'I'm making an educated guess. Look. It's definitely a man with a suitcase and this isn't exactly the type of area where people fly to the Caribbean on a whim at this time of year, is it? He's heading in this direction, therefore, it stands to reason that it's got to be Jeremy.'

I held my breath until I could be certain.

'It is him! Thank God,' I sighed, when I could finally make out his glasses. (He said that flying interfered with his contact lenses.) 'Now where's the bloody taxi? The taxi was supposed to be here at ten past ten as well. Oh, bloody hell! I knew everything would go wrong for me . . .'

'Stop panicking before I cave your head in and steal your place. Taxi drivers are always late. It's part of their job description.'

'I know. I'm sorry. It's just that, after the way things have been going for me lately, I can't quite believe that I'm really going to pull this trip off. Something always goes wrong for me. If I have any luck at all, I usually end up paying double for it.'

'Sit down for a minute and listen to the voice of reason.' Emma dragged me away from the window and forced me to sit down at the kitchen table. 'The way I see it, Ali, you've more than paid for this holiday in advance. In the last two months you've lost an appendix and a fiancé. Don't you think that each of those disasters adds up to at least a week in the Caribbean in the big scheme of things? Nothing will go wrong.'

'Do you really think that?'

'If you're still not convinced, I could take your place.'

'No,' I protested, just as the doorbell rang. 'You are right. I do deserve this holiday, don't I? Everything will be perfect, won't it? How do I look?'

'You look as though you've been up all night arguing with an ex-boyfriend and spent the morning in tears.' I made a grab for my vanity case. 'Only joking,' said Emma. 'You look fine. Shall I let him in?'

'I suppose you'd better.'

Jeremy really looked the part. Though outside the grey February sky was threatening drizzle, Jeremy was dressed in readiness for the blazing sun and an azure sea. He was wearing a cream linen jacket over his faded blue jeans. On his head was the kind of Panama hat that can be rolled up into a tube to pack away when the holiday's done. He took it off when the door opened and swept it in front of him as he bowed.

'Wow,' I said involuntarily.

'Ready for the off?' he asked.

'Have you got the camels ready for all her baggage?' asked Emma sarcastically.

'Luckily I passed a taxi downstairs. He says he's waiting for us. Ali darling, you say goodbye to your friend while I lug this lot down to the car. Don't be long.' He left dragging my vanity case behind him with some difficulty. (I needed a lot of sun protection, you understand. There's ginger in my genes.)

'Oh, Emma, this will be OK won't it?' I asked.

'It will be like a dream,' she told me once more. 'Just get out there and enjoy yourself. Once you're on the plane, not even the True Romance Police from *Complete Woman* will be able to get you anymore. Now, hurry up and get in that taxi. It's very hard for me to keep consoling you on your amazing luck, you know. Especially when I'm just going to be stuck here with Fattypuss, waiting for Ashley to finish stitching up builders and pulling children's heads out of saucepans.'

'And you know what to do if anyone from work calls?' I persisted.

'I'll tell them that you're in bed and you're not allowed visitors. Doctor's orders,' she said. 'Rest assured, I'll fend them off for you.' With a little bit of arm twisting, she was certain that she could persuade Ashley to write me a sick note on my return.

'Emma, you're a star,' I told her. 'You're the very best friend a girl could have.'

'Just remember that when you're buying me a present.'

Jeremy had left nothing behind for me to carry but the little string rucksack that contained my most important worldly goods. My wallet, my passport, and of course, our tickets. I gathered that little lot up and kissing Emma three times for luck, I finally made it through the door.

But I couldn't truly relax until we had got through passport control and onto the plane. I was utterly convinced that Amanda the editorial assistant would pop up at Heathrow, just to wish us a happy holiday from the *Complete Woman* gang, and our cover would be blown when she playfully asked to see David's passport photo and saw that he was really called Jeremy Baxter.

But she wasn't there. She was probably busy interviewing some B-list celeb about the close relationship she had grown to have with her horses since parts in *The Bill* had dried up. Instead, we were met by a smiling air stewardess who plucked us out of the queue waiting to check in.

'You're in first class, silly,' she told me. 'No need to queue with this rowdy bunch.' She whisked us straight into a private lounge and the formalities were over in seconds. I couldn't believe it. We were flying first class. It was fantastic enough just to be in the first class departure lounge sipping chilled champagne and not fighting for a coffee at a Burger King concession with the hoi polloi. That didn't stop me from shredding a drinks mat with nerves however.

'It's OK,' said Jeremy, quickly relaxing into the atmosphere as if he had been born to it. 'No-one can get us now. We're going to Antigua, Ali. Please don't spoil the whole flight by worrying.'

'I'm sorry. I just don't know when I'm going to realise that this is for real. I'm absolutely convinced that I'm going to wake up in my bed at home any second. I probably haven't even come round from the anaesthetic they gave me for my appendectomy yet. Or perhaps I really died on the operating table and all this is just the afterlife.'

Jeremy laughed. 'No, it's definitely not the afterlife, because with the disgraceful thoughts I've been having ever since I met you, I certainly won't be able to get into heaven if I die now.'

'What thoughts?' I probed.

'Bad ones. Hey,' he leaned in close. 'Do you fancy joining the Mile High Club this afternoon?'

'Oh no,' I said hurriedly. 'What if there's an emergency or something? I'd never live it down if they had to drag us out of the loo while we were, you know, entangled.'

'You worry too much about what people might think,' Jeremy told me. 'You should be like me, Ali. A free spirit. Unrestrained by social convention.'

'Mmmm. I don't know how you do it,' I said admiringly. 'I always worry what the neighbours might think.'

'You can be sure that they'll be thinking the worst anyway, so my philosophy is, you might as well prove them right.'

Though in the end, we didn't bother with the Mile High Club after all. We were too busy drinking the complimentary champagne and eating canapés. Added to that was the fact that the minor soap opera star sitting in front of us hogged the loo with her Italian-looking boyfriend from ten minutes outside Heathrow to at least halfway over the Atlantic, forcing the rest of the first class passengers to cross their legs or, worse, cross the class barrier and use the economy loos. I didn't like to ask for her autograph after that.

Ten hours later, jelly-legged with jet lag (not to mention the free booze that I had been more than making the most of), Jeremy and I stumbled into the arrivals lounge of the tiny airport at St John's in Antigua, pushing our cases on a predictably errant trolley.

CHAPTER TWENTY-FOUR

'Do you think we should get ourselves a cab?' I asked as we ambled out into the sunshine, but before I could spot a free taxi, Jeremy had spotted a smartly dressed man with a board that bore the name of our hotel. The man was wearing a proper chauffeur's uniform complete with hat and gold braiding and he smiled widely at everyone just in case: he obviously didn't know who he was actually waiting for.

Jeremy strode up to him. 'Hello, I think we're staying at your hotel. Santa Bonita?'

'What your name, please?' asked the man.

I could see that Jeremy was scanning down the list written on the driver's clipboard. 'Whitworth,' Jeremy announced finally. 'Mr and Mrs Whitworth. That's us.' The driver smilingly relieved Jeremy of our cases and ushered us into the back of his waiting car. But it wasn't any ordinary car. It was a white limo, specially polished for the occasion and finished off with a pink satin ribbon on the bonnet.

'You are the Most Romantic Couple in the United Kingdom?' the man asked. I was too dazed by the opulence of the limo to even manage a nod. 'Antigua salutes you,' said the chauffeur. He clicked his heels together and doffed his cap in a bizarre military parody.

'Ohmigod,' I muttered into Jeremy's shoulder, as we sank into the white leather seats of the car. 'Antigua salutes us. I feel such a fraud.' I daren't even look out of the frosted windows in case a welcoming party had been assembled to wave us into town.

'Ali,' murmured Jeremy comfortingly. 'Relax, will you? We'll be at the hotel in ten minutes and then we'll finally be on our own.'

'It is a very great honour to drive you to Santa Bonita,' the driver was telling us as he sped along the sparsely surfaced road. 'I have had many famous people in my car. Princess Margaret, Joan Collins and now you.'

'Not quite in the same league,' I said nervously.

'My car is the one that they always use whenever anyone really famous is in town,' the driver continued regardless.

'Jeremy,' I squeaked. 'I don't think I can stand much more of this.'

But he was already popping open the half bottle of champagne which had been so thoughtfully provided in the limo's minibar. He handed me a glass, then used the electric controls to wind down the windows on both sides of us.

'Smell the ocean,' he told me. 'Look at the sunshine and the palm trees out there. Is this paradise or what?'

Children playing in the dust at the side of the road looked up as the huge car passed them. They waved happily to us. But all I could think was, if only they knew. If only they knew the truth. No-one would be happy for us then.

But soon we were at the hotel. The driver leapt out of the car to help me out too. Liveried porters were already waiting on the bright marble steps to whisk our luggage away. The smiling manager shook Jeremy warmly by the hand and planted a wet kiss on mine.

'We are very honoured to have you both here,' the platitudes started again. 'We have reserved you the very best room.'

But first there was the register signing to get over. I was sure I must be visibly shaking as we stood at the check-in desk, just waiting for those dreaded words. 'Please may we see your passports?'

'Mr Whitworth, your passport please,' asked the manager.

He handed over both his passport and mine with a big smile on his face.

'Jeremy, what are you doing?' I thought as I dug my nails into his hand. The manager opened up the little red booklet that bore Jeremy's real name and his eyebrows knotted together in confusion.

'Jeremy Baxter?' he said very slowly. 'Mister Jeremy Baxter.' Perhaps he would think that Jeremy had somehow had his passport switched in customs, I prayed. But no, the face was right.

'Jeremy Baxter?' Jeremy repeated as if the revelation had confused him too. 'Let me see that.'

He took the passport back and studied it with a frown that soon blossomed into a wide, wide smile.

'Ha! I don't believe it. I am David Whitworth, I promise you!' He turned to me. 'Darling, can you believe I must have picked up my twin brother's passport by mistake again. I can't believe we managed to get through customs at Heathrow. Still, doesn't really matter, does it?' he winked at the manager, while simultaneously slipping him a fifty dollar note. 'We're the same in every respect apart from our names. Except that I'm the more romantic twin, of course. When our parents divorced, Jeremy took our father's name but I sided with my mother.'

The manager nodded warily.

'If you could just sign the register,' he said.

Jeremy signed David's name with a flourish. David himself had only just been able to manage a signature in joined-up writing.

'Thanks for being so understanding,' Jeremy continued. 'I'll pop down to the British Embassy first thing in the morning to see if I can't sort this dreadful mess out.'

At last the porter picked our bags up again and led us to our room.

Our room, rather our hut, was incredible. The bath in the *en-suite* was easily as big as the swimming pool at the last hotel I had stayed at. And when I opened the minibar, I found another complimentary bottle of champagne inside.

'Open it up then,' said Jeremy.

'No. We should save it for a special occasion.'

'But this is a very special occasion,' he reminded me. 'You and me, alone at last, in our fabulously well-appointed beach hut in Antigua.' He wrested the champagne bottle from my grip and proceeded to unwrap the foil. Pop! The cork exploded out of the bottle and ricocheted against the lampshade.

'Get the glasses, then,' Jeremy laughed.

I hadn't thought of that. And I couldn't find them quickly enough, so in the end we had to drink champagne out of the tooth mugs I found on the bathroom shelf. I didn't mind too much. It seemed more romantic somehow.

'I can't wait to have a dip in the sea,' I told Jeremy as I gazed dreamily at the rolling waves, sitting on our balcony, sipping champagne from a plastic cup.

Jeremy nodded. 'Neither can I. But I think we should test out the bed first. And I know exactly what I'm going to do with the rest of this champagne . . .'

Funny how those Jackie Collins' books forgot to mention that it just gets really sticky.

CHAPTER TWENTY-FIVE

So we didn't get to paddle that afternoon and that evening at dinner we were in for a bit of a surprise. Instead of being ushered towards a small secluded table on our own, we found ourselves being directed towards a huge round table laid for eight.

'Er, we are the UK's Most Romantic Couple,' Jeremy hinted.

'That's right,' said the Maître d'. 'Follow me please. We have a place for you right here.'

Jeremy shrugged and we followed the Maître d' to the big table.

'Here.' He pulled out my golden chair for me. At the head of my place setting was a little white card adorned with scrawly pink writing. 'Most Romantic Couple (UK) Woman' it said.

'Have you got one of these?' I asked Jeremy, showing him my little card. 'Not very romantic, is it? Most Romantic UK Woman. Hang on a minute.' I noticed another. 'Who's sitting next to you?'

'Most Romantic Couple (Aus) Man.'

'I don't believe it. I've got Most Romantic Couple

(USA) Woman on one side and Most Romantic Couple
(Can) Woman on the other.'

'They've obviously got a job lot of us in.'

'Amanda didn't mention this,' I protested.

'No,' said Jeremy. 'I'll bet she didn't. But never mind.
We can insist on a table of our own tomorrow night. I'm
sure the rest of the romantic world will feel exactly the
same way about wanting some time alone. Especially
on Valentine's Day. It could be a bit of fun to meet them
though. I wonder what they'll be like.'

'I wonder,' I murmured, as I saw a couple who looked
as though they might be about our age walk into the
dining room. He was wearing a white Western-style
suit with a rhinestone covered waistcoat and a matching
Stetson. She was wearing an Elizabeth Walton-style
Sunday best dress in pink chiffon and sequins. Jeremy
turned to see who I was gawping at.

'Are you thinking what I'm thinking?' he asked with a
grimace as he too copped an eyeful of the All American
nightmare.

'Oh my, what a simply darling little restaurant,' the
girl trilled as, naturally, she and her other half were
led across the floor to join us. When they finally got
to the table, having admired every place setting and
table arrangement along the way, Mr Romantic USA
and the Maître d' had a small battle over who should
pull Ms Romantic USA's chair out for her. As it was,
Mr Romantic USA won and jerked the seat back so suddenly that his missus nearly ended up on the floor. Not
that she'd have felt a thing through the myriad layers
of that skirt. In my stretchy little black number from
Miss Selfridge, I suddenly felt rather underdressed by
comparison.

'Hi y'all,' drawled Ms Romantic USA while she straightened herself up and tried to fix her tiara back in place. Yes, now that she was up close I could see that beneath her bright blonde candyfloss hair there really nestled a small, glittering tiara! 'I'm Shelly Adamson and this is my fiancé Luke Connolly. Did you guys win the *Complete Woman* Most Romantic Couple competition too?'

I nodded.

'Isn't that sweet? Don't you think that's sweet, Luke? They've put all of us here together tonight. I see that I'm going to be sitting next to Mr Romantic (Aus). Where's that, honey? Is that somewhere near Arkansas?'

'I think they're from Australia, actually,' said Jeremy helpfully.

'Oh, my God,' Shelly exclaimed. 'Did you hear his accent, honey? Say something again. Are you guys from England?'

'Yes, we are,' said Jeremy, giving it the full Roger Moore as 007 treatment this time. 'I'm David Whitworth and this is my other half, Alison Harris.'

'Where exactly are you from?' Shelly asked me.

'Somewhere near London,' I said, knowing that Brindlesham would probably mean less than nothing to her.

'Wow. London. Do you know Hugh Grant by any chance?'

I had to bite down hard on my tongue to stop myself laughing when Jeremy told her that we did indeed know both Hugh and Liz, though Liz and I hadn't been too friendly since she borrowed my best Versace dress to go to a party and managed to drop red wine all over it.

'Didn't even offer to pay for the dry-cleaning,' Jeremy continued. Shelly's jaw was on the table. I gave Jeremy a kick beneath it.

'That's a lovely tiara,' I said to change the subject.

Shelly touched it affectionately. 'Why thank you. I won this in the Most Romantic Couple heats in Tucson, Arizona. We were up against three hundred other couples that night. All of them lovely people, just like you. But I have to say we were far and away the most romantic. Some of them didn't even hold hands. Luke here won a tie pin.' He showed up the tie pin, which was stuck in his waistcoat, since it wouldn't have looked right on the bootlace tie. I couldn't actually see it. Jeremy later claimed it was a little rhinestone heart with a cupid's arrow. There were so many rhinestones on Luke's ensemble, I thought he must have mugged the Follies Bergères.

'Didn't you get a tiara?' Shelly asked me next.

'I told you you should have brought yours, darling,' said Jeremy. 'It's similar to yours, Shelly. But bigger. And I think Alison's may have had rubies.'

I delivered a warning shot to Jeremy's foot with the heel of my new Pied A Terre sandals.

Thankfully, the most romantic people in Canada and Australia turned up before Jeremy could go any further. Chad and Penny Spencer from Ontario were pretty sweet. Like Luke and Shelly slightly watered down. But Mark from Australia was simply gorgeous. Unfortunately so was his half-Italian fiancée, Marguerite, and they only had eyes for each other. Not that I would really have strayed from Jeremy's side anyway.

'Alison knows Hugh Grant,' said Shelly reverently when the introductions had been made.

I smiled stiffly. Jeremy was just too good at this lying lark. And I told him so later that evening, when the Maître d' rather embarrassingly called us all up onto the dancefloor to start the evening's dancing with an anniversary waltz. Whirling round out of time in Jeremy's arms, I said, 'You really are being cruel to her you know.'

'So what,' he said. 'Shelly will go back to Little Hole, Nebraska or wherever it is they come from and dine out for years on the story. "We met some people who know Hugh Grant," ' he mimicked. 'She loves it.'

'I think you're being patronising.'

'No I'm not. She'll never know otherwise, believe me. I'm just giving her a little piece of a dream. That's all. Just a little piece of a dream.'

I smiled. It did seem pretty harmless then.

But when the band had packed up for the night, Shelly was still raring to go, pressing me for more details of my falling out with Liz. When it was clear that I wasn't going to come up with any more juicy titbits – I simply didn't have the imagination for it – Shelly said, 'It's so sweet that you're being so discreet about her even after the way she took such a liberty with your Versace.'

I allowed myself to bask guiltily in her high opinion of me.

'I have an idea,' she said then. 'We have champagne in our room.'

'We've finished ours,' said everybody else.

'Well, Luke and I wanted to save ours for a special occasion and I think that this is it. Right now. Here we are, the eight most romantic people in the world altogether in Antigua. Isn't it wonderful? I say that we go back to our room and read each other the elegies that got us where we are today.'

Jeremy and I shared a tortured glance. I had been under the impression that elegies were for the dead.

'Come on,' Shelly said, mustering us with her best cheerleading powers. 'I want to hear them. I need to know what we're up against this week.'

'Up against?' I asked.

'Yes,' she said. 'In the grand final. The competition to find the most romantic couple in the world. I hope you've all been practising.'

'For what? What do we have to do?'

We seemed to be the only couple who hadn't heard about this little development.

'We have to prove the strength of our love of course,' Shelly explained patiently. 'Aw, you're kidding me aren't you, Alison? You do know what we have to do really?'

Jeremy's face went slightly paler.

'We have to answer questions about each other's preferences and then talk about the things which keep our love going strong through the bad times. If you get an answer wrong. For example, if you say that his favourite kind of jelly is blackcurrant when it's really loganberry, then you're out. No second chances. Not that any one of us girls here would make a mistake that fundamental, of course.'

'Of course we wouldn't,' I agreed. But I didn't even know Jeremy's phone number off by heart yet, let alone his favourite kind of jam.

'Oh, it's going to be such a lot of fun,' Shelly clapped her hands together.

'Sounds like a bloody stupid idea to me,' said Mark from Brisbane.

'Now, don't you be such an old sourpuss,' said Shelly. 'Come on. I want to hear what you girls all wrote about your men. I'll start.'

I heaved a sigh of relief. With a bit of luck, the American version of the competition wouldn't have had a word limit on entries and we'd all be dead before I had to read mine out. Not that I could anyway. I hadn't exactly kept a copy.

'I knew from the moment I first set eyes on Luke,' Shelly began, 'that one day we would grow old together and find ourselves at fifty on the front porch of life . . .'

Jeremy yawned ostentatiously. So ostentatiously that Shelly paused.

'Jet lag,' I explained.

Shelly nodded and continued. 'No challenge in my working life could possibly give me the same satisfaction as making sandwiches for my fiancé to take to work . . .'

Marguerite nodded.

'No public honour could be so great as the right to wear his engagement ring on my left hand.'

Penny gave a hearty sigh.

'Are these girls from Planet Stepford?' Jeremy whispered in my ear.

'Looks like it. Have you got a gippy tummy yet?'

He looked at me in confusion. But he wasn't the only one who could make up a good story in times of utter desperation.

'Shelly,' I interrupted. 'We'd really love to hear the rest of your elegy but I think that David's suffering . . .'

All eyes turned to discover what from.

'No, no, no. Of course he's not bored,' I reassured them. 'It's just the heat and the rich food. Interferes with his natural functions. You know how men are.'

Shelly covered her mouth with her hand in case he was infectious. 'Then you had better go and take some rest,' she told Jeremy through her fingers. 'You don't want to spoil the whole holiday. Missing you already,' she added with a hand-covered smile.

Jeremy nodded bravely and as we left, I was sure I heard Shelly say, 'Those Englishmen. Always suffering in silence. It's those stiff upper lips they have, isn't it?'

So ended our first night at the lovely resort of Santa Bonita. Jeremy and I lay on our ocean-wide bed, staring up at the fan that slowly chopped the air above us to keep us cool.

'Recovered from your tummy upset yet?' I asked him as I rolled across to kiss him goodnight.

'Certainly have,' he said as he wrapped me in his arms and began to kiss me all over and I mean all over, though there was no champagne to lick off this time. An hour later, panting with exertion, we rolled apart once more.

'You were a lioness tonight,' Jeremy told me.

I roared obligingly. Then wished that I hadn't. The walls of that hut must have been really thin, because I was sure I heard Shelly wishing goodnight to her man.

'Goodnight, Luke.'

'Goodnight, Shelly.'

We were staying next door to the Waltons.

CHAPTER TWENTY-SIX

The second day of our holiday was of course February the 14th. Though in the excitement and panic of going to Antigua I had completely lost track of the passing time. When I woke up on the morning of the sunniest Valentine's Day I had ever seen, Jeremy wasn't in the bed beside me. Instead, a small envelope lay on the pillow with my name written upon it in swirly writing.

I sat up suddenly. No-one had ever left a note on my pillow before. In fact, no-one had ever left me a note anywhere before, apart from my boss at Hudderston's, to tell me that I needed to order more staples. My stomach lurched up into my mouth as, barely awake, I opened what could only be a 'Dear John'.

'I know it's twenty years later, but I'd like to say yes to being your Valentine.'

I began to laugh with relief at the reference to the card I had sent Jeremy in 1979. At that moment he walked back into the hut, dripping from an early dip in the sea, and carrying a pink conch shell that covered half my face when Jeremy held it to my ear so that I could hear the waves.

'Happy Valentine's Day,' he said, as he kissed me good morning.

I couldn't help crying then, as I always do when something really wonderful happened. Just a little sob. I'm a sap like that. I'm afraid I just can't help thinking forward to a time when the happy moment will be but a distant memory. I also miss people in advance, sulking about them going away for a week before they leave then hardly noticing the difference when they've actually gone.

'I haven't got you anything,' I told him, wiping the tears from my eyes. 'I'd completely forgotten in my hurry to get ready for this trip.'

Jeremy put the conch shell into my hands and smiled handsomely. 'I don't need presents. I've got you.'

It was perfect. So perfect. I thought I was going to explode with happiness.

Meanwhile, in the hut next door, Shelly and Luke had obviously woken up. We heard Shelly shriek with delight and when we next saw the United States' most romantic couple at breakfast, she was dressed from head to toe in hearts. Pink heart-shaped earrings. A red heart-printed dress. There were even fluffy hearts on the tops of her little white socks.

'Isn't this outfit just the sweetest?' she asked me. 'Luke chose it all himself. I'm so lucky to have a man with such amazing taste.'

Amazing was the word for it, but I just smiled. It was hard to be sarcastic when faced with such blind faith in romance. Besides, if Jeremy had turned up that morning with a pair of heart-patterned pedal-pushers instead of the conch shell, I probably would have put them on too.

I wrote my postcards on the second day, because there's nothing worse than beating your postcards home, especially if you're sending one to your housemate so that you actually see it arrive while you're picking off the last of your tan over breakfast.

Anyway, even though I had been on the island for less than twenty-four hours, it wasn't as if I didn't have anything to write about. I could have written a whole book on the beauty of the place. I kept looking at the sparkling sea, then rubbing my eyes, as if it just wasn't possible that water could be so blue. Or the sky. Not a cloud. Not a whisper of wind to spoil the day.

'Dear Emma,' I wrote. 'Life just couldn't get any better. Jeremy woke me up this morning, Valentine's Day, with the gift of a perfect conch shell he had found on the beach for me. I feel as though I am living in a dream-world. Please give my love to Fattypuss.'

I stuck to the usual platitudes when writing home, including 'Wish you were here' on the card I sent to my parents. My mother would have been upset if I hadn't made some pretence at missing her. I wondered how Grandma's birthday party was going. But not for too long.

When I had licked the last of the stamps I needed I found that I had one card and one stamp left over.

'Got anyone you need to write to?' I asked Jeremy. He was stretched out on a sun-lounger with his new paperback novel protecting his beautiful nose from burning up.

'No,' he told me. 'I don't even want to think about anyone back home, let alone write to them.'

It seemed a shame to waste the postcard though, particularly as I had already licked the stamp.

I don't know quite what came over me then, but I decided that I would send the spare card to David. It wasn't to gloat, you understand. At least that's what I told myself. I was simply sending him a card to suggest that there were no hard feelings on my part and that perhaps when I did get back from Antigua we really might start to think about becoming friends again. If he was especially nice to me.

'Dear David,' I wrote. 'Well, here I am on the sun-drenched island of Antigua. It's eighty degrees in the shade, really hot stuff! The only thing I have to worry about is where my next *cock*-tail is coming from. See you soon. Love, Ali.' At first I didn't put any kisses at the bottom, but then I added two. It seemed petty not to.

I took the postcards to the lobby and handed them to the duty receptionist to post. Then, chores done, I stripped down to my borrowed pink bikini (Emma had come to the rescue) and flopped into the pool with a triumphant whoop of joy. I flopped so triumphantly that the water splashed out of the pool and all over Jeremy's paperback.

'Do you have to be quite so exuberant?' he asked.

I did. I was having the time of my life. If you can't be exuberant while you're sitting in the sunshine, I asked him, when everyone back home is fighting to work through gales, when can you be? If you can't be exuberant when you only have to click your fingers for a pina colada to arrive at your side, you may as well holiday in a morgue.

Sensing defeat, Jeremy put down his book and joined me in the pool. I managed just one and a half lengths before I felt the urge to swim up and wrap my arms around him. He kissed me on the nose and I felt like I was floating on something far more magical than water.

'Are you glad you came?' I asked him prettily.

'Ask me again in half an hour,' he said, hauling me back out of the pool and dragging me off in the direction of our beach hut.

Our second night. We made our way down to dinner and were about to take our places at the big round table when the Maître d' came over with an apologetic mutter and told us that the sea view table had been promised to someone else that night. Now, I would have gone quietly, happy to be in a corner with Jeremy, alone. But Mr and Miss Romantic America were outraged.

'Someone else,' Shelly shrieked. 'Whaddya mean? We're the most romantic couple in America. Who deserves this view more than we do?'

'Candida Bianca,' said the Maître d' quietly. I didn't even catch what he had said first time, but I guessed it must have been pretty impressive when Shelly's mouth dropped open so that she looked like one of the shoal of grouper I had seen on that afternoon's snorkelling trip.

'The Candida Bianca?' she asked.

Then my mouth dropped open too. And Luke's and Jeremy's and the mouths of anyone else close enough to eavesdrop on this incredible revelation.

'She's staying here? In this hotel? You're kidding me? The Candida Bianca?' asked Luke, with the kind of reverence my mother reserved for talking about the Pope.

'She stays here every year, and I'm afraid that this is her favourite table in the dining room,' explained the man in charge.

'That's fine,' said Shelly, throwing her hands up in defeat. 'You tell her she can sit on my fiancé's knee if she wants to. She is such a great actress. I don't believe she's really here. Please give her our very fondest regards.'

'Yes, and mine,' said Jeremy, his eyes still glistening with that look that children get in the run-up to Christmas. Then he brought out a scrap of paper from his pocket and thrust it at the Maître d' asking if he would be so kind as to ask Miss Bianca to sign it, to Jeremy, if she had a moment. Or the inclination.

'I heard she never signs autographs,' said Shelly in warning. 'Not since that guy threatened to kill himself and President Clinton if she wouldn't marry him.'

'That was terrible,' I said, remembering the newspaper reports of the incident well. She had been walking out of a smart Hollywood restaurant with Kevin Costner. Some madman had asked for her autograph, thrusting a piece of paper in front of her nose. On it, he had written his demands: 'Marry me or the president dies.' In green ink, a true sign of madness. Then he flashed open his jacket to reveal enough semtex to blow up the whole of Los Angeles strapped to his body with gaffer tape.

'I don't know how she carried on after that,' said Shelly in awe.

'She was just born to act,' said Luke. 'She is the most incredible actress since . . . er, since . . . since the most incredible actresses you can think of really.'

'Have you seen *The Twelve Days of Christmas* yet?' asked Shelly. It had been released in England at the end of November. Candida Bianca played an angel, setting the world to rights, reforming muggers and bringing broken families back together for the holidays. I had insisted on seeing the film with a rather reluctant David in tow. I wondered briefly if things would have been different had I let him see the Jean Claude Van Damme blood-fest instead.

'I liked her best in *Terminator Seven*,' said Jeremy.

'No, no, no. She definitely gave her best performance in the screen version of Sir Cliff Richard's *Wuthering Heights*,' Shelly protested.

But the discussion was cut short when we were ushered to the table next to the kitchen door, as at the other end of the room, and even as we sat down, the beaded curtain was lifted aside for the guest of honour. The room went silent, even cutlery stopped clinking against porcelain when Candida Bianca walked in. The star of last summer's three hottest movies. Hollywood's highest paid female star of the moment. She was so stratospherically successful that she made Julia Roberts look like the office junior of the movie world.

'She is so beautiful,' murmured Shelly.

'She's shorter than I expected,' I said, but no-one seemed to hear.

The room continued to stand still as everyone watched their heroine glide across the carpet in a pair of impossibly high-heeled iridescent gold shoes, to go with the sparkling beaded dress she wore. It was actually less a dress than a second skin, clinging tightly to her pneumatic curves; it was the perfect accompaniment to the honey-gold tan that made her teeth look even whiter than Hollywood white. Her long black hair, worn loose for her role as a Latino temptress in *August Moon*, was tied up in a graceful, glossy chignon, as it had been for her latest role as a hot-shot lawyer. She had been dubbed La Chameleon, for her ability to look perfectly cast whether she was playing white trash or a Jewish princess. Whatever she was playing, she always looked beautiful.

But most surprising of all was that she entered the restaurant alone. She sat alone at her table, back to the room, facing the sea, ordered with a whisper and then proceeded to watch the twinkling lights on the bay until her meal came.

Everyone at my table could watch only Candida Bianca.

'Want to swap sides?' Jeremy asked me after our first course. 'You might get a stiff neck from sitting in the draught from that window.' I swapped gratefully, not thinking for a moment that Jeremy could have such a dastardly ulterior motive as wanting a better view of Candida Bianca.

As she neared the end of her meal, we watched on tenterhooks as the Maître d' asked Candida whether she would sign Jeremy's scrap of paper. Her forehead crumpled into a frown as she took the scrap, then the Maître d' pointed in Jeremy's direction and Candida looked up, caught his eye and actually smiled. She smiled straight at my boyfriend. Then she scribbled something onto the paper and left the dining room with a little wave in his direction.

Jeremy was jumpy as a cat with fleas as he waited for the Maître d' to bring the scrap of paper back to us. When he did, we crowded round to see what she had written. Shelly said that she had done a graphology course and would be happy to analyse the signature for us.

'What colour has she written in?' Shelly asked.

'Red,' said Jeremy.

'Oooh, that's very passionate. Red represents sensuality. A good sign.'

'She just took the pen that the Maître d' handed her,' I protested.

'What does it actually say?' asked Mark, Mr Romantic Australia by name but ever the practical sheep farmer at heart.

'Er, just her name,' Jeremy said, looking somewhat unnaturally flustered as we others fought to have a look at the sacred superstar signature.

'And her room number!' Mark suddenly boomed. 'Way-hey! You're in there, mate.'

'Excuse me,' said his girlfriend, Marguerite, speaking up on my behalf. 'Aren't you forgetting someone?'

'Er, sorry, Alison,' said Mark.

'Is it really her room number?' I asked Jeremy as I struggled to keep the jealousy from my voice.

'No,' said Jeremy. 'Of course it isn't. She's just written the date under her signature, that's all. See, 14th of the 6.'

'But it's February now,' said Shelly.

'Did she write 6?' Jeremy blushed. 'She must have meant a 2.'

Well, I was convinced. After all, gorgeous as Jeremy was to me, I didn't really think I needed to protect my interests from the clutches of a woman who could have had Brad Pitt for breakfast. What would she want with a lowly computer programmer from England? Even if he did hold the whole of Eastern Europe in his hands . . .

'Well, she seems pretty friendly. I'm going to ask for her autograph tomorrow night,' Luke decided.

'No, you're not,' said Shelly adamantly. 'You're going to leave her alone. I'm sure she just wants her privacy.'

'Hear, hear,' said Marguerite, Penny and I.

CHAPTER TWENTY-SEVEN

'Hi.'
Next morning, I was sitting by the pool, feeling rather proud of my budding tan, and the fact that my belly was looking more gently rolling tundra than hillock at the moment, when I was joined by Candida Bianca.

'Mind if I join you?' she asked.

It was a difficult one. Of course I didn't mind being joined by a celebrity, but at the same time, I knew my satisfaction with my newly, reasonably decent body was going to be pretty short-lived once she slipped off her robe and revealed whatever dental floss piece of bikini she had chosen for that morning.

'Where's your boyfriend?' she asked me as she untied her sandals.

'Scuba diving,' I told her.

'And you're not joining him?'

'I don't like to get my hair wet,' I joked, but she seemed to have taken me seriously so I added, 'Makes me feel a bit claustrophobic actually. I did try to learn once, in a swimming pool, but I just know that if I ever came face to face with a shark or something horrible like that I would shoot up to the surface too quickly and get the bends.'

'The bends? What's that?' Candida Bianca asked.

'Nitrogen in your brain I think,' I bluffed. 'Makes you feel like you're pissed apparently.'

'What? Angry?'

'No, pissed in the English sense. Drunk.'

'Sounds like fun.'

'It can kill you.'

'I'd like to learn to dive anyway,' she said, unpacking her beach bag to reveal a Harvey Nichols' beauty department's worth of expensive unguents. 'Do you think your boyfriend would teach me?'

'Well, I don't think he knows that much about it himself. He's just learning too.'

'Pity,' she said, shrugging off her robe. Iridescent pink dental floss this time, with bra cups the size of Dairylea triangles, on breasts the size of generous Edams.

'You two been together long?' she asked.

'Not really,' I said. 'About a week if I'm truthful.'

'A week!' she shrieked. 'And he's brought you to the Caribbean already? That's really something. Though Brad Pitt did fly me to Rio for our second date, I suppose. Whatever does your boyfriend do, to enable him to make such incredible gestures?'

'Actually, it was my gesture. I brought him.'

'Wow. Then what do you do?' she asked, rolling onto her elbow to look at me while she heard my reply.

'I'm a . . .' I hesitated. Candida Bianca wouldn't want to talk to a lowly secretary who'd won a poxy competition. 'I'm an engineer,' I said instead. It was almost true. I had worked with several in my time. And lying was becoming so natural . . .

'Wow,' Candida cooed. 'That's so . . . so noble of you. I really admire women who are prepared to throw off feminine convention and get their hands dirty for a change. Have you invented anything I might know? Or are you one of those brave people who work in a nuclear power station or something like that?'

'I deal with pipes mostly,' I said nonchalantly. 'Hydraulics. Tubes and stuff.'

'Oh.' She visibly wilted at the thought of having to listen to any further explanation. 'That's nice. And what about your boyfriend?'

'Computers. In the eastern bloc. He's actually based in Warsaw.'

'Oh, Germany? How lovely.'

'It's Poland, actually.'

'Wow,' she said again. 'You guys really are brains and beauty. I mean to say that you're the beauty of course,' she added just a little unconvincingly.

'Well, thank you. But I have to say that I don't feel particularly beautiful next to you, Miss Bianca.'

'Oh, call me Candida,' she purred. 'And don't ever let me hear you say that silly thing about not feeling beautiful again. It isn't a skin deep thing. Real beauty comes from the inside. Sometimes I feel like a dog myself. You just have to think positive and you'll glow with something far greater than superficial beauty.'

'Try explaining that to any man I've ever met,' I snorted.

'But don't you see that your boyfriend already knows

it? I wouldn't care if all my hair fell out tomorrow if I could have just an hour of the happiness you two so obviously have together.'

'Really?' I was incredulous. 'But you've dated Brad Pitt and all those other famous stars. Every girl in the universe envies you.'

'Empty experiences, darling. Mostly set up by my agent for PR purposes. There's always some up and coming male star in Hollywood who needs to avoid a sudden gay relationship scandal. No, you don't know how lucky you are to be normal, Alison. Real, honest, decent men are just too afraid to approach me half the time. They'd have a surprise if they did. I get asked out on a proper date so rarely that I'd say yes to the pizza delivery man if he asked me.'

'I don't believe it,' I said. 'I'd love to be famous.'

'Be careful what you wish for,' said Candida. 'In case it just happens to come true.'

It was very difficult to concentrate on sunbathing next to the world's most beautiful woman. Every thirty seconds or so I would think that a cloud was passing over the sun as every man, woman and child staying at the Santa Bonita resort made some spurious excuse to saunter over to our side of the pool and linger, casting a shadow over Candida and me, as she tanned and I blushed at the thought of them making unflattering comparisons. Inner beauty isn't immediately obvious in a bikini.

I couldn't wait to write more postcards. I spent a good deal of the afternoon imagining Marvin's stunned and disbelieving face when I told him that I had actually sunbathed next to a living, breathing movie star, and, more importantly, that she had told me that she actually envied my simple, uncomplicated life. She was so nice. She let me share her Estée Lauder sun-cream. It's always a surprise when famous people are nice, isn't it? You can't help imagining that anyone who's ever been on TV becomes a monster as soon as the camera is off, swiping at little children with manicured claws if they dare ask for an autograph.

Despite her terrible experiences with the President Clinton nut, Candida seemed happy to sign anything for anyone that afternoon. At one point, she even had the good grace to sign some disgusting Italian man's left buttock. He said that he was going to get her signature tattooed over so that he could remember the moment forever.

'Pervert,' Candida commented in a whisper as he swaggered back to show his mates the biro scrawl.

'Do you think he'll really get a tattoo?' I asked her.

'Well, if all the men that said they were going to did, my name would be more popular than "Mum" in the tattoo world. I don't think so. This week I'm their favourite star, they say they've watched all of my films . . . next week they'll be telling Danny Devito exactly the same.'

'I don't think anyone would ask him to sign a buttock.'

'You'd be surprised. Anyway, when is that boyfriend of yours coming back? Aren't you worried that he might have been eaten by sharks?'

'He said he'd be a couple of hours.'

'It's been that long already, surely,' she said, checking the time on the Cartier watch she had taken off and placed on the floor beneath her lounger so that the strap mark didn't interfere with her perfect tan.

'You seem more worried about him than I am,' I laughed, nervously.

'Oh no,' she said, slipping her sunglasses over her eyes so that she was inscrutable once more. 'I'm just interested to hear about this diving.'

Well, Candida certainly asked questions about diving when Jeremy finally came back from the sea with a big red mark on his nose where the snorkel mask had been. Unfortunately Jeremy was too gob-smacked to tell her much, but he agreed readily when she asked if she could be his partner on a dive the next morning.

'You'll look after me, won't you?' she asked, patting him on the arm.

'Nnngh,' said Jeremy.

It was only when we got back to our room that the magnitude of that conversation by the pool seemed to sink in.

'She wants me to look after her on a dive,' said Jeremy.

'Yes,' I said, somewhat jealous. If only I hadn't had that irrational fear of man-eating sharks, I could have gone along to chaperone.

'She wants me to look after her on a dive,' he said again.

'You just said that,' I replied.

'You don't mind, do you, Ali?' Jeremy asked. 'No, of course you don't,' he continued before I could form an answer. 'Imagine the amazing stories we're going to have to tell people when we get back home to England.'

'Yes, imagine,' I said. Though I would have been happy enough just to say that Candida Bianca and I had shared a bottle of Factor 8.

From next door, Shelly and Luke's room, there suddenly came the sound of voices being raised.

'You will not ask her!' Shelly was shrieking. 'You're here to celebrate our romance, not chase some silver-screen tart. You're ruining my Valentine's Day.'

Jeremy and I shared an amused glance as we listened to Luke trying to make amends.

'I won't ask her for her autograph, Shelly, I promise I won't. I don't know why I even dared think about it.'

'You're lucky I'm not Shelly,' I told Jeremy then. 'Sounds like she would string you up by your air hose.'

'Yes, I'm lucky to be with you,' he said, wrapping his arms around me. 'If it were any other girl, Alison, you know that I wouldn't have said yes to taking her diving. I'm meant to be here for you. But Candida Bianca . . . It's such a rare opportunity. You have to understand . . .'

'You don't have to say it,' I said, shaking him off and heading for the shower. I tried in vain to wash out my jealousy with two whole sachets of hotel shower gel.

'It's all right,' I told myself as I scrubbed furiously at the rough skin on my heels. 'They're just going diving together. If Brad Pitt were diving here too, she would definitely go with him instead.'

But I couldn't fight that stab of pain when I came out of the bathroom to catch Jeremy at the mirror, checking his reflection in a snorkel mask.

CHAPTER TWENTY-EIGHT

That night was Limbo Night at the resort's own Beach Bar. I wasn't desperately keen to join in, since I was barely flexible enough to touch my own knees let alone shimmy through a six-inch gap, but Jeremy was insistent. He wanted to see everything, and make the most of this all-inclusive business by trying every cocktail on the menu. We joined Luke and Shelly at a table reserved specially for the world's most romantic lovers. Ms Canada had sunstroke and Australia's Mark had wimped out having made the most of the free cocktails since breakfast.

'I had heard that Australians like their alcohol,' said Shelly primly. 'But I've always tried to resist classing people by racial stereotypes. Still, if he keeps it up, it'll be less competition for us on the night of the grand finale,' she added with a smile. 'You're looking very brown, Alison. I didn't think the English tanned.'

'I spent the afternoon by the pool, with Candida.'

'Candida Bianca? You mean she was by the pool as well.'

'Yes, right next to me.'

'But not with you, surely,' Shelly probed.

'She let me borrow some of her sun-cream.'

Before Shelly could articulate her surprise, the place fell into the usual silence that heralded the arrival of Candida in that evening's fabulous dress.

This time it was red. A silken slip of a thing, with a diagonal hem, that fluttered like a flame around her perfect legs. She shook her head when the Maître d' offered her her usual table and made a bee-line for us, instead.

'Oh my God, she's coming over here,' Shelly muttered into her napkin as Candida walked through a crowd that parted like the Red Sea around her and took what would have been Marguerite's place were she not nursing Mark through a bout of alcohol poisoning.

'I hope you don't mind me joining you,' the megastar said sweetly. As if anybody ever did. Shelly just gulped air like a frog.

The cocktails flowed like water all night that night. Every time I put an empty glass down on the table, Jeremy reminded me that we were on an all-inclusive deal and it was my duty to make the most of it. So the cocktails kept on coming. Blue ones, pink ones, green ones. Fruity, fiery and creamy ones. Tall ones and short ones, all with a variety of cocktail stirrers and paper umbrellas, until the surface of the table started to look slightly wobbly and I knew that whatever I did, I mustn't stand up.

'Come to the bathroom with me,' Shelly said suddenly, hauling me to my feet and dragging me behind her to the ladies.

'It's OK! It's OK!' I protested, as the room swirled around me. 'I'm not really drunk at all.'

'What?' said Shelly as she positioned herself in the best place at the mirror and started to reapply her lipstick.

'I said I'm not drunk,' I mumbled.

'You surely are,' said Shelly flatly. 'But that is your business. Now, what do you think she's up to?'

'Who?' I asked.

'That Candida woman, of course. What is she doing, joining us for dinner when she could have had the best table in the place to herself?'

'She said she wanted company.'

'Huh. And I think I know exactly whose company she wants. She can't take her eyes off him. She's been undressing him in her mind ever since she sat down at the table with us. Well, I'll tell you what, she's going to have to quit messing around because I don't care how much her nose-job cost, I'm going to flatten that pretty little ski-jump right to her face if she does it once more.'

'Eh?'

'She's been making eyes at my Luke, Ali. All night. I was starting to feel like I was the gooseberry out there. She's driving me crazy. What should I do about it? You've got to help me out.'

'She wasn't making eyes at him,' I tried, hoping that I might be able to calm her down. 'You must have been imagining things. What would she want with someone like Luke, anyway?'

'What do you mean? What would she want with someone like Luke? Are you joking with me? He's the most romantic man in America. Officially. And I know when a woman wants my fiancé. My imagination is perfectly under control and I know what I saw with my very own eyes. You've got to help me, Ali. You've got to suggest that we all move places around the table so that we can better talk to the people we haven't spoken to so far, then you've got to sit right between her and Luke, so that she can't start playing footsie or putting her hand in his lap. I can trust you to do that can't I, Ali?'

She shook me so that the ceiling seemed to lurch dangerously towards my head.

'Well, there's no way I'll be playing footsie with Luke,' I said when the room stopped moving.

'Good. Now, do you want to sort yourself out before we go back into the restaurant. I'll hold your hair back while you puke if you like.'

'No, I'm fine, really.'

'You look a little bilious. I'm quite happy to help you, Ali. I've been bringing on my vomit since high school. How else can one keep slim and yet still pretend to have a sensual appetite?'

I felt sick at the thought. I had never actually brought a chunder on. Instead, I refused her kind offer and staggered back out into the restaurant with my alcohol quota still very much intact. But so much for Shelly's seating-plan plan. Only Jeremy remained at our table. Candida had already spirited Luke onto the dance floor to join her in a particularly filthy looking merengue.

'Why didn't you stop him?' Shelly shrieked when she spotted her beau.

'Stop him what?' asked Jeremy.

'From dancing with her.'

'Why don't you just go and interrupt them yourself?' he asked.

'I will,' said Shelly, setting her jaw. 'You know what. I will.'

'Got to see this,' said Jeremy, as Shelly flounced onto

the dance floor. 'Come on.' He hauled me to my feet and manhandled me out there after her, to stagger around the fight in an approximation of a waltz.

'Excuse me,' said Shelly, baring her teeth like an irritated Jack Russell. 'If it's OK with you, Miss Bianca, I'd like to dance with my fiancé.' She injected the word with such venom you might have thought she was using a different f-word altogether.

Candida stepped away with her hands up. 'Feel free, I was just about to sit down anyway. My feet are killing me in these shoes.'

'Hope they give you bunions,' said Shelly to the star's retreating back.

Jeremy and I did two more spins around the dance floor but my head was in such a bad way that when Jeremy told me that he thought he should ask Candida to dance, since she was starting to look lonely after two minutes off the floor, I was almost pleased at the prospect of a nice quiet sit-down. Jeremy escorted me back to the table and settled me safely in a chair.

'One more for the road, I suppose,' I agreed when a cocktail waitress asked me if I wanted a Brain Haemorrhage. I downed the disgusting Baileys and grenadine concoction in one, then I put my head down on my folded arms as Jeremy led Candida out onto the dance floor and was asleep before they'd made one trip around the room.

The music still played inside my head. I dreamed of a swirling room. Of concerned faces crowding round me as I started to spin myself. I was spinning, spinning, out of control. Then:

'Oh, my God! Will somebody deal with this woman?' Shelly was shouting.

I was vomiting all over my bare arms and onto the floor.

Thank goodness someone in that room had trained as a nurse. She quickly pushed all others aside to clear my air passages and had her boyfriend help Jeremy carry me back to our room.

'What happens now?' I heard Jeremy ask as if he were a long way off into the distance.

'You just have to leave her until she sleeps through it. If she's in this position, she can't do herself an injury if she vomits.'

'Is it OK if I go back to the party?' Jeremy asked.

'You go. I'll look in on her later on,' the nurse kindly said.

Then everything went black and fuzzy.

CHAPTER TWENTY-NINE

When I next woke up it was fairly late in the day. I rolled over to face Jeremy in bed, except he wasn't there. His pillow looked undented.

I sat up suddenly, but was quickly pinned back down again by the mother of all headaches. I couldn't exactly remember what had happened but all the evidence pointed to one shandy too many. Dried sick stained the front of my Jean Paul Gaultier sundress (another acquisition from Emma's trendy wardrobe).

'Uugh.'

I crept into the bathroom and started to spruce myself up. My watch, which somebody had kindly placed on the washstand, told me that it was eleven o'clock. I had slept right through breakfast. I decided that the housekeeper must have been in to make up Jeremy's side of the bed while I dreamed my drunkenness off.

Grateful for my shades to cut out the light, I made my way down to the pool. When my entrance seemed to inspire almost as much awe as the magical nightly appearance of Candida Bianca in evening dress, I knew that whatever I had done the night before, I must have done it in spectacular style.

'Why is everybody staring at me today?' I asked Shelly.

'They are probably just concerned,' she assured me. 'You overdid it just a little at the beach barbecue.'

'I guessed as much. What happened after I left?'

'Well, Candida was up to her usual tricks. She did a couple of turns around the floor with David, then she set her sights on Chad. Like dancing with an octopus, he said it was. I don't know why she can't go for the single men. There are plenty of them around here.'

I stole a glance at the Italian Stallions, playing with a beach ball, hairy chests rippling like cornfields in the breeze. 'Maybe she isn't actually looking for anything more than a dance,' I suggested. 'If she dances with the men who are already attached, then nothing more can happen, can it?'

'Well, whatever you think, I will be keeping Luke under close observation from now on,' said Shelly, scanning the pool for her puppy dog. 'That woman is dangerous, Ali. I'm telling you. She's poison.'

Then Miss Poison herself sat down next to us.

'Oh, hi Candida,' Shelly trilled. 'Can I just say what a fantastic dress you were wearing last evening?'

'Why thank you. Would you like to have it?'

'What? Moi?' Shelly clutched her hand to her heart. 'Are you serious? Me have your dress?'

'Sure. I can never wear the same dress twice. Imagine what the press would say.'

'Imagine,' I sighed.

'What about you, Ali? You'd look fantastic in that

pink dress I wore on Tuesday. Would you like to have
that? It's vintage Versace.'

'Wow,' I couldn't help myself. 'But it's OK, you keep
it,' I told her. 'I'd need to get shoes to go with it . . .'

'Have mine,' said Candida generously. 'I'd say we're
about the same size.' She stretched out her leg alongside
mine so that we could compare the size of our feet. I
quickly tucked mine beneath me. My crusty toenails
were no match for her pedicure in the latest cult colour
by Chanel.

'Come round and fetch them from my room whenever you like.'

'That's so generous,' said Shelly. 'So very kind.'

'Think nothing of it. You girls want a drink, I'm going
to the bar?'

'Make mine a margarita,' said Shelly.

'Coke,' said I.

As soon as Candida was out of earshot, Shelly started
again. 'And what do you think that is all about?' she
asked. 'Offering us her cast-offs as some kind of consolation prize for trying to steal our men.'

'We didn't have to accept.'

'Are you kidding? That red dress she wore last night
wasn't off the peg at Nordstrom, you know. No, I'll
take the dress, but I'm not dropping my guard for one
moment. I've heard about these Hollywood women.
She probably expects us to turn a blind eye to her
escapades if we accept her presents. Probably expects
us to treat it as a honour that she wants to sleep with
what's ours.'

'Perhaps she's just a generous soul.'

*   *   *

We were certainly making the most of our holiday. Every day, from dawn till dusk, was like a scene from a Hollywood movie. Breakfast in bed. Cocktails by the pool. The sun beating down on the sea as Jeremy and Candida scuba dived and I snorkelled in the shallows, trying to pet the big, rainbow-bright fish which swam fearlessly around me, until it was time to go back to the restaurant and eat some of their less fortunate cousins.

I felt like a princess. No, better than a princess, since I wasn't having to fight off the waistline criticising paparazzi while I lounged on the sand.

Our fellow romantic winners seemed to be having an equally good time, but in their own special way. Mark and Marguerite started every morning with a jog along the beach. (They might have been the World's Fittest Couple too.) Chad and Penny did a spot of bird-watching. And Shelly kept Luke well occupied. After breakfast, they would go straight down to the pool. He would oil her all over with factor twenty-five sunscreen, then he would spend the morning moving the parasol which shaded her every five minutes so that her face was never fully in the sun.

'Keep young and beautiful,' she warned me once while I slathered on the factor nil cooking oil I had bought at the airport. Hell, I wasn't likely to get another holiday like this in a hurry, I reassured myself. I was going to go home with a tan even if it was my last.

CHAPTER THIRTY

Then suddenly we had just two days left to go. The first layer of my tan was already flaking off so I planned to spend my last 48 hours baking. Jeremy wanted to get in as much diving as he could, with Candida of course. I had trained myself not to mind, since she spent every evening with us talking about Hollywood men she had big crushes on, and my wardrobe now boasted a Versace.

But Candida wasn't alone by the pool and ready to go diving that last but one morning. Squinting through my sleep-bleary eyes as we walked across the empty garden to the restaurant, I thought at first that she was sitting on one of the loungers with a man. The youngish looking chap had a clipboard, and he was ticking things off while Candida lounged and lolled and looked terribly bored by it all. Her face changed dramatically when she spotted me with Jeremy. She waved a long brown arm in our direction and beckoned us over. I just about managed to hide my surprise when she introduced us to Loretta, her personal assistant. A girl.

Loretta grunted hello, rearranged the straps on her

short denim dungarees and dragged a hand through her bleached crew-cut hair in a masculine fashion.

'I can't come diving today,' she told a horribly disappointed Jeremy. 'Loretta has flown out here to harangue me. She doesn't think I should have been diving at all. Says it isn't covered by my life insurance. Honestly, Alison, you have no idea what a drag it is to be a successful actress. I can't be away from work for five minutes. Can I?' She looked at Loretta accusingly.

'Jerry says that we have to sort this French contract out by tonight or you'll lose it altogether,' Loretta complained.

'Maybe I don't want to do his crumby little film anyway,' Candida spat. 'Well, would you want to spend a month in Paris shooting the life story of Coco Chanel, Ali? I'm only playing her until she starts to get all middle-aged and doggy. Demi Moore's doing the rest.' She smiled her disarming smile, as though she was unaware of how bitchy her comment had sounded. 'Besides, Paris is in Europe. What is there to do in Europe for heaven's sake? I don't have any friends there. And the food? They don't have Granola, you know. It's all snails and horse-meat. Yuk.'

'You have us in Europe,' Jeremy piped up suddenly. Candida turned on the full beam again.

'Why yes, I do. How far is London from Paris?' she asked suddenly.

'Three hours by Eurostar,' I said helpfully.

'And you'll be in London?' she asked us.

'Well, not exactly. Brindlesham is on the outskirts. And David will be in Warsaw again.'

Candida's face fell. 'But that's in Germany, isn't it?' she asked hopefully.

'No. Poland. But it's just a short flight away from Paris,' Jeremy said soothingly. 'I could show you around.'

I could see Candida's brain working as she hovered with a biro over the dotted line on her contract to play fashion's greatest doyenne.

'What was that other job?' she asked Loretta suddenly. 'The cold one.'

'The one in Warsaw?' said Loretta with a look of surprise. 'The last days of the Tsars. I thought you weren't interested in all that "highbrow stuff",' she added mockingly.

'I never said that,' said Candida. 'Does it clash with the Coco Chanel business?'

'Absolutely. They start shooting on the exact same day.'

'Then send my apologies to Jerry, but tell him that I want to make something arthouse instead. Tell him I want to make sure I'm not typecast as a fashion bimbo.'

'Coco Chanel was hardly a fashion bimbo,' I said in surprise.

'She was hardly Versace either,' Candida replied. 'Loretta, send Vadim my tape again and tell him that you turned the part of Anastasia down on my behalf by mistake. I'd love to play the Tsarina. Tell him I've fired you as well while you're at it.'

Loretta took the notes down dutifully.

'I meant that last bit,' said Candida, when she caught a hint of a smile on her PA's face. 'I can't abide incompetence. You guys had breakfast yet?' she asked me and Jeremy cheerfully. Then she linked her arm through Jeremy's and Loretta and I followed them inside.

For someone who had just been fired, Loretta seemed to get an awful lot of errands to run over that breakfast. There were letters to write, contracts to chase and the right suntan lotion to source. I wondered what Loretta was doing working for a woman like Candida. With her funky, ethnic nose-ring and her bleached, cropped hair, Loretta looked as though she would be more at home giving a reading of the latest in anarchic poetry in some basement bar rather than running about looking for the right lipstick for a woman who was only one step up the intellectual evolutionary chain from a toy poodle. But Loretta took the gibes Candida rained on her like a mother ignoring the bleatings of a spoilt child. I longed to get Loretta on her own and ask for the real gossip about her boss. Shelly would be delighted with any dirt I could share.

Later that day, I had my opportunity. Jeremy took Candida diving again, and after I had cursed my fear of being twenty feet below the surface of the sea with an unfriendly underwater native one more time, I took up my position by the pool again. Loretta was sitting beneath a sun umbrella, with her nose covered by a bright stripe of zinc block, despatching letters and instructions to every part of the civilised world with the help of her laptop, mobile and modem.

'Hi,' she smiled widely when she saw me. 'Thanks so much for persuading your man to take her off my hands for a while.'

'Oh, he didn't need persuading,' I said, a little rue-fully. 'Have you been working for her long?'

'Too long. It started out as a short term thing. While I waited for someone to be wowed into submission by my first screenplay. But that didn't exactly happen and now

I seem to have landed myself with a life-long sentence and no chance of parole.'

'How did you get a job as assistant to a film star?'

'By looking like a dyke,' she said flatly. 'Her Majesty Candida had a dozen applications from people who would have made better assistants than me, but she didn't want someone who would show her up. I guess I'm like the coalface for her sparkling diamond.'

'Don't put yourself down. Even Candida says that beauty comes from the inside.'

'She says that to every ugly person she meets.'

'Oh.'

'But don't worry about me, Ali. I used to get something from this fucked up working relationship too. I fancied her like mad before I actually started working for her.'

'You fancied her?' the shock must have registered on my face.

'Yeah. I know she's a terrible bimbo and all that, but I've always been a sucker for a pretty face,' she smiled.

'Me too. On boys though.'

Loretta laughed.

'Everybody loves Candida, don't they? She really does have it all, doesn't she?' I said, as I settled back onto my sunbed.

'Including athlete's foot,' said Loretta, punching yet another number into her mobile. 'Excuse me for a moment, Ali. I have to call the only pharmacist on this godforsaken island and find out if he has any fungicide.'

He didn't. Loretta clicked off her mobile and flung it onto the sunbed on her other side.

'Well, that's me fired. Again.'

'I thought she fired you this morning.'

'She reinstated me after breakfast when she couldn't work out how to send an e-mail herself.'

'Does she fire you often?'

'Every other day. I just can't wait until I'm in a position to accept one of my enforced resignations.'

'I find it really hard to believe that she's such a difficult person. I mean, she's been lovely to us, and we're only ordinary people.'

Loretta snorted.

'She's flesh and blood, too, Ali. She never does anything out of niceness. And if I were you I would watch her around that boyfriend of yours.'

I raised my eyebrows. 'My boyfriend? But she's dated Brad Pitt.'

'Just because a girl gets to eat caviar from time to time, doesn't mean she stops liking roast chicken.'

I was rather offended by the chicken part of that. But I guessed that Loretta meant well.

'Drink?' she asked me then.

'Why not?' They were free after all.

Like a magical genie, a waiter soon appeared at our side with a tray loaded down with candy-coloured cocktails and a bowl heaped high with peanuts. Loretta dived straight into the nuts, tipping a huge handful into her mouth and talking while she chewed.

'Oh, yeah,' she assured me as she downed another cocktail and warmed to her theme. 'Hollywood is simply crawling with queers. Name a sex symbol and I'll name you his boyfriend. Go on. Go on. Anyone at all,' she dared me.

'I don't think I want to know. You'll shatter my illusions.'

'Illusions were made to be shattered. It's much more fun when you know what really goes on beneath the make-up and the bright lights. Listen, I've got to tell you this story about Candida. It's quite ironic really, when you know that Candida is the Latin name for thru . . .'

Suddenly, Loretta's eyes widened in horror. Then she began to cough. Nasty, pent-up little coughs that told me she was choking on a half-chewed nut. I waited politely for her to get over it and continue with her story. But after thirty seconds or so, I realised that she wasn't about to finish.

'Want some water?' I asked her, handing her my glass. Loretta was still hacking violently, her face growing red with the exertion. She took the glass and attempted to take a sip, but could only spurt the water straight back out again. I gave her a stiff whack between the shoulder blades but she simply fell forward and began choking in doggy position on the floor instead.

'Help? Somebody? Is there a doctor round here?' I called. I had a nasty feeling of *déjà vu* and hoped that it might extend to the arrival of a helpful vet. But while a circle of people had already gathered around us, it was clear that they knew far less about the business of saving someone's life than I did.

Yes. I had almost forgotten how much I actually knew. The Heimlich manoeuvre. We had been shown how to do it at Ashley's first aid class. Thank goodness Emma had forced me to attend. The sea-scout practising on me that day had almost squeezed my lungs out through my nose but I had quickly absorbed the principle.

Knowing that if I got it wrong I was going to look like

a prat but realising that if I didn't even try, I was almost certainly going to have a corpse on my hands, I got behind Loretta, pulled her into a semi-upright position and brought my fists together just beneath her breast bone. Then, one quick hard hoik and a half-chewed peanut sailed through the air at an impressive velocity to land in the suntanned cleavage of a horrified Italian beach-babe.

Loretta stopped choking and started gasping in an altogether more manageable manner. She rolled onto her back and looked up at me with blinking, disbelieving eyes.

'You just saved my life,' she murmured.

I shrugged my shoulders and sneaked an embarrassed glance at the Italian woman inviting her boyfriend to fish out Loretta's projectile.

'I don't know how I can ever, ever repay you.'

I shrugged again. 'I'm sure you'll think of something.'

'Alison, you're amazing. So modest. You know that if we were American Indians my life would now belong to you. You could do anything you wanted with me.'

'That's quite alright.' I wondered if this was a roundabout way of asking me to kiss her. But before I could find out, Candida and Jeremy returned from their dive. Everyone had been so absorbed in my life-saving antics that they didn't notice the diva striding across to us, Bond-girl style, complete with diving knife strapped to her thigh. Parting the crowd, Candida stood over her PA and dripped sea water from her gorgeous long hair into the poor girl's face.

'Uugh. What happened to you?' she asked. 'You look all green about the face.'

'I was choking on a nut,' Loretta explained breathlessly. 'Ali here saved my life.' She gave me a puppy-eyed gaze.

'Did you get the stuff I asked for?' Candida asked, without missing a beat. I noticed that she was not mentioning in front of Jeremy what exactly it was she had asked for.

Loretta shook her head. 'The chemist didn't have any. He offered to make up a herbal solution, though.'

'Herbal solution? Do I look like I'm interested in witch doctor crap?'

'No,' said Loretta in a small voice.

'Then Ali really needn't have wasted her time bringing you back to life. You're fired, Loretta.'

'Does that mean I can fly back to LA now?' Loretta asked hopefully.

Candida looked about to boil over. 'No. You're still on a week's notice. Make sure you get that stuff flown in.'

Then Candida flounced off in the direction of her beach hut, with Loretta following behind like a scolded puppy.

'It must be a nightmare, working for Candida,' I commented when they were out of earshot.

'It must be very difficult to find staff who don't try to take advantage of a woman in her position,' Jeremy replied. 'Candida told me that girls usually only want to work for her as a way to meet Brad Pitt. That's why she hired Loretta. She's a lesbian.'

'That doesn't give Candida an excuse to treat her so badly.'

'She doesn't. Loretta gets a private health plan and three weeks paid holiday a year.'

'Well it's better than being a child slave in India, I

suppose,' I said sarcastically. 'But I wouldn't put up with the way Candida behaves for that.'

'She has a very stressful lifestyle.'

'Yeah. Swimming pool, diving, beautician.'

'When she's on set,' Jeremy corrected. It was clear that he wasn't going to join me in a bitch-fest so I gave up. 'I hope she gets that Warsaw job. She's really excited about playing such a meaty part.'

I put my sunglasses on and pretended to read my bonkbuster.

Jeremy was obviously star-struck, but I had seen a different side of Candida and, in my opinion, it didn't matter how many times she had to reshoot a love scene with Brad Pitt, there was no excuse for being such a cow. I scanned the pool for Shelly and Luke. They had been going to spend the day exploring some of Antigua's other three hundred and sixty five beaches. Luke was interested in seeing some of the red-breasted booby birds that lived along the shore apparently. Shelly was only really interested in shopping, but, she assured me, it was important to let Luke do exactly what he wanted to every so often. Give and take, she said. It was the secret of a great relationship.

I sneaked a sidelong glance at Jeremy's gorgeous profile. He hadn't even attempted to speak to me since I picked up my book. Putting it down again, I reached a hand across to his sunbed and gently caressed his bronzed arm. But he brushed my hand away.

'Little bit burnt,' he explained. It didn't look all that red to me, but I decided that I had better leave him alone for a while in any case. Shelly had told me something about men needing to be allowed to sit alone in their 'caves' from time to time, revelling in their solitude.

This was probably one of those times. But I couldn't help hating Candida for being the cause of the first angry-ish words that ever passed between us.

Thankfully, an hour later, the cloud seemed to have passed. Instead of complaining that he didn't want me to touch his burned arm, Jeremy suggested that I rub in some aftersun. I did so joyfully, taking extra special care to do it lovingly when Candida and Loretta re-emerged and wandered across to join us.

'I got it,' Candida announced. 'I got the job in Warsaw.'

Jeremy's eyes widened. Loretta shot me a knowing glance.

'Vadim said that he couldn't really have contemplated having anyone else in the part. He's giving Gwyneth her marching orders tomorrow. I'm sure she'll just be relieved that she doesn't have to dye her hair. And I'll be in Warsaw at the end of the month. Do I need to have any vaccinations for going that far?'

'This is fabulous news,' said Jeremy, throwing his arms around Candida and swinging her round.

'I'm very, very sorry,' said Loretta to me.

CHAPTER THIRTY-ONE

I had fallen asleep with a paperback over my eyes when somebody asked, 'Can I buy you a margarita?'

It was Luke.

'No,' I told him. 'You can't.'

Luke recoiled slightly, before I reminded him. 'It's all inclusive here, remember.'

Luke guffawed and shovelled a handful of peanuts into his mouth.

'That'll make you thirsty,' I said.

Luke nodded. He raised a finger to summon the barman, but had to point to the drink he wanted because if he'd opened his mouth he would have sprayed us all with shrapnel.

'Where's Shelly this afternoon?' I asked him.

'Oh.' He gulped a slug of his beer. 'She's in the beach hut. She's getting some sleep for tomorrow night.'

'Really. What's so special about tomorrow?' I yawned.

'It's the competition,' said Luke, as if I was an idiot.

'Oh yes, the competition.' I had been suppressing

that thought and almost completely succeeded in blocking it from my mind.

'I don't know what she'll do if we don't win,' Luke continued. 'I mean, she's set her heart on us being the most romantic couple in the world and all.'

'I'm sure you are,' I reassured him.

'I don't know,' Luke muttered, then: 'Ali, do you think you and I might go somewhere and talk for a while?'

'What?'

'It's just that you seem like you're a really nice person and right now a nice person is what I really need.'

'Oh.' I smiled awkwardly. 'That's sweet. I suppose I could spare you ten minutes in my busy schedule of laying about. Where do you want to go?'

'Down on the beach, perhaps. We could walk up to the sunbeds and back. No, hang on. I'm forgetting myself. Where's David?'

'Scuba diving. I think he's becoming a fish. I can give you a few minutes.'

'That's real kind of you.'

He was quite sweet. In fact there was something about Luke that reminded me of the real David. Maybe it was the way he could put away more peanuts than the average elephant without seeming to need to swallow between huge handfuls.

I gathered up my beach towel and wrapped it around my waist as a makeshift sarong. We headed down towards the edge of the water, where the sunbeds lay in strangely regimented order for such a laid-back kind of place.

'What do you want to tell me?' I asked, to get

the ball rolling. He probably wanted to know what fantastic going-home gift he should buy for his future bride, or something sick-making like that. Luke took off his baseball cap and started to wring it between his hands.

'Ali, me and Shelly can't be the world's most romantic couple any more,' he began. 'Because I think I'm falling in love with you.'

I choked on thin air.

'I tried to stop myself, but I can't,' Luke continued. 'Every time I see you I get that thump, thump, thump feeling inside my chest. I haven't had that with Shelly in years now. Shelly only ever wants to talk about how the wedding's gonna be and when we're gonna start having a family, but you, you're not like that. You're wonderful, Ali. You're just so full of life. So exciting.'

He lunged towards me, lips puckered.

'Luke,' I held him back. 'You don't know what you're doing.'

'I do,' he protested. 'I've made my decision. It's better to live one day as a sheep than a lifetime as a tiger.'

'I don't think you mean that,' I said. But I didn't bother to point out his mistake. 'Listen Luke, Shelly will make hamburger of you if she finds out about this.'

'I don't care. I can't go on living this lie any longer.'

'Please do,' I asked him. 'At least until this holiday is over. It's one thing deciding that you don't love Shelly any more, but it's quite another to lay her open to the ridicule of the whole world while you're at it. After all, you're supposed to be entering a worldwide competition as America's most successful love match tomorrow night.'

'So you want me to keep quiet until tomorrow night?' Luke asked. 'Then can we be together? I've got this aunt in Reno. She has a caravan there, where we could hide out until things between me and Shelly are properly settled. It's empty. We could move in straightaway.'

'Er. I don't think so,' I said, still having to push him away.

'Don't you like the idea of a caravan? I know you English girls. Home is your castle and all that.'

'It's not the caravan part,' I assured him. 'There's David as well, remember. I still love him.'

'Ali, you know that's a lie.'

'What?'

'I feel real bad telling you this, but it's been obvious to the rest of us from the start that you and David don't really even know each other. He doesn't love you. I can tell by the way he looks at you. He may love the idea of being here with you but he doesn't have that softness in his eyes that says it will work out back home. Forget him, Ali. I can show you what real love is all about.'

'Luke,' I said, giving him one last shove that landed him bum-first on the sand. 'You are really talking rubbish. Now why don't you just go back to Shelly and give her some of your soft-eyed crap. I love David and he loves me. But I will never, never love you.'

'You don't mean that. I know you're saying that because I've taken you by surprise . . .' Luke called after me as I made a slow exit in the foot-sucking sand. 'David doesn't love you, Ali. He's been getting it on with Candida.'

I stopped in my tracks. 'What? You're just saying that to get a reaction. Forget it, Luke. I'm a one man woman.'

Poor Shelly, I thought, lying in the beach hut, getting her beauty sleep. She had no idea. As I passed the hut she shared with her hopeless fiancé, she emerged, face covered in an avocado-green pack.

'Hi, Ali. You getting ready for tomorrow night? You know, I couldn't find a drugstore on the whole of this goddamn island. I had to get the guys in the kitchen to give me some real avocado for this mask. You want some? I got plenty left.'

'No thanks. I've already eaten,' I told her.

'For your face, dufus!' she laughed. 'You should try it. Luke is always telling me that one of the things he loves most about me is the softness of my skin.'

I forced myself to smile.

'Hey, I hope we didn't keep you guys up last night,' she continued. 'We were playing cards with Mark and Marguerite until well past eleven and the walls of these places are awful thin.'

'Oh, you didn't keep us up,' I reassured her. If she was worried that we might have heard them playing cards, then surely she would have heard that Jeremy and I weren't asleep at all.

'You know,' she said to change the subject, 'avocados aren't the only miracle product in nature's beauty cabinet.' Shelly was poised to impart some more of her all-American wisdom but we were suddenly interrupted by Luke, red-faced from racing up the beach, no doubt terrified that I had gone straight to Shelly to tell her what I thought of the rat that he had revealed himself to be.

'Hi, honey,' Shelly beamed, instantly putting his mind at rest. 'I was just telling Alison about my avocado face pack. But hell, I shouldn't be letting you see me like this,' she added, pushing him away playfully. 'Seeing your fiancée all covered in a face pack hardly makes you want to be the world's most romantic man does it?'

She laughed her tinkling chandelier laugh and disappeared back into the cool darkness of the hut. Luke went to say something to me, but I stopped him by raising my hand.

'Let's forget it ever happened,' I whispered.

'But it's true what I said about Candida.'

'I'm especially forgetting you said that.'

Luke nodded in resignation and turned to follow Shelly. In the past, when anyone had given me the all-men-are-bastards line I had thought that they were overreacting, but seeing Luke, America's Most Romantic Man, lighting up Shelly's face again just moments after telling me that he loved me, I felt pretty sure that the all-men-are-bastards generalisation could be applied to about 80% of the species. Jeremy wasn't among them of course. The bit about Candida had been made up. Just over lunch she had said she had a crush on the director she would be working with in Warsaw.

I told Jeremy about the incident as soon as he came back from scuba diving.

'Ha,' he laughed. 'I could have told you that about Luke days ago. I could tell by the way he looked at you.'

'What do you mean? I thought you guys couldn't read emotions anyway.'

'That's a clever myth,' Jeremy explained. 'Gives us an excuse when we go trampling all over a woman's.'

'And the Candida thing? Is that true?'

'Don't be crazy, Ali. What would she want with me? She's in love with that hot-shot director.'

Exactly, I thought. Jeremy and Candida? It just wasn't a possibility. Luke Connolly was mad.

'Did you see any good fish today?' I asked to change the subject.

'One or two,' he said. 'Thought we might have seen a shark but it was quite far in the distance.'

'How big?' I gasped, eyes widening.

Jeremy stretched his arms out as far as they could go.

'Candida remained quite calm.'

'Only because she was with you. You're so brave,' I cooed. 'All you need to do now to make you the most perfect man in the world is learn my preferences on the jelly flavour front.'

'Shit. The big competition. I'd forgotten all about that.'

'We don't have to enter if you don't want to,' I told him. 'We can be indisposed.'

'No way,' Jeremy protested, as he searched the drawers next to the bed for a pad and pencil. 'You better start telling me what I need to know about you. There's ten thousand pounds at stake, you know.'

'Yes. But how can we possibly win it anyway? We're up against three couples who have known each other for ever. Shelly probably even knows exactly how many hairs Luke has on his head. We've got no chance against the likes of them.'

'Ali, let's not waste time thinking about whether we've got a chance or not. What's your favourite colour?'

'Blue,' I suppose.

'Great, that's mine too. I won't forget that one. What's your favourite animal?'

'Cats.'

'I like dogs.'

'Dogs. Really? I never had you down as a dog person.'

'Much better than flea-ridden felines,' he snapped. 'What's your favourite TV soap?'

'Hang on a second,' I said, slipping myself onto the bed beside him. 'I'm just trying to get over the fact that you prefer dogs to cats. Can't we think about this later?'

I ran my hand gently over his shoulders.

'Ali,' Jeremy protested. 'Not now. If we put our minds to it, this could be the easiest ten thousand pounds we have ever earned in our lives. And I need the money to . . . er, never mind.'

I sat up again disappointedly. 'OK,' I said. 'But to be honest, I don't think they're going to want to know this stuff. This is so basic and we're taking part in the grand final. I think they're going to want something more juicy. We need to make up some stories. The history of our grand affair. How we met. Passionate arguments we've had.'

'Arguments? But we're meant to be the most romantic couple.'

'I know,' I said. 'But don't you think it's romantic to have fights sometimes too? All that kissing and making up. How about this for one? You were struggling to come to terms with the depth of your feelings for me. You thought that you would be overcome by love, swept up by it and eventually dashed against the jagged rocks of abandonment. We were apart for a whole week before you realised that you didn't care if you would end up being hurt one day. To have loved so wholly just once was all that mattered.' I was pretty moved by the idea.

'That's great,' said Jeremy, scribbling the basic points down. 'Now what about if we had one when you borrowed my car and smashed into another car while you were parking.'

'Oh, thanks a lot. Do you think I can't park?'

'Well, it's more realistic than your tale. Women crash cars all the time.'

'How about the row we had over the fact that you sometimes act just a little too much like a male chauvinist pig?'

'You'll ruin my image.'

'Oh, this is mad, isn't it,' I told him. 'Let's just pretend we've never had a row in our lives.'

'Well, that's sort of true.'

'What do you mean, sort of?'

'You seemed a bit tetchy with me when I came back from diving this morning.'

'Only because you went straight back out to dive again in the afternoon. You spend so much time in the water that you're starting to look like a prune. And you spend so much time with Candida that people are telling me to watch my back. I think I had every right to get a bit tetchy.'

'Oh, Ali,' Jeremy enfolded me in his arms. 'I didn't mean to upset you. I just got carried away with having a famous friend. We'll spend the rest of our holiday together.'

'Huh,' I snorted. 'All twenty-four hours.'

'Candida won't be diving tomorrow. That director, Vadim, is flying out here tonight.'

'Good,' I said, 'then you won't have to worry about her being lonely.'

Jeremy shook his head (and if I had been less lovestruck I might have noticed he shook it sadly). 'No,' he said. 'I suppose I won't.'

CHAPTER THIRTY-TWO

The big day dawned. The Grand Final of *Complete Woman International*'s search to find the most romantic couple in the world was just eight hours away.

As an extra special treat, an internationally renowned hairdresser had been flown in from Florida to make us all look our best for the photos. Or at least, to make the girls look their best. I think Jeremy was quite disappointed to be left out. Mark from Australia wouldn't even let shampoo near his ultra-manly hair, let alone other less necessary styling products.

Shelly and I sat side by side under the kind of hairdryers that had been banned in the rest of the world since the sixties. She was excited. No hint at all that things weren't all well between her and her beau. I guessed Luke must have taken my advice.

'It's been so interesting meeting you lovely guys,' she told me warmly, with the air of someone who thought that she had already won the race. 'So many of our friends back home, the couples that we know, they don't take their relationships so seriously. They don't respect each other like Luke and I do. Meeting you guys has reaffirmed my faith in romance.'

'Thanks,' I muttered. I didn't really feel like getting into a conversation, but luckily Shelly was the kind of girl who could easily be set off on a soliloquy. 'So,' I couldn't resist it. 'What do you think your secret is?'

'Well,' she began, popping out from beneath her drier so that she could address me head-on like a missionary. 'Have you heard of positive imaging?'

I shrugged.

'It's like this, Alison. What you want, you can have. You can have anything at all. But you have to want it hard enough. You have to want it so hard that you are able to visualise it. Almost touch it in your mind's eye. I first got to hear about it on the television. There was a guru. She was talking about her new book and she said that she knew she was going to be able to finish it as soon as she could picture the cover in her mind. After that, she set about imagining the covers of all her books before she even started to write them. She made them real in her mind first. Now she's a millionairess. Do you follow me so far?'

I nodded.

'Well, when I saw what positive imaging could do for her, I decided to try it for myself. I didn't know Luke at all in those days. I had just seen him working in the body shop of his father's garage. I thought, wow, he's cute. But I never imagined that he could be mine. I swear, girls all over my town suddenly lost the ability to drive around lampposts when Luke became a mechanic. I know you probably can't imagine it now, seeing us looking so right together, but I had so much competition I thought the game was lost.'

'Really?'

'Yeah. So I started to try this positive imaging thing. At first, it was for a bit of fun. I imagined myself walking into the garage to ask about getting my car serviced. I imagined Luke looking back at me with a spark of recognition in his eyes that I could be the girl of his dreams. Two weeks after our first proper date I imagined us getting married and three years later, he proposed.'

'So it doesn't have instant results, this method of yours?'

'Love isn't instant, Ali.'

Unless it's true love, I thought, thinking of the moment it had hit me that Jeremy was the man of my dreams. It had been at my parents' party, when we were standing at the sink together. I hadn't known at the time, but now I knew clearly that what I thought had been wind caused by undercooked vol-au-vents, had in fact been the first rumblings of desire.

'Good luck tonight,' said Shelly, as she was allowed out from beneath her drier and went to mug up on Luke's personal habits.

'Good luck,' I replied. But I meant it.

Alone under my drier I turned Shelly's words over in my mind. Positive imaging, eh? It sounded too good to be true. But it wouldn't cost anything to try it, I figured. And if it didn't work, no-one need know, so I closed my eyes and tried it for myself.

I imagined the final of the Most Romantic Couple

Competition. I imagined a pedestal, like you see at the Olympics, with different levels for the couples who came first, second and third. I imagined Chad and Penny in third place. Luke and Shelly taking the silver. And right on the top . . . Well, you can guess it wasn't Marguerite and Mark.

I imagined the feeling of ten thousand pounds in my pocket and Jeremy's hand in my own. I imagined him whispering something in my ear. 'Let's do it for real,' he was saying. 'Let's really tie the knot.'

'Yuck. Just full of knots.'

I was rudely awoken by the hairdresser. 'You really haven't been taking care of your hair in the sun,' he complained. 'Have you never thought about wearing a sun hat?'

'Not much call for a sun hat in England,' I shrugged.

'No, I suppose not. But you know, if you took a little more care you could almost have tresses like Candida Bianca. Now she's got the most beautiful tresses in the world.'

'What would it take to have a body like hers too?' I wondered out loud.

'Settle for the hair, dearie,' the hairdresser said bitchily as his comb tugged painfully at my scalp. 'You can cover a multitude of sins with Lycra.'

The hotel's fabulous Sea View dining room had been totally rearranged for the final of *Complete Woman International*'s Most Romantic Couple competition. The tables had been cleared away from an area in front of the wide, panoramic window where stood just one solitary chair. The hot seat. The walls had been covered with swags of red velvet, dotted with gold-painted hearts so that it looked like the Queen of Hearts' palace from *Alice in Wonderland*.

The competition was due to start at eight. At seven-thirty, I joined Shelly, Penny and Marguerite by the bar, where we were to be briefed by Marjorie Pine, *Complete Woman International*'s executive editor with responsibility for every issue of the magazine world-wide, as she kept reminding us. Amanda had sent a fax to me that afternoon, saying how sorry she was not to have been able to fly out herself to see my finest hour.

'I want a good clean fight,' Marjorie Pine laughed, showing her long, yellow teeth. 'Remember that what-ever happens here this evening, you are all winners. Each one of you is one half of a fabulous relationship that to you is the best relationship in the world, no matter who takes home the crown tonight.'

We nodded as though she had just revealed some profound truth. Shelly's eyes were glittering madly with the thought of victory regardless.

'Now, if you'd each like to fill out these question-naires,' Marjorie said, handing us each a sheaf of paper and a *Complete Woman* complimentary biro. 'The first round will involve partners matching answers on per-sonal issues. When you've finished those we'll retire to a waiting room so that there can be no communication between you girls and your other halves before the competition begins. We wouldn't want any cheating, would we?'

We sat down at four bar tables and began to fill the questionnaires out. When I looked up at Shelly she was chewing the end of her pencil, poring over some answer as if she were completing a physics A-level. It started out pretty simply. Favourite colours, animals and TV soap. Good job we'd covered all those. Then it went on to the slightly trickier stuff. His mother's maiden name. Good job Hilary Barton-Baxter had been feminist enough to be double-barrelled when they lived next door to us during the seventies.

At the other end of the hotel, the boys were filling out similar forms. I wondered if Jeremy would be able to remember my brand of deodorant and thought strong Natrel Plus thoughts in his direction. Then Marjorie Pine collected our papers together and we retired to the dismal little windowless room where we would have to wait until the hotel audience was assembled. I wondered if Candida would be watching the competition or if her hot-shot director would have whisked her somewhere private for the night. A television crew from Florida was recording the competition for the newly formed 'Romance' satellite channel. When Marjorie mentioned the name of the compere for the evening, Shelly clapped her hands together in delight. The rest of us had never heard of him.

'Perfect,' she gushed. 'Aidan Hobbs is my favourite TV presenter of all time. I think this is a good omen for us.' She meant for her and Luke, of course.

By the time we were finally called out onto the stage, it seemed as if the competition was already over. Certainly there was no doubt in Shelly's mind that she and Luke would come away with the crowns that night. And the money. I was a little irritated by that, since I had already been on a pretty extensive mental shopping spree.

Shelly was first onto the stage. She was wearing her Valentine's Day dress, the one that had more hearts than a sacrifice to that goddess Kali in *Indiana Jones and the Temple of Doom*. Shelly bounced out onto the stage and gave a practised twirl. I stepped out rather more carefully since I couldn't see a thing for the bright lights that glared straight into my face.

'Alison Harris, The Most Romantic Woman in the United Kingdom,' boomed Aidan Hobbs, as I took a shaky bow. There was a polite ripple of applause, punctuated by someone shouting, 'Go girl, go!' I squinted at the front row of the audience and there was Candida, sharing her table with a man who looked like a cross between Cyrano de Bergerac and Mahatma Gandhi. Her Svengali film director, without a doubt. Loretta was sitting on Candida's other side, looking utterly bored as she fanned herself with a menu. But Candida beamed straight at me and gave me a thumbs-up sign. I straightened myself up immediately. Suddenly I was filled with a new confidence. Candida was wishing me luck in a Romantic Couples competition. Why would she do that if she was after my man?

Jeremy was announced next. He too shuffled onto the stage like a deer straight into the glare of car headlights. I made a grab for his hand. 'Candida's here to wish us luck,' I whispered. Jeremy stared into the crowd and focused his attention on Candida's new man.

'He's a complete potato head,' Jeremy hissed to me.

'Who?'

'That director guy.'

'I know he's not exactly Mel Gibson. But look at

the chemistry between them. Sexual attraction often follows when people are impressed by somebody's art. What did you say my mother's maiden name was when you filled in the questionnaire, by the way?' I asked then.

'Smith,' Jeremy whispered. 'That is right, isn't it?'

'No. It's not. But I put Smith too, just in case.' I squeezed his hand hard. The other couples had joined us on the stage and the competition was about to begin. Jeremy still stared ahead into the crowd. I assumed he was just nervous and dug him in the ribs when the first round got under way and it was his turn to take up a bow and shoot an arrow into a papier-mâché cupid's heart.

CHAPTER THIRTY-THREE

I almost fainted with surprise when I discovered that Jeremy and I had actually made it to the final.

'And with just one more round to go, we have two couples head to head with twenty-five points apiece,' shouted Aidan. 'They are Shelly Adamson and Luke Connolly representing the United States of America and David Whitworth and Alison Harris representing the United Kingdom of Grand Bretagne!!!'

The crowd applauded us. I looked across to Shelly with the intention of sharing a friendly smile but she was looking straight ahead at the trophy which stood on a table at the back of the room. No doubt she was visualising holding it aloft. Visualising victory. Visualising herself as one half of the Most Romantic Couple in the World. I tried to visualise myself in her place just as hard.

'What do we get for coming second?' I asked Jeremy defeatistly when the vision refused to take shape.

'We are not going to come second,' he said. He was staring at the trophy as well.

I wondered what on earth the final round of the

competition could be. We had answered just about every possible question on each other's faults and foibles. Been through the mother's maiden name bit. I had even correctly guessed Jeremy's blood group, which was a good job since my attempts at hitting the papier-mâché heart with an arrow had resulted in a nasty nick to Jeremy's ear.

The compere's face twisted into a wicked grin as he contemplated what now awaited us. 'How will we choose between these two lovely couples?' he asked. 'There can be no doubt that there's a lot of love going on here. They've told us how well they work as teams. Now let's see them prove it. Gentlemen . . .'

He waved towards the window.

Outside, the guys who looked after the pool stepped forward and started to roll back the covers. It was always covered over in the evenings, in case someone had one too many pina coladas and decided to go skinny-dipping. Loretta also said that the pool contained that chemical that went purple if you peed in it should such an occasion occur during the day.

'What's going on?' I asked Jeremy.

Shelly too, had lost her concentration while she wondered what was to happen next. A swimming competition? I hoped not. But the pool was no longer full of water. Instead, the surface of whatever it now contained had a distinctly custardy texture.

'Do you think we're going in there?' I asked worriedly.

'Only if we lose,' said Jeremy.

'This round is called,' began Aidan Hobbs triumphantly, 'How Deep is Your Love?'

'Ohmigod,' cursed Shelly. 'We're going in.'

'Out there. Hidden in the depths of our pool of passion is just one golden envelope,' the compere continued. 'A golden envelope which actually contains the prize that these good people have been aiming for all evening. Now all they have to do is find it and, as the saying goes, the finders will be the keepers.'

His assistants were already ushering us out of the restaurant and towards the edge of the pool. I took off my clip-on earrings (a present from Candida – I was itching to get them valued as soon as I got home). Shelly looked down in horror at her hand-sequinned evening dress.

'I'm gonna ruin my outfit,' I heard her hiss to Luke.

'Shelly,' he said manfully. 'We've come this far. I'll buy you a new dress when we get home again, honey. I promise.'

Jeremy held my hand tightly. 'We need to have a strategy,' he whispered. 'We'll take one end each and meet in the middle. You start over there.' He pointed at the deep end.

'Jeremy,' I shrieked. 'That's the deep end. I'll drown!!'

'No you won't. There are loads of people to drag you out if you get into trouble. Just take a deep breath and jump on in. Feel your way along the bottom until you need another breath, then come back up, take another deep breath and start again on the next stretch of pool.'

'You make it all sound so easy,' I said sarcastically.

'It is. We've got just as much chance as them. More even. Shelly won't want to get her hair wet. Let alone covered in that muck.'

I wasn't too keen on the idea myself. The stuff in the

pool looked like custard but heaven only knew what it really was.

By now the audience too had filed out into the hotel garden. As I took off my shoes and looked for somewhere safe to put them, I felt the touch of a hand on my arm.

'I'll look after your shoes for you.' It was Candida. 'Good luck.' She kissed me on the cheek. Then she kissed Jeremy. He stood very stiffly as she brushed her lips against each of his cheeks. 'Good luck to you too.'

Almost shaking Candida off, Jeremy rushed to the shallow end of the pool and took up what he considered to be the optimum position for an effective sweep. I took up my own position at the deep end.

'On your marks,' the compere shouted. 'Get set!'

Shelly wobbled on the edge of the pool, still wearing her high heels. Luke had at least taken off his Stetson.

'Go!'

The shouts of the crowd were suddenly deafening. Jeremy jumped straight in and disappeared below the pink. I hesitated for a moment, making sure that he didn't come up for air horribly disfigured by something caustic in the blancmange before I ran to the other end and gingerly let myself down the steps and into the mire. Shelly was just up to her knees in the shallow end, her face already a picture of desperation as she dabbled in the goo for the envelope like my mother looking for a ring in a sink full of cold washing-up water. No such luxury for me. As soon as I let go of the ladder, I went into the pink stuff right over my head. I struggled back up again and took a deep breath through my custard-filled mouth.

Why had Jeremy taken the shallow end, I cursed. He was at least a foot taller than me.

I struggled back to the ladder and clung to it grimly. Part of me protested that this was incredibly stupid. But ten thousand pounds was at stake. And at the other end of the pool, Shelly was still weeping but industrious.

I closed my eyes and let myself drift to the bottom. I thrashed around with my arms as I fell, after all, who was to say that the envelope was at the bottom. I was feeling pretty weightless myself.

Coming back up for air, I gasped like a grounded fish. My head was spinning and the crowd around the pool merged into a blur of shouting faces. I couldn't see any of my fellow competitors for the blancmange in my eyes. Then Jeremy's head popped up.

'Got it?' he yelled.

'No!' I yelled back.

'Then keep going. Come on. Dive, girl, dive.'

Back down again into the murky pink deep.

Was this what it was like to be in the womb, I wondered? More likely, it was what it felt like to be a dying fly in someone's Angel Delight. I seemed to take ages to sink this time. When my feet hit the bottom, I had to go straight back up again to breathe anyway.

'What are you doing?' Jeremy shouted when he saw me clinging onto the ladder again. It was all right for him, his head never went beneath the surface. But at least he was working his way towards me.

'One more time, Ali,' he yelled to me. 'You know you can do it. One more time.'

I ducked my head under. I was exhausted. So what if I hadn't found the envelope? This dive would definitely be my last. My lungs felt ready to burst. I am going to die down here, I thought. I am going to die in a swimming pool full of synthetic, strawberry gunk for the sake of ten thousand measly pounds. I would almost have been happy if Shelly or Luke had found the envelope then. Anything to get out of this terrible game.

Then, as if by divine intervention, my hand touched the sharp edge of what could only be the envelope. No sooner had I touched it, though, than I had pushed it a little further out of reach. Though I really, really needed to take another breath, I decided to go for it one last time. I thrashed out in the direction of that elusive prize. My fingers closed upon it and I kicked off from the bottom of the pool to get to the surface. But my escape met with some resistance. Mine were not the only fingers clinging on.

I wanted to scream with frustration. I couldn't even see who my opponent was. Perhaps it was Jeremy. But the odds were that it wasn't. I could feel the envelope slipping from my grasp. The only way that I could ensure that Jeremy and I took the money home was for me to fight for it now. I kicked out in the pinkness. My feet made contact with someone soft and suddenly the envelope was all mine.

'I've done it!' I broke through the surface holding the envelope aloft. 'I've done it! I've done it!' Hands appeared from all sides to pull me out of the swamp. I lay at the side of the pool, clutching the envelope to my chest and trying desperately to get the muck out of my lungs and some air in.

Gradually the others surfaced. They looked bewildered as they were pulled out of the pool, and desperate when they realised that the competition was well and truly over.

Shelly exploded with a wail of despair. Luke sat beside her, trying and failing to get her to shut up. Jeremy staggered up the side of the pool to collapse alongside me. He was discreetly clutching his balls.

'I did it!' I said. Lack of oxygen had left me somewhat dazed.

'Yeah, you did it,' he said, licking some pink stuff off my forehead. 'I might even be able to forgive you for kicking me in the balls.'

'Well done, Ali,' Candida gingerly kissed one of my pink cheeks. 'I knew it would be you.'

Jeremy turned away from her and concentrated on rinsing out his hair.

'Well done, Ali,' said Loretta. 'Though I thought I was going to have to do the Heimlich on you at one point.'

'I've got a fine pair of lungs,' I told her. 'My mother always said so.'

Just a brief rub down with a towel, then we took to the podium.

'Congratulations, Alison Harris and David Whitworth!' The compere shouted. 'You are *Complete Woman International*'s Most Romantic Couple in the entire world!!!!'

'Hurrah!!!' screamed the crowd.

Shelly burst into tears again immediately. Jeremy and I just looked at each other. We were still slightly stunned. Marjorie Pine led the applause and soon the whole room rose to give us a standing ovation while the *Complete Woman International* lackeys prodded us towards the stage to pick up our prize.

'I can't understand it,' Shelly was wailing. 'They haven't even set a date to get married to each other. How can that be romantic?'

Even as I looked at the cheque in my hand, I had to agree that it hardly seemed fair. How could romance be measured by the ability to find an envelope in a vat of blancmange? I mean, I'd even managed to kick the supposed love of my life in his family jewels in the process.

'Waaah! It's just not fair!!'

Shelly and Luke didn't pick up their 'World's Second Most Romantic Couple's Prize' that night. Under the circumstances, Marjorie decided that Shelly might prefer to have the consolation prize hamper of fresh fruit and flowers delivered to her room.

But in her haste to get away and lick her wounds, Shelly missed the coup of the holiday. Aidan Hobbs was wrapping the competition up with a few gags about future in-laws when Vadim Caravaggio asked if he might take the stage.

Probably hoping for a film part, Aidan stepped down without a murmur and Vadim took the mike. He was considerably taller than Aidan and had to bend down so that he looked like a nosferatu bending over a virgin's corpse.

'Tonight has been all about romance,' Vadim began. 'And while I don't wish to steal the glory of this wonderful moment from the Most Romantic Couple in the World, I'm sure that in the spirit of true love, they won't mind me taking this opportunity to make a little announcement of my own.'

The crowd was silent with expectation.

'Many of you here will know and love my charming companion Miss Candida Bianca. Candida and I have known each other for several years now, and during that time I have been privileged to come to know her not just as a screen idol, but as a woman. A living, breathing woman with a heart of pure gold.'

I looked across at Loretta in time to see her roll her eyes towards heaven.

'Since the moment we met, Candida has been one of my best friends, and for the past six months, she has also been my lover.'

Gasps all round. *Hello!* had always contested that she had a wild and unassailable crush on Brad Pitt.

'And tonight, I am incredibly thrilled, delighted and ecstatic to announce that Candida Bianca has consented to be my wife . . .'

Ta-daa!

'Wow!'

The spotlight swivelled to catch her in its one-eyed glare. Candida shrugged her shoulders and seemed, oddly for her, to shrink into herself. Vadim bounded down from the stage to sweep her up in his arms. Aidan Hobbs pressed her to take up the mike and say a few words herself.

'Thank you,' she muttered quietly. 'I guess the drinks are on me.'

Despite the fact that the drinks didn't have to be on anyone – this was Antigua's premier all-inclusive resort – the crowd flooded towards the bar, sweeping up Candida and Vadim as it went, until only Jeremy and I were left, all alone, by the pool, with my tiara and an envelope full of dosh.

'My God,' I said. 'I wasn't expecting that.'

'Neither was I,' said Jeremy.

'Shall we go and join them. Toast the other happy couple?'

'Think I'll just wash my hair first,' said Jeremy.

I happily trotted behind him to our hut.

CHAPTER THIRTY-FOUR

And so we had come to our very last night in Antigua. After an hour long shower to get the custard out of our hair, Jeremy and I decided that we would take one last moonlit stroll along the beach that had almost become our own. As we rounded the headland, we stopped and sat down on the soft sand from where we had the best view of the glittering lights in the harbour in front of our hotel.

'This has been such a magical holiday,' I began. 'I can't believe it's nearly over. I've had such a wonderful time.'

'Me too,' Jeremy assured me. 'But not just because we've been here. It's been most magical for me because I have been here with you, Ali.'

'Do you mean that?'

'You know I do. And that part of the holiday doesn't have to end when we get off the plane at Heathrow, you know.'

'But you've got to go back to Warsaw in a week,' I said sadly.

'Yes. But I don't have to go back alone.'

I looked at him disbelievingly. 'Jeremy,' I murmured tentatively. 'What are you suggesting to me?'

'What do you think I'm suggesting? Listen, I know that Warsaw sounds like an awful place but it really isn't as bad as you think. Sure, you can't get a suntan quite like the one we've got here, but we'll be together. And one day soon we'll return to Antigua to start a family.'

I rubbed at my ear. The one that had felt as though it was full of water since that first afternoon in the pool. Something must have been distorting his words.

'Start a family?' I murmured.

'Yes. You and me. I know we're still young, Ali. And I know that you've been hurt in the past. But I feel that this is the right moment for us, don't you? You're the right girl for me. I've never met anyone that I felt so free to be myself with. I just know I've got to be with you for the rest of my life. Ali Harris,' he paused significantly. 'Will you marry me?'

By the time the question had got through my waxy deposits and hit my auditory cortex I was answering Jeremy with a kiss. Simultaneously, the Most Romantic Couple Competition firework display started by the pool and a glittering rocket seared across the sky from the bay. As it burst into a huge green and red carnation of glittering light above our heads it seemed to be blessing us. An omen.

'Yes,' I told him. 'Yes, of course I'll marry you.'

We tumbled back onto the sand, kissing more passionately than we had ever done before. However many lies we had told in the past two weeks, we were definitely not pretending to be the World's Most Romantic Couple that night.

CHAPTER THIRTY-FIVE

For the first time in my life, I didn't feel sad as I packed my case at the end of a holiday. Except that it wasn't just my case any more. It was our case. Jeremy said so. He had started the packing and thrown all our things in together.

'We're not going to be one of those dreadful "his and hers" couples,' he told me. 'What's mine is yours now and vice versa.' I felt like singing with joy when I heard those sweet, sweet words.

As we waited to board our plane back to Heathrow at the tiny airport, I caught sight of Luke and Shelly checking in for their own flight home. Shelly was wearing dark glasses and a big floppy straw hat so that her face was totally obscured, as though she was trying to leave the island incognito. In fact, I only knew for sure that it was her because there simply couldn't have been that many pink gingham luggage sets in the world.

Shelly and Luke stood silently next to the passport control desk. I saw him try to give her an affectionate peck on the cheek but she shrugged him off irritably.

'Not taking the title of the United States Most

Romantic Couple very seriously are they?' Jeremy commented, as he too saw the altercation.

'Oh don't,' I said. 'It's quite sad really. Shelly had her heart set on the world title.'

'Well, I don't think they'll last long enough to fight for it again. They're not really meant for each other.'

'What do you mean?' I asked him. 'What makes you think that?'

'Well, promise me you won't take this the wrong way, but that night, when you were sick and had to go back to our room, Shelly accosted me down on the beach and made me quite a proposition.'

'You're joking?'

''Fraid not. She just kept on and on about how much she had always wanted an Englishman for a lover. How Luke was just an insensitive brute only interested in watching baseball and mending his Chevvy. She wants a real romantic. She even asked me if I knew some poetry.'

'Wow,' I said, remembering my own brush with one half of the USA's Most Romantic Couple. 'So it really was all a facade.'

'Yeah. Not like us.'

'We started out as a facade,' I reminded him.

'But it's the real thing now, isn't it?'

I was so happy, I could have flown home under my own steam.

But our kiss was interrupted by a tap on my shoulder. It was Candida. Loretta hovered in the background, bowed down by the weight of a presidential party's worth of bags.

'Hi. I'm not interrupting anything, am I?' Candida asked.

I smiled magnanimously. She could break up that

one kiss because I knew that I would be kissing Jeremy Baxter for the rest of his life.

Candida rifled through her plush leather Kelly bag, the only thing she was carrying, for something to give us. Finally, she pulled out a little leather-bound notebook and scribbled something with her Mont Blanc propelling pencil.

'Just in case you're ever in Los Angeles,' she said, handing the scrap to Jeremy and looking him deep in the eye.

'Thanks,' he said. 'I'd give you my number in Warsaw but I'm sure you'll have far grander places to stay when you start filming.'

Candida fixed him with a particularly coquettish gaze. 'I'm sure that your place has its charms.'

'Quite,' I said, linking my arm through his. I know it must have looked petty and possessive, but I told myself that I was just eager to make sure we didn't miss our flight.

'You flying home today too?' Jeremy asked Candida, as I started to drag him away.

'Yes,' she said. 'Same flight as Luke and Shelly, I think.'

'Jeremy, they're boarding our flight now,' I told him. They were. Honestly.

'You'd better go,' said Candida. 'I'll see you guys around.'

'Oh, and congratulations on your engagement,' I called after her.

Candida raised her hand in a pretty weak wave.

'Do you think we will see her again?' I asked when Candida finally headed off in the direction of the check-in desk for the flight back to Florida. I couldn't help smiling as I watched Shelly wrap her arm possessively around Luke's back at Candida's approach.

'I doubt it,' Jeremy grunted. 'Real stars like her just play at being friends with people like us.'

'Do you think so? Oh, well. At least I got a real Versace dress out of the whole experience.'

'Yeah,' said Jeremy vaguely. He seemed to be dragging his feet as we got closer to the departure gate.

'Come on,' I chivvied him one more time. 'I don't want to miss our flight. We'd be stuck here for another week before the next one came.'

'Stuck on this beautiful island? What a drag,' said Jeremy sarcastically.

I can't say I was desperate to get back home myself but I had a vague recollection of having things like a cat and a job to go back to, so we finally boarded our shiny jet and left the magical island in the comforts of first class. As I watched Antigua shrinking to a little, blue and green postcard picture while the plane rose higher and higher, our time there had already started to feel like a wonderful dream. At the other end of the flight London loomed like a big, grey splodge of reality. Though a very much better reality than I had left behind now that it had Jeremy in it. For the foreseeable future. Forever.

When we touched down at Heathrow, the weather was typically appalling for the time of year. Determined grey sleet battered the huge picture windows of the terminal as we drifted, still dressed in shorts and sun hats, to pick up our luggage from the baggage carousel.

'Ah well. This is it,' said Jeremy as he manfully pushed our luggage trolley through the green channel in customs. 'The end of our holiday but the start of our new lives. How do you feel?'

'I feel like I'm the luckiest woman in the whole world,' I told him sincerely. 'The only thing that could make me happier would be if Mum and Dad were in the arrivals lounge with a big cheque from our Lottery syndicate.'

'How shallow,' Jeremy laughed.

In fact there was no-one there to greet us. It was odd, since my family are pretty big on airport scenes. But perhaps Mum was still annoyed that I'd got out of Gran's birthday tea. All the better, I thought, as Jeremy and I kissed in the cab back to Brindlesham. I didn't want the rest of the world to intrude on us just yet.

'Back to your place?' Jeremy asked, as the taxi sped us through the city boundary.

'Yes,' I said firmly. 'No, make that my Mum and Dad's. I want to tell them the good news. Tonight.'

'Good idea,' Jeremy squeezed my hand. 'And then we'll go and see my folks. I just know that Mum is going to be over the moon to land a daughter-in-law like you.'

'Do you really think so?'

'Of course. I couldn't have done any better.'

'Charming. My Mum will probably pass out with joy when we tell her. She never really much liked David . . .'

Jeremy put his finger to my lips. 'Sssh,' he said. 'Now that the holiday's over, we've no need to mention that particular name ever again. Agreed?'

'Agreed,' I nodded happily.

'Though I have to say that I'm eternally grateful to him for staying out of your life just long enough so that I could take his place.'

Yes, David, I thought. Thanks for that. Whoever thought that the cloud that marked the end of my relationship with David Whitworth would have such a huge lump of solid silver beneath?

But I should have known that everything had been going just a little too well when I saw the police car parked at the top of Mum and Dad's driveway.

As we paid the taxi driver and unloaded our bags from the boot, I continued to chatter blithely to Jeremy, not thinking for one moment that the patrol car had anything to do with my family. As far as I was concerned, the police were probably staking out the dodgy rabble that had moved into number thirty-three. My mother, who was usually quite tolerant of fraud and other minor misdemeanours amongst her friends and neighbours, had phoned the police to tip them off about the Trustcott family's out-of-date road tax disc after one of their wild-looking children put chewing gum in Berkeley's fur.

'They've come for me,' Jeremy joked as we rang Mum and Dad's doorbell. Then he put his arm around me and nuzzled my ear. We were going to be the perfect picture of togetherness when Mum finally opened the door.

Instead we were met by Jo.

'Deep shit, Ali,' was all she said. 'Deep shit.'

CHAPTER THIRTY-SIX

The police car was indeed something to do with my family. More importantly, the two burly-looking policemen who sat drinking tea at the kitchen table were something to do with me.

'Ali,' said my mother desperately. 'The police are here.'

How could I have missed them? They filled up most of the kitchen in their regulation winter jackets. Seeing me arrive, the younger of the two retrieved his helmet which had been sitting like a tea-cosy on the middle of the kitchen table and put it on. All the better to arrest me in.

'What's going on?' I asked. I was relieved of my holiday bags by one of my sisters and sat down opposite the two strangers to await an explanation.

'Miss Alison Harris?' asked the bigger of the two men. 'Otherwise known as Ali Harris?'

'That's me,' I replied. 'What's happened? Has my cat been run over? Is my flat OK?'

'Miss Alison Harris, you are under arrest under suspicion of a charge of grievous bodily harm. You do not have to say anything . . .' he continued, exactly as they do on TV. 'But it may harm your defence if you do not mention now something which you later rely on in court.' The whole world started to spin sickeningly around me. 'Anything you do say may be given in evidence.'

'Hang on a minute,' interrupted my mother, as she tried to prise the policeman's hand from my arm, while he simultaneously clapped my wrists in a pair of shining handcuffs. 'Grievous bodily harm? Have you gone mad? Look at her, for heaven's sake. She's not a violent criminal. She's not big enough to hurt a fly. Let her go. You've obviously got the wrong girl. Tell him he's got the wrong girl,' she pleaded with my Dad.

'I'm afraid not,' said the policeman. 'Come with us, please, Miss Harris.'

'Where are you taking her?' shrieked my mother as I was led out into the hallway. 'Where are you taking her? Don't worry, Alison,' she called to me. 'This is all a terrible mistake. We'll rescue you as soon as we can. Get the car out, John. Alison, we're going to follow you to the station.'

'This must be a dream,' I murmured to myself, as I was manhandled out of the house and towards the waiting police car. I wondered if the sleeping tablets I had taken to get me through the long flight home were having dodgy side effects. Really dodgy side effects. I mean, me, arrested on a charge of grievous bodily harm? What an insane proposition! Oh, how Jeremy would laugh when I finally woke up and told him about this nightmare.

But right then, in the real world, his handsome tanned face drained of all its colour, as flanked by my hysterical parents, Jeremy watched me being driven away.

I had been dying for a cup of tea since our plane touched down at Heathrow. Never in a million years did I expect that I would get my first cup of PG Tips at the Brindlesham police station. As I sat in a miserable, bare-walled interview room waiting for the duty solicitor to arrive, the over-strong brew congealed in its plastic cup. I knew I wouldn't be able to touch a thing until somebody came into the room with a big smile on his or her face and told me that there had been a serious administrative mistake and that they were really after someone else.

When they did, I told myself, I would sue the bloody Brindlesham Police Force from there until Christmas.

But pretty soon the duty solicitor arrived and I heard the full details of my charge once more, with the in-flight alcohol almost totally worn off and reality slowly dawning. My solicitor, the elderly Mr Wagstaff, looked barely competent enough to tie his own shoe-laces as he sat a couple of feet behind me while the officer in charge of the investigation read out the charge. I, Alison Harris, was accused of inde-cent assault occasioning actual bodily harm, when, on the 2nd February 1998, I did apply a caustic sub-stance to the genitalia of one David Ainsley Devereux Whitworth with the intention of causing him grievous bodily harm.

'But it was only Hot Stuff Heat Rub!' I shrieked. Mr Wagstaff leaned forward and placed a quieting hand on my arm.

'I'd like to request a few moments with my client,' he told the inspector. The tape was switched off while Mr Wagstaff explained my current predicament to me. Best keep quiet, he suggested. And the bottom line?

Never ever cross a man who has a Police Inspector for a big brother.

As you can probably imagine, David's mother, Maureen Whitworth, had hated me from the very start of our relationship, since I was, in her eyes, nothing but an adulterous fast piece who had de-throned the lovely Lisa, queen of cross-stitch and batch baking, future mother of the kind of children that never shouted for sweets at supermarket tills. David's father was fairly ambiguous in his feelings towards me, but erred on the disapproving side for the sake of his marriage.

David's younger sister Marie would bring up the subject of Lisa at every possible opportunity. Every conversation I had with Marie would run along the lines of, 'I've got terrible thrush today, Ali. Lisa never used to get thrush. She always took such good care of her diet . . . and David's.' Even the dog's ear infection provoked a conversation about Lisa's amazing way with little fluffy animals.

Yes, apart from David, his elder brother Barry was the only member of the Whitworth family who seemed to rate me slightly higher than the average serial killer.

If I called round the Whitworths' house to discover that David wasn't home from work yet (he had to go back to live with his folks while Lisa sorted out selling the starter home they had bought together), I would be left standing on the doorstep unless Barry was in. It would always be Barry who invited me over the threshold and made me a cup of tea. Barry was probably the only member of that family apart from David who actually knew what I did for a living. He would always ask about my exciting secretarial life in the engineering industry and in turn he would regale me with long and convoluted stories about Brindlesham's criminal low-life, or at least the ones that I had known at school.

When David and I announced our engagement, I knew that I was resigning myself to life with the mother-in-law from hell, but that realisation was slightly counter-balanced by the fact that I would be getting the brother-in-law of my dreams. Barry Whitworth was funny, warm and generous. He would always make me welcome. And with a bit of luck, he would last far longer than his mum.

That all changed, of course.

One day, while David was still looking for a place of his own, I decided to pay him a surprise visit at his mum's. When I got to the house, it looked as though I had called at the wrong time even though I knew that David had one of his flexi-days off and had said that he would be at home all day. It was winter, four o'clock-ish. Dark already. But there were no lights on in the house. I rang the doorbell anyway, since having come that far, I thought I might as well be sure. The bell rang out in the empty hallway. Nothing. I rang it once more for luck. Then, just as I was about to leave, a light was flicked on in the hallway and Barry lumbered towards the door.

'Who the fuck is it now?' he grumbled as he pulled

back the latch, but when he saw me, his face broke into a generous smile. 'Hello, lovely,' he said. I could tell by the way that his hair was sticking out at all angles that I had dragged him from his bed.

'Is David in?' I asked.

'No,' said Barry. 'But you can come in and wait for him, if you want.'

I had done it so many times before, I agreed without question. Normally, Barry would lumber back to bed to continue sleeping off his hard nightshift, leaving me to help myself with the kettle and the biscuit tin. But this time, he joined me for a cup of tea instead.

'Shouldn't you be in bed?' I asked.

'Nah. I've been asleep for four hours already this afternoon. I want to talk to you.'

'I don't want to keep you up,' I told him.

'Darling,' he said. 'You could keep me up all night.'

From that very first innuendo I knew that something was awry. Barry had never said anything like that to me before. Instead, his comments had always been confined to the brother-in-lawly, if you know what I mean.

Anyway I made the tea and carried Barry's Postman Pat mug through into the sitting room. His parents were away, visiting David's batty grandmother in the north – the only pensioner more loathsome than my own toxic gran. David's sister always went to night-school for a Spanish class on Mondays. I had timed my visit for minimum family contact and I had got it. Barry and I were very much alone.

'Did David say when he was going to be back?' I asked desperately, when Barry squeezed his manly bulk into the chintzy two-seater sofa beside me.

'He didn't say. But I don't suppose it will be anytime soon. He said that if you turned up I should look after you . . .'

I gulped tea nervously as Barry slung his arm along the back of the sofa behind my head. It seemed a matter of mere seconds before that arm was resting along my shoulders. Next thing I knew, Barry was pulling me towards him, his lips puckered up like some dreadful cartoon character waiting for a kiss.

'I've always fancied you,' Barry told me.

'Eeek!' I said. Or words to that effect.

'Come on, Ali, just a little kiss,' he pleaded as I twisted desperately within his manly grasp. 'David won't ever know.'

'No, Barry, I can't,' I protested, as Barry's hot wet lips collided with my burning cheek. 'Please don't kiss me. I don't want to be unfaithful to David.'

'I'm not asking you to be unfaithful,' Barry told me roughly. 'I'm only after a one off shag for heaven's sake.'

He didn't get one, needless to say. By the careful application of a cup of scalding hot tea to his groin, I managed to distract Barry for just long enough to evade his sticky grasp and I was soon on the other side of the room, defending my honour with my Benetton rucksack.

'Aw! Fucking hell,' said Barry. 'What did you do that for?'

'I didn't mean to hurt you,' I lied.

'You got me up for this, you bitch. I could have you done for fucking GBH!'

'Really? And have me tell everyone at the police station exactly why I needed to defend myself?' I retorted. (As if they would have believed me, as I was currently discovering.)

I fled the house just as David arrived home. I didn't even let him get inside, but made him take me to the pub forthwith. I struggled all night long to bring myself to tell him how his brother had tried it on with me but never quite got around to spilling the beans. Fortunately it seemed, neither did Barry. That evening I kept David away from the house until I felt sure that Barry would have left for his nightshift once more.

Barry never mentioned the incident again, but from that day onwards I had one less ally than usual *chez* Whitworth. Now, however, that terrible night in the Whitworths' chintzy sitting room was coming back to haunt me in truly nightmarish style.

'It's most unusual for the Crown Prosecution Services to decide to intervene in this kind of domestic incident,' Mr Wagstaff mused as he flicked through the papers pertaining to my arrest. 'Most unusual.'

Not when the chief witness for the prosecution was related to the local police inspector, I thought wryly. David's brother must have encouraged him to bring a charge against me. Grievous Bodily Harm by way of the severe psychological damage imposed upon him when I Hot Stuff Heat Rubbed his dick all those weeks ago. David couldn't even have spelt the charge on his own.

I couldn't understand it.

'But he got up and walked away,' I told my solicitor. 'Believe me, I didn't do that man any physical damage at all.'

'I'm sure you're right, but we're not talking about physical damage any more. Mr Whitworth is claiming that he has been unable to maintain an erection since the incident. Every time he tries to have sex, he says that he is haunted by an image of your evil face and it quite puts him off the idea of making love to another woman.'

'If only he'd suffered from that before all this happened,' I thought out loud. 'So what's going to happen to me next? And when can I go home?'

'I'm afraid you won't be able to leave the station just yet, Alison. You'll probably be bailed on the condition that you stay well away from Mr Whitworth. And then the matter will be taken to the magistrates' court. With a bit of luck, the magistrates will decide that there is no case to answer and that will be the end of it. The whole matter certainly seems ridiculous to me. But these things can go either way,' he added, sucking his teeth. 'I don't want to get your hopes up.'

'No danger of that,' I told him. 'My hopes are hiding in my boots right now.'

Mr Wagstaff approximated a smile.

'I'll do my very best for you, Alison. Whatever happens, I'm sure I don't need to tell you that if you are bailed tonight, under no circumstances must you bring yourself to the attention of the police in any other way until all this is sorted out.'

'I haven't come to the attention of the police in twenty-five years,' I said indignantly, neglecting to mention the horror of Top Shop or the time when the local bobby came round to tick me off in front of my parents about roller-skating in the school playground during the summer holidays.

'Good. Now you just relax and have another cup of

tea,' said Mr Wagstaff helpfully. 'Meanwhile I'll try to grease the wheels of justice.'

He left me alone again and soon another cup of thick brown stuff masquerading as a tasty beverage was slopped onto the table before me by a spotty police constable who looked as though he was a fifth-former on work experience.

I looked at my watch. I had been at the police station for almost three hours. Twenty-four hours earlier I had been kissing the palm tree outside our beach hut goodbye. As I've said before, what a difference a day makes. This time, just twenty-four hours had taken me from the Caribbean to the clink.

CHAPTER THIRTY-SEVEN

I had thought that I couldn't be held at the police station against my will for longer than a couple of hours. So much for my legal knowledge, gained almost entirely from watching *Murder One* and *Inspector Morse*. After much whispering in the corridor Mr Wagstaff came to tell me that, as far as he was concerned, the worst had happened. I wasn't going to be bailed that night. Instead, because of the seriousness of the charge against me, I was going to be held until the earliest possible opportunity for me to appear before a magistrate. In the eyes of the police, apparently, I was a danger to the public at large.

'You mean, they're not letting me out tonight?' I whimpered.

As Mr Wagstaff nodded I seemed to hear a bell tolling in my mind.

'They can't do this to me!' I wailed. 'I want to see my mum and dad.'

'Just try to get some sleep,' said Mr Wagstaff.

'How can I get some sleep? I'm worried out of my mind.'

Mr Wagstaff just shrugged and asked the officer on duty to let him back out into the corridor. As the metal door of the cell I had been moved into clanged shut behind him, I started to shiver uncontrollably. Partly through cold. (I was still in my shorts, not having been given time to change into something more sensible for February in a bare-walled cell.) But mostly I shivered through fear. I had led a pretty sheltered life up until that point. My years at St Olive's High School for Girls had prepared me for a variety of emergencies that could be averted with a bit of skilful darning, but for nothing so seedy as spending the night in the slammer.

Not that I could sleep at all on that hard bed with its itchy grey blankets. The tales of terrible inmates with which Barry had regaled me all those years ago back when we were still friends, suddenly seemed horribly real. Closing time brought in a bevy of drunken brawlers. A football match held earlier that day had turned out badly for the supporters of Brindlesham FC (not that it ever turned out otherwise), and a fight had broken out on the High Street. Now the protagonists of the warring factions of supporters were being held in cells on opposite sides of the corridor and the fight continued verbally, with insults and tuneless songs hurled backwards and forwards for hours. If I hadn't been a girl, the duty officer said, he would have put some of them in with me. I was quite an inconvenience to them, taking up a whole cell on my own.

'Well, why don't you let me go home?' I asked him.

'What? A dangerous lunatic, like you?' he replied. Stinging from his insult, I lay down on the hard bed and pulled a blanket right up to my ears. Where was my knight in shining armour? How long would it take someone – Mum, Dad, Jeremy, anyone – to convince the police that I didn't really need to be locked up? Apart from David Whitworth, I literally had never hurt a fly in my life. In fact I was the kind of girl who constructed elaborate spider ladders to rescue the blighters from the bath rather than flush them straight down the plughole as Emma did.

Finally, exhausted by lack of sleep, jet lag and worry, I started to drift away into a fitful doze. But just as I was dropping off, the little window in the door of my cell was flipped open and someone shone a bright light right onto my face.

'Just checking that you're not killing yourself in there,' someone laughed cruelly.

'Far more likely that I'll die of sleep deprivation,' I snapped back.

Just five hours later, at six o'clock in the morning, I was woken again with my breakfast. Congealed scrambled egg and two pieces of toast that sprang back into shape like rubber if you tried to fold them. I couldn't help thinking back wistfully to that last breakfast on Antigua. Fresh pineapple cut into thick chunky slices. Big smiling slabs of melon, with juice that dribbled down your chin when you bit into it. As I chewed the reconstituted egg, a tear ran down my face and into the corner of my mouth.

'Oh, Mum. Oh, Dad. Oh, Jeremy,' I cried. 'Somebody please come and rescue me.'

Then the door to my cell was thrown open, and for the first time in my life, I was overjoyed to see someone as short and ugly as Mr Wagstaff.

'You're in luck,' he said. 'You can see the magistrates this morning. Right away. Tidy yourself up.'

That was a tall order. I didn't exactly have access to the full range of primping products I need to make myself look even half decent after a good night's sleep, let alone a night on a concrete bench. A female officer accompanied me to the prisoners' bathroom and I had a quick, cold shower with some scratchy soap. After that, I had to put my shorts back on, and my sandals, still itchy with sand. Then I was led the short distance across the road from the police station to the magistrates' court in handcuffs.

Fortunately, the magistrates, as I had hoped, looked a pair of kind women, more inclined to sentence someone to duty on the cake stall at the WI fete than community service. And despite the fact that I looked as though I had just escaped from an amateur dramatics production of *South Pacific* on acid, I was released on bail pending committal for trial.

When I finally was allowed to go, after handing in my passport so that I couldn't flee the country (apparently the fact that I had just come back from Antigua made that highly possible), Dad and Mum were waiting at the police station, together with Jeremy, who had insisted on coming too, to collect me. When I saw Jeremy again, I couldn't help bursting into tears. It was a mixture of relief and joy. The twenty-four hours I had been kept in the cells at the station seemed like the longest twenty-four hours in history. More importantly, it was the longest time Jeremy and I had spent apart since flying to Antigua.

'Thank goodness you're here,' I said, flinging my arms around Jeremy's neck.

'Hmm. Well there's no need to look pleased to see your poor worried parents as well,' said my mother. 'I've been up half the night sick with fear.'

'Oh, I'm sorry, Mum,' I said, flinging my arms around her and my father too.

'What happened?' Jeremy asked urgently. 'We heard you were being charged with attacking someone. They've got it all wrong, of course. Tell me they have. They're letting you off the charge, aren't they?'

I shook my head sadly.

'They didn't get it wrong?'

'Well, they did get it wrong,' I told them all. 'I swear they did. But they're not letting me off yet. I've got to come back again next week. I'm only out on bail.'

'A daughter of mine on bail!' my mother shrieked, as she pressed the back of her hand to her forehead in a dramatic swoon. 'Just like a common criminal.'

'I'm not a criminal, Mum. You know that. It's all just a ridiculous misunderstanding. Mr Wagstaff says he'll sort it out.'

'Who on earth are you charged with attacking?' asked my father.

'David. David Whitworth.'

'David? But he's a grown man. How could you possibly have attacked him?'

'Let's just say I went for his Achilles Heel,' I told them flatly, almost smiling at the euphemism but not quite finding it funny enough to share at that point.

When we got back to the house, my younger sisters

tumbled out to meet us on the driveway. For once, their main concern wasn't what gaudy nick-nacks I had picked up for them in duty free. Instead they had tactfully decided to leave searching my suitcases for pressies for a little while. In fact Jo, who had been doing screen-printing during her obligatory creative arts period at school, had a present for me instead.

'It's still a bit wet,' she explained, as she handed me the voluminous white T-shirt. 'I started it as soon as Mum said what was going on but I really expected you to be in a bit longer to give it a chance to dry out.'

'Thanks,' I said, unfurling the T-shirt so that I could see the full glory of her design. 'Alison Harris is inocent!' it said, in big drippy letters. I wondered if she had missed the extra 'n' out of 'innocent' by mistake or deliberately, so that she could fit the exclamation mark in instead.

'I was going to make them for the whole family,' she continued. 'But they've let you go now so I won't have to bother.'

'I'm only out on bail, Jo,' I explained. 'This fiasco is far from over yet.'

'A daughter of mine on bail,' sighed Mum once more.

'But it will be over soon, my love,' said Jeremy comfortingly. 'We'll get the best lawyers in the land to make sure that this ridiculous farce never even gets as far as court.'

'We can't afford the best lawyers in the land,' I whined. 'I don't think we can even afford Mr Wagstaff for much longer.'

'You're not using Mr Wagstaff of Wagstaff and

Chivers?!' my sister Jane exclaimed. 'Oh, Ali, he's an absolute disaster. When some friends of mine used him to help them move house, he did a search on the wrong property and the whole deal fell through. Not only that, but he charged them for the time he took to make the cock-up in the first place.'

'This gets worse and worse,' I said, sinking into the sofa and accepting a cup of tea thrust at me from one side and a chocolate biscuit from the other.

'We've got to look on the bright side,' Jeremy twittered. 'When we flew back from our holiday yesterday, we were both on cloud nine, weren't we?'

I looked up into his shining eyes and nodded. 'We were. We really were.'

'We had plenty to celebrate then and none of that has changed.'

'You mean?'

'Yes. I think it's time to make the announcement, don't you? Might help everybody sleep just that little bit easier tonight.'

'You say it,' I whispered.

'No, we'll say it together.'

We both took deep breaths and counted to three, then blurted out variously, 'We've got engaged / we're getting married.'

Mum just look confused.

'We've decided to get married,' Jeremy said more slowly, clutching my shaking hand.

'Oh!'

Mum's face crumpled up like a discarded hankie and she burst into tears.

'That wasn't quite the effect we were after.'

'Mum,' I said, wrapping a comforting arm around

her shoulders. 'Mum, it's good news. We're in love. We're getting married. Isn't that fantastic?'

She nodded and blew her nose loudly. 'It's wonderful. Really good news, darling. It's just that it's all come as a bit of a shock. I don't know how much more excitement I can take today. I might have to take one of my pills. John, take me upstairs,' she told my father.

'Dad? Are you pleased?' I asked.

He nodded, but didn't actually say anything. Then he shook Jeremy's hand perfunctorily and helped my mother to her bed.

'Well, that went down like a bacon sarnie at a Jewish wake,' I muttered. 'What do you think, Jo?' She had remained downstairs and was rifling through my suitcases. She pulled out a sarong patterned with gaudy tropical fish and held it against her.

'I think this is lovely.'

'Actually, Jo,' I said, pulling it away from her grubby mitts. 'I wasn't referring to the shopping. Besides, that's for Emma. This is for you.' I pointed out a T-shirt printed with the name of our hotel.

'Great,' she said unenthusiastically.

'Well, if you don't like the design, you could always paint over it.' Jo snatched up the T-shirt and left us alone.

'This is brilliant,' I said sarcastically. 'Wonder if your mother is going to be this pleased as well?'

'She'll be happy enough,' Jeremy assured me.

'When will we tell her?'

'Er, perhaps not just yet. We'll wait until we've found out more about this ridiculous charge you've been landed with, shall we? I think if my mum had to hear as much news as your mother had today, she'd need to take more than a pill to sort her out. She's very highly strung.'

'Aren't all mothers?' I asked.

'It doesn't matter,' said Jeremy soothingly. 'What matters is you and I. That we're happy. And that there are no secrets between us. Ali, I think I need to know exactly what happened between you and David Whitworth now. The whole truth.'

'Sounds like I'm in court already,' I joked.

'You know what I mean. Tell me everything. Not just the bits you told the solicitor. I want to be able to understand what's going on.'

'Well,' I said, bracing myself for disaster. 'It happened like this.'

'I'll stand by you,' Jeremy said determinedly when I had finished telling him the full story. Well, it was almost the full story. In the end, instead of the Hot Stuff Heat Rub aspect, I told him that I had kicked David in the balls, accidentally, while we were having a row. I know it's even more violent, but somehow it sounded less sexual than rubbing something in and I didn't want Jeremy to know that I had been sexual with David so recently.

'I'm so lucky to have you,' I murmured into Jeremy's hair as he gave me the hundredth of many reassuring hugs.

'We'll get you through this, Ali. The man's an idiot. He's obviously overreacting. Thousands of men get kicked in the balls every day. But how many of them go and prosecute?'

'Those with policemen for brothers,' I said sadly. 'Oh, Jeremy, are you serious about standing by me?'

He nodded.

'I don't know what I'd do without you.'

'Well, I'm afraid you'll have to practise for a little while,' said Jeremy then. 'I got a call from the office this afternoon. The place is in a mess. They want me to go back to Poland right away.'

'How right away?' I asked him desperately.

'Right away, like tomorrow morning.'

Waaaah!!! I didn't think I had any tears left in me that day, but I did.

CHAPTER THIRTY-EIGHT

I couldn't even see him to the airport. Next day, while Jeremy was boarding a plane that would take him back to Warsaw, I was waiting to see Mr Wagstaff again, in a room full of men with lots of tattoos and not very much hair who looked as though they could really do some damage to a grown man like David Whitworth. When a chap with the *Titanic* on his tattooed forearm asked me what I had done, I told him I was just delivering some sandwiches to the office.

'You have options,' said Mr Wagstaff, when I finally got to see him.

What a relief.

'At the end of next week,' he continued. 'You will have to appear at the Magistrates' Court again, and this time you will be formally charged. This is the point at which you have to make a choice. You can either be tried at the Magistrates' Court, or ask to go to Crown Court. At the Magistrates' Court you'll be tried by a trio of fuddy-duddy old geezers who will probably convict you because you've never done an exotic hand-job on them.'

I winced. It gave me a very peculiar and unpleasant feeling to hear a man of Mr Wagstaff's age and position say 'hand-job'.

'At Crown Court,' he continued, 'you will appear in front of a jury. There could be lots of people among that jury who will understand exactly how you felt when you administered the Hot Stuff Heat Rub to Mr Whitworth's private parts. On the other hand, the jury could be full of women like your Grandma who won't understand at all.'

'She approves,' I told Mr Wagstaff quickly.

'Well, make it like my Grandma then. She'd have had you locked up for even knowing where a man's genitals were before marriage.'

I managed a small laugh. 'Great. Sounds like a choice between being buried alive or boiled in hot fat. So what's the third option?'

'There isn't one. Crown Court or Magistrates' Court. That's it. Comprendez?'

Nope. I still didn't really understand the difference. 'Well, I guess it has to be the Crown Court,' I said confidently. 'I mean, at least I've got a chance of getting off that way, haven't I? Normal people will be sympathetic towards me when they hear what David is really like.'

'Yes. But if you don't get off . . .' Mr Wagstaff drew in breath in a way that suggested I was about to be horrified. 'We're looking at a charge of indecent assault occasioning actual bodily harm here, Alison. At the very least, we're looking at indecent assault, a very serious charge indeed. A Magistrates' Court can impose a maximum sentence of six months in prison and a maximum fine in the region of five hundred pounds. But if we go to Crown Court?' He made that uncomfortable sucky noise again. 'You could be looking at five years minimum.'

'Five years?' I gasped. 'My God. I'd be in my thirties by the time I got out.'

'You could make it three years with good behaviour. But it is still a long time.'

'This is like a game of Russian roulette,' I wailed. 'What you're telling me is that I could either get off scot-free or go down forever?'

'So what's it to be?' said Mr Wagstaff lightly, as if I had just said 'So it's Harvey Nicks or Harrods'.

I started to chew the fingernails I had always been so precious about again. 'Well, if I go to Magistrates' Court, you reckon I'll definitely be convicted, right?'

'I think so. Unless you're a mason.'

'Then it seems to me that I have to go for trial by jury. Even if the consequences could be worse. I mean, at least that way I've got twelve chances of someone in that jury being sympathetic towards me. Not just two or three. And I am innocent, Mr Wagstaff. I swear I am.'

Mr Wagstaff nodded. 'I'm sure you are. But innocence isn't always the best defence, I'm afraid. We may do OK. After all, you're a very personable girl, Alison. You've never been in trouble before. You're intelligent, smartly dressed, attractive.' He loosened his tie and I gripped the arms of my chair tightly, praying that I wasn't about to be hit upon by my solicitor. But Mr Wagstaff quickly stopped looking at me through his narrowed, shifty eyes and began to make feverish notes again. 'Yes, I think I can groom you into a model citizen, Alison Harris.'

At a cost.

CHAPTER THIRTY-NINE

That afternoon I had to go into work. There was no escaping it. Julie had been calling the flat non-stop for the past fortnight and Emma was running out of patience with her role as my protector. Besides, she warned me, it was just a matter of time before my impending court case came to light. Julie was an avid reader of the court file which appeared in the local newspaper, and she had bedded enough policemen to make it possible that she was, in fact, an official part of the police public relations training programme.

'She'll find out,' was the general consensus.

So I went back to work, clutching the sick note which Emma had written out on a form she had stolen from Ashley's briefcase. He had refused to write the note himself, which Emma said had made her doubt his suitability as a boyfriend. Unsuitability which was quickly forgotten when he gave her another anatomy class, if you know what I mean.

The in-tray on my desk at Hudderston's looked like the lower reaches of the Himalayas. My computer screen was covered with a thick layer of dust into which someone had scrawled the word 'Skiver'. Julie was waiting for me, power-dressed in purple Karen Millen and a pair of surgical-looking boots.

'Back at last,' she trilled. 'Feeling better? I must say you're a terribly funny colour for someone who's been in bed for two weeks.'

'Jaundiced,' I squeaked.

'Mmm. I'd pay good money to get that jaundiced at the Tanning Shop,' she replied. My heart raced with the terror of having been caught out, but Julie was already sorting out the most important pieces of work from my mountainous pile and the discussion seemed to be over.

'You've got a doctor's note, of course,' she said.

I handed her the envelope.

'I don't want it. Give it to Mrs Webber in personnel, when you've got a minute.' Then she left me alone, practically imploding with relief. Mrs Webber in personnel was almost a hundred years old and as blind as a bat. She'd never notice that my note was forged.

I picked up the first report to be typed and switched on my machine. No-one suspected I had been on holiday. I just had to keep my head down and plough on through. And I wouldn't take another minute off work until my magistrates' hearing on the following Friday morning.

Then the phone rang on Julie's desk. She picked it up and her face took on a curious expression. She buzzed through to me. 'It's some woman from a magazine. She says she wants to know how your holiday went.'

'My holiday?' My voice shook like coward yellow jelly. 'It must be Emma having a joke.'

'Funny joke,' said Julie.

'She has a surreal sense of humour.'

'Well, are you going to take this call or what? I haven't got all day.'

'OK,' I squeaked. I watched Julie from the corner of my eye to make sure she put down the phone before talking to my caller. It was Amanda of course.

'How was it?' she shrieked. 'Did you have a fabulous time? Did you swim with dolphins? How did you like the food? And I hear you won the international competition. Darling, I'm so proud of you both. We've decided that we want to do another fashion shoot for our summer holiday issue to celebrate. The World's Most Romantic Couple.' I could almost see her gesticulating with the thrill of it all. 'Want to do it tomorrow, sweetheart? While you've still got a tan?'

'Bleeurgh . . . I . . . er . . . I.' I'd completely forgotten about *Complete Woman*.

'Can't talk eh? I understand. I'm always rushed off my feet first day back at the office after a holiday. Call me when you've got a minute. March issue's out today by the way. You're on pages 14 to 16.'

She rang off. Leaving me clutching the phone as if it might morph into a life belt. The March issue was out already? If anyone saw that magazine I would be finished. Who bought it? I looked around the office, doing a mental head count of the girls and wondering who might trip me up. I thought I was in the clear when I remembered that Irene had a *Complete Woman* pin-up special of the doctors from *ER* blu-tacked to the cupboard above her desk.

So less than an hour back at work, I had to ask Julie if I could have an hour off.

'What for?' she asked, deeply irritated. 'Can't you wait till lunchtime?'

'No. I need painkillers. Now. I need to pick up my prescription.'

Thank God she didn't want to risk having a corpse in the office. She let me go and, rushing straight past the chemist's shop, I headed straight for the nearest newsagent to Hudderston's. And the second nearest. And the third nearest. Within an hour I managed to visit thirteen paper shops, bought 115 copies of *Complete Woman* and spent £230.

I was indeed on pages 14 to 16, five different poses and four big paragraphs about my love life. Jeremy looked fantastic, I thought, as I lovingly fingered his image. I looked scared. But not as scared as I was of anyone at Hudderston's seeing the spread. I allowed myself to keep just one copy, hidden safely at the bottom of my bag. The rest were consigned, in pieces, to a number of skips and bins about town. There was always the possibility that Irene would pick up her copy at Tesco's but I had done all I could do for now. I would have to get Emma to drive me to all the local superstores that night.

'Christ, you look like you've been running a marathon,' said Julie when I fell into the office again, panting desperately for breath. 'Sit down. We don't want you going into hospital again.'

Right then, a week in a mental hospital sounded just fine.

CHAPTER FORTY

That week passed like a sloth with arthritis as my date at the Magistrates' Court drew nearer. Jeremy phoned me nightly. And Irene daily bemoaned the fact that she couldn't get hold of a copy of *Complete Woman* for love nor money in our poxy little town.

Jeremy's calls kept me hanging onto life. Whatever horrors I had to face during a day at Hudderston's evaporated when I heard the telephone ring each night at nine o'clock on the dot. Emma bought herself a mobile phone because she got fed up of me hogging the house line for at least an hour at a time and was convinced that she was missing Ashley's calls. But on the very night Emma bought her new Nokia home, Jeremy told me that he couldn't talk to me for as long as usual.

'I'm going out tonight,' he said.

'Oh?' He usually moaned that there was nothing to do in Warsaw.

'Candida's here.'

'Candida?'

'Yes. She's started to make her film.'

Candida was in Warsaw. In the turmoil that had
been my sorry life since returning from Antigua I had
almost forgotten that Candida was due to start filming
in Poland. But in any case, I certainly hadn't expected
her to call Jeremy when she did get there.

'She called you?' I squeaked.

'Not exactly. She got Loretta to give me a buzz.'

That felt slightly better.

'Well, please give her my regards,' I said. Then,
'Things still OK with that fiancé of hers?'

'What? Vadim, I think so.'

I went to bed that night only mildly concerned.

Two days later, I walked into the office to find Irene
and Julie bent over a copy of the *Sun*, ooo-ing and
aah-ing as though they were seeing the Dead Sea
Scrolls for the first time.

'It can't be him,' Irene was saying with wonder in
her voice. 'It just can't be. I've known him since he was
a little lad. He always had darker hair than that.'

'It is him, Irene,' Julie protested. 'I'd recognise him
anywhere. He's obviously just had highlights. Well,
who would have thought it. Jeremy Baxter and her.'

I froze. My first thought was that somehow the pictures taken for *Complete Woman* had been syndicated
to the *Sun*. My cover had been blown and I was about
to get the sack in spectacular style. But that couldn't
have been the case. When Julie saw me, she smiled
and called me over.

'Alison,' she said. 'You can sort this argument out.
Is this or is this not "Boil-face Jeremy Baxter"? The
one from junior school.' She jabbed at the paper with
a vermilion nail.

I took a deep breath and focused on the picture

which had been the cause of their debate. Was it Jeremy? It certainly looked like him. The guy had his hair. His nose. His sunglasses even. But he was partially obscured by the girl in front of him. The girl who was standing with her back to the camera and her hand on the boy in question's shoulder.

'Who is Candida's mystery man?' the caption beneath the picture asked.

'Candida?' I murmured. 'Is that Candida Bianca?'

'Yeah!' Julie snorted. 'The film star. I couldn't bloody believe it. Can you? Boily Baxter and Candida Bianca? I didn't see that coming when he used to hang around the bus stop waiting for me to come home from school.'

'He waited at the bus stop for you?'

'Yeah. He had a crush on me,' she said in the throw-away manner she seemed to reserve for delivering bombshells. 'But I was too busy with Andy McIntyre. At least he had a motorbike. Jeremy just had O-levels and a bicycle back then. So do you think he's shagging her?' Julie asked, referring once again to the picture.

'I don't know,' I said, as calmly as I could.

'She's kissing him.'

'Yeah,' said Irene, unwittingly coming to my emotional rescue. 'But she could just be kissing him hello, couldn't she? You know how those paparazzi can make a big deal out of something perfectly innocent.'

'Like Fergie sucking that bloke's toes?' Julie shrieked. 'You know what, I almost wish I'd got off with Baxter now. Then I would be able to say that I had him first.'

'Probably not even him,' said Irene, slipping back to her desk at the approach of our boss.

I hoped not. I really hoped not.

I didn't have to tell Emma about the incident. She had bought a copy of the *Sun* on her way to college and knew all about it when she called me at work. She took Irene's view.

'He told you he was seeing her the other night. It's innocent, Ali. You know.'

But Jeremy didn't call on time that night. In fact he didn't call that night at all. I tried to reach him on the numbers that I had for him, but I couldn't make myself understood to the bored-sounding Polish receptionist at his office and no-one answered the telephone at his home. I spent the night in agony. For once, there was something worse on my mind than my impending day in court.

When he finally rang, I was so wound up with waiting that I immediately burst into tears.

'What's wrong?' he asked.

'There's a picture of you in the newspaper,' I sniffed.

As I explained what I'd seen, he just tutted and gave a hollow little laugh. 'Paparazzi,' he sighed, as if they had dogged him his whole life. 'We just went to the opera and then to a restaurant. They'll make a story out of anything.'

'The opera? But you told me you hate all that wailing crap,' I sobbed, testing him with his own words.

'It's not all wailing crap, Ali,' Jeremy protested. 'Candida tells me I've just been listening to the wrong ones. Wagner's *Ring Cycle* was really rather good. If a little long . . .'

'Did Vadim go too?'

'No, he was busy with the crew checking out locations. But he didn't mind that I took Candida out and neither should you.'

'I guess not,' I sniffed.

'No guessing about it. Shit. Listen. There's the doorbell. I've got to go, darling. I'll call you on Thursday night.'

'Thursday!' I protested to no-one. Jeremy had already rung off. Thursday was two days away.

There was no-one to console me but Fattypuss. Emma had gone out with Ashley. Marvin had recently met a rather nice dancer of South American origin and was on his way out to learn how to cha-cha when I caught him. When I rang home, there was no-one in but Jo, and she was dyeing her hair and wouldn't talk in case she got the timing wrong. I sat at the window and looked out into the dark street. Who had been ringing Jeremy's doorbell? Was it the gas man? Or Candida? I needed someone to tell me that even if it was Candida, everything was still all right. Jeremy still loved me. And he would still be flying home in time for my appearance in court, wouldn't he?

My court appearance. I picked up the telephone and my fingers hovered over the digits that made up David's number. I hadn't thought to call him since the whole nightmare began. Perhaps if we just talked he might see his way to dropping the charges. I couldn't believe that he was really psychologically damaged by the whole affair. He had obviously been annoyed about the night before the holiday. Now that he was back in Lisa Brown's arms and seemingly

happy there (Emma had seen them picking out curtains in Debenhams), perhaps he could be persuaded
that I deserved my happiness too.

Three. Four. Two. I dialled the first three digits
slowly. Then punched in the last four digits like a
maniac before I could bottle out.

Ring. Ring.

'Hello?'

It was Lisa.

I crashed the receiver back down into its cradle. She
wouldn't know who had called.

I had of course forgotten about 1471.

CHAPTER FORTY-ONE

'**D**arling ... are you going to tell me what is going on?'

Amanda had caught me on my way out of the door. I clutched the phone tightly and wondered if it was too late to pretend that I was in fact Emma.

'Am I or am I not looking at a picture of David in yesterday's copy of the *Sun*?'

'Eh?'

'Yes! With Candida Bianca. Have you seen a copy? Candida and her mystery man. It really looks like David, but I told myself, he's not in Warsaw. He's hard at work in sunny Brindlesham, busy saving up cash for his impending wedding to the lovely Alison. Tell me I'm imagining things, sweetheart, and I'll let you get on.'

'You're imagining things,' I assured her. 'Someone showed me the picture at work. It's not David. It's just someone who looks very much like him. I guess I'm lucky that Candida Bianca doesn't live in Brindlesham or she'd be after him like a shot,' I added with a very forced laugh.

'Mmm. It is quite a coincidence. You do know that Candida was staying at Santa Bonita all the time that you were there?'

I coughed. 'I had heard that, but, you know, she kept herself pretty much to herself.'

'That's not what I heard,' said Amanda slyly. 'Sugar, if you can let your Auntie Amanda in on a little secret regarding your fiancé and this stella superstar, I might be able to help you get a few little piccies of your own into the paper to help soften the blow of your split. I've got a direct line to Max Clifford . . .'

'There's nothing to say.'

'I know it's embarrassing, being jilted . . .'

Didn't I know it.

'But the sponduliks I'm thinking about could keep you in retail therapy for years. When do you think it happened, darling? Did you know about this while you were on holiday? Did he tell you what was going on before the picture appeared in the *Sun*?'

'There's nothing to talk about. It's perfectly innocent. And I've got to go to court . . . I mean, work.'

'OK. You go to work. I can't force you to make piles of money out of your pain.'

'I'm not in pain,' I said as I slammed the phone down, knocking the phone off the table as I did so to land straight on my toes.

It was just what I needed before my appearance in the Magistrates' Court. The make-up I had so carefully applied to give the impression that I was at once both someone who was feminine and competent was soon running down my face in thick, candy-stripes of mascara, blusher and gloss.

I was still sitting at the bottom of the stairs when

Emma woke up at half-past nine. She needed her sleep, she said. It was hard work being a student. I heard a sharp intake of breath when she saw me slumped by the telephone stand. She rushed down to be with me and didn't bother to hide her disgust at my appearance.

'Christ, you've got Louis Vuitton under your eyes,' she exclaimed. 'Do you know what time it is? Your mother warned me to make sure that you didn't forget about your appearance. Good job I'm skipping lectures again. Do you want some coffee? You ought to eat something before you go out, you know. I'll make some toast.'

I took the toast, slightly overdone, gratefully. Then I let Emma choose a new 'going to see a magistrate' outfit. The one I had put on first thing was now crumpled and covered with tears. Thank God my best friend, like my mother, didn't believe I could stand on my own two feet.

I had to patch up my make-up on the bus to meet Mr Wagstaff. I couldn't have done much of a job, I guessed from his wince when he saw me.

At the Magistrates' Court, I waited to be called with Mr Wagstaff and a selection of the tattooed thugs I had last seen in his office.

'Now you know what you've got to do?' he asked me for the tenth time.

'I'll go in there. They'll ask me my name and describe the offence again and I'll plead not guilty. Then they'll tell me when I have to go to court.'

'Are you sure you're going to plead not guilty? Are you sure you've told me absolutely everything? Are you sure there isn't another side to this story that could get you into very serious trouble indeed when the prosecution calls its witness?'

'I'm innocent,' I told him tearfully. He pulled out his hankie so that I could blow my nose, but he was looking at me in such a way that suggested he had seen this all before. No doubt even the man with 'I love Pit Bull terriers' tattooed across his cheekbone could turn on the waterworks if so required.

'I'm innocent and the jury at the crown court will find me innocent because I'm telling the truth,' I persisted.

'OK,' said Mr Wagstaff. 'But remember what I told you, if we take this to Crown Court, then there is no turning back. If you're found guilty there, you will be looking at a very, very serious sentence indeed.'

'I'm not going to be looking at any sentence,' I sniffed defiantly. 'David Whitworth has blown this out of all proportion. And I've got witnesses to prove it too. There's Emma, my flatmate, she was listening at the door when David came to beg me to go back with him the night before I left for Antigua. She heard him say that I hadn't done him any permanent harm that night. He was prepared to forgive me then if I took him to the Caribbean.'

'And she would be prepared to say all this in court?'

'Emma would do anything for me,' I said triumphantly. Though I knew that I was probably setting myself up for a lifetime's worth of favours in return.

Then I was called. Feeling like Marie Antoinette regretting her comment about the cake, I followed the clerk into the court. The Magistrate I faced this time, an altogether more serious stipendiary magistrate who sat alone, was a portly man who didn't look quite so kind as the old women I had faced before. In fact, he rather looked as though he got off on fining people for letting their dogs foul their own back gardens.

'How do you plead?' the clerk of the court asked me.

'Not guilty,' I whispered.

'What was that?' he asked. 'Guilty?'

'No. Not guilty,' I repeated, making sure there could be no mistake this time.

So I demanded my right to a trial by jury. The Magistrate went quiet for a while and shuffled a huge pile of papers. Mr Wagstaff kept pointing out the opportunities in the process at which the magistrate could decide that I had no case to answer but he didn't and I was duly given the date for my Crown Court trial.

It would take three months to come round. Three whole months. It was a very long time to have such a thing hanging over you. The only consolation was that if my appetite remained affected as it had been for that long, I might be able to wear a bikini if I was free for the summer holidays.

'Keep your chin up,' Mr Wagstaff told me as he slid into the driver's seat of his smart new BMW. 'I'm doing my very best for you.' Then he drove off, leaving me standing alone outside the court house while he went to assure some other poor sucker that everything would be all right. If they liked prison food. I started the long walk back to my house, feeling deeply introspective. I walked extra slowly, figuring that the longer I was away from the phone, the more chance Jeremy would have to ring and make everything better again.

CHAPTER FORTY-TWO

I couldn't believe it when Jeremy called that night to tell me that he would be flying in from Warsaw the very next day, which was Saturday. I must have thanked the Lord about a thousand times for my wonderful boyfriend. He said he had to see me the minute he landed. I said I would be at the airport. No, better than that, he said, he would drive straight to The Aspidistra, which was halfway between my home and the airport and meet me there. Save me the drive, he said. So thoughtful.

I was awake with the birds next morning and spent all day doodling Jeremy's name on the side of the *Radio Times* while I watched all the Open University sociology and politics programmes in the hope that I would see someone whose predicament seemed worse than mine. There was a talk show just before the children's programmes started, where a girl blubbed that her mother had run off with her boyfriend, but I have to say that with her perm it was hardly surprising that she lost out to someone twenty years her senior.

By contrast, I decided that that night I was going to

look a million dollars. I hung Candida's red Versace dress from the shower curtain while I bathed so that the steam would make the creases drop out. I spent an hour on my hair and plastered my lips with seven coats of lipstick, so that I would remain picture perfect no matter how many times he kissed me.

I was ready to go out at half-past five, though Jeremy and I weren't due to meet until eight. I actually sat in the car on the driveway for five minutes at six o'clock and toyed with the idea of driving to the airport to meet him there anyway. It would save him getting a taxi to the restaurant and heaven knows we needed to save all the money we could with the terrifying prospect of my legal costs. But I thought better of it. I didn't know the details of Jeremy's flight for a start, or even which terminal he would be flying into, so it was perfectly possible that I would miss him and end up having to wait even longer to see him for my troubles.

So, I hung on until seven o'clock, then I floated to the restaurant, as light-hearted as a girl with a ball and chain in the back of her mind could possibly be. Trust Jeremy to be thoughtful enough to book a table at my favourite restaurant to cheer me up. We would have a nice long chat about our wedding plans, I told myself, brightening still further at the thought, as I let the Maître d' of The Aspidistra relieve me of my coat.

Jeremy had yet to arrive.

I got myself a drink to steady my butterflies. This would be the first time that Jeremy and I had had a 'reunion' of sorts. I was very much looking forward to it, but I felt I still needed to loosen up a little. Blot out my troubles. A double vodka and tonic arrived at the table forthwith.

By half-past eight I wasn't feeling quite so excited. The waiter kept hovering by the table, trying to get an order from me. I was sure that he even raised his eyebrows disbelievingly when I said for the third time that I was waiting for someone to join me. Perhaps his flight had been delayed, I thought. Half an hour later, I was thinking, perhaps he's had a crash.

But just as I was wondering whether I ought to call the airport, I heard the crunch of car wheels on the gravel driveway of the restaurant and looked out through the window to see a vast limousine swing up to the front entrance. A vast limousine that soon disgorged my boyfriend. I was so astounded that instead of the sweet nothings I had planned, the first thing I said to Jeremy was, 'How on earth did you afford to hire that?'

'Free limo service with the flight,' he said as he squeezed himself into the chair opposite me after barely pecking me on the cheek in greeting.

'What? With economy class Aeroflot? You're kidding. I thought you were lucky if you actually got a seat on the plane, let alone a lift home in a stretch limo.'

'Look, don't worry about it, OK. It wasn't your money.'

That ruffled my feathers a bit.

'Mineral water,' Jeremy barked at the waiter.

'Aren't you going to have something a bit stronger? It is a celebration of sorts, isn't it? Seeing each other again after all those horrible weeks apart.'

'I need to keep a clear head.'

'How long are you here for?'

'Just until tomorrow.'

'Is that all?' I started to miss him in anticipation already.

'It's long enough.'

'Remember this dress?' I asked him, fishing for a compliment to lighten things up.

'Yes, it's Candida's. Have you ordered yet?' he asked, changing the subject straightaway.

'No,' I told him. 'I was waiting for you.'

'I'll have the chicken salad. No dressing.'

I almost laughed. 'Chicken salad with no dressing. Isn't that a bit dull? Why don't you have a steak?'

'I'm watching my health,' he replied. 'You should think about doing the same too, you know.'

'Well, my diet's been the least of my worries lately,' I muttered. 'I can barely hold down water. Oh, Jeremy, I can't tell you how much I've been looking forward to seeing you again. Hearing your voice last night, after that awful morning in court, made me remember that it's all going to be all right in the end. Just seeing your face makes me feel so much happier. Only you can make me feel better these days.'

And after that little outburst, I could resist no longer. I got up from my seat and flung my arms around him, plastering kisses all over his face and head like a deranged puppy dog.

But when I pulled away from him to take my seat, I had an awful feeling that that night, Jeremy wouldn't be making me feel better at all. He had that look in his eyes. The one that I had seen in David's eyes on that terrible Christmas Day in the hospital. Jeremy was distracted. Desperate. Needing to say something that I really wouldn't want to hear.

Though he never got round to saying it that night.

He ate his salad. He refused dessert. He ordered coffee. No milk or sugar. Decaffeinated. And then he excused himself to the little boys' room. I drank my coffee. Milk and two sugars. Extra strong. I drank his coffee. He didn't come back.

At first I gave him the benefit of the doubt. I mean, maybe he had constipation. I had heard all the horror stories about Polish food. Then darker thoughts started to gather at the back of my mind. I had recently developed the imagination of a Stephen King. What if he had slipped in a puddle of something unspeakable on the bathroom floor and knocked himself out on a urinal? What if, even as I unwrapped the foil-covered chocolate mints that came with the bill, he was drowning, face-down in a lavatory pan?

The restaurant started to empty, as two by two the guests gathered up their coats and left in a flurry of air kisses. The waiters hovered by the till, shining up wine glasses and cutlery in readiness for the next day's diners. The bill for our meal lay folded in front of me. The Maître d' wandered past and looked pointedly at the slip of paper that I hadn't even bothered to look at. Jeremy had told me the night before that this would be his treat.

'Ahem,' a waiter coughed discreetly. 'I'm afraid that the restaurant will be closing for the night in ten minutes time, madam.'

'Er, yes,' I squeaked. 'I know that. It's just that I'm waiting for my boyfriend to come back from the bathroom. I don't suppose you could pop and see what's become of him, could you? He doesn't usually spend such a long time in the loos.'

One of the waiters standing by the till, covered his smile and gave a cough to choke a giggle.

'But monsieur has already left,' said the man who was talking to me. 'He left almost an hour ago, madam. He said that he had received a bleeper message calling him into work and that you would be staying for coffee alone.'

'He what?' I didn't even know he had a bleeper.

'You mean, he didn't tell you?'

The look on my face must have told the waiter all he needed to know.

'Oh, madam. I am so sorry.'

'You're talking rubbish.'

I got to my feet and ran to the men's room. I had to pass the exit on my way there, but I still wouldn't believe that Jeremy could possibly have slipped out without telling me. I wouldn't even start to entertain the idea until I had banged open every cubicle door in that room and left one elderly gentleman in particular feeling rather embarrassed.

'He can't have left me!' I wailed.

'Er, would you mind closing the door on your way out,' said the gentleman I had interrupted while evacuating his bowels.

I stumbled back out into the restaurant, where the Maître d' was still waiting for me with the bill.

'Madam, if I could beg your kind attention . . .'

'Wait,' I pleaded. 'He's got to be round here some-where. Perhaps he stumbled into the ladies' room by mistake. He wouldn't have gone home without me. I know he wouldn't. And he certainly wouldn't have left this jacket,' I added, pointing triumphantly at the Giorgio Armani creation which was still hanging from the back of Jeremy's chair. That jacket was Jeremy's pride and joy. If he could have got away with it, I'm sure he would have worn it inside out just so that everyone could see the label.

I was just about to wreak havoc in the ladies' room when the telephone rang. It was a mobile phone. Jeremy's mobile phone, ringing from the pocket of Jeremy's jacket.

'And he wouldn't have left his phone,' I said with something bordering on hysterical relief. The phone continued to ring out accusingly, its ugly tone disrupting the calm ambience of the restaurant almost as much as I had been.

'If you wouldn't mind answering it, madam.'

'But . . . I don't know if I should. I mean, it's his phone.'

'Then turn it off. This is a mobile phone-free zone, I'm afraid.'

'All right. I'll answer it.'

I pulled the damn thing out of Jeremy's pocket and looked at it in confusion for a clue as to how it might actually open. After another five rings, the waiter took the phone from my hand and opened it himself.

'Hello,' I said tentatively, when he handed the phone back to me. 'Jeremy Baxter's phone.'

'I know,' said the voice at the other end of the line. 'I am Jeremy.'

'Jeremy,' I giggled hysterically. 'Where on earth are you? I was beginning to worry. I bet you're calling me from the lobby, aren't you? Well, the joke's wearing a bit thin on the waiter, so you'd better come back in here and rescue me right now. Where are you?' I scanned the restaurant to see if I could see him hiding behind a potted plant, à la his namesake, Sir Jeremy Beadle.

'I'm on my way back to the airport.'

'What?'

'I'm about a mile from Gatwick,' he sighed. And thirty miles from me! 'I'm sorry to do this to you, Ali, but I'm not coming back. Not tonight.'

I must have gone very pale indeed. The waiter stepped forward to support me, then pulled out a seat and made me sit down. 'Jeremy,' I said, regaining just a little composure. 'What's going on? Have you got to get back to Poland for work or something?'

'No. It's just that I could see how the evening was panning out and I thought that this would be the best way to end things.'

'The evening?'

'No. Things. Us. To end us.'

'Aaaagh!' I shrieked. 'Please tell me you're joking.'

'Alison, I'm afraid that I've never been more serious in my life.'

'Jeremy, please stop messing about. The last thing I need right now is for you to start acting the silly bugger.'

'Alison, I'm telling you that our relationship is over.'

'But we're engaged!'

'That's over too.'

'No,' I whined. 'You can't end things. Not like this. Not over the telephone. It's so cowardly. It's so mean. Come back here at once.'

'I could have sent you a fax instead,' he protested. 'Look, I've got to go. The phone in this limo starts to cut out as soon as we get under the flight paths. Look after yourself, Ali. Oh, and you can keep that mobile if you like.'

'No. No. Noooo!!' I wailed with anguish but he was already gone. I tried to call him back at once. I punched 1471 into the mobile until I was blue in the face but it wouldn't give me a number. It had to be a joke. It just had to be a joke. I dialled 192 and tried to get a number for the airport so that I could demand that the next plane to Warsaw didn't take off until Jeremy and I had sorted this out.

'A-hem,' the waiter interrupted me. 'Since we've established that sir won't be coming back to the restaurant this evening, I wonder if perhaps you could spare just a moment to consider our unfinished business?' He fluttered the bill like a little fan.

'Christ! I don't think I've got enough money,' I warned him, when I clocked the ridiculous amount. I rummaged deep in my handbag and came up with a furry cough sweet and two tenners. I was at least thirty pounds shy of the total.

'How could he do this to me?' I asked nobody in particular. 'How could he do this to me? He was supposed to be supporting me in my hour of need. Cheering me up. Not pushing me to the brink of bloody suicide.'

'Madam, if you would like to step into my office.' The Maître d' shuffled me out of the way of his other guests. 'I am sure that we can come to some sort of arrangement. Perhaps you have something that you could leave with us as security while you go to find the rest of the money. Your passport, perhaps?'

'My passport? You must be joking. I'm on bail. My passport's with the police.'

That didn't exactly inspire his confidence in my ability to find the rest of the dosh.

'Then your driving licence, perhaps.'

'I haven't got that with me either.'

I was almost blind from crying. Now I flung myself at the Maître d's feet and begged him to let me wash up or something.

'That won't be necessary,' he said, prising me from his knees. 'We do have a dishwasher. Perhaps, under the circumstances, we might be able to waive some of madam's bill this evening. You've obviously had a bit of a shock. I'll tell you what. I'll take the mobile phone and we'll say no more about it. Oh, and the money that you do have.'

But he had to prise that phone from my stiffly-gripped hand, as though he was prising a lock of Jeremy's hair from me. Apart from the Armani jacket he had left behind which I had no intention of letting go, it was my last point of contact with him. What if he tried to call me back, to tell me that it was all just a horrible dream?

'He can call you at home,' said the waiter, as he parted me from the phone with a final, determined yank.

He summoned me a taxi then, obviously keen to get me off the premises before I put the last remaining diners off their food. He wouldn't let me drive my own car for fear I'd scratch the gateposts on my way out. So, bodily bundled into the back of the taxi with my coat still only half on, I curled up on the seat and cried out my heart. I couldn't believe that Jeremy was deserting me. Why? Why? Why? Was it because he was concerned for his bloody reputation as the chief of

Eastern Europe in the face of my impending court case? What about the conversation we had had at the airport in which he had the cheek to accuse me of worrying too much about what other people thought when I refused to join the Mile High Club? Thinking about how happy I had been too, as we set off for Antigua, made me feel so much worse right then.

The taxi driver let me bawl for a good ten minutes before he asked me where I wanted to go. Sweet man. He didn't even run the meter while I cried.

'I've got to stand on my own two feet,' I whispered to myself like a mantra as the taxi sped me home. Unfortunately, my legs felt like jelly and I collapsed in a soggy heap at the bottom of the hallway as soon as I got into the house, and there I stayed with only Fattypuss to warm me, until Emma came back from Ashley's house to get a fresh pair of knickers the next day.

CHAPTER FORTY-THREE

'You have got to pull yourself together,' Emma said as she manhandled me out of my coat and into my dressing-gown. 'And you've got to start right away.'

Thank God it was Sunday and I didn't have to go to work. I installed myself on the sofa and refused to move while I listened to Emma's pep-talk.

'My life is falling apart,' I wailed periodically.

'It is not,' said Emma flatly. 'You've still got your family. And your health.'

I was rapidly losing my mental health.

'Jeremy has left me,' I wailed.

'Jeremy is just running scared. He'll probably call and apologise when he realises what an idiot he's been.'

'Do you think so?'

'Yeah. And then you'll have to decide whether you want to take such a schmuck-head back or not.'

I sniffed and took a handful of the Pringles that Emma had dug out of her emergency supplies.

'There's still the court case to get through.'

'I know. But I was talking to Lorna in Boots yesterday,' Emma said through a mouthful of crumbs. 'She says that she wishes you luck.'

'What? Lorna?'

'Yeah. And she's well in with David's gang so I think that should give you some idea of how a jury is going to react. You'll get off, Ali. You only have to tell them how he dumped you on Christmas Day and they'll be queuing up to Hot Stuff Heat Rub him themselves. In the meantime, just chill out. Live a normal life. Get up. Go to work. Come home. Eat Pringles. Three months will pass before you know it.'

We polished off two tubes of Pringles that night. One original and one cheese and chive. And two bottles of wine to go with them. One red. One white. I slept like a plank and would have slept right through my alarm if Fattypuss hadn't woken me up with a present.

'See,' said Emma as I scraped the remains of a vole into the pedal bin. 'Fattypuss loves you. Everybody is on your side. When you get to court, they'll turn out in their hundreds to support you.'

I didn't expect to see a party of people gathered in my honour quite so soon as that morning however. When I got to work – it took me three attempts on the bus because I kept having to get off to throw up – it seemed as though everyone who had ever worked at Hudderston Heavy Engineering Co. was squashed into the admin office where I whiled away my days dreaming of death's sweet release.

When I walked in, the room suddenly went silent.

Even the big ugly grinding machines that provided a constant background growl and whine to the working day were quiet. People parted as I passed them by on the way to my desk. A desk which I hardly recognised since someone had kindly removed every last piece of paper from my in-tray and piled the extra work into Bridget's.

'All right, everybody?' I asked.

I was met with silence. Even Julie just looked down at her desk diary and said nothing. Then Mr Chivers, the factory foreman, poked his head around his office door and summoned me straight to him before I even had a chance to take my coat off.

'What's up?' I asked innocently. 'Sorry I'm a bit late. I was feeling sick. I had to get off the bus a couple of times.'

'That's OK,' he said to my surprise. 'Er, Alison. I wonder if you might sit down.' He pulled my seat out for me.

In front of him on his desk, I could see my personnel file. Mr Chivers picked up the flap and studied something on top of the pile of papers I had accumulated during my years at Hudderston's. He took a deep breath. 'Well, Alison,' he exhaled. 'I have to say I really don't know where to begin.'

'Try the beginning,' I said facetiously.

'Yes, I suppose that would be a start.' He reached into my file to pull something out. It was a copy of the *Sun*. He turned to page six. It was a copy of the *Sun* containing a picture of me!

He linked his fingers in front of him and leaned forward on his desk earnestly while I studied the open paper in horror. For a second, he was distracted by something outside his office, and when I glanced round, I could see that a crowd had gathered outside the frosted glass panels that served as walls to cut him, the boss, off from the hoi-polloi. Suddenly, I knew how it felt to be a goldfish.

'What is this about?' I squeaked.

'Exactly. What is this about?' echoed Mr Chivers. 'Perhaps you should read the caption.'

The photograph was an out-take from the *Complete Woman* shoot. I was wearing the blue shift dress that I had liked so much. Jeremy had his arms around me and he was looking into my eyes with great bucketfuls of love.

'The look of love,' the caption said. 'As Alison Harris and David Whitworth are pronounced the United Kingdom's Most Romantic Couple. But just two weeks later, lovely secretary Alison lost her fiancé David to Candida Bianca when the couple met Hollywood's brightest star at Antigua's Santa Bonita resort.'

'It's not jaundice, you've got, is it?' said Mr Chivers. 'It's a suntan.'

'I . . . I . . .' I couldn't begin to protest.

'You told Julie that you had complications as a result of your appendectomy. You told her that you had septicaemia and wouldn't even be able to get out of bed for two weeks. Next thing we know we're reading about your Caribbean holiday in the *Sun*. And I don't like to be made a fool of.'

I just stared at the photograph of me and Jeremy looking so happy. Then I stared at the picture beside it. Jeremy and Candida Bianca, looking even happier. The caption to that picture said that it had been taken on Sunday morning, as the couple shared a romantic breakfast in a Warsaw cafe. No wonder he had been in such a hurry to get back.

'What do you have to say for yourself?' asked Mr Chivers.

'I just can't believe it. It says here that she's not going to marry Vadim any more.'

Mr Chivers shook his head in frustration. 'What are you talking about? Aren't you even going to say you're sorry? Pretending to be sick so that you can take extra holiday is a very serious matter, you know. And as for your sick note? Don't you realise that forging a doctor's signature could see you ending up in court?'

I pushed the paper away from me and sank back into my seat, my eyes filled with hot, stinging tears.

'Alison? Alison? What have you got to say in your defence?'

What did I have to say in my defence? Suddenly it hit me that I was about to lose my job. I got to my feet and glared down on Chivers with what I hoped was a look of withering disdain. 'I was in love, that's my defence,' I cried. 'Haven't you ever done something stupid for the love of the person you want most in the whole world? I needed that holiday with Jeremy. I don't care what you think about my methods for getting the time. I'm handing in my resignation right now.'

'Alison!'

'Don't try and change my mind. I know when I'm not wanted. It's clear that you aren't a kind enough man to understand, Mr Chivers, and I don't want to work for a heartless worm. You can stuff your rotten job. I never liked working here anyway. I hate this factory and I especially hate you, Mr Chivers, thinking you're trendy with that disgusting shiny suit of yours and your bloody Mickey Mouse tie. You like to think you're one of the lads, don't you? But all the girls call you Mr Shivers behind your back because that's what you send down their spines. I've waited four long years to tell you that you ought to buy a wig that fits, and you should see a dental hygienist before you kill any more of the office plants.'

With that, I stormed out dramatically, leaving Mr Chivers gulping pathetically for air as if I had just punched him. As I passed her, even Julie was gasping with surprise at the ferocity of my attack.

'You can keep my desk tidy if you like,' I told her.

It was only when I got outside the building that the magnitude of what had just passed became clear.

I had just given up my job. The job I had held down for four years. If I had managed to limp on to five I would have been given a free Marks and Spencers gift voucher. I had thought that I was calling Chivers' bluff but standing outside the factory gates, it became horribly clear that in actual fact I had played straight into his sweaty hands.

If I'd grovelled, perhaps he would have felt obliged to give me another chance. I could imagine the uproar I had left behind. The gossip would keep Irene and Julie fuelled up for a fortnight. Perhaps Bridget would have a quiet week or two until the scandal surrounding me died down.

Perhaps I should have grovelled, I thought as I sank down onto a filthy bench covered with pigeon shit. It would have been painful but the fact was, I needed a job to pay my solicitor's fees, and how was I going to get another one with a possible conviction hanging over my head like the sword of Damocles?

*   *   *

Shock swept through my body like waves, reminding me of the nausea I had felt moments before my appendix burst. In the dustbin beside the bench, I saw a recently-dumped copy of that morning's *Sun*. I pulled it out and flicked to the photo that had been my Nemesis. Amanda must have called the *Sun* and told them the story. I could have strangled her with my bare hands.

But in a moment of rare lucidity I remembered the conversation we had had the previous week and the fact that she had promised she could get me money for a story like this. I'd just lost my job. And I needed money. I dug my last fifty pence piece out of my tattered purse and made for a pay phone.

'*Complete Woman*,' she trilled. 'How may I help you?'

'Amanda,' I sobbed. 'It's Ali. You've got to help me. I think you were right. I want to tell the whole story now.'

'Oh. And which story would that be?' she asked me frostily. 'Seems you've been telling quite a lot of stories lately.'

'What do you mean?'

'I just had a call from my contact at the *Sun* telling me to get my facts straight before I ring him with a lead. Then I get a call from the *Brindlesham Herald* asking for more pictures of Jeremy Baxter. Jeremy Baxter, I said. Who the hell is he? What on earth is that about, Alison?'

'I can explain.'

'You don't need to. I know now. I've been on the phone to Candida's agent for the last half hour. That wasn't your fiancé that you took to Antigua at all, was it? You were dumped by the real David Whitworth and so you bribed Jeremy Baxter to pretend to be your man.'

'So? I was in love with Jeremy and now I find out that he's gone off with her. There's still a story to be told, isn't there? What about the money you got for talking to the *Sun*? You owe me half of that.'

'Au contraire, Alison. I'm afraid that you owe *Complete Woman* ten thousand pounds for attempting to defraud the judges of a major international competition.'

She slammed the phone down. Ten thousand pounds. Was she serious? I hoped not. I had given the money to Jeremy to invest and I could hardly call him up right then.

CHAPTER FORTY-FOUR

'Woe is me,' I wailed as I tumbled in through the front door.

'Alison!' Emma careered down the hall towards me. 'What on earth is going on? The phone's been ringing non-stop. I've been talking to the *Sun*, *The Times*, even the *Brindlesham Herald*. They all want to know about you and David. I told them that the case doesn't come to court until the end of the month.'

'You mentioned the case.'

'Yeah, and the bizarre thing was that even though they were ringing up about David, the whole indecent assault case thing seemed to be news to them. I couldn't understand that. What's going on, Ali? I'm worried that I've told them something I shouldn't have done.'

She had indeed. It was just a matter of hours before the first copies of the *Brindlesham Herald* hit the newsstands with the damning headline – 'Brindlesham Bobbitt!'.

What a scoop for a local rag that had carried three front page stories about lost cats in the first two months

of the year alone! Brindlesham Boy dumps psycho for
a film star, and what a film star! What a psycho! If
the story hadn't been about me, I might have enjoyed
counting up the number of words they had found to
avoid the use of 'penis'.

At least the *Brindlesham Herald* couldn't taunt me
with pictures of Jeremy or Candida. The photograph
they had of me had been taken when I won the art
prize at secondary school. I was wearing my tie in the
trendy narrow knot I had sported the year before I took
my GCSEs.

'Britain's own Lorena!!' proclaimed the headlines
inside. 'Pretty young secretary Alison Harris (26) looks
the picture of innocence in this picture of her as a
schoolgirl at Brindlesham's own St Olive's High School
for Girls. But while the wicked young woman was
enjoying a steamy holiday romance in the Caribbean,
her fiancé David Whitworth was piecing together the
tatters of his life after the love affair that has left him
permanently disabled!'

Where do newspapers get their facts from? I wondered angrily. For a start I was still only 25 and David
Whitworth was most definitely not my fiancé. I could
only read the report a sentence at a time, because my
blood was so close to boiling.

So David had been heartbroken, had he? According
to the *Brindlesham Herald*, I had left him for a third party
in our relationship, then bitterly launched my attack
on him, because, while I didn't want him for myself,
I didn't want him to have anyone else.

'Lies, lies, lies,' I protested out loud.

My anger grew around me like an impenetrable shell
of fury. Up until then I had been simply dazed by the

things that were happening around me. Now I was ready to lash out at the next unfortunate to cross me.

'What can I do about this?' I asked Emma, slapping the paper onto the coffee table in front of her.

'Ignore it,' she said helpfully.

'It was you who put them onto the court case story.'

'When they rang up asking about David I assumed they already knew.'

'Couldn't you have guessed that they really wanted to know about Jeremy after all that Candida stuff in the *Sun*?'

'Well, I'm sorry if I'm not quick enough to keep up with the web of lies that you've been spinning round yourself for the last month,' she shouted back. 'I was trying to help you. I defended you on the phone. I told everyone who called that you acted out of self-defence.'

'Fat lot of good that did me. I've been made out to be like some kind of Hannibal Lecter.'

'I was really trying to help you, Ali,' said Emma, slipping her arm around my shoulders.

I shrugged her off. 'I'm not talking to you any more.'

Emma sprang away, looking hurt.

Then the doorbell rang and I used the excuse to escape her kicked puppy dog gaze.

Marvin stood on the doorstep, flanked by his new dancing partner Chico. In his hand he carried a copy of that despicable *Brindlesham Herald*.

'Not very nice, is it?' he said insightfully. 'And where did they get that photograph? You look like you're auditioning for Bananarama.'

'Aaaagh.' I slammed the door in his face. 'Go away, you evil queen,' I shouted. 'It's not funny. None of this is funny. You're reading about my life.'

Marvin shouted through the letter box. 'Does that mean we can't come in?'

'There must be someone I can sue?' I continued to rant. 'All this stuff is libel, surely.'

'If you want to bring a libel case you have to able to prove that what they're saying isn't true,' said Marvin, still through the letter box. He was also a big fan of *Murder One*.

'It's so unfair,' I wailed.

'Let us in, Ali. Chico here did a law degree. Maybe he can give you some advice.'

'I don't want you to come in,' I sniffed. 'You're only here to make fun of me.'

'We're here to be your friends.' For a moment the letter box was shut, then it opened again as Marvin pushed through a tissue. I took it without thanking him and blew my nose hard.

'Attagirl,' said Marvin. 'Feeling better already, I'll bet. Now let us come inside.'

I opened the door reluctantly.

'Phew,' said Marvin. 'You don't look much cop tonight.' Chico nodded in agreement, though I can't say I thought much of his fun-fur salopettes either. 'Ali love, this is Chico.'

'I recognised him from your description.'

'Yeah? Well, why don't you go and make him a nice cup of tea,' he suggested, as he craned his neck towards the front room. 'Is Emma in?'

'She's through there.'

'Both of us want milk but no sugar. Run along.'

I trudged into the kitchen and put the kettle on. I shouldn't be so hard on my friends, I told myself. They really did want to support me. They weren't the type of people who would just turn up to gloat.

Then I heard a piercing shriek of laughter from the sitting room.

'What is it now?' I asked suspiciously, as I stood in the doorway with an empty teapot in my hand.

Marvin stuffed something down the side of the sofa guiltily. Emma stifled a giggle and Chico looked at the ground.

'What is it?' I demanded, marching over to the sofa and pulling the swiftly-hidden paper out.

It was a copy of the next morning's *Sun*.

'Where did you get this?'

'I was in London tonight. You can get the next day's papers from a stall outside Charing Cross.'

'And what was so funny about this one?'

I flicked open to page three and knew. There I was. In all my glory. It was a picture taken during my fortnight in Antigua. I was wearing a sunny smile and no top.

Suddenly the *Brindlesham Herald*'s account of my misspent life was about to seem like Enid Blyton. I held that copy of the *Sun* with shaking hands.

'Is this the face of Britain's Most Dangerous Woman?' the headline asked. 'Alison Harris shows the form that helped her exert such a fatal attraction on insurance salesman David Whitworth and Candida Bianca's new man, model Jeremy Baxter.'

Where on earth had that picture of me come from?

'Ali Harris, page three girl,' said Marvin admiringly. 'You've got to be pleased with that.'

'Pleased? I'd be more pleased if my tits just dropped off,' I shouted. 'This is libel. This is slander. It's going to ruin my image in front of a jury. If this doesn't stop, I'm going to have been found guilty before I even get to court. It must be illegal.' I picked up the phone and began to dial Mr Wagstaff.

But Mr Wagstaff was in a meeting. His secretary promised that he would call me back straightaway. That would be the next day, since Mr Wagstaff was the kind of provincial solicitor who would have knocked off at five on the dot, even if he was representing the Kray twins.

Emma took the *Sun* from me and flicked to page three again. 'This is so hilarious. My flatmate on page three. Whoever would have thought she had it in her?'

CHAPTER FORTY-FIVE

I was glad that my misfortunes were making everybody else so happy. When I was telling people the story of my disaster, I could almost believe that it was funny myself, but the fact was, I was in deep trouble. I lay awake, staring at the ceiling, occasionally willing it to turn into the thatched roof of that distantly-remembered beach hut in Antigua. A wish which would never be granted.

I tried not to think about the case. I tried to keep my spirits up by promising that when this whole shambles was over, I would take a trip around the world. Then I would plan my imaginary itinerary, complete with prospective dates and that would start me off on the downward spiral again. How could I possibly set a date for a holiday when I didn't know how long I might have to spend in prison?

Prison. What a horrible word. What a terrible place. All I knew of women's prisons I had gleaned from *Prisoner Cell Block H*. In real life, the only person I knew who had actually been inside was a boy from the year above me at junior school who had done three months for persistently having no car insurance. But he was hard. He had tattoos on his eyelids before he went down. What would become of sweet, little, innocent me?

Pretty soon, my imaginary walk down a sandy beach was interrupted by a vision of me on a very different walk. This time, I was walking in through the gates of Holloway prison. I could see the women who were already there checking out me and the other new arrivals who tumbled out of the police van onto the tarmac behind me. The old-timers were no doubt planning hideous ways to make my acquaintance.

Would I be allowed to live out my sentence quietly, I wondered? Would I be able to spend time alone in my cell learning how to knit and catching up on the classics I had always meant to read? Or would I be picked on in the showers, forced to become the slave of a bigger and far butcher woman in return for her protection?

Would my protector make me kiss her? That was probably the least of my worries, I decided with a shudder.

At breakfast, Emma noticed that I was looking even less optimistic than I had done the night before and asked me what was wrong.

'No point dwelling on it,' she assured me. 'You've not been sentenced yet and you'll probably get off. Best to get on with life as normal,' she added flippantly.

But what was normal now? I dreaded the thud of the newspaper on the doormat.

* * *

The papers were late but a letter from *Complete Woman* came by registered post. Having taken receipt of it, Emma propped the letter against the toaster so that I wouldn't miss it when I had finished chucking up in the bathroom. I was surviving on the traditional 'Just been dumped, tea and toast diet'.

'Dear Ms Harris,' the letter began. It seemed like no-one was using my Christian name anymore. 'It is with great regret that we have to write to you regarding your disqualification from *Complete Woman International*'s Most Romantic Couple Competition on the grounds that your companion on the prize holiday, one Mr Jeremy Baxter, was not the man you described in your original winning competition entry. Additionally, in view of the adverse publicity generated by your impending court case and with regard to your former fiancé, we find that we have no choice but to strip you of your "Most Romantic" title and ask that you return your winner's sash to this office by registered post. We shall be writing to you shortly detailing the further action which will have to be taken regarding the grand prize . . .'

'They're going to ask me to pay for the holiday, aren't they?' I said worriedly.

Emma placed a sympathetic hand on my shoulder. 'I'm sure they can't do that,' she replied. But I could tell by her voice that she was about as convinced as I was. 'OK,' she admitted. 'So you might have to cough up, but you'll only have to cough up for half the trip. Jeremy owes the rest. How much can it possibly be, anyway?'

'Try five thousand pounds.'

'For two weeks in a beach hut.'

'A beach hut frequented by some of the most glitter-ing stars of stage and screen. It had air-conditioning.'

'Five thousand pounds,' Emma murmured. 'I don't think I've ever seen that much money in my life.'

'Fifteen thousand pounds with the prize money as well. What am I going to do?' I whined again.

'We'll think of something,' she said, picking up the paper, which the paperboy just poked through the door. 'Let's see what Justin Toper has to say in his horoscope column.'

'Good news?' I asked, when she seemed to have had enough time to read the whole paper, let alone what Justin had to say about the week ahead for Libra.

'Do you want me to read what your stars say? Or do you want me to tell you the truth?'

Emma pushed the tabloid across the table towards me. It was folded open at a picture of David, looking pained.

'Britain's Bobbitt even taunted me from the other side of the world,' said the caption. Underneath the picture, I discovered that they had reproduced the postcard I sent to David from Antigua, with careful highlighting over the words 'hot stuff' and a nice bit of editing so that the next sentence read 'The only thing I have to worry about is where my next cock is coming from!'.

As if that wasn't bad enough, the unravelling of my disastrous so-called love life continued overleaf. But this time, the narrator of the gossip was someone I didn't know at all. At least, I didn't recognise Shelly without the Waltons' dress she habitually wore to dinner. The *Sun* had her pictured in a fringed Western bikini.

'British Bobbitt's love slave begged me to help him

escape!' screeched the headline. I skimmed quickly through the story as though that might make it hurt less. 'Charming computer expert Baxter made love to me beneath the Caribbean moon while psycho Harris slept off massive booze binge.'

'Where do they drag them up from?' Emma asked. She had been reading over my shoulder. 'I mean, who are they kidding? When did Jeremy have time to get it on with her? You told me you were holed up in your love nest all week.'

'If only,' I sighed. 'There was just one night. One night when I had too many margaritas and had to be put to bed by eleven. Jeremy told me that he went for a moonlit walk on the sand, but he said that he went all alone.'

Emma's face grew serious for a moment but then she forced a smile back onto her lips. 'In which case he probably was on his own. This is made up, obviously.'

'I wish I was so sure.' I remembered how frosty Shelly had become towards me after that drunken night. I had assumed that it was just because of her inherent prudishness and dislike of puke, but now I knew differently. And as I read on, I knew for sure that she was telling the truth.

'He told me that he loved me in Polish,' the girl wrote. 'Many men on holiday try to seduce the girls they meet, but this time I thought it was different. This time I thought it was true love. If only we could get rid of his evil girlfriend.'

'He told me that he loved me in Polish too!' I whined.

'Oh, Ali,' Emma wrapped her arms around me and

stroked my hair. 'Oh, Ali, I should never have shown you this. I thought we could have a laugh about it. I thought that it would be a pack of press lies that we could tear to pieces to make you feel better.'

'How could Jeremy do this to me?'

'I don't know,' said Emma. 'I mean, normally I'd say it's just the way men are, but I still can't quite get my head around it. When you came back from Antigua, I thought I had never seen a man so much in love as Jeremy appeared to be with you.'

'It wasn't me,' I said sadly. 'It was the freebie holiday and the nice big cheque.'

'Don't think like that.'

'What did I do to deserve this? It's bad enough that he's been running around with Candida, but Shelly too?'

'Oh, Ali,' Emma sighed.

'I can't stand this,' I told her suddenly. 'I'm going out for a walk.'

I got up and shrugged on my coat. 'Don't wait up.'

'Ali!' Emma chased me to the front door. 'Ali, where are you going? Don't you dare go anywhere near the canal. He isn't worth it, you know. Nobody's worth throwing away your life for.'

'I'm not going to top myself,' I shouted back cheerily. 'I'm just going to buy some fags.'

Out of town shopping had done for the corner shop in our town so I had quite a walk ahead of me. The only place open within half a mile of our house was the all night garage by the end of the dual carriageway. As each of the little local businesses folded, they seemed to have been incorporated into the nasty neon warehouse of a shop behind the petrol pumps. At least at the twenty-four-hour garage you could get just about everything except the kitchen sink. But you could send a fax to order one of those if you needed to.

'Twenty Marlboros,' I muttered to the girl behind the desk.

The girl didn't even look up from her copy of the *Sun*, which, to my distress, was open at that page. She reached down the fags from the shelf behind her and placed them in front of me.

'How much?' I asked.

'Two sixty-nine,' she muttered gracelessly.

I reached into my pocket and pulled out my change. Not very impressive. I figured that I had about three pounds, but when I actually counted it out, I discovered that I actually had only two pounds fifty and an assortment of Antiguan small coins. The girl was still reading her paper, tracing the lines with her finger so that she didn't lose her place while she mouthed the words. I shoved all the coins I had down in front of her, said thanks and turned to leave.

I was almost off the forecourt when the commotion started.

'It's her! It's that psycho out the paper!' someone was shrieking. 'She's trying to run off without paying.'

Next thing I knew, the air was filled with a fair old cacophony of sirens. The cashier had set off the emergency bell and I was being bodily lifted from my feet by two men that I would far rather have had protecting my body than apprehending it.

'Hey, what do you think you're doing?' I shouted, as they marched me back to the garage, across a forecourt full of gawpers, with my feet kicking the air as if I was some kind of cartoon baddie who had just tried to rob a Wild West bank in Toon Town.

'I've called the police,' the cashier told the men breathlessly. 'They say they'll be here any minute. They said we shouldn't try to approach her in case she's armed.'

'Armed? What on earth are you talking about?' I protested. 'I'm not armed, you idiots. I just came out for a packet of fags, not a fight. When the police get here I'll have them arrest the pair of you for GBH,' I warned my burly captors. 'You're hurting my wrists.'

The men laughed. ''Fraid you'll have to put up with it, darlin',' the bigger one said. 'I think the police will agree that we're only using the kind of force necessary to apprehend the likes of you. You psycho.'

'Yeah,' said the smaller one. Though he was a good foot shorter than his mate, he had a meaner look, like a Pit Bull fresh from a fight with a badger. 'Women like you give my missus ideas.'

'Good ones by the look of you,' I told him.

''Ere, you shut your mouth,' said Mr Pit-Bull. 'Or I'll shut it for you.'

Thank God the police arrived just then.

'What's all this about?'

It was Inspector Heath, one of the men who had arrested me when I got back from holiday, flanked by two other policemen in the full riot gear get-up. I wondered if that was because they had got the call from a garage, or because they were coming for me.

'Alison Harris,' Inspector Heath said in his schoolteacher's voice. 'What on earth have you been getting up to now?'

'Nothing!' I protested.

'Yeah, right,' said the cashier sarcastically. 'She tried to rob me, she did. These kind gentlemen stepped in to prevent any violence.'

'I did not try to rob her!'

'Alison, you'll have a chance to speak down at the station,' Inspector Heath warned me. Then he turned to the cashier, 'Ms . . . Adams,' he read her badge. 'I'll have to take a statement.'

Meanwhile, I was bundled roughly into a police car for the second time that month.

'You again!' said the driver.

'Watch it,' I warned him. 'I'm armed.'

Immediately, the two officers flanking me prepared to attack.

'Don't worry,' I told them. 'It's only a tube of Bonjela. I've got an ulcer from all this stress.'

'Don't joke with us, Alison,' the driver said seriously. 'These men are highly trained weapons in themselves.'

I took a good look at them. Both thirty-something. Both with the kind of paunches that would give a woman in the seventh month of pregnancy cause for concern. And I thought that the coffee and donuts thing only happened in New York.

Mr Wagstaff was waiting for me when we arrived at the station. Not because he'd hurried there to be with me, you understand. He was visiting the bloke with the *Titanic* tattoo who had just been caught in the Mayor's flowerbeds with an armful of rare Royal Worcester.

Mr Wagstaff shook his head pitifully when he saw me. 'What did I tell you about keeping out of trouble?'

'I am not in trouble. I got some Antiguan and English coins mixed up, that's all.'

'You need a good spanking you do,' said my solicitor. I made a mental note to ask for legal aid and another duty solicitor as soon as I got the chance. 'Alison, I can't defend you if you don't try to defend yourself. I've heard reports that you've been calling the chief witness for the prosecution.'

'Who?'

'Mr Whitworth.'

'I never did.'

'Next time, before you dial his number, remember to dial 141.'

This time it was Emma who came to fetch me from the police station. I had made Inspector Heath swear that he wouldn't tell my Mum that I had been in again, even though the situation had been rectified quite calmly. Inspector Heath told the cashier that she should have given me the opportunity to rectify my mistake with the foreign coins. Apparently she hadn't dared ask me because of the hard-drinking, violent image of me she had got from the tabloids.

I was allowed to exit the station from a back door since a hack from the local paper was hanging around in reception, tipped off by one of the cashier's lardy heroes, no doubt. I had been lucky so far that the press hadn't been camping outside my door, since they seemed far more concerned with getting a quote about Candida from the Baxters. Anyway, I ducked down in the back seat while Emma drove past the front of the station like a bat out of hell, so fast in fact, that I half expected a dozen bobbies to pile out of the station door and arrest us for speeding. What a great way to round off the evening that could have been.

'Perhaps you should get out of town for a while?' Emma suggested that evening. 'Go to Wales or somewhere like that. Somewhere where no-one will recognise your face.'

'Too late for that,' I told her sadly. 'Hiding myself away is what I should have done the first time David chucked me. That way I wouldn't have been here and vulnerable when Lisa went on her bloody self-assertiveness course in Hastings and I'd never even have met flaming Jeremy Baxter.'

'No good wishing you could turn the clock back,' said Emma helpfully.

'Didn't anyone ever tell you not to say things like that to dangerous criminals?'

'Anyway, since you've been out,' Emma continued blithely, 'I've been thinking about ways you can earn money to pay off the money you owe *Complete Woman*. The papers are interested in this case, right? So you should tell your side of the story to one of them, in return for some nice hard cash.'

'Nice idea, but I'm kind of under a court order at the moment, darling.'

'Does that stop you from selling your story?'

'Since I'm doing my very best not to get banged up for the next five years, I guess it probably does.'

'What about close friends of yours? What if someone told your story for you?'

'Like who?'

Emma shrugged.

'I don't know. But I wasn't thinking of volunteering myself,' she added quickly. 'Ashley would just die with embarrassment. Someone in your family perhaps?'

'What? Like one of my sisters? They wouldn't piss on me if I was on fire.'

'There's got to be someone who can help tell your side of the story.'

'No-one I can think of,' I muttered. 'Just forget about it.'

Though in fact, at that very moment, someone very closely related to me indeed was telling all.

CHAPTER FORTY-SIX

'That's it. I don't care if she does write us out of the will. She's betrayed our family!' screamed my Mum. 'My own mother. Seventy-two years old and just look at her, lying on that chaise lounge thingy in a see-through negligee like she's bloody well got something to show off about.'

'I dunno. Hope I've inherited her legs,' said Jo, treading on very thin ice.

'I can't believe she said all this rubbish,' Mum continued as I stared in horror at my half-dressed grandmother and Jo scanned through the text.

'My hot-headed granddaughter gets it all from me,' said glamorous granny Renee Marlene.

'I didn't know Marlene was her surname,' Jane chipped in.

'It bloody isn't,' said Mum. 'That was the name she used when she thought she had a chance of making it big as a cabaret singer in the working men's clubs. I've never been so humiliated in all my life,' she continued.

'Join the club,' said I.

'Well if she thinks she's keeping the money she

earned from this filth, she's got another think coming.
Get your coat, Ali. We're going round that home right
now to sort this out.'

When we got to Daisy Knoll retirement home, it was
pretty easy to find out where Gran was. She hadn't
exactly gone into hiding since her tabloid debut. No,
far from it. She was sitting in the best chair in the day
room, surrounded by dribbling admirers. I know, the
men in there were always dribbling, but this time they
appeared to be dribbling with intent.

'A word, please, Mother,' said Mum, making sure that
all Gran's admirers were reminded that she still was a
grandma as well as Renee Marlene, star of stage and . . .
well, star of the stage at the Royal British Legion club.
Once. When the comedian they'd actually booked had
to go home with food poisoning. 'Where's the money?'

'See? Didn't I tell you,' Gran said sadly to one of her
companions. 'They don't care about me. It's all about
money. They just want me out of the way so they can
spend their inheritance.'

'I'm not talking about our bloody inheritance,' Mum
snapped. 'You've sold just about everything you ever
had anyway. I'm talking about the newspapers, Mother.
Where's the money from that?'

'I didn't get any,' Gran replied indignantly.

'You liar, they must have paid you something for
betraying your own flesh and blood.'

'They didn't. I said I didn't want anything. I wasn't
going to do it at all, but the young man said I might have
a career ahead of me as a model. He said I could keep
the photos he took, for my portfolio.'

'A model,' Mum sneered. 'For what, for heaven's sake? For the dinosaur models in the sequel to *The Lost World*.'

'He said that there's a growing demand for women of a certain age.'

'By that they mean girls who are twenty-seven or twenty-eight,' I explained patiently. 'Not seventy-two, Gran.'

'You're just jealous, both of you,' Gran spat. 'You wish it had been you on them pages.'

'But it was me, Gran, don't you see?' I protested. 'You talked about my love life to the press.'

'Love life, pah! That's a laugh. I had to make most of it up.'

'Well, I wish you hadn't bothered. I'm awaiting trial for indecent assault, Gran. This kind of publicity is the last thing I need.'

One of the residents, who had been dragging himself nearer the fracas on his Zimmer frame, got one of his legs tangled up in a knitting bag then and went arse over tit into someone else's thousand-piece jigsaw.

'Look what you've done,' said Gran, to distract me from my argument.

'I wasn't anywhere near him.'

'So? He was trying to leave the room because you were shouting at me.'

'I wasn't shouting,' I said, trying to keep my voice down.

'It was peaceful in here before you two came in shouting the odds. Can't you see we're all old people here? We need our peace and quiet.'

'Don't try and change the subject,' my mother interrupted. 'You've betrayed the family.'

'The family! Ha! You only bother with me because you want to know what's in my will. Well, I'll put you out of your misery, Josephine. I've left it all to your sister. Every last penny. Because when she comes round here she acts like she's pleased to see me. The only person in your family who's ever pleased to see me is the dog.'

A murmur of agreement rustled around the room.

'That's probably because the dog likes to sniff things that are decaying, you rotten old bag,' said Mum.

My mouth dropped open.

'I'll tell you why my sister always looks so happy to see you – it's because she only has to see you twice a year. She doesn't get you every single bloody day of the week, week in week out, moaning on about your varicose veins and your itchy piles . . .'

'I do not have piles,' said Gran, going crimson in front of her admirers.

'You certainly do. And then there's your bloody bedsores and your uncontrollable wind . . . Do you want me to go on? Embarrassing, isn't it? Having all your secrets revealed in public. And that's what it was like this morning when our Ali opened the newspaper to find two whole pages of you going on about her love life. You can keep your fucking inheritance, because as far as I'm concerned, that's not the kind of behaviour I want associated with my family at all.'

With that, Mum turned and stalked out of the day room, leaving the entire collection of Daisy Knoll residents on the verge of a communal coronary.

'She doesn't mean it, Gran,' I said comfortingly, patting the old woman on her Frank Usher clad arm. 'She'll probably run back in and apologise in a minute.' But there was no sign of that. Through the huge windows of the day room I could see Mum getting into her car and firing up the engine. Then, with a face like thunder, she sat and waited for me to join her.

Let me explain my latest predicament. Even though Gran had betrayed me to the press, choosing sides at this point was like having to choose between Genghis Khan and Vlad the Impaler. I knew that when Gran and Mum made it up again, which they would do soon enough, I would come off badly, whatever, as the cause of their row.

So I flipped a mental coin and decided to go with Mum. Besides, I actually still had to tell her that the rumours she had heard about Candida and Jeremy were true and that the wedding was off.

'I'm writing you out of the will too!' Gran shouted from the day-room patio as I legged it to the car park.

'Great,' I said, slipping into the car beside Mum. 'At this rate, there'll be no-one left on my side. Even Jeremy's deserted me . . .'

'What?'

Never tell your mother that a wedding's off when she's pulling out onto a dual carriageway.

'The swine!' my mother was still shrieking uncontrollably as she pulled the car into a handbrake turn in the driveway of our family home, having narrowly avoided a twenty-car pile-up while she cursed the Baxter family name in seven different languages. 'How could he do this to you?'

'I've been asking myself exactly the same question.'

'You were supposed to be getting married.'

'That doesn't seem to mean anything much these days,' I said ruefully.

'I didn't ever like him,' said my father later from behind the shield of his newspaper.

'What?' asked my mother and I.

'I didn't ever like him. Always poncing about talking about how he's head of Eastern Europe and all that and showing off about his fancy car. I could see straight through him the first time he came round.'

Now this was unusual. My father rarely spoke when we girls were in full assassinatory swing, let alone to pass a judgement.

'Well fan-bloody-tastic. Why didn't you say this before?' I asked.

'Didn't think it was my place to. I don't want to interfere.'

'Well I bloody well wish you guys would interfere from time to time,' I said in exasperation. 'You know, before I get engaged to these losers, rather than waiting until I've been dumped to tell me that his eyes were too close together or that he just had a funny way about him that made you know it would all end in tears. Isn't that what parents are for? To stop you from making these ruinous mistakes?'

Dad retreated behind his paper again.

My mother, for once, leapt to his defence. 'Your father's right. We don't want to interfere with these things. When I have told you that I don't like your boyfriends in the past, it only seems to have made you all the more determined to throw yourself after them. What if we'd turned against Jeremy and he had gone and married you after all . . . He might not have let us see the grandchildren.'

'You mean you would have let me marry the wrong man?'

'If that was what you wanted, dear. Cup of tea?'

'I don't think a cup of tea is going to make things seem any better right now, Mum,' I told her.

'You're right. After the day I've had, I need half a bottle of whisky and a good punch up. That'd release some pent-up frustration.'

'I think I'd better go home,' I said.

'No, Ali. Not yet. Your father and I have got something important to tell you,' Mum announced.

'I think I'll just check on the shed,' said Dad. Strangely Mum nodded her consent.

'What is it? I thought you said that you and Dad had something important to tell me.'

'I think I can speak for your father.'

I waited to hear the latest piece of terrible news that would push me over the edge from purgatory into oblivion. But it didn't come. 'Your father and I have been trying it out. And it doesn't hurt at all.'

'Well, great,' I said, just a little confused. 'That's means you must have been doing it right.'

'No. You don't understand, darling. We've been trying it out with the Hot Stuff Heat Rub. It doesn't hurt at all. Just tingles. Your father and I are respectable people, pillars of the community. And we're prepared to stand up in court and tell the world that Hot Stuff Heat Rub can be part of a healthy and normal sex life.'

I choked on my chocolate hobnob. The idea of my parents having a sex life at all was bad enough. But a healthy and normal one? They had three daughters for heaven's sake!

'What do you say? We want to support you in your time of need, darling.'

'Yes. But Mum . . . I mean, what would the neighbours think.'

'The neighbours? Pah! I've learned a thing or two about neighbours today. And I happen to know for a fact that Mrs Baxter has more than one pair of suspenders in her closet. We're all adults, Alison. People don't just stop having sexual lives once they're married, you know.'

'I thought that was the whole point.'

I prayed that my solicitor would think it was as bad an idea as I did.

'Just stay out of this, Mum,' I said firmly. 'I don't want you or Dad anywhere near the witness stand. I know you're trying to help, but the best thing you can do now is make me a cup of tea and keep clear of the whole situation.'

CHAPTER FORTY-SEVEN

Fat chance.

Later that night, I got a rather distressed phone call from Dad. Turned out that when he got back from the shed, for the first time in his married life he discovered that Mum wasn't waiting in the kitchen to berate him . . . And the reason? It was because his wife was being held in the police cells.

'And your sisters too,' he said forlornly. 'They didn't know I was still in the shed . . . Your sister says that she tried to phone you but you had that silly machine on.'

I played back my answer-machine messages while I got ready to meet Dad at the station to try to bail my family out.

'We're in the clink,' it was my sister Jo. 'And it was all in aid of you, Alison, so you had better get down here pronto and bail us out.'

'What on earth happened?' I asked Dad when I met him on the forecourt of the station.

'Something about a fight. Mrs Baxter and her daughter came round to the house for some reason. I think

it was to ask if you could return Jeremy's Giorgio
Armani swimming trunks. Well, your mum just saw
red and went for her. Pulling her hair out. Scratching
and kicking. Jennifer Baxter joined in on her mum's side
and after that your sisters had to get involved.'

'But why?'

'To defend your honour,' said Jo proudly, after they
had been released with a warning. 'She came round our
house accusing you of being a Jezebel, tempting her
precious son into marriage with your skimpy bikinis
and fancy holidays. She said you wanted to turn him
into a sex slave. She read that in the papers. I told her
that if you wanted a sex slave you wouldn't have gone
for someone with boils on his knob.'

'Thanks, Jo. I'm sure that went down really well.'

'That woman's got a nerve,' said Mum. 'Anyway, as
soon as I saw her I knew I was going to hit her, no matter
what she said. Always acted like she's too good for the
likes of us, she has. She didn't know that I saw her, at
my own anniversary party, running her finger along the
mantelpiece to check for dust. Well, I told her today, that
it's a bit rich her checking my house for dust when she's
got a whole built-in wardrobe complex full of skeletons.
That daughter of hers was done for shoplifting once,
you know.'

Jo smirked. 'Wasn't Ali . . .'

Mum slapped her. Jane sat silently in the back of the
car, between my mother and Jo, the hard-nuts.

'I'm not happy about all this violence,' she said solemnly.

'Oh, Jane,' Jo exclaimed. 'But you were the best of us
all. When it looked like Mum and I were going to lose
the fight, Jane leapt in with one of those fancy martial

arts kicks of hers and took the pair of them out in one move.' Jo did a little demonstration with her hands. 'I always knew that prancing about in the garden every morning would come in handy one day.'

'It's meant to be a peaceful art,' Jane explained. 'It's supposed to be a form of meditation, not used like boxing.'

'Whatever,' said Jo.

'Listen,' I said, turning round to the three of them in the back seat. 'I'm very grateful for what you did today, standing up for me and all that but, in future, I think that you guys had better keep your noses clean. Don't rise to provocation. This kind of behaviour isn't going to do my court appearance much good. Do you want David's barrister to be able to say that I come from an unruly and dangerous family?'

'Yeah,' said Jo.

'Button it,' said my mother. 'Ali's right. There's to be no more fighting, girls. Though I have to say that I'm very proud of you both and if any woman deserved to lose a handful of hair this afternoon it's that Baxter woman. I'll give her dust on the mantelpiece.'

'Wild Women in Worcester Street' was the headline in the local paper. And most of the nationals.

I warned my family that I didn't ever want to hear the name Baxter again.

Emma, unfortunately, didn't seem to think that the embargo extended to her. I was reading the report of my family's disgrace in the street outside their house when Emma came home, looking breathless and excited.

'I've got something to tell you,' she panted as she unpacked her shopping bags. 'How are you feeling today?'

'Terrible. Devastated.'

'Oh, well perhaps I shouldn't say.'

'Say what?'

'Doesn't matter.'

'No, Emma, you can't do this to me. You can't come home and say you've got something to tell me and then not tell me anything.'

'OK. Sit down.'

'I am sitting down,' I said irritably.

'OK. I'll sit down.' She took a chair opposite me. 'No. I can't say.'

'You've got to say, or I'll kill you.'

'I think I've worked out how that photo of you with no top on got into the papers.'

I leaned forward on the table, to better hear what she was about to come out with next.

'Jeremy is back in town.'

'What? He's supposed to be in Poland.'

'He must be on holiday.'

I felt suddenly boiling hot, then freezing cold. I put my hand to my mouth to pre-empt a wave of nausea. 'He's back. Do you think he's heard about my trial date? Do you think he's left Candida and come back to support me through it?' The clouds in my mind parted for just a second.

Emma reached across the table to take my hand. I knew then that the news was bad.

'Er . . . He wasn't on his own, Ali. That's the whole point. He was with someone else. A woman.'

'His mum? His sister?'

'Uh-uh,' she shook her head. 'Remember that skinny posh tart from the magazine?'

'Amanda?'

'That's the one. It was her. Hanging on his arm like a handbag she was.'

'You're pulling my leg. You don't even know what she looks like.'

'Unfortunately, I do. I read *Complete Woman* once. Under duress. It was definitely her. I followed them into Betty's.'

'Emma, tell me you didn't?'

'Well, it's a free country and I wanted a cup of tea. I sat right behind them. Jeremy didn't notice me, or if he did, he pretended not to. Though I guess I have changed a bit since February.'

Emma had recently dyed her hair pale blue to mark the beginning of summer.

'Anyway, I couldn't help overhearing their conversation. Jeremy was talking so loud, seemed like he wanted the whole place to hear. So, she said to him, "I've got you two weeks in Florida lined up for next month. They loved the pictures. And I'm going to be the stylist." Then he said, "Oh darling, how clever of you. Who's the photographer? I don't want any old snapper now that I'm going to be the new Boss boy."'

'Boss boy?'

'Model. For the Boss campaign. God, Ali, it made me sick. They went on for half an hour about how good his portfolio was and how he would soon be putting the wind up that bloke who posed in nothing but a tie for Versace. Jeremy Baxter, a model. Can you imagine it?'

'Unfortunately, yes.'

'Anyway, don't you see what I'm getting at?'

'You're breaking my heart again.'

'It's obvious that Jeremy and Amanda are swapping favours. He got the fashion shoot. She got . . .'

'Him?'

'No. She probably wants him, sure. But he's shacked up with Candida and what Amanda got instead was an exclusive on Britain's Lorena Bobbitt. You wanted to know how they got pictures of you in your bikini? It's simple. Jeremy supplied them.'

'No.'

'Makes perfect sense to me, Ali.'

'But he was so upset about that. Apparently he told his mother that the newspaper coverage was the reason why he couldn't marry me.'

'A great excuse. But now you know the source of the press leak, you can get him into some real trouble. I think it's contempt of court, or something. Aren't you happy?'

'He wouldn't have done that to me,' I murmured, shaking my head.

'Ali, I could tell from the very first time I met him that he was the kind of bloke who would do anything to anybody. I mean, even while I was watching him with Amanda in Betty's. She was gazing at him like a sodding puppy but he didn't even look at her. He kept looking at his reflection in the mirror, like he can't believe his luck that he's grown out of those boils. Then, when Amanda went to the ladies, Jeremy slipped the waitress his phone number. He is pond scum. A pimple on the face of humanity.' Emma was enjoying herself.

'I wish you hadn't told me about all this,' I said sadly.

'He deserves to be punished.'

'I don't know if I can face even seeing him again.'

'He hated Fattypuss.'

I needed no better reason to blow the whistle.

'I'll call Mr Wagstaff in the morning.'

I had another prison dream that night. This time was worse than ever. As I was led from the van to the heavy, iron-studded oak gates that would separate me from the folks that I loved for eternity, with no time off for good behaviour, I couldn't help noticing that the prison warden awaiting me had a familiar pink gingham handbag hanging incongruously from her uniform-clad shoulder.

'Well, well, well. Miss Alison Harris,' she said, in an oddly un-English drawl. 'I've been waiting for you.'

She tilted back the brim of her prison officer's hat and grinned at me through horrible cerise-painted lips.

'Take her to the blancmange room!' ordered Shelly, America's Most Romantic Woman and Holloway prison's newest and most terrifying guard. I was led away, screaming like a stuck pig, to a fate far worse than lesbian frottage in the showers.

The guards took off my handcuffs when we arrived at the pink-painted door. They pushed me against it so that I could look through the tiny barred window and see what lay ahead.

'But I'll drown,' I pleaded. The room was six feet deep in strawberry whip.

'Ha ha ha. Do you think I care?' asked Shelly. 'After what you did to me?'

'But I didn't mean to do anything to you, Shelly. I liked you. I thought you'd win the competition. Honest I did.'

'Silence, bitch. You stole what was rightfully mine.'

She bound my mouth shut with a heart-patterned bandanna.

'Now, I'm willing to give you just one more chance. Somewhere inside that room is a golden envelope. And inside that golden envelope is a golden key. The golden key that opens this door, Alison. Find that key and you're outta here. Don't find it and you'll rot in jelly!!! Ha ha ha!!'

Then she opened the door to the cell and pushed me inside, with barely time to take a deep breath before I was plunged into the gunk.

Blindly, I thrashed about me. I had done it before, I told myself. I could do it again. I could find the envelope. I could escape from this hell. I just had to be methodical. Only methodical ain't easy when you're blinded by pink goo.

My hands grabbed at nothing. My ears and throat were filling with strawberry gunk. My nose was plugged shut with blancmange. I was never going to find it. I was going to die there. At least my sentence wouldn't be long. I would soon be with the angels in heaven . . .

'For God's sake, Ali. Wake up!!'

Emma shook me awake. I was strangling myself in my own duvet.

'I heard you knock the lamp off your bedside table,' she explained. 'You were holding your breath or something. Your face was going blue.'

I sat up in bed, panting and clutching at my throat. Emma passed me a glass of water.

'I was going to throw this over your face if you didn't come round,' she explained.

I took the drink gratefully and swallowed it in three greedy gulps. 'I'm finished, Emma,' I told her when I was able to speak again. 'If I have to go to prison I'll die of fear. If the nightmares I'm having already don't do for me first, that is.'

'I don't know what to say,' said Emma, unusually lost for words. 'I told you things couldn't get any worse last week, but they did.'

'Yeah. Thanks.'

Fattypuss, who was never the type of cat who actually went out hunting at nights, slinked out from behind the curtain and insinuated herself onto my knees.

'How did I get into this much trouble just by loving someone? Loving someone shouldn't be so very hard.'

'Yeah, but you didn't just love a someone,' Emma pointed out. 'You loved a man.'

'I'll never make that mistake again. Next time, I'll fall for a woman. I'll meet a lovely girl and become a lesbian. That'll be much better.'

Emma took her arm from around my shoulders again and began to fiddle with the tassels on the edge of one of my cushions.

'I don't think you can become a lesbian just like that,' she told me.

It would be a matter of hours before I got my chance to ask.

CHAPTER FORTY-EIGHT

A phone call in the middle of the night. Emma answered, thankfully. But it was for me. I knocked Mickey Mouse off the bedside table when I went to pick up the receiver, and it took another two minutes of fumbling about in the dark to find him again. I wondered who on earth it could be. Perhaps it was Jeremy, calling to tell me that he had made a terrible mistake. It was usually calls from abroad that came at such ridiculous times. Well, I was right on that count.

'Ali?' asked an unfamiliar voice.

'Who is this?'

'It's me. It's Loretta. Remember?'

'Loretta?' For a moment I didn't remember her at all. Then her bleached blonde crop and dungarees came into my mind's eye and I felt a stab of pain. After all, it was her boss who had marked the beginning of the end for me and Jeremy.

'Alison? Are you OK over there? I've been hearing terrible things. I hear you might be going to prison. I want to help you, Alison. You saved my life in Antigua. Now I want to do anything I can to put things right.'

'It's too late. How can I get Jeremy back? He's fallen for the most beautiful woman in the world, and to make things worse, she reciprocates the way he's feeling. I've lost him forever.'

'I'm not talking about Jeremy any more.'

'Well, what else could you help me with?'

'With your court case.'

'How do you know about that?' I asked in surprise.

'It's in just about every newspaper I pick up. Besides Jeremy tells Candida everything and Candida sometimes tells me. Indecent assault on a member of the oppressive sex, eh?'

'I didn't do it. Well, I did do it, but I certainly didn't mean to hurt him as much as he claims I did.'

'I know. And the chances are, you didn't. Listen, I want you to meet a friend of mine. She's in London this week, at the feminist film festival.'

'Is she a lawyer?' I asked.

'No, she's a film producer.'

'What help will that be to me?'

'I don't know yet. But she's usually pretty good at finding solutions to this kind of shit.'

'In America maybe. But I'm going to be tried by a British jury, Loretta. A life sentence is pretty much a forgone conclusion for what they think I've done.'

'Just see what you think of her. I'll get her to call you tomorrow. Look, I can't tell you how sad I am for you, Alison. You're a truly decent person. If Candida hadn't crossed your path, perhaps Jeremy would still be there to support you. Not that the support of a man is worth anything. Anything at all.'

I was almost ready to agree with her.

'We sisters have got to stick together. I'll try and make it over for your case, if it gets as far as court.'

'Oh, it will.'

'We'll see. Candida gave me my marching orders again this morning, and with a bit of luck, she'll have meant it. And if it's any consolation, I don't think that Jeremy is going to last too long with her either.'

'You mean that?'

'He made some kind of comment about her ingrowing toenail. And if there's one thing I've learned, it's that goddesses don't like to learn about their own imperfections. Listen, I've got to go. Sounds like she's on the warpath.'

In the background I could just about make out Candida shouting, 'Where's my fucking conditioner?'

'Listen, you'll love my friend,' Loretta whispered. 'She'll be with you tomorrow morning.'

'Loretta, I . . .'

But she was gone. She hadn't even told me the name of the woman I was expecting.

'What was that about?' Emma asked.

'Someone I met on holiday. Wants to offer her services.'

'In what way?'

'Exactly.'

CHAPTER FORTY-NINE

'Hi. I'm Marcie Guttenberg, feminist film producer,' said the woman who had muscled her way into our kitchen, pushing her specs a little further up her nose as she settled into a chair with Fattypuss on her lap. She was Loretta's friend, she told me, then she announced, 'I'm here on behalf of the Sapphire Society.'

'Sapphire Society?'

'Yeah. It was meant to be Sapphic but the totally phallocentric guy at the printers thought that we'd made a spelling mistake. Anyway, I'm here to shake you warmly by the hand on behalf of all my sisters in the worldwide feminist and lesbian communities.'

She took my hand in both of hers and made like she was making a margarita.

'What you have done, Alison, is strike a blow for womankind. You have triumphed over the oppressor.'

'Not yet I haven't,' I said grimly. 'Court case starts in two days.'

'Ah, yes. Your sisters send their best wishes for that. But in our hearts, whatever the outcome, we want you to know that as far as womankind is concerned you have already won. You have shown the women of this misogynistic world that passivity is not the only way forward. That closing your eyes and putting up with male oppression is not the only way to get through this patriarchal life.'

'I have?'

'You have. And we salute you.'

She started searching in her Prada rucksack for something.

'We'd like you to have this,' she said. 'To bring you luck in court. And to remind you of what it is we are fighting for.'

I accepted the little package with a weak smile.

'What is it?'

'You'll see.'

I opened the box up and there before me was a little golden penis on a stick-pin. It looked pretty floppy.

'It's for your lapel. Like a shrivelled head,' Marcie explained. 'A trophy.'

'Uh, thanks.'

'Here's to the next one.' She tapped her clenched fist against my own in a gesture of solidarity.

'I don't think there will be an opportunity for a next one.'

'That's the spirit,' Marcie laughed. 'You know, you have a beautiful cat.'

Marcie Guttenberg was difficult to get rid of. Fattypuss adored her. And Emma didn't help things by bringing cup after cup of camomile tea to slake the woman's thirst. She must have needed it, talking nineteen to the dozen as she regaled us with stories of revenge and mutilation that even Emma's bloodthirsty doctor Ashley might have found hard to stomach.

'You mean she tied it to a helium balloon,' said Emma. 'That's fantastic. I would have loved to have seen his face.'

'Yeah. And he didn't ever get it back. Lorena Bobbitt should never have told those policemen where she threw that dick she cut off. I mean, the man's now making a living as a porn star, for heaven's sake! If that doesn't defeat the object of the whole damn exercise, I really don't know what does.'

'Do you think David will become a porn star?' Emma asked me mischievously.

'Don't be ridiculous,' I said. 'He can't act.'

'Honey,' said Marcie. 'For a feminist icon, you've sure led a sheltered life. I bet he's already getting himself an agent. We have to stop this rot, Alison. We've got to help you win this case.'

'I have a solicitor for that,' I said.

'I think I can come up with something a little more effective,' Marcie assured me.

After Marcie left, Emma ticked me off for being a little less than positive about her visit.

'She wants to help you. She's a nice woman.'

'She a nutter. And her patchouli oil perfume gave Fattypuss a sneezing fit.'

'I liked her.'

'You would.'

'You could do worse than have her as an ally.'

'Emma, what's she going to do? You know as well as I do, that for all her pontificating today she will probably just stand outside the courthouse with an obscene banner and make the jury think that I'm not just a jilted lover but an insane anti-man terrorist. I think it's best that I stay as far out of her way as possible. If she calls again, you'll have to pretend that we've had the number changed or something. I don't know why Loretta put her in touch with me. I mean, with respect, what use are all the good wishes in the world to me right now?'

'It's nice to know you've touched someone's heart. And don't you like the brooch she gave you?'

'Put it this way, I'm not going to be wearing it in court.'

But what does one wear when one has to appear in court on a charge of indecent assault occasioning actual bodily harm? As I stood in front of my wardrobe, the night before my case was due to begin, I wished that I still had the services of Amanda from *Complete Woman* to call upon, but no doubt it was against *Complete Woman* policy to dress the accused.

'Emma, what do you think?'

'Wear that little black number you got for your twenty-first birthday party,' she suggested. 'After all, it could be those nasty blue trouser suits for you from here on.'

'Thanks very much. That's just what I need. My own best friend doesn't think I'm going to get off.'

Emma jumped up from the bed to hug me. 'Oh, Ali! I do think you're going to get off. Honest I do. I wouldn't joke about the blue trouser suits if I thought that you were actually going to have to wear them.'

'Right.'

'Wear your navy blue suit,' she said more helpfully.

'Your job interview one. That looks smart and respectable. No one would ever believe you were capable of
atrocities against mankind in that outfit.'

I pulled the suit out of my wardrobe and hung it from
the door.

'And the pale green shirt,' Emma continued. 'Bit of
colour but not too much. Stylish yet serious. And what
are you going to do with your hair?'

'Hadn't even thought about it.' It was true, I hadn't
thought about my hair for a very long time. The
ends of my grown out layers were still bleached and
frayed from those distant calm-before-the-storm weeks
in Antigua.

'You need to wear it up,' Emma decided. 'I'll do it for
you. French plait, I think. Not as severe as a bun but still
very neat and tidy. I'll try it now.'

She began to fiddle about with my hair and suddenly
I couldn't stop myself from crying. Big fat tears rolled
down my cheeks and plopped onto the green shirt
which I still held in my hands.

'Hey,' Emma said. 'Watch the shirt, you've got to
wear that tomorrow.' Then, with slightly more concern,
she asked, 'What is it, Ali? Can I help?'

I shook my head and sniffed violently. 'No. No-one
can help. Oh, Emma, I feel like I'm Mary Queen of Scots.
I feel like it's my last night on earth and I'm preparing
to have my head chopped off in the morning.'

'Ali,' said Emma seriously. 'You mustn't think like
that. Tomorrow will be fine. You will be magnificent.
No jury in the world will convict you of assaulting
David once they've actually met the swine. I give you
my guarantee that you will get off. Once you tell them
how David dumped you on Christmas Day, while you

were languishing in hospital, and then tried to worm his way back into your life for a freebie holiday, they'll be lining up to stone him to death.'

'It was like that, wasn't it? I mean, he did deserve it, didn't he? I didn't really just overreact, did I?'

'Of course you didn't. And everyone will see that. Look, you're the one who's been wronged around here, darling. Besides, David looks far shiftier than you do.'

CHAPTER FIFTY

But we hadn't reckoned on David having access to the style gurus of the world. According to the grapevine, all the top men's magazines were falling over themselves to dress him for the trial and when I was brought into the court, in handcuffs, I was almost confused by how fabulous he looked. I got the kind of feeling that I thought I would have walking down the aisle to marry him. Only this time, he definitely wasn't setting out to make an honest woman of me.

The case was called Regina v. Harris

'All rise!'

Now this was the bit I remembered from the movies. The judge swept in, swathed in robes and topped off with a spectacular wig. I was so taken in by the outfit that it took me a moment to register that my judge, Judge Olivia Maxwell-Harris, was a woman. When she took her seat, she was so short that her head and shoulders were barely visible over the top of the bench.

The clerk of the court, a little man whose robes had obviously been made for his big brother then called me into the dock.

'You're going to be arraigned,' my barrister warned me. It sounded painful and I was shaking like a leaf as I took the stand.

'Alison Harris,' the clerk began. 'It is charged that on the 2nd February 1998, you did indecently assault Mr David Whitworth with the intention of causing him Actual Bodily Harm. How say you, are you guilty, or not guilty?'

'Not guilty,' I squeaked. I heard a stifled whoop from my sister Jo in the public gallery. The clerk nodded and I was allowed to stand down again.

Then the jury was sworn in, one by one. I tried to gauge their mood and moral preferences while Mr Tailforth, my barrister (Mr Wagstaff would have been way out of his depth – no kidding) briefed me on how I should behave. There were seven men and five women. That was bad news for a start, since I figured that any red-blooded man would almost certainly find himself on David's side of the fence. Of the women, only two looked like the kind of girls I could be friends with. One of them, an older lady with thick bi-focal lenses in her glasses, was staring at me as if she needed to remember every line on my face for a neighbourhood watch drawing she would produce when she got home. Of course, it might just have been her bi-focals that were giving me that impression.

'I think we have a sympathetic jury,' said Mr Tailforth.

'You're kidding,' I snorted. 'At least ten of them look as though they agree with hanging for bicycle theft.'

'Alison. Try not to let your opinions be reflected in your behaviour today. I don't want to see a sulky schoolgirl up there when you take the stand. I want to see a confident, mature young woman who played a practical joke that went just a tiny bit too far.'

'When will I have to get up there and say what really happened?' I asked him.

'We may not even get our chance today,' Mr Tailforth warned me. 'The prosecution goes first. And they're calling four witnesses.'

'Four? I don't get it. Who?'

My barrister shushed me as David's man stood up to present the case.

'Ladies and Gentlemen of the jury, what we have here is a clear case of indecent assault with intent to cause malicious wounding. We will be calling four witnesses.'

'Four,' I said again. 'I don't understand. There were only two of us in the room that day. Where has he got four witnesses from?'

Mr Tailforth flicked through the details of the prosecution's case in the notes before him. 'Medical opinion, character witnesses.'

I scanned the rows of seats behind the prosecution to see who they might be calling. There was a shuffly looking bloke in an ill-fitting suit. Probably the medical expert, I thought hopefully. I wouldn't have trusted him with Fattypuss.

But there, in the row behind him, my eyes met with someone I hadn't expected to see. Andrew. Andrew from Marvin's dinner party. Andrew, the one who got 'stung'.

'Oh my God,' I murmured. 'They can't be calling him. This is the end.'

'The defence calls upon David Whitworth to take the stand.'

David swaggered – no, make that limped – up to the stand and took the oath. As he envoked Almighty God, I waited for the thunderbolt, but none came. Then his lawyer started the ball rolling in David's favour by asking him if he felt comfortable standing up in the stand – in view of his physical condition.

My brief rolled his eyes.

'So, Mr Whitworth, perhaps you would like to begin by describing your relationship with the defendant, Ms Harris. How you met, perhaps? The early days of your relationship. And its subsequent deterioration to the sorry position we find ourselves in today.'

'Well,' David cleared his throat. 'When I met Miss Harris, I was actually already engaged to someone else, Miss Brown. I didn't want to get involved with someone else, but Alison, I mean Miss Harris, had a powerful personality even then and I felt that I was being coerced into something that I didn't really want to do.'

Then followed the story of our first blissful months together. Only I barely recognised them. I had pursued him rabidly, according to this tale. There was no mention of the fact that I had refused to see David for a week, to give him a chance to sort out his feelings for Lisa. Instead I was portrayed as horribly jealous, waiting for him every lunchtime outside his place of work. No mention of the fact that he wanted me to be there. That he said I made the best sandwiches . . .

And our engagement? I had asked him to marry me of course. No mention of the night that he went down on one knee in the middle of the park and shoved a ring-pull onto my finger in lieu of the real thing. David made himself sound like a man truly beleaguered. Hounded by a girl with only one thing on her mind.

'And the first hint that Miss Harris might have a dangerously violent temper?' asked David's barrister.

'Leading question,' shouted Mr Tailforth, jumping to his feet but the judge simply waved him back down.

'That came late last year,' said David solemnly, 'when Miss Harris visited my family home while I was out for the evening. My elder brother, Police Inspector Barry Whitworth, was at home on his own. Miss Harris forced herself upon him and, when she was spurned, she tried to use violence to get her own way.'

'You didn't tell me about this,' whispered my brief urgently.

'Well, I'm sorry if I didn't manage to pre-empt all of David's lies,' I hissed back.

'We'll hear more about that from Police Inspector Whitworth himself later on,' said David's brief, smugly. 'And finally, if you could describe, in your own words, the morning in question. Saturday, the second of February . . .'

Now this was a work of pure fiction.

I had begged David to go to Antigua with me, he claimed. He had refused. He didn't want to be unfaithful to Lisa. I had accosted him in the hallway, where he stood fully clothed, and shoved my hand down his trousers to rub on the Hot Stuff Heat Rub.

'That's rubbish!' I cried.

Judge Maxwell-Harris told me to be silent.

'That's rubbish,' I said, more quietly this time. 'He didn't even say that he was in bed with me at the time.'

'We'll get our chance in a minute,' Mr Tailforth promised me.

But it wasn't to be. When David's brief had finished with him, Mr Tailforth got up again and rearranged his gown, in readiness to begin his questioning. At which point, David decided to have an asthma attack, which quite clearly wouldn't pass until all danger of cross-examination was over.

David was led away and Mr Tailforth returned to me, sighing with exasperation.

'History of asthma, your ex-fiancé?'

I shrugged.

'I didn't think so.'

Inspector Barry Whitworth came next.

I had never seen him looking so smart. When I had seen Barry in his uniform in the past, it was usually after a hard night playing darts at the station while on cell duty. Then he would be sweaty and his special unthrottleable tie would hang loose. Now, taking the stand with his official hat tucked under his arm, he looked like Tom Cruise playing the good naval officer in that movie about a court marshal. Mr Tailforth looked at me and winced.

Barry took the oath like a pro, and under the prosecution brief's careful guidance, he poured forth a story of that night at his house, which even almost convinced me, though it was quite unlike the truth.

'Unusually for me,' Barry continued. 'I made a very poor judgement of character when I met Miss Alison Harris for the first time. That night, I faced a battle for my virtue far worse than any fight I have ever had with one of the more traditional criminal fraternity.'

'Thank you Detective Constable Whitworth,' said his brief, turning to the jury and smiling as he did so. 'That will be all.'

Mr Tailforth got to his feet and cleared his throat dramatically.

'I'll tear this one to pieces,' he promised.

'Detective Constable Whitworth,' Mr Tailforth began. 'You are six feet tall are you not?'

Barry straightened himself up, 'Six foot one as a matter of fact.'

'And looking at you from here, I'd say that you must weigh in the region of fifteen stones.'

Barry sucked in his stomach.

'Fourteen and a half.'

'While my client here is only five feet two inches in height and weighs, at most, nine and a half stone.'

I sucked in my stomach but managed to resist the urge to inform the members of the jury that I was nine stone max on a bad day.

Mr Tailforth stepped from the box and put his fingers to his chin in a gesture of thought. 'A grown man,' he thought aloud, 'of six feet in height, who arrests dangerous and often armed criminals for a living, scared of a girl almost a foot shorter than him and just about half his weight?'

A couple of the girls in the jury shook their heads.

'I didn't think so. I rest my case.'

'Is that all you're going to say to him?' I asked, when Mr Tailforth swaggered back to me again.

'Trust me. It was enough to get them thinking.'

I wasn't so sure.

CHAPTER FIFTY-ONE

U p in the public gallery, Marvin, Emma and Ashley shared Marks and Spencers' salmon sarnies as they watched the events unfold. When I looked up at Emma she had an expression on her face which reflected the way I thought the case was going. That is to say badly. When she caught sight of me looking at her, however, she gave me a cheery thumbs-up.

I was sure that David and his brother had charmed the jury. After all they had shown all the traits that attracted me to the Whitworth brothers in the first place. They had been quiet-spoken, charming, eloquent. They looked like the kind of boys you wanted to take home to your mum. And Tailforth had done little to squash the image they created.

Who was on next?

'The prosecution calls Miss Lisa Brown.'

My nemesis.

Lisa looked different from usual. She was wearing a pretty little pink number with huge gilt buttons which made her look almost fragile. Her hair, usually scraped back so severely before, was in a looser style now, with little tendrils that hung down upon her cheeks. It was clear that someone had been advising her to be a little less *Dynasty* when she took the stand.

And she very nearly didn't, tripping over the step into the box in her new high heels.

'Lisa Brown,' the witness squeaked when the clerk of the court asked her name.

'Do you promise to swear by Almighty God to tell the truth, the whole truth and nothing but the truth, so help you God?'

'I do,' Lisa squeaked again.

'Tell me about your relationship with Mr Whitworth, Miss Brown. From the beginning, when you first met each other.'

Lisa beamed stiffly. 'We met at a Deacon Blue concert,' she began. 'My brother introduced David to me because he had known him since school. My brother was very careful about introducing me to people,' she added for good measure. 'He was always looking out for me. Making sure that I didn't get mixed up with the wrong kind of people. I knew straightaway that David wasn't from the wrong sort of people though.'

'And what are the wrong sort of people.'

'Oh, you know. The kind of people who use violence against someone else when they don't get their own way.'

'And David wasn't like that.'

'Oh no. David was the gentlest man I had ever met. He loves children and animals,' she added. 'We had the perfect relationship. We liked the same things. We shared the same values. We had the same vision of our future lives.'

We had the same script-writer, I added mentally to her list.

'I thought that we would be happy forever,' she continued. 'We were going to get married and start a family,' Lisa suddenly dabbed at her eyes.

I glanced over to the jury and noticed to my horror that the three women in the front row were sniffing discreetly too. The men were just transfixed by Lisa's tragically heaving bosom.

'I had chosen the dress and booked the reception. Everything was in place. Then I had to go to Bosnia. On a mercy mission. For the orphaned children. It was part of my civilian police worker training.'

Mr Tailforth groaned.

'I was going to be away for a long time. Two weeks. David gets lonely. I rang home every day, but you know, it's just not the same as being together. That's when she made her move. She saw that David was lonely with me away and made advances to him while I was helping the poor orphans of the former Yugoslavia.'

'She being?'

'Alison Harris.'

'And would Miss Harris have known that you were away from Brindlesham?'

'Oh, yes. My mission was well-documented in the local press.'

I couldn't help wondering where Lisa picked up a word like documented. Crown Court seemed to bring out the verbosity in everyone.

'When I got back, it was as if David had been replaced by someone else. As if someone had sucked out the soul that I had been in love with and put another, less loving soul in its place.'

How tragically familiar this sounded.

'It was as if she had put a spell on him. But since then, I realise that it was probably just that he was afraid of her violent temper.'

'Objection, your honour!' shouted Mr Tailforth.

'Overruled,' said Maxwell-Harris.

'It took him two whole years to find the strength to come back to me,' Lisa concluded. 'And that was when she decided to maim him for life.'

'Your witness,' said David's brief. But before Tailforth had even made it to the stand, Lisa was having a funny turn.

'I think I'm going to faint,' she murmured. 'It's ever so hot in here.'

'This is ridiculous!' Tailforth shouted.

'I think my witness needs medical attention,' David's brief replied.

The clerk of the court rushed forward to help Lisa down from the stand. She smiled bravely at him for the benefit of the jury, then rushed to the back of the court, where she was congratulated by my one-time future mother-in-law.

And the case was adjourned for the night.

'This is terrible,' I groaned when Tailforth and I were alone in the hallway. 'You haven't even had a chance to talk to any of his witnesses properly.'

'No,' said Mr Tailforth. 'It's not all lost. We've still got our turn to come. Now that he's started to bring your good character into disrepute, we can let all hell loose against him. Who do you know who can dish the dirt? Ex-girlfriends?'

'The only girlfriend he ever had before me as far as I know is Lisa, and as you saw this afternoon, she's very much on the prosecution side of this case.'

Mr Tailforth scratched his moustache. 'Mmm. And you're sure he's never made a pass at any of your friends?'

'They haven't told me if he did.'

'Harder than I thought. Looks like we're just going to have to go on what you say. Were there ever any incidents when Mr Whitworth was violent towards you?'

'Well, he once threw a golf club in my direction when he lost a game of crazy golf at Brighton, but I don't think there was any malicious intent.'

'What do you mean?' said Tailforth, eyes brightening. 'The man sounds like a nutter.'

'And he once threw my cat down the stairs . . . after she'd peed on his new suede jacket.'

'Perfect. Animal abuse. It's well-known that that kind of behaviour leads to worse things later on.'

'What could be worse than throwing a cat down the stairs?' I asked. Though in fact David had only thrown Fattypuss from the second stair of the flight, and she had landed perfectly and hissed at him for good measure upon doing so.

'Will that do it?'

'It might help. English juries are terribly uptight about animals.'

'But apart from that?'

'I don't know. But I should get a chance to question both David and Lisa Brown properly tomorrow. I'll find the hole in their story if there is one and pick the case to pieces.'

'You sound optimistic.'

'Never say die.'

I gave him a weak thumbs-up sign as he left me to go home.

CHAPTER FIFTY-TWO

But behind the brave face I was about as optimistic as Eeyore. 'I'm finished,' I told my family that night. 'I know I am. This is my last night of freedom.'

My Mum threw a comforting arm around my shoulder but I could tell that she was feeling the same way. By the time David had finished giving his evidence he had had a halo floating over his head. I, by contrast, was fast becoming a Jezebel. A sluttish whore with unnatural physical urges that manifested themselves in violence if I didn't get enough sex. When I took the stand the next day I knew I would have a very long and difficult task ahead of me. It would be like having to crawl back into the jury's good books over the Sahara desert.

'They'll know that he was lying,' said Mum. 'When they hear your side of the story, they'll soon realise that he was exaggerating. Ooh, I'd like to get up there myself and give evidence about all the times he made my favourite daughter cry.'

Jo and Jane looked up in surprise.

'Oh, you're all my favourite daughters,' Mum back-pedalled. 'But Alison needs all our support now. What did you think of the trial today, Jo?'

'I thought that David came out of it looking like a saint and smelling of Chanel number five. That's made of roses,' she added, in case we didn't get the reference.

'Thank you,' said Mum, before Jo could do any more damage. 'Jane?'

'Well, he did give a pretty good show,' Jane said carefully. 'But I think that the women in the jury will have seen through the facade. Especially that asthma attack . . . And Lisa's fainting fit. I mean . . .'

'Great,' I said forlornly. 'But that still leaves me with a minority on my side. I'm going down. You guys had better be prepared to smuggle loads of cigarettes in when you come to visit me at Holloway.'

'Cool,' said Jo. 'I've always wanted to go inside there and have a good look round. Who do they keep locked up there, Ali? Anyone famous?'

'No-one I want to mix with. Oh, Jo, I should have listened to you when you said that his eyes were too small. You were right. David Whitworth is mean. Why does he want to put me through all this? He's got someone new. I'm left with nothing.'

'Yeah,' said Jo. 'But he has lost the use of his dick.'

'So he says. And if he hadn't already lost the use of it, I would be first in line to chop it off,' said Mum.

My father, who had been attempting to read a newspaper throughout this conversation winced.

I went to bed early. Fattypuss padded across the room and lay on my chest in a gesture of solidarity. I had made

Emma promise that she would look after the cat well while I was inside and not try to put her on a diet in an attempt to make her look less like Bagpuss and more like the Siamese cross she was supposed to be.

'I wish I could take you with me,' I told the purring flea-bag.

But since the British prison system doesn't even allow babies to stay with their mothers after the age of six months or so, I figured that being allowed to take my geriatric cat with me was probably out of the question.

The only thing that could save me now was for someone on the prosecution's team of witnesses to drive home via Damascus.

CHAPTER FIFTY-THREE

After a frugal last breakfast of Marmite on toast, I hugged Fattypuss almost to death while I waited for the taxi to take me to court.

I wore my sentencing outfit. The little black dress that had last seen an airing at my twenty-first birthday. It was probably a bit over the top, with its diamante straps, but I wanted everyone to remember me looking my best. Needless to say, by the time I got to the door, I had rather spoiled the effect by getting myself covered in cat hairs.

Emma was unusually quiet as we were driven into town. My parents, who were already waiting for me in the court lobby, looked as if they hadn't slept too well themselves. My sisters hugged me and I was sure that even Jo had a tear in her eye.

'Don't kiss me,' said my mother. 'It makes me think you're not coming back.'

'We've got to say goodbye properly,' I insisted. 'Just in case I don't.'

'Can nothing persuade that wicked man to drop this case against you?' said my mother loudly as David's brief shuffled into court. 'He's depriving a mother of her eldest daughter. Her comfort and joy. Her grandmother may not even live to see the day when she's released.'

'Sssh,' I hissed. 'How is Gran anyway?'

'She's talking to us again,' said Jo. 'She rang up to say she's got a photo shoot for *Golden World* today. That's that old biddies' magazine they give away free at the post office. Otherwise she'd be here.'

'She wishes you luck,' Jane added.

We were interrupted by Mr Tailforth then. 'Feeling ready to win?' he asked me. My whole family looked at him in disgust. This was no time for jokes. The only possible positive outcome as far as we could see was that I would be sent to an open prison.

Mr Tailforth motioned me forward. As he did, my mother threw me her jacket. 'Put that on,' she said. 'If you've got any chance at all, you don't want to blow it with those stupid diamante straps.'

Inside the courtroom, David's brief lolled in his chair as though he had already won. Barry and Lisa sat behind him. Lisa was dressed in another Jackie O-style suit. In tangerine this time. She was wringing a paper handkerchief into shreds between her hands. She looked nervous. Her cheeks were surprisingly white instead of their usual Lancome pink. I suppose she was concerned about her cross-examination which should be the first task of the morning. She couldn't exactly fake another fainting fit.

'Are you going to be especially cruel to her?' I asked Mr Tailforth hopefully.

Soon the room was silenced again as Judge Maxwell-Harris swept majestically to her chair. She addressed the room briefly, recapping the previous day's events and reminding the jury what was expected of them. We were to pick up where we had left off. That is, Lisa was to go back on the stand.

When she was called, she got to her feet about as steadily as a new-born giraffe. For a moment, she seemed utterly unable to take a step forward. I saw David's mother give her a smile of encouragement. She looked at her as if she had never seen her before in her life. Then she made a terrible snorting sound as she held back a sob.

'What on earth is the matter with her?' I asked Mr Tailforth as Lisa had to be helped back into the stand by a pair of ushers.

'I have a reputation for harshness,' said Tailforth slightly proudly.

'I can't do it,' Lisa squeaked in the direction of David's barrister. 'I don't want to take the stand again. You've got to let me go.'

David's barrister seemed to be considering the possibility of asking whether Lisa could stand back down, but Judge Maxwell-Harris was determined that no more time should be wasted by sickly prosecution witnesses.

I looked up at the gallery. Emma and Marvin were leaning forward over the barrier to get the best view. Ashley was there too. Perhaps David's barrister would call for a doctor and Ashley would be able to prove that Lisa was just pretending to be sick so that she didn't have to tell the truth about me and her boyfriend.

'Miss Brown,' said Judge Maxwell-Harris impatiently. 'Do you think you might be ready in a moment?'

Lisa put her hand to her mouth as if she was about to be sick.

'Please don't let her get away with this,' I begged God. 'Please make her be well enough to be cross-examined.'

The clerk stepped forward with the bible.

'I can't do it!' Lisa pleaded.

'Miss Brown,' said Judge Maxwell-Harris, 'you will do it or I will have you charged with contempt of court.'

Talking of which, I spotted another familiar face in the gallery. Amanda from *Complete Woman* was there with her reporter's notebook, unaware that the wheels of justice would soon be rolling in her direction, even if I had to put them in motion from behind a locked door.

With a sob in her voice, Lisa finally took the oath. She was allowed to sit, but she certainly wasn't going to be allowed to stand down until some questions had been answered.

Tailforth drew himself to his full height and cleared his throat like a man who meant business. As he walked up to the stand, Lisa's eyes widened in fear. But I wanted her to suffer, because it seemed certain that I soon would be.

'Miss Brown,' Tailforth began. 'Yesterday, we all heard the heart-warming story of your relationship with Mr Whitworth up until the night of February 2nd 1998. Today, I would like to ask you about more recent aspects of your relationship with the prosecution's chief witness. And much as I hate to dwell on the sordid, I'd like to start with the last time you had sexual relations . . .'

'What?'

'The last time you had sex,' Mr Tailforth repeated. 'Or would you prefer, the last time you "made love"?'

Trembling so much that it was making her dangly earrings shake, Lisa started to speak.

'We had a wonderful love life,' she began, barely audibly.

'Speak up, Miss Brown,' said the Judge.

'I wanted to save myself for marriage, you understand, but once David and I became engaged, I decided that it wasn't worth waiting any longer.'

'You say that you "had" a wonderful love life. When did things change, Miss Brown?'

When I came into the equation of course.

'But when you got back together following the end of Mr Whitworth's engagement to Miss Harris, things were as they once had been again?'

Lisa nodded.

'Until?'

'The 2nd of February,' she whispered.

'And ever since that morning, when he claims that he was assaulted by Miss Harris, would you confirm that Mr Whitworth has been unable to maintain a satisfactory erection?'

Lisa's face contorted at the question. The 64 million dollar question. Had he, or had he not, been able to function 'as a man' since that terrible night, Tailforth repeated.

'Er . . .' said Lisa.

'Perhaps you don't understand the question,' said Mr Tailforth cruelly. 'Has Mr Whitworth been able to make love to you, as a man?'

I held my breath as I waited for her to speak. Time seemed to expand like a rubber band. Up in the gallery, my family and friends were in danger of tumbling into the courtroom as they craned to hear Lisa answer.

'He has,' Lisa blurted suddenly.

David's brief's face registered a look of surprise. So did mine.

Mr Tailforth continued calmly, sensing that Lisa was about to crack. 'You mean that he has been unable to maintain an erection?'

'No,' Lisa squeaked. 'I mean that he has been able to function as a man since February the 2nd.'

David's brief shook his head and groaned, 'No!'

'But surely you mean in a day to day, "going about his business" sense,' Mr Tailforth persisted. 'And not in the bedroom.'

'No. I mean in the bedroom. David Whitworth made love to me the very night after he last saw Ali Harris.'

'With penetration.'

'With everything.'

A snigger went around the public gallery.

'He's been lying to you,' she blubbed. 'He wasn't hurt by what Alison did to him at all. It didn't affect his performance one little bit. In fact, when David's brother told him that he might be able to sue Alison and get some money out of the whole fiasco, David's performance in the bedroom went through the roof, if you know what I mean. And not just with me.'

David's brief's eyes pleaded with her to shut up. Beside him, David's solicitor was scribbling frantically, a smile he couldn't suppress stretching across his face like a slice of melon despite the fact that their case was crumbling like year-old Parmesan.

'We're home and dry,' Tailforth's assistant scribbled on a note to me. And though the jury still had to make its mind up, I felt the muscles in the back of my neck begin to unknot themselves as Lisa continued to spill the beans all across the courtroom floor.

'A week after Alison put Hot Stuff Heat Rub on David Whitworth's penis, we were still having it away up to three times a night.' She allowed herself a small, proud smile. 'All that stuff about him not being able to get an erection because of the psychological damage she had inflicted on him was a lie. There was no damage at all. In fact, when he went to the doctor for an examination to be used in the evidence against her, he got me to rub some Hot Stuff Heat Rub on him in the car just before we got to the surgery. So that he would be walking funny when he went in.'

David's mother gasped and I heard a thud as she fell off her chair in shock. But Lisa hadn't finished.

'When I got home from work last night there was a strange car parked outside our house. It was a flash car. A big Mercedes or something. Now I don't know anyone with a car like that, so I assumed it belonged to David's solicitor. I let myself into the house, but David wasn't in the kitchen, or in the living room. He was upstairs. And when I walked in on him, there was a woman between his knees on the bedroom floor. She was giving him a blow-job!'

I clapped my hand to my mouth to stifle a laugh.

David's mother screamed.

'I pulled her away by the hair. She didn't half scream. And then I slapped her around the face. Who the fuck are you? I asked her. David told me to let go of her hair but half of it had just come off in my hand anyway. It was one of those false bits. A hair-piece. The whole of her plait. Well, as you can imagine, I chased her out of my house and back into her car, which was the Merc of course. When I got back in, I expected David to at least say that he was sorry or something, but he didn't. He was in a complete rage.'

'A complete rage?' mused Tailforth. 'And why was that?'

'He said I'd probably just ruined his career.'

'His career? What? His career in insurance?' asked Tailforth in mock innocence.

'No, his career as a film star. In pornography.'

There was a moment's silence while it sank in.

Then David's mother had to be carried out of the court.

'As a porn star?' Tailforth asked once more.

'Yes,' Lisa sobbed. 'That woman. That false-haired tart giving my boyfriend a blow-job, was the owner of this country's biggest porn production company. Stiff Upper Lip Films, David said it was called. She said she wanted to make a film about David's life story. She was giving him a blow-job to make sure his performance on celluloid wouldn't be a flop!'

There was an explosion of laughter from the gallery. And soon the whole courtroom had erupted in a fit of the giggles.

'What's so funny?' asked Lisa innocently.

Judge Maxwell-Harris restored order at once.

'Hardly the actions of a man who has been living in fear of what a jealous woman might do to his nether regions, don't you think?' asked Mr Tailforth.

'That's right,' Lisa sniffed. 'So much for him being too frightened to let anyone touch him. David Whitworth asked me to lie for him, your honour. But I can't lie when the good name of my fellow woman is at stake.'

A huge cheer went up from the gallery then. It was the Sapphire Society of course. And all around them, the crowd began a hesitant round of applause. Lisa looked towards me for reassurance that she had done the right thing. I managed just a tiny thumbs-up. David's sister was on her feet.

'She's lying. She's not telling the truth,' David's sister protested.

Judge Maxwell-Harris made her sit back down.

'It's the real story,' Lisa concluded. 'David Whitworth is a lying bastard and you can tell him from me,' she addressed Judge Maxwell-Harris, as she ripped off her diamond ring, 'that our impending engagement is off.'

With that, Lisa left the witness box without being dismissed, and ran out of the courtroom as fast as her orange kitten-heeled shoes would carry her.

'It's all right,' said Mr Tailforth, when someone made a move to retrieve her. 'I don't think there's any need for further questioning.'

I looked up at the gallery. A row of friendly faces giving me the thumbs-up. Even Amanda looked faintly pleased with the way things were turning out. Though I was far from through ruining her life.

'We would like to request a recess,' said David's brief.

I bet they would, I thought.

CHAPTER FIFTY-FOUR

So, our destruction of David's case was pretty straightforward after that. The golden boy, seduced by an evil ex-girlfriend, tragically injured while trying to escape her wicked clutches, was all but forgotten. Here was the truth. A hopeless womaniser, driven by the promise of a free holiday, drove his shy, insecure ex-fiancée to try to salvage the last vestiges of her self-esteem by an action she did not for one moment think would have a permanent effect. And the fact was that it quite obviously hadn't.

As great moments go, I don't think I'll ever have such a great moment in my life again as the moment when David Whitworth realised that he had been rumbled. My heart soared when Judge Maxwell-Harris agreed with Mr Tailforth's submission that there simply was no case to answer and, giving David a hard stare, told him that he was guilty of a very serious crime indeed, blackening the good name and reputation of a fine, upstanding young pillar of the community like me. I could have punched the air when she warned him that further action might be forthcoming. The case was dismissed and I stepped out into the sunshine feeling elated in a subdued kind of way, as though I had spent the past few months behind bars anyway.

Marcie Guttenberg and her Sapphire gang were waiting on the step, carrying banners which proclaimed me to be a heroine for womankind. Champagne corks popped and I was drenched in the froth that was sprayed all over my head. Flowers were pressed into my hands from all sides and into Lisa's hands too. After all, it was her brave testimony that had really saved the day.

As it turned out, my real knight in shining armour was Marcie Guttenberg. As the Sapphire Sisters bore me aloft to the car park, Marcie explained that not every lesbian fitted in with my narrow stereotype and that the glamorous owner of Stiff Upper Lip Films was one of them. It was Marcie who had arranged for David to be in the throes of that kind sister's enticement just at the moment when Lisa walked through the door. At Loretta's prompting, of course. I shouldn't forget her.

'Who are these strange women?' Lisa asked me, as she wiped a smudge of Marcie's militant red lipstick from her cheek.

'They're the Sapphire Sisters,' I told her. 'And I think that kiss means you're an honorary member.'

'I don't know if I want to be,' she said. Same old Lisa creeping through.

'Make the most of the adoration, I say,' I told her. 'Don't think either of us are going to be getting much action from the opposite sex for a while.'

'Oh, why did this have to happen to me?' Lisa suddenly broke down. 'I loved him. He loved me. We were going to get married. What am I going to do now?'

'Join my club,' I told her. 'We'll get over this together, Lisa. I promise you we will.'

My parents were throwing a party in my honour that night. The outside of their house was decorated with a huge banner proclaiming, 'Ali Harris is innocent'. Spelt properly this time. The neighbours were all crammed into the sitting room in the dark, pretending not to be there when Dad brought me to the house. Unfortunately, I'd seen the lights go out as we pulled into the drive so I wasn't able to act too surprised.

'Everybody's here,' said Mum, as she ushered me into the party. The neighbours (minus the Baxters, of course) and all the maiden aunts. Gran had her place of honour in Mum's usual seat and they were wearing matching dresses. Yellow meringues this time.

'Do you get it?' Mum asked, as she stood beside her own mother and they were joined by my sisters in a pair of sunshine coloured lycra inner tubes. 'It's yellow. For "tie a yellow ribbon round the old oak tree". It was in case you went down. To let you know that we wouldn't forget you whatever.'

I couldn't help crying then. Big tears of relief rolled down my cheeks and plopped into the gin and tonic which had been helpfully placed in my hand.

'We knew you didn't do it, Alison,' said Mr Griffiths slapping me heartily between the shoulders. 'I mean, you always acted like a lady whenever you took me home. Even when I was drunk enough to be taken advantage of. I would have given evidence in support of your honour you know . . .'

'Thank you,' I told him. 'Thank you all.'

What a laugh it was, though. The room was full of people who might never have spoken to my mother again if I hadn't got off that charge.

'Let's have a sing-song,' piped up Gran. 'What about Jailhouse Rock?'

I had hoped that my notoriety would start to fade as soon as the court case was over, but during the rest of that week I had calls from publicity agents all over the country. Did I want to speak to the nation on *Radio Middle of Nowhere*? Would I give an interview to the *Out in the Sticks Somewhere Times*? There were bigger things too, though. I got one call from an American film producer. For a moment I could see myself as the next Sandra Bullock, then he explained the plot of his film. It was a recreation of my last night with David of course, and the film, which would go straight to video, would never be seen in our local Blockbuster.

I turned everything down. Celebrity is one thing, but notoriety is another and I didn't need it. Besides, I had another court case coming up. And if I jumped on the publicity bandwagon, it might seem a bit odd that I was pressing charges against Jeremy Baxter and the assistant editor of *Complete Woman* for libel, defamation and slander.

Yes, I'm afraid poor old Jeremy's luck was going from bad to worse. I was staying out of his way, pending the libel hearing, but Emma did see him once more. In the accident unit of the hospital where this sorry saga started.

Emma was waiting for Ashley to stitch up some drunken Saturday night fighter so that they could catch the last showing of *Blade Runner: Director's Cut*. (Yep, Ashley and Emma have passed the six month mark though she still doesn't understand blood pressure.) Jeremy was waiting to be seen by someone like Ashley.

He wasn't alone. He was with Amanda. The *Complete Woman* herself. He had a tablecloth wrapped around his head like a makeshift turban. Emma didn't like to walk straight up to them to find out what was wrong, but the nurse on reception had no qualms about informing her that the chap in the tablecloth turban had had a terrible accident with his hair. Turned out that, while having a romantic dinner with the queen of twee, Jeremy had leaned too close to the candles on the centre of the table and set his heavily lacquered fringe on fire. Went up like a nylon nightie apparently and things only got worse when Amanda reached for her brandy to put the conflagration out. Heaven only knew if Jeremy's luscious locks would ever grow back again. Whatever, it seems like Jeremy's catwalk career is going to be on hold for a while, unless Jean Paul Gaultier decides that the singed look is in. And Candida went straight back to Vadim.

Meanwhile, David has gone underground. His brother Barry is awaiting disciplinary action for inciting a sibling to waste police time. Lisa got a transfer to the switchboard of another police station and has started to go out with a fireman. She didn't reply to the Sapphire Sisters' request that she be the cover girl of their summer newsletter.

And me? Well, you'll be amused to learn that I got an interesting letter through the post this morning. It was from *You and Your Kitty*. Don't ask me why I did it, but I entered their Christmas anagram competition while I was languishing in hospital all those months ago and this morning I discovered that I've won a lifetime's supply of cat food.

Not much use to me anymore. You see, Fattypuss upped and died last week. One minute she was hissing at Berkeley from the safety of my bedroom windowsill, the next she was the wrong way up in the flowerbed. First time ever she hadn't managed to land on her feet.

So, all tears and sniffles, I called the editorial assistant at *You and Your Kitty* and told her the sorry news. The whole office was distraught, as you can probably imagine.

'I don't think I can bring myself to get another cat just yet,' I sniffled. 'Any chance I could just have the money?'

There wasn't of course. Three hundred and sixty five tins of gourmet guppy goulash were already cluttering up the *You and Your Kitty* office as they waited to be collected. And that's how I ended up spending the afternoon at the local cat sanctuary. I thought I would donate the food to them, you see.

I had to wait a long time to be attended to. There was a kitty emergency going on in the back. Apparently, some cat that had been dumped on the doorstep only two days before, was suddenly having kittens. It happens quite a lot, explained the receptionist. People dumping cats that are just about to give birth.

'What will happen to them?' I asked.

'Well, if they're cute they'll be homed. If they're not,' she made a slashing motion across her throat.

'You won't really have them put down?' I said in horror.

'More mouths to feed,' she said.

Anyway, while I was waiting to be attended to, a rather wonderful looking man walked into the waiting room. He was handsome in a gentleman farmer kind of way, all strong curly hair and great thick forearms. He marched up to the desk and attracted the receptionist's full attention straightaway. I'm afraid I just couldn't help straining to hear what he was about.

'I've given her 50 mils,' he said. 'She should sleep for another three hours or so.'

'Oh, thank you Doctor Farringdon. Mrs Smith will be ever so relieved that you managed to save her Miffy.'

Mr Gorgeous got ten extra lushness points instantly when I discovered that he was a vet! As Julie had once pointed out, even more money than a doctor and no scantily-clad female patients to catch his eye. Unless he had a thing about sheep, of course.

'Right, I'm off,' he told the receptionist. 'If you need me, give me a call.'

Then he turned to leave. But on the way out he caught my eye and hesitated by the door.

'Do I know you?' he asked.

I straightened myself up automatically.

'Me? Are you talking to me?' I squeaked.

'Yes. I'm sure I know you from somewhere.'

I shrugged. 'Well, I guess I have been pretty prominent in the local paper of late.'

'No. That's not it. I never read that rag. I'm sure we

met at a party. Or a club? Yes, a club! Now it's all coming
back to me.'

And it was coming back to me too. The girls' night out
I couldn't escape from. The gorilla. The epileptic fit. The
handsome vet who sorted everything out.

'You ran off.'

'I didn't mean to.'

'I was worried about you. You looked like you were
in shock.'

'I was embarrassed. But I've learned first aid since,
as a result,' I added in an attempt to save face. It was
almost true.

'That's good. I thought you looked kind.'

'Oh, she's very kind,' interrupted the receptionist.
'Look what she just brought in.' She showed Dr
Farringdon the cat food.

'I won a competition, but my cat just died,' I
explained.

'What a coincidence. One of my patients has just had
five kittens. Want to take one home?'

'Oh no,' I said. 'I mean what about the vet's bill.'

Dr Farringdon smiled. 'We could come to some
arrangement. In The Rotunda? Over a beer.'

I'm going to wear that red Versace dress . . .

Well, you didn't expect me to end up with Black
Beauty?

Flatmates

To Mum and Dad

ACKNOWLEDGEMENTS

Special thanks are due to David Garnett, Peter Hamilton and Helen Pisano for their professional guidance and support. Thanks also to my agent Antony Harwood, my editor Kate Lyall Grant and to Kate and Lee Arnold for the bridesmaid experience. Love and gratitude to Ryan, Vicky, Ed, the two Janes, Jools, Bill, Anna, Tom C., Nick, Laura, Kim, Gerry(!), Rico, No. 17 and Collin for their support, their printers and numerous free dinners. Finally, extra big thanks to Guy 'Biscuit-boy' Hazel for believing I could do it without reading a word and to Mum and Dad for not making me get a proper job.

CHAPTER ONE

How to make fatal pesto:
1. Prepare as ordinary pesto.
2. Leave dirty plate in the sink for up to a week.

The screaming started shortly after seven o'clock one ordinary Saturday night. Kerry, who was upstairs in the bathroom, froze in the act of brushing her hair and strained to catch the words stirred into the cacophony of terror. It was hard, for as usual the screaming was accompanied by the fervent whirring of a fast rotating wheel . . .

Fiona was on the exercise bike again. She usually started an argument then, as if speaking over the sound of the spinning gave her an excuse to raise her voice.

'I'm not saying it's you,' she was screaming. 'But it only takes a couple of seconds, for heaven's sake . . .' There was a sudden bleep and the whirring stopped. The bike stopwatch had measured twelve minutes exactly. 'No, I don't think I'm being pedantic, Linzi. You know dried pesto sets like glue and it's always me who has to come in after a hard day at work . . .'

Yes, thought Kerry, stress that.

'. . . to face an archaeological dig before I can find a single plate clean enough to put my toast on. It's not even as though I can scrape the remains of your lunch easily into the bin because that is always overflowing. Why do you always have to cram the pedal-bin to the point that when I try to get the bag out it splits and goes all over the floor? I got sodding spaghetti rings all over my new Pied-à-terre sandals last week. I certainly never eat spaghetti rings and I know that Kerry . . .'

Oh no, thought Kerry, putting down her brush. Don't bring me into this.

'I know that Kerry feels the same way about . . .'

Kerry bounced down the stairs and into the open-plan living room, stopping Fiona mid-flow before she could implicate her more.

'I've had my hair done,' Kerry said quickly to change the subject.

Fiona and Linzi broke off from arguing just long enough to say 'that's nice'.

'I only went in for a trim but then I decided "what the hell", I'll have the lot off. If I don't like it it'll always grow back, won't it? What do you think?'

Linzi looked up from her little nest she had made with her duvet on the sofa and smiled her approval. There was a tuft sticking up from behind Kerry's ear that made her look like a mandarin duck.

'*Très* Suzi Quatro.'

'Yes. Lovely,' added Fiona, grudgingly. Kerry had broken her stride. Fiona jumped off the exercise bike with an exaggerated sigh and went to slam a lasagne into the microwave. The volume on the television was turned back down again. The pesto incident was over, and this time there were no fatalities. Just.

Never ever ever live with your friends. You may well ask 'Who better to live with?' but, rest assured, there are millions of better people who you don't yet even know. Take Fiona, Linzi and Kerry; friends since their first day at senior school when Linzi borrowed Kerry's compass to stick Fiona in the thigh. Twelve years down the line, they felt ready to make it something more. To make the commitment of sharing a house. They thought they knew and liked each other well enough. Little did they know that all those hours spent fighting over who had the best collection of Bros posters had done nothing to prepare them for the agony of the itemised phone bill.

They had been at number 67, Artesia Road for almost a month. It was their first Greater London address. In fact, it was the first house they had seen in London, chosen in a blind panic because the letting agent had assured them that hundreds of people were queuing up to spend 75 per cent of their take-home pay on a place so compact and bijou that even the carpet lice had claustrophobia. And only seventeen minutes from the nearest tube station, the nice young man had stressed . . . If you were Linford Christie. Not that you could actually guarantee transport when you got that far since the nearest tube was on the Northern Line, which is the only part of the London Underground system that still runs on batteries. Not Duracell, of course.

The letting agent gave the girls just twelve minutes to make a life-changing decision.

But the house itself was OK. It was a thirties mid-terrace affair that had been refurbished by its owner in the late eighties and looked it. The two front rooms had been knocked through to create one marvellous cavernous living space that had plenty of potential for parties but would soon prove impossible to heat. A three-piece suite in bachelor-grey Draylon dominated the room and the walls had been stripped down to the bare brick for a rather chi-chi rustic effect. The kitchen was nice, though, and there was even a washing machine (with an overflow straight on to the terracotta tiled floor for convenience, which Fiona discovered to her horror on the day the pipes froze and the resulting flood ruined her brand-new suede boots).

Upstairs, number 67 was a rather peculiar mixture of bachelor-pad black and Laura Ashley. Linzi fell in love with the bathroom, which had two sinks, stripy wallpaper and a bulb-surrounded mirror. It put her in mind of post-sex soap opera scenes. Of cleaning your teeth while your hero is having a shave. The three bedrooms, however, were more accurately described as two bedrooms and a box room – no, make that a shoe-box room – the two bedrooms having double beds and space to put your pot-pourri; the box room being just too small to accommodate a single bed and still allow you to swing your hamster.

Bedrooms provided the focus for the first shared-house debate. Fiona and Linzi felt that the distribution of spoils was obvious. They were both dating. Kerry was not. So Fiona took the front room with the pink curtains and newish carpet. Linzi had the one at the back with the flowered wallpaper and the rocking chair and Kerry moved into the box room, with its dirty white walls and the crusted remains of the previous tenant's Blu-Tack. The fact that Linzi chucked her Latin lover, a visiting Italian language student, a week later, did not seem to offer an opportunity to re-examine the status quo. Kerry had to send most of her belongings back to her parents' house in Bristol and Fiona very kindly suggested that she should perhaps pay a whole pound less rent per week. And they would think about changing rooms at a later stage. Honest.

Anyway, where she slept at night was the least of Kerry's worries when she moved into Artesia Road. She wasn't just starting out in a new house; the Monday after moving in she started a new job as a trainee booker for a voice-over company called Verbal Tix. It wasn't exactly what her biology degree had prepared her for but the tiny Soho office looked nice enough and the money they were offering was OK for a beginner. Kerry thought it might be a route into television and dreamed of being discovered when having to step in and record a radio ad because one of her clients had gone sick.

Fiona had strolled into her rather more high-powered job straight after graduation. No one was surprised when she took up her position at the Japanese First Orient Bank and declined their generous offer of a year's deferred start to 'find herself' beforehand. She had never been the type to dream of six months' slumming it in India and the starting salary they offered her was the stuff of a politician's arms deal dreams. Linzi, on the other hand, had yet to join the rat-race proper. She had just finished another course in alternative therapy (was it shiatsu this time?) and was waiting for 'something to grab her, careerwise'. Her television producer parents were divorced and guilty and it seemed that she would be getting a double allowance for the rest of her golden life anyway. However, a month into the Artesia Road period there were rumblings that her father thought that, at the age of twenty-four and three-quarters, it was time Linzi got herself a 'proper job'. She signed up with a temping agency that specialised in supplying secretarial support to the advertising industry and tried to be out when they called.

So, things went happily enough for a while. The complicated telephone pad system where you had to write down who you called and for how long quickly went by the by, as did the rota for doing the cleaning and the washing-up.

Sometimes there might be a war of attrition over the pesto problem but Kerry would usually step in and wash up before the crockery, piled high in the sink, went crashing to the floor; and, when their periods weren't synchronising in a huge hormonal scream of a week, the girls would sometimes even sit around and think that they were lucky to be living with their pals. It saved bothering to go out and meet them after all . . .

Blind Date came on and Linzi turned the volume of the television back up to get the full force of the 'jokes'. Unable to get comfortable on either of the remaining armchairs, which were comfy in name only, Kerry wandered aimlessly into the kitchen where Fiona was scientifically prodding her lasagne with the tip of a sharp knife. She put the kettle on to make herself a cup of tea but the tea-bag jar was empty, again. The curly-edged rota on the fridge door suggested that it was Linzi's turn to refill it. Kerry would have to have coffee instead.

'Do you want a coffee?' she asked Fiona, who had decided that the lasagne was still half-cooked.

'No,' said Fiona. 'I've given coffee up.'

'Oh. Even decaff? Why?' Kerry asked disinterestedly.

'It aggravates your cellulite.'

'But you haven't got any cellulite.'

'I assure you I have.'

'Please don't start that again,' sighed Linzi. She had appeared at the kitchen door with an empty mug found beneath the sofa which was only slightly green at the bottom with mould. She rinsed it out beneath the cold tap until it looked almost hygienic. 'I'll have a coffee please,' she told Kerry. 'I don't give a toss about my bum.'

Fiona shot her a dangerous look. The kind of look that only the painfully thin can give the painfully thinner. As it was, neither of them needed to worry about their bums, thought Kerry sadly as she ladled coffee and sugar into two mugs. At school they had been known as the 'Twiglet Sisters'. Kerry herself had been 'Podge'. Now she had long given up preventative measures with regard to her own posterior and was relying largely on the magic of Lycra to get by.

'No, look at this!' Fiona was grabbing a thimbleful of thigh and roughly pulling it out to demonstrate her 'obesity'. 'I'm all wobbly!!!'

'For heaven's sake, Fiona, you couldn't make a fairy's pin-cushion out of that. You're not fat. You've got thighs like a pair of nutcrackers.'

'Nutcrackers? What do you mean, nutcrackers? Are you trying to say that I've got bandy legs?'

This was fairly typical of Fiona. If you told her she looked nice, she would only ask you why you hadn't said that yesterday. Now she was staring at the gap between her denim-clad thighs, trying to decide whether early ballet lessons had really turned her into some kind of physical freak. Linzi threw her a musty Christmas walnut that lived alone on the spice shelf and shouted, 'Crack that'. She was hardly renowned for her tact.

'So, what are you two doing tonight?' Kerry asked hurriedly to avert the brewing row.

'Nothing much,' shrugged Linzi.

'I'm going out with Tim,' said Fiona.

'Now there's a surprise.'

Tim was Fiona's boyfriend, a merchant banker with a regime of work hard, play hard and fall over after twelve pints on an average Friday night. Kerry and Linzi didn't really like him. Linzi even claimed to have seen him snogging a fair-haired gatecrasher at the Artesia Road house-warming party they'd had, but Fiona had countered that Linzi needed glasses and the incident had never been mentioned again. At least, not to Fiona's face.

'I've got a party to go to,' Kerry added casually, as she poured boiling water into the mugs. 'But I don't know whether I want to go or not.'

'Where is it?' asked Linzi.

'Battersea.'

Kerry stirred the coffee clockwise until all the nasty floating brown bits were dissolved.

'That's not far,' said Linzi.

'Well, distance isn't actually the issue. It's just that I won't really know anyone there.'

'Whose party is it?' Linzi asked. She had just fetched a tomato out of the fridge and was eating it like an apple. As she bit into it, pips spilled out and dribbled down the front of her shirt. 'Oh no.'

Linzi reached over the sink to grab a piece of kitchen roll. Fiona turned from the chopping board, where she was dicing a carrot into calorie-counted chunks, to see what was going on and her eyes suddenly widened with rage.

'For goodness' sake, Linzi!! You're wearing my shirt again. My bloody Nicole Farhi shirt. When did I say you could borrow it? No, don't do that!'

Linzi was already damping the kitchen roll beneath the warm tap and moving to apply her now wet-wipe to the stain. Fiona snatched the damp ball of paper from her hand.

'It's pure silk. It's got to be dry-cleaned . . .'

Here we go again. Kerry tactfully sneaked away from the kitchen and stole Linzi's place on the sofa. She needed more sugar in her coffee but she wasn't prepared to risk going back into the fray.

'Take it off!!' Fiona was shrieking.

'You never wear it!!' came Linzi's reply.

'Take it off!!'

'It doesn't even suit you!'

'What do you mean? It looks perfect with my hair!!!'

God, thought Kerry, was it always going to be like this? She had hoped that such kitchen-sink nightmares would end when she moved away from Bristol and her sisters. But, no. This was worse. And her mother wasn't even around to intervene. Kerry flicked through the television channels with the remote control. There was a buzz at the door. It was Tim. He'd come early. Hearing the sound of his baritone voice, Fiona switched suddenly from screaming harridan to sweetness and light and whisked him straight upstairs to her lair. Talk about saved by the bell. Linzi slunk back into the sitting room when she was sure that the worst of the danger had passed.

'Lend me a shirt for tonight will you, Kerry? I'm meeting Eddy in the pub at ten and everything I own is in the wash.'

'You can wear my black one from Oasis,' Kerry said graciously. 'But only if you promise to come to this party with me first.'

Linzi looked down at the pink stain on Fiona's pale blue silk. The Nicole Farhi was unwearable and she didn't have a thing in the world of her own that didn't smell of fag ash or armpit.

'And I'll let you off that tenner you owe me from last weekend.'

What choice did Linzi have?

'Battersea, wasn't it?' she replied. 'Shall I call a cab?'

CHAPTER TWO

You've heard of the Bermuda Triangle of course. But I bet you didn't know that there's an area of Clapham Common that has exactly the same effect on passing cars. The taxi company that Linzi called to get a ride from Balham to Battersea promised a quick service, friendly drivers and nice clean vehicles. It didn't, however, promise that it would actually get you anywhere near your chosen destination in that double-quick time.

Clapham Common seemed to be a stumbling block for most of the minicab drivers of Balham. Inevitably speaking barely a word of English, they would turn up on time, claim to know where they were taking you, perhaps even point out the road you were looking for in their battered *A to Z*, and three-quarters of an hour later you would be on the wrong side of Clapham Common, getting out of the car to walk the rest of your journey, to the tune of approximately fifteen pounds.

'He's going the wrong way, isn't he?' Linzi hissed nervously. Indeed, he was. The cab driver had bypassed Battersea and was heading straight for Wandsworth instead.

'Queenstown Road?' Kerry reiterated hopefully.

'Yes, I know, Quinston Road,' said the driver with a sigh. He drove on towards Wandsworth Common and turned the stereo up pointedly.

'Kerry, he is still going the wrong way,' Linzi persisted. 'Why don't you tell him?'

'Why don't you tell him?' Kerry rejoined.

'Because I don't know the address of the party.'

Kerry cleared her throat, but that didn't stop her next sentence coming out as a strangled gasp. 'I said Queenstown Road,' she gurgled.

'Yays, I know it,' said the cab driver again, fixing her with a fierce glare in the rearview mirror. 'Quinston Road, I know. I know.'

'I don't think so, actually,' Linzi interrupted. 'It's over on the other side of the Common, mate. You're going the wrong way.'

Linzi leaned over into the front passenger seat and snatched up the grubby *A to Z*. She flicked through the tattered pages angrily. Most of central London was missing or had been Sellotaped back in upside-down. She eventually found what she was looking for, with no help from the largely absent index, and jabbed at it with a vicious finger. 'Look, Queenstown Road, mate. There. It's in Battersea. You're taking us the wrong bloody way.'

'I not know this area,' the cab driver protested. 'I only come to England for to do my cartography degree.'

'Oh, Christ on a bike,' sighed Linzi. 'You obviously haven't had time to go to many of your lectures, have you? Look, turn right here. At this next corner.' She tried to get him back on course. 'And when you get to those traffic lights, turn left, then take a left again.'

The driver threw a right at the lights.

'Left, I said.' Linzi pointed wildly. 'Left at the lights . . . Oh, bloody hell. This is ridiculous. Stop the car,' she shouted. The driver pulled up abruptly without bothering to turn into the kerb. Linzi opened her door and pulled Kerry out on to the pavement after her. The taxi was now blocking the traffic, a queue of irate drivers already forming behind.

'Three pounds fifty. Three pounds fifty!!!' the driver protested with an open hand. He wasn't going to move until he got paid.

'You can sing for it, mate,' Linzi told him, flicking the V-sign as she stalked off down the road. Kerry froze at the taxi's door and fumbled for the right money. She had a solitary fiver in her faded Body Shop 'Save the Endangered Species' purse.

'I got no change,' said the cab driver rudely when she handed the crumpled note over.

'Have it,' Kerry whispered in a fluster. The man in the huge car behind the taxi was sounding his horn and making her too nervous to wait for any change. The cab driver slowly folded the note into his wallet and tutted. Kerry had to run to catch Linzi up.

'We should have walked in the first place,' Linzi muttered.

'Three pounds fifty indeed!! He's got a nerve asking for that. How much did you give him?'

'I gave him a pound,' Kerry lied.

'That's a pound too much. You're soft in the head, you are, Kerry Keble. The whole point of taking a cab is that it gets you to where you want to go with no hassle. You're not supposed to have to navigate as well. He should have given us a pound for teaching him a new route.'

'He's not from the area,' Kerry whined. 'And the one-way system can be really confusing if you don't know it.'

'Its not his job to be confused,' Linzi sighed. 'Honestly, Kerry, if you don't stop being such a soft touch I'm going to go straight home right now, shirt or no borrowed shirt.'

'I just didn't see the point in getting angry with him, that's all,' Kerry squeaked. But her voice was lost in the din of the Saturday-night traffic heading down Queenstown Road and into town.

The girls finished their journey to the party on foot in almost half the time it had taken them to circumnavigate Clapham Common in the cab driver's old blue Astra. They recognised the venue because one happy reveller was already hanging out of a downstairs window, puking his guts out, and the creamy yellow splashback of his vomit very nearly got Linzi on her suede knee-high boots. Fiona's suede knee-high boots to be more precise. The ones that had already barely survived the washing-machine disaster.

'Kerry, this had better be a good one,' Linzi hissed as she skipped out of the way of the chunder fountain.

She couldn't guarantee it. Kerry suddenly wished she had come alone. At least then she knew that she wouldn't have moaned to herself all the way home. Linzi was so difficult to please. She and her trendy aromatherapy friends were an entertainment Gestapo, unimpressed by anything falling short of Elvis Presley coming back from the dead to hold a reunion party for the great and the good at the Grosvenor House Hotel. A house-party in Queenstown Road was hardly likely to cut the mustard. Blinking back the urge to run back to Artesia Road and bury herself under her duvet, Kerry quickly pressed the doorbell, which was hanging loose from a single wire.

*   *   *

The party was being thrown by one of Kerry's clients at 'Verbal Tix – your one-stop voice-shop'. Lance Sylvester had been a big name in the early eighties. He had played the teenage tearaway son in a television sit-com that had run for almost three years. During that time his roguish face had graced the gossip pages of the tabloids daily and he'd been voted a 'top-ten hunk' by the readers of *Just Seventeen*. On her first day at Verbal Tix, as she leafed idly through the details of the artistes who she was going to be representing, Kerry had been thrilled to find the career résumé of Lance Sylvester among them. And she had been ecstatic when he called in that morning to say that he would drop by the office to meet her later that very day. When Lance turned up, however, Kerry barely recognised the man who had played such an important part in her third-form fantasies. He was shorter than she had imagined and his hair, dyed bright blue for his role in *Family Affair*, had all but fallen out. As had half of one of his front teeth which he couldn't afford to get capped. Lance had barely worked at all since a couple of criminal cameos for *The Bill* in 1989. It was obvious that he drank like a fish these days and his hand felt just like one when he tried to rub it across Kerry's backside.

'Ignore him and he'll go away,' was her boss Leon's advice.

But he didn't. Lance Sylvester popped up at the office every day, as early as his hangover would allow, in the vain hope that someone wanted him to do his American accent for a cornflakes commercial or something paying even half as well. And Kerry knew that if she didn't go to his birthday party, Lance would make her life a misery by harping on about how good it had been for at least the next five weeks, if not for the rest of her days on this earth. Her head ached with the nuisance of it all. There's nothing like having to enjoy yourself under duress.

As he opened the front door to Kerry and Linzi, Lance was already in a state of advanced inebriation. 'Where have you been, Kelly-man?' he slurred as he slumped against the door-frame with a bourbon bottle clenched in his hand. 'The party's been going on since three o'clock this afternoon . . . Hey,' he perked up, suddenly noticing Linzi, 'you didn't tell me you were bringing your sister.'

'Linzi, this is Lance Sylvester. Lance, this is Linzi, my house-mate.'

Lance took Linzi by the hand and kissed it theatrically.

'I've been on the telly, love,' he told her as his mouth twisted into a leer. 'Fancy a shag?'

Linzi graciously forced out a laugh.

He ushered them into the purple-painted hallway. Kerry with a wave. Linzi by the old hand-on-bum control. She removed his fingers from her bottom casually, as if she were dealing with someone below the age of three who didn't really know any better. But she made sure she cracked them as she did so, and when Lance hopped in front of the girls to guide them into the fray, he was blowing on his digits as if they might be broken.

'He is disgusting,' Linzi hissed to Kerry. 'And he's wearing a Level 42 T-shirt, for God's sake.'

'I think he knows the drummer.'

'Yeah, right. Look, let's find a phone, call a proper cab, and go to meet Eddy now. What do you say, Kez?'

'I say I've just got to say "hi" to my boss before we can go.'

'Say "hi" to your boss?' Linzi mimicked. 'You absolute bum-licker. Make it quick, eh?'

'I'll see what I can do.'

Lance led them into the sitting room, where the party had already fragmented into little cliques which hung around the walls as though the centre of the floor might be carpet over quicksand. Almost blind in the ineffective ambient lighting, Kerry nearly tripped over Lance's girlfriend, who looked at the arm belonging to Lance which had wound its way around Kerry's waist as though she might have been able to help it. Tactfully, Kerry wriggled free of Lance's octopus grip and he made a dangerous sideways lurch, until his empty hand hit a table which put a rather abrupt stop to his listing.

'Drink?' he asked. At least, that was what it sounded like.

They nodded politely.

They weren't going to survive this party without it.

Lance stumbled off in the direction of the kitchen, taking the bottle of Chardonnay they had bought for personal consumption with him. They wouldn't see that again.

'Can you believe that people still have this stuff on their walls?' Linzi was off on a rant already, this time picking literally

at the woodchip wallpaper. It had been painted over with a
very dark red emulsion that made the room look like the
lair of Count Dracula after a night of projectile vomiting and
each picked-off chip revealed a nasty, bright white wound
beneath. Kerry tried to slap Linzi's hand away as Lance re-
emerged from the kitchen with a different bottle and two very
smeary glasses. Linzi casually leaned her hand over the bald
spot she had so recently made and even managed a wink of
thanks.

'Nice place you have here, Lance,' she told him.

'Fanks,' he slurred. 'I interior-designed it myself.'

'Yes, it's very interesting. Very . . . um, vibrant. I can see that
your personality is stamped all over the place . . .'

Kerry rewarded Linzi's flattery with a sharp dig in the ribs.
But she needn't have worried because Lance had missed out
on Linzi's lack of sincerity altogether. 'I'm gonna do the dining
room next,' he told her excitedly. 'In maroon with a gold trim.
It's gonna look quite baroque, don't you think.'

'Oh yes. *Très* baroque,' said Linzi sweetly.

Lance poured each of the girls a glass of the very best
Lambrusco Frizzante. Linzi held hers stiffly, without taking so
much as a sip. She claimed she was waiting for the bubbles to go
down but when Lance had to leave them to answer the door, she
poured her drink straight back whence it had come. A cigarette
end was already floating in the bit that remained at the bottom
of the bottle. 'I'm not drinking that piss,' she told Kerry in no
uncertain terms. 'And this is the kind of party where it probably
is piss. Lance looks just the type who would urinate in a bottle
for a laugh.'

'Oh, he's all right really.'

'All right really? That man is one down from a rat. What did
he do with our Chardonnay?'

'You didn't have to come with me,' Kerry protested.

'You said that if I did, I wouldn't have to pay you back that
tenner I owe you from last Friday. I had to come, Kerry, because
I don't get paid until the end of next week. Besides, I quite like
this shirt.' She smoothed the clingy black material down over
the waistband of her jeans.

'Yeah, it suits you,' Kerry said grudgingly. She hadn't worn it
at all since bringing it back from the shop. It had been bought

in a bit of a hurry and when Kerry got it home, she discovered that she couldn't do the middle button up.

Kerry took a sip of her Lambrusco and decided to her horror that Linzi was probably right about the piss. She put her glass down discreetly on a table covered with the detritus of a buffet. Two cans of Special Brew in a Threshers bag nestled behind a washing-up bowl full of potato salad. At least Kerry hoped it was potato salad. She fought shy of picking up a fork and finding out. Linzi snatched up the abandoned cans with glee. 'I hope Lance wasn't saving these for later,' she laughed. She handed one over to Kerry. 'At least they're still sterile and sealed.'

It didn't taste that much better than the piss but, at eleven per cent or whatever the alcohol content of the damn stuff was, Kerry figured that by the time she had finished the first half of the can, she wouldn't be able to taste the second half anyway. Linzi leaned back against the woodchip and continued to survey the party with a jaundiced eye from her sartorial highground. She tutted in despair at a forty-something gothic in lacy leggings who was picking over the remains of the cheeseboard. Nothing and nobody had met with Linzi's approval so far that night.

'Have you spotted your boss yet?' she moaned. 'Because I am more than ready to go.'

Lance staggered past again. This time, his eyes were barely open. He was wiping his nose and sniffing hard.

'Having a good time, girls?' he asked.

'Yeah, yeah. Great time.' Though obviously not as great as the time he was having, thought Kerry. 'Where's Leon?'

'Leon's over there,' Lance told her, waving an arm in the vague direction of the other side of the room. Kerry strained through the smoke to catch a glimpse of her boss. He had indeed appeared and was standing by the window, flanked by two smaller guys. One of them was wearing a beanie cap on his largely bald head. That must be Sam, Leon's boyfriend. Leon had mentioned him a few times, and though he hadn't really described his paramour's physical attributes at great length, his anecdotes about him were usually preceded by 'that bald bastard'. Leon himself looked incredible, as usual, in a dark blue velvet jacket over straight cut jet-black jeans. He had said that he was going to get his hair cut that weekend and the shorter look made the most of his textbook handsome face. Leon was the best thing about

Kerry's job. He was unlike any boss she had met before. You could actually have a laugh with Leon . . . not to mention the fact that she fancied him like mad.

'There he is,' Kerry whispered. 'That's my boss.' Linzi made a face that suggested she approved.

'Whooah! He's a bit gorgeous, isn't he?'

'I'm afraid so. And utterly unavailable.'

'Never say never, Kez.'

Catching Kerry's eye, Leon motioned them over, looking almost relieved to see another familiar face. When they reached him, he kissed Kerry on both cheeks. She stepped backwards with a blush. The sweet smell of his expensive aftershave clung briefly to her skin.

'This is Sam,' Leon said, introducing the bald one of his companions. Suspicions confirmed. 'And this is Andrew.' Sam and Andrew acknowledged the girls briefly but were quickly back in conversation between themselves.

'Great party, eh?' Leon asked.

'I think the answer to that question has to be "eh",' said Linzi.

'Oh, yeah. Leon,' Kerry interrupted, 'this is my housemate, Linzi. I bribed her to come with me.'

'I didn't think we paid you that much,' Leon laughed. 'How long have you been here?'

'Ten minutes.'

'We've been here since eight,' Leon said, rolling his eyes. 'I didn't think that Sam would want to stay for one second but then he bumped into Andrew and now I can't persuade him to leave. Andrew works for Sony. I think Sam's angling for a three album deal.'

'Any chance?' asked Kerry.

Sam was a singer. He had actually been the voice of a small frog on the soundtrack of the latest Disney cartoon and now he was trying to break into the dance scene.

'I think not,' Leon smiled dryly. 'Little does he realise that Andrew is low down in accounts.'

'Perhaps he just fancies him,' said Linzi, not realising her *faux-pas*. Kerry stared at her meaningfully but Linzi wasn't even looking in her direction anymore. The front-door bell had just rung again and, ever hopeful, Linzi wanted to see who was coming in. 'Wow,' she murmured suddenly. 'Things are looking up.'

Linzi drew Kerry's attention to the back view of a tall, dark-haired man, wearing jeans clinging tighter than a skin graft, who was leaning over an unsteady three-legged coffee table while attempting to roll a spliff. He was more than a little drunk, and the paper kept slipping from his fingers and unfurling again to lie flat. He tucked his long curly hair behind his ear to stop it from breaking his concentration and began the operation once more. Linzi affected a mock swoon. Kerry tipped her head to one side in appraisal and had to agree, 'Not bad from the back.'

'Not bad? He's incredible, Kez!'

Leon was looking in the same direction now, to find out who or what had attracted their attention.

'Oh, no,' he groaned. 'Please tell me it's not Gaetano.'

'Gaetano?' the girls echoed at once.

'His parents are Italian,' Leon explained.

'How exotic,' said Linzi.

'He's up his own arse,' said Leon.

'Wish he was up mine,' Sam quipped as he passed them by with an anaemic-looking sausage on a stick.

'So, you know him?' Linzi asked excitedly, clutching the lapels of Leon's velvet jacket. 'He's completely gorgeous. You've got to tell me everything you know.'

'I don't really know him, Linzi. We've only been introduced a couple of times,' Leon said warily. 'Sam knows him far better than I do.'

'What does he do?' Linzi asked Sam.

'He's a drummer,' said Sam.

'A musician?' asked Linzi.

'Well,' Leon murmured for the benefit of Kerry, 'he's certainly someone who bangs things. But he's only a drummer in the evenings. By day he works in some trendy clothes shop on the Kings Road.'

'He's the most amazing man I've ever seen. You've got to introduce me to him,' Linzi begged.

'Well, I don't really . . .'

'Introduce me or I'll die . . .'

As it was, Gaetano's attention had already been attracted by the bizarre sight of a girl sinking to her knees at the feet of

Leon Landesman. He raised a beautiful eyebrow quizzically as Leon beckoned him across. Gaetano walked towards them with the feline grace of someone who had been brought up on the catwalk. In fact, the proudest moment of his life had been almost getting a casting for a Dolce & Gabbana shoot.

'Look at that walk,' Linzi swooned.

'He used to be a model,' Sam chipped in lasciviously. 'Once did an underwear catalogue that I keep under my pillow for lonely nights.'

Linzi licked her lips to buff up her lipstick and slowly rose to her feet again. 'I like him more and more.'

'Gaetano, this is Linzi,' Leon said smoothly. 'She was just demonstrating the flexibility of her knees.'

'Very impressive,' Gaetano murmured.

'I like to keep myself limber,' said Linzi.

Kerry covered her mouth with her hand and hiccuped back a laugh. Sam turned away in disgust.

'Are you a dancer?' Gaetano continued.

'Are you asking?' asked Linzi.

Kerry rolled her eyes.

'If something good comes on then maybe we could . . .'

The heat that flared between them was palpable. Kerry looked at her watch as an excuse to avert her gaze. It was almost ten. 'Aren't we supposed to be meeting Eddy in the pub?' she asked in desperation.

Linzi stared at Kerry as though she didn't understand her. 'Eddy? Oh, yeah. Eddy. You can go if you want but he won't be on his own, so you really needn't worry about standing him up. I'm staying here.' She turned her attention straight back to Gaetano. Linzi wasn't about to leave now. Poor old Eddy was already the flavour of last week. Subject closed.

The ear-splitting music suddenly shrank to a slow, sensuous grind. Linzi snaked her way out into the middle of the room to dance with her hands on Gaetano's slinky hips. Kerry turned back to Leon, who was smiling sadly. Sam and Andrew had left the room altogether while Leon's attention had been focused on introducing the girls to Gaetano.

'Well, I guess I must be staying then,' Kerry told Leon. 'Fancy another drink?'

He shook his head. 'Not for me. I'm driving. But I think I

spotted another can of Tennants Extra over there by the buffet. That is what you're drinking isn't it?'

'Oh, yeah.' Kerry blushed when she remembered the can she had been holding. It rather lacked the sophistication of a real Martini with olive. 'I think I've had enough of this actually,' she said, shaking the dregs. 'It's horrible when it starts to get all flat and warm.'

Leon nodded. 'I can't touch the stuff myself.'

'I thought South Africans were weaned on lager.'

'There's lager and there's lager, Kez.'

Kerry went to put the empty can down and nearly missed the table. Either that stuff was seriously strong or she was getting pathetic in her old age. When she had righted herself, she saw that Leon was looking at his watch again. Obviously pretty bored. Kerry searched the deepest recesses of her brain for something remotely clever to say. Leon gazed over her shoulder to the spot where he had last seen Sam. Pinching herself on the thigh through her pocket in an attempt to restore some semblance of sobriety to her head, Kerry flipped through a mental Rolodex of suitable party subjects to broach with your homosexual boss. She never had this kind of trouble when she was at work.

'You look really pissed off,' she announced suddenly. It wasn't exactly an accomplished opening gambit.

Leon turned back towards her with a weakish smile.

'Do I? I don't feel pissed off,' he said.

'Well, you're doing a good impression of someone who is. Come on, Leon. This is meant to be a party. Smile.' She jigged about on the spot and was vaguely aware that she sounded like the kind of person she often wanted to punch. 'Party! Party!' she added lamely.

'It isn't exactly where we planned to be tonight,' Leon sighed.

'Really? I thought that Lance Sylvester's soirées were the only place to be any night.'

'Right,' said Leon. 'If the alternative is purgatory. You know, it was a year ago tonight that I first met Sam at the "O" Bar. So I guess you could say that today is our anniversary, though he didn't stop sleeping with his last boyfriend until we had been seeing each other for three months.'

'Oh.'

'Yeah. Sam got me a surprise present,' Leon continued. 'He

bought us two tickets on Eurostar to Paris. He's got a friend there who was going to lend us his apartment in Pigalle for the weekend. Sam had it all planned. Dinner on a boat floating down the Seine. Champagne breakfast looking out on the Eiffel Tower. He was really excited about it.'

'I would be too. What went wrong?'

'I couldn't go. I can't risk travelling through customs at the moment.'

'Why not? South Africans don't need a visa to go to France do they?'

'Getting into France wouldn't have been the problem, Kez. The problem would have been getting back in here. I've got two days left on my visa.'

'Two days? You're kidding. Then what?'

'I don't know. I'll think of something.'

'You'll have to get married to a British citizen,' she joked.

'That's the best idea I've heard so far,' Leon sniffed. 'But I can't see the union of Mr and Mr Landesman going down too well with immigration. Can you? Look, let's stop talking about this or I'll go into a decline. This is, after all, a party and you don't go to a party to stand in a corner and moan. Let's go and moan in the kitchen instead. By the way, Kez, what have you done to your hair?'

'Oh,' she put a hand to her tuft. 'I had it cut this afternoon. Does it look really bad?'

'No, it doesn't look bad at all. In fact it really suits you. I didn't know you had cheekbones. And I love that shirt. Green brings out the colour in your eyes.'

'Really?' Kerry felt her throat tightening at the thought of Leon looking at her closely enough to notice anything more about her eyes than that she had the usual two. 'Do you think so?'

'Yeah, they're totally emerald. Look, I think I will have another drink after all. Do you want me to get something for you?'

Kerry shook her head. His flattery had left her barely able to talk. When he disappeared into the kitchen, she sneaked a look at her reflection in the darkened window. Cheekbones? She'd certainly never noticed those either. While she was checking out their existence, Leon returned from the kitchen empty handed.

'Changed my mind. There's nothing drinkable left.'

Kerry still hadn't quite regained her composure. She looked at her shoes and wished she had cleaned them. 'You've had your hair cut too,' she said suddenly.

'Yeah,' said Leon. 'Highlights my receding hairline.'

Soon it was after two in the morning. There was nothing left to drink and the party had degenerated to the stage where people were sleeping over most of the horizontal surfaces. The host himself had passed out in the bath a couple of hours earlier, much to the disgust of his female guests who became too shy to use the loo. Leon glanced at his watch for the millionth time, and scanned the room once more for Sam, who was still nowhere to be seen.

'I think I might head off soon,' he told Kerry. 'Do you want a lift?'

She nodded eagerly. 'If you've got enough room . . .'

'There'll be enough room. Sam seems to have left without me.'

'But what about Linzi and Gaetano?'

Linzi and Gaetano were sitting on the window-sill. They had danced themselves into a near frenzy of lust and now Linzi was sensuously tracing the lines of Gaetano's palm with her fingers. She was probably telling him, 'You're going to wake up next to a beautiful dark-haired girl.' It was an old and over-used trick but still one of the best.

'I'm afraid we'll have to leave them behind. I've only got one spare helmet.'

'Spare helmet?' said Kerry.

'Yeah, I ride a bike. You knew that?'

'I think I remember you saying so but . . . I mean, when you asked me if I wanted a lift, I assumed you must have a car as well. I've never been on the back of a bike, Leon. I wouldn't know what to do.'

'You don't have to do anything. You just have to hang on to me. It's easy.'

Kerry looked at her thin cotton trousers.

'But I'm not wearing leathers. What if I fall off?'

'You won't fall off. I'm not wearing leathers either, am I? I'll take it really slowly, I promise.' Kerry still looked uneasy. 'You don't have to if you really don't want to, though.'

'No, no,' Kerry protested, feeling her heart begin to flutter against the roof of her mouth. 'I'd love to have a go. Got to live dangerously some time. I'll just tell Linzi where I'm going.'

'I don't think she'll miss you.' Leon steered Kerry away from the window where Linzi and Gaetano were now quite seriously entwined. Linzi had given up tracing the lines on his palm and was instead languorously tracing the outline of his left ear with her long, wet tongue. 'You ready?' Leon reached below the table to find the helmets he had stashed there earlier. 'It's Sam's,' he sighed. 'So you might find it a little bit big.'

'How will he get home?' Kerry asked.

'As far as I'm concerned,' said Leon, 'he can walk.'

Leon's fox-eyed Yamaha 750 waited patiently outside Lance's house like a sleek horse seen through an acid haze. Leon put on his helmet, and helped Kerry fasten hers beneath her chin. Then he climbed on and waited for her to clamber up behind him. She felt a little strange about putting her arms around his narrow waist, but when he fired the engine up she had no choice but to cling on so tightly through fear that she probably left fingermarks.

CHAPTER THREE

Leon took the long way home and by the time they had circled Clapham Common about six times Kerry was almost enjoying herself. At one point, she very nearly opened her eyes wide enough to look at the view. But the best part of the journey by far was its end. As Leon turned the bike into Artesia Road, Gaetano and Linzi could be seen stumbling towards number 67, leaning heavily on each other for support. Leon pulled the bike into the kerb with a growl just behind them and helped Kerry climb off to stand, jelly-legged but proud, on the pavement.

'You OK?' he wrapped an arm around her shoulders and tipped her face towards him. 'You look completely white.'

'Nice bike, man,' Gaetano gave the bike a cursory once-over and muttered something about the Triumph Bonneville he had been restoring for the past eight years. Linzi, who knew nothing about wheels except the colours that she liked them in, was duly impressed. Kerry took off the borrowed helmet and tried to shake her hair loose as casually as if she rode a bike to the corner shop on a daily basis.

'That was great, Leon, thanks,' she said. Now that it has stopped, she added to herself.

'You fancy a quick spin?' Leon asked Gaetano.

'I think he might want to come in for a coffee first.' Linzi wanted to get Gaetano in off the street. She could see her charms fading rapidly beside the sleek shiny lines of the Yamaha. Leon declined the coffee and Gaetano reluctantly declined the ride, much to Linzi's joy and Kerry's disappointment. Gaetano shrugged and mentioned "some other time". Leon got back on to the bike and was gone with a roar before Kerry realised that he had finally said goodbye.

'I can't believe I did that,' she murmured.

'Neither can I,' said Linzi. 'You're usually such a chicken.'

Gaetano returned his attentions to the next best thing after a motorbike. Linzi purred. She had won. It appeared that he would be staying for the duration of the night, after all.

Now it was beginning to rain. The three remaining revellers huddled for shelter in the tiny porch of number 67 while Kerry fumbled to find her keys at the bottom of her deep, black PVC bag. Linzi never remembered her keys, whether she was out with one of her housemates, or not. Her subsequent tendency to wake the whole house up in the middle of the night had been the source of many a bitter breakfast argument.

'Hurry up,' Linzi complained as Kerry pulled out a set of keys only to discover that they were the keys to her office when she tried to get them in the door. 'I'm freezing to death out here.'

Gaetano obligingly wrapped his arms around her to keep her warm, then he tucked his freezing fingers beneath the hem of Linzi's borrowed shirt and she shrieked with the shock of his cold touch on her warm flesh. 'Stop it! No! No! No!'

'Sssh!!' Kerry put a finger to her lips and eased open the door. 'I don't think you ought to risk getting any further on to the wrong side of Fiona tonight.'

'Oh, she won't have heard that,' Linzi nearly managed to whisper. 'Not over Tim's snoring. You must have heard him snoring, Kez. Poor you. It's wonder you can sleep at all, having to have the room next to them . . . I tell you what, I'm sure Tim's related to this pig my grandad once had down on the . . .'

'Ssssh.' Kerry put her finger to her lips again. The sound of tinkling laughter from the sitting room suggested that Fiona and Tim were not yet in bed.

'My grandfather used to keep pigs,' Linzi was explaining to Gaetano. 'Big fat pink ones with black spots. Gloucestershire Old Spots, I think they were called. So I know a lot about them.' Gaetano was so entranced with the pig story that he almost tripped over the front step.

Kerry was right. Tim and Fiona weren't in bed. Instead, they were huddled together on the sofa beneath a duvet. When her housemates walked into the room, Fiona giggled and clasped her section of the cover tightly beneath her arms. They were obviously naked beneath the Habitat-covered quilt. Linzi moved to steer Gaetano immediately up the stairs to her room. Kerry averted her eyes and rushed to the kitchen to get one last glass of water before she followed them upstairs herself. It was so embarrassing, Kerry thought, as Fiona and Tim continued to whisper and giggle. Why couldn't they have stayed in Fiona's room instead of flaunting their sex lives all over the house?

But suddenly the sofa lovers were on their feet, with the duvet still wrapped around them, swaying unsteadily from side to side like a giant, drunken sausage roll.

'Ladies and gentlemen,' Tim boomed loudly, as he swung a champagne bottle and prepared to pop the cork. 'Please be upstanding for the bride and groom.'

Linzi and Gaetano stopped halfway up the stairs and peered down over the banister. Kerry stood quietly in the doorway of the kitchen, sipping from her glass.

'What?'

The cork exploded loudly from the champagne bottle and ricocheted against the bare brick wall.

'Please raise your glasses!' Tim continued. They were staggering about in their duvet cocoon. Fiona was giggling, trying hard not to fall out. 'Ladies and gentlemen . . .'

'What on earth have you done? What's going on?' Linzi ran back down the stairs to hear the news.

Fiona raised her glass triumphantly.

'Tim and I are getting engaged.'

Two more bottles of champagne later, Kerry finally dragged on her plaid pyjamas and slipped between the cold covers of her narrow single bed. If she stretched herself into a star shape she could almost touch all four walls of the tiny room at once. It had become a bit of a ritual, just to check that her life hadn't shrunk a little since the morning. It hadn't. Unless her arms were getting shorter too.

What an evening it had turned out to be. The last thing anyone had expected was for Fiona and Tim to get engaged. The odds on were only just shorter than those on Kerry winning the lottery. Things had been more than a little one-sided between the future Mr and Mrs Harper lately. In fact, Kerry couldn't recall

Tim having phoned Artesia Road at all since they'd moved in. Instead, Fiona was always chasing him around, calling him up, going over to his place. Oh well. It was nice to see Fiona happy for once. So happy that she hadn't even protested when Gaetano fished his gear out of his pocket and skinned up a celebratory spliff in the strict no-smoking household. In fact, Kerry was sure that Fiona had almost smiled indulgently when Tim got completely ratted and asked Gaetano to be his best man.

Kerry sighed. In the next room, she could hear Fiona and Tim giggling again, then moaning, then groaning in the throes of mutual ecstasy. It was a wonder that Tim could even get it up after all the champagne he had drunk. From the other end of the house, Linzi was giving out a strangely high-pitched scream. Kerry pulled the duvet up to her neck and tried to cover her ears with the stretchy white Alice band she used to prevent her fringe from causing forehead zits in the night. Alone in the box room again, while all around her the world was making love. That, it seemed, was the story of her life.

The last time Kerry had slept with a man had been during her final term at university. That was almost three years ago now but the episode with Andrew was probably best forgotten anyway. She had met him in a seminar on osmosis when he asked if he could borrow a piece of her notepaper. They went for a coffee after the lecture and said 'goodbye' at four o'clock the next morning. Kerry thought she was heading for a perfect romance. She fancied him like mad and they even seemed to have a lot in common. He was the only man she had ever met who liked Roxy Music for a start.

It all fell apart when they decided to go to bed after six weeks of fairly chaste snogging.

Once he had undressed her, Andrew had put a pillow over her face and tried to carry on fumbling.

'Hey, what are you doing?' Kerry had thrown the pillow off. Trust her luck to land herself with the Southampton suffocator. 'Are you trying to kill me or what?'

'No,' he told her quite plainly. 'It's just that if I cover your face up I can pretend that you're Sonia.' Sonia was his ex-girlfriend. 'I'm sorry, Kerry, but it's the only way I can get a hard-on.'

Kerry made her excuses and left.

It had been a long time before she could think about that

particular disaster and laugh, though Linzi and Fiona laughed about it on a regular basis of course. Kerry hoped she would never be that stupid again. The next man for her would be someone really special. Someone without all that emotional baggage. And someone who was at least reasonably gorgeous. Leon had the right face for a start.

Leon Landesman, Kerry sighed to herself. If she had to draw a picture of a perfect man . . . He was six feet tall, not too big, like the six-foot-five rower called Ryan who had given her a crick in the neck. He was dark and handsome, not preternaturally pale like the ginger-haired accountant with no eyebrows that Fiona was forever trying to persuade her to date. He rode a motorbike, not an embarrassing push-bike with Kelloggs Frosties stickers like the bloke she had accidentally picked up by the broccoli in Safeway. And he was gay. Not camp as a row of tents but gay as a gay thing none the less.

Kerry screwed up the picture she had been painting in her mind.

Was it really too much to ask for? A man who was handsome, witty and straight? Didn't Linzi have any spares? Kerry suddenly saw herself ten years down the line, alone in a basement flat with three mangy cats. Perhaps she should have stayed with Andrew? After a few months she probably would have been grateful for the pillow-thing herself. Or Ryan? Had he really been that bad? All that stretching up to kiss him was probably good for her posture. And what did she have against ginger hair? That accountant probably wouldn't have any hair at all eventually.

Kerry wondered if she still had the telephone number of the deputy warehouse manager with the Frosties-stickered bike. These were desperate times.

'I just don't want to be on my own,' she murmured to whoever it was that was supposed to listen. 'Please don't let me end up on my own.'

Number 67 had at last fallen silent. Kerry rolled on to her back and looked up at the shadow of her round paper lampshade. She wondered how long it could possibly last; this barren plateau in her love life, this plateau in the decline of Fiona and Tim. And Linzi with Gaetano? Sleeping with him already? That girl was such a tart . . . Oh well. Kerry closed her eyes and began to count sheep.

But moments later it started again. This time on the other side of Kerry's bare-walled room. Kerry stuffed her head beneath her pillow. Now even the weirdoes next door were having their annual shag.

CHAPTER FOUR

For Kerry, the arrival of Monday morning was almost a relief.

Sunday had been unbearable. Woken at seven by the renewed sexual celebrations of the newly engaged Fiona and Tim. Put off her breakfast by the tantric tongue tangling of Gaetano and Linzi. Unable to concentrate on the Sunday papers because of the creaking bed directly above the dining table. Unable even to go for a walk across the Common without being reminded that she was on her own by the good people of Clapham with their bloody public displays of affection.

She considered calling Leon. He had given her his home number for emergencies. She could ring and claim that she thought she had dropped her credit cards while she was on his bike, then perhaps casually suggest that they meet in town for a cup of tea. A great idea – though in the end she decided against it. But not until she had almost dialled Leon's number so many times that she knew it off by heart.

So once again, Sunday night for Kerry Keble was Marmite on toast in front of the *Antiques Roadshow*. But with the volume on the television turned up so loud, to drown out the clamour of squeaking bed springs above, that the rock guitarist from next door actually popped round to complain.

Yes, Monday morning came as a relief.

The tube ride to work was eventful.

Unsurprisingly, the Northern Line was experiencing delays due to a defective train at Hampstead and Kerry had a fifteen minute wait in Clapham before the journey even began. She positioned herself right at the end of the platform, knowing

that the carriages which stopped there would be emptiest and
that she might even, if she was very lucky, get herself a seat.
She had a new romantic novel to read in her bag and couldn't
wait to crack the spine and dive right in. Kerry didn't like to
read on the platform because she was worried about nutters
who might try to push her on to the lines. She figured that it
wasn't a totally irrational fear, since it was something she often
felt like doing herself on a Monday morning.

When the train arrived, she could hardly believe her luck.
Everyone in the end carriage was crammed into the space by
the doors while the seats that lined the walls appeared to be
completely empty. The passengers were obviously all waiting
to get off. Kerry stepped forward to claim her chair. The train
stopped. The passengers piled out. Kerry and the people behind
her piled on. They scrambled for the chairs and Kerry was
relieved to feel her bum make contact with the soft blue foam.
Success. She had made it. She had her coveted seat.

The guard announced that the doors were closing and the
train sped into the dark tunnel like a rat into its hole.

It very quickly became apparent why so many people had quit
the train at Clapham South.

'What are you bloody well looking at?'

Kerry peered up from the refuge of her paperback and found,
to her horror, that the question was being directed at her.

'I said, what are you bloody well staring at, eh?'

Sitting opposite Kerry was an old woman wrapped up in three
coats who appeared to have a tea-cosy crammed down on her
head. It was literally a knitted tea-cosy. Kerry could see the hole
that had been meant for the spout. In the seat beside the old
woman, with a tea-cosy of his own through which protruded
his fluffy ears, sat a matching dog. The little brown dog had
his chin on the back of the seat and was dozing, dribbling in
his dog-dreams over the shoulder of the smartly-dressed man
to his right.

'I said, what are you bloody well looking at, young lady?' Mrs
Tea-cosy asked once more.

'I . . . I . . .' Kerry was gobsmacked. Was she supposed to
answer? 'I wasn't looking at you,' she said in a panic. 'I was
just reading my book. Really, I was.'

'Yes,' the old woman narrowed her eyes. 'I know all about you and your books . . . You're taking notes about me aren't you? All of you are,' she waggled her finger at the commuters up and down the carriage. 'You all get money off the Government to do it, I know. Money off the Government to take your itty bitty little notes.' The man with the dog dribble on his shoulder was trying to suppress a smile.

'Do you want to see my stitches?' the woman asked menacingly, leaning forward across the aisle that divided her from Kerry and breathing strongly alcoholic air straight into Kerry's face. Kerry's eyes fixed in horror on a stamp-sized flake of something she assumed to be dead skin caught up in the woman's hair. 'You want to see my stitches,' the woman continued. 'I know. You all do.'

Kerry looked frantically to her fellow passengers for support, but they were all looking in different directions. Staring into space. Not about to get involved. It was as if she wasn't there.

'No, no, thank you, I really don't want to see your stitches.' Kerry opened her book again and tried to concentrate on the words which now appeared to swim like fishes before her eyes. The woman continued to rant about her surgical appliances, rocking backwards and forwards so that the cider smell of her breath hit Kerry in foul waves.

'You do, don't you?' Mrs Tea-cosy pulled on the coat-tails of a middle-aged man who was strap-hanging. He tugged the corner of his Burberry raincoat free from her greasy grasp and continued to read his paper as if nothing had happened.

'Excuse me,' he ventured politely, when she tried the trick again.

The old woman's dog raised his head from the neck rest and looked around slowly as if he had seen it all before. 'Don't you start ignoring me,' the woman raised her voice. 'I said, you want to see my stitches, don't you?'

The man made no indication to suggest that he did.

Which obviously made Mrs Tea-cosy even more upset than the fact that the Government was tailing her. Suddenly, she snatched the man's newspaper from his hand and began to hit him with it about the pin-striped knees. He jumped backwards from her vicious aim, at the same time knocking into a startled young woman who had been teetering on high heels behind him. She shrieked as she tumbled and laddered her tights. The man helped her to her feet while Mrs Tea-cosy continued to rain angry blows on his head with the *Daily Telegraph*.

'Ugh! Hay-yelp,' the young girl started screaming and the fat dog too was suddenly galvanised into action. Mrs Tea-cosy didn't relent in her beating. Her dog began to bark at the man as though he were the assailant and Mrs Tea-cosy the assailed. The crowd who were strap-hanging along the aisle parted like the Red Sea and crammed themselves back-wards into the spaces by the doors. Kerry pressed herself back into her own seat as far as she could go, eyes wide with terror.

'Get off me.' The man being hit with his own paper obviously couldn't decide whether or not to throw a punch. His arms wavered between positions of defence and attack. 'Get off me, you stupid old woman.'

Both the woman and her dog were on their feet now and the woman was reaching inside her greasy coats. The next thing Kerry knew, the woman had one of her breasts squeezed naked between her red-mittened hands and was waving it at anyone who cared to look and see.

'Look at my stitches,' she cried to the sky.

The other passengers let out a collective gasp.

'Oh, man, that's disgusting,' said a young black guy who up until then had been laughing through his chewing gum.

The train pulled slowly into the station and the doors opened. Once again, the entire contents of the end carriage poured out on to the platform and tried to cram themselves on to the train a little further down.

The crowd moved along with murmurs of amusement and disgust. Kerry shoved her novel back into her bag and followed the complicated signs to the Bakerloo Line. She wasn't amused, or disgusted. She was worried. How long before that mad old woman was her? All alone in the world and showing her tits to plain strangers.

When she got into the office, she recounted the story to Leon. He laughed all the way through. Then Kerry told him about the surprise engagement announcement. He laughed all the way through that too. Especially the bit about having to listen to a variety of happy couples shagging the night away. Kerry laughed with him, but when she stopped she felt oddly hollow again. Was this really her life she was talking about?

Then the phones began to ring.

'Good morning, Verbal Tix . . .'

Verbal Tix was a relatively new company. The big chief, Serena Winterson, had worked at a huge talent agency for many years, until she got sick of the pitiful commission structure and defected to form Verbal Tix with a number of dissatisfied artistes in tow. Now almost a year old, the company had expanded to employ four people. Leon was in charge while Serena had time off to drop yet another baby. Then there were the three bookers; Celestine, Joshua and Kerry, the new recruit. Leon had interviewed her and offered her the job as he walked her out of the office. They had hit it off straightaway. Kerry liked Josh too but Celestine was proving more difficult to get to know.

Kerry had the desk opposite Leon. On her first day it had been totally clean and empty, but one month into her contract, the drawers were overflowing with showreel tapes and sweet-wrappers, and a selection of fluffy little gonks with googly plastic eyes had formed a defence line between her and her new boss. Kerry's blotter was covered in so many scribbled numbers that she could never find the really important one she had just written down. All numbers were meant to be entered into the database on the computer, but that, despite the extensive experience she had listed on her CV, was one area of modern life that Kerry did not feel inclined to embrace. She could, however, work the switchboard, which foxed both Leon and Celestine. So most of Kerry's working day was spent taking calls and logging vital numbers on her blotter and on Post-its, which always got lost on the floor.

'Hello, Verbal Tix.' No rest for the wicked.

'Yes, hello,' said a plummy voice. 'I'd like to book Lance Sylvester to do three advertisements this afternoon.'

'I'll just check his availability for you, sir.' Kerry put her hand over the receiver and mouthed 'Someone wants Lance Sylvester' across the desk to Leon. 'Make out he's quite busy,' Leon mouthed back.

'This afternoon?' Kerry said to the caller. 'I'm afraid that might be a problem. He's quite busy today. How long would you like him for?'

'Quite busy, eh? What a load of bollocks?' The plummy accent slipped. It was Lance himself on the phone.

'Oh, ha ha ha, Lance,' muttered Kerry. 'If you keep calling me up like this you're only stopping the people who might really want to give you a job from getting through.'

'Sorry, Miss Keble,' he whimpered like a schoolboy then laughed his nasty dirty laugh. 'So, did you enjoy yourself at my party, darlin'? Got any scandalous gossip to tell your Uncle Lance?'

'I don't think so.'

'You got a lift home with Leon,' he reminded her conspiratorially. 'With your legs wrapped around him on the back of that bike.'

'I had to hang on somehow . . .'

'Ha ha ha. Anything happen? Eh? Eh?'

'Lance. No. You've got a one-track mind. Besides . . . you know,' she stuttered.

'Stranger things have happened, I say. Ask Celestine.'

'Lance!!! Look, I've got another call coming through. I'll call you back if anything comes in for you. OK?' Kerry put down the phone and started to chew her pencil. 'Stranger things have happened.' Just what did he mean by that?

At lunchtime, Leon asked her to join him for a sandwich at Pret-à-manger. He paid. But Kerry could hardly take the time to enjoy his generosity or his company because she was so desperate to get back to the office and ask Celestine about Lance's latest insinuations. Stranger things have happened? Was Lance suggesting that Celestine and Leon had got it on? Leon linked his arm through Kerry's as they walked back to the office. He was chatting about Sam and Kerry couldn't find an opportunity to probe about anything else. At Verbal Tix, Celestine was on the telephone to an important client. Kerry willed her to put down the phone. A bubble of excitement was rising in her stomach and she knew that she wouldn't be able to do a thing until she knew the whole story. If Kerry had a ghost of a chance with Leon Landesman she wanted to snatch it right away.

Fiona had been at work since the markets opened at seven o'clock in the morning, and the night before she had had just two hours sleep. But for once she didn't feel tired at all as the big hand crept towards eleven. When Maureen the tea lady came round with the trolley, Fiona bought two Crunchie bars and ordered a nice strong coffee. Maureen had raised an eyebrow.

'So you're off your sugar-free flapjacks then?'

'Life's too good to eat birdseed,' Fiona told her. Cellulite didn't matter anymore. Nothing mattered anymore. Somebody loved her. Somebody was about to prove that he loved her. They were going to take Tuesday afternoon off to choose the ring. Fiona picked up the phone to call Tim's office and doodled a heart on her blotter while his phone rang. It rang and rang. Tim had probably already gone out to lunch with a client. Fiona put down the phone and coloured in the little blue heart.

'Doodling hearts now? You look like you're in love,' Maureen observed as she poured out a strong cup of tea for Fiona's neighbour.

'I am. I am. I am,' Fiona sighed. But she was waiting until she had the ring to tell everybody just how much.

'Well, let's hope that love can conquer this,' said Pete, as he handed her a memo from the powers that be. Pete smiled smugly. He had the desk opposite Fiona and had been in unspoken competition with her from day one. 'Mr Hara wants to see you,' he told her with no small degree of satisfaction. In Pete's considered opinion, you only got a message to make an appointment with Mr Hara, head of the whole conglomeration, if you were on the way out.

'Do you want me to call him for you?' Pete asked eagerly. 'Tell him that you're wetting your pants?'

'Thank you, Peter, but no,' replied Fiona. 'I'll just finish this Crunchie and then I shall call him myself.' Nothing was going to spoil her second day as a fiancée. Especially not Peter Harris. She pushed back her chair and put her feet up on the desk, having first speared the memo from Hara on her spike for receipts.

'Good afternoon, Miss Davenport. I'll just let Mr Hara know that you're here.' Hara's secretary broke into a rare smile.

Miss Koto was known to the boys on Fiona's floor as the 'Komodo Dragon'. She was a hard-boiled woman, who had come from Japan with Mr Hara when he was put in charge of the London offices. Koto was in her early forties or maybe younger but she'd led a very hard life. Rumour had it that she was jilted at the altar by a dashing young army officer, who with embarrassment later committed hari-kiri. Naturally, the deserted bride had been devoid of the milk of human kindness ever since. When Ms Komodo Dragon smiled at you, it didn't necessarily mean that you were favoured. More likely, she knew that your head was about to roll and was actually suppressing the desire to laugh at your pathetic disposable face.

'Go straight in, Miss Davenport,' Ms Koto said, waving her towards Hara's office with a pencil that had been sharpened on a Samurai sword.

Fiona took a deep breath and took hold of the handle on the polished wooden door. She had had enough time to start worrying now. The only other time she had been in Hara's office was when she first started at the bank. On that occasion she had been crammed into the room with twenty other graduate recruits. She had been right at the back and had barely heard a word of Hara's quiet pep talk. Instead she had been looking at the management books that lined his office shelves, at least half a dozen of them written by himself. Mr Hara was a frighteningly successful man but when Fiona walked into his office on this occasion, he rose from his chair behind his desk the size of a football pitch and surprised her by strolling across the room to shake her warmly by the hand.

'Miss Davenport,' he said in his lispy Japanese accent. 'How lovely to see you again. Sit down. Sit down.' He motioned her towards the black leather sofa which flanked one side of the room. Fiona sat in one corner of the sofa. Mr Hara sat in the other. Fiona crossed her legs demurely at the ankle. Was this the new human approach to giving an employee the chop?

'Tea?' he asked.

Fiona refused politely. She didn't really want to be holding anything she could spill in her slightly shaky hands. Hara smiled at her and nodded. Fiona nodded back and hoped she hadn't nodded too deeply because she knew the Japanese had some kind of code about that. Hara took a deep breath and began.

'Well, Miss Davenport, you are probably wondering why I have asked you here today.'

Wondering, thought Fiona. Now she was really wetting her pants.

'Though you may not have seen much of me during your time

here with First Orient Bank, rest assured that I have my finger on the pulse of everything that goes on in the London office and, in particular, I monitor the progress of my graduate recruits with very great care indeed . . .'

Fiona nodded.

'Very great care indeed,' he repeated.

Fiona nodded again.

'I suppose you could even say that I have my spies . . .'

Fiona just nodded. She had a sudden flashback to one terrible lunchtime when she had been spotted blubbing in the loos by the Komodo Dragon. Tim had just cancelled their three-year anniversary date in favour of an old boys' rugby dinner at his college in Cambridge. Fiona felt the first prickles of a cold sweat gathering beneath her fringe. Had that one awful moment sealed her fate? Apparently the Dragon was the kind of woman who thought that taking a whole day off to go to your father's funeral was weak.

Hara continued, 'And we've noticed that your progress has been somewhat different from that of the other employees in your year . . .'

Different? She was finished. 'Well, I haven't . . .' Fiona began to prepare her excuses. Hara raised his hand to cut her short.

'In fact, so different, that I have decided to offer you the placement in our New York office because I feel that it is time for you to spread your wings . . .'

'I . . . I.' Fiona was astonished. She couldn't possibly have heard him right. The New York placement? It was the most prestigious trainee placement that the First Orient Bank offered. And Hara was offering it to her? Everyone had assumed that it would go straight to Peter Harris. 'New York?' she squeaked.

'Yes. New York,' said Hara, with a quizzical smile at her disbelief. 'And you should also be thinking about making applications to do an MBA as well. First Orient Bank has close links with Harvard . . .'

Fiona couldn't close her mouth. 'Harvard,' she murmured.

'Yes, Harvard,' repeated Hara. 'The placement begins in two months' time, Miss Davenport. You would be based out there for six months. Of course the bank will provide funds for your resettlement and take care of your British affairs while you are away. Miss Koto will be pleased to help you with all the necessary documentation.' Mr Hara paused and smiled. He laid a cool, slim hand on top of Fiona's which were clenched tightly together in her lap. 'Of course, I am assuming that you want to go . . .'

Fiona nodded. 'Oh, yes. Of course I do,' she lied. The time to get out of this mess was later. 'But I had better go back to my desk now,' she muttered, shell-shocked. 'Got to get some figures finished for this afternoon.'

'Certainly. Conscientiousness is what we like to see.'

Mr Hara rose to show her out of the room. In the reception area, the Dragon looked up from her typing and smiled. It was a real smile this time, one that even involved her eyes.

'Well done,' she mouthed.

'Yeah,' said Fiona. 'Yeah. Thanks.'

When Fiona returned to her desk, she was chalk white. The New York placement. What a disaster! She knew that what the choice really boiled down to was six months away from Tim or the end of her career. Pete and his cronies Simon and James were already waiting by her desk like vultures, eager to hear the bad news. Seeing Fiona's stony pale face, they assumed that they had got what they wanted. A head had rolled.

Simon handed her a cup of tea, ready made. Milk and two sugars. Not her usual drink at all.

'I thought you might need this,' he told her. 'It's nice and sweet. My mother always said that it's just the thing to drink when you've had a nasty shock.' His voice was full of unnatural concern.

'Thanks,' said Fiona. 'I guess I have had a shock.' She sipped at the tea silently. Simon perched on the edge of Peter's desk. James leaned forward across her monitor to stare. They watched her swallowing slowly as if that cup of tea would be the last thing ever to pass her quivering lips.

'For Christ's sake, what did old man Hara say to you?' Pete couldn't wait a second more.

'He said,' Fiona whispered into her polystyrene cup. 'He said that he wants me to go to New York.'

Linzi was almost horizontal on her desk. The only thing moving was her index finger, which was pressing the mouse to flip over the cards in yet another game of Solitaire. What time was it? She looked at her Mickey Mouse watch. It was only two minutes later

than it had been two minutes ago. Still two hours till lunchtime.
Still seven hours till knocking off time. And about ninety-six
hours until the end of the week.

Linzi was shaken out of her reverie by the sound of a pile of
papers dropping heavily on to her desk. Cymbelline, the graduate
trainee, tried to attract Linzi's attention with a discreet cough.

Linzi pretended not to hear.

'Duncan wants this lot typed up straight away,' Cymbelline
told the top of Linzi's head. 'We've got a presentation to the
client at eleven. And, by the way, it would help if you could
use the approved layout first time, this time.'

'Yes, sir,' Linzi saluted Cymbelline's retreating backside. She
was wearing the creative department uniform of tight-fitting
black trousers and high-heeled suede boots. She really shouldn't
have been. Not with those thighs.

Linzi wearily flicked through the papers that Cymbelline had
given her and opened the word processing package on her desk-
top PC. The approved layout indeed, Linzi snorted. Ellington,
Froggett and Splinter had a special system for their presentations
and every letter, proposal and invoice had to be typed in precisely
the same way. Linzi had caused a complete débâcle in her first
week by using Times New Roman instead of the approved
Century Schoolbook to type a memo to the TV department
head. Big deal? It seemed it was. Linzi complained that nobody
had told her anal retention was a company policy. Was she
supposed to guess?

Bing! The word processing package announced that it was
ready to play with the cheerful little beep that made Linzi want
to push the computer on to the floor with her boot. Every single
time. She entered her password. 'TITS.' Apparently it had been
chosen by the girl who worked there before. Well, thought Linzi,
she must have been a 'right larf'.

God, so this was the heady world of advertising? The creative
department of Elton John, Frog-spit and Sphincter. Six lads
from 'oop North' and a couple of Sloaney just-out-of-schoolgirls
gathered daily around a glass-topped table to put toilet jokes into
the copy for everything from bank accounts to 'boil-in-the-bag'
chicken. Caroline, the boss at Linzi's temping agency – Advertising Angels – had promised that this would be a stimulating job.
Linzi had had more fun sticking her fingers into electric sockets.

She read the yellow Post-it note that was stuck to the top page of the pile to be typed.

'Darling Linzi, approved lay-out, please. And when you've finished this you can come and sit on my face.'

Oh, ha ha ha. A Post-it with extra wit from Duncan the wag. Duncan the wank. The creative department head with the perm straight out of eighties *Brookside*. Linzi took the Post-it note and stuck it into her diary to keep as evidence for the day when she would sue his saggy-trousered arse. If this wasn't sexual harassment then she didn't know what was and the Post-it note was more tangible than the leery winks and the 'accidental' bottom pinch he had given her as she tried to put more paper into the photocopier. Linzi certainly hadn't bothered to wear a skirt to the office after her first unhappy day in this job.

The computer had been standing unused while she sorted through the papers. After three minutes the screen-saver kicked in. 'GET YER TITS OUT!!!' scrolled across the screen in slow motion. Somebody must have changed the saver while Linzi was in the loo. She clicked her mouse angrily to get rid of it. Did they do this to Cymbelline? she wondered. Probably not. In the one lunchtime that Linzi had joined her workmates for a drink, Cymbelline had downed three pints and thrown two of them straight back up again. Cymbelline was one of the lads. Though with red lipstick, of course.

Linzi began to type the first page out. Fourteen point, bold font for all headings. Twelve point, not-bold font for text. She was about halfway down the page and heading for her top speed of forty words a minute when she felt a hand on her shoulder and stumbled on the space bar. Bugger. It was him.

'You've spelt that wrong . . .' he said.

Linzi tried to find the spelling mistake in the words that flickered before her. Nothing was obviously wrong.

Duncan elaborated. 'Penis only has one "n".'

'I'll go back and spell-check it when I've finished,' Linzi said without looking up.

'Ooooh, what's wrong with you today? Get out of the wrong man's bed, did you?'

Linzi took a deep breath. 'I didn't find your Post-it note to me tremendously funny, Duncan,' she said through tight lips.

Duncan rested his belly against the back of her chair. Linzi

closed her eyes and gritted her teeth against the mental picture
of the tuft of hair that was habitually pushed out between
the bottom buttons of his too-tight shirt by copious rolls of
excess fat.

'Writing that kind of thing could count as sexual harassment,
you know,' she elaborated.

'Woo-oh! Big words! Sex-u-al ha-rass-ment,' he mimicked
her voice. 'Oh, get a sense of humour, Linzi. You know that
I wouldn't touch you with a bargepole anyway. You're far too
skinny for me.' He leaned forward and squeezed her hard around
the waist. 'Look, I can get my hands right around you.' Linzi
turned on him with a snarl. 'Ooooh!!' Duncan backed off with
his hands in the air, shielding his face and crying 'No. Please. Help
me!!! The woman's gone mad!!' He appealed to his audience for
approval. Cymbelline obliged with a sycophantic laugh.

'It's not funny,' Linzi hissed.

'Everyone else in the office thinks that it is,' Duncan replied
in justification.

Linzi bashed at the keyboard blindly until Duncan leaned
heavily against her backrest and the sudden jolt made her skip
a key. 'I can't type while you're looking over my shoulder,' she
told him flatly.

'Looks like you can't type anyway,' Duncan replied. 'How
much do we pay you? Seven pounds an hour? Too much for
someone who doesn't even know how to bloody well spell. I'll
have to ask that fat cow at Advertising Angels to send us a proper
girl next time . . .'

'I can spell.' Linzi ploughed on with the typing. 'Customer
profile (fourteen point, bold) . . . We must remember that the
typical consumer for Butcher's new Soup-in-a-Mug is likely to
be a young single mum with only a small weekly budget for food.
It is likely that she will not be terribly well educated . . . (twelve
point, not bold)' Ellington, Bigot and Splinter.

'When you've finished that, my petal,' Duncan rested his chin
on her shoulder. She could feel his hot stinky breath against her
ear. 'If you think you'll ever finish it – I need you to send a
courier up to Sarah's house with this.' He propped an 'E, F and S'
embossed envelope between Linzi's keyboard and monitor. 'Call
her and tell her when to expect it. I need ten woolly jumpers
for tonight. Patrick Farnham is having a leaving do after work

at the Dog and Duck . . . You can come if you like.' He stood
up and turned towards his office. 'Though I don't suppose you
ever "come" do you, Miss Iron Knickers.' He slipped back behind
the glass partition that separated his creative greatness from the
proles before Linzi had time to respond. Cymbelline stifled a
snigger.

Linzi paused in her typing and stared at the envelope. Then
she looked up and glared across the open-plan office straight at
Cymbelline. Cymbelline quickly ducked her glossy-haired head
behind the cover of her monitor to escape the evil eye.

'Woolly jumpers' was the code for coke and Duncan wanted
ten grams of coke at sixty pounds a gram, which meant that
the envelope sitting in front of Linzi contained six hundred
pounds in cash. In fifty pound notes probably, since Duncan
would never carry anything less. It was disgusting, sticking that
amount of money up your nose. Linzi briefly considered picking
up the envelope and walking straight out with it. But that was
too easy. Instead she picked up the dirty white telephone and
dutifully dialled first the courier company and then the dealer.
To the courier, she gave the reference of the client to whom
Duncan would make that morning's presentation so that the
trip would be written off against their fee. To Sarah, the dealer,
she gave an estimated time of arrival for the 'wool' of a quarter
to midday and Sarah promised to have finished her 'knitting' by
twelve.

According to Cymbelline, Sarah the dealer had a new top-
of-the-range BMW and sent her five-year-old son to a private
school so her 'jumpers' must have been the most popular outfits
in town. Sarah was always polite on the phone, friendly but
businesslike. Linzi tried to imagine how she must look. A mother
and a coke-dealer? What kind of a woman would step into such
a nasty little world with a tiny child in tow? The kind of single
mother who couldn't afford 'Soup-in-a-Mug' on her Income
Support perhaps?

When the deal had been sorted out, Linzi dialled Gaetano at
his shop, thinking that the sound of his voice might cheer her
up. He wasn't there and Linzi didn't leave a message with his
assistant. Then she called Caroline at Advertising Angels and
begged her to find her a different job.

'Heaven's above, Linzi,' Caroline sighed. 'That's a three-month placement you have there. You've got job security. I thought that you wanted security for a while. You've only been in the job for a week and a half. Give it another chance. It's three months' work, my darling.'

'Exactly,' said Linzi. She just knew she wouldn't last that long. She wondered for a moment whether she should tell her temp controller that Duncan thought she was a 'fat, old cow'. No. Pointless. Caroline would probably put that down to 'jolly japes' before spending the afternoon blubbing in the loo. It wouldn't actually spur her into action.

'Please,' Linzi begged.' Just keep an eye out for something that might suit me a little better, would you, Caroline? I'll do almost anything and you know that I'm reliable. I just don't feel quite right here.'

Cymbelline paused before Linzi's desk en route to the coffee machine.

'Personal phone calls?' she asked, not-at-all-quietly.

'Yeah. It's the Pope actually. I'm confessing my murderous thoughts. Do you want a word?' Linzi covered the mouthpiece and held out the phone.

Cymbelline waddled on by with a tut.

'Stick with it, darling,' Caroline told Linzi when they resumed the conversation. 'Even the most extrovert people among us can sometimes find that we take a little longer than we expect to settle in. Oh, whoops. I've got another call coming through. Speak to you later, sweetheart. Mwah! Mwah! Cheery-bye.'

'Cheery-bloody-bye.'

Cymbelline returned from the kitchen with a trayful of drinks. One for every member of the team – with the exception of Linzi, of course. When she leaned over to put down the coffee she had poured out for Duncan, he hooked a finger into the V-neck of her shirt to get a better look at her cleavage. Cymbelline emerged from his little glassed-in office blushing like an overblown rose.

'Don't get many of those to the pound!' Duncan called after her.

'Obviously don't get many brain cells to the pound in this place either,' Linzi sighed. 'Where's my coffee, Cymbelline?'

'In the machine,' Cymbelline replied.

Linzi finished the pile of typing just before the deadline and all in the approved layout. Duncan took it from her with a grunt,

and went to his meeting without reading it. Linzi wished that
she could have been there when they got to the section in which
she had added her own special opinion that Soup-in-a-Mug was
'reconstituted cack'. Ten minutes later, the cocaine arrived. Same
ingredients as Soup-in-a-Mug, but slightly more expensive. Linzi
signed the courier's delivery slip and took the coke straight into
Duncan's office without opening the padded envelope. He had
instructed her to leave it in the bottom drawer of his desk. She
opened the drawer and stuck the jiffy bag full of powder beneath
his collection of football and girlie mags and the neatly folded
issue of *Guardian 2* in which Duncan was hailed as one of
advertising's 'brave new yobs'. 'Breaking new ground' according
to the interview. Duncan spent more time breaking wind. Linzi
closed the drawer with a smile at the thought. Next, she went
back to her desk and picked up her bag.

'Where are you going?' Cymbelline asked.

'I'm going to lunch,' said Linzi.

'But who's going to cover the phones?'

'You can, Simper-leen.'

Leaving Cymbelline looking like a goldfish which had suddenly found itself on the dry side of the fishtank, Linzi headed
straight for the lift. Cymbelline was probably calling Advertising
Angels to complain about her even as she reached the ground
floor. So what, thought Linzi. She had no intention of going back
to Ellington, Froggett and Splinter. Never ever ever again.

When she got to the phone box on the corner of Soho Square,
Linzi dialled the police and quietly tipped them off about the
quantity of coke in Duncan's bottom drawer.

CHAPTER FIVE

Getting home from work early meant that Linzi had plenty of time to get ready for that evening's date with Gaetano and since the house was empty, because Kerry and Fiona were still out treading their hamster wheels, Linzi was doubly pleased that she could use Fiona's expensive body oil stuff in the bath without having to ask.

Linzi soaked for almost an hour, topping the water up with extra hot until her fingers got so crinkly that she began to worry that they might not plump back out again in time for her date. She slapped on some of Kerry's best Clarins' moisturiser, just in case, and then made sure that she rinsed the bath clean of all evidence of body oil theft. Last time, Fiona had cottoned on that someone was using her Clinique when she slipped on the slick it had left behind while having a shower. She had almost pulled the shower rail off the wall in an attempt to stop herself falling. It wasn't funny. At least that's what she said.

Linzi raked through her underwear drawer to find a set of lingerie that if it didn't match exactly at least matched in colour. The choice wasn't inspiring. Black or chewing-gum grey. She plumped for the black and reminded herself that she was going to have to do some washing one of these days. Luckily, she had been saving a once-worn Wonderbra for special occasions. So, foundation work done, she set off on a tour of her housemates' wardrobes to find something suitable to sling over the top.

Fiona's wardrobe first. Linzi opened the polished walnut doors wide and stood back. This could be the wardrobe of someone who did night shifts in a dry-cleaner's shop for a hobby. Every shirt, skirt and running-vest hung from its very own padded

coat-hanger, and every loaded coat-hanger was covered with
a plastic dry-cleaning bag to fend off the dust. The order was
absolutely rigid. Like a rainbow, the clothes ranged from red on
the left to blue on the right. Black and white basics had their own
section at each of the spectrum's ends. This strict organisation
made it very difficult to steal from Fiona's wardrobe. She could
see at twenty paces whether something had been tampered with
and would be waiting by the front door to snatch her best shirt
off your back before you could take off your coat and make your
excuses.

Besides, thought Linzi, it would be a bit of a risk borrowing
something from Fiona that night. Linzi was going to watch
Gaetano's band playing in a North London pub she had never
heard of but which was apparently quite a prestige venue on
the rock circuit these days. DKNY is hardly the kind of thing
you want to wear to a heavy metal gig, so Linzi closed the
walnut doors of Fiona's wardrobe once more and tried to make
sure she hadn't left any incriminating fingerprints on the bright
brassy handles.

Kerry's wardrobe was a different matter altogether. For a start,
she couldn't fit a proper wardrobe into her tiny room. So, most
of Kerry's stuff had migrated out on to the landing and to help
solve her storage problems she had bought one of those canvas
portable wardrobes on a tent-pole frame which was bulging at
the sides like an old man's best dress-shirt. Linzi sometimes
felt guilty that Kerry had got such a bum deal when it came
to bedrooms but Kerry rarely complained and had once even
claimed that she liked it. Looking in through the slightly open
door now, Linzi could almost see why. Kerry's room was like a
little nest, practically all bed. Cosy. But not really enough room
to entertain a visitor.

Linzi unzipped the floppy fabric door of the portable wardrobe.
Three crumpled T-shirts sprang out straight on to the floor as if
they had just been waiting for a chance to escape. This wardrobe
was chaos. Linzi wasn't even sure that there were actually any
coat-hangers in there at all. She pulled out a couple of pairs of
jeans in an attempt to make some working space for her search
and quickly concluded that this collection was the result of at
least five years' panic buying. A pair of flared green jersey-knit
palazzo pants? Purleese? Linzi had never seen those before. And

that orange tube skirt? A real throwback from the eighties (which was probably the last time Kerry had been able to fit into it, she thought unkindly). Linzi draped the offending items over the banister and continued to hunt for something vaguely wearable beneath the frumpy frills and furbelows. No wonder Kerry was always wearing those black jeans of hers.

Linzi spotted a corner of promising red fabric and tugged it out to find that it grew into a skirt of that special proportion, the one that can make even Kate Moss look as though she has fat knees. Linzi held it against her body and snorted. She was surprised to see that it came from somewhere as trendy as Miss Selfridge. Then she piled everything that lay across the banister back into the canvas coffin and zipped it up again, at least as far as the zip would go before it got caught on something inside and jammed.

Linzi retired to her room with the red skirt and a belt she had pinched from Fiona. She rolled the skirt up at the waistband and fastened it in place with the belt. With her own black jumper over the top the ensemble looked almost stylish. Fiona had a lipstick that might even match the skirt. Linzi helped herself to a couple of generous smearings and made sure she was gone before anyone got home to complain.

As she struggled up the road with three carrier bags full of shopping, Kerry caught a brief glimpse of Linzi as she dashed out of the house. She looked wonderful as always. She had such a stylish way with clothes. And, of course, thought Kerry sadly, the figure to carry it off. That red skirt she had been wearing was particularly cool, though. It reminded Kerry of the Miss Selfridge number she had consigned to the back of her wardrobe after just one disastrous airing at a twenty-first birthday bash when she had a snog with a boy who turned out to be her cousin. After supper, Kerry mused, perhaps I'll dig that old thing out and give it another try.

She was glad that for once nobody was in when she got home. It meant that she could soak in the bath for as long as she liked and perhaps even borrow some of Fiona's bath oil stuff.

Fiona had been waiting at the bar of the Pitcher and Piano for almost three-quarters of an hour. When she arrived, the place had been almost empty, but now, with all the offices in the vicinity chucking out their inmates, it was packed with people trying to drink away that Monday feeling. If one more person jostled her at the bar, Fiona thought angrily, she would throw her drink straight over him to save him the bother of spilling it.

Finally, Tim appeared. His head was easily visible above the sea of little people beneath him. As he moved across the room, the crowds parted before him as if they recognised something infinitely superior to themselves in his bearing. Fiona's stony face cracked into a smile as soon as she saw him. She was engaged to that six-foot-four god of a man. Not bad work at all for a girl from Bristol.

'Sorry I'm late,' he told her as he kissed the top of her head.

'It's OK,' she grinned and lied. 'I've only been waiting five minutes.'

'Good job I didn't come on time in that case,' Tim replied without a hint of a smile.

Tim commandeered Fiona's space at the bar and ordered them both a fresh drink. As the barman fiddled about with his taps and tried to find a couple of clean glasses, Fiona just gazed at the back of Tim's neck. At the way his hair curled down on to his collar. At the little raised mole she had wanted to kiss so many times but resisted because she felt that it might be embarrassing for him if she drew attention to it. As he leaned on the bar, Tim's pinstriped suit jacket was stretched tightly across his broad shoulders. This is the man I'm going to marry, Fiona murmured to herself. Tim turned around and caught her silently moving her mouth.

'Sorry, Fi. Didn't catch a word of that. Too noisy. God, it's packed in this place tonight. Why do we keep coming here, eh? Oh look, Wooders and Minky are over there by the door. Hey, Wooders!!!' He waved hello. 'We'll go over and have a chat with him in a minute.'

Fiona nodded compliantly. Tim's best pal from college, Wooders, was her biggest rival for his affections.

The barman put a pint and a half of Guinness down in front of Tim, then presented him with his change and a receipt in a small white dish. Tim scooped up all the little coins and shoved them straight into his back pocket. 'I hate it when they give you your change like that,' he told Fiona. 'What do they expect? A bloody tip?'

Once again, he had forgotten that Fiona hated Guinness. Tim put the half-pint in her hand and began to stride off in the direction of Wooders. The crowd parted before him and closed straight up again behind him, so that Fiona reached Wooders and Minky almost three minutes later than Tim had.

For one of the premier rock venues in London, the Forget-Me-Not and Firkin had a dire record with regard to its provision for ladies' conveniences. Linzi stood with her feet on either side of an unidentified puddle and leaned over the cracked sink full of murky water and fag-ends to reapply her lipstick in a horribly smeary mirror. Gaetano's band had just finished their set. It had been met with what seemed like approval from the audience, though it may just as well have been a collective fit brought on by the erratic strobe lighting. Now Monster Munch were packing up their equipment and loading it into the van so that the Professor, as their bassist was called, could drive it home before coming back to the pub again sans wheels to get slaughtered with impunity.

Gaetano was already waiting outside the ladies' when Linzi emerged repainted. He wrapped his arms around her and pressed a kiss to her newly coloured lips. The sweat from his face wiped off half her foundation.

'What did you think?' he asked excitedly. 'Those last two songs went down well, I reckon. The Professor said that the guy from Malibou Records didn't turn up until then so it doesn't matter if the set was a bit crap.'

'I thought it was all brilliant,' Linzi smiled. She stroked his earlobe lovingly and fiddled with the little silver ring that was stuck right through it. 'Almost as brilliant as your solo performance on Saturday night.'

'Foxy lady!!' Gaetano murmured.

He kissed her again, this time simultaneously bringing his thigh between her legs so that she could wriggle up and down against it. Linzi rubbed against him like a cat. She couldn't wait to get him home. She had been longing for this moment since she had reluctantly let him out of her bed to go to work that morning.

'What are we going to do now?' she whispered hotly into the hollow where his shoulder met his neck.

Gaetano took his leg away from her crotch and fished a fag out of the top pocket of his leather waistcoat. He didn't offer one to Linzi. 'Well, we're going to wait here until the Professor gets back from dropping the van off at his old man's garage. Then we're going to have a few jars and just see what develops. We'll probably hang around here while Mutant Phlegm are on. They're pretty good. Our biggest rivals.'

'Oh.' Linzi was more than a little disappointed. Their first real date and she was already taking second place to a bunch of men who could BO for Great Britain. 'I was thinking that we could perhaps go and get something to eat later on. Just the two of us?'

Gaetano smiled at her as if she had just told him a joke. 'I'm not hungry.' He kissed her on the forehead.

'But I am,' Linzi protested.

'Do you want me to get you some crisps from the bar?'

'No, don't bother.'

The Professor reappeared all too quickly. He had changed out of his Terrorvision T-shirt into something equally unsavoury without sleeves. He had combed his hair too and pulled it back into a frizzy ponytail with a brown elastic band. Linzi didn't like to think of the potential for split ends when he tried to pull it back out. The Professor got the first round in and the band retired to a table which, according to a little beer-stained card sign, was specially reserved for 'artistes'. The man from Malibou Records had told Socks, the band's guitarist, that he enjoyed the show, apparently. However, he didn't have time to stay for a chat and a drink, which was a pity.

'Yeah, and I really liked that bit in "The Virgin is Bleeding" when Socks cut the crap and went for the reverb,' the Professor was telling the boys. 'The crowd went berserk, man!! We are nearly there, man. I tell you, nearly there. This time next year, we'll be wearing our own T-shirts.'

Linzi wondered where he had borrowed the one he was sporting tonight.

'You'll have to stand at the back for the publicity shots though, Professor,' Gaetano told him. ''Cos we don't want to scare any children.' The rest of the band laughed. The Professor looked as though he had heard that one before and hoped he wouldn't have to hear it again. Linzi's heart went out momentarily to the teddy-bear of a man.

'Yeah, Merlin had better go at the front,' Socks thought aloud. ''Cos he's like the singer and all, isn't he?'

Only just, thought Linzi.

'But Gaetano's the most handsome,' she suggested sycophantically.

Bingo! Gaetano turned to Linzi and gave her an affectionate squeeze on the knee. Then his hand moved up Linzi's leg and beneath the edge of her borrowed skirt. 'Can we go back to your place, please?' she whispered desperately. Gaetano looked uncomfortable.

'No, it's best if we go back to yours tonight. But I've got to finish this pint yet.'

Kerry stretched the lead on her CD player as far as it would go and then turned the volume up full blast so that she could hear it clearly while she was taking a bath. She had used some of Fiona's bath oil and topped that up with her own bubbles so that now the bathtub looked like the kind of tub you see on fashion shoots where the model is just sticking her pink-painted toenails out of the foam and staring at the camera with a look of terrible coyness.

Kerry had put on her Roxy Music Live CD. She could only risk doing that when Linzi the Trend Controller was out. This was going to a great bath. Kerry had bought a microwaveable vegetarian curry with rice from Safeway and the minute that was ready she would take it upstairs and jump right in. Bryan Ferry, Biryani and a bathful of bubbles. What girl in her right mind needed a man?

Though she wouldn't have said 'no' if the man on offer was someone like Leon.

That evening, the tube had been out of service at Leicester Square due to 'customer action', which meant that someone must have thrown themselves on to the line, as they always seemed to do so selfishly during the rush-hour. When Kerry re-emerged to make a beeline for Oxford Circus instead, Leon had been passing by on his way to the car park. He had offered her a lift home on the back of the Yamaha. Kerry couldn't accept because she was wearing a pencil skirt, but Leon had been concerned and that was enough to make her subsequent tube journey home almost bearable. She had hardly even flinched when a pixie-faced infant picked his nose and wiped the sticky findings on her jacket as the train pulled into Victoria. Leon had offered her a lift home. God was in his heaven.

The steam from the bath had frosted up the mirror. Kerry drew a heart around her face and started to wipe away the condensation from its middle. When the mirror was clear again, she noticed the white head of a spot nestling treacherously between her eyebrows. It must have been there all afternoon. All the time she was sitting right opposite Leon. She huffed on the mirror in disgust to frost it up again.

Wooders was giving Tim the low-down on the old boys' match he had missed that Saturday. Apparently, someone they knew from college had broken his nose. And bled all over his cream Ralph Lauren jumper, the poor lad's girlfriend, Minky, added to Fiona as an aside. The match hadn't gone as well as the boys hoped and that in no small part, said Wooders, was due to Tim's absence. What was his excuse, eh? Fiona's attention drifted from the best way to get stubborn blood stains out of lambswool as she waited for her moment to step into the spotlight.

'Where were you when we needed you?' Wooders jabbed Tim hard in the side.

Fiona stepped closer to Tim and wound her arm through his, ready to make the tableau of a perfect couple when Tim announced their big news.

'I had to go into the office and finalise some details on this project I've been doing,' Tim said. 'It's a pretty big deal actually, and if I get it right it'll be mega-bucks for my bonus. You know how it is.'

'Yeah, right. That accounts for your day. But what excuse do you have for missing the post-match training, you woman?' Wooders continued.

'I was just too tired after work, man,' said Tim. 'I'll make up for it next week though. Twelve pints at the Iron Horse. I betcha.'

'Twelve pints? You'll be on your knees, mate. Fifty quid says you don't make it to eleven.' Tim and Wooders shook on the arrangement. Then Fiona opened and closed her mouth like a goldfish while Wooders and Tim did a bit of friendly punching-each-other-in-the-guts to reaffirm their allegiance. Too tired to go out on Saturday night? What was Tim on about? Why hadn't he told Wooders that he had been too busy getting engaged to play rugby?

'Are you OK, Fiona?' Minky asked, recognising a face she pulled quite often herself when her boyfriend was pretending that she was part of the furniture.

'Yes. Fine,' Fiona lied but she desperately followed the rest of the conversation between the boys, waiting for the crucial turn to what had really happened that weekend. It didn't come. The boys sank another two pints and Wooders made his excuses. Minky followed Wooders to the door. Tim made some comment to the effect that Wooders was jumping straight into a sick man's bed, then he finished his pint and put the empty glass down on the lid of a shiny grand piano.

'You ready, Fi?'

She had finished her half-pint hours ago.

'Yes. I suppose.'

Fiona shrugged on her coat and tried to follow in Tim's wake to the door.

Linzi stared at the clock above the bar, willing the barman to call time. The gig had been dissected right down to the opening chords of their cover of The Stones' 'Gimme Shelter'. The Professor had drunk himself to sleep. Socks was still holding forth on the advantages of Fender over Gibson or something like that. Gaetano's hand had occupied the same position between Linzi's legs for the past half-hour. She had almost forgotten that it was there apart from the occasional flickering movement of his fingers which was meant to pass for affection.

The barman rang his brass bell to call last orders. Socks said he had to 'shake hands with the governor'. The Professor started to snore.

'Why's he called Socks?' Linzi asked when the man in question had disappeared into the gents.

'Don't know,' said Gaetano. 'He's been called that for as long as I can remember. Might be something to do with him wearing odd socks to school one time.'

'That's original. And Merlin?'

'Because he's magic on the mike.'

'Yes,' observed Linzi. 'He certainly knows how to make himself disappear when it's his round. And why is the Professor called the Professor?'

'Because he's clever. He's the only one of us that got any "O"-levels. He went to university to do a degree in pharmacy and all that. The idea was that when he finished he'd be able to make his own acid and sell it to us cheap but now he just spends his days in Boots in Kentish Town telling grannies how to insert their suppositories.'

Linzi snorted.

'That must be nice. And how about you, Gaetano? How come you haven't got a nickname like the others?'

'Because I'm too cool to have a stupid tag. Believe me, Linz, if we get noticed I'm going to ditch those idiots straight off. The Professor's only in the band as it is because he's got access to his dad's Transit van. He can't play bass to save his life.'

'Oh. That's harsh. I thought he was quite good. Very enthusiastic.'

'Too enthusiastic, if you ask me. That's why he always comes in too early on the chorus of "The Virgin is Bleeding".'

'Practice makes perfect.'

'He's the exception that proves that rule.'

'Enough bitching,' Linzi put a finger to his lips tenderly. 'I think he's waking up.' The Professor stirred slightly in his sleep. 'Anyway, can't we go soon? Only it's pretty late now and I've got to get up early in the morning.'

'What for? I thought you chucked your job in today.'

'Yeah. And tomorrow I've got to start looking for a new one, haven't I?' She leaned towards him and kissed him gently on his long black eyelashes. 'Besides, we've still got a bit of getting to know each other to do.'

Gaetano squeezed her upper thigh. 'I'll just tell Socks we're going.'

But Socks had already got one last pint in.

'We'll just finish this,' said Gaetano. 'And then I promise you, we're gone.'

The live concert version of 'In Every Dream Home a Heartache' was Kerry's favourite song of all time. It was right at the end of

the album. Kerry would get out of the tub when it finished. She
wasn't feeling too great as it was. The combination of the curry
and the hot bath had brought her out in a ferocious sweat and
she was feeling rather drained.

So drained that she had to pull the plug out of the bath and
lie there until all the water had disappeared before she could
even think about moving again. She wondered what time it
was. The phone hadn't rung all evening. Linzi and Fiona were
probably out with their respective men. Kerry didn't want to
think about how long it had been since she last went out with
a man after dark.

That afternoon, she had cornered Celestine in the loos in an
attempt to find out exactly what Lance meant by 'stranger things
have happened'. Celestine just kissed her teeth and said that
Lance Sylvester was a no-good stirrer but upon the application
of a little more pressure she had buckled.

'I expect he means the Christmas Party,' she said at last.

'Was it a good one?' Kerry asked.

'It was a complete disaster,' Celestine replied. 'We were all in
this really posh restaurant, right? Josh couldn't come because
he had flu so we had a space in the reservation and we let
Lance come along to make up the numbers since he's practically
a permanent fixture here as it is. Anyway, Serena's husband got
so drunk he could barely see and then accused her of having an
affair with Leon.'

'But that's ridiculous. Leon's gay, isn't he?'

'Supposedly,' said Celestine. 'But sometimes he acts like he's
not sure.'

'Staying at my place tonight?' Fiona asked as she and Tim waited
for a train going their way to arrive at the tube station. Tim cleared
his throat and gobbed a big ball of phlegm on to the live line.

'No thanks, I think I'll go back to mine. I need to change
my shirt.'

'I've got one of your shirts at my place,' Fiona persisted
hopefully. 'You left it last week. I've washed it and ironed it.'

'Which one is it?'

'White with blue stripes.'

'I feel like wearing the pink one. I'll give you a call at work
tomorrow.'

'At work? But we've both got the day off, haven't we? You said we were going to go shopping and buy the ring tomorrow.'

'Oh yeah. I did. Sorry, Fi. I forgot to tell you. I've got to work tomorrow. On this project. Nobody's going to be getting any time off for the foreseeable. We'll go into town on Saturday, OK?'

'OK.'

What choice did she have? The train arrived and Tim guided her safely inside a carriage. When they reached Stockwell station, he got off there and left her alone on the train to complete her journey. Fiona waved goodbye until her journey took her on into the tunnel. Tim had only looked back once.

Fiona had to dig her fingernails into the palms of her hands to stop herself from crying. She had decided that Tim had not mentioned their engagement in the pub because he was waiting until he had bought the ring, but that thought was of little comfort to her now that she was on her own. Tim was as distant as he had been for the past couple of months again. In fact, though she couldn't bear to admit it, his sudden proposal had been as much of a surprise to her as it had been to her flatmates. When he said that he had something to ask her that Saturday night, it could just as easily have been whether she wanted to call their relationship off.

Perhaps it was his work. Fiona knew how easy it was to let a bad day in the office spill over into after-hours. She was the closest person to him and as such she was bound to get most of the fall-out. Yes, that was what it was. He did love her really. It was his work.

But the protective bubble of their engagement had already burst. She hadn't even had time to bring herself to tell Tim about New York. A treacherous little tear sneaked its way on to Fiona's cheek. The girl sitting opposite looked at her curiously and drew her boyfriend's attention to the damsel in distress. She whispered something in her boyfriend's ear and smiled smugly, safe in the knowledge that she was loved without needing symbols to prove it. Fiona dug her nails harder into her hands. She mustn't cry. She mustn't cry. She didn't want to look like some kind of idiot in front of all these people. But her lungs were ready to explode with a sob. The train couldn't reach Clapham South quickly enough.

*   *   *

While Kerry was lying like a flat fish at the dry bottom of the bath, the doorbell rang. She leapt to her feet and, suddenly taken by an attack of dizziness, reached straight for the shower curtain for support, ripping the plastic coated fabric from two of its plastic hooks. Bugger, that was half their deposit gone, again. She struggled into her dressing gown to confront her midnight visitors.

Gaetano and Linzi tumbled on to the floor of the sitting room in a kissing heap. Kerry fled back up the stairs to be out of their way.

'Wow,' said Gaetano as he watched Kerry's flight from his vantage point on the carpet. 'Is it my imagination or are Kerry's legs bright purple?'

'Who gives a shit about Kerry's legs?' Linzi silenced him with a kiss. 'Come upstairs and fuck me, you stallion.'

Gaetano followed her dutifully into the bedroom. Since she had hold of his collar, it was clear that he wouldn't be going anywhere else that night. She had her hand down his trousers almost before she closed the door behind them. His penis was as limp as three-day-old lettuce.

'Oh no, Gaetano. I just knew you were drinking too much!'

Fiona waited at the top of the road until Gaetano and Linzi were safely inside number 67. She gave them two more minutes to get to Linzi's bedroom, then she let herself into the house and washed down two Nytol with a quarter-bottle of white wine someone had left unfinished in the fridge.

CHAPTER SIX

Tuesday always seems to go more slowly than Monday. It must be something to do with the fact that you've already been over all the previous weekend's gossip and yet the next weekend is still far enough away to make it seem slightly premature to be thinking about your next lie-in. In short, it's a bit unreasonable to expect any Tuesday to be a real blinder.

'Good day everybody?' Kerry asked as she walked through the door and threw her fake-fur-collared coat across the back of a chair.

Stupid question. Linzi was already installed on the sofa with the duvet tucked around her and a jar of Nutella balanced between her knees, which she was attacking with a tablespoon. Fiona was getting in a couple more minutes on the exercise bike while she waited for her jacket potato to be cooked in the microwave. They were both focused on the television and didn't even seem to notice Kerry coming in.

'I take it that's a "no", then.'

'Huh?'

'I just asked whether everybody had had a nice day at work . . . Oh, never mind. It doesn't matter. You obviously didn't.'

'I didn't go to work today. I quit my job,' Linzi announced suddenly.

'You did what?' Fiona stopped pedalling and stared. 'You didn't tell me.'

'I quit my job yesterday. I couldn't stand it any longer.'

'But you had only been there for a week and a half. What do you mean, you quit?'

'I mean I packed up my desk and walked out into the free

spring air. It was the worst job I have ever ever had to do, Fi. Can you believe that my boss got me to send a courier out to fetch his cocaine and then told me not to think about getting a habit myself because with my lack of skills and experience I'd never be able to earn enough to support one?'

'Nice guy,' said Kerry.

'He was a piece of shit.'

'But the rent is due at the end of the week, Linzi. How are you going to pay? None of us can stand our jobs, but do we quit a week before the rent is due?' Fiona was on a rant again and the louder her voice grew, the faster she pedalled.

'I thought you loved your job, Fi,' Kerry tried to change the focus. 'Counting all that money every day.'

'I do not "count money" every day.' Fiona was offended. 'I work on new international business projects and as a matter of fact I've just been offered a six-month placement in New York.'

'New York? Wow.' Linzi popped up from beneath the duvet like a tortoise at the sniff of a lettuce leaf. 'Wow! That's brilliant. When are you going? We'll be able to come and visit.'

'No you won't. Firstly because you never have any money and secondly because I'm not going to go,' Fiona told her flatly. 'I don't want to.'

'Why not?' Linzi was disbelieving. 'I would cut off my legs for a job in the States.'

'Then you can cut your legs off and have it. I don't want to leave London.'

'You don't want to leave Tim,' Kerry said perceptively.

'We've just got engaged,' Fiona protested. 'If I go away now everything will be ruined.'

'Why? Six months is nothing when you've promised yourselves to each other for a lifetime. It's the Big Apple, Fiona,' said Linzi. 'Just think of the shopping. Macys, Saks, Bloomingdales and all those other ones.'

'Christ. That's about all you ever think about isn't it? Shopping? I'd have to leave everything behind. My friends, my family, just about my whole bloody life. Macys just doesn't mean that much to me, funnily enough.'

'Well, your family live just two hundred miles away now and you only ever see them when Tim's got something better to do at the weekend,' Linzi reminded her. 'New York is only six hours away, Fi. Stop being so wet and go for it.'

'I am not being wet.' Fiona stopped pedalling. 'Just tell me what's wet about not wanting to go through the palaver of uprooting myself and going to a foreign country where they just happen to have the highest murder rate in the world? I don't think that's wet. I think that's pretty sensible.'

'And you could get knocked over by a bus on Balham High Road tomorrow . . . It's the chance of a lifetime so why not live a little . . .'

'What, you mean like you, Ms Career Girl? I don't see you getting on your bicycle and cycling to Heathrow.'

'If I could find the opportunity, I would take it. One day, when you and Tim have finished redecorating all the bedrooms of your semi-detached, you're going to turn around, take a good look at his beer gut and wish that you had done it.'

Fiona opened her mouth but didn't appear able to say anything sharp in return. Kerry hovered halfway across the room, as if she knew that Linzi had thrown a grenade and was waiting for it to explode. But Fiona still didn't say anything. Instead, she jumped off the bike with an exhalation of exasperation, picked up her handbag and sprinted up the stairs. From downstairs, the two girls heard a strangled sob amplified by the acoustics of the bathroom.

'What did you have to say that for?' Kerry asked. 'You know she's sensitive about Tim's gut.'

'He isn't.'

'Do you think she's all right?'

'No.'

'I'll go up and talk to her.'

'About what, Kerry? She doesn't seem to have anything in her life except Tim these days. I remember when we used to talk about going off and working in a place like New York. All three of us together. I remember a time when Fiona was going to be the next prime minister and you were going to be the next Sigourney Weaver. If Fiona doesn't take that place-ment in the States then she really is the Stepford wife I think she's turning into. Six months in New York! I would kill for a chance like that. And knowing that bank of hers, she'll have some huge relocation package built in. She should try working in some of the places I've had to work in since I've been temping. You would think that it was still the Middle Ages if you met some of the men in the advertising industry.'

'Oh, yeah,' Kerry suddenly remembered that Linzi had quit. 'What happened to you?'

'I had to report my boss to the police for dealing in Class A drugs.'

'Fair enough. So you're not going to go back?'

'Put it this way, I don't think he'll have signed my time sheet.'

About an hour later, Fiona crept sheepishly back down the stairs and squeezed herself into the corner of the sofa that wasn't occupied by Linzi and the duvet. She was clutching a dusty bottle of red wine.

'I've been saving this since Christmas,' she said. 'It's a peace offering. Do you want some?'

'Go on then,' said Linzi. Kerry brought three glasses from the kitchen and sat cross-legged on the rug since the floor was infinitely preferable to the chairs.

Fiona cleared her throat. 'Listen, I know you both think I'm stupid for not wanting to go to New York, but I assure you that it's not as simple as not wanting to leave Tim behind. I mean, I'd have to leave you guys behind as well . . .' Kerry smiled at the sneaky flattery. Linzi punched her on the arm. 'And I really am frightened about the murder rate . . .'

'Most people are murdered by someone they know,' Kerry chipped in cheerfully.

'Great. Thanks. So now you're saying that I wouldn't be able to make any new friends either in case one of them turned out to be the nutter who has it in for me.'

'That nutter could be Tim,' Kerry continued. 'Has he asked you about taking out life insurance yet?'

'I know,' Fiona laughed. 'You're right. It is a pathetic excuse. But it's strange, isn't it? I never thought that opportunity could be such a double-edged sword. I don't want to go to New York, but I know that if I don't take the placement, First Orient probably won't bother to renew my contract at the end of the year.'

'Are you so unsure that Tim would wait for you?' Kerry

suggested reasonably. 'You just got engaged, after all. That proves that he's committed.'

'You didn't just decide to tie the knot because you're up the duff?' Linzi asked flatly.

'No, Linzi,' Fiona reeled in indignation. 'I am not up the duff. Look, if you two stop hassling me, I promise I'll think about it for a bit longer. I haven't even mentioned the placement to Tim yet. He'll probably insist that I go anyway, so that he can have a final fling.' Her mouth smiled but her eyes stayed decidedly unhappy as she raised her glass. 'Not bad stuff this, is it? Happy Tuesday everyone.' The others returned the toast. 'Linzi,' Fiona began again. 'Just out of interest, what are you going to do about this month's rent?'

Linzi would call both her parents, of course, and apply pressure to each by implying that the other would provide for their only child if he or she did not. Linzi's parents had been divorced for almost fifteen years now but the war still went on. In her wildest dreams, she thought that it was perhaps because they still harboured some deep feeling for each other and were longing to get back together.

When the issue of money was resolved, the girls got on to far more important matters. Fiona's mother had recently reported that one of the girls' old classmates had dropped her third sprog in as many years. Guessing who the father might be took up the best part of an hour. Then the demolition of yet another packet of Boasters sparked a great diet debate.

'I've got a brilliant idea,' Fiona said suddenly. 'Instead of just talking about how we're going to get fit the whole time, let's set ourselves a goal and really, really go for it. One of the guys at work was telling me about a half-marathon that he's going to run. It's still a couple of months away so we've got plenty of time to get fit. It's only thirteen miles and you don't even have to run the whole way. What do you think?'

Kerry looked worried.

Linzi didn't even bother to look up to see if Fiona was joking, but remained flat on her back on the floor with her half-full wine glass balanced on her curvy belly.

'Linzi, what do you think?' Fiona persisted.

'I think the whole idea is perverse.'

It was the kind of answer Fiona had expected.

'I'll sign us up,' she continued regardless. 'It's twenty-five pounds each to run but you get that back if you raise enough sponsorship money. It's for some cancer charity, I think.'

'Twenty-five pounds, Fi? I don't know . . .' Kerry began. 'I'm expecting a bit of credit card damage this month. And it'll be painful.'

'Your credit card bill or the marathon?' asked Linzi.

'Both,' Kerry wailed.

'Rubbish. It'll be brilliant fun and besides, you both need to get into shape . . .'

Fiona divided the very last of the Bordeaux between their three glasses.

'Get into shape? But I like the shape I'm in,' Linzi protested. 'What do I want to change it for?'

Fiona sighed as if they were just pretending not to know why. 'Because you are both going to be my bridesmaids, aren't you?' she asked them impatiently.

'Your bridesmaids?'

'I'm getting married, remember? Linzi, you'll do it, won't you?'

'OK,' said Linzi disinterestedly. 'As long as you swear we won't have to wear peach.'

'I swear it. I was thinking along the lines of jade anyway. And you, Kez? You're on for it, aren't you?'

Kerry shrugged. 'I suppose so. Always the bridesmaid, me.' She drained her glass sadly. Fiona's wedding would make Kerry's third bridesmaid job in two years. She wondered how many more times she could get away with it before she would never be able to be the bride. 'OK,' Fiona raised another toast. 'We'll start training tomorrow night.'

'Actually,' said Linzi. 'I can't. I've got a date.'

'Not Gaetano again?' asked Kerry. 'How was last night?'

'Brilliant,' Linzi replied. 'He's fantastic. I'm so glad you made me go to that crappy party with you, Kez. Turned out to be the best move of my life. I borrowed your red skirt by the way. Hope you don't mind.'

'No,' Kerry lied. 'Of course I don't.' At least her wardrobe was having a love life.

CHAPTER SEVEN

Kerry picked up the TV supplement and grazed through the listings of the last few programmes for that night. Nothing doing. It was Saturday night, after all. Most normal people were out enjoying themselves in clubs and pubs and bars. Kerry, however, was having to miss a party because she had tried to jazz her hair up with some 'wash-in, wash-out' hair-dye and now she had "Passionate Pecan" tiger stripes all the way down her face and her back. Fiona had warned her not to use the stuff in the shower but it was odd that while it washed happily out of Kerry's hair, which was now back to its usual pale mouse-brown again, any skin that the stuff had touched remained bright red. Kerry's grandmother would have told her that it was God's way of saying 'Stay brown'.

Kerry stuffed the last of the Choc-Chip and Hazelnut Boasters into her mouth in two bites and took her empty mug out to the kitchen. The credits of the film she had been watching played slowly across the screen. When she had rinsed out the mug and left it soaking – since Fiona could throw a convincing epileptic fit over tea stains on the crockery – Kerry switched the television off and headed up the stairs. There was really nothing left to do but go to bed.

The doorbell rang while she was in the bathroom, right in the middle of cleaning her teeth. She spat the toothpaste out into the sink with a curse. It was bound to be Linzi. Why couldn't that girl ever remember to take her house-key? The doorbell rang again. Occasionally, if you left her outside for long enough, Linzi would find her key in the bottom of her bag and let herself in but tonight she obviously couldn't be bothered, or she was genuinely locked out. Kerry wiped her mouth dry on a slightly damp towel.

'Hang on. Hang on,' she muttered. 'You're just bloody lucky that some of us have nothing to do on a Saturday night.'

Kerry opened the door abruptly, causing the late-night caller to jump back a couple of steps. She stared at her visitor for a couple of seconds before she realised that this wasn't someone she particularly wanted to catch her in her Alice band and tartan PJs.

'Leon?'

'Yeah, it's me,' he nodded sheepishly. 'Look, I'm sorry to come round so late, Kerry, but I didn't know what else to do. I had a row with Sam this afternoon and he kicked me out of the flat. When I went back to make it up to him I found he'd had the locks changed. I've got nowhere to sleep tonight. Any chance I could borrow your floor?'

Kerry was already back inside the house and halfway up the stairs to collect her dressing gown.

'Yeah,' she called. 'Of course you can. Come on in. Can you put the kettle on?'

Leon slunk into the house and closed the door quietly behind him. Kerry could hear him going into the kitchen. She rubbed her eyes to make sure that she wasn't asleep, then, reassured yet rather worried by the fact that she wasn't, she made a surreptitious dash for the bathroom, whipped off the Alice band and checked the extent of the Pecan streaks. Wasn't it just Sod's Law that the hair-dye disaster had happened today of all days? Her cheeks were still faintly orange and her hair was a mess. She dragged a comb through her fringe and then wrapped a red bandanna around it. No, that looked ridiculous. It even accentuated the pale tangerine pallor of her skin. She ripped the bandanna back off again. Should she stick some foundation on perhaps? She heard Leon cough nervously in the silence downstairs. Bugger, bugger, bugger. He would have to take her as she was. At least she had managed to half-clean her teeth.

She floated back downstairs with her dressing gown wrapped tightly over the tartans. Leon was sitting on the very edge of the sofa, still wearing his coat.

'Do you want me to take that for you?' she asked him.

'No,' he said. 'I've been out in the freezing cold all bloody day. I need to get some circulation back in my body before my arms drop off.'

'You poor old thing. I'll make the tea.'

'So, what did you row about this time?' Kerry asked as she unscrewed the tea caddie. She heard Leon sigh painfully in the other room.

'Its a disaster,' he called back. 'Do you remember that Andrew guy who was at Lance's party?'

'The one with hair like shredded wheat?'

'Yeah, that's the one. Well, looks like your friend Linzi was right after all. Even after Sam found out that Andrew couldn't get him a record deal, he still went ahead and slept with him. When I tackled him about it this afternoon, Sam told me that he actually thinks he might be in love with the man. He thinks we've outgrown each other lately and says he needs space to mull things over.'

'And he's kicked you out on to the street while he does it?' Kerry emerged from the kitchen with two steaming mugs. Tea with milk and two sugars for Leon, which was how he had it at work. 'That's a bit of a liberty. I thought it was your flat anyway?'

'Well, it's rented but my name is on the agreement.'

'Oh.'

'The locksmith obviously didn't bother to ask.' Leon slipped his padded jacket off his shoulders. Beneath it, he was wearing only a tight sleeveless vest. The top of his left arm was black and blue. Kerry decided not to mention it.

'So, since it is your flat, why don't you just go to the police and get them to demand that he lets you back in?'

'I don't want to get them involved,' Leon sighed. 'Not that they'd do anything about it anyway. A couple of queens scratching each other's eyes out? They've got better things to think about. Besides, what if they ask to see some identification, Kez? I've already overstayed my visa by a week. I didn't want to get anyone else involved. Especially you. I'm sorry, Kez. It's really late. I should have called first.'

'I don't mind,' she said brightly. 'I was just going to have my Horlicks anyway. You're more than welcome to stay and on Monday morning we can talk about that pay-rise you owe me.'

Leon managed a laugh. Then he recoiled suddenly, clutching at his chest.

'What's up?' asked Kerry.

'Just wind, I think. I stopped for a curry on the way over.'

She wondered if he was bruised across the ribs too.

'Listen, Leon, do you think Sam is serious about Andrew or might it just be that he's hedging his bets for when you have to go back home?'

'To be honest, I've been trying not to think about it. I suppose it might be that.'

'Then why don't you suggest that he goes back with you?'

'To South Africa?'

'Yes. I had a friend from school who fell in love with a Kiwi. When his visa expired she went back to New Zealand with him. They got married and now they live in Auckland and Bristol on alternate years.'

'It's a bit different, Kez. Even if Sam does come back with me, it would just be extending the problem. We could never get married, could we? He would have to come home eventually. Besides, he wouldn't come to South Africa in the first place. He's already said as much. I mean, it's hardly the kind of country where two gay guys can hold hands in the street. Sam loves it here. He's trying to break into the music scene. He thinks South Africa doesn't have one. No, the only solution is for me to stay here and the only way I can do that is by getting a British passport.'

'How are you going to do that?'

'I'm not sure yet. Something will hit me. Look, Kez,' Leon said suddenly. 'Would it be OK with you if I went straight to bed now? I don't think I can keep my eyes open for very much longer.'

'Oh, sure . . . Don't you want to finish your tea first?'

He put the full mug down on the coffee table. 'No. I just want to go to sleep.'

'OK.' Kerry hadn't even thought that far ahead. A brief mental picture of her tiny room with its single bed flashed into her mind. He couldn't stay in there. And she had no spare linen for the sofa. She got to her feet and fiddled with the waist-tie of her dressing gown.

'What's up?' asked Leon.

'I'm just thinking where I can put you. I haven't got any bed-stuff for the sofa.'

'I'll share your bed,' Leon said casually.

Kerry's mouth must have dropped open.

'If you don't mind.'

'No, it's not that . . . It's just that . . .' Kerry began to stutter.

'I'll keep my clothes on,' Leon promised.

Kerry giggled. If only he knew how little she would mind his taking them off. Suddenly she was struck with inspiration. 'OK,' she said. 'I'm fine about it if you are.'

'Kerry, I've shared a single bed with a bird-eating tarantula before now. To share a bed with you would be sheer luxury.'

Kerry remembered the words of Celestine in the ladies' loo. 'He acts like he's not sure.' Was she about to get a love life? Breathing quickly, she led Leon upstairs to Fiona's bedroom, passing it off as her own.

'Nice room,' he said, appraising the twee miniature Monet prints that Kerry thought rather naff.

'Thanks.'

She sat down on the edge of the bed, her chest heaving expectantly as she waited for him to untie her dressing gown like the foil wrapper around an exotic chocolate. It didn't happen. Instead Leon slipped straight beneath the clean white duvet, without taking off his vest or his jeans first, and fell asleep almost instantly, leaving Kerry gazing up at the flower-patterned lampshade which hung from the ceiling, still wearing her dressing gown and her pyjamas.

When she was sure that he wouldn't wake up if she moved, she rolled over on to her elbow and looked down on to his face. There was always the morning, she figured. He had said that he was tired.

Kerry snuggled down beside him again and sighed with pleasure as he draped a heavy arm across her body. Who would have thought that she would end this disastrous Saturday with Leon in her bed? Well, in Fiona's bed. Kerry prayed that Fiona and Tim wouldn't have a row that night.

CHAPTER EIGHT

Fiona knew that something was up when she saw that her bedroom door was not exactly the same distance ajar as she had left it the night before. She hoped that Linzi hadn't been raking through her wardrobe again. She was tired of having to argue with her about who had the right to wear her own brand-new trousers first. All she wanted to do now was get beneath the warm duvet and catch up on the sleep she had missed while squished into a single bed at Tim's. She pushed open the door and slung her overnight bag down by the dresser.

'Oh, Christ,' she muttered.

It seemed that she wasn't going to be jumping straight under her duvet after all. Her bedclothes were piled up over two distinct body-sized humps. She recognised Kerry's light brown hair spilling out over the pillow. God only knew who the other hump was. Without saying a word, Fiona crept out of her room again and opted instead for a nice cup of tea and the sofa.

Fiona didn't say anything about the matter until Leon had left the house to pick up the Sunday papers. When she did speak, the first thing she said was 'I thought he was gay.'

Kerry flushed. She sat next to Fiona on the sofa and hugged her knees beneath her dressing gown. 'So did I. I guess he must be "bi" instead.'

Fiona's eyes widened like saucers. '"Bi"? So, tell me more, Kez. What happened?'

'He turned up shortly after you left for Tim's,' Kerry lied. 'I couldn't believe it. We had a couple of drinks and then he asked if he could stay the night. I couldn't ask him to sleep with me in my single bed, could I? So I had to pretend that your room is mine. I'm sorry, Fi. I was desperate.'

'That's OK,' Fiona said graciously. 'It's a bit risky though, isn't it? I mean, sleeping with your boss has to be a fast one-way route to disaster.'

'Oh, we don't have a conventional boss/employee sort of relationship anyway,' Kerry assured her, wishing that they had done something to be worried about. 'Verbal Tix isn't like that.' She picked up the teacup which Fiona had just placed on the floor and put it to her mouth to take a sip.

'Hey,' Fiona protested. 'You had my bed last night and I let you off about that, but you can make your own bloody cup of tea!!'

'Sorry,' Kerry put the cup down again double-quick. 'Anyway, Fi,' she remembered her manners. 'How was your Saturday night? You look done in.'

'Yeah. I could have done with going straight to bed when I got home,' Fiona replied pointedly. 'Last night wasn't too bad though. Tim had some kind of drinking contest with his mate Wooders at the Iron Horse. He drank eight pints of Stella and then he was sick all over the table so the landlord asked us to leave. Needless to say, I took the opportunity to get Tim home straight away. The contest had started at six and was over by seven so by nine o'clock he had been through his hangover and was almost sober again . . . I told him about the New York placement then,' she added, almost as an after-thought.

'You did? What did he say?'

'He helped me to write this.' Fiona unfolded a scrappy piece of paper from the pocket of her jeans. 'I'm going to type it up before I send it, of course.'

'What is it?' Kerry scanned the first few lines. 'Oh, Fi. I don't believe it. You're not going to go, are you?'

Fiona shook her head. She was twisting something on her finger. The new engagement ring. 'No, I'm not going to go. Tim and I have been thinking about having a June wedding. No point in messing around with a six-year engagement, is there?'

'No, I suppose there isn't.' Kerry folded the letter back up and gestured that she wanted to see Fiona's ring. Fiona stretched her left hand out delicately and tipped her fingers from side to side so that the brilliant solitaire diamond glittered blue and yellow in the light. It was almost as big as a peanut.

'It's beautiful.'

'Thanks. It's a little bit loose,' Fiona told her. 'So I'm going to have it adjusted to fit. But it is lovely, isn't it? Tim insisted that we buy it from the shop where his grandfather bought a ring for his Gran. He said that it's actually family tradition for engagement rings to be handed down from generation to generation, but his mother threw hers into the gutter when she and Tim's father got divorced. They never did find it.'

Kerry smiled. 'It's fabulous, Fiona. And I hope you'll have better luck than Tim's mum. OK.' She slapped her hands down on her thighs and pushed herself up from the sofa. 'If you're not going to let me drink your tea, I suppose that I had better go and put some clothes on. Leon will be back any minute.'

'Then it's hardly worth getting dressed again, is it?' Fiona observed.

'I'm not like Linzi,' Kerry laughed as she tackled the stairs two at a time. 'Some of us like to get out of bed at least once every twenty-four hours.'

From Linzi's bedroom came some mutterings in Italian and a high-pitched squeal. Gaetano had stayed off the juice especially that weekend. Now Linzi didn't expect to see sunlight again until Gaetano went to work on Monday morning.

Leon returned to number 67 and let himself into the house with Kerry's key.

'Nice man in that shop at the top of your road,' he told Fiona.

Fiona smiled. The man in the paper shop was a screaming queen.

'I'm sorry to be getting in your way like this,' Leon continued. 'I'm just going to see if Kerry wants to go for lunch and then I'll be gone.' Kerry had reappeared, resplendent in her best Sunday dress, and was already putting on her coat.

'We can go to the pizza place on the other side of the Common,' she told Leon excitedly. 'I think it's half-price on a Sunday.' She ushered him back out into the street, winking at her housemate as she did so. Fiona retreated to her bedroom with relief.

Leon Landesman was no bisexual. What had Kerry been on about?

CHAPTER NINE

The telephone rang. And it was Sunday night, so it was bound to be one of their mothers. Kerry let the phone ring until the answerphone kicked in and waited until she heard the unmistakable voice that belonged to her very own mum.

'Oh, I hate these stupid answering machine thingies,' Mrs Keble began after the bleep. 'I never know what to say when they come on . . .'

'Makes a change,' said Kerry as she picked up the receiver and cut the answerphone short.

'Oh, so you are there, Kerry. I let the phone ring seven times,' she said accusingly.

'I was upstairs, Mum. I was drying my hair. I couldn't hear it ringing,' Kerry lied.

'Have you been using that conditioner your sister sent you?'

Kerry studied a split end which she held tightly between her fingers. 'When I remember.'

'Kerry, you must try to remember. You want to look your best for the wedding, don't you?'

'Oh, yes,' said Kerry sarcastically. 'The wedding. Is that still going ahead?'

'Of course it is. It's going ahead next weekend! Why do you have to sound so bored by it the whole time, Kerry? You really upset Michelle when she called you last Thursday. She said you kept changing the subject each time she tried to ask you when you'd be able to come back for your final dress-fitting. The wedding is less than seven days away now and the sleeves aren't even sewn on your dress yet. Auntie Angela needs to check you haven't grown since last year.'

'Grown?' That was a nice euphemism for putting on weight. 'Tell Angela to model my dress on that old toilet-roll holder of yours. That's what she usually does, isn't it?'

'Kerry!!'

Angela had made the bridesmaids' dresses for the wedding of Kerry's elder sister Miranda to her dream plumber Steve. The dresses for Michelle's wedding were being cut from the same pattern, but using a different colour fabric. Turquoise this time, instead of overblown English Rose pink.

'You've got to come home for a fitting, Kerry,' her mother persisted. 'And Michelle also needs to know if you have decided yet how you want to have your hair done. She's booked you an appointment at Smart Cuts for eight thirty . . .'

'The night before?'

'No, on the morning of the day, of course.'

'But the wedding's not happening until three in the afternoon.'

'I know. But there's the bride to do and then you three bridesmaids and me. Pat needs plenty of time in case anything goes wrong.'

'What can she do with my hair anyway?' Kerry moaned. She was the only one of the three Keble sisters to have inherited her father's unruly mousy mop.

'That's why Michelle sent you the conditioner. You're supposed to be getting it under control.'

'I could have it fluffed up like candyfloss to complement the meringue dress, I suppose,' Kerry mused.

'Kerry, I can see there's no point talking to you about this today. Honestly, you haven't changed a bit since you were a little girl. It's your sister Michelle's big day and all you can think about is self, self, self.'

Kerry didn't bother to argue. But Michelle's Big Day? That was pushing it. Kerry would lay bets that this wasn't going to be Michelle's one and only wedding. After all, Richard was the third guy she'd been engaged to since her sixteenth birthday four years before.

'Anyway, I saw Mrs Davenport in town the other day and she told me that her Fiona has just got engaged to that lovely boyfriend of hers. You didn't mention that when I called last week. Her mother says that they announced it two weeks ago.'

'They announced it last week actually and I'm very sorry I didn't get on the phone to you straight away. Maybe I've just got wedding-itis.'

'Oh, Kerry-love, don't talk silly,' her mother's tone softened. 'It will be your turn one day very soon and then you'll see what all the fuss is about. Talking of which, have you decided who you'll be bringing as your escort yet? I've got to give the stationers the table plans for the reception this week so that they can do the calligraphy. Your "other half" is the only gap I've got left on the top table . . .'

'Oh, mother,' Kerry sighed. 'You know I haven't got an "other half". Can't you just close the gap up?'

'Absolutely not. It would ruin my seating plan. You could always ask Nicholas Faddy. He's such a nice, polite boy and you know that he still holds a torch for you, even after all these years of rejection.' Nicholas Faddy had had a crush on Kerry since junior school, which meant that he spat at her regularly until puberty hit and then started writing her poems.

'It's a bit short notice, Mum. And besides, I haven't spoken to him in two years.'

'Then he'll be delighted to hear from you, Kerry.'

'OK. OK. I'll call him in a minute and I'll let you know what he says tomorrow. All right?'

'Good, that's settled then, except for the final fitting.'

'Couldn't I just take my measurements here and call you with those as well?'

'No, Kerry, you cannot. You've got to be here on Friday morning. Apart from anything else I need to know what you think of my outfit in case I have to take it back to the shop. I went to Berketex again and I was going to have a blue version of the suit I wore for Miranda's do but then Richard's mother turned up and announced that she'd gone for the blue herself. And she did that after we discussed outfits and agreed that blue is most definitely more my colour than hers.'

'That's shocking, Mum,' said Kerry as she began a thorough examination of her fingernails.

'Well, if she wants to look washed out in the photographs . . .'

Almost the instant Kerry put the phone down, it began to ring again. Suspecting that it was her mother calling once more to ask her whether she wanted roses and gypsophila in her hair or just the gypsophila, Kerry almost let it ring. But then she decided that it was probably best to get any more wedding agony over with straight away.

'Yes,' she said rather aggressively.

'Oh, I'm sorry, Kerry,' said Leon. 'Have I called at a bad time?'

'No, no. You haven't.' All sweetness and light again.

'I was just calling to say thank you for last night. For letting me stay and for listening to my ramblings all through lunch. You're a real star, Kerry. I hope you managed to get some sleep with me snoring next to you.'

Kerry felt a flush creep across her body.

'I slept like a log,' she squeaked, despite having spent half the night praying that he would try to keep her awake some other way.

'Good. Anyway, I'm staying with a friend in Willesden tonight so I thought that I should also call to ask if you could try to be in work a little earlier than usual tomorrow, to open up the office for the others, since I haven't the faintest idea how long it will take me to get in.'

'No problem,' Kerry replied. 'I'll be there.'

'I'm sorry to ask all these favours of you, Kerry. I really owe you one. If there's ever anything I can do in return. Except give you a pay-rise, that is,' he pre-empted the usual joke.

'Well, actually,' Kerry smiled. 'There might be something. What are you going to be doing next Saturday?'

As she put down the phone a second time, Kerry felt a malign presence looming behind her. Fiona tapped her smartly on the shoulder. She was dressed from head to toe in royal-blue Lycra, a professional looking pair of trainers on her feet.

'Come on, Kerry,' she said brightly. 'We've got to start training for the race.'

Kerry protested. It was the Sabbath.

But Fiona was insistent. 'If you want to be able to finish this race at all you're going to have to start training now. I'm going to run around the Common. You're going to come with me.'

'What about Linzi?' Kerry moaned. 'How come she's excused?'

Fiona said nothing but looked skywards. The creak of a bed rocking on floorboards again.

'She seems to think she's getting enough exercise already.'

CHAPTER TEN

Caroline Murray of Advertising Angels took off her glasses, closed her eyes and pinched the bridge of her nose in a very weary fashion indeed. Linzi Adams had swallowed her pride and squeezed herself into the hard chair that was jammed into the tiny space between Caroline's desk and that of the other temp controller. She smiled broadly, Caroline just shook her head.

'Well, Linzi Adams, I must say that this is a very pleasant surprise. And what can I do for you today?'

'Got any work for me?'

'You just jettisoned a three-month placement at Ellington, Froggett and Splinter,' Caroline hissed.

'I had to. It didn't suit me. Did they make much of a fuss?'

'No,' Caroline sighed. 'As a matter of fact, they asked if you would go back but I couldn't get hold of you in time because your telephone was engaged all day. I had to put someone else in. Seems like they had a bit of a débâcle at E, F and S after you walked out. Now, this is between you and me, Linzi,' Caroline leaned forward so that her ample bosom displaced her papers to the outer edges of the desk, 'but I know someone who works in another department at the agency who tells me that the dear chap you were working for was found with half a pound of heroin in his desk. Half a pound!! Of heroin!! I never would have thought it of him. Would you? Now, it looks as though he's going to be dismissed. In fact, he will probably end up doing time. So naturally, with him gone, the creative department was in utter disarray and they needed a temp more than ever.'

She leaned back again to gauge the effect upon Linzi of this shocking piece of gossip.

Linzi affected a look of surprise to stifle a blossoming smile.

'But anyway, you've missed that job altogether now. The new girl I've put in there loves it. And they've asked her to stay for the full term.'

'That's a shame,' said Linzi. 'For me, I mean,' she added quickly. 'Not her.'

Caroline put her glasses back on and began to flick through her files. 'Now, Linzi. We are still supposed to be looking for a full-time position for you, aren't we?' Linzi nodded. 'And I've got an updated version of your curriculum vitae here.' Caroline opened Linzi's cardboard folder and looked at the CV with tightly-pursed lips. 'Ah, yes. You're the one with a degree in psychology. Two-one. Not much call for that in the field of advertising these days.'

'So you keep telling me.'

Caroline leaned forward again and pushed her glasses up into her fringe. 'Oh, Linzi dear, what are we going to do with you?' she said with a sigh of concern. 'I think it's time that you and your Auntie Caroline had a wee chattette about your qualifications and training.'

'We've been through this before, Caroline. I've done all the training courses you offer. Freelance, Lotus Works and Ami-Pro,' Linzi counted them off on her fingers. 'I can use just about any computer package now.'

'Exactly,' said Caroline.

'Huh?'

'Bit of a clever clogs, aren't we?' Linzi screwed her eyebrows together. Clever clogs? Caroline reached right across the desk to take her hand and rubbed it comfortingly. 'Oh, darling. You mustn't take that as an insult. Mustn't, mustn't, mustn't. But in today's harsh *employmental* climate, being good at everything quite often doesn't work to your advantage. After all, nobody wants to employ someone who might be after their own job within a fortnight.' Caroline squeezed Linzi's fingers. 'And this is the problem that we have with you . . . It's not just your psychology degree, Linzi. You've got diplomas in shiatsu and aromatherapy too. When I send your CV to a client who's looking for an office junior, they're going to take one look at this lovely long list of qualifications and put you straight to the bottom of the pile.'

Linzi was agog.

'Well, why don't you put me in for an office "slightly more senior" job?'

Caroline looked unamused. 'We all have to start at the bottom, Linzi.'

'Oh.'

'What I want to suggest to you, sweetheart,' Caroline continued, 'is that we adopt a new strategy. Let's reinvent Linzi Adams and make her the most sought-after girl in town.' She squeezed Linzi's fingers so hard that Linzi expected to see blood spurt out of the ends. 'OK?'

'What do you mean? Reinvent me?' Linzi was suspicious.

'Well,' Caroline picked a fat red marker out of her desk tidy and popped off its lid. 'We might as well start here.' She drew a thick red line through the section of Linzi's CV that read 'qualifications'.

'You've crossed out my degree!'

'That's right. And all these awards,' the pen hovered over some of Linzi's proudest achievements. 'Just a little bit scary. And we hardly need to tell them about your voluntary work, do we? You raised the money to buy a water-pipe for Africa? Not really all that relevant to any of our clients.' She scored away at Linzi's CV like a hairdresser asked for a crop after a week of doing only shoulder-length bobs. When she had finished, she handed the piece of paper back to Linzi. The only things recognisable beneath all that red ink were her name and her date of birth. 'And we need to change your work experience. To make it show that you can handle responsibility but at the same time not too much. Ever worked in a pub, my dear?'

'No,' said Linzi quietly.

'Waitress in a restaurant, perhaps?'

'No.'

'Oh dear. Well, I'm sure you'll think of something.'

Linzi was in shock. It would take a few moments before she could summon up the energy to be angry again. She stared at her decimated curriculum vitae. Caroline wanted her to leave out her degree. Three years of hard work. Three years of sweaty swotting wiped out in a stroke of red biro so that some fat ad exec would think about letting her make his tea.

Caroline put the red marker back in the green plastic pot and crossed her arms on the table again.

'Now. What you'll need to do is go through to the training room and type your new improved curriculum vitae up on one of the machines. Make me a couple of copies and then I can put you in for these jobs that I have here.' She fanned out a selection of postcards as if they were exotic trips on *Blind Date*, then picked out one to read. 'I have a feeling that you will like the sound of this one, Linzi. It's for a secretary in a marketing company. Nine thousand pounds a year and a free lunch twice a week. Doesn't that sound nice? Yes? The word processors are through there.' Caroline pointed to the way out. She was already looking for the file of the next poor girl, who was standing shyly at the office door, about to lose her PhD in the cause of Advertising Angels.

'OK, Linzi sweetheart. Bye-ze-bye. Off to the typing room with you. Leave it with Stephanie when you're finished.'

Linzi rose from her chair and walked towards the training room like a zombie. Of course! What a fool she had been to think that hard work and qualifications would get her anywhere in this game. She sat down in front of the machine that ran the Ami-Pro tests and opened up a new word-processing file. She began to type her CV out again automatically, keeping nothing of the old Linzi but the barest details of her identity. Out with the A-level results. Tone down those GCSEs. She printed out a copy and read it through. The humiliation was absolute.

'Never hide your light under a bushel,' her grandmother always used to say. She was a senile old bat for the most part, but for once, Linzi thought, perhaps she had been right. Linzi's light hadn't just been hidden, it had been unplugged. And all so Caroline could stuff her in some crappy job and pocket the fat commission. Linzi scrolled through her CV until she got to the section labelled 'work experience'. Was she going to make up some job in a pub? No way. She could do better than that.

A smile spread across Linzi's face as she typed out the details of her extensive experience as a lap-dancer, listed 'frottage' under her interests, and delivered the amended manuscript to the vacuous Ms Ash on the front desk who scanned the document officiously without batting an eyelid. As far as 'Advertising Angels' were concerned, thought Linzi, they could go straight to hell.

But a tour of central London's remaining major recruitment agencies failed to turn up much in the way of a job that Friday morning. Linzi was OK until they got to the typing tests, but as soon as they saw her measly max of forty words a minute it was 'don't call us time' again. After all, as the woman at the Brook Street Bureau said, 'just what is a psychology degree without shorthand?' Perhaps Caroline had been right.

Linzi mooched down Oxford Street, window-shopping as she went. There was a fantastic Romeo Gigli sweater in the window of Selfridges, but she had to get down to the Mr Byrite store near Tottenham Court Road before she could find something that was actually within her price range. Pretty soon, all that sticking her nose on windows had made her desperate for a drink. If she could afford one, she snorted. She really needed to make some money.

She had mooched as far as Soho. Gaetano had once told her that his family owned a cafe on Dean Street. His mother and uncles worked there most days (his father had done so too, until his operation) and some of his younger cousins took over at the weekends. Linzi turned down Dean Street and felt a funny warm sensation spreading through her limbs as she neared the cafe with its tattered brown sunshade overhanging the dirty street. It was exactly as Gaetano had described it. It had to be the one. Gaetano told her that he had cleared coffee cups and wiped tables in his school holidays. The thought of him two feet smaller and without his itchy stubble made Linzi feel weak at the knees.

She gazed up at the canopy with its faded words, 'Carlotta's Café', and wondered how many times Gaetano had unfurled that sunshade. She touched the part of the frame that she could reach, excited to be touching a part of her lover's past.

'Carlotta's Café,' she murmured again and stepped inside.

Behind the shining counter, two men made sandwiches, cutting and buttering with the speed and precision of machines. A small woman, almost as wide as she was tall, was pouring out cappuccino into polystyrene cups for two builders in dust-covered jeans. Only the very top curls of her hair-do bobbed above the coffee machine. She was talking quickly, with a thick Italian accent. She was the kind of proprietress who remembered the names of everyone who came into her shop.

'*Alora*, Dennis, that'll be three pounds and fifty pee to you today. How are your kids? All right? And your wife, she is OK too?' Dennis nodded and handed over the cash. 'OK, darlin' I see you tomorrow again. *Ciao*, Dennis, bye-bye.'

This must be Gaetano's mother. Now that Linzi could see her around the corner of machine she noted with delight that this woman had her lover's deep brown eyes. The man in front of Linzi asked for tea to take-away.

'No sugar for you, innit?' She gave her customer a radiant smile. Linzi couldn't wait to talk to her. She looked so warm. So different from Linzi's own perfect professional mother and her friends. Gaetano's mother was the sort of woman who would only kiss you on both cheeks in the street if she actually meant it. 'OK.' She fixed the plastic lid firmly on to the polystyrene cup. 'Careful you don't spill it, eh. I see you tomorrow, my love.'

'Who's next, please? *Ciao*, bella.' It was Linzi's turn to be served. 'And what can I do for you today, young lady?'

'A cup of tea, please. To drink in.'

'You want sugar? No. OK. You go sit over there and I bring it over to you in a minute.'

The coffee machine let out a huge plume of steam. Gaetano's mother shouted to the kitchen. A boy came out. He was a few years younger than Gaetano, but the look was already there. He pouted as he filled the hissing cauldron. His lips were the same as Gaetano's. He mumbled, 'It's OK now,' in the same displaced Italian-in-London drawl.

Gaetano's mother bustled out from behind her counter. She had to come down a step to enter the seating area of the café and Linzi was surprised to see just how short she really was. She put the cup and saucer down in front of Linzi without slopping a drop and simultaneously whipped a cloth out of her apron pocket.

'Those builders are too messy boys,' she complained as she whisked away the spilled sugar and salt from the wood-effect vinyl covered table. 'I don't know what their mothers teach them at home, eh? No manners.' She turned to walk back to her post behind the coffee machine. A queue of gasping Soho workers was winding almost as far as the door.

'I think I know your son,' Linzi said, suddenly placing a hand on the woman's arm to stop her from racing away. The woman turned back towards Linzi with a smile.

'Which one? Is it my Luigi or my Gaetano?'

'Gaetano.'

The woman rolled her eyes heavenwards. 'Oh, Gaetano! That boy to me! He is just like his father . . . a devil. You know him from your school? Yes?'

'No, not from school,' Linzi laughed. 'In fact I only met him a couple of weeks ago. I suppose you could say I'm his girlfriend though.'

'His girlfriend?' the woman's lip quivered almost imperceptibly.

'Yes. My name's Linzi. I expect he's probably mentioned me to you.'

'Oh, no.' The woman leaned back with her hands on her hips. 'He has not a mentioned you to me. Not by your name. Was it a your place that he stayed last Sunday night when he was supposed to be having his dinner at home with his family?'

Linzi giggled shamefully. 'Oh, whoops, sorry about that. I guess he must have forgotten.'

'So it was your place.' The woman's eyes narrowed and she leaned forward to hiss in Linzi's ear. 'You English girls don't care anything about the family do you? Does your poor mother know that her daughter in London is a whore?'

'I'm sorry.' Linzi wasn't quite sure she had heard correctly.

Likewise the members of the coffee queue who all turned their heads to see what was going on.

'I said you are a whore, young girl. Sleeping with my son. Sleeping with any man before you are married to him. You English girls are all the same. You don't have any morality. You think that a man will respect you after you have let him do everything he likes on the first night that you meet? Ptoo-ey!'

Gaetano's mother spat straight on to the table that she had only just wiped clean.

'Get out of my café, bitch. I don't need any custom from a woman like you. And you stay away from my Gaetano!!'

Linzi gathered up her bag and left without bothering to question. She ran towards Leicester Square and couldn't stop her cheeks from blushing furious red until she was on the tube and almost at Charing Cross. Her ears were stinging with embarrassment. She had been called a whore in front of all those people, and worse than that she had been called a whore by the mother of the man that she thought she might be falling in love with.

CHAPTER ELEVEN

That Friday Fiona's parents were in town on one of their flying visits. They had tickets to see a show that evening and would be staying with friends overnight, but between one and three they had time to see their darling daughter. When she broke for lunch at work, they were already waiting for her downstairs in the glittering marble lobby of First Orient. Her mother kissed her lightly on both cheeks then wiped away the little lipstick mark that she had made with her handkerchief. Fiona's father smiled his slightly silly smile.

'Your father has booked us in at The Chop House,' Mrs Davenport began excitedly as she bundled Fiona into a waiting taxi. 'So I do hope you're not going through one of your funny vegetarian phases, dear, because apparently the menu is all rather meaty. Such a shame Tim couldn't join us. What's his excuse this time?

'He's got to work straight through lunch, Mother. His team are on the verge of completing a very important project.'

'What's all that about?' asked Fiona's father gruffly.

'I'm not sure, Dad. He never really tells me much.'

'Been at that firm for almost two years now, hasn't he?' Mr Davenport mused. 'Time he was moving on if you ask me. Time he spread his wings. Got to bump up the take-home a bit now that the pair of you are going to take the plunge.'

'Oh, yes, darling,' Mrs Davenport trilled. 'I almost forgot. You must let me see the ring. Oh wonderful, you did go for the solitaire in the end. How lovely. Just so classy, aren't they? Looks a little bit big though, Fi. You should get it adjusted before you go and lose it. I know what you're like about losing things. Look, Hugo. Tim's bought the ring.'

'Yes, I know he's bought the ring, dear, but has he set the date? That's what I need to hear.'

'Hugo, you haven't even looked at the ring,' Mary Davenport reprimanded. 'Don't pester the poor girl about the date today. We've got plenty of time to sort that out. But has he, dear?' Mary asked her daughter conspiratorially. 'Have you decided when the big day might be?'

'Oh, I don't know, Mum,' Fiona was a little embarrassed. 'Tim's been a bit too busy to discuss that kind of thing in any detail.'

'A summer wedding would be nice though. June? Or July? No hurry.'

The taxi had pulled up outside the restaurant. The family Davenport bundled out of the car and into the lobby. They were shown straight to their table by a young Australian girl who presented the menus with a flourish. She announced the specials with idiosyncratic intonation.

'Get everywhere these colonials,' said Hugo, when the waitress had left them to choose at their leisure. 'All over London now. That chap in the garage was a Kiwi, wasn't he, Mary?'

'I think they do a lot of travelling, Dad.'

'Do too much flitting around, these young people. Though there's not much at home for them except sheep, I suppose. Right, I'm ready to order. Where's that bloody girl gone now?'

'Hugo,' Mary tutted. 'We're not ready yet. Keep your voice down.' After the army and a few years on the trading floor, Hugo Davenport found such on instruction very hard to obey.

'How's Angus, Mum?' Fiona asked.

'Oh, Angus sends his love. Obviously he couldn't come up to town today because he's slap bang in the middle of his finals. I think he's a little bit worried, the poor lamb.'

'Nothing to be worried about,' Hugo boomed. 'He knows he'll pass them with flying colours. If his sister can do it . . .'

Mary shot Hugo a look that changed the direction of the conversation immediately.

'He's had quite a few job offers from the management consultancy firms he's applied to. He thinks that he might go for the one at Atherton Bros. They offer the most holiday time apparently,' Mary smiled. 'I think that's swung it.'

'Lazy little bugger that he is,' said Hugo.

'Well, I must say I can't blame him,' defended Mary. 'He'll have to work terribly hard as it is, Hugo.'

'It's no kind of attitude to have if he wants to get on,' Hugo continued. 'A man's got to take his career seriously. None of this fannying about for five years before going off to have a baby.'

'Your father's secretary has just gone on maternity leave,' Mary added by way of an explanation.

'Oh.'

'But how about you, dear? How's your little job at First Tokyo?'

'First Orient, Mum. My little job's fine.'

'I expect you can't wait to get home every day to make your wedding arrangements now. Have Kerry and Linzi said whether they want to be bridesmaids?' Fiona nodded. 'You'll have to be careful with the colour you choose for their dresses. Linzi will be easy. She's got such wonderful skin and striking dark hair. But Kerry? She might be more difficult to match. Perhaps you could get her some of that wash-in, wash-out hair-dye stuff for the day?'

The waitress had reappeared, armed with an electronic device to take down their orders which looked like something out of *Star Trek* and, by the trouble she was having in getting it to work, was probably technologically of the same era. In the end, she admitted that she would have to resort to old-fashioned memory.

'Not entirely sure she took all of that in,' Hugo muttered as the girl headed off in the direction of the kitchen. 'That's well-cooked for my steak!' he boomed after her. All eyes turned to see who was making such a fuss. Fiona pretended to be fascinated by the shape of the pepper pot.

After lunch, Mary and Fiona left Hugo alone in the dining room while they went to powder their noses. It was Davenport girl-speak for going somewhere to discuss things unmentionable in front of the men, such as gynaecology and career aspirations. Fiona caught her mother's eye in the mirror as they both reapplied their lipstick in exactly the same way. First step, a careful line around the cupid's bow, then both lips together and press hard to distribute the lipstick evenly over the rest of the mouth. Fiona was struck not for the first time by how much she looked like her mother these days. It wasn't just genetic. Fiona could barely pass a mirror without remembering her mother's early warning that she had to keep herself looking nice at all times, for the men. First to get one and then, when you'd got one, to make sure he didn't stray. It was a full-time occupation.

'Are you excited, dear?' Mary asked again. 'About becoming Mrs Timothy Harper?'

Fiona nodded. 'I suppose I am.'

'Oh, it'll be wonderful, sweetheart. He's such a catch. A real Prince Charming.'

'Yes, Mum, so you say.'

'Such lovely blond hair and so very tall,' Mary mused. 'And he's doing well in his career. You know I'm very pleased, Fiona. I couldn't have asked for a better son-in-law. Beats any of the royal family hands down.'

'Mum,' Fiona interrupted before her mother could start reminiscing about the time she had danced with the Prince of Wales. 'Mum, what do you really think about me getting married at twenty-four? Are you sure I'm not too young? I know you married Dad when you were nineteen, but have you ever thought that you might have missed out on something?'

'Missed out on something? Like what, darling?' Mrs Davenport looked very curious indeed.

'Like seeing the world, Mum. Travelling a bit. Perhaps even working overseas?'

'Working overseas? Heavens.'

'Yes. You could have gone to India and taught English there like Auntie Jane did when she finished her degree. What if I did something like that?'

Mrs Davenport screwed the lid back on to her lipstick and dropped it into her bag. 'Well, Fiona, I suppose I must admit that there are times when I think that your father is a belligerent old bugger, but if I had waltzed off to India at the drop of a hat instead of marrying him, I might have ended up with no belligerent old bugger at all to keep me in my dotage. Like your Auntie Jane.' Pleased with her answer, she linked her arm through her daughter's and led her back out to the table where Hugo was subjecting the bill to some extreme scrutiny.

'Think they've over-charged us for the mineral water,' he told his wife.

It was exactly like something Tim would have said.

When her parents had been safely dispatched on a tour of the best shops in Knightsbridge, Fiona returned to her desk and took a slightly dog-eared envelope out of her handbag. It was the letter to Hara, telling him that she couldn't take up his offer of the New York placement for 'reasons of a personal nature'. She dropped the letter into the sack of the spotty boy who collected and delivered the internal post. There was to be no turning back now. Or was it no going forward?

CHAPTER TWELVE

Kerry had been waiting three long Underground minutes for the train to arrive. Just how long is an Underground minute, she wondered, since her reasonably accurate watch had counted at least six to London Underground's three. While she was pondering this, the intercom suddenly crackled ominously into life.

'Ladies and gentlemen. I would like to apologise for the delay to your service this morning. This is due to passenger action at Kentish Town. Your next train should arrive in approximately three minutes. I said, your next train should arrive in approximately three minutes. London Underground apologises for the delay.'

The commuters up and down the platform murmured their disappointment. Kerry sighed and moved back to lean against the tunnel wall. She and Leon would be leaving for her sister's wedding straight after work that evening so she was carrying a case full of clothes for the weekend, not to mention the bumper bottle of conditioner that Michelle had sent Kerry to deal with her frizzies. When she left the house the suitcase had seemed light enough, but now the cheap fake leather-covered handle was cutting into her fingers and she longed to put it down. She didn't like to because she had once seen a woman have her bag snatched after doing the same. Though who would want to steal her case, Kerry reasoned with herself. The lads who hung around Balham tube station asking people the time until they found a Rolex to pinch had offered to upgrade her Casio digital to a Timex.

It still hadn't quite sunk in that Leon had actually agreed

to come to the wedding at all. He had been in a surprisingly good mood all week. On Monday afternoon he had gone back to his flat with the reinforcement of a big friend and demanded that Sam let him in. Sam, apparently, had been quite reasonable for a histrionic nutcase. He agreed that Leon should probably be allowed to get over the split in his own flat and had taken his own stuff to his mother's house. Leon had his suspicions that Sam had in fact gone straight over to Andrew's, but he wasn't going to dwell on it. No, he said, much to Kerry's joy, he was going to enjoy this weekend with his favourite colleague instead. He had never been to an English wedding before and he was really looking forward to it.

The electronic noticeboard flashed up 'CORRECTION' and the passengers looked towards the renewed message with the stoical patience of cattle. 'Edgware via the Bank'. Damn, thought Kerry, she needed Charing Cross. The next Charing Cross train wasn't even shown.

But then, suddenly, in the manner that occasionally makes you think that travelling by tube really isn't that bad after all, the commuters of Clapham South were granted a special visitation from the gods of the underworld and the next tube arrived. It was two whole Underground minutes early. And just to ice the cake for Kerry, this surprise train was going to be travelling via Charing Cross.

'Praise the Lord.'

Kerry was stepping forward to board the train when the shouting started. As she put one foot on the train she was suddenly knocked off her feet by a flying commuter, causing her to land chin first on the hard wooden-slatted floor

'What the f . . .' She scrambled to her feet and turned to glare at the man who had knocked her over. But, even as she did so, he was falling on his face too. He hadn't meant to push into her. But he was being pushed.

Behind him, stood a small man with a broom handle at the end of which was attached a battered boxing glove.

'Get on the train! Get on the train!' the man was shouting manically as he pushed the commuters into carriages with his home-made super-shover. 'Get on the train. Quick, quick. Get on before the doors close.' He punched a girl in the back with his boxing glove. Another commuter flew involuntarily into the carriage, pleading 'But I want Bank, not Charing Cross.'

The train was delayed for three London Underground minutes while the police came to fetch the man with the poker. By the time they had restrained him, the intercom was announcing that there would be a delay again, due to passenger action at Clapham South. Of course, the train now standing at the platform would be diverted via the Bank. Kerry decided it was time to ask Leon if he was serious about teaching her to ride a motorbike.

Leon had hired a car for the occasion of driving back to Bristol, since he sensed that Kerry wasn't too happy about tackling the M4 on the back of his Yamaha. They left the office at three o'clock, in a fairly vain attempt to avoid the mass Friday-night exodus from London. Celestine had been a little bit grumpy about being left to hold the fort, since Josh had done a sicky, but Leon promised her that she could take Monday morning off in lieu. When it was time to go, Leon picked up Kerry's bag. His knees buckled a little under its unexpected weight.

'What on earth have you got in here?' he complained.

'Nothing much. Girls' things, you know. Extra knickers. Hairspray and stuff.'

'Hardly travelling light, are you?' he laughed.

'Well, I need everything I've brought,' she replied.

The traffic crawled out towards the M40 and, through the centre of London, they were frequently overtaken by pedestrians. Fortunately, Leon had the foresight to bring some tapes to keep them amused. He asked Kerry to make the choice and pointed to a Tesco carrier bag bursting with cassettes which he had stowed behind her seat. Kerry fished out 'Boys and Girls' straight away.

'Brilliant! Can I put this on?' she asked eagerly.

'Sure.'

'I didn't know you were into Bryan Ferry?'

'Neither did I, but you went on about him so much, I thought I'd give him a second chance. It's a bit schmaltzy, Kez. Don't think I'll listen to your musical opinion in the future.'

Kerry pushed the tape into the cassette deck joyfully anyway. At least he had listened to her once.

'It grows on you,' she assured him as the opening chords began to issue weakly from the speakers in the back.

'So does ringworm,' said Leon. 'I'll play you some proper music later. Now tell me, before I have to ask your mother, who is it that's getting married again?'

'It's my younger sister, Michelle,' Kerry told him for at least the third time that day. 'I've got two sisters. Miranda's older and she's already married to a guy called Steve. They thought they ought to do it before they christened their second child. That was last year and I was bridesmaid then, too.'

'Fun?'

'A nightmare. You have to wear a stupid dress all day and everyone keeps telling you that it'll be your turn next. Except that it wasn't to be, because Michelle beat me to it.'

'Who's she marrying?'

'Richard. He's OK. They've been going out for a couple of years. Before that she was engaged to Jason, but he wouldn't set a date for a wedding so she chucked him.'

'Sounds harsh.'

'I think it was for the best. He worked as a fishmonger and it wasn't much fun having him around the house on a hot day. Not to mention the fact that he used to beat her up.'

'That's bad news.'

'Yeah, I told her that the first time she came home with a black eye. But Michelle and some of her friends . . . they've got this strange attitude. They think that if someone's jealous or violent it's only because he feels so strongly for you. They stand around in the ladies' saying things like: 'Ooh, he's lovely. He only beats her up at weekends.' Richard's not like that, thank God. But I sometimes get the feeling that Michelle rushed into their relationship because being with Jason made her feel like she couldn't cope on her own.'

'Could she?'

'Of course she could. She's a really bright girl.'

'Like you.'

Kerry blushed.

'How old is she? Your little sister.'

'She's twenty-one.'

'That's young.'

'Listen, in my family they think you're on the shelf once you hit twenty-four. That's why I had to drag you along to be my "other half" today.'

Leon snorted with laughter. 'I take it you haven't told them much about me, then?'

'Leon, I don't tell my parents much about myself.'

'Aren't you close?'

'Oh, we're close enough. It's just that they worry so much. Every time I go home it's: Are you saving up for that mortgage? Have you sorted out your pension plan? Have you got a boyfriend? I know that they just want me to be settled down so that they don't have to worry about me any more. But the thing is they don't have to worry anyway. I mean, I'm doing all right.' Leon nodded. He was convinced.

'But when I spend any length of time at home I end up thinking that they're telling me how it really is. Maybe I should have a mortgage by now. Maybe I should have a pension. Maybe I should have a man. I see those down-and-outs that sit near our office and start thinking that it could be me if I don't get things right before it's too late. Lost and lonely. With no one to talk to but a whippet with mange.'

'I think we all think like that sometimes.' Leon turned the car on to the motorway. 'But it doesn't happen to most of us even though most of us fuck things up once or twice in our lives. Hey, I'm really looking forward to this wedding. Aren't you?' He deftly changed the subject. 'I can't wait to meet your mum.'

Two and a half hours later, they hit the driveway of the Keble family home in Bristol. It was teeming with strangely clean and well-polished cars. Even Kerry's father had decorated his old white Mondeo with a pink ribbon that came down across the bonnet in a Victory V. The windows of the house were already decked with rosettes and flowers in readiness for the morning. There was no mistaking that something was going on.

Mrs Keble was standing on the front step before Leon had time to finish parking. Her hair was in curlers, covered over by her one and only Hermès headscarf, a twenty-first birthday present from a glamorous maiden aunt. The faces of Kerry's cousins and her nieces crowded at the windows now, displacing the decorations as they fought to catch a glimpse of Kerry and her legendary new beau.

'Hello, Kerry Love.' Mrs Keble kissed her last spare daughter so hard on both cheeks that Kerry felt her Mum's pink lipstick being pressed into her pores. 'Did you have a lovely drive, dear, all the way from London?'

All the way from London? London was less than three hours away, but it was the furthest any Keble girl had ever gone. Or any Keble at all for that matter, not since Uncle Tony went North in dubious circumstances.

'And this must be Leon?' Mrs Keble was talking through an orchard of plums. 'It's very nice to meet you at last. We've heard so much about you from our Kez.'

'Mum!'

Leon raised an eyebrow to Kerry while Mrs Keble gave him the lip stamp treatment as well.

'Come on in, you two young lovers. Miranda, get the kettle on. Your little sister's home. Michelle's having a facial with that mobile beauty salon girl,' Mrs Keble said in a stage-whisper as they passed the dining room. 'So you had better not go in there. Don't want to catch her with a green face.'

'Hi, Kerry!' Michelle the bride-to-be called out from beneath her cucumber face pack. 'I'll be out in a minute when me pores are done. Hi, Kerry's new man!!!'

Kerry's new man? Leon was struggling to keep anything like a straight face.

'Earl Grey or Tetley?' Mrs Keble asked another prospective son-in-law. 'Then we'll sit down and you can tell us all what's happening in *Neighbours* back home.'

'Mum,' Kerry sighed. 'Leon's from South Africa.'

Michelle had decided to spend her last night as the penultimate Miss Keble at the Keble family home. It was a bit of a joke, since she had been living with her fiancé Richard for the past eighteen months, but Michelle was superstitious like that.

It was a full house. Leon had to share the sitting-room floor with cousins Malcolm and Derek and for the first time in about fifteen years, Kerry found herself sharing a bed with her sister. They went up to bed at ten o'clock on the strict instructions of their mother who was concerned that Kerry's under-eyebags would never go down, despite having kept her under a pair of cucumber slices for an hour that afternoon. Kerry lay to the left of the bed. Michelle lay to the right with her arms on the outside of the covers so that the duvet dipped and divided them down the middle. They said 'good night' and closed their eyes. Each waited for the breathing of the other to slow into the familiar pattern of sleep.

'Are you asleep yet, Kez?'

'No.'

'I'm not keeping you awake, am I?'

'No.'

'Are you excited about tomorrow?'

'Nn . . . yes.'

'I'm not . . .'

There was silence for a moment.

'What do you mean, you're not excited about tomorrow? It's your wedding.'

'I'm terrified, Kez.'

'Oh. That's to be expected, Chelle,' Kerry tried to sound comforting. 'It's your big day isn't it? The spotlight will be on you. Don't worry though. While you're up at the altar pledging your troth most of the congregation will be concentrating on my arse in that meringue of an outfit.'

'Don't you like your dress?'

'Put it this way, I don't know if I'll be wearing it out next weekend.'

'I hate my dress, Kez.'

'What do you mean? You're the bride.'

'I mean, I hate it. I'm going to look like a bloody cotton-wool ball when I go down the aisle.'

'But you chose it . . .'

'I didn't, Kez. Richard's bloody mother chose it. She insisted on coming with me when I went to Pronuptia. I wanted something a bit more, you know, a bit more modern. No sleeves. Quite straight. A sheath dress or something like that. But she kept on making me try on these dreadful puffball things instead. Kept on about how lovely I looked and how it was as if I was the daughter she never had. She said that mine was going to be the perfect wedding that she had always dreamed of arranging.'

'Oh.'

'I didn't know what to do. I tried on this dress that I really liked and she just sort of screwed her face up like she'd smelled something horrible. She said it wasn't decent, having your arms on show like that when you're getting married in the house of God.'

'And so you bought the puffball?'

'No. I didn't. She bought the puffball. She said she had been saving up to buy a wedding dress for her future daughter since she got pregnant with Richard in 1969. She was devastated when she found out that she couldn't have any more children after him and so she kept on saving for her future daughter-in-law's wedding dress instead.'

'And did she choose the bridesmaids' dresses as well?' Kerry was horrified.

'No, Mum suggested those. She thought it would be cheaper to use Miranda's old patterns and we got the material from that fabric shop in town after all the stock had been ruined in a flood. That's why it's a slightly different colour on the bodice. I'm sorry, Kez. I know it's not exactly your style.'

'It's just a dress,' Kerry told her. 'And by this time tomorrow night it'll be wrapped up with its mothballs again. You've got to think of your dress as one of those little things sent to try you, Chelle. I guarantee that by the time you and Richard are having rugrats you'll be saving up to humiliate your own first daughter-in-law.'

Michelle made a funny snorting noise in the dark. Kerry wasn't sure whether it was the beginning of a laugh or a sob.

'Oh, Kez.' It was a sob. 'It's not just the dress. That's just the tip of the iceberg. Since her husband died, Richard's all she's got and she keeps on interfering. She's already come round our house and had him put a dado all the way down our hall. I hate those things. And she's coming to the hairdressers' with us tomorrow morning. She's going to make me have all my hair cut off to show that I'm a married woman, like those Russian brides, I know it. It's the beginning of the end for me, Kez. I'm never going to be able to be myself again. You don't know how lucky you are. You're living in London. You've got an exciting job. You're going out with an incredible-looking man. You wouldn't believe how much I envy you!'

Kerry smiled in the dark.

'Michelle, things are never quite as they seem. You wouldn't believe how much I envy you.'

'How can you envy me?' Michelle sighed. 'I spend all week filing boring car insurance claims and all weekend traipsing round garden centres and DIY shops in search of the perfect trellis. I didn't want to work in insurance. I wanted to be a dancer on a cruise ship. Or a nanny in America. Even a gaucho in Argentina once when we did about them in Geography. I wanted to see something of the world. OK, so we're going on honeymoon to Majorca but Richard has said that'll be our last holiday for five years because we've got to start saving for when we have children. I'm twenty-one years old and I haven't even seen the Niagara Falls.'

'Linzi says they're not as big as you think they're going to be anyway.'

'That's not the point. The point is, she's seen them and I haven't.'

'But Michelle. It's not all bad. I mean, you've got security with Richard. You've got your own house. You've got a car. You've even got a washing machine. You've got a start in life. It's three years since I got my degree and all I have in the world amounts to a double duvet and a broken sandwich toaster.'

'Life's not about having things, Kerry. It's about doing things. It's taken me signing away a week's wages every month on a washing machine and tumble dryer to realise that. Our house could burn down tomorrow, but Linzi's memories of how small Niagara Falls seemed will be with her for ever.'

'But even if your house did burn down, you'd be able to replace it from your insurance,' Kerry reasoned, as she totally missed the point. 'You have got insurance, haven't you?'

'Of course we've got bloody insurance, Kerry. I am marrying Mr Anus after all.'

'Mr Anus? That's no way to talk about your future husband.'

'I believe you dubbed him that after he insisted that we get a doggy bag at Pizzaland.'

'Oh, yeah. I think I did. But I like Richard, Michelle. I really do. I think you'll be good for each other.'

Michelle sighed and rolled over on to her side.

'I wish I was so sure. Hang on to your independence, Kerry, or you could spend the rest of your life wandering round B & Q in your spare time like me and Miranda do. I don't want to go through with this bloody wedding. I've been trapped into it by our folks and his mum. You are the only one of the three of us sisters that can escape all this shit now.'

*   *   *

But at three o'clock the next day, the prize puffball and her attendant meringues strode proudly down the aisle.

When they reached the altar, Kerry stepped forward to take Michelle's bouquet. Michelle met her eyes with a smile. All the misgivings of the night before seemed to have melted away in a dream of forever love. Michelle turned her gaze to Richard, who was so nervous that he looked as though he was trying to hold in a fart when he smiled. Richard was a kind and gentle guy, thought Kerry. Michelle was going to be all right with him.

Kerry ushered the younger bridesmaids into their seats by the aisle. They were level with her mother, who was sitting next to Leon. Mrs Keble sniffed discreetly as the vicar began his spiel about the sight of God. Leon fished in his pocket and brought out a clean, ironed handkerchief, which he lent her to dab at her eyes. He was the perfect escort, smiling, smarming, singing out loudly for all the hymns.

While the bride and groom signed the register, the choir sang 'Wonderwall' and the organist tried to keep up. The vicar had originally said that only hymns could be played in his church, but Richard's mother had slipped him a couple of hundred quid for the vestry fund and the musical policy had been mysteriously changed. Unfortunately, that money covered the painful rendition of 'Lady in Red' as the bridal party proceeded out of the church as well.

But it was a beautiful wedding and Mrs Keble was staggering with emotion as she walked proudly back up the aisle on Leon's arm. Either that or the cooking sherry.

CHAPTER THIRTEEN

The wedding reception was being held in the banqueting hall of a local hotel, Hawthorne House. As children, Kerry and her sisters had often played in the ruins of Hawthorne House as it then was. It had been decimated by a fire in the twenties which was supposedly started by the cook's eldest son when he found out that his father was in fact lord of the manor. In the mid-eighties property boom, the red-brick shell had been bought and restored to its former glory by the Post House Group, and where once there had been grass poking up through singed flagstones, there was now that familiar carpet – dark blue pile with an attractive golden monogram. Michelle had always said that she intended to live in Hawthorne House when she grew up. A night in the honeymoon suite was almost a wish fulfilled, Kerry guessed.

There were three wedding parties at Hawthorne House that day. When the Keble party arrived, they were ushered straight out on to the rolling lawn for their complimentary glass of feeble Bucks Fizz. It wasn't the most glorious of days and Kerry was starting to wish that she had a little more puff in her sleeves to keep her warm. The official photographer had a set-to with the manager because the party which had arrived shortly before the Kebles were taking too long with their photographs and hogging all the best scenic spots.

By five o'clock, Kerry felt grinned out. Her sister and her new husband finally got to have their photocall on the precarious swing by the ornamental lake and the Keble party were called inside for the wedding breakfast. Breakfast? Ha ha. Kerry's stomach had been on the verge of rumbling throughout the service. She had only been able to have one piece of toast that morning because Angela had cut the dress just a little on the small side. Mrs Keble reminded Kerry that it was her own fault, since she hadn't managed to attend a single dress-fitting since the very first one almost eighteen months before.

As chief bridesmaid, Kerry sat to the right of the best man. Leon had been placed three spaces down, between Michelle's new grandmother-in-law and Kerry's Great Auntie Jean. He was still smiling and nodding while Jean probably told him about her problem waterworks. While the waiters were pouring out the first of many glasses of champagne, Leon turned and caught Kerry's eye. He winked at her and raised his glass. She felt herself blush and got some bubbles up her nose.

'That your boyfriend, is it?' Derry the best man asked as he broke a bread roll into a pile of clumsy crumbs. 'Bit flash, in't he? Saw his car outside. Still, I 'spect they're all like that up in the big city, mind.'

'It's not his car,' Kerry explained. 'He just hired it for the weekend. He usually rides a Yamaha 750.'

Derry's eyes widened. 'Bloody hell. I knew he was a flash bugger. That's one of the fastest bikes you can have on the road.'

Kerry knew it too.

'How come you didn't ride up on that then?'

'I wouldn't have been able to fit my suitcase on the back of it.'

'What? I wouldn't let no bloody woman's bag stop me from riding a Yamaha 750,' Derry commented through a mouthful of bread. 'I'd have told you to take the bloody train and I'd meet you here.'

'I guess that's why Carina broke off the engagement,' Kerry replied acidly.

'She was unfaithful to me.' Derry was hurt. 'And after I painted her name on the side of my Escort and all.'

The wedding breakfast segued almost without event into the speeches. One of the younger bridesmaids threw up in the loos and Kerry was dispatched to deal with it. When she returned, feeling a little queasy from the experience herself, her father stood up to give his speech as 'father of the bride' and ended his little monologue of Michelle's most embarrassing childhood memories with 'Two down, one to go'. He even publicly offered Leon a fiver to take Kerry off his hands. Derry said he would do the job for just three pounds.

From the Hawthorne House Hotel, they proceeded to the 'wedding disco' at the Lions' Rugby Club. The lobby to this draughty hall was still caked with mud brought in by that afternoon's rugby practice but the hall itself had been really tarted up for the occasion. All the plastic tables had had their cigarette burn scars covered with pink paper tablecloths. At the centre of each cloth was a pink and white floral arrangement to which was attached a helium-filled balloon. A fair arch of balloons graced the buffet table. But when Michelle walked into the room she burst into angry tears.

'I told her to match the balloons to the bridesmaids' dresses,' she wailed.

'They had a special offer on the pink,' comforted her new husband.

Michelle and Richard missed the first dance while she reapplied her tear-stained face in the toilets.

The guests who hadn't been quite important enough to warrant an invitation to the wedding reception proper drifted into the rugby club between seven and eight. They brought with them a terrifying posse of small children who drank too much fizzy orange and started to run around as though somebody had taken part of their brain circuitry out. Leon and Kerry were sitting at a table with Great Auntie Jean.

'There'll be tears before bedtime for that lot,' she remarked. And sure enough, even as she spoke a three-year-old lad in a blue velvet waistcoat collided head-on with a little girl in pink jeans. The adults recoiled from the sickening crack.

'See? What did I tell you?' said Great Auntie Jean. She was the kind of person you wouldn't want to sit next to on an aeroplane.

Pretty soon, Mrs Keble rolled up to their table. She was still wearing her hat, which had been firmly pinned to her head that morning though it was beginning to slip to one side. 'Oh my goodness,' she said in a stage whisper. 'If Richard's cousin Cheryl doesn't take control of her children, I swear I don't know what I'm going to do. I'll give them bloody cracking their heads together. That little kiddy ripped a cloth off the buffet table just now and ran off with a bowl full of crisps. How are you doing, Jean?' she softened her voice a little. 'Has our Kerry's Leon been looking after you? He's a lovely boy, isn't he? From Down Under, you know. Did you recognise his accent?'

Leon smiled obligingly as she ruffled the top of his hair drunkenly. Kerry just prayed that her mother wouldn't pinch his cheeks.

'Isn't he nicely dressed?' She talked about him openly in his presence. 'Not like our Miranda's Steven. I ask you, Jean. His own sister-in-law's wedding and he turns up without a tie. I had to borrow one off some old chap who was in the churchyard putting flowers on his wife's grave. Amazing, isn't it, how obliging people are when they know you've got a wedding on?'

'You should have said, Mrs Keble,' Leon piped up. 'I was carrying a spare tie myself just in case I spilled something down this one.'

'Oh, Leon,' she plopped down in the chair beside him and placed a hot hand on his knee. 'This man is such an angel. I tell you, Jean, I was just about to burst into tears as our Chelle came down the aisle looking so beautiful, when Leon pulled out a handkerchief. And not just a paper one. It was cotton and pressed. I suppose you must have noticed, Leon, how our Kerry just shoves toilet paper up her sleeve. Honestly, I don't know where I went wrong with my girls.'

'I don't think you went wrong at all, Mrs Keble,' Leon smiled. Kerry tried to hide her reddening face on the pretence of getting an irritating bit of gypsophila out of her fringe. Leon's besotted boyfriend impression was completely spot on.

'Thank you, Leon. You're such a comfort to an old woman.'

'Not an old woman, Mrs K.'

'Oh, you cheeky monkey.' Then she did pinch his cheeks. 'Right, come on, our Kerry. You're Michelle's chief bridesmaid so you're supposed to be helping me and your father to entertain her guests. Go and see if you can't control Cheryl's little menace will you? Since it doesn't look as though she intends to take him in hand herself.'

Kerry rose from her chair dutifully. 'Mum, you do know that Leon and I have got to drive back to London tonight, don't you?' Leon stalled her with a wave of his hand.

'Not until your lovely mother and I have had a dance.'

By the time Leon had done the rounds of all the ladies of a certain age, it was out of the question that they would be driving back to London that night. Kerry's mother insisted that they stay over until the next day and Leon, to Kerry's surprise, raised not one word of protest. When it came to bedtime, Mrs Keble took Kerry aside and said that, since Michelle had gone on her honeymoon to Majorca and this was the nineties and all, she had no objection if Leon wanted to take up Michelle's side of the bed in her absence. Kerry protested feebly on the grounds of decency, since that was what she thought she was supposed to do, but Leon seemed only too happy with the arrangement.

'I couldn't spend another night with your cousins,' he told her when they finally got behind closed doors. 'They spent the whole time having farting competitions in their sleeping bags. Honestly, I felt inadequate.' He crawled into the saggy double bed beside her. The springs had been knackered for as long as Kerry could remember. 'I think we're going to get a bit of roll-together in this,' Leon commented. 'Hey, is that you in that picture?'

He pointed at a photograph of the three sisters in primary school uniform which stood in a dusty frame on a shelf.

'Yeah, that's me in the middle. Stopping the other two from kicking the living daylights out of each other. They used to fight all the time.'

'I can't believe that. You've got such a lovely family, Kerry,' Leon whispered. 'But then, someone as nice as you had to be brought up by nice parents, I suppose.'

'Like my mother says,' replied Kerry dryly, 'she doesn't know where she went wrong.'

'They're all so friendly. They really welcomed me into the fold.'

'I'm sure they're just like any other family, really.' Kerry was feeling strangely embarrassed by the flattery.

'Not mine,' Leon sighed. 'Do you know that this June it will be three years since I last saw my mother? And my father? I can't even remember how long that's been. I've got an older sister, but I haven't seen her either. She sided with Mum when we fell out and refused to return any of my calls. I was quite surprised about that.'

'What did you fall out about?'

'What d'you think? Me coming out of the closet, of course. Me doing "unnatural things" with some sailor I met in Cape Town. Mum just tried to deny it at first. Then, when I told her that I was actually going to move in with him, that was it. She cried for three days and then cut me off without another word.'

'Shit, that's rough. But why do you think your mum was so upset? I mean, I think that my parents would stand by me whatever I did.'

'Believe me, I thought the same. I suppose Mum might have been embarrassed. We lived in a very small town. And I think she was worried about not having any grandchildren too. My sister never had a boyfriend in all the time I can remember. She's destined to die an old maid. I suppose Mum thought I was the only hope for the continuation of the Landesman family line.'

'I'm lucky I've got two sisters to do all that for me. Miranda had Hayley before she left school. But did you ever have any girlfriends?' Kerry asked casually.

'Yeah, I had a few. In high school I went out with this girl called Janine for almost five years. It started when we were twelve. Mum thought that she was going to be the one. After we split up I would come home every other night to find Janine and my mother sitting at the kitchen table plotting how they could get us back together. I felt bad about that. I mean, I don't dislike girls even now. And I would love to have children one day.'

Kerry could almost hear the beating of her heart.

'It's just that I'm attracted to the whole person,' Leon mused. 'I think gender is pretty irrelevant if everything else is there. You know, if you've got total empathy with someone.'

Kerry nodded in the dark.

'Unfortunately, since I hit eighteen I've tended to find that total empathy only with the boys,' Leon added with a faint laugh.

'But it's not impossible that you might turn straight again,' Kerry whispered hopefully. 'I mean, if you found a girl you had total empathy with?'

'Turn straight? Well I suppose you should never say never,' Leon laughed. 'If I found the right girl.'

'Leon, what are you going to do about your visa?' Kerry asked when he had fallen silent again.

'I was trying not to think about that.'

'You're always trying not to think about it. You're going to have to sort it out soon. I mean, I'm sure it'll show up that you're still working illegally when the company gets audited.'

'I don't think the tax office is connected to immigration.'

'Look, it's better to sort it out now than be caught a year down the line. If they have to deport you you'll never be allowed back into the country. Ever. We might never see you again.'

'I'm not ready to go home yet.'

'You might not have to. You could say that you were planning to get married to someone British and that you need a bit more time to make sure you're making the right decision.'

'Married to who, Kez? Are you offering?'

'Are you asking?'

Leon snorted. 'That's a pretty ridiculous offer but thanks all the same. Look, I'll see you in the morning, Kez. I'm knackered now.' He put out the bedside lamp.

'I don't want you to have to go,' Kerry whispered in the dark.

'What?' Leon murmured in his half sleep. He lay his arm across Kerry's waist and began to snore in her ear.

It wasn't until late that Sunday evening that Leon finally pulled the hire car up outside Kerry's door. He undid her seatbelt buckle for her and sat back to wait for her to let herself out. The engine was still running.

'Thanks for coming to Bristol with me,' Kerry said shyly. She wanted desperately to invite him in for a last cup of tea, but she had had his undivided attention for almost a whole weekend now. He probably had other things to do.

'My pleasure. You know that I really enjoyed it anyway. It was something different and your Great Auntie Jean was a real scream.'

'She thought you were lovely too,' Kerry told him. 'She asked me when the big day is going to be after you caught the bouquet.'

Leon blushed. 'Yeah. I don't think I was supposed to have done that. It's a "girls only" thing, isn't it?'

'My cousin Jenny was a bit disappointed, I have to say.'

Leon looked at the bridal bouquet which was wilting fast on

the back seat of his car. He reached over and fetched it. 'Here. I don't think I've got much use for this.' He handed the roses to Kerry. 'You could dry them out to preserve them. Hang them upside down until the petals go crispy. There's something else you should do to them to make them last forever but I can never remember what it is.'

His fingers brushed lightly against Kerry's as he passed her the bouquet.

'I'll try that,' she murmured.

The engine was still running. Leon straightened himself up in his seat again. It was a sign that he was ready to go. Kerry pushed down on the handle of her door and put one foot out on to the pavement. 'Thanks again,' she told him. 'You really made my weekend.' Then she leaned over the gear stick and planted a soft kiss just to the side of his mouth. She was sure that his lips puckered to meet hers. Taking her heart in her mouth, she kissed him again.

'I'll see you tomorrow morning,' he told her. 'Nine o'clock sharp.'

'OK.' She clambered out of the car.

Kerry stood on the pavement with her bags around her feet and waved until the tail-lights of his hired car had turned the corner and were gone. She looked at the bouquet in her hand. One of the heavier roses had already dropped out of the soggy oasis base and lay like a dead butterfly in the oily puddle at the side of the road.

CHAPTER FOURTEEN

'Kerry, I need to have an urgent word with you.' Fiona didn't even wait until Kerry had taken her coat off. 'You just won't believe what Linzi has done now.'

Kerry racked her brains for the answer. 'Let me guess,' she began. 'She turned the heating on outside designated hours? Left pesto in the sink for three days?'

Fiona's upper lip twitched angrily. 'No, it's far worse than that.'

'Worse? Don't tell me. She left a tap running for the whole weekend?'

'Ha ha ha.' Fiona wasn't in the mood for a joke. 'No. You're not even close. She's moved Gaetano in.'

'Moved Gaetano in?'

'She's moved Gaetano in.'

Fiona pointed to the four pairs of men's shoes that had joined their boots beneath the hat-stand to illustrate her point. 'He turned up on Friday night with a car full of bags and boxes. He says that his mother has thrown him out of her house. Can you believe that she objects to him going out with a girl who isn't Italian? Anyway, Linzi let him straight in to stay without even asking whether it would be OK with you and me. She said that he was going to go and see his mother on Saturday morning to try to sort things out. But it's Sunday night now, Kerry. And Gaetano is still here. In fact, I don't think he's been out of the house at all since he arrived.'

Kerry surveyed the room, looking for further signs that a cuckoo had indeed been making itself at home in their nest. An ashtray overflowing with the dog-ends of roll-ups balanced precariously on one arm of the grey Draylon sofa. A dented, empty lager can lay on the floor beside it.

'And he smokes in the house.' Fiona followed Kerry around as she walked from lounge to kitchen and kettle to fridge, whispering all the time like a latter-day Iago. 'And he has about as much clue as Linzi about the ethics of taking your turn with the washing-up. We talked about this before we even moved in, Kerry. We decided that boyfriends staying overnight is OK, but no one is allowed to actually move someone in on a permanent basis.'

'Not that I could move anyone into my room if I wanted to,' Kerry muttered.

'OK, so I know it's a bit small, Kez. But we'll swap rooms in a couple of months, I promise. It's just that . . .'

'I know. I don't have a proper boyfriend. And you and Linzi do. You see, if Linzi had the small room, Gaetano wouldn't be here.'

'Ha ha ha. But the fact remains, he is here. And what are we going to do about it?'

'I'm not going to do anything. It's only been two days and I'm sure it's just temporary,' Kerry sighed. 'Linzi will have fallen out with him by the end of the week if he even stays that long.'

'Do you really think so?'

'Of course. You know what Linzi's like with men. Gaetano will be old news by next Saturday.'

Linzi's bedroom was above the kitchen. With the sound of the kettle boiling, Kerry and Fiona had almost missed the rising squeak and creak, but now the kettle had stopped its furious bubbling, they found their attention being drawn to the ceiling. To the sound of a badly made bed rocking frantically on creaking floor boards. Kerry and Fiona groaned simultaneously.

'Do you still think he'll be out before the end of the week?' Fiona asked.

'We've got to tell her to get that bed fixed,' said Kerry.

'I swear she's never been in love for this long before,' Fiona whined. 'I'm sure she thinks that he's the one for her.'

They resolved to tackle the question the next morning at breakfast. But breakfast came and went without event. Linzi had called in sick for that week's temp job and returned to her warm bed and lover before the subject of unwanted guests

could be properly broached. Fiona and Kerry walked together to
the tube.

'If he's going to be staying for more than a week, we'll have
to work out his share of the rent and the bills,' Fiona began.
Kerry just shrugged. 'Oh, how selfish of me. I almost forgot to
ask,' Fiona continued. 'How was your little sister's wedding?'

'Romantic,' Kerry admitted.

'Lovely! Tell me all about it from the start. What were the
dresses like?'

Kerry couldn't wait to get to work.

Fiona was feeling particularly intolerant of Linzi's misdemeanours because she hadn't seen Tim all weekend. The Old Boys'
rugby team was having its annual reunion do and as an ex-
captain of the college side, Tim was, of course, obliged to go.
Fiona didn't expect him to come back before all the drinking
games were done but she was a little disappointed that he hadn't
even phoned to say 'hi' by Sunday night. On getting into the
office, the very first thing she did was check her voicemail to see
if he had called. No new messages since Friday afternoon. She
picked up her handset and dialled Tim's desk at BFO Schwartz,
the merchant bank.

'Tim,' she said automatically when the phone was picked up
at the other end.

'No, Tim's not at his desk. This is Ryan.'

'It's Fiona, Ryan.'

'Oh, hi, Fi. How's tricks?'

'Well as can be expected on a Monday morning, thanks.'

Ryan had the desk opposite Tim. They got on very well.
Apparently they had a mutual friend who had been at Ryan's
prep school and in Tim's tutorial set at Cambridge or some such
spurious connection like that. Once or twice, Tim, Fiona, Ryan
and Ryan's girl of the moment had been on a double date. He was
thickset and handsome with curly blond hair. In fact, not unlike
Tim but without the cauliflower ears. Ryan might have been
just Fiona's type if she wasn't already engaged to his workmate.
'Where is he, then?' Fiona asked impatiently. 'Throwing his guts
up in the loo, I suppose.'

'He's not coming in today,' Ryan replied.

'Oh really. Did he call in sick?'

'No, he booked a day's holiday at the beginning of last week.'

'He didn't tell me.'

Ryan spluttered. Fiona sensed that he knew he had put his foot in it, right up to the ankle. 'Oh, no. You must be right, Fi,' Ryan back-pedalled. 'He must have called in sick before I got in this morning. I was getting him mixed up with one of the other boys. Yes. That's it. Tim's sick. Rugby this weekend, wasn't it? I expect he's throwing up right now.'

'Thanks, Ryan. I sincerely hope he is.' Fiona put the phone down and blinked back the prickle of tears gathering behind her eyes in disbelief. She prayed that Ryan had been wrong. She couldn't believe that Tim would have taken a day's holiday when they were meant to be saving up all their leave for a nice long honeymoon. She dialled his home number. He wasn't there. Perhaps he was still in Cambridge. Fiona couldn't concentrate on her screen and managed to accidentally delete all the hard work she had done on Friday afternoon.

Tim called her shortly after lunchtime. He claimed that he had dawdled back from Cambridge with Wooders that morning, having called work at the crack of dawn to tell them that he was sick with food poisoning. He arranged to meet Fiona after work at a bar near her office. He hadn't proposed the meeting readily and Fiona put down the phone with a strong sense that he would rather have stayed at home and nursed his head. But she didn't give him the opportunity to cancel and at half past five she made a dash for the loo to put her face straight, adding an extra coat of mascara. Linzi had once said that she could tell by the thickness of Fiona's mascara whether she thought she was just about to be dumped. Fiona sniffed back the thought. But it was true. She only bothered to accentuate her good points when she wanted to warn Tim to be grateful for what he had. This make-up truly was her war-paint. A knot tightened slowly in her stomach which didn't let her loose until Tim walked into the bar and hugged her hello. Then he ordered a couple of Diet Cokes. A sure sign that he had made a new week's resolution never to drink again. Ever.

'Did you have a good weekend?' Fiona asked automatically.

'Oh, it was a great match,' Tim began. 'And, as ever, I was the man of it. We showed those young pups a thing or two about rugby, I can tell you. They were absolutely pony and crap, Fi.

No wonder the college has slipped right down in the league. Apparently they've got this strict new entrance system which means that the undergraduate applicants are chosen purely on academic merit these days. How can they expect to get a decent rugby team together with a policy like that? Bloody ridiculous if you ask me.'

Fiona wasn't in the mood for an education policy debate. Instead, she went straight for the jugular.

'I called you at the office this morning and Ryan said that you had booked today off.'

'No,' said Tim patiently. 'I called in sick.'

'He said that you had booked the day off,' Fiona repeated as she angrily stirred the ice and lemon around in her Diet Coke with a straw. 'Taken a day's holiday.'

'OK. I did. But so what?' Tim couldn't be bothered to try to hold out under questioning while his head still thumped like a Kiwi warrior's dance hall floor. 'I booked a day off. Big deal.'

'So, when we were supposed to be buying the engagement ring you told me that you couldn't get any time off because of this terribly important project you've been working on. And after that, we decided that it would be a good idea to save up all our leave for an extra long honeymoon anyway. Then you go and blow a whole day on messing around with that bloody idiot Wooders.'

'Calm down, Fi. It was time off in lieu, I swear. Besides I'm sure that I mentioned it to you last week.'

'You did not.'

'Sheesh!!' Tim blew his floppy blond fringe out of his eyes. 'It won't happen again, Herr Führer. I promise.'

'Have you even told him yet, Tim?'

'Told who what?' Tim leaned back in his seat and spoke into his glass, misting it up as he did so.

'Have you even told your best friend that you just got engaged to me?'

Tim put his glass down noisily. 'Of course I have.'

'I don't believe you,' Fiona countered. 'When did you tell him?'

'I told him on Friday. When we were driving down to Cambridge. I told him in the car.'

'And what did he say?'

'He said that he was very pleased for us both and that he wishes us a very long and happy marriage.'

'Rubbish. He wouldn't have said that. Wooders would have said that you were out of your mind, Tim. He hates me. I'm the last girl on earth he would want you to marry.'

'One, he doesn't hate you, Fiona, and two, perhaps there is just a vague possibility that he really is pleased for us.'

'Ha ha ha, Tim.' Fiona wasn't convinced. 'Look, I've told Mr Hara that I'm not going to New York because we're getting married this summer and now I want you to set a date. I want you to tell all your friends that we're engaged and then set a date on which we will be married come hell or high water. It doesn't mean anything, this bloody ring, if we're not allowed to tell anybody about it.' She took the ring off and held it threateningly between her thumb and forefinger right in front of his face.

Tim's forehead was wrinkled with panic. 'Fi, I'll tell everybody at the next rugby practice, I promise.'

'And we'll set the date?'

'Of course,' he gulped. 'When for?'

'June, like we discussed when we were deciding whether or not I should go to New York,' Fiona announced. 'June the fifteenth to be more exact. It's a Saturday and it'll be my parents' silver wedding anniversary on the same day.'

'Christ, Fi. June the fifteenth? It's a bit short notice. Can't we . . .'

'Set the date or call this wedding off altogether, Tim Harper. There's your choice.'

Fiona didn't hang around to hear him choose but flew off in the direction of the ladies' as if the hounds of hell were on her tail. She waited three minutes, hyperventilating over a toilet bowl and trying not to cry. Why had she given him an ultimatum, she asked herself in despair. Tim was the type of idiot who would call her bluff on principal. She reapplied her mascara, poking herself in the eye as she did so and instantly making it look as though she had been crying even though she had just barely managed not to. When she finally re-emerged, with the blood thudding in her head as though she had just finished a five mile run, Tim had been joined at their secluded corner table by Wooders. Fiona wondered whether she should walk straight out again. She couldn't believe that Tim had told Wooders where they would be on their quiet evening out after spending the whole weekend in his company. Tim muttered something quietly to which Wooders responded by spitting out a mouthful of beer and slapping Tim heartily across the back.

'Good God, Tim!' Wooders shouted so that the attention of every customer in the bar was drawn to their corner table. 'You're out of your tiny little mind!!!'

Fiona stalked hurriedly across the room and stood before the table with her clenched fists resting on her hips.

'What's going on?' she snapped.

Tim smiled sheepishly. Wooders continued to snort with laughter.

'I was just telling Wooders that we're getting married in June.'

CHAPTER FIFTEEN

The phone rang. Linzi was pretending to be out, but Gaetano answered the call and forgot that he was meant to say that Linzi wasn't in. It was Caroline, from Advertising Angels. She proudly announced that she had arranged an interview for Linzi at a very smart advertising agency in the West End. The position was for a personal secretary to one of the directors and they were offering ten grand to start and a twenty-five pound Next voucher after five years' continuous service without sick leave.

'So, you see,' said Caroline triumphantly, 'I know you weren't very happy about it at first, but my idea about toning down your CV worked after all. You've got an interview, darling. Don't you think your Auntie Caroline always knows exactly what she is doing?'

'Yeah, thanks.'

But Linzi was puzzled. Hadn't they seen the bit about frottage?

'I have had to put a couple of other girls forward for the job of course,' Caroline continued, 'but I don't mind telling you that I think you have by far and away the best chance of success. I've pencilled you in for three thirty. You'll be interviewed by Mr Gerrard himself. He's a lovely man. I'm sure you won't find him scary at all. But you will remember to take your nose ring out won't you, darling? I'm not sure how old Mr Gerrard is, since we've only spoken on the phone, but my guess is that he is in his middle years and I think we both know that body piercing generally does not go down too well with men of a certain age. Have I made myself clear, sweetheart?' Linzi grunted an affirmative.

'Good. Right, you'll need the address. Do you have a pen? You do. OK. Here it is. I think you'll find that Tottenham Court Road is the nearest tube. Better make sure you're there a couple of minutes early in case of emergencies. Don't want to have to nip out for a tinkle halfway through the interview, do we?' Linzi rolled her eyes. 'OK, darling. Wishing you the very best of British. Don't forget to call me the minute you get out to tell me how you've done. Mwah-mwah. Bye-ze-bye.'

'Bye-ze-bloody-bye.'

Caroline had already hung up.

'Got an interview?' Gaetano asked.

'Yeah,' Linzi told him. 'Don't think I'm going to go through with it though.'

'Why not?'

'Because it will be crap, G. Because every single job interview that stupid woman sends me to is crap. She doesn't need to send out girls. She should just send out loo-rolls. I'm not going to go.'

'I think you should,' said Gaetano without looking up from his paper.

'Oh, yeah. And why's that?'

'Because you need a job, that's why.'

'Why do I need a job? I get my allowance and my dole. I think I can cover the rent until my housing benefit comes through.'

'You said yourself that your father has threatened to cut off your allowance if you don't get yourself some work before the end of the month. You don't have to do it forever, Linz, just show willing for a while.'

'You're supposed to be on my side.'

'I am on your side. Look, Linz, falling out with your family isn't much fun, you know.' He was going misty eyed over a full-colour illustration of a plate of pasta smothered in rich tomato sauce. 'Just make out like you're trying for a little while and your father will be off your back again before you know it.'

'You're worse than the people at the dole office.'

'And it'll give you something to do while I'm at the shop this afternoon.' Gaetano put down his paper and pulled Linzi towards him for a hug. 'Besides, just think of all the presents you'll be able to buy for me with your first big wage-packet.' He nuzzled into her ear.

'And when are you going to buy something for me?'

'When I'm rich, *cara mia*. When the band has its first number one album, I'll buy you a diamond-studded speed-boat and take you around the world.'

'I get sea-sick,' said Linzi flatly, as she freed herself from his arms.

Linzi decided to borrow Kerry's navy-blue suit to wear to the interview. Fiona's black DKNY number would have been more stylish and a far better fit, but Fiona had already read the riot act to Linzi that week over Gaetano's extended residence and at that moment, to wear her clothes without permission just didn't seem like such a great idea. Linzi did, however, borrow a pair of Fiona's smartest Pied-à-terre shoes. Fiona's shoes were easier to get away with because she had yet to work out an infallible footwear filing system.

The Soho offices of CPIDG Ltd (named, very creatively, thought Linzi sarcastically, after the directors' initials) were rather fantastic. The receptionists looked as though they were supermodels dressed by Armani and sat behind a burred oak desk that was as big as a small boat. As she waited on the edge of a buff leather sofa, Linzi began to wish she had taken the risk and come DKNY after all.

'Miss Adams,' said the receptionist who moonlighted as Naomi Campbell's body double. 'Mr Gerrard will see you now. Take the lift to the third floor and someone will meet you there.'

At the third floor, Linzi was met by a vision of a boy in black leather jeans. He took her to the anteroom of Gerrard's office and asked her whether she wanted tea or coffee. When she asked for coffee, he offered cappuccino or espresso. She went for espresso for fear of getting a milk moustache. The leather-vision told her that they had proper coffee machines on every floor of the CPIDG headquarters.

As she waited for her summons, Linzi watched the beautiful people of CPIDG drift by. It seemed that everyone was smiling. A man in his forties bent down to pick up a bundle of papers a young girl had dropped on the floor without even pausing to think of the opportunity to get a quick flash of her knickers. By the time Mr Gerrard poked his heard around the door, Linzi had almost forgotten how pissed off she had been on the way there and decided that she wanted a job in this place, even if it was just making the tea.

She got out her best interview technique and shook him warmly by the hand.

'Sit down,' he implored her, as he pulled out a chair. 'Linzi, isn't it? George Gerrard's my name, but you can just call me George.'

He resumed his position on the other side of the desk, and looked down at a piece of paper in an Advertising Angels folder. It was her creative CV. He quickly refreshed his memory of it and smiled broadly.

'Ah, yes,' he said. 'Frottage. Perhaps you should start by telling me some more about that.'

Linzi had to admit that she'd only seen pictures.

George Gerrard was nothing like the man Linzi had expected to meet that afternoon. He was not, as Caroline had suspected, in 'his middle years'. Rather he was only just the wrong side of thirty and his body was resisting all temptation to spread. He was dressed in a beautifully cut suit, possibly Paul Smith, and a white shirt with a Nehru collar that circled a tanned and well-muscled neck. As he spoke to Linzi about her CV, he rolled up his sleeves to reveal a Breitling diving watch on one brown wrist. Linzi wondered idly how deep he could go.

'Well,' said George, when Linzi had admitted that the three GCSEs on her CV were in fact supplemented by four A-levels and a degree, 'I think that's about all the questions I have for you, Linzi.' She made a move as if she was about to stand up and shake his hand goodbye. 'No, hang on, I've got one more.' He leaned back and tapped his silver pen against his pearl-white bottom teeth while he decided whether or not he should risk asking it. 'Do you fancy coming for a drink?'

'A drink?' Linzi exclaimed, as if it were the hardest question she had ever been asked. 'With you?'

'Yes. With me. Why not? It's a beautiful day and I fancy having a quick half before I head home. I think you should come with me. We need to build up some kind of a rapport if we're going to be working together.'

'Working together?'

George was already slipping on his jacket. 'Come on.' He opened the door to his office so that she could pass on through

before him. He let his temporary secretary know that he would
be out for the rest of the day and then guided Linzi into the lift.
She wasn't sure quite what to say. Had he just offered her the
job? It seemed as though he had. Her heart was beginning to
do little skips of delight. After everything he had told her about
the company and her prospects should she join them, she found
that she couldn't wait to accept it. And he would be such a great
guy to work for, far better than that chauvinist moron at E, F
& S. George Gerrard seemed really keen that his PA should
have the opportunity to get on within the company rather than
moulder behind a monitor. Even the ice-maiden receptionists
waved goodbye cheerily as George and Linzi stepped out into
the street. He was obviously well liked by the other employees.
She had a job. Gaetano would be thrilled. And maybe even
Fiona would get off her back for a bit. She was so excited that
she found it difficult to cross the road and stepped out in front
of a moped.

'Hey, careful,' George yanked her back on to the pavement.
'My car's over there,' he pointed towards the multi-storey car
park.

'We're going in the car? I thought we would be going for a
drink around here.'

'You're not in a hurry, are you?' She shook her head. 'Then I
thought we'd get out of town. Who wants to sit outside a central
London pub on a day like today? Breathing in all that crap in
the air.' He pulled an exaggerated face of distaste. 'No, I know
a great place down by the river. It's got a beautiful garden and
more importantly, it's also got real ale.'

He opened the passenger door of a navy-blue BMW 325i. It
had a soft top, which he rolled down. 'Don't get to use this often
enough in England,' he commented. 'And these days I hardly
ever get the time to drive down to my place in the South of
France.'

'The South of France?'

'Yes. Near Cannes. Do you know the area?'

'Vaguely,' Linzi lied.

'Thought I might take my lap-top and my new PA down
there for a bit. Got to take advantage of the communications
revolution.'

'Absolutely.' Linzi settled back into the deep leather passenger seat and ran her fingers ponderously over the polished wooden dash. She really couldn't believe her luck. What a great day. What a great guy.

They drove to the pub by the river and sat at a picnic table right on the bank until the sun began to creep down the sky. Midges danced in the air, suddenly buoyed up, then dropping down in the thermals. Each time he went to fetch them a drink, George came back to sit a little closer to Linzi. Now they were side by side, just an inch or so between them. George was flipping a beer-mat between his fingers.

'So, do you think you could work with me?' he asked her.

'Oh, yes,' said Linzi. 'I think we'd get on very well indeed.'

'Good. Do you want another drink? They've just called last orders.'

'No. I think I really ought to be getting back home. Will you be OK to drive? You've had a few . . .'

George laughed. 'Do I look drunk? I'll be fine. I'll drive you back to town, no problem. Where abouts is it that you live, again?'

'Clapham South. Well, it's Balham really. Just doesn't sound quite so good.'

'Ah yes. I know it. Do you live on your own?'

'No, I share with a couple of friends. Fiona and Kez.' She didn't bother to mention Gaetano, but George still looked a little disappointed.

'Will they be at home tonight?'

'I don't know. I think so.'

'Shame.' George swilled the last dregs of his pint around in his glass and then swigged it back. 'A real shame,' he repeated. Linzi felt a strange creature with pins for feet jogging up her back and subconsciously scanned his left hand for signs of ownership. There were no signs. 'Come on,' he said, getting to his feet suddenly and grabbing her hand. 'Let's get you back to Clapham South before curfew.'

This time, he put the hood of the car up. It was very different to be sitting next to him in the dark. As he pulled out of the pub gates into the narrow country lane and changed gear, Linzi felt his knuckles brush lightly against her leg. Suddenly, the rough material of her borrowed skirt seemed very, very thin indeed.

When he placed his hand fully on her thigh, Linzi felt as though she were on fire.

'George!' she said, her voice rising in surprise. 'What are you doing?'

'You've got beautiful legs, Linzi,' he told her flatly.

'I don't think you should be . . .'

'Don't think I should be what?' He moved his hand slowly towards her crotch, bunching up the skirt beneath his hand. His fingers rested right at the top of her thigh. Linzi's body responded with a fully blown hot flush. 'Do you really mind?' he asked.

'Well, I . . . No.' Her reply was almost a sigh.

'Will your housemates be at home?' he asked again.

'Probably,' Linzi squeaked. His fingers brushed against the cotton of her knickers.

'Damn. I can't really stay then.'

A lump rose in Linzi's throat. He wanted to stay at her place? Well, he could have stayed, but Gaetano was probably already warming up his side of the bed. 'No,' she told him, covering his hand with hers and pressing it hard against her pubic bone. 'I guess you can't.'

George took his hand from between her legs to take a narrow corner. Linzi found to her surprise that her body already ached in the absence of his touch. George was scanning the side of the road, looking for a place to pull in and park. He found a spot by a five-bar gate and by the time he had turned off the headlights, his tongue was in Linzi's mouth.

'Oh, yes,' Linzi murmured as he struggled into the passenger side of the car on top of her and tipped her soft leather seat back as far as it would go. She could already feel that he had a hard-on beneath his beautifully cut trousers. His kiss was so rough. So different from Gaetano's. It took the breath right out of her body and bruised her lips until she felt they might be bleeding. He had his hand up her skirt again now and had pulled her knickers to one side. Linzi groaned with delight and arched her body upwards against his.

With his free hand, George tugged down the zip of his flies and worked his wood-hard penis free. Linzi slid her hands in between their bodies and touched it. Then George pushed her skirt up until it was around her waist and tried to force her legs apart.

'No way,' Linzi protested. 'Not without a condom.'

'Damn,' George swore. 'I haven't got one.'

Linzi pushed his body away. George crossed the gear-stick barrier again and slumped panting in the driver's seat.

'Aren't you on the pill or anything?'

'That's hardly the point, is it?'

'I suppose you're right, but God, Linzi, I really want to fuck you right now.'

'You do?' Linzi felt strangely flattered by his desperation.

'There could be other opportunities,' she said coquettishly, stroking his wilting penis gently as if to make up for his disappointment.

She leaned across the transmission tunnel and guided his dick into her mouth. George sighed as though he was relieved. Then he put a hand on the back of her head and pushed her down further so that his stiffening shaft went deeper into her throat.

'Yes, yes,' he murmured. 'Suck me harder. Yes, baby, do it like that.'

'Well, give me some space to breathe,' Linzi spluttered.

She elbowed her way upright and took a huge breath.

'You OK?' he asked impatiently, his hand already on the back of her head.

'Sorry,' said Linzi insincerely. 'It's just that you're so very big.'

He pushed her down again and since there was nothing else for her to do in that position, she sucked him as far into her mouth as she could without gagging. George's breathing grew deeper and deeper. She prayed that he wasn't going to be the kind who liked to think about football teams and prolong the occasion. Luckily, it was mere seconds before George began to moan more urgently. She felt the bottom of his penis twitch and knew he was about to come.

'Whoah!!' Linzi turned her head away as the white arrow shot from the jerking head. It made a graceful, glittering arc in the air before landing with a splatter on the polished dashboard.

George didn't even bother to tell her whether it had been good. Instead he got a handkerchief out of his pocket and feverishly began to wipe the dashboard clean.

CHAPTER SIXTEEN

'And what time did you get in?' Fiona asked the next morning. 'Old lover-boy was going up the wall. I thought he was going to walk out on you. He didn't though, worse luck.'

'I went for a job interview,' Linzi told her smugly.

'What? Until two o'clock in the morning?'

'Yes, until two o'clock in the morning. My future boss asked me to go for a drink with him afterwards, that's all.'

'Oh, sounds very friendly. I bet Gaetano really loved that.' Fiona bit into her toast with a wink and slid out of the kitchen as Gaetano walked in. He didn't even kiss Linzi hello.

'I'm going to work now,' he announced curtly.

'OK, G. I'll see you later on. Yeah?' Linzi stretched up on tiptoe to plant a kiss on his cheek but Gaetano turned his face away 'Charming,' she muttered once he had left. 'It was him who told me that I needed to get myself a job.'

'Yeah,' said Fiona, removing her margarine tub from Linzi's grasp. 'You do. What time is it now?'

'Seven thirty.'

'Cool. I've got a late start today so I think I might try to find out what all the fuss over this *Big Breakfast* programme is about.' Fiona ambled towards the television. Linzi flew out of the kitchen to stand in front of it.

'Don't!'

'What?'

'Don't watch the *Big Breakfast*. It's rubbish, Fi. Honestly. It'll spoil your morning and if I start watching television now, I'll never get anything done today.'

'Linzi. What are you talking about?' Fiona tried to get past her. Linzi employed her best netball marking tactics to keep Fiona back. 'And why is there a tea-towel over the screen?' Fiona, who had always been placed in goal attack, zipped past Linzi easily and whipped the cloth away.

'Shit,' Linzi gave up her defence. 'I'm sorry, Fi. I was going to get it fixed later today. I will get it fixed. I promise. I swear. I think it's only the buttons that are a bit bashed in anyway.'

'What?'

Fiona gazed in disturbingly quiet annoyance at the control panel of her television. It had indeed been caved in, as had the little speaker below it.

'I'll have it good as new by this afternoon. No, better than that. I'll get you a completely new television,' Linzi burbled. 'I mean, this set must be getting on for ten years old by now. It's ancient. I'll get you something state of the art. Absolutely brand-new. Flat screen. Surround sound?'

'With what, Linzi?' Fiona asked coldly. 'With what? You've got no money to replace this. Besides, it's not that the television's worth all that much, what's really upsetting is the fact that this damage is hardly accidental. Someone appears to have kicked it in. Did you do it?'

'Fi . . . I . . .'

'Gaetaňo did it, didn't he?' Fiona narrowed her eyes.

'Well, yes,' Linzi squirmed. 'But it was my fault really. He just got a bit wound up while he was waiting for me to come home from the interview and we had a bit of a row and . . .'

'He thought it would be a good idea to kick my television in to show you just how much he missed you? That's great. But what confuses me is how on earth he managed to miss the screen with his big feet?'

'Fiona, I've told you that I'll pay for the damage. I can't do anything more.'

'No. You won't. Gaetano broke it, so he should replace it and when he's replaced my television he should get out of this house before I get mad and kick him in. He's a bloody thug.'

'He's got nowhere else to go,' Linzi pleaded.

'I don't care. Why can't he get a bedsit like anyone else in his position? Tim would never impose on us like this. When he first came up to London he lived in a horrible little place in Hackney and had to share a single loo with sixteen other residents.

Gaetano just lazes about here, using all the hot water, eating all the food and never washing up and as if that wasn't enough, it now appears he feels free to rearrange the furnishings.'

'So, Tim's a saint and Gaetano isn't.'

'No. I didn't say that. Tim acts like a grown man, there's the difference. Oh, this is just bloody typical. I've got a late start at work and now all I want to do is go in and get behind my desk as quickly as possible. You've got to get rid of him, Linzi. I don't care how you do it.'

Fiona left her toast unfinished and flounced back up the stairs to fetch her briefcase. She walked out of the house without bidding Linzi goodbye. Instead she hissed 'Sort it out' as she closed the door.

The shouting had woken Kerry up. When she managed to struggle out of bed, she found Linzi in the kitchen, sitting on the work-surface next to the sink with a knife in the toaster.

'What are you doing?' Kerry shrieked. 'You'll electrocute yourself.'

'That's what I'm trying to do,' said Linzi dryly, though she was actually just salvaging a wonky piece of toast that had got itself stuck on the filaments and was starting to burn. 'Honestly, Kez, I don't think I can do anything right these days. I went for a job interview last night and because I came back late, Gaetano kicked the television in a rage and spent the night sleeping with his back to me. Then this morning, I have to face rage number two from Fiona because Gaetano has ruined her telly. She's told me that I've got to kick him out but he's got nowhere else to go. I don't know what to do. I'm just stuck in the middle. What do you think, Kez?'

In reality, Kerry thought that the house was way too small for the four of them and was getting a little bit tired of finding her toothbrush already wet when she went to use it. But she didn't say so. She could see that Linzi was nearly on the verge of tears and had a very strong aversion to being responsible for pushing someone over that verge. 'I don't mind,' Kerry reassured her. 'I understand that he can't go home yet and I hope that one day someone will do me as big a favour as you've been doing for him. Just keep him off the furniture, eh? And get him to bung Fiona fifty quid for the damage. Anyway, I'm sure she'll forget all about this morning once she's talked wedding guest lists with the wonderful Tim.' The girls swapped comedy grimaces.

'Yeah. Guess we'll have to be measured up for the bridesmaid dresses soon.'

'I'd rather be measured for my coffin.'

Kerry had restored a smile to Linzi's face, but the way that week had been going, it was no surprise that it ended in a screaming match. Kerry was still lying in bed when the countdown started, enjoying the Saturday morning pleasure of knowing that you could hit the snooze button on your alarm clock for just about as long as you liked if you felt so inclined. The morning noises had begun. Somebody had got up and had themselves a shower, and from the deep hacking smoker's cough, Kerry guessed it was Gaetano. A few minutes after that, the front door opened and slammed shut behind him. The house was silent for a short while again, unless you counted the screaming of next-door's two young children which could have penetrated six-feet-thick stone walls.

Eventually, yet another high-pitched rendition of 'Mummy, I didn't do it,' rising to a full-lunged keening scream, drove Kerry from her little bedroom and downstairs to the kitchen. En route, she picked up the post. A red envelope addressed in her mother's neatest hand and a postcard from her honeymooning sister in Majorca which she must have sent the moment she touched down at the airport to make sure that it arrived on time. 'Wish you were here,' the postcard said. A strange note to write from your honeymoon suite.

As Kerry waited for the kettle to spring into life, Fiona padded down the stairs behind her. She too must have heard Gaetano go out, because she was wearing her stripy nightie and fluffy Garfield slippers. She hadn't come downstairs in such a state of undress since the day their unwanted lodger first moved himself in.

'Making coffee?' she asked sleepily.

'Yeah,' said Kerry. 'There's not much milk though.'

'That's OK. I'll have it black. No sugar.'

'I thought you'd given coffee up?'

'I've taken it back on.' A recent report had shown that caffeine helps your body burn more calories in a resting state.

'He's used all the hot water again, you know.' Fiona usually gave the day five minutes before she started a diatribe about Gaetano. 'Selfish beast. I can't bear having a bath when it's tepid.'

'I've put the immersion heater on already,' said Kerry.

'Costs us a bloody fortune,' Fiona muttered. 'When Tim stays he only uses the cold tap.'

'Yes, well. Tim's obviously a nutter.'

Kerry poured out their extra-strong shots of instant life and shoved the last crust of a mouldy brown loaf into the toaster. 'We need some more bread,' she observed.

'It's Linzi's turn to buy but I'm not eating bread any more anyway,' Fiona replied. 'I think I may have an allergy to yeast and that's what makes me get so bloated the whole time.' She patted her washboard-flat stomach, then moved yawning to the sink and started to feel her way along the window-sill, lifting up the sorry-looking shrivelled plants in their pots without really seeing them.

'What are you looking for?' Kerry asked.

'My engagement ring,' Fiona replied through a yawn. 'I forgot to put it back on after I did the washing-up last night.' Her hand continued to creep along the sill like a blind man's. 'That's funny,' she said. 'It's not where I usually leave it.' She took the cup of coffee that Kerry offered while she knitted her brows together in deep thought. 'Perhaps I left it in the bathroom? No. I wouldn't have.' She took a sip from the scalding coffee and then put the cup down on the draining board. She leaned over the sink, careful not to let the ribbons around the neckline of her nightie drag in the cold dirty water of the night before, and scanned the sill more thoroughly. Nope. The ring definitely wasn't there.

'Maybe it dropped into the sink while you were washing up?' Kerry said helpfully, as she scraped a burnt layer off her toast and into the bin. The last slice was too precious to waste.

'I sincerely hope not.' Fiona rubbed nervously at the place where the ring had once been. Then, rolling up a sleeve and closing her eyes, she stuck a hand into the full sink with no small measure of distaste and felt around in the cold, food slime at the bottom. She spiked her finger on a forgotten fork and recoiled, wincing. 'This sink is just too disgusting,' she muttered. 'We've got to rewrite that cleaning rota.'

Kerry watched Fiona trawling through the sludge with the kind of squeamish joy you get when watching a gory horror film. Disappointed, Fiona pulled her hand out of the mire and rinsed it thoroughly clean beneath the hot tap.

'Nope. It's not in there,' she sighed.

'Perhaps you should have pulled the plug out.'

'Then it would have gone straight down the sink, stupid.'

'Oh, yeah. But hang on. You say that you washed up when you got home from work last night and, knowing the way you are about sinks, you would definitely have pulled the plug out when you finished. Right?' Fiona nodded. 'Which means that this water here is left over from Linzi's after-dinner attempt at household hygiene. Perhaps the ring went down the sink before Linzi even started to wash up.'

'Well done, Sherlock,' Fiona rolled her eyes. 'That's really good news.'

'Don't worry. If it has gone down the sink, it'll probably be stuck in the U-bend. That's what it's for. To catch stuff. When I was little, my mum lost one of her favourite earrings down the sink. Dad unscrewed the pipe and it was just sitting there in the U-bend. It had a little bit of sludge on it, but otherwise it was OK.'

Fiona had already opened the cupboard beneath the sink and was looking in despair at the twisty white pipe beneath.

'That's where it'll be,' Kerry pointed at the relevant curves.

'I just don't believe this,' Fiona moaned. 'It took me an age to persuade Tim to buy it, and now, less than two weeks later, I've managed to lose the damn thing.'

'Don't panic. We'll find it in there and Tim need be none the wiser.' Kerry was rather excited at the prospect of being proven right and once again asserting her position as the 'practical one' in the house.

'Are you sure we should be doing this?'

Kerry put a dirty pan beneath the U-bend to catch anything that might be lurking in the pipe. 'Trust me,' she said, 'I've never done this before in my life.'

But the U-bend provided no answers, just a horribly sulphuric smell adding fuel to the girls' theory that the previous tenant had dissolved his estranged wife in acid. An extensive search of the flowerpots on the window-sill proved equally inconclusive. As did the bathroom theory. And likewise a foray around all the possible flat surfaces in the sitting room. Fiona's composure was slipping. She collapsed on to the sofa, still in her Garfield slippers, and took her head in her hands.

'What could I have done with it, Kez? We've looked everywhere. I can't think of anywhere else it could be.'

They went through the possibility that she could have lost it somewhere outside the house. But it wasn't possible. After doing the washing-up, Fiona hadn't moved from her seat in front of the patched-up television until it was time to go to bed. There had been nothing to go out for. Tim was in Cambridge. On an old boys' rugby training weekend, again.

'The last time I saw it,' Fiona said painfully once more, 'was when I put it down on the window-sill before I did the washing-up. I wouldn't have let it fall into the sink. I know I wouldn't. I'm always so careful. It's got a thousand-odd pounds worth of diamonds stuck into it.'

Kerry didn't think this was the right time to mention that Fergie had managed to mislay half of the Crown Jewels at some American airport.

'Tim is going to kill me.'

'That'll save me having to buy a wedding present.'

Fiona wasn't amused.

'Kerry,' she whined, 'stop mucking about and help me out. As far as I can see, the only other possible answer is that I did leave it on the window-sill but that someone else had taken it by the time I got up this morning.'

'Don't be ridiculous. Nobody's been in here except the people that live here and why would any of us want to steal your engagement ring?'

At that moment, Linzi sloped into the sitting room wearing her boyfriend's best Motley Crue T-shirt. 'Hi guys. Has anyone seen Gaetano this morning? Nope? He must have already gone out. Can't believe the bastard didn't kiss me goodbye again.'

Fiona gave Kerry a very knowing look.

By the time Gaetano came back from the market with a new leather jacket draped over his arm, his guilt had practically been sealed. When he let himself into the house, with the extra key that Linzi had cut for him, against Fiona's express request, he found the girls lined up along the sofa like a police inter-view panel. Fiona sat in the middle, still wearing her Garfield slippers.

'I cannot believe that you actually think . . .' Linzi lamented.

When Gaetano walked into the room the girls fell suddenly silent.

'Morning ladies. Looking lovely as usual. Do you want to see what I just picked up at the market? It was a real bargain.'

He opened the plain white plastic carrier bag to show the girls his new leather coat.

Fiona burst into tears and fled up the stairs.

'Jesus,' said Gaetano. 'What's the matter with her?'

'Nothing,' Kerry and Linzi said in unison as they followed swiftly after her. Gaetano was left alone in the middle of the sitting room with the leather jacket hanging half out of its bag.

'Are you going to ask him or do I have to?' Fiona hassled Linzi upstairs in her bedroom.

'No way, Fiona. I am not going to ask my boyfriend if he has stolen your engagement ring. It is a waste of time. He wouldn't have done that to you. I can't believe that it even crossed your mind that he would.'

'Well, I must admit that it didn't cross my mind that Gaetano would be the type to cave in my television set until he actually did it. What other explanation do you have for my ring's disappearance?' Fiona countered. 'Last night it was on the window-sill in the kitchen. This morning my ring is gone and Gaetano has a new leather jacket.'

'Oh, come on. If he had stolen your ring do you think he would be stupid enough to go out, sell the ring, buy himself a new wardrobe with the proceeds, then come back here and show it to you the very same morning? You've gone mad, Fiona. Are you sure you've checked everywhere in the house?'

'I have looked everywhere,' Fiona was finding it difficult to keep her voice down. 'My engagement ring is not in the house. It is probably sitting in some East End pawn shop right now and you're so blinded by lust for that stupid Italian that you're refusing to see the truth.'

'The truth? For God's sake, Fi. Whose kind of truth is that?'

Kerry, who had been sitting on the edge of Fiona's bed trying to keep out of it, suddenly looked towards the door and widened her eyes in a desperate gesture to get them to shut up. The door creaked open. Gaetano stood in the doorway, the new leather jacket still grasped in his hand.

'What's going on?' he asked. 'What are you all whispering about? It's something to do with me, isn't it?'

'Yes. No,' the girls chorused at once. Fiona rose slowly from her seat at the dressing table, rubbing the spot where her ring had once been like some tragic Shakespearean heroine. 'Gaetano,' she cleared her throat, 'have you seen my engagement ring?'

He shook his head.

'Are you sure? Only, last night I put it on the window-sill in the kitchen while I washed up and this morning, when I went to find it, the ring wasn't there.'

Gaetano shrugged.

'We've searched everywhere in the house . . . Have you taken it?'

'Fiona!!!' They could practically see the smoke pouring out of Linzi's nose.

'What do you mean, have I taken it?' Gaetano asked quietly.

'I mean, have you moved my engagement ring? Did you see it on the sill and put it somewhere else for safe-keeping perhaps?'

Linzi shook her head in despair. She didn't dare look at Gaetano but she knew only too well the furious expression which would at that moment be forming in his eyes.

'What you're really asking is whether I have stolen it, right?' Gaetano stared straight at her. Fiona nodded automatically and stared back, her chin jutting out proudly. 'And the answer to your question is no. Of course I haven't taken it. I've got no need to go stealing things like your poxy little ring, Fiona.'

'It is not a poxy little ring,' Fiona said indignantly. 'It is worth more than two thousand pounds.'

'And I can win two thousand pounds on a single night at the greyhound track. I've got no need to steal anything of yours, you bitch,' he hissed. 'Unlike you, I've got my pride.'

But Gaetano moved himself and his pride out of number 67 that very night. Had she been able to, Linzi would have followed him. But, since he was going back to his family home and she already knew exactly what Gaetano's mother thought of her,

it didn't seem like such a good idea. However, she arranged to
meet him at the pub as soon as he had dumped his stuff. In view
of the mood he had been in since she stayed out all night at a 'job
interview', Linzi didn't want to leave him alone to brood for too
long. Fiona decided to go to Tim's house for the evening. Kerry
was just relieved to have them both out of the house. Despite
the fact that in the confusion caused by the missing ring they
had both completely forgotten that it was her birthday.

Kerry opened the red envelope from her mother. Inside was
a floral card printed with 'Happy Birthday Darling Daughter'
in gold and signed by Mum, Dad and The Dog. As she opened
it, a twenty pound note fluttered to the floor. For a moment
she considered blowing it on two bottles of vodka and drinking
herself into Monday. What a miserable way to turn twenty-five
that would be.

But then the phone rang. She picked it up on the second
ring.

'Hey, what are you doing in on a Saturday night, Cinderella?'

Her heart did a little back-flip of joy.

'And it's your birthday isn't it?'

'Leon?'

'That's me. How come you're not out partying, Birthday
Girl?'

'Oh, I don't know. There was a bit of a disaster here today.
Fiona has lost her engagement ring and she's blaming its disappearance on Linzi's boyfriend. You know him. Gaetano.'

'Mmmm. Of course I know him. Have to say I wouldn't be
surprised . . .'

'Whatever. Anyway, they were too busy arguing with each
other to remember what day it was.'

'And they forgot your birthday? Those people you live with are
unbelievable, Kerry. They're supposed to be your friends,' Leon
sighed. 'But listen, my darling, all is not lost. I just called to say
Happy Birthday. Didn't expect you to be in really but Jeremy and
I are going to Heaven tonight. Do you want to come along?'

'Heaven? Sure. What's that?'

'It's a club. You'll love it. We're on the guest list. I think Jeremy
used to sleep with the guy that's doing the lights so we won't
have to pay to get in.'

'But I'm not on the guest list, am I?'

'You will be by tonight, Cinderella. Look, I can't yack on, because I'm using Jeremy's phone. Can you believe I got cut off? I gave Sam the money to pay the bill last month but he obviously put it towards the joint bank account of Dolce & Gabbana instead. I'll meet you outside the club at ten o'clock. Its near Charing Cross. You know that alley that goes down to Embankment? Wear something funky, birthday girl. Wear that green shirt of yours. I'll see you at ten.'

'Yeah. See you then.'

Kerry put down the phone. It was already eight o'clock. Two hours hardly seemed anywhere near long enough to get ready for an evening with Leon.

CHAPTER SEVENTEEN

Two hours wasn't anywhere near long enough to get ready for an evening with Leon.

When Kerry got off the tube at Charing Cross, she was half an hour late. She scanned the queue for Heaven nervously, praying that Leon wouldn't have gone inside without her. It took a couple of minutes before she caught sight of him with great relief. He was standing near the front of the queue, wearing a pair of white jeans and a tight black vest beneath his silver puffa jacket. His companion, who must be Jeremy, was a tall shaven-headed man in tartan trousers and a tight white T-shirt. Smooth-finished was obviously Leon's type.

Leon seemed very pleased to see Kerry. He kissed her on both cheeks and pulled her into the queue beside him. A thin-faced man standing behind them tutted at her intrusion and she was sure she heard him mutter 'fag hag'.

'Take no notice of that bloody queen,' Leon whispered. 'He's been driving us nuts for the last half-hour. Keeps telling his mate the story of how he once met Boy George at some rave. But darling, I said, haven't we all?' The thin-faced man fumed quietly.

The queue shuffled forward three or four steps before the bouncer fastened the red rope gate behind the lucky few once more.

'I can't believe this queue,' Leon's friend complained. 'How long have we been here? Twenty-four bloody hours?' He picked up Leon's wrist and pushed up his sleeve to look at his watch. 'Oooh, that's a nice piece, Leon. But what happened to your Tag?'

'Sam borrowed it . . .'

Jeremy raised an eyebrow.

'And then he put it in the wash.'

'I thought that they were meant to be waterproof.'

'Yeah, they are. I don't think they're designed to take Persil Colour though.'

'How come we're waiting in the queue?' Kerry asked suddenly. 'I thought that we were going to be on the guest list.'

'Darling,' said Jeremy. 'This is the queue for the guest list. I certainly had no idea that Marvin knew so many people and to be frank with you, I'm gutted. I'm also Jeremy, by the way.'

'I guessed you might be. I'm Kerry.' She extended her hand and retracted it somewhat awkwardly when Jeremy looked at her overly polite gesture with surprise.

'You're the birthday girl, aren't you?' he continued. 'Leon tells me that all your nasty friends have forgotten you today.' She blushed bright crimson. Had he introduced her as 'Kerry-no-mates'? 'But we're going to make sure that you have a wonderful time tonight, aren't we, Leon?'

Leon nodded. 'We certainly are.'

'If we ever actually make it inside, that is,' Jeremy added with a sniff. 'Who would have thought that this little shit-hole would become quite so popular with our set?'

The queue moved forward again. Leon and Jeremy slipped beyond the barrier. The bouncer stopped Kerry with a rough hand against her chest before she could follow.

'Wait there,' he said gruffly.

'But she's with us,' insisted Leon. 'Her name's on the list.'

Genghis couldn't have cared less. 'Are you a lesbian?' he asked her bluntly. Kerry felt her mouth fall open. She hadn't expected this. Was she supposed to be? It suddenly struck her that she hadn't seen a single other girl in the queue.

'I'm with them. I'm on the guest list actually,' Kerry squeaked.

'I didn't ask if you're on the list, I asked if you are a lesbian.'

'Oooh, don't be so personal . . .'

The bouncer was suddenly joined by a seven-foot-tall version of a young, black Danny La Rue. 'Come on through here, dear,' the transvestite smiled and lifted the red rope from her path. He fingered Kerry's furry fake ocelot collar enviously as she passed through. 'I do like your coat. Where's it from? Can I try it on?' he asked, already plucking the coat from Kerry's shoulders. It was a small price to pay to get past Genghis Khan.

But putting the said coat away was only slightly more straightforward than getting through the door. The queues for the cloakroom wound almost right around the dance floor and when Kerry finally did get to the front, the boy in charge of hanging up the coats didn't seem to want to know. Seeing three boys in sailor suits push in front of her, Leon finally came to her rescue and handed Kerry's coat over himself. The cloakroom attendant handed Leon a ticket with a wink.

'This place is weird. It's like I'm invisible because I'm a girl,' Kerry said in disbelief as they waited again at the bar.

'I can see you and you look divine.' Leon gave her a hug. 'I'll admit it must seem a little strange here but you'll soon settle in. It's a great place to people-watch.' He jerked his head towards a blond twenty-something Adonis who was standing on the shiny bar and grinding his pelvis against an aluminium pole erected expressly for the purpose. The blond was wearing nothing but a black leather G-string and some painful kind of harness made from heavy silver chain. Leon sighed. 'No wonder they call it Heaven.'

Kerry looked up at the taut brown buttocks gyrating inches away from her head. 'Yeah. I see what you mean,' she replied. But she felt a pang of jealousy that Leon could be interested in something she most definitely was not and would never be. Whatever happened to the 'whole person thing' Leon had talked about at Michelle's wedding? Leon handed her a beer and a bottle of Evian.

'Is this for you?' she asked, looking at the Evian.

'No,' he said. 'But I've got one for me as well.'

'I didn't really want any water.'

'You will in a minute. Come on. I said we'd see Jeremy over there as soon as we got served.'

They pushed their way through the crowd towards a tiny tunnel between the bar and the cloakrooms that was lit with fluorescent purple light and papered with pictures of variously naked and strangely-clad male torsos. As they moved forward, people stepped aside to let Leon pass, but they moved only grudgingly for Kerry. It was as if she didn't know the magic word. She bumped into the greased up biceps of someone twice her size but when he turned around to say 'Sorry' it sounded as though he had just taken a suck from a balloon filled with helium.

Jeremy was already in the tunnel, deeply involved in conversation with a man who looked almost as out of place as Kerry did in his pale blue jeans and neatly tucked-in chambray shirt amongst all that glitter. The man disappeared into the crowd again before Kerry and Leon reached them. Jeremy was grinning. He gave Leon the thumbs-up sign. 'Got three,' he mouthed.

'How much was it?' Leon asked.

'Fifteen each.'

'Not bad, I suppose. I'll pay for Kerry's.'

'Pay for my what?'

'For your birthday present, of course,' Leon smiled.

'Oh Leon, you didn't have to get me anything.'

'Well, just have it now before I change my mind and keep it for myself. Reach for my hand like you're going to hold it. Don't look at what I've given you until you're in the loos and behind a locked door. I know you, Kerry Keble, you're indiscreet. You'll get us thrown in jail.'

'Hey? What do you mean? What is it?' Kerry asked excitedly.

'Its an "E",' said Jeremy in a stage whisper. 'Ecstasy. You must have done one before?'

'No, I haven't actually,' Kerry told him prissily.

'Oh, then this should be a real laugh. You'll have a great time tonight, my dear.' Jeremy put his hand up to his mouth and, though he didn't seem to have put anything into it, he swallowed, then gave a little shimmy of delight. 'It'll make you feel sublime.'

'I don't know if I really want to do this,' Kerry started to tell them.

'Don't be such a chicken, Kerry,' Leon told her. 'You'll be OK. Everybody does it here. It's the only way I can stand this stupid music. You won't have visions or anything like that. It'll just make you feel really mellow and like you want to dance all night. I promise you, you'll have a great time.' He pressed the small white tablet into Kerry's hand. 'You can just take half of it if you want.'

'No way,' Jeremy butted in. 'That's when people start to have bad trips. You've got to take the whole thing at once.' Kerry looked from one to the other in confusion. She knew plenty of people who had taken ecstasy but had never thought that she would be one of them. Now she had been handed a tablet by her boss. The school drug-talk pictures of pushers and broken down heroin addicts sitting in the gutter seemed a thousand miles away from this glittery reality.

'Do you take this stuff often?' she asked Leon.

'Often enough. I took one at your sister's wedding to help me get through the reception.'

'Leon!! You didn't!' Kerry's jaw dropped to her chest.

'I'm afraid I had to. How else do you think I managed to dance with your Auntie Jean for so long? I could have used some acid as well that night to be honest with you.' Leon's face cracked into that familiar friendly smile. Kerry couldn't believe that he had taken ecstasy at her sister's wedding. She hadn't noticed him behaving particularly oddly then.

'Look,' Jeremy continued his lecture. 'It's no worse than drinking alcohol, right? And you won't feel half so out-of-control as you do when you're pissed. Just remember to keep drinking water so that you don't dehydrate and you'll be fine. Oh, damn it. Leon, I forgot to get some chewing gum again.'

'Good job one of us is on the ball.' Leon fished a packet of Spearmint Wrigley's out of his pocket and handed a bendy stick to his friend.

'Leon, you're a true life saver. I tell you, there's nothing worse than waking up the morning after a fabulous night out with a mouth ulcer the size of a saucer. You'll need some of this stuff too, Kerry. It's in case you start to grind your teeth.'

'Grind my teeth?' Kerry stood between them, still holding the tablet tightly in one fist and now the stick of chewing gum in the other. 'That sounds terrible. Is there anything else should I know about this stuff?'

'Nothing. Just get on with it, Kerry,' Leon insisted. 'The night is slipping away.'

'I'll go and take it in the loo,' she told them. 'Swallowing tablets always makes me gag.'

'OK. Be quick.'

She left them in the tunnel and headed for the ladies.

Once safely inside a cubicle, Kerry opened her fist. The tablet

Leon had given her was as small as a contraceptive pill, a pill she had been taking every day for the last three years though she hadn't had the faintest whiff of a shag in all that time. What was the difference, she asked herself, between taking a prescribed tablet that fucked up her ovaries every day of the month and taking one illegal tablet, once only, that at the very worst would make her dance all night? She stared at the little white circle which was stamped with a tiny dove. Ecstasy had been used in some bona fide medical cases, hadn't it? That meant that it must be safe in moderation and surely one tablet was moderate. But then again, Miss Sensible butted in, what if it had been cut with something terrible? Something like those horse tranquillisers that made you instantly paralysed from the neck down. She'd heard about that. And the thought of being unable to stop herself from grinding her teeth wasn't particularly appealing either.

She could just flush it down the loo and pretend to have taken it. Kerry could dance about like a loon with the best of them.

But how long could she seriously hope to pretend to be deliriously happy for?

And how long would they actually expect her to pretend to be deliriously happy for?

Kerry unscrewed the lid of her water bottle.

'It'll be OK,' she told herself. She put the tablet on the tip of her tongue. 'I'm here with Jeremy and Leon. Loads of people are taking E. I bet Linzi does it every weekend. Everything will be OK.' She swallowed the tablet, feeling it sliding slowly all the way down the back of her throat as if it were the size of a frozen pea. Then she drank half the bottle of Evian straight off to prime her kidneys for the dehydration, just in case. She'd gone and done it now.

When she came out of the cubicle, Kerry looked at herself carefully in the mirror, paying particular attention to the size of her pupils. She looked exactly the same as she had done a few minutes before. Exactly the same. Nothing had happened yet. She sneaked a glance at the other girls waiting patiently in the queue. No one seemed to be regarding her any differently than before. She wondered how long she had before the insignificantly tiny tablet started to take effect.

When she found Leon and Jeremy again they were jigging

from foot to foot on the spot, like two greyhounds in the trap at the start of a race, raring to go. They smiled widely. Leon mouthed 'You've been ages. You OK?' The music seemed louder already, though that might have been simply because they had turned the volume up. Leon led the way out on to the dance floor. Kerry unwrapped her chewing gum and started chewing. She took another swig of water. It seemed really easy to dance.

'It's like putting on the "red shoes", isn't it?' Jeremy commented. 'You know, the "red shoes" in that film that made the girl dance until she died from exhaustion?'

Kerry nodded. It had been one of her favourite films as a child.

'It's going to be a good night tonight. I can tell. I can smell it. I can feel it in the air. Who-ooh!!!' Jeremy stripped off his T-shirt and started to samba his way deeper into the crowd. 'Watch out sailors, dancing queen coming through.'

'I'll stay right next to you,' Leon promised as Jeremy disappeared. 'Are you still feeling all right?'

Kerry smiled and nodded. 'I think so.' He had touched her arm and the place where his fingers had brushed her skin was still vibrating at that touch. She was getting into the music in a way she had never imagined possible before. The bass notes seemed to be coming from somewhere inside her. She chewed her gum harder and grinned.

'Yeah, yeah. I think I'm OK.'

CHAPTER EIGHTEEN

When Linzi arrived at the pub where she had promised to meet Gaetano for a drink, he was already there, sitting at a table by the jukebox, with two unfamiliar girls. When she joined them, Gaetano didn't bother to introduce her or make any attempt to bring her into the conversation. Linzi nursed a pint of lager silently until the girls decided they should leave to make sure that they got into the club they wanted to go to. As they were leaving, the taller and more attractive of the two leaned across the table and kissed Gaetano very firmly and unashamedly on the lips. Her long blonde hair fell across his smug face like a curtain.

Linzi fumed.

'Thanks for introducing me to your friends.'

Gaetano shrugged and took a swig from his pint.

'Who were they?'

'Fans of the band.'

'Yes? Well, she certainly seemed to be a very big fan of yours.' Linzi sneered at the retreating back of the taller girl, whose short black skirt was clinging for dear life to the flesh of her thighs just below her buttocks.

'You're not getting jealous, are you?' Gaetano asked, as he tried to suppress a proud grin.

'I think I'd have every right to be if I was.'

'You are getting jealous.'

'I am not. But I am supposed to be your girlfriend, Gaetano. You could show me just a little more concern.'

'Oh, really,' Gaetano sneered. 'So, if you're my girlfriend, why didn't you show me some concern and stand up for me this afternoon when your stupid friend accused me of stealing her engagement ring?'

'I did stand up for you.'

Gaetano snorted into his drink.

'Well, what was I supposed to do, G?' Linzi protested. 'Other than say that you didn't do it? Call for forensic tests? You hardly handled the situation very well yourself. You know that Fiona has had it in for you since the day you ruined her television.'

'And whose fault was that?'

'What are you suggesting? That it was my fault?'

'If you hadn't stayed out all night putting yourself about to get some stupid little job, I wouldn't have been so angry when you finally got home.'

'I wasn't putting it about.' Linzi felt her cheeks flushing red. 'I was having a friendly drink with my future boss. He offered me the job and then he asked me to have a drink with him to help us to get to know each other. What was I supposed to do? You can hardly refuse your new boss's first request, can you?'

'You could have gone for one drink and been home long before you were,' Gaetano hissed.

'We got talking. We were getting along really well.'

'You don't talk to your secretary all night without wanting something more from her than her typing speed. Did you give in to his second request as well?'

'Gaetano, we've been through this a dozen times. I thought that we'd sorted it out. Nothing happened between me and that man.'

'I don't know if I can trust you any more.'

'Trust me? What about you? How can I trust you?' Linzi tried to change the angle. 'I walk in here tonight to find you sitting with another girl who kissed you like she knew you very well indeed when she got up to leave.' Gaetano shrugged. 'Perhaps we should go back to your place now so that I can kick your television to pieces in a blind rage. Or perhaps your mother's television. After all, there wouldn't be much love lost there.'

'Leave my mother out of this,' Gaetano said quietly.

'Why? She hasn't kept her nose out of my business so far,' Linzi snarled.

'You know what, Linzi? I'm beginning to think that what my mother says about you might be true. You English girls really don't have a sense of decency. You've got no modesty. Shouting at me and making a show of yourself in a public place. When it comes down to it, none of you are any good to a man. You deserted me today on the word of your mad friend, instead of standing by me when she accused me of common theft.'

Linzi was open-mouthed. 'Gaetano! How dare you say that? You know that I believe you . . .'

'I'm not so sure.' Gaetano drained his pint and got to his feet. 'I'm going now. I said I would meet the Professor in the Dog. You can go back to your stupid friends if you want.' He stalked towards the door. Linzi gathered up her coat and skipped after him.

'Wait, G. You can't just walk out like that after saying all those things to me.'

'Just try and stop me.'

Gaetano crossed the road outside the pub and headed for the Dog and Duck. As they reached the other pavement, Linzi managed to get just close enough to him to grasp the sleeve of his leather jacket.

'Get off me,' he spat.

'Gaetano. Come on. This isn't fair. Why won't you listen to me for a minute? Why is it always you that's right?'

'Get off me,' he hissed in warning.

'No, I won't get off you. I want to sort this out now. I'm sick of your black moods. I've had to put up with Fiona getting at me the whole time and now you're having a go as well. I was doing you a favour, letting you stay at my place. You spoiled it. You were the one who didn't make an effort to fit in. You wrecked the television. Honestly, I don't think I've met anyone so childish in the whole of my life.'

Linzi's head was flying backwards before she felt the back of his hand make contact with her cheek. When she regained her balance, her face was stinging as though it had been branded with a red-hot iron. She clasped a cool hand to her burning skin. Gaetano was frozen to the spot in front of her. His hand hovered in mid-air.

'Oh, my God. You hit me?' Linzi said the words as though she couldn't quite believe they were true. 'You hit me. You fucking bastard. You hit me.'

Gaetano just stared.

Linzi brought her fingers down across her lip. 'I'm not bleeding am I?' She took her fingers away from her face to look at them. They were clean but the pain in her head had grown so bad and so quickly that she though she might black out at any moment. 'God, I can't believe you just did that,' she murmured. 'I don't think I ever want to see you again.'

But Gaetano had taken hold of her arms now. His face was creased into a terrified frown. 'God, Linzi. I'm sorry. I didn't mean to do that to you. You forced me to. Are you OK? I'm sorry. I'm really sorry. You made me do it. Say that you believe me.'

Linzi's jaw hung slack. She had never been hit before in her life. Not even as a child. Her parents were far too liberal. Whenever she read about such things happening in *Cosmo* she would close the magazine with a snort, unable to see why those stupid battered women hadn't run away at the first slap. Why they just stood there and waited to become a human punchbag. Now she was just standing there too.

'You hit me,' she whimpered again.

Gaetano was crying now. The fat tears ran down his cheeks and into his open mouth which was still wailing lame excuses. 'I didn't mean to do it. I was too drunk to stop myself,' he wailed. 'I didn't want to hurt you, Linzi. I swear I didn't. You made me do it, Linzi. You made me . . . I was angry because I love you.'

'I really, really love you. I really, really love you.' An hour and a half after taking her first E, this single thought was beating through Kerry Keble's head in time with the music. 'I really, really love you.' She gazed straight at Leon. He was dancing with his arms above his head. His eyes were closed. His mouth curled upwards at the corners in a beatific smile. 'I really, really love you.' Kerry felt the same smile stretch across her face until her head was almost split in two by a grin. She wanted to tell Leon what she was thinking. That she really, really loved him. It seemed so important that he should know right now. She reached out and took hold of one of his hands. He carried on dancing as he leaned in close to hear what she had to say. Both still dancing. Never missing a beat.

'I really, really love you, Leon,' she told him.

'Hey, yeah,' he cracked his chewing gum. 'I really love you too, Kerry.'

He kissed her, right on the mouth, then he raised his hands high in the air and turned in a little circle. Jeremy moved back towards him until they were almost bumping hips. They pulled Kerry in between them and danced like a skin sandwich for a bit. As they were dancing like that, Leon kissed Kerry on the top of her head. Kerry in turn planted a wet kiss on Jeremy's bare chest just above his left nipple. It made him squeal.

CHAPTER NINETEEN

Tim was cooking. A rare occurrence. Fiona assumed that he was donning the apron to cheer her up after the most terrible day of her life. She had called him in Cambridge and hearing how distressed she was about the disappearance of her ring, he had actually excused himself from another night of drinking away the benefit of the rugby match he had played that afternoon. If he hadn't, Fiona told him, she didn't know what she might have done in her grief.

Now Tim was chopping an onion silently while Fiona sat at the kitchen table and nursed a glass of chilled rosé.

'I can't believe it,' she began again. 'I was always so very careful with that ring. I took it off every single time I washed up to protect it from the suds and made sure that I put it on again afterwards. I can't think how I could have forgotten. Maybe it slipped my mind when the telephone rang as I was drying up. It was a call from Mum. She wanted to know if it would be all right to invite some of the neighbours to the wedding. I said, yes. That's OK with you, isn't it?'

Tim shrugged.

'Anyway, we searched absolutely everywhere. Got the cushions out of the sofa, everything. Checked beneath the sink. The only possible explanation is that the ring isn't in the house at all. You should have seen Gaetano's face, Tim. He looked so embarrassed when I confronted him.'

'I would be embarrassed too if someone accused me of theft,' Tim reasoned as he tipped the onions into a saucepan.

'Only if you had something to hide.'

'How can you be sure it was him, Fi?'

'Because if he was innocent, Tim, he wouldn't have left the house in such a hurry, would he? He would have stood his ground. And that's another dodgy thing. I mean, Linzi kept on and on about how Gaetano couldn't possibly go home because of the row he had had with his mother and then, as soon as it suits him, the supposed dragon welcomes him back into the nest with open arms. He is as guilty as sin. I don't know how Linzi can live with herself.'

Tim was raking through the drawer for the tin-opener. It wasn't where he had left it. In fact, whenever the tin-opener went missing it usually turned up somewhere really bizarre. Like on the shelf in the bathroom. He had a suspicion that it was something to do with his housemate, another guy who worked at BFO Schwartz. He was a little older than Tim, a bit higher up the company and often stayed away on business. When he was around, Tim tried to avoid him.

'You need to be able to trust your housemates,' Fiona continued. 'If you had done to Linzi what Gaetano's done to me, I know exactly whose side of the argument I would have come down on.' She turned the wine bottle around and studied its label. Tim didn't comment. Probably, like Fiona, he knew that in such a situation she would have been at his side in a shot.

'Is it covered by the insurance?'

Tim sighed. They had been through this on the phone that afternoon and five or six times since then. 'Yes, it is on the insurance. Are you trying to catch me out on this or something?'

'No. But are you really sure, Tim? Doesn't your credit card just cover things for a few days after you've bought them?'

'The ring is covered, Fiona. You don't think I would have spent that much money without taking out some kind of insurance, do you? I mean, you could chuck me next week and hurl the ring into the gutter just like my Mum did. Then where would I be?'

'You're not insured in case we split up, are you?' Fiona was horrified.

'No, of course not,' Tim smiled. 'You can't get insured for that kind of thing.'

'I sincerely hope you haven't looked into the possibility.'

Tim snorted. There was the germ of a great business idea there.

'How long do you think it will take for a claim to go through?'

Fiona continued. 'It's strange, but I feel naked without it already. Sometimes, when I'm not thinking about it, it almost feels as if the ring is still there. I was just getting used to it. But we don't actually have to wait for the money to come through before we get a new one, do we? If you use your credit card again we could get one on Monday and you won't have to pay for it until the end of next month. We could meet up at lunchtime. Now that we know what we're looking for it shouldn't take us half as long as the first trip to the shops did.'

Fiona's voice was momentarily drowned out by the frantic sizzling of the onions as the oil heated up and began to cook them transparent.

'Monday lunchtime?' Fiona repeated hopefully. 'What do you think, Timbo?'

Tim shifted his weight from one foot to the other and continued to stir the onions around in the pan. He didn't turn to look at her as he began, 'I don't know, Fi. My credit card's nearly right up to the limit as it is. I might have some kind of emergency this month and if I've filled up my card, I'll be stuffed. You can wait a while, can't you?'

Fiona rubbed at the naked base of her middle finger.

'You mean until next month?'

'Or the month after?' Tim said hopefully. 'That would be better for me.'

'But Tim,' Fiona whined. 'We'll be right into preparations for the wedding by then! I can't go through my whole engagement without having a ring to wear!'

'Fetch a couple of plates out of the cupboard, could you?' Tim commanded.

'We could get it on my card and you could pay me back. Or you could get your credit limit extended. You've had a pay rise. It shouldn't be a problem.'

Tim took the cold plates from her hands and put them under the grill to warm up as he cooked.

'How about that?' she asked hopefully.

'Let's talk about it later,' Tim replied. 'I'm burning the onions.'

'You want onions on this?'

Linzi sat on the hard plastic bench beneath the unforgiving UV light in an all-night café. Gaetano was at the counter. Getting their hot dogs. The man behind the counter seemed to be taking ages with the unnaturally orange sausages. Gaetano didn't want to be away from Linzi for too long. In case she decided to give him the slip.

Linzi was playing with the salt cellar. Pouring out a few thousand grains of salt at a time and forming them into a pattern. She made a heart, then smashed it into nothing with her finger. Gaetano sat down opposite her and placed her hot dog where the heart had been seconds before.

'Say something to me,' he pleaded. 'You haven't said anything to me since outside the pub.'

Linzi picked a long, stringy piece of burnt onion from the top of her hot dog and folded it into her mouth. What was she doing here? She wanted to go to the bathroom and look at her cheek. Check out the damage. It was still stinging like crazy. She picked up the ketchup, squeezing the unyielding plastic bottle momentarily distracted her from the pain.

'Oh, come on, Linz. You know I'm sorry. I've said it a thousand times. What more do you want me to do? You know that I'm not normally like that. I'd never have hit you if you hadn't got me so fired up. I was jealous about that guy who took you for a drink. You're the most beautiful girl I've ever met, Linz. I don't want to lose you to some flash bastard, that's all. I'll never meet anyone better than you if you go. You're beautiful even when you're crying . . .'

Linzi looked up from her hot dog, which she had no intention of eating, and met Gaetano's eyes for the first time since it had happened. His gaze penetrated hers desperately, begging for forgiveness.

'If we weren't in the middle of a café, I would go down on my knees for you right now,' Gaetano insisted. 'I swear I would.' Linzi looked unimpressed. 'Ah, what the hell. I will.' Gaetano slid from his seat until he was on his knees on the dirty floor beside her. He buried his head in her lap. Two beery middle-aged men in Arsenal shirts told him not to do it. Not to propose.

'Linzi,' Gaetano continued in a low whisper that she had to bend over to hear. 'I need you. I know that we've only known each other for a short time, but if you call things off now, I don't know what I'll do without you. You're part of my life now. I've been making all my plans around you. I can't carry on if you're not there.'

'Gaetano,' Linzi murmured. 'You can get up on your seat again. Everyone's watching you, you're ruining your trousers and I think that I've just about got the message.'

'Are you still going to go?' He scrambled back into his seat. His eyes were wet with tears.

Linzi reached across the sticky table and took his hand. 'No,' she told him. 'I'll give it one more chance.'

Gaetano lifted her hand to his mouth and kissed it extravagantly. 'You won't regret it, Linzi. We're going to be perfect together. I promise you.'

The men at the counter shook their heads sadly.

'All downhill from now on, mate,' the fatter guy said wisely.

When he had eaten both their hot dogs, Gaetano drew a couple of hundred pounds out of a cashpoint and insisted that they make it up immediately in a rather bland Covent Garden hotel. Later, when he had fallen asleep, Linzi listened to the white noise of the air-conditioning and wondered whether she had done the right thing. She looked at Gaetano's face. Relaxed, relieved, reformed. She decided that she had.

After all, even her mother's King Charles Spaniel had been allowed three bites before it was put down.

CHAPTER TWENTY

Jeremy had been right. It had been a great evening, possibly one of the greatest nights in a club Kerry could ever remember, but she was still pretty glad when Leon announced that he'd had enough and wanted to go home, saving Kerry the embarrassment of being the first to flake out. There was no queue at the cloakroom window now and the attendant even managed a smile as he handed Kerry their coats. In fact everybody seemed to be smiling. Leon collected a couple of flyers from Kerry's transvestite heroine on the way out.

'Coming again next week?' Leon asked Kerry as he helped her to slip on her coat, for which the transvestite had offered fifty pounds in cash.

'Maybe,' Kerry replied.

'So you had a good time?'

'I did.'

'You feel OK?'

'OK? Leon, I feel like I've been plugged straight into the mains.' The music was still pumping in her head even though they were outside now. It felt as though her brain was shimmying against her skull.

'That's good,' Leon told her. 'But take it easy now, yeah? For a moment earlier on I was pretty worried about you.'

'I was just a bit scared, that's all. I didn't know how I was going to react, did I? I don't normally "do drugs".'

'Do drugs?' Leon laughed. 'You make it sound like we spent the evening shooting up heroin. Where's Jeremy gone now?' Jeremy was lingering by the cloakroom, extracting a phone number and a quick tongue wrestle from a man twice his width and half his height. Kerry winced. It didn't look terribly romantic. Just rough.

'Jeez. That man has such bad taste,' Leon commented.

Short Fat Baldy disappeared back into the crowd and Jeremy came skipping out into the street after Leon and Kerry, wearing a gormless, pleased expression on his face which Kerry had no doubt had often lived on hers. Especially lately.

'Strike three,' Jeremy said exultantly. 'Three telephone numbers in one night. Am I the hottest thing in this place or what? And how did you two fare, my dear little children?'

'You know I'm not in the mood for casual affairs any more,' Leon reminded him.

'Which means that he couldn't even manage to pull a muscle,' Jeremy translated. 'And how about you, Birthday Girl?'

'I was hardly in the market,' Kerry laughed.

'What on earth do you mean, Kerry-darling? There was a girl in the bar upstairs who was the absolute spit of kd Lang.'

'Jeremy,' said Leon. 'I don't think kd Lang is exactly Kerry's type.'

They wandered up the narrow road that led to The Strand. Leon and Kerry linked arms. Jeremy walked along in front of them, weaving from one side of the pavement to the other, doing the occasional pirouette, feeling, he claimed, 'as light as a feather'. The sky was clear after a cloudy day and though you couldn't see many of the stars because of the dreadful ambient light central London gives off, Kerry had a feeling that there were a lot of them up there. They were all twinkling down at her, wishing her a 'Happy Birthday'. And it was.

'Where to now, folks?' Jeremy asked, when they had reached The Strand and stood at the edge of the pavement as though they stood on the bank of the Thames. 'Anybody ready for a bit of rough Trade?'

Trade was the place where everyone who was anyone went after Heaven. It didn't start until most other clubs had finished and it went on way past dawn.

'I don't think so,' said Leon. 'I'm not sure we'll be able to get Kerry in for a start. They've been having a crack down on girls lately. Besides, I could use some sleep tonight.'

'So I'm on my own,' Jeremy pouted.

'I guess you are.'

'Then cheerio, *mes chers*.' He kissed them farewell on both cheeks and disappeared in the direction of the nearest black cab, sharing a fare with a couple of guys who were wearing matching blue feather boas. In the meantime, Kerry's legs had given in and she was sitting on the edge of the pavement. Leon crouched down and lifted her up by the armpits.

'Can't stop there,' he told her. 'We've just got to make it across Trafalgar Square to the Nightbus. Then you can fall asleep if you like.'

'But I need to sit down now, Leon. Please,' Kerry pleaded. 'I don't think I've ever danced so much in my life. My legs are broken. I swear they are.'

She swayed dangerously. Leon himself was too tired to hold her up for very long.

'OK,' he conceded as his knees buckled beneath her weight. 'Plan B. We'll get as far as the fountains. Then you can splash your face to wake yourself up a bit and we'll catch a cab home instead.'

'No, no more water!!!' she wailed.

'Just for your face,' said Leon. 'You don't have to drink it.'

'Are you coming back to my house with me?' Kerry asked pathetically.

'I think I better had, don't you? I don't suppose you can even remember the right address.'

'I can. It's 67, Archeesia, I mean, Artesia Road.'

'Right.'

The traffic lights changed and they limped across The Strand to Trafalgar Square. All around, people were gathering at the Nightbus-stops but the square itself was almost empty. Leon walked Kerry as far as the nearest fountain and helped her clamber on to the marble wall that surrounded it. She trailed a hand in the cold, black water and tried ineffectively to splash her face once or twice, getting more of it down her neck than on her cheeks. Then she shut her eyes and leaned back so far on the narrow wall that Leon thought she was going to fall in. Thinking that it was probably a good idea to get her away from anything potentially fatal for a while, Leon led her instead to the foot of Nelson's Column and the great bronze lions that guarded it. There, he popped her on to the wall, then quickly climbed up beside her and took her icy hands in his to warm them.

'Where's your circulation gone, Kerry? You're scaring me now,' he said. 'Are you sure you're feeling OK?'

'I'm just really tired,' Kerry whined. 'And I feel a bit sick from drinking all that water. I just want to go home.'

'We will in a minute, I promise.' He rubbed her hands briskly between his palms until they began to tingle and Kerry pulled them away. Then she leaned back into him and tried to tuck herself inside his coat to keep warm. Leon pulled one arm out of its sleeve to make it easier for her.

'Can we go home now?'

'Not while you still look like you might be sick. No taxi driver is going to pick us up until you've had a bit of air and come round. The quicker you look sensible, the quicker we can go.'

'I'm always sensible. My mother says so.'

'Yes, I'm sure she does. But your mother also keeps saying that I'm an Australian.'

He tried to do the puffa jacket up around Kerry's back but had little success. Instead he pulled her closer into his arms. 'Warmer now?'

'Mmm. Cuddle me,' she murmured. 'People will think that we're in love.'

Leon gave a grunt of amusement. 'I suppose it is kind of romantic this, isn't it?' he mused. 'Sitting in Trafalgar Square in the middle of the night.'

'Mm-hmm,' Kerry agreed.

'Sometimes,' Leon continued, 'when you're living in London you can start to forget just how beautiful the city really is. I mean, look at the National Gallery now. And that church over there. Look at all these lovely buildings around us. London is as beautiful as Paris ever knew how to be tonight. Except that I never did get to see Paris, did I?'

He looked up at the sky a little sadly.

'And it's a full moon, Kez. Means that the lunatics are out.'

'You've made me into a lunatic,' she mumbled. She tried to look up at the moon with him but contented herself instead with burying her nose further into the shoulder of his puffa jacket. Leon smoothed her hair away from her forehead and smiled.

'You know what, Kez? You're one of the best people I've met since I've been living in this country. You're so sweet and caring. You really would do anything for anybody, wouldn't you?' Kerry nodded into the quilted shoulder. 'I mean, you're about the only person round here who really cares about what's going to happen to me if I can't renew my visa. Sam's deserted me. Even Jeremy will soon find himself a new best friend, whatever he says to the contrary.'

Kerry nodded again. 'I don't want you to go back to South Africa,' she mumbled.

'Join the club,' Leon sighed. He tipped her face towards his so that he could look into her eyes. 'Kerry,' he bit his lip. 'You know what you were saying the other week after your sister's wedding? About what you'd do to help me out? Did you really mean that?'

Kerry nodded. Then added, 'What did I say again?'

'You said that you would marry me if that's what I had to do to stay in the UK.'

'What? I said that? I didn't?'

Kerry suddenly came back to life as if one of Nelson's lions had blown smelling salts straight into her face. She pulled away from Leon to stare at him and swayed backwards dangerously.

'You said that you would marry me so that I could get a visa. Remember?'

'Leon!! Of course I do. But I thought you weren't interested in doing that. You said it was a stupid idea.'

'I've changed my mind.'

'Are you serious? Why?'

'I don't know what else I can do, Kez. I've checked every possible avenue and I think it's the only one left open. Would you really do that for me? Would you get married to me so that I could stay here in England?'

'Oh God, Leon. I'd love to. Yes, of course I would! Yes, yes!!!'

'It's not a proper proposal,' Leon reminded her tactfully but Kerry threw her arms first around Leon's neck and then jumped up to hurl her arms around the nearest all-seeing lion. 'Yes, of course I'll marry you. I can't wait. Oh, Leon. You and me. It's going to be such a laugh.'

'Kerry,' Leon looked concerned. 'Hang on a minute. You know what this means, don't you? You know that we're going to have to live together until immigration are off our backs and if we get caught out you'll be in just as much shit as me. You could even end up in jail for helping an illegal immigrant stay in the country.'

'Leon, of course I know all that. But we're not going to get caught out, are we? It's going to be brilliant. A match made in heaven.' Leon raised an eyebrow. 'I can't believe you asked me. My mum is going to be ecstatic. She already has you ear-marked for a son-in-law.' Kerry hugged him again and kissed him all over the face. Leon held her at arm's length for a moment. 'When are we going to do it?' she asked.

'Well, I suppose we've got to do it as quickly as we can. My visa gets more out of date every day.'

'We've got to have a party after the ceremony.'

'I . . . er . . .'

'Leon, we've got to have a party. It's got to be convincing, hasn't it? Oh, this is so incredible. And do you remember how it was you who caught the bouquet at my sister's wedding? That was an omen, Leon. An omen.' Kerry got to her feet and climbed astride the lion as though it were a horse. She punched the air with a fist.

'You're going to be able to stay here for ever,' she laughed. 'And I'm going to be married. Before Fiona! I can't believe it. She'll be sick with envy. This is the craziest birthday I have ever had. I'm afraid I'll have to have an engagement ring, Mr Landesman,' she reminded Leon gravely.

'Of course,' he said. 'I'll sort it out. But I want you to think about this seriously, Kez. Really, really seriously before you make up your mind.' She nodded, but he wasn't sure that she'd heard what he'd said.

'Shall we go and get that cab now?' he asked.

Kerry didn't look as though she was about to puke anymore.

'Yes. I feel perfect now. Completely perfect.'

Leon slipped down from the wall and braced himself to catch Kerry when she jumped. As she landed, she wrapped her arms around his neck and hung on tight.

'I had a great time tonight,' Kerry told him sincerely. 'I would have had a crappy birthday if it wasn't for you and Jeremy. Especially you. Thanks, Leon.'

'My pleasure entirely.'

'I can't wait to tell the girls about the wedding.'

Leon put a finger to her lips. 'No, Kerry. Not yet. I don't think we should tell anyone what we're going to do until everything is arranged.'

Kerry frowned. 'Really?'

'Really, Kez. You've got to promise me that you won't.'

'OK. I promise, fiancé of mine.'

Leon took his finger away from her lips and kissed them instead.

CHAPTER TWENTY-ONE

The sound of the postman woke Linzi up at half past ten. She stumbled grumpily downstairs. He was delivering something that Fiona had ordered from a catalogue (probably books about how to live with phantom cellulite), a bank statement for Kerry and a letter in an embossed cream envelope for herself. Linzi recognised the emblem of CPIDG excitedly. It had to be the letter confirming her appointment as assistant to George Gerrard. She bounded up the stairs two at a time to her bedroom where Gaetano was still sleeping, having crept in without Fiona's knowledge the night before. Linzi ripped the envelope open as she leapt on to the warm bed beside him.

'It's a letter about that job,' she told him.

Gaetano opened his sleep puffy eyes just the merest crack.

'I don't know why I feel so nervous,' Linzi said as she unfolded the crisp cream letter inside. 'I mean he near as hell said that the job was mine and we got on so well. It's bound to be a letter of acceptance.' She scanned the first few lines and her face suddenly clouded over. 'My God. I don't believe it. The bastard. How could he? He's bloody well gone and given the job to someone else. But he promised it to me. He promised it to me.'

Gaetano was not quite awake. 'Did you get it then?'

She scrunched the letter into a screwed up little ball and hurled it in the direction of the open door. 'No, I bloody well did not,' she bawled. 'After all that bullshit he gave me at the pub it's gone to someone whose "qualifications more accurately fitted the job description". I don't understand it. He told me that I didn't need any specific qualifications. He told me that I was perfect for the job. What a fucking, bloody bastard!!'

'Hey, calm down, *cara mia*.' He pulled her back down under the duvet. Gaetano wasn't ready to get up.

At a quarter to one, Gaetano managed to drag himself out of the pit. Linzi was downstairs, eating toast disconsolately as she flicked through the previous day's *Evening Standard* and checked out the depressing columns full of secretarial jobs, nearly all requiring shorthand despite the none-too-recent invention of the Dictaphone.

'Look at this,' she complained bitterly. 'They want a graduate with fluent French to do the nine-to-five for eight grand a year. They'll be bloody lucky.'

'It's more than the dole,' Gaetano commented.

'Only just. Shit. Shit. Shit.' Linzi dropped her toast butter-side down on the carpet. She had forgotten to sign on. Again. 'Do you think they'll let me sign on this afternoon instead?'

Gaetano shook his head. 'No way, man, that's your money gone for at least a fortnight.'

'Why didn't you remind me I had to go in this morning?'

'You didn't tell me to remind you.' He picked up the piece of toast that Linzi had dropped on the floor and fitted it into his mouth in two bites, carpet fluff and all.

'I can't go on like this any more.' Linzi was in a foul mood. 'How is anyone supposed to live on thirty-seven pounds a week anyway? We can't even get any Marmite for the toast! If my father could only see how he is forcing me to live . . .' Gaetano slung a comforting arm around her shoulder. 'I mean, your mother threw you out of the family home for having sex before marriage and she still sent you an allowance even though you've got a full-time job and she wasn't talking to you.'

Gaetano shrugged. 'Well, I guess family is just more important to the Italians.' He looked at his watch. 'Shit, I said I would cover for Louis at the café this afternoon because I don't have to go into the shop until tomorrow.' He shrugged on his jacket. 'I'll see you tonight, at the Duke of York. I'm meeting the Professor at seven to get set up for the gig. *Ciao bella!*' He blew her a kiss.

She hated it when he said that. He reminded her of his mother.

With Gaetano gone, Linzi uncrumpled the letter from CPIDG and read it through one more time. Qualifications? That was a laugh. It was more likely that she lost the job because she had let that chauvinist bastard come all over his precious dashboard. Well, if George Gerrard thought he had heard the last of Linzi Adams he was very much mistaken. She rang the switchboard of CPIDG and, to her surprise, the receptionist put her straight through to the director.

'George, this is Linzi Adams. You may remember me from last week? I *came* for an interview with you.'

'Linzi,' he knocked her off her stride by being disarmingly charming from the start. 'Of course I remember you. How are you, my dear?'

'Not too great this morning as a matter of fact. I just received a letter on your headed notepaper. I thought you said that I was going to get the job.'

George Gerrard cleared his throat. 'Did I say that, Linzi? I think there seems to have been some kind of misunderstanding.'

'Oh, really. And which bit of the sentence, "You've got the job" did I misunderstand?'

'Linzi. In the first place I did not formally offer you the job, and in the second place I think that under the circumstances it would have been most inappropriate for me to do so.'

'What? Inappropriate? Why?'

'Well, I think that we may perhaps have overstepped the mark when it comes to interviewer/interviewee relationships.'

'We overstepped the mark? I think it was more the case that you pushed me over it. Look, Gerrard, I could make a very serious complaint about this you know.'

'And it would be your word against mine. A company director and a failed job applicant. Who do you think they'd believe?'

'You really are scum,' she hissed.

'Linzi, there really is no need for things to get nasty. It must have been obvious to you that I was very much attracted to you and I realised during the course of our evening together that an attraction that strong could put an unnecessary strain on the working environment.'

'Oh right. So you would have given me the job if I hadn't been so good at giving blow-jobs?'

'Linzi, calm down. I'll make it up to you. I promise.'

'Oh, you'll give me the opportunity to retrial will you? Perhaps if I swallow this time instead of making you come all over the dashboard things will be different.'

'Linzi! I can't give you the job here but I promise I'll make it up to you.'

'How?'

'Sit by the phone. I'll get someone to call you back within half an hour.'

'Really . . . and . . .'

George had already hung up.

The phone did ring again exactly thirty-one minutes later. But it wasn't George Gerrard. It was Caroline from Advertising Angels.

'Linzi, darling!!'

'Oh, it's you. You'll have to be quick, I'm waiting for a call.'

'Now, now, Linzi. I'd be grateful if you could sound a little happier to hear from your favourite Auntie Caroline. Especially when she's the bearer of such good news for you.'

'You are? Go on. Thrill me.'

'Linzi, you really do have something of an enthusiasm problem this morning, don't you?'

'So would you if you'd just been turned down for yet another poxy job.'

'CPIDG?'

'Yes.'

'I know, my dear. But it's not the end of the world, is it now? In fact, I've just had that lovely Mr Gerrard himself on the telephone. He says that he found it terribly hard to choose between you and the girl who eventually got the job but in the end she just tipped you on shorthand and typing speeds.'

'Right,' Linzi snorted. He hadn't given her a typing test.

'However, Mr Gerrard was so impressed with you that he has been ringing round his friends in a desperate attempt to place you elsewhere. He'll have me out of a job one of these days. Ha ha ha! Anyway, he's done it. He's placed you. He has a lovely friend at Manatee Records who is simply gasping for an assistant. Mr Gerrard has recommended you most highly and you'll start on Monday morning. If you want to, that is. He's gagging to meet you.'

'I'll bet he is,' Linzi sneered. 'How much?'

'Oh, negotiable,' Caroline breezed. 'I'll call you just as soon as I know. You do want the job don't you, Linzi? It is the music business we're talking about here. Very exciting. You can even wear smart casual clothes to work.'

'Smart casual clothes? You should have said,' Linzi sighed sarcastically. 'Caroline, I'll see how it goes.'

'Good, good. And you know where the Manatee office is? Right near Hyde Park!! Wonderful for lunchtime in the summer. You see, I knew we'd find a place for you if we just kept trying. George Gerrard was terribly impressed, you know. I wonder what you did to make him take such a shine to you?'

'Yes,' muttered Linzi. 'I wonder.'

When Linzi arrived at the Duke of York that evening, the only other person in the bar was the Professor. He raised his half-pint glass in greeting and gestured her towards him. He was wearing his dirty blue jeans and a faded Little Angels T-shirt with a big rip under one of the arms for ventilation.

'They're not here yet,' he said, stating the obvious. 'They said they'd be here half an hour ago. I had to set up all the gear on my own. But it looks as though it's not going to matter whether they turn up at all anyway. The place is totally empty and we won't get paid if the bar doesn't do well enough.'

'Don't be such a pessimist, Professor. It's only half past seven,' Linzi consoled him. 'People will start pouring through the door in an hour or so, I promise you. Most of them are still getting home from work.'

'I hope you're right. You know, I could have been working tonight,' the Professor said flatly. 'Could have earned sixty-odd quid doing a bit of locum work in the East End.'

'Locum work. Really? I thought only doctors did that?'

'And chemists,' the Professor explained. 'You know how there has to be a late-night chemist in the area? Well, if the shopkeeper doesn't want to do it himself, he can get another chemist in to do it for him. Usually someone who's just qualified and hasn't got a shop of his own, like me. It's all right sometimes. Depends on the area you end up in. You don't want to be doing somewhere near King's Cross after dark.'

'I can imagine,' Linzi nodded. 'Too many drug addicts trying to supplement their prescriptions, I suppose?'

'Yeah,' the Professor drained the last of his drink. 'They come in after methadone and jellies.'

'Jellies?'

'Temazepam. Sleeping tablets. You can melt them down and inject them. It's all right, actually. They leave most of the really interesting stuff though.'

He ordered another pint for himself and one for Linzi.

'But I don't know how much longer I can stand being a chemist, you know,' he told her now that buying her a drink had bought him the right to moan. 'I didn't think that it would take us this long to get a record deal for Monster Munch. I mean, we had loads of interest last month and we sent off all those demo tapes but we haven't heard a thing back from anyone. The majors are only interested in something that's going to be a banker with the first single. The only way we're ever going to get a record out is if we do it ourselves and try to get our own airplay.'

'You mean take it round the clubs?'

'Yeah. I've got plenty of contacts. The only problem is that it'll cost us a couple of grand to get a single cut. I don't have that sort of money to spare and Gaetano certainly doesn't. He spends everything he owns on grass and clothes.'

Linzi smiled ironically. Gaetano had pleaded poverty that very weekend.

'Two grand isn't so much. There has to be some way to get that kind of money, Professor. If you're serious about it. Couldn't you go to a bank? You could pretend to be setting up a label and get a small business loan?'

'Get real, Linzi. A chemist, a clothes shop manager and two out-of-work sparks getting together enough money to put out a record? They'd laugh us out of the bank.'

'And I thought I was cynical,' Linzi commented.

'Anyone who isn't cynical, is stupid,' the Professor told her seriously. 'I'm rapidly coming to the conclusion that crime is the only business that pays these days.'

'Well, you just carry on being cynical, Professor,' Linzi smiled. 'But by this time next week things could be very different for us all.'

'How come?'

'I've got myself a job.'

'Oh, well that's great for you,' the Professor said without enthusiasm. 'Where?'

'At Manatee Records.'

'Manatee Records? You're kidding.'

'I'm not. I'm starting on Monday morning. I'll give myself a couple of days to get to know a few people, then I can take the Monster Munch tape into work and force the people who matter to listen to it.'

'That's really good of you, Linz. It'd be a real help.'

'I'll stand right over them until they sign you.'

'That'd be fantastic.'

At that moment the door to the bar swung open. Gaetano and Socks walked in carrying two battered guitar cases and the mike stand.

'Shit,' Gaetano muttered as he noted that the bar was very, very empty. 'What happened to the audience?'

'Never mind about the audience,' Linzi piped up. 'I just got a job at Manatee Records.'

'That's great, man,' said Socks, dropping his guitar case and punching her on the arm. 'Our own industry insider. Linzi, you're brilliant!'

Gaetano picked Linzi up and swung her around.

'You're a star, Linz. I knew you could do it.'

For a moment it didn't matter that even their singer had failed to turn up to the gig.

CHAPTER TWENTY-TWO

K erry's plan to bring peace to number 67 by cooking a house
   meal had been scuppered. As she filled the refrigerator with
the goodies she had just picked up from Safeway she noticed a
note stuck to the door. Fiona had scrawled, 'Gone to Tim's'.
Beneath that Linzi had written 'Gone to the pub'. Both of them
knew that Kerry had intended to cook that night and had gone
out regardless. Kerry tore the note down with a huff. She was
desperate to tell them about the impending wedding (in strictest
confidence, of course). The news was burning such a hole in
her brain that she thought she might start stopping people in
the street and telling them soon. And to make matters worse,
neither Linzi nor Fiona had remembered her birthday either. So
much for her two best friends in the world.

Kerry's foul mood was compounded by the fact that Sam
had dropped by the Verbal Tix office that day. He was looking
for Leon, who was out with the newly-returned Serena seeing
the bank manager with regard to Verbal Tix's ever-expanding
overdraft. Sam had decided to wait for his return and made
himself at home on the corner of Kerry's desk. He told her that
he intended to get Leon back. That he'd realised what a terrible
mistake he had made by running off with Andrew. Sam was sure
that the minute Leon saw how sorry he was, their relationship
would be back on again immediately. And deep down, Kerry
knew that Sam wouldn't even have to pretend to be sorry to
reinstate himself in Leon's heart.

Sam said he had tried to call Leon a hundred times but it
seemed that he had decided to unplug his phone. Kerry raised
an eyebrow.

'Is he missing me?' Sam asked. 'I don't suppose he is. He's been out two Saturdays in a row. Kerry, has he told you whether he's started dating anybody else?'

Kerry shrugged. 'He doesn't really tell me much about that kind of thing but I think that he is interested in someone.'

'Oh, God, no.' Sam bit his lip. 'Tell me it's not that awful Jeremy.'

'No, it's definitely not Jeremy.'

'Who is it then?'

Kerry bit her lip and tried not to look smug as she announced, 'I think it might be a girl.'

'No!!! Not again!!!' Sam left the office straightaway in tears, begging Kerry to let Leon know that he had been there. Not again? Kerry basked in Sam's parting words. Not *again*.

Leon returned just moments later, having left Serena to browse through Mothercare. He must have passed Sam unknowingly in the street. Leon looked hassled. 'You'd think that we'd asked him for the money to set up a gay brothel. Anybody called?' he asked.

'No,' Kerry lied. She concentrated on her screen so that Leon wouldn't be able to look into her eyes. Thank goodness Celestine had decided to go home with a migraine. Josh hadn't made it in at all that day. 'Not a peep from anyone.'

Later that afternoon, Leon called British Telecom and tried to get his telephone line reinstated. Not until he had paid his bill in full and with interest, he was told. Sam had run up a bill of four hundred pounds calling an ex-boyfriend in Canada.

'It's so annoying,' Leon complained. 'Anybody could be trying to get hold of me.'

'Including immigration. Besides, if they couldn't get hold of you at home they would ring you at work, surely,' Kerry reasoned.

'Sam wouldn't. In case Serena picks the phone up. They hate each other's guts. He thinks that she messed him about on some soundtrack deal.'

Kerry remembered what Celestine had said about the alleged affair, combined with Sam's parting words and wondered if that was the real reason. If it was, then there was definitely hope for her.

'I miss him like crazy, Kez,' Leon continued. 'We were together for a very long time.'

'If he was all that bothered about you he would have come round by now, wouldn't he? Serena or no Serena.'

'Yes,' sighed Leon. 'I suppose you're right. You know what, without Sam I wonder if it's worth my while staying here in England at all. I'd be putting you in such an awkward position for nothing . . .'

'Not nothing, Leon. You'd be able to stay with your friends,' Kerry reminded him, desperate for a scrap hinting at affection. It was the first time he had mentioned the wedding since the weekend and he sounded as though he was unsure about going through with it already.

Leon smiled wistfully and murmured, 'Yeah, my friends. There's always them.'

At home in the empty kitchen, Kerry stabbed a potato named Sam right through its potatoey heart.

Fiona knocked on the door of Tim's flat with a peculiarly nervous sensation in her stomach. She hadn't called him first to let him know that she was coming round. She heard his moccasined footsteps padding down the hallway towards her. He opened the door and met her with a look of rather worried surprise.

'Fi? Hi. I thought you were staying in tonight.'

'I know, I was going to but Linzi decided that she was going to stay in as well and so the atmosphere was pretty tense.' She was still standing on the doorstep. 'Well, are you going to let me in or do I have to stand out here in the cold all night?'

'Oh, of course. Sorry.' Tim stood aside and Fiona wandered straight towards the sitting room taking off her coat as she went. She began to tell Tim the story of her day but she stopped abruptly when she walked into the sitting room and discovered that Tim was not alone. Minky Bingham was perching on the edge of the navy-blue Ikea special sofa, nursing a half-full glass of red wine.

'You know Fiona, don't you, Minky?'

Minky smiled shyly. 'Yes, I think we've met before.' She put her glass down on the scratched-up coffee table and straightened her little skirt so that it barely covered her knees.

'You're Adam's girlfriend, aren't you?' Fiona asked pointedly.

'Well, I was.' Minky shuffled her court shoes on the rattan rug. 'I'm afraid we split up last weekend.'

'Oh, I'm sorry to hear that.'

'Thanks. But I think it was for the best. No point prolonging the agony, is there?' She sneaked a look at Tim, who was avoiding Minky's eyes as he brought Fiona a drink.

Fiona installed herself in the armchair opposite Minky and made no further attempt to prolong the conversation. Minky took two more sips from her glass.

'Listen Tim,' she said suddenly. 'Thanks awfully for the wine but I really ought to be going now. Got an early start in the morning. I'm doing a presentation for some tanning shop clients. I work in PR,' she explained for the benefit of Fiona. 'Beauty PR.' She gave her long blonde hair a gratuitous flick and started to stand up. 'I'll see you soon, no doubt. Down at the Pitcher and Piano probably. Seems to be where everyone ends up after work these days.'

Fiona smiled tightly.

Tim helped Minky to put on her jacket and escorted her to the door. He was gone a long while. Fiona strained to hear their too-quiet whispers, desperately fighting the urge to take a peek out of the window and find out what was going on. When Tim came back into the sitting room and took the chair opposite her, Fiona was suddenly aware that he hadn't even kissed her hello.

'I didn't know that you knew Minky all that well, Tim?' Fiona began.

'She lives quite near here.'

'I seem to remember her saying to me that she lived in Fulham which isn't all that near Stockwell, if my geography's not too bad.'

'She was on her way to see a friend in Clapham,' Tim explained. 'She just popped in to say "hi" en route. That's all.'

'Right, Tim,' Fiona sneered. 'And you weren't expecting her at all which is why you've got a fucking great chocolate gâteau defrosting on the kitchen table. Not even you could be planning to eat all that on your own.'

'Christ, Fiona. Are you sure you don't work for MI5?' Tim muttered as he lit a cigarette from a packet of Marlboro Lights which Minky had left on the arm of the sofa.

'I thought you'd given smoking up.'

'I had. But I've just started again.'

'So, had you invited Minky to stay for dinner or not?' Fiona persisted.

Tim took a long, thoughtful drag on the cigarette before addressing Fiona in an uncommonly quiet tone of voice.

'Look, there's something you need to know, Fi, and that is that you do not have the right to barge in here and tell me what I should be doing every moment of my life and who I should be doing it with.'

'What?'

'If I want to have Minky over for dinner then I will.'

'Then you had invited her over for dinner?'

'I had, yes. Big deal. Call the police if you like.'

'Why didn't you tell me?'

'As I mentioned just a moment ago, I didn't think that I had to tell you everything.'

'Instead, you just let me barge in here unknowing, making me look totally stupid in front of her. She must have been embarrassed too. There was absolutely no need for her to leave so suddenly unless the pair of you were up to something.'

'Fiona,' Tim groaned. 'I think you made her feel pretty uncomfortable.'

'I did not make her feel uncomfortable. Look, Tim, I don't want to get into an argument about this. I just want to know why we can't share these little things with each other. After all, we are supposed to be engaged. Engaged to be married.'

'Yeah,' said Tim cagily. 'And that's another thing we need to talk about.' He took another deep drag on the Marlboro Light and stood up to look out through the window.

'What do you mean?' Fiona panicked. 'Another thing we need to talk about?'

'I mean,' Tim began without turning back to face her. 'I mean, I feel like you've twisted my arm over this whole June wedding thing, Fi. I made a bit of a hasty decision under pressure and now, with the ring having been lost and all, I think perhaps we should take a couple of steps back to the way we were before.'

'What? You mean put the wedding date off again? We can't, Tim.' Fiona began to count off the reasons on her fingers. 'I've already talked to my parents about it . . . Mum's looking into the possibility of using the same church, where she and Dad . . .'

'No, stop there. Please. What I mean to say is, let's take a step back to the way things were before we were engaged. It wouldn't be so very different.'

Fionas lower lip began to tremble violently. 'What are you saying, Tim?'

'It just might make me feel a bit happier if we dropped the whole engagement thing for a while. I don't think I'm old enough for all this commitment yet. We're both at vital stages in our careers and I think we should be devoting more time to that right now.'

'Careers, Tim? But you just told me to turn down a six months placement in New York so that we could get married this summer,' Fiona shrieked. 'That was my career. Hara went insane when I told him . . . I'm finished as far as First Orient's concerned.'

'I didn't tell you to turn the placement down, Fi,' Tim replied calmly. 'You made that decision yourself. I just helped you to write the letter.'

'I thought you didn't want me to go.'

'I don't know. Maybe I didn't. Maybe I did. I really didn't want to influence your decision either way.'

'How can you say all this now? Now that I've thrown away the New York placement, which means that in all probability I've also thrown away my whole career, and I've told my family and all my friends that we're getting married in June. If you call the wedding off now, Tim, I will die of embarrassment.'

'Embarrassment isn't fatal, Fi.'

'Tim, if you go ahead with this crazy plan of yours, you know you will ruin my life.'

'If we go ahead with this wedding, I think you know as well as I do that it will ruin both our lives. Look, I really am sorry that I let things get this complicated before I realised what a mistake we were making.' He looked steadily at a spot on the floor. 'But I can't carry on like this in the hope that things might get better. I thought it might make a difference but marriage won't change anything between us if we shouldn't be together. I'm sorry, Fi. I really am.'

'Believe me, Tim,' Fiona hissed as she rose unsteadily to her feet and tugged on her coat. 'You don't know what sorry is. But you will.'

'Fi, sit back down. You don't have to go right now.'

Fiona headed for the door. 'Call me when you've come to your senses.'

She stormed out into the night and walked all the way from Stockwell to Clapham Common, crying with every painful step. Tim watched her go from the front door she had left open and prayed that she wouldn't do anything stupid. But he didn't follow her to make sure.

CHAPTER TWENTY-THREE

There was no way that Fiona was going to be able to go into work the day after Tim told her it was all over. She lay in bed, awake but unmoving from five in the morning until one in the afternoon. When she finally managed to drag herself downstairs she called her office and told them that she had twenty-four hour flu. Her supervisor sympathised, there was a lot of it going around.

She couldn't eat anything. It was difficult even to get a cup of tea past her dried out lips. When she could bring herself to look in a mirror, she could barely see her eyes, so puffed up were her eyelids with all that crying.

She sat by the phone for half an hour while her fingers hovered over Tim's number. Maybe he had calmed down a little now and was already regretting the terrible mistake he had made. He wouldn't call her from work to tell her that, of course, because they would need to have the kind of conversation that you didn't really want your workmates to listen in on. They had split up once before and he had called her the second he got home from work the next day to make things better.

Besides, it was natural that he should be nervous about the step they were taking together, wasn't it? They had promised each other the rest of their lives. Those boneheads in the rugby team had probably been giving him some stick about being under her thumb. God, how Fiona hated the rugby boys. All men together until they needed someone to cook them dinner or iron their shirts. And anyway, Tim wasn't under her thumb. She let him have plenty of freedom. She didn't mind him having Minky Bingham round for dinner, it was simply the fact that he felt he had to keep it a secret from her which was a problem.

And she had her own life outside him, she reminded herself. There was the half-marathon for a start. She could do with devoting a little more time to preparing for that. Yes, when Tim called that evening, as he inevitably would, Fiona wouldn't try to prolong the argument, she would get straight in there with the solutions. They could cut down on seeing each other to just once or twice during the working week so that they weren't so tired and irritable when they got together. She would train for her marathon and when that had finished she would start training for another one. Or perhaps she could do some voluntary work. She could help out at the dog's home or something. Yes, that was the key. Separate interests. She should go out with her friends more often, too. Kerry was usually at a loose end on a Saturday night.

By the time she had told herself all this, Fiona was almost convinced that the previous night's argument with Tim was the best thing that could have happened. She took a shower and lay down on her bed for half an hour with an ice-mask over her eyes to bring down the swelling. Then she listened to some happy music and flicked through an old copy of *Brides*.

Outside, the sun was shining. It seemed like the perfect moment for the new Fiona to start her regime. She forced down a bowl of Weetabix while she laced up her trainers. Yeah, she just needed to become a little more independent, that was all. Tim didn't really want to call the wedding off, he just wanted to make sure that Fiona knew the status quo before they took the plunge.

She bounced out on to the sunny pavement and touched her toes a couple of times.

He would be so proud of her if she finished this race in good time.

When Fiona reached the other side of the Common, she stopped sprinting and swung forward to put her head between her knees and catch her breath. Her chest ached as if it were about to burst. She put it down to the combination of having run and having cried so much the night before. Maybe she should take it easy on the way back? Right now, she needed a drink and a sit down. She went into Burger King and ordered a huge Diet Coke.

'Hey, Fiona.'

She turned around to see who was calling her name and immediately wished that she hadn't. Sitting by the cloakrooms, flanked by two of his dodgy-looking long-haired friends, was Gaetano. And he was all smiles.

'How come you're not at work today? Surely you're not doing a sicky?' he asked loudly.

'Sort of,' replied Fiona. She changed her order from eat-in to take-away. The counter assistant looked pained.

'I'll have to key it in again,' he whined.

'Don't bother,' Fiona told him. 'Just give me a straw and a bag.'

'Come and sit here with us.' Gaetano was still talking to her. Fiona was just waiting for the subject of the ring to be brought up and for things to turn nasty. 'Fiona lives with Linzi,' Gaetano was explaining to his friends. As if he hadn't already told them all about her – the wicked witch of Artesia Road. 'Move up so she can sit down, Professor. Be a gentleman.' The tall dirty-looking blond with his baseball cap on backwards obliged. Fiona stopped by their table in passing but didn't sit down.

'Thanks, but I really can't stop today. I'm right in the middle of writing up a project for work and I ought to get back to it. I'll see you around.' She managed a sweet smile for Gaetano's companions before heading for the door in double-quick time. She heard a commotion behind her. Gaetano was putting on his jacket.

'Hang on, Fiona,' he called after her. 'I'll walk back that way with you.'

She pretended not to hear and as soon as she had cleared the door she started to run. Seconds later she was flat on the floor face-down in the icy spilled contents of her drink. 'Oh God,' she murmured.

She just wanted to close her eyes and disappear. Everything hurt. Everything. Especially her chin.

'Bloody hell, Fiona,' Gaetano had caught her up. He was panting. Even jogging the few steps between Burger King and the prostrate Fiona was too much for him. 'Are you all right?'

'I don't know,' she groaned as she tried to lift her face from the paving slabs. 'I think I've got concussion.'

'You just took one hell of a fall.' Gaetano helped her until she

was in a sitting position on the kerb with her feet in the gutter.
A small crowd had already gathered around them. Fiona put a
finger to her stinging lip. It was bleeding.

'Oh God, no. Why did this have to happen today?' she fought
back the urge to cry.

'Let me have a look.' Gaetano gently turned her face towards
his. 'You've cut your lip pretty badly. Perhaps we should get you
to casualty.' An elderly woman with a shopping trolley and a
small dog nodded.

'He's right, you know,' she told Fiona. 'You might be con-
cussed.'

'No, really. I'm all right. I really am.' Fiona pushed the
concerned hands away. 'I'll be fine. I just need to have a sit
down for a minute. Got to get my breath back.'

'Well, while you're down there,' said Gaetano, 'perhaps you
ought to do up your shoelace.'

'Thanks, smart-arse.' As she reached down to tie her treacherous lace, her elbow complained like crazy. When she turned
it towards her for a better look at the damage she saw that the
white sleeve of her sweatshirt was stuck to her skin with bright
red blood. 'Oh, shit,' she muttered. 'I've ruined my top.'

'We've got loads like that in the shop,' Gaetano comforted her.
'I'll get you another one cheap. Come on. Up you get.' He tucked
his hands beneath her armpits and lifted her to her feet.

'Are you going to take her to the accident unit?' the old
woman asked.

'No, she doesn't live far from here. I'll take her straight home.'

'You want to be more careful,' the woman told the limping
Fiona as Gaetano escorted her across to a low wall. 'All the silly
exercising young girls do these days and then they wonder why
none of them can have babies. Running themselves into trouble,
they are.'

'You're right,' Fiona replied. 'I promise I'll never jog again.'

Satisfied that the young girl had learned her lesson, the old
woman and her dog waddled off in the direction of the bank,
leaving Fiona sitting on the wall feeling very much like Humpty
Dumpty must have done after the plunge.

'Ready to go?' Gaetano asked.

Fiona put her hand to her forehead. 'No, I'm not. Can't you
just leave me here to die?'

He couldn't. Gaetano offered Fiona his arm.

'Honestly, I'll be fine in a minute. Just go back to Burger King with your friends, will you?'

He wasn't about to give up.

'If you try to get back home on your own, you might collapse in the middle of the Common. Who'll help you then? Come on, Fiona. Let me walk you back. I promise I won't try to steal any of your jewellery.'

Fiona narrowed her eyes at him.

'Did you find the ring?' he asked casually.

'No. I didn't.'

'It'll turn up when you least expect it. These things always do.'

Fiona glared but Gaetano tucked his hands under her armpits anyway and physically set her on the path home. Realising that she was not going to get away from him now, Fiona shook herself free of his hands so that she could at least limp alone. She walked as purposefully as her bruises would allow, looking straight ahead, answering questions only. She was not going to make conversation. Gaetano's innocence had been protested but not proven.

'So, they let you work from home now?' Gaetano asked jovially. Fiona nodded. 'Must be nice. Means you don't have to get on the tube in the morning.' Fiona nodded. 'Linzi's got herself a job at last.' Fiona nodded. 'Hope she can stick at it for a while. Might help my band to get a record deal. Christ, Fiona. Are you just going to nod at me all the way home?'

Fiona turned to Gaetano. Her face was horribly creased, as though she was trying to hold something from the *X Files* back behind her cheeks.

'Look, I didn't steal your fucking engagement ring, all right, if that's what you're thinking?' Gaetano was suddenly defensive. 'I don't want all this frosty stuff. I just wanted to do you a favour.'

'Oh, God!' Fiona sobbed suddenly. 'I'm sorry. It's not you. Really it's not. I'm just having a bad day and I want to be on my own. Just leave me here, will you? Leave me alone.'

She collapsed on to a moss-covered bench and covered her eyes with balled-up fists. Gaetano crouched beside her and tried to pull her hands away. 'Shit, Fiona. Are you sure you don't want me to take you to casualty? Are you in serious pain?'

'Yes, I am,' she wailed. 'But there isn't a doctor in the world who can make me feel better!! Go away from me. Go away.' She swatted at him with her hands.

But Gaetano didn't go away. Instead he sat down beside her and shrugged his shoulders.

'Why do these things always happen to me? Why doesn't he love me any more? All I ever did was try to make him happy.'

'You talking about Tim?' Gaetano ventured perceptively.

'Of course I'm talking about Tim,' Fiona snapped. 'Nobody else has ever loved me, have they? But now he's gone and got himself another woman. And I've already made out our wedding invitation list.'

'It's not the end of the world, Fiona.' It seemed like the right thing to say.

'It is the bloody end of the world. I've been jilted by my fiancé, Gaetano. Don't you understand? My mother is going to go insane.' Gaetano nodded this time. He knew about mothers. 'I've told everybody that I'm getting married. I've even turned down a job in New York because of it. They're all going to laugh at me. I'll be the biggest joke in London. They probably already think I've made the whole engagement thing up because I haven't got a ring. I can't go on without him. I can't go back to work. I can't even face my friends. He's ruined my life. Absolutely ruined it and all for some tart with a name like a hamster.'

'What's she called?' Gaetano couldn't resist finding out exactly what a hamster's name was like.

'She's called Minky,' Fiona sneered. Gaetano thought it was a better name for a rabbit. 'Minky Bingham. Minky Binky Bloody Bingham. And she's the fastest bike outside the Tour de France.'

'You got her phone number?'

Fiona shot him a look.

'I'm sorry, Fiona. It was meant to be a joke.'

'Ha ha ha. Well, it wasn't a very funny one. You see, you've started making a joke out of my misery already. Pretty soon everybody will be sniggering about me behind my back. Bob Monkhouse will probably dedicate a whole show to "Fiona Davenport, jilted of Balham". This kind of thing is supposed to happen to Kerry, not me.'

'Hey, come on, let's keep going.' Fiona was beginning to rant and Gaetano was getting twitchy. 'Look, you're even attracting a crowd.' A group of pigeons was strutting past purposefully. Gaetano fished a Burger King napkin out of his jacket pocket and gave it to Fiona for her nose. 'Come on.'

'Do you think he still loves me?' Fiona asked later as they staggered on past the bandstand. 'What's going on in his mind?'

'I can't tell you what's going on in Tim's mind,' said Gaetano, wishing they'd never started this conversation. 'Most men don't even know what's going on in their own.'

CHAPTER TWENTY-FOUR

Back at Artesia Road, Fiona locked herself in the bathroom while she changed out of her jogging gear and surveyed the damage caused by her fall. She dabbed antiseptic lotion on the worst of the grazes, bringing tears flooding back to her eyes. Despite their pleasant enough conversation as he helped her to cross the Common, she was not especially happy to be alone in the house with Gaetano. Something about him put her on edge. It was nothing to do with the missing ring even. She had felt it the second time they ever met. And it was worse now that she had blurted out the story of last night's row to him. She hoped that if she took long enough in the bathroom, Gaetano would be gone by the time she emerged again. Then she heard music strike up from the direction of Linzi's room. He was making himself at home.

Fiona steeled herself. She paid rent on this house. If she was uncomfortable in his presence then she was perfectly entitled to ask him to leave. She knocked on the door to Linzi's room, feeling only slightly more composed now that she was wearing trousers which covered her sticky knees. When Gaetano didn't answer – the volume was too loud – she went straight ahead and pushed open the door.

'Ahem.'

Gaetano swivelled around with the look of a cornered rat. He was using the cover of Linzi's prized signed Boney M album as a flat surface upon which he could roll up his joint. When he remembered that there was no one but Fiona in the house, he visibly relaxed again.

'We're a non-smoking household, actually,' Fiona told him stiffly.

'I know,' Gaetano shrugged. 'I was just making this one for the walk home.' He licked the length of a Rizla to make it sticky and continued to construct the T-shaped skin regardless. 'You feeling any better?'

'Yes, thanks. Did you find what you wanted? The CDs Linzi borrowed?'

'Dunno. I haven't really looked yet.'

'Look, Gaetano,' Fiona began. 'I'm afraid you'll have to turn the music down while you're searching. I can't begin to work with that noise going on.'

Gaetano fished in his pocket and brought out a little plastic bag with what looked like a very shrivelled dandelion head inside. He opened the bag and sniffed its contents, a wide smile spreading over his mouth as he did so. 'Wow. The wonder of skunk. You should smell this.' Fiona recoiled. 'No? But it's really great. I could get high just sniffing it.' Then Gaetano took a cigarette out of his packet and broke off the filter. He applied a freshly licked thumb to the seam of the cigarette body and the paper rolled apart obligingly to reveal a naked sausage of tobacco beneath.

Fiona stepped across his cross-legged body with some difficulty and turned the stereo down herself.

'Hey,' Gaetano looked disappointed. 'What's the matter with you? I would have turned it down myself in a minute.'

'But I need to start working now. I'm sorry.'

'You're strange, Fiona. One minute we're walking along having a conversation like we might even actually like each other and the next minute you're biting my head off again. No wonder Tim's pissed off with the idea of marrying you. You need to chill out more.'

'Chill out?' Fiona sneered. 'You mean like you? You mean get stoned and lie on my back all day laughing at the pretty woodchip patterns on the ceiling? Is that "chilling out"?'

Chuckling to himself at the mere thought, Gaetano began to crumble the skunk on to his delicately-arranged Rizlas, taking great care not to let any stalk or seeds contaminate the mix. 'Yeah. Something like that.'

'Well, for your information, some of us don't have time to "chill out",' she spat the words with extra contempt. 'Some of us have work to do.'

Gaetano twisted the end of the fat spliff so that it looked like a skinny miniature icing bag. Then he looked around to find something from which he could make the roach. The spare flap of his Rizla packet had gone that way days ago. Instead, he plucked a greetings card off Linzi's cluttered pinboard and ripped a little rectangle out of the back.

'Don't you think she might have been saving that?'

'She won't mind. It's just an old card. Unlike you, Linzi doesn't think with her anus.'

'You're the only anus round here.'

Gaetano snorted and turned his attention back to the very delicate job of inserting the roach into the open end of the spliff. At first, it seemed that he had made it just a little too big. The roach was removed to be more tightly rolled. He tried it again and Bingo! Gaetano held the completed spliff between his thumb and forefinger and admired it as if he had just blown the thing in molten glass. 'Perfect,' he murmured. 'You still here?' Fiona stood in the doorway with her hands on hips.

'It is my house.'

Gaetano brought out his personalised Zippo.

'You can't light that thing up in here. This house in a no-smoking zone.'

'I'm in Linzi's room, she doesn't care if I smoke.'

'Linzi isn't here.'

Gaetano flipped the Zippo up into the air and caught the flint as it came back down. A flame sprang up obediently and he applied it to the end of the spliff so that the twisted paper burned away. Then he put the smouldering joint between his teeth and held the flame to it again until the tobacco caught and it began to burn properly. Fiona stared as he dragged on it deeply and then exhaled a plume of thick grey smoke.

'You want some?' He held it out to her.

'No. Thank you. I don't.'

'It'll make you feel less uptight. Honestly, Fi, the world's a better place with skunk.'

'I don't think you know how silly you sound, Gaetano.'

'I don't think you know how silly you look standing there with your hands on your hips like you're forty years old. Try something different for once.' He held the joint towards her. 'Act your age, not your bust size.' That was just thirty-two.

'Gaetano, why do you have to make this difficult for me?'

Fiona tried to reason. 'I let you into the house to look for your CDs, now all I want to do is get on with my project in peace. In silence.'

'Hang on a minute,' he replied. 'I thought I was the one doing you a favour. I made sure you got home safely, didn't I? Now I need a rest from that walk. You haven't even so much as offered me a cup of tea in gratitude. I'll keep the music down.'

'You won't. You never did.'

'OK, have one toke on my pipe of peace and then I'll go away. You know it's breaking Linzi's heart that you and I don't get on so well.'

'It breaks my heart that you and she do get on so well.'

Gaetano took another drag on his spliff then held it towards her.

'I've never smoked before.'

'Sure you have. Everybody has.'

But Fiona really hadn't ever smoked before. Not even a single B & H with the girls behind the caretaker's shed at school for fear of an embarrassing expulsion. Now she took the spliff from Gaetano and held it gingerly between her thumb and forefinger.

'I should throw this straight out the window,' she said, waving it in the direction of the closed curtains.

Gaetano looked worried. 'Please don't. That would be such a waste. Just have one drag. Go on. Be a devil.'

'Tim doesn't like me to smoke.'

'Tim, Tim, Tim,' Gaetano mimicked. 'Then if I were you, I would smoke forty a day. Men like a wayward girl.'

'Do they really?' she asked a little desperately.

Gaetano nodded. 'Yeah. That's what I like about Linzi.'

'I don't think that Tim would be terribly impressed . . .'

'You'd be very surprised. A little bit of subversion might be exactly what he is looking for. You're getting old before your time, Fi. If you ask me, this row you guys had about the wedding was about his last-ditch attempt to have a bit of fun before settling down. If he thinks he can have fun with you, then Bingo! Wedding's back on.'

'Do you really think so?'

'Listen. My father ditched my mother two weeks before their wedding. She went out on the town with her sisters that night and sent him wild with jealousy by dancing with another man. He was on his knees the very next day. Begging for forgiveness. And my elder brother, born eight and a half months later, is the only blond in the family.' Gaetano laughed.

'Tim won't be made jealous if I have a smoke.'

'No, but Tim is expecting you to mope around, Fiona. If he calls up tonight and you're caned, you'll sound happy. He'll be round like a shot to find out why.'

'Really?'

'Try it.'

'Oh, this is ridiculous.' But Fiona put the damp end of the spliff to her lips anyway and closed them tightly around it. The grey smoke continued to whirl out from the end like a ghostly dancer. She hadn't yet inhaled.

'I don't even know how to do this,' she said, taking it back out of her mouth again.

'What you've got to do,' Gaetano explained. 'Is take it really gently. Really slowly. If you rush you'll only end up coughing.' He placed a hand on her shoulder, like a doctor showing his patient how to inject insulin for the first time. 'Just inhale a little bit and hold the smoke in your mouth.'

Fiona obliged. Her cheeks blew up like a cornered puffer-fish. Gaetano's mouth slid into a smile. 'Now, when you're ready, breathe in naturally and take the smoke down into your lungs. Just breathe as if you were on a hillside, taking in fresh air.'

Fiona raised her eyebrows frantically and shook her head. Fresh air? It was like sucking on an exhaust pipe. Her cheeks were still stretched out to twice their normal size.

'You can do it, Fi. Just breathe in naturally. The smoke will be really cool by now. It won't hurt. Breathe naturally.' he demonstrated the flow of air with his hands. 'I sound like an ante-natal class, don't I?' He took the spliff from Fiona's hand and inhaled once more himself. 'Like that.' He forced the smoke out again between clenched teeth.

Fiona was going slightly pink. She had yet to breathe at all. Finally she could hold the air in her mouth no longer and exhaled like Old Faithful, sending the smoke straight back out into the room. None of it had touched her lungs.

'I can't do it, Gaetano,' she panted. 'I've never smoked. It's just not me. I'll only end up having a choking fit. And I've got to get on with my work.'

Gaetano drew on the spliff again and passed it back to her patiently. He was on a mission now, and if it was the last thing he ever did, he was going to get Fiona stoned. It should be a laugh in more ways than one. He took her by the elbow and guided her hand back up to her lips. 'One more time,' he told her. 'Remember the attraction of subversion.'

She turned her head away from the approaching roach like her mother's terrier when it refused to take antibiotics.

'I can't smoke it. I really can't. Isn't there anything else we could do? You can make it into cakes can't you? I've heard that lots of times. I think I've got some flour and stuff downstairs.'

Gaetano shook his head. 'You're thinking along the right lines, Fi, but you can't do that with this stuff. It's grass, isn't it? If you try to heat it, grass just burns. You need the resin to make cakes.' He nudged her elbow upwards. 'Try one more time. It'll be really worth it. I've never had such a good feeling as the one I got the very first time.'

Fiona licked her lips nervously. 'OK. One more time and then I'll give up.' She slipped the roach between her lips once more and sucked some smoke into her dry mouth. 'I must breathe naturally, I must breathe naturally,' she chanted to herself. Holding the smoke in her mouth for a moment longer, she breathed in through the nose to fill out her chest. She felt the smoke and air rush on down, flooding the tiny chambers of her lungs, and her eyes widened with surprise. She breathed out again and saw a faint plume of smoke escape via her nose.

'Yeah, that's right.' Gaetano gave her a one man round of applause. 'What did I tell you? I knew you could do it, Fi. Welcome to your misspent youth.'

'God, I feel weird. I'm going all light-headed.'

'Not yet you aren't. It's just the shock of christening your lungs. Have another go now, while you've got the hang of it.' He tipped her elbow upwards and the spliff went back into her mouth. Fiona followed the steps she had learned before. Into the mouth, cool the smoke down, air through the nose, and down into the lungs. She couldn't help smiling as she completed the steps without coughing her guts up on to the floor. She held the spliff away from her and looked at it in admiration almost exactly as Gaetano had done.

'You're right,' she told him. 'This stuff's amazing.'

Gaetano laughed. 'I told you so.' She passed him the spliff and he gave it the same doe-eyed look of love. 'But it's such a bad habit. Once you start, you can't think why you never did it before.'

'I didn't because I was scared.'

'We've established that,' said Gaetano. 'You're scared of a lot of things, Fi. But you're not so scared now, are you?' He inhaled deeply and exhaled two perfect little smoke rings that floated off across the bedroom like lost halos.

CHAPTER TWENTY-FIVE

Linzi must have really tried George Gerrard's patience. He had indeed found her another job, but what kind of job was this? Linzi had been more than a little pissed off when she arrived at Manatee Records to discover that her 'truly covetable position' was in fact in the company's dingy basement post room. Hardly the best place to begin her Monster Munch promotion campaign. That morning she had franked three and a half thousand postcards to announce the imminent release of a new single by the heavy metal combo Dyer Ria. To alleviate the boredom she had readdressed the card bound for the PR department at Radio One with her home address and scribbled 'Dear Kez and Fi, Wish you were here . . . instead of me.'

At lunchtime, the pink-haired girl to whom Linzi was meant to be reporting, came down to the post room and looked at the pile of cards left to be franked with a critical eye.

'How's it going?' she asked through her chewing gum.

'I'm surviving,' Linzi lied.

The pink-haired girl bit her lip, unconvinced. 'We've got to get a whole load of cards out for Tineka Bovary's new album this afternoon. I'd better call for someone else to come in and help you.'

'I'll manage,' said Linzi valiantly. The only thing worse than being holed-up in this dingy basement would be being holed-up in the dingy basement with someone else.

'I don't think so,' said the pink-haired girl. 'I'll call the agency.'

Three-quarters of an hour later, Linzi was joined by Freya from Sydney, who was willing to do just about anything to get the money together for her European tour.

'Hiya.' She was unnecessarily cheerful. 'I was sent here to help you by Advertising Angels.'

'No good looking so happy to be here,' Linzi informed her. 'We've got to get through all this lot before they'll let us go home.' She waved her arm in the direction of ten brown-cardboard boxes, each one of which was filled with a thousand postcards. 'Do you know how to use a franking machine?' Freya nodded quickly. 'Good. Then you can get going on these. I need a fag.'

Freya got to it. She didn't know that Linzi wasn't her boss. Two boxes of postcards later, Linzi let her in on the secret. Two cigarettes later than that, they were fast on the way to becoming firm friends. Freya told her how excited she was to be in the UK. And everyone had been so kind. Particularly Caroline at AA.

'But what I don't understand is,' Linzi began to tell her, 'why all you Australians want to come to England in the first place. I mean you've got everything out there. Sunshine, sandy beaches. The latest series of *Neighbours*. And you decide to give all that up and come to London instead. And it's a dump. I mean, where do you live when you're over here? Earl's Court, I suppose.'

'Actually, I'm sharing with some friends in Hackney.'

'Hackney?' Linzi gasped. 'You couldn't pay me to live there. It's so dirty and rough.'

'Oh, we've got a really lovely place there though. Three bedrooms and a sitting room.'

'How many of you are living there?'

'Just eight at the moment.'

Linzi's jaw dropped. 'Eight?'

'Six flatmates and two dossers. I'm just dossing because I only came over from Bangkok last week, so I've got the mattress on the landing. But Finola is going back to New Zealand next month so I'll be able to move into her room then and share with Sandy.'

'Share a room? Doesn't that drive you up the wall? I'm sharing with just two girls in a three-bedroomed house and most days it seems like the place isn't big enough for the three of us. How on earth do you all manage to get in the bathroom before you go to work?'

'Oh, we've got a rota for that,' Freya said cheerfully. 'It starts at six a.m. Unfortunately the dossers get the worst bathroom spots so I'm in at ten past six.'

'Ten past six?' Linzi wasn't sure she had ever seen that particular time of day unless she had forgotten to go to bed the night before. 'Ten past six?' she asked again as if Freya had got her figures wrong. 'That's mad. Why on earth do you want to put up with that?'

'It's worth it,' said Freya dreamily as she slit open another box of postcards. 'It's the only way I can afford to stay in London while I save up to do a tour of Europe. I really want to see the whole of the world before I die.'

Linzi fed the first of a million postcards into the franking machine. She hadn't seen that much of the world herself. Just France on half a dozen family holidays before the family split up. A few Greek islands. Amsterdam on the obligatory student smoking weekend. And a month travelling in the States after finals. On the front of the postcard she was franking, the popstar to be promoted was standing in the foamy surf that crashed against the white beach of an unspecified Caribbean island. Yeah. It would be nice to travel. See the world. If only she had the money.

'If you'd like to go Down Under sometime,' Freya told her happily, 'you could always use my place in Sydney as a base. My flatmates are really cool about houseguests.'

'Then you'd better give me your address today,' said Linzi. 'Because I don't think I'm going to come back here tomorrow.'

Freya duly scribbled down her address on the back of a Tineka Bovary postcard and Linzi responded in kind. Linzi folded her postcard and stuck it into the back pocket of her jeans, wondering if she'd ever get to use it. Not unless the DSS started to hand out international travel grants, she thought dryly.

'Are you really not going to come back tomorrow?' Freya asked.

'I don't think so. I thought that I might be able to meet some influential people, you know, push my boyfriend's band. But I haven't seen daylight since I got here, let alone the A & R department.'

'What kind of music is it?'

'Heavy metal, I suppose,' Linzi said apologetically. She reached into her bag and fished out the Monster Munch tape she had brought with her. 'You can have this if you want it,' she told Freya. 'Do your ear-drums some damage.'

'Thanks. It looks really interesting. But Linzi, don't you think you're giving up just a bit too soon? Won't Caroline be mad?'

'Doubtless, she'll be livid. But you can tell her I said "bye-ze-bye".'

CHAPTER TWENTY-SIX

Fiona was now completely prone at the foot of Linzi's bed. Gaetano was lying on the bed itself, occasionally passing the spliff down to Fiona who would take a deep toke in-between attempting to plait the fringed edge of Linzi's orange bedspread.

'No, I'm sure I'm better off without him. I mean, he would never do anything like we're doing now. I don't think he'd even breathe in if he walked into a room where someone was smoking a spliff. He is so uptight I'm sure he only shits twice a year. It was him that made me like I was, Gaetano. I was a nightmare, I know it.' She passed the spliff back up to Gaetano. 'I gave you and Linzi such a hard time.' Gaetano reached his hand down towards Fiona and she knitted her fingers through his.

'You're not so bad,' Gaetano said soothingly. 'Anyway, like you said, Tim will probably call you when he gets home from work tonight and everything will be back to normal before tomorrow. You know it will.'

'Do you think so?'

'I know what men are like. He would never have asked to marry you in the first place if he didn't have very strong feelings for you. Even though he's now retracted the offer, that doesn't take away from the fact that he made it and that, at that moment in time, he really felt something for you which won't just have vanished into mid-air because of all this trouble.'

Fiona sat up and rested her chin on the edge of the bed. 'What?' Her brain was having trouble keeping up.

'I mean, he probably still loves you, Fi, doesn't he?'

'I really hope you're right.'

Gaetano had been looking at the woodchip on the ceiling but now he turned so that he was facing Fiona. He exhaled carefully, so that the smoke didn't go straight into her eyes. Fiona locked her eyes on his. Linzi had been right about them. Gaetano's eyes were like two big chocolate buttons, slightly melted to a gloss by the sun. Gaetano casually licked his full red lips. Fiona moved imperceptibly closer, so that there was less than an inch between their trembling mouths.

'I'm not so sure that I even care if he loves me or not any more,' Fiona murmured. 'After all, there's plenty more fish in the sea.'

'And I'm a halibut,' replied Gaetano.

Fiona laughed.

Gaetano took hold of the back of her head and pulled her mouth down upon his.

CHAPTER TWENTY-SEVEN

Linzi bumped into Tim on her way back from the tube to Artesia Road. He was fresh from work, still in his suit, and carrying a huge bunch of bright red roses beneath his arm.

'Hello, Tim,' said Linzi. 'You must have done something really bad to turn up with those.'

He looked a little embarrassed as he spun around to see who was addressing him. 'Oh, hi, Linzi.' He waved the bunch of roses at her as if they had suddenly appeared beneath his arm by magic and he had nothing to do with them being there. 'Fi and I had a little bit of a fight last night. I called her at work and they said that she had twenty-four hour flu, so I think I must have upset her pretty badly.'

'Either that or she really has the flu,' said Linzi.

'I don't think she was coming down with anything yesterday.'

'Did you call her at home?'

'If she's in, she didn't pick up the phone.'

'Probably sulking. Or shopping. Retail therapy. Harvey Nicks is marginally cheaper than seeing a psychiatrist.'

'Look, Linzi,' Tim said suddenly. 'I don't mean to put you in an awkward position or anything but what do you think of us? I mean, what do you think of me and Fi? Do you think that we ought to get married or what?'

'Oh, whoah,' Linzi backed off with her hands in the air in a gesture of surrender. 'Don't try to get me involved in some heavy debate about marriage before I've had a drink.'

'But, Linzi, you live with her and you know me well enough. What do you think about us?'

Linzi sighed. 'Fiona is one of my very best friends, Tim. Obviously, I think that the man who marries her has got himself a really good catch. Anyway, you've been together for four years. You should know whether you like her enough to marry her or not by now.'

'Yeah, you're right,' Tim nodded. 'We've been together for ages without too much hassle, haven't we? No reason why it should all change when we get married, eh?'

'Not in theory.'

'Could even get better?'

'Could do. I don't know.'

They had turned into Artesia Road but there were no lights on in number 67. Linzi glanced up at the bedroom windows. No sign of life up there, either. That was odd. Perhaps Fiona really had given up moping about Tim and gone out to meet some friends, though she hadn't exactly kept up with anyone but Linzi and Kerry since meeting the man of her dreams, so which friend would she have gone to see? Linzi really didn't know. 'You're more than welcome to hang on here until she comes back,' Linzi told Tim. 'She'll be really pleased to see you.'

'I hope she will,' Tim said sadly.

Linzi put her key in the chubb lock. It was already open, which was very strange. Fiona never went out without first making sure that the house was fastened up tighter than Fort Knox. Relationship disaster or no relationship disaster. She must be in and asleep. Linzi didn't let Tim know what she was thinking.

'Make yourself a cup of tea. I'm sure you must know where everything is by now. You can put the television on too . . . As long as it's not rugby.'

Tim forced a smile. One of the reasons that he didn't come round to Artesia Road so much any more was the ban Linzi had put on television sport, which was heavily enforced by the other girls. 'Yeah, Tim. You know you're doing the right thing.' Linzi put a hand on his arm as she passed and gave him a little squeeze. 'Besides, Kerry and I have already bought the bridesmaids' dresses.'

Linzi heard the sound of giggling as she turned at the top of the stairs.

'Shit, someone's in!'

The voices were coming from her bedroom. Linzi froze on the

landing, not really sure that she wanted to investigate. Were they being burgled? She almost screamed to Tim to give her backup.

'Ow, what was that?' The burglar had just stubbed his toe.

There was definitely someone in there. 'Tim, come quickly!' Linzi called.

Tim bounded up the stairs, taking them two at a time until he reached the top.

'I think there's someone in my bedroom.'

He had already picked up the poker that stood unused in the fireplace and now raised it up in readiness to bring it down again on someone's head. He put his hand on the doorknob and the world seemed to hold its breath. Linzi crammed her fingers in her mouth as she got ready to stifle a scream.

'Tim! No!'

Fiona appeared in the doorway with her arms raised to cover her head in defence. Gaetano ducked down behind her. The rod slipped out of an astonished Tim's hand and over his back to the floor.

'Tim?'

'Fiona?'

'What are you doing in my room?' Linzi asked.

'What are you doing with him?' asked Tim.

But Tim didn't wait around for an explanation. Instead, he was out of number 67, Artesia Road with the speed of a hurricane, ingloriously stuffing the peace-making roses in the dustbin as he passed.

'Tim, Tim.' Fiona ran out on to the empty street after him. 'Wait for me. Hang on, Tim. Let me explain.' But he had sprinted off around the corner and she couldn't follow him that far in her bare feet.

When Fiona gave up the chase and came back inside, Linzi was sitting halfway down the stairs. Gaetano hovered a few steps behind her, subtly buttoning up his shirt.

Linzi stared at her dishevelled housemate and her sheepish-looking boyfriend. 'OK. Is someone going to tell me just what is going on?'

'I got Fiona stoned, that's all,' began Gaetano. 'We bumped into each other at Burger King and I asked if I could come over and pick up some of the CDs that I left here. I was rolling a joint for the walk back and Fiona asked if she could have some.'

'Fiona wanted a smoke?' Linzi asked incredulously.

'Yeah,' Gaetano shrugged. 'I thought it was strange too, but I guess she was feeling a bit down what with the row with Tim and all. But I didn't know she'd never smoked before so she got completely caned after two tokes. She fell asleep on your bed and that's what must have happened to me too. It was skunk, Linz,' he added, pulling out the bag to prove it. 'It must have been pretty strong stuff.'

Fiona repeated the story almost word for word. Between sobs. Then she tried to call Tim, but he either hadn't made it home or wasn't answering his phone. Later that evening, when Linzi finally managed to get past his answerphone on Fiona's behalf, Tim told her in no uncertain terms that he didn't believe their excuses at all.

'But you believe me, don't you?' Fiona pleaded with Linzi when she put down the phone.

Linzi nodded. She did. She had to.

'Look, Fi,' she said softly. 'I think that your best bet is not to call Tim for a while. Give him a chance to cool down. He obviously wanted to make it up with you after last night. Give him a day or so and he'll be straight back on the phone.' But something told her that Tim had no intention of giving Fiona the benefit of the doubt. Fiona had made his big decision for him. She had quite unwittingly let him off the hook.

For his part, Gaetano decided that it might be a good idea for him to risk his mother's wrath and spend the night at Artesia Road with Linzi.

CHAPTER TWENTY-EIGHT

When Kerry got home from work that evening, she thought at first that the house was empty. Fiona had retired to her room to sob. Linzi and Gaetano were reaffirming their commitment to each other in the bedroom. But Fiona crept downstairs again when she realised that Kerry had come back home and Kerry knew the moment she saw Fiona's red-rimmed eyes that something very serious indeed had gone wrong. Her first line of action was to put the kettle on. Then Fiona began to tell the story. She got as far as sobbing that Tim had broken off the engagement before her intermittent sniffing and wailing became so loud that Kerry didn't have a hope in hell of finding out why.

'He'll call tomorrow, I'm sure,' Kerry reassured her absent-mindedly. They had broken up before. Tim would come crawling back as he always did. After all, getting himself a new girlfriend might actually require making some effort. Right now, Kerry had something far more worrying on her mind than the end of Fiona's doomed engagement.

That afternoon, Mrs Keble, Kerry's mother, had called her at Verbal Tix. At the moment she called, Kerry was on the cappuccino run but her mother felt she knew Leon well enough after the wedding to leave a very delicate message for him to pass on.

'She wants to know if you've seen your sister Michelle,' Leon told Kerry as she tried to get the plastic lids off the polystyrene cups without scalding herself to death.

'Of course I haven't seen my sister,' Kerry replied. 'She's on her honeymoon, isn't she? I shouldn't imagine she's even seen daylight since she got to Majorca.'

'Oh dear. You'd better call your mum,' said Leon.

Mrs Keble explained the dilemma in a whisper. It appeared that Michelle was no longer on her honeymoon at all. She had disappeared. When Richard woke up alone in the room that morning he assumed that she had gone for an early swim, but when she didn't come back after an hour, he got up to join her and found that she had left him a note on the kitchenette table. It said quite simply, 'Richard, I can't go on like this.' She had taken all her belongings with her in the smaller of their two new leather suitcases, which had been a generous wedding gift from Auntie Jean.

Richard had searched the whole of the resort and when that course of action drew a blank, he simply had to inform the island police. He didn't see how Michelle could have got too far since he had their tickets home and all the holiday money. However, a routine check of the airport revealed that she had indeed left the island that morning, flying back to Gatwick. She had paid for her ticket with a credit card! Visa! Imagine that! Richard didn't even know that she possessed a credit card and he certainly wouldn't have allowed her to get one because he doesn't agree with that kind of thing.

'She should have landed at Gatwick at one o'clock this afternoon,' Mrs Keble continued. 'It's gone five o'clock now, Kerry. Are you sure that she's not with you?'

'I haven't heard a word, Mum. Honest I haven't.'

'Are you sure, Kerry, because so help me God if you're keeping her hidden from us and her husband, I'll give you such a hiding. And her and all, when I catch up with her. You can tell her that. Worrying us all to death, she is. It's so selfish. I've had Richard's mother round here all day. She can't stop crying. Your father's gone out to the garage to fiddle with his car and he says he won't come back in till everything's sorted out, not even for his tea. If Michelle is with you, Kerry, you just better make sure she knows how selfish she's being. You can't leave your husband on your honeymoon!'

'Mum, if I see her, I'll let her know that she ought to get in touch, but I promise you, she isn't here with me.'

'Oooh, I don't know what I've done to deserve such terrible daughters,' Mrs Keble sighed. 'Your other sister was round here last night saying that she wants to leave her Steve. None of you can stick at anything for long.'

'Mum, I've got to go. I'm at work. Remember?'

'Leon won't mind you talking to me. He's a lovely lad. Now listen, Kerry. Make sure you call me the minute you get home to let me know whether she's been at your place. And don't you ever go causing me trouble like the other two have. Try and stick with something. Hang on to that Leon. There aren't many men like him about these days.'

'You're right, Mum,' Kerry sighed. 'You're right.'

Kerry reported the conversation to Leon.

'Bloody hell,' he snorted. 'She's not going to be too happy when we get a divorce, is she?'

Kerry smiled sadly. They hadn't gone through with the ceremony yet and Leon was eager to plan the end of their marriage already. That afternoon he had told her that he was prepared to pay her two thousand pounds for her involvement in the scam. Kerry refused. She wasn't doing it for the money.

When Fiona had finished a first sniffly draft of the great engagement break-up story, Kerry picked up the phone and dutifully called home to file her report on Michelle. It took her almost half an hour to persuade her mother that she was telling the truth when she said that Michelle hadn't been in touch. As she put the phone down again, even Kerry was beginning to feel a little concerned for her sister's safety. Where could she have gone? As far as the family could tell, Michelle knew no one outside Bristol except Kerry.

It was while Kerry was worrying about this that the doorbell rang and she opened the door to find Michelle herself, brown and bedraggled but still smiling, on the front step.

'My God, you're in trouble,' Kerry told her sister. After an unwarranted ear-bashing from their mother, Kerry was in no mood to return Michelle's joyous hug.

'I know, I know,' Michelle said wearily. 'I just tried to call Mum from the callbox at the top of your road but she's engaged. Probably yacking on to Richard's mum about what they could have done to end up with such terrible children.'

'Actually she was yacking on to me about what she'd done to end up with such terrible children. She's worried sick, Michelle.

We are all worried sick. What on earth happened? Where have
you been?'

'My marriage broke up,' Michelle announced dramatically as
she dropped her bag in the hallway and threw herself on to the
sofa with a sigh. Fiona looked up from her tea and momentarily
felt that perhaps hers wasn't the worst life in the world.

'Your marriage broke up? But it's less than a fortnight old for
goodness' sake.'

'I know, Kerry, I know,' Michelle sighed. 'But even as we were
getting on the plane I realised that we weren't going to last the
honeymoon.'

'What? How did you know that?'

'I can't really explain it.'

'You're going to have to try.'

Michelle straightened herself up in her seat and began. 'Well,
I think that the main problem was that nothing was different. I
mean, just little things like the fact that Richard still insisted on
taking the window seat on the plane and putting all his rubbish
on my tray while we waited for the stewardess to collect it.'

'Oh, for heaven's sake. If he always did that, where was the
problem?' Kerry didn't understand.

'I suddenly realised that I'd married him because I thought
that it would make things better. But it hadn't. I thought it might
make us more of a partnership but it was obvious that was just
a distant dream. I still felt like I was Richard's donkey, not his
wife. Make us a cup of tea, will you, Kerry? I'm gasping.'

'I don't know if you deserve one.'

'Oh, give me a break.'

'You hardly gave Richard one, did you?'

'I gave it nearly two years of living in sin and a few days of
full-blown marriage, Kerry. How much more of a break can you
give a man? I was miserable. Even the sun and sangria didn't help
to cheer me up. When we went out for dinner he would always
insist on eating something we could have got in any number of
places back home and he moaned like mad when the waiter at
this one place said they had no HP sauce. I wanted to see the
local sights, eat paella and go a bit Spanish. He just wanted to
sleep until the bars opened and then watch the football from
home on satellite television. We weren't matched, Kez. We
never were matched, we never will be and no piece of gold is

going to make enough of a difference. In fact sometimes,' she added dramatically, 'it was almost as if that wedding ring was cutting off the bloodflow to the rest of my body.'

'God only knows what Mum is going to say about this.'

'I don't care what other people are going to say any more. Especially Mum. That's how I got myself into this mess in the first place. Caring too much about appearances and not upsetting Mother. Now I've been unfair to myself and to Richard. You know, I opened a separate bank account without telling him six months ago and then I went and got myself a credit card. I've been gearing myself up to leave him for ages. I just didn't realise that that was what I had been doing.'

'So that's how you managed to fly back here without your ticket. That really confused him.'

'Everything I do confuses Richard.'

'But Mum said that your flight would be in at one o'clock. It's nearly nine now. Where on earth have you been all day?'

'I've been at the Australian Embassy,' Michelle announced. 'I've been getting myself a visa and a work permit.'

'Michelle!'

'I'm flying out to Hong Kong tomorrow night. I got a courier flight so it's dead cheap. Then I'm going on to Sydney.'

'You're going to Australia?' Kerry was almost hysterical.

'It's only the other side of the world, Kez. Stop acting like you're our mother.'

'Oh God, Michelle. You had better call Mum right now. She is going to go insane.'

'Exactly. And I can't face that tonight. I've had one hell of a day already. You call her instead, Kez. Please. Tell her that I'm here with you and that I'm safe. Tell her that I'll talk to her tomorrow morning before I fly. But you can also tell her not to bother driving over here to try to make me change my mind because I'm not going to and I don't trust Dad's driving skills in the dark.'

'You've gone nuts, you have. Completely bonkers.'

'Maybe I have. But I feel much better for it.'

'If Mum has another go at me because of you, Michelle . . .'

Kerry flew into the kitchen to grab the phone and break the news. Michelle finally noticed Fiona's red eyes.

'What's up with you, Fi? You look like you've been crying all day.'

'I have. Tim's broken off our engagement,' Fiona sniffed pathetically.

'I guess I should say I'm sorry,' Michelle began. 'But believe me, Fi, you just had a lucky escape.'

CHAPTER TWENTY-NINE

Linzi traced the outline of Gaetano's nipples through the soft black hair on his chest. He had been lying on his back for the past half-hour, just staring up at the ceiling. When Linzi snuggled into his side he made a half-hearted attempt at a hug.

'What's up with you?' she asked finally.

'Nothing. I'm just thinking.'

'How can it be nothing if you're thinking about it?'

'I mean it's nothing that you would find interesting. I'm just thinking about the band, that's all.'

'What about it?'

'You don't want to know.'

'I do now. The sound of your brain ticking over is keeping me awake. Come on, G, spill the beans.'

'It was right, you know,' Gaetano began, 'what The Professor was saying in the pub the other night.'

'About what?'

'About promoting the band. We can't just sit around waiting for someone to sign us up any more. We're going to have to go for it by ourselves. We've got to put a CD out on our own label.' He sighed heavily. 'It's the only way. You remember Mutant Phlegm? They put out an EP last year. Apparently they got back everything they paid for it and generated enough interest to get themselves a deal.'

'Good for them. But where will you get the money from to make the CD in the first place?' Linzi protested. 'The Professor said that it would cost you at least a couple of grand to get the thing pressed and that's before you've even thought about distribution and promotion.'

'Listen to you. A whole day in the music industry and you're spouting all the terms already.'

'Then you'll be pleased to know that it was my last day in the music industry.'

'What do you mean?'

'They put me in the bloody post room. I'm not going back there again.'

'Oh, great. That's one less contact than we had this morning. We've got no chance of getting in via an A & R man now.'

'I'm sorry, G.'

Gaetano sighed. 'It doesn't matter, Linz. I'm sure it wouldn't have made that much of a difference anyway. Monster Munch are just too off the wall. Those A & R men never have enough vision to introduce something really new. We've got to put something out ourselves. We've all got to pull together. The Professor has got some money saved up. Merlin's a bit of a wash-out financially but Socks could sell his car.'

'Socks sell his car? You've got to be joking. He loves that car more than his own mother.'

'His mother's dead.'

'Oh, I'm sorry,' Linzi said reflexively.

'It doesn't matter. They never got on. He bought the car by selling her bungalow. But even he will have to see that when we hit the big time he can buy himself a thousand bloody cars like that rust heap.'

'And what about you, what have you got to sell?'

There was silence for a moment except for the sound of Gaetano breathing in and out. Finally he answered. 'Nothing material, I admit. But I've got my expertise, haven't I?'

'Your expertise?' Linzi repeated slowly and, she hoped, not too incredulously.

'Yeah. I've got an amazing plan. You remember what we were talking about with the Professor the other night?'

'What?' Linzi yawned. 'How Zildjian make the best possible cymbal?'

'No, apart from that. Before then. When we were talking about his job?'

'Surely you're not going to train to be a pharmacist?' Linzi laughed. 'You'll be retiring before you make enough money for the CD.'

'No chance. What use is a degree to anybody these days anyway?'

Linzi rolled away from him with a snort. 'Quite.'

'Look, I wasn't trying to get at you but it's a fact, isn't it? You've got to do something a bit different to get ahead now. Do you want to hear my plan, or not?'

'Go on. Amuse me.'

'It's not about amusement, Linzi. This is serious stuff. If you don't think you can handle anything heavier than licking stamps in the post room of a record company, then it's best you don't get yourself involved.'

'Me get involved? I have no intention of getting involved. Since when have I been a member of Monster Munch?'

'You're my girlfriend, Linzi. You're supposed to be behind me all the way.'

'How many paces is that?'

Gaetano rolled over onto his side, increasing the physical distance between them. Linzi reached out in the dark and put her hand on his silhouetted shoulder. She knew that she was taking out her frustration on him for her shitty day at Manatee and for the incident with Fiona that she had claimed she didn't even believe took place. 'Hey, come on,' she whispered, 'you just touched a raw nerve with your comments about the post room, that's all. Of course I want to hear what your plans are. Of course I want to help you in whatever way I can.'

Gaetano rolled onto his back again. He reached over to the bedside table for his packet of cigarettes and lit one up. His face looked stony with concentration in the brief glow shed by his flaming Zippo and the tip of the cigarette. Linzi stroked the top of his arm, hoping to smooth the hardness away. 'Come on, spit it out,' she murmured. 'What's the big plan?'

'OK. But you've got to tell me that you love me first, yeah? So that even if you decide that you don't want to be a part of this, you won't ever tell anyone what I am about to say.'

'Of course I won't. I love you.' Linzi was aching to hear the story now. He had never been so serious in all the time she had known him. 'Just tell me what you want me to do.'

'Linzi,' Gaetano said slowly. 'We are going to do a robbery.'

'What?' Linzi sat bolt upright in the bed. 'A robbery? We? I think you had better elaborate.'

'OK.' Gaetano elaborated. He had hatched the big plan while listening to the Professor talking about his job. The Professor was always taking on locum work whenever he had a spare evening, trying to supplement his wages and then ploughing the proceeds back into the band. Some of the shops he worked in had been robbed before. People had got away with thousands of pounds' worth of controlled drugs and had never been caught. Not just once but dozens of times. The smaller shops in particular had minimal security systems. They were cheaply installed and easy to disable. Sometimes the Professor would have only one assistant to man the tills while he made up the prescriptions and most of the time that single assistant would be some stupid young girl. There was one shop in particular which would be very easy pickings. He was due to do a night's locum work there later in the week.

'The Professor reckons that he can put the cameras out of action before we arrive,' Gaetano concluded.

Linzi's heart was pounding against the walls of her chest.

'We're going to rob a pharmacy?'

'I can get a car,' Gaetano whispered. 'You can drive it for us. You can drive, can't you?'

'Yes, I can. But you're not really serious about this?' Linzi murmured to his shadow.

'Of course I'm serious about this, Linzi. I don't want to be a loser working in a clothes shop for the rest of my life. I want to be a somebody. I want to get Monster Munch a record deal and this is the way to make the money to do it. Are you going to help me or what?'

'No way am I. What you're asking me to do is illegal and dangerous,' Linzi said flatly.

'Well, I can't deny that it's illegal,' Gaetano began. 'But it won't be dangerous, Linz. No one will get hurt. The Professor will pretend that he doesn't know what's going on and he'll persuade the shop-girl to co-operate. There'll be no violence, no blood and no risk of getting caught because the Professor will have dealt with the cameras and the panic button to the police station.'

'The panic button to the police station? You didn't mention that. Oh my God, Gaetano. You're being ridiculous now.'

'I told you, the Professor will have disabled it. If there even is one. He says that it's easy, just a matter of unscrewing the buzzer. No one will notice. It'll give us extra time.'

'But what's in it for me?' Linzi continued. 'I'm afraid that the glittering future of Monster Munch is a little too abstract a concept for me to want to end up in prison for it.'

'You won't end up in prison, I swear. And you'll get a cut of the money. A quarter if that's what it takes to get you on board. It'll be about a thousand quid. You could do another course.'

Linzi smiled. 'No thanks. My shiatsu days are over.'

'It could be a lot of money.'

'It would have to be a lot of money to make me take that kind of risk,' Linzi snorted.

'C'mon Linzi. There must be something you're dying to do. All you need is that elusive grand and you can go and do it.'

'You said a quarter. How many of us would be involved?'

'Three.'

'Then why wouldn't the money be split three ways?'

'Because three-quarters of the cash has to go towards putting out the single, of course.'

'I think my help would be worth more than a quarter.'

'OK, a third. Will you do it for that?'

'Well,' Linzi mused, remembering that afternoon's conversation with Freya. 'I was thinking that I might try to travel a bit this year. I've hardly seen anything of the world except France and the Greek islands. But I was also thinking more along the conventional lines of working hard and saving up to pay for the trip.'

'Saving up? You're going to have to get better at holding down a job if that's your plan,' Gaetano pointed out.

'Not fair. I could hold down a job easily if someone would give me something exciting to do.'

'Isn't my idea exciting enough for you?'

'I said "exciting", not "terrifying".'

She felt Gaetano move so that his leg was across hers. He nuzzled her ear beneath her hair and whispered. 'If Monster Munch make it big because of this, I'll take you anywhere you want to go, first class.' Linzi laughed out loud. Gaetano put his hand down between her legs and began to gently massage her crotch. 'So you'll be our driver?'

Linzi bit her lip. 'I didn't say yes.'

She felt Gaetano's leg slip off her own again. 'Look, I'll think about it, OK?' she said to salvage his affection. 'But you've got to give me more details first. You know, I can't really believe you're asking me to do this at all. It's like going out with someone in the Mafia.'

'Hey, you. Shut your mouth.' Gaetano put on his best God-father accent. 'Some of my favourite relations are in the Mafia.' Linzi smiled. His mother could certainly have put the frighteners on a wimp like Joe Pesci.

'When would we have to do it?' Linzi asked after a while in a quieter, more serious voice.

'The Professor is going to be working in this shop on Saturday night. It's in North London. A rough area. There'll be hundreds of natural suspects in the housing estates around the shop and if it gets as far as an identity parade, the Professor says he'll pick out the first bloke he sees who looks anything like the A & R man from Malibou.'

'Gaetano, you're nuts.'

'Yeah, but you love me for it.'

CHAPTER THIRTY

When Kerry arrived at work the next morning, Leon insisted that she leave again straight away to sort her family obligations out. Mrs Keble had been on the phone the minute the Verbal Tix office opened to tell Leon exactly what was going on and Leon was both sorry for her and anxious not to get on the wrong side of his future mother-in-law (though they had yet to detonate that particular bombshell).

'At least make sure she gets to the right terminal at Heathrow,' Leon instructed Kerry. 'She could be gone for ages. She's your little sister. You've got to keep in touch.'

Kerry wasn't really all that bothered about giving Michelle a good send-off. She was angry that her younger sister seemed able to cause such chaos and still get away with it. When Mrs Keble's first fit of hysterics had passed and she had persuaded Michelle to talk to her in person, she seemed to forgive her youngest daughter everything. In fact, when Michelle handed the phone back to Kerry, Mrs Keble even said 'She always was the bravest of you all. She'll make something of herself Down Under. I know she will.'

What happened to the selfish, irresponsible and often impossible girl who had left her husband weeping in their honeymoon suite?

Kerry and Michelle shared a largely silent taxi-ride to Heathrow.

'Which terminal?' the taxi driver asked. Michelle looked at her ticket blankly.

'I can't see it, Kerry. Which terminal do you think we want?'

Kerry took the ticket from her and scanned it for the relevant information.

'Four,' she announced. 'Terminal Four.'

'Thanks,' Michelle took the ticket back. 'I didn't have a clue what I was looking for. You always were the practical one, Kez.'

'And you were always the exciting one,' Kerry sniffed.

'Yeah, right. Don't exaggerate. Look, Kez. You will come and visit me, won't you? When I've got myself settled in? You'd love it in Australia. I'm sure you would. Nicky Hazel said that she didn't want to come back after her year out there.'

'Nicky Hazel didn't have all that much to come back for.'

'Leon wouldn't miss you for a week or so, would he?'

'No, I suppose he wouldn't. You get yourself settled in and I'll see what I can do. Though I don't suppose I've even earned any leave yet. I've only been at that job for two months and I've already had to take two days off because of you, what with the wedding and making sure you get to the right terminal today.'

'I'm eternally grateful. You know you're my favourite sister, Kez.' Michelle squeezed her hand. 'I always looked up to you. All through school.'

'Yeah, well. In that case, don't do anything I wouldn't do.'

'I'll see you in Australia then.'

'I said perhaps.'

'Look, Kez. Try to be happy for me, won't you? I expected Mum to be the difficult one but I feel like you're the one who is most pissed off with me over this whole thing. You wouldn't have wanted me to rot away in St Paul's with Richard for the rest of my life, would you? I'm going to take control of my own destiny now. You're going to be proud of me. You'll see. Everyone's got to follow their dreams. At the end of the day, you're the only person with your own best interests at heart.'

'I know you're right, Michelle. It's just that it's all so sudden. And I'm worried that you'll be disappointed when you get there.'

'In some ways, I won't care so very much if I am. It would be far worse to live with the question of what might have happened. Nothing ventured, remember, Kez?' Michelle sniffed a little sadly. 'You said that to me when I first met Richard. When I didn't know whether he fancied me or not and he was too shy to ask me out.'

'I remember.'

'Well, I ventured then, didn't I? I asked him out and discovered that he did fancy me after all. I know it's all gone a bit pear-shaped now, but we had some happy times together and I got you to wear a stupid dress at the end of it.'

'Yeah. I won't ever forgive you for that.'

The taxi driver pulled up outside the terminal. Kerry helped Michelle to drag her bright new rucksack into the departures lounge.

'Is this going to be enough for a whole year?'

'You've got to be a portable girl at times like this, Kez. You don't really need that much stuff to survive.'

Kerry shrugged. But it was hard to imagine how Michelle would cope without her hairspray and curling tongs.

Kerry took the tube back from Heathrow to Clapham South. She had kissed her little sister goodbye at the gate which led to the duty free shops. As she passed through the gate, Michelle suddenly remembered that there was something she had to ask Kerry to take home for her. She pressed her wedding and engagement rings into Kerry's hand.

'Give them back to Richard, could you?'

Kerry nodded.

'It's funny, isn't it?' Michelle continued. 'To think of these two things as symbols of commitment when, in reality, they don't mean anything without the right feelings behind them. Why do so many people seem to spend their lives chasing a little piece of gold, eh?'

'Who knows?' Kerry sighed.

'So long, sis.'

One last kiss goodbye.

'I'm off to chase some sun.'

Now, Kerry fished the two rings out of her top pocket as she sat on the tube. The glittering sapphire and cubic zirconia cluster and the plain gold wedding band. She remembered the first time she had seen the engagement ring. It had been Christmas Day, two years earlier. Michelle's smiling face. Richard's shy request for her hand. She remembered how jealous she had been of them then.

Kerry slipped first the engagement ring and then the wedding band on to the fourth finger of her own left hand. Well, not so much slipped, as wedged. Michelle had much more slender fingers. Kerry turned her hand to watch the ring glitter as she had seen Fiona do with her ring so many times when she thought no one was watching. You couldn't really tell that the cubic zirconia weren't real diamonds. The stones were so pretty. And the gold was so smooth.

Kerry's gaze wandered momentarily from the brilliant rings to the tips of her fingers. She noted with disgust her chewed and stumpy nails. She would have to have a manicure before her big day.

CHAPTER THIRTY-ONE

The next Saturday was a big day for all the girls at 67, Artesia Road. After a week of pleading phone calls, Tim had finally given in to Fiona's demands for a summit meeting and had agreed to see her that very evening to talk things through just one more time. Linzi seemed to be unusually on edge and would sigh and snort with irritation every time someone went near the phone. She said that Gaetano was planning a special evening and she was anxious to know the details. The moods of both Linzi and Fiona were still preventing Kerry from announcing her surprise engagement but she was looking forward to a Saturday almost as good as the last. Leon was taking her along to a Gay Pride march.

The party atmosphere began on the tube. Kerry and Leon could feel their hearts speeding up to follow the beat as they sailed down the escalator at Tottenham Court Road surrounded by a sea of Carmen Mirandas all blowing into their new pink plastic whistles. The noise was hellish. Leon looked a little embarrassed. He turned to Kerry, who was standing one step above him and said, 'No wonder we've got a bad name.'

He turned to face the direction of the escalator again. Kerry stared at the back of his head, at the way his hair swirled in two different directions at the crown. She wanted to kiss it. When they reached the bottom of the escalator, the crowd on the platform surged towards an incoming train. Leon grabbed Kerry's hand and helped to pull her on board. Once in the carriage, he didn't let go, but squeezed her hand tightly as they were pushed backwards against the wall by the sheer volume of revellers.

'If we get parted,' he told her, 'get out at Bethnal Green and wait by the exit.'

'OK,' said Kerry. 'I'll see you there.' But there was no way she was letting go of his hand.

Linzi's telephone vigil was rewarded when the Professor finally called at half past five to confirm the address of the shop where he was working that night. There were just two security cameras in Patel's Pharmacy and General Goods Store. One at the front of the shop and one in the pharmacy itself. The Professor was alone as he had hoped, except for the daughter of the chemist who owned the shop. Manjri Patel was dressed in a bright orange and gold sari and hid the fashion magazine she was reading beneath the counter as though it were a girlie mag whenever the doorbell rang and someone walked in.

The Professor made her acquaintance pretty briefly, then installed himself in the pharmacy on the pretence of checking supplies. The layout was the same as that of any chemist's shop he had worked in before. Pills and potions lined up alphabetically along the shelves. Weighing scales. A pill counter that counted the tablets quite accurately if you dropped them through so slowly that you might as well have counted them out yourself. A list of stolen prescription pads to look out for was scribbled on a Post-It note stuck to the computer that printed out the bottle labels. The controlled drugs were kept in a locked cabinet that was further complicated by a code. The Professor fingered the unfamiliar key which now hung from his belt. Each time the bell sounded when the door opened, his heart hammered against the inside of his chest.

While Manjri dished out another packet of Fisherman's Friends, the Professor gazed at the security camera which filmed the pharmacy. He followed the cable down from the camera to the socket where it was plugged in. All too easy to get to. It was basically an ordinary video camera. A proper cowboy job. The Professor kicked the switch off as he walked through to the main body of the shop. He didn't even have to bend down. Manjri wasn't disturbed by the click.

'What a way to have to spend Saturday night, eh, Andrew?' she said when he emerged into the main shop to see if the camera there had been immobilised too. He was too absorbed in his mission to answer her question.

'I said,' she repeated, 'this isn't much of a way to spend Saturday night, is it?'

The Professor looked at her smiling face a little guiltily. He didn't think it terribly wise to tell her that things were only going to get worse.

'There's a really good band on at the Forum tonight, as well. "Radioactive Survivors". Have you heard of them?'

The Professor nodded. In fact, he knew and loved every song they had ever done. Hardly thought they'd be Manjri's kind of band though. 'Yeah,' he said. 'Did some song about bleeding wounds didn't they?'

'That's the one. Though I have to say that "Stigmata" is far from my favourite track off their new album. Bit too gory. Even for me.'

'So, you're into heavy metal?' the Professor asked. He had dreaded having to force himself to make conversation. To act normal. At least she was making it easy for him with the topic she had chosen. 'You don't look like you are.'

'Well, I don't go out in this, do I?' Manjri said, holding the folds of her beautiful sari out like butterfly wings to reveal the battered sixteen-hole Doc Martens she wore beneath. 'I have to go to my friend's house to change first. Our Dad's a bit traditional,' she explained. 'Especially when me or Sangita are working in the shop. He likes his neighbours to think that he's got two perfectly respectable little Hindu daughters. No conversation with the opposite sex before marriage. That kind of thing.'

'Is he really strict?'

'To be honest,' Manjri admitted, 'he's not so bad now that I've left school and I suppose he was only ever trying to look out for us in the wicked Western world.'

'You've got a really strong London accent,' the Professor commented inanely.

'Yeah? Well, I grew up here, didn't I?'

A little old man, with a back so curved that he was almost polo-shaped, came into the shop at that point and asked for some Kaolin and Morphine. The Professor retreated into the pharmacy. This was something that Manjri could deal with alone. When she had bagged up his purchase and counted the old man's money out into the exact amount of coppers and five pence pieces, she poked her head through the door and tried to pick up the conversation.

'So, as I was asking, where do you usually go on a Saturday night?'

She caught him nervously chewing at the skin on the side of a fingernail. 'Eh? Oh, I go to gigs sometimes. Maybe to a club.'

'If you like my kind of music, perhaps we could go somewhere together one night next week,' she added hopefully.

'Yeah,' said the Professor. 'That'd be nice. I'll give you a ring here, shall I?' The doorbell sounded again and Manjri popped back into the shop like the sunshine girl popping out of a weather house. She was nice. Really nice. It was a pity that, after tonight, the Professor knew he would never be able to see her again.

Pride's headlining acts had finished and it seemed as though everyone who was anyone was now crammed inside one of the sweaty dance tents, so that the only dance anyone could do was one which involved jumping up and down on the spot. Kerry was completely exhausted. She felt as though she had lost three stones in weight that afternoon and was in desperate need of a drink. She had been separated from Leon by two huge guys who were both dressed as brides in matching white dresses and veils. Wedding fever was in the air. When she caught a glimpse of Leon again around the edge of one man's puff-sleeved elbow, she was more than a little relieved as he gestured that he too was ready to leave although it was still only nine in the evening.

They fought their way to the exit. Kerry made it first and collapsed against the springy side of the tent. On the grass around the marquee lay beautiful young people in combinations of boy/boy, girl/girl, boy dressed as girl and so on, catching the last of the evening sun. A girl with cropped hair dyed pink and a ring through her eyebrow gave Kerry a beautiful smile. Just as she was returning it, Leon broke free into the open air.

'Oxygen!! At last!!' He leaned against the tent next to Kerry and the guy-ropes strained disturbingly. 'I don't think I have ever felt this hot in my life.' He took hold of the bottom of his T-shirt and pulled it off over his head. Kerry tried not to look at his chest. 'Phew, that's better. You OK?'

'Sure. I'm fine.'

The pink-haired girl raised an eyebrow quizzically in Kerry's direction. When she got no response, she shrugged her shoulders and walked away. Kerry wondered whether she had actually just scored.

'Jeremy is having an After-Pride party later on but I really don't know if I can be bothered to go now,' Leon continued. 'Do you want to?'

'I guess I might,' said Kerry. 'If I'm invited.'

'Of course you're invited. He loves you. Especially now that you're my fiancée.'

'Did you tell him? I thought we weren't supposed to tell anybody yet.' In fact they had barely talked about it between themselves since the afternoon when Leon said that he had no reason to bother staying on now that Sam had gone for good.

'I had to tell Jeremy,' Leon explained. 'He got drunk and rang up blubbing. He said that he wouldn't have a friend in the world when I went back to South Africa. When I said that I wasn't going to go back to South Africa, he wanted to know how I'd wangled it, of course. He wants to be best man. I've told him I'll think about it. Only thing is, he's so bloody camp, it might be a bit of a giveaway that I'm gay too.'

'But we are going ahead with it?'

'Of course we are. Didn't think I'd jilt you at the altar, did you?'

Kerry smiled with relief. 'I was hoping not. I've already chosen my dress.'

'Don't go too over the top.' Leon looked concerned.

'Won't it look a little odd if I don't?'

'I suppose so. Talking of which, I've got something totally over-the-top for you back at my place. Want to make a move?'

'What is it?' Kerry asked excitedly.

'Wait and see. Though I'm sure you've already guessed. You definitely ready to go?'

'Definitely. Apart from this mysterious present, I'm desperate for the loo and the queue over there at the Portaloos is ridiculous.'

Leon shrugged. 'That's because hardly anyone goes into the loos at Pride for a quick slash.' Kerry winced at the thought. Leon slipped his T-shirt back on. 'Feel a bit skinny with all

the beefcakes round here,' he explained. 'Come on. Let's go.'
He started off in the direction of home.

As they walked towards the tube station, Leon linked his arm
through hers. The gardens of the grotty flats which flanked the
park were full of local residents, leaning menacingly against
their garden gates, occasionally pausing in the slow necking of
a warm beer to hurl abuse. A bald-headed man wrestled with
his muscular dog on the lawn. It wasn't the kind of place Kerry
would have wanted to find herself in after dark and alone.

'Bloody perverts,' shouted a woman with a naked and fairly
grubby baby tucked under her arm like a bundle of rags.

'Charming,' laughed Leon. 'I hope her baby grows up gay.'

'You sound like a wicked stepmother,' Kerry observed.

'No,' Leon protested. 'I thought I was your Prince Charming.'

CHAPTER THIRTY-TWO

Linzi was feeling more than a little bit sick as she waited outside the Esso garage in the car Gaetano told her he had borrowed from a mate. It was a white Ford Escort. Common enough for the area. But it had a thick red 'go-faster' stripe down both sides and 'Speedy' written in curly red letters on the bonnet. Linzi wondered if Gaetano had told his friend why he needed to borrow the car. When he got back in on the passenger side with a bar of chocolate in each hand, it was the first thing she asked him.

'Don't be stupid, Linz,' he told her. 'I said I was taking you for a romantic night out, didn't I? When the job's done, we'll dump it and I'll tell Lance that it got nicked from a car park while we were having our meal.'

'Lance?'

'Yeah, Lance Sylvester. The man who brought us together. He'll be glad of the insurance money now that Verbal Tix is going down. OK, worrier?' He kissed Linzi on the end of the nose and pressed a Mars bar into her hand. She put it straight onto the dashboard.

'I don't know how you can eat anything right now,' she said.

'I need my strength.'

They drove erratically to Patel's Pharmacy. Linzi stalled the car at some traffic lights and had to fight back tears when it wouldn't restart first time. They turned into the narrow side street at three minutes before ten. The Professor was expecting them at ten exactly. Gaetano told Linzi to do a U-turn and drive back in the opposite direction for a little while. It wouldn't do for them to get there before the Professor was ready and have to hang about just asking to be recognised.

Gaetano had lost his smile now. He held the specially prepared bobble hat with its ragged cut-out eye-holes tightly, screwing it up like a dishcloth in his sweaty hands. He was wearing a jacket he had bought from a charity shop that afternoon. His jacket, his trousers and even his socks were black. Everything completely black and plain. Not a distinguishing mark on him. Unlike 'Speedy' the car.

Linzi turned back into the right road. Two minutes to go. She felt as though she might be about to get a migraine.

'Are you sure you want to do this, Gaetano? We could turn back now. What if the Professor hasn't been able to turn the cameras off? What if there's a customer in the shop?' Linzi began to babble. 'There has to be a better way to get the money.'

Gaetano looked at her with a frighteningly expressionless face.

'Linzi. Shut up. There'll be no customers to worry about because the shop will be about to close. The alarms will have been disabled and so will the cameras. I've known the Professor since school. He would never let me down. He wouldn't dare.'

Linzi wondered whether the Professor had ever been put in such a difficult position before but she clammed up and dutifully pulled the car to a standstill near the kerb outside the chemist's shop. She kept the engine running, like she'd seen on any number of films. Gaetano pulled the woollen hat down over his face.

'Good luck,' she murmured, though it hardly seemed appropriate.

'Thanks, bella.'

Gaetano leapt out of the car and seconds later he was springing through the open door of Patel's Pharmacy and General Goods Store.

'Come on. Tell me what the present is.'

'Wait until we get back to the flat. God, I bet you are a nightmare at Christmas.'

Leon lived near the City. He had a third floor flat in a modern development with a gym downstairs and even a doorman. 'You'll have to excuse the mess,' he muttered as he struggled with his key in the lock. 'I didn't have time to sort the place out before coming to meet you this morning. And I didn't expect to have anyone back here tonight or I'd have hidden my pants beneath the sofa.'

But the room that he opened the door on to looked immaculate. The walls were painted plain white. Along one stood a huge blue sofa with deep squashy seats dotted with red and green cushions. The opposite wall was flanked with thousands of pounds' worth of matt black stereo equipment. A bright woollen rug formed the centrepiece on a polished wooden floor.

'Wow,' Kerry breathed. 'No wonder you don't want to leave London.' She was slightly embarrassed now that Leon had been anywhere near Artesia Road, with its furniture borrowed from two different but equally tasteless generations. However, the embarrassment was quickly replaced by delight. After all, this palace was where she would have to live after the wedding. 'You've done this place up beautifully.'

Leon was dead-heading some of the sunny orange flowers which stood in a vase on the coffee table. 'It was all Sam really. He studied interior design before he decided to become a singer.'

Suddenly, Kerry wasn't sure she liked that blue sofa so much. Maybe it was a little bit too chic.

'I wasn't even all that keen on renting the place until Sam pointed out the possibilities,' Leon continued. 'It's really light. In the daytime, of course.'

'Where's your loo?' Kerry asked.

'Oh sorry, Kez. I forgot you were busting.' Leon pointed her in the direction of the half-finished bathroom. 'Mind that pile of tiles under the sink. I can never get myself into the right mood to start grouting. Though the landlord's promised us a bundle off the rent if I do.'

Kerry wasn't listening. 'When I come out again, I want my present.'

She carefully negotiated the DIY booby traps and sat herself down on the cold loo seat. The bathroom was being decked out in tiles which were the same blue as the sofa, mixed in with a few slightly lighter ones so that the overall effect would be like a reflection of the sky in the sea. The white bathtub sparkled, as did the sink. Towels the same colour as the lighter tiles hung in a fluffy array from a shining chrome rail. Kerry went to wash her hands and studied her face in the mirrored bathroom cabinet. At some point that day she had caught the sun and had a little white stripe on her nose where her sunglasses had been. That was a pain, but over all, she decided, she just looked a little healthier than usual. She dragged her comb through her hair and scrubbed at her teeth with a finger loaded with toothpaste.

She could hear Leon moving about in the background. There was the sound of a tap being turned on. A kettle being filled. He walked across the bright wooden floor of the sitting room in his squeaky trainers and switched on the wide-screen television. For a moment, Kerry allowed herself to day-dream about their future together. When they were married she would hear these sounds every night.

Kerry looked at the bathroom cabinet again, but this time she wasn't interested in her reflection. She wondered whether the cabinet door would make a noise and give the game away if she tried to open it. Slowly, she tugged at the little silver handle. Only the merest well-made click. She opened the cabinet door wide.

Kerry wasn't sure what she expected to find. More toothpaste. Indigestion tablets. Proplus. A packet of Nurofen. Three bottles of aftershave. Eternity. Obsession. Egoïste. She knew that he wore Eternity. A tube of KY jelly.

'What are you doing in there, Kerry?' he called suddenly. 'Having a bath?'

'Nothing. I'll be out in a minute.' She flushed the loo hurriedly and closed the cupboard while the sound of rushing water would hide the guilty noise. Then she splashed her face with water in an attempt to cool it down. Obsession and Egoïste? Had Sam left them behind, or was he back? Leon hadn't really mentioned him for days but the sudden re-emergence of the wedding question suggested that something had changed Leon's mind.

Leon had installed himself on the sofa. When Kerry came into the room he pointed at a mug of tea he had already put in front of her place. He had sugared it perfectly. She murmured her thanks.

'There's never anything on television on a Saturday night, is there?' he complained. 'I suppose we're all supposed to be out strutting our funky stuff. I hope you wanted tea. I've got some stronger stuff out in the kitchen but I figured that you probably feel as dehydrated and knackered as I do. I'm getting too old for this partying lark. It's time I settled down.'

'You sound like my mum.'

'I'm probably nearly as old as your mum. No, today was fun, but I can't do it every weekend any more. I used to. Sam and I would go to Heaven until that finished and then straight on to Trade. God, we didn't get home until Sunday afternoon sometimes. Though I think that E had more to do with my staying power than youthful stamina then . . .'

'I had a good time,' Kerry told him.

'Good. I'm glad you weren't bored.'

'The bands were really great.'

'Not really. Honestly, they drag the same old queens out year after year. If I have to see Erasure one more time I swear I'll go straight.' Kerry smiled weakly. 'At least we didn't have to sit through Jimmy Somerville. I used to date a guy who looks like him. Talk about love being blind.'

Kerry slipped off her shoes and curled her feet up under her bottom. 'Are we going to go to Jeremy's party later on?'

Leon sighed. 'Not me. I don't think I can move from this seat again tonight. You can go if you want to. I'll give you the address. It's in Hackney. Chris and Ian will be there. You know them. Remember?'

'Oh, yeah.' Chris had advised her to get her hair straightened. Professionally. 'I don't think I'll bother if you're not going to.'

'Sorry. But I think I'll go straight to bed when I've finished this. I'm just an old wuss, Kez. I'll call you a cab if you like.'

Kerry whispered to hide her disappointment. 'Yeah. Thanks. But I want this present you've been talking about first.'

'What? Oh, yeah.' Leon reached beneath the cushion. 'I was just pretending that I'd forgotten.'

Leon passed the small golden cardboard box over to Kerry. She read the carefully matched gift-tag. 'To my dear, dear friend Kerry, All my love, Leon.' Then she pulled gently at one end of the ribbon so that it unfurled. Inside the box was a smaller, velvet-covered jewellery case.

'I thought as much,' she grinned widely as she opened that up.

'Oh, it's nothing.'

'Nothing?' It was as if the light reflected by the ring inside that box was illuminating Kerry's face. She picked it out and held it up for a closer look. 'Nothing? Leon, this is beautiful. It's the most beautiful thing I've ever seen. Put it on me.'

'What?'

'Put it on my hand for me. I want to do this properly.'

'If you insist.' Leon took the ring from Kerry and slid it on to the appropriate finger. She held her face out for a kiss and closed her eyes. He placed a dry peck on her cheek.

'Oh, Leon. This is so incredible,' Kerry murmured. 'The best thing ever.' She was looking at the ring again now, turning her hand so that shards of light struck the wall. 'And it looks so expensive. Fiona will be so jealous.'

'Yes. Well, I thought you could sell it afterwards since you don't want to take any money now. You can buy yourself something useful. Put a deposit on a bike.'

'But I'll never sell it,' Kerry replied indignantly. 'Don't talk like that. This is my engagement ring.'

Leon smiled stiffly. 'Shall I call that cab for you now? I promised I'd go into the office early tomorrow to help Serena with some figures.'

'Oh, I don't remember you planning that.'

'She called last night.' Leon was already dialling for a cab. 'Artesia Road. What's your post-code there, Kez?'

'Hang on,' Kerry took the phone gently from Leon's hand. 'There might not actually be much point in your calling a cab. I'm not sure I've got my house-keys.'

'What?'

'I had a root round my bag while I was in the bathroom.' Kerry picked up her bag and made a show of looking inside it again. 'Bugger. Looks like I was right,' she smiled sheepishly. 'No keys. I'm locked out.'

'Won't your housemates be in?'

'I'm not sure. I was hoping I could stay with you. I know Linzi's gone to a party tonight and Fiona may have gone home to see her parents for the whole weekend. Would it be OK if I stay? I want to make you breakfast as a thankyou for this, anyway.' She waved her newly ringed hand at him.

'Honestly, Kez. You're doing me the favour where that's concerned.' Leon was already searching the back of the sofa for her keys.

'Where else have you been in here?' he asked her.

'Only the bathroom.'

'Well, I don't think I saw them in there. Where did you last see them?'

'I put them in my pocket when I left the house this morning. Perhaps they dropped out at Pride. It could have happened when we were in the dance tent. I was getting knocked about quite a bit, perhaps they fell out then.'

'You'll never find them again if that's the case,' Leon sighed. 'Do you want to use my phone and call home? It's pretty late. Someone might be in by now.'

'Oh, yes. Thanks.' Kerry picked up the phone and began to dial. But while she dialled she held her thumb over the button that cuts the caller off. She pretended to let the phone ring. Once, twice . . . five times. 'Doesn't look like there's anyone in,' she told Leon as she replaced the receiver.

'Why don't you leave a message, then they can call here and let you know when they get back.'

'Oh yeah,' Kerry picked up the phone again. 'But what if they don't get back until really late?'

'I don't mind,' Leon said flatly through a yawn. 'And the cabs run all night.'

Kerry dialled her number and kept her finger over the cut-off button once more. This time, when she figured that five rings had passed, she waited for the duration of an imaginary answerphone message and left a message in return. 'Hi, girls, it's Kerry. I've managed to lose my keys. Can someone call me at Leon's place? Soon as you get in. Thanks. Bye.'

Leon had gone through to the bathroom. She heard him open the mirrored cabinet. 'Nope. Nothing in here,' he called. 'Perhaps we should check with the man downstairs, in case you dropped them on the way up here and someone's handed them in?'

'I'm sure I didn't,' Kerry replied.

'And you haven't been in the kitchen, have you?'

'No, I haven't.' Kerry was disappointed. It was nice that Leon cared enough to help her look for her keys, but now he was getting just a little too keen to find them. Why couldn't he just let her stay with him and promise to have another look for the damn things in the morning?

'Well, you must have dropped them at Pride,' he was saying

now as he delved into the airing cupboard and emerged with a couple of blankets. He dumped them next to the sofa, then disappeared into his bedroom and came back with a pillow. 'So they're lost for ever. You'll be all right out here, won't you?' he asked rhetorically. 'It's not that cold tonight and the sofa's really comfortable. I've spent many a night on it myself,' he added with a little snort. He pressed the pillow into Kerry's arms. 'Good night, Kez.' He didn't even kiss her on the cheek before he went back to his wide double bed.

Kerry sat down on the edge of the sofa with the pillow still clutched in her arms. What was wrong with him? As she lay back on the cushions and stared up at the ceiling, she could hear him turning over in the next room, groaning and moaning a little as he tried to get comfortable in his ocean-wide bed. He had given her just two sodding itchy blankets. He really didn't want her there at all. No, she was misinterpreting his tiredness, that's all. When he was tired at work he was exactly the same. Monosyllabic, matter of fact, wanting to be left alone. The next morning over breakfast everything would be all right again. She would go out and buy croissants. She thought that she had seen a decent shop on the corner as they turned into Leon's road.

She took one last look at the new ring adorning her left hand. It must mean that she was allowed to tell the girls and her mother at last. And the people at work. Lance would be surprised.

Kerry draped the blankets across her fully clothed body. The heat of the day was just a memory now, disappearing up into the clear sky. That week, London had been like the Sahara Desert. Baking in the day and freezing at night. With only her new ring to keep her warm, Kerry wrapped the blankets around her and pulled them right up to her chin.

CHAPTER THIRTY-THREE

'Get down on the floor, you fucking Paki!'

The Professor caught the look of horror in Manjri's eyes as she fell to the floor beneath a single blow from Gaetano's fist. Instinctively, he ran out into the body of the shop to see whether she was OK. Gaetano pushed him away from her roughly.

'Keep away from her, fuck-face. Just open the bloody till.'

Jesus! Gaetano was playing the armed robber for all he was worth.

'What? Fuck!!!'

Gaetano elbowed the Professor in the back. He couldn't be sure but it felt as though Gaetano might even be holding a knife against the thin material of the white chemist's coat. He was really going the whole way. 'Open the fucking till!!!' he shouted again. The Professor opened the till hurriedly and laid the contents bare before him.

'Get some bags.'

He pulled a handful of carriers out from a drawer and shoved them helplessly in Gaetano's direction. Gaetano began to load the bags with that day's takings. Notes first. Scrunching them up as he grabbed. Then he tipped up the drawer to empty out the coins while the Professor watched and actually felt afraid.

'How much do you reckon is in here?' Gaetano asked, not forgetting for a moment to sound ferocious.

'I don't know,' the Professor said feebly. 'Maybe three hundred. I'm not sure.'

'Three hundred? Christ. I thought you said there would be more.'

'Yeah. Well, it's been a quiet night, man . . . I . . .'

Gaetano silenced his friend with a stare. Beneath their feet, Manjri was moaning. She had curled into a little ball, almost wrapped herself around the Professor's ankles.

'Andrew,' she groaned.

The Professor shrugged his shoulders.

'Sort her out, will you man? Fuck. This is hardly worth it.' Gaetano slammed the till shut. 'We need some more stuff. What's in the pharmacy?'

The Professor's eyes widened.

'Tell me what's commercial,' Gaetano demanded. 'Tell me what I can sell.'

The Professor looked down towards the poor girl who was climbing her way up his trousers legs. Blood trickled from her nose to her upper lip.

'I . . . I . . .' he stuttered. 'I'm not sure.' Seeing the girl move, Gaetano swung the bag of money, heavy with coins, straight into her face to set her back on the floor again, catching the Professor's legs at the same time so that he almost buckled on top of her. 'Come on, for fuck's sake, man,' Gaetano was heading into the pharmacy, pulling packets off the shelves as he went and shoving them straight into his bags. 'Hurry up.'

'What's this?' he asked, waving a package at the Professor who could not free his ankle from Manjri's grasp.

'It's for cystitis,' the Professor told him. 'You don't want to bother with that.'

'Well, what the fuck do I want to bother with then? I don't bloody know, do I? What's cystitis anyway? Get that fucking girl off your feet and come through here, will you, you fucking idiot? You're the pharmacist. Tell me what to take.'

Manjri was beginning to right herself again. She was on her knees now, slowly dragging herself up by the waistband of the Professor's trousers. He sagged a little under her weight, his hands hanging helplessly by his sides as he wondered whether he should try to help her or help his friend. Gaetano stood in the middle of the pharmacy, knees slightly bent, ready to spring into action. He looked like a snarling IRA hitman on a supermarket trolley dash.

'Tell me what to take,' he snarled.

The Professor licked his lips and tried to speak. Manjri was still groaning. He looked at her face. One side of it was all

blood now. Her brown skin shiny red. 'Take . . . take . . .' he
stuttered.

'Take what? Take what? For fuck's sake, man. Tell me what
to take. We haven't got much time.' Gaetano clutched at the
carrier bags full of cash until his knuckles started to go white. He
scanned the shelves desperately for a name that he recognised.
The Professor still said nothing. He was transfixed with horror as
Manjri loosened her bloody grip on his trousers and slipped back
on to the floor. She was completely out of it. Unconscious.

'Take what the fuck you like,' the Professor screamed suddenly. 'You've nearly bloody killed her. You promised me no
one would get hurt.' The Professor fell to his knees and tried to
get a better look at Manjri's bleeding face. He put his fingers to
her bloody neck and tried to find a pulse.

'You promised me no one would get hurt. I think she's dying
man, for fuck's sake!!! You've fucking killed her.'

Gaetano swept his arm along a shelf and caught as many of
the falling packets as he could in an open bag.

'You're a fucking idiot,' he told the Professor as he stormed
back into the shop. 'A fucking, bloody idiot.' The Professor
looked up only to be cracked hard in the nose by an angry
fist. He buckled and landed heavily on his wounded assistant
before Gaetano grabbed him by the hair and pulled him almost
upright again.

'I'll fucking see you later, you twat.'

Then he hurled the Professor back to the floor and booted him
in the side of the head for good measure.

Gaetano burst out into the street where Linzi was still waiting
in the Escort, having seen nothing but the dusty dashboard in
front of her. She pushed the passenger door open as he ran
towards her and leapt into the car. Then she slammed her
foot down hard on the accelerator and skidded away from
the scene of the crime before Gaetano even had the door
closed.

'Drive, drive, drive,' he shouted as he pulled off the mask.
'Don't stop at the fucking lights, you stupid cow . . .'

Linzi had been slowing down for an amber signal but instead
she put her foot to the floor and roared on through, eyes shut
tight. Behind them, the scream of brakes and horns told her just
how close she had been to disaster.

'Oh God, Oh God,' she whimpered. 'Did you do it? Did you do it?'

'Just keep driving, for fuck's sake. Go faster. Everything's OK.'

They drove until they were out of the City, then dumped the car on the forecourt of a deserted factory and legged it to the nearest tube. As they had been driving, Gaetano had transferred the contents of his shopping bags to an anonymous black sports holdall. He dumped the face mask and jacket in some innocent punter's dustbin.

At twenty-five past ten, the black leather bag sat between Gaetano and Linzi on the southbound Victoria Line. They spent an unnatural amount of time not looking at it and not mentioning it to each other.

CHAPTER THIRTY-FOUR

It was no good. Kerry couldn't get to sleep on the sofa. She stood up and folded the blankets carefully, then she walked silently across the immaculate room and hovered outside Leon's bedroom door. She could hear him breathing, even the tiny whistle as the air passed out through his nose. She put her hand on the door handle and gently pressed it down. Please, please, please, she begged as the door opened without a protest of hinges. Please let me be doing the right thing.

He was fast asleep. The sound of the door swishing across the plush carpet didn't disturb him at all. Kerry crept across the room to the foot of his bed. He was sleeping on a futon and where the street light filtered through the flimsy curtains she could see that his bedclothes were purest white. He was sleeping on his back, with his head turned slightly to the left, his thick black hair in stark contrast with the white pillow. His broad brown shoulders were naked against the cotton.

Kerry walked up the side of the bed and stopped to look at his face. She had never experienced such a strong feeling of love for anyone before. All she wanted to do was bend down to kiss his lips and after that the world could just disappear for all it mattered to her. The fingers of his right hand, lying on top of the sheets, twitched a little as he dreamed. Kerry sat down on the edge of the futon and stared. What was he dreaming about? Did he ever dream about her as he slept?

Taking a deep breath, Kerry picked up the edge of the duvet and slid herself beneath it. Leon murmured and rolled a little further towards the other side of the bed but still he didn't wake up.

Kerry lay next to him, facing towards him, watching his profile in the weak orange glow of the street light. 'Leon,' she whispered. 'I think I love you.' He didn't seem to hear her. 'I mean really love you. I'm not just pretending so that you don't have to go.' That said, albeit unheard, she slid down the bed so that her head rested on the pillow and closed her eyes. Satisfied that he wasn't going to be woken by her presence, she allowed herself to drape an arm over his chest.

In the street below Leon's window, a passing drunk staggered into a car and set off its alarm. Leon woke up.

'Ohmigod.' He sat bolt upright and sprang backwards from the figure which lay beside him in the bed. He turned on the bedside light and got a good look at the intruder. 'Kerry! It's you. What do you think you're doing in here?'

Kerry had fallen asleep. Now, at the sound of his voice, she too woke with a start and suddenly realised that she was in deep shit. Leon just stared at her, the duvet pulled around him like an embarrassed child. He was naked beneath it. 'You're meant to be in the other room.'

'I know. I know. I didn't think you'd mind though,' she squeaked. But Kerry was terrified by the tone of his voice. She had never heard him speak like that before and he definitely wasn't amused.

'Come on,' he told her just a little more softly. 'You've got to get out of here.'

'I . . . I . . . I was scared,' Kerry began pathetically. I couldn't get to sleep out there. I thought that I might have a better chance of dropping off in here with you.'

'But you haven't got any clothes on,' Leon exclaimed.

'I don't sleep in my clothes.'

'Kerry. I don't want to sound harsh or anything but you can't sleep in here with me. You've got to go next door.'

'Why can't I?'

'What do you mean, "why can't you?" This is my bed, Kerry, and I want to be in it alone. You can't sleep with me. Especially not naked.'

'You slept in the same bed as me at my house.'

'That was different. There was nowhere else for me to sleep at your house. And I was wearing all my clothes.' Leon got up from the futon now, protectively covering his nakedness with a pillow, and shrugged on his dressing gown. 'I'm sorry, Kerry. One of us has got to sleep next door or you have got to go home. Haven't your housemates called yet?'

'No, they haven't,' she whimpered.

'Jeez.' He ran his fingers through his thick hair irritably. 'Why don't you try them again? Just in case they didn't pick the message up.'

Kerry hid her eyes behind her hands. She could feel the unfamiliar coldness of her new ring against her eyebrow and at the thought of it she felt tears begin to prick the back of her eyes. Her cheeks were burning. Leon was sitting in the chair by his dressing table now, just staring at her in his bed as if she were the most disgusting thing he had ever seen.

'Why don't you want to sleep with me?' The voice which came out of her mouth belonged to a stranger. It was a pathetic, frightening sob. Leon's mouth dropped open in a mixture of horror and sorrow as tears began to force their way out on to Kerry's cheeks. 'I thought you liked me,' she continued. 'I thought we got on really well. And we're going to get married.'

Leon pulled his dressing gown tighter around his body. Kerry dropped her hands from her eyes and started to sob openly. Her shoulders lurched up and down as she cried uncontrollably.

'Oh, my God, Kerry, what is wrong with you?' Leon threw her the box of tissues which had been sitting unused on his dressing table for months.

'I thought we could get things together.'

Leon snorted. 'How, Kerry? How could we get things together? I'm gay. You've known that since you met me. It's not you I'm not interested in, it's women in general. You know that.'

Kerry sniffed loudly. 'But you told me that you'd had girl-friends before.'

'Yes, when I was a teenager. Before I admitted to myself that I am gay. None of the relationships I had before that actually meant anything to me. I'm gay, Kerry, that's the bottom line. Here, blow your nose.' He had got up from the chair and was sitting on the edge of the futon again. He fished a tissue out of the box and handed it to her gently. 'You haven't been feeling like this all along, have you? Tell me you haven't.'

But Kerry nodded solemnly.

'Oh no. Whatever made you think that I would be interested in seeing a girl again?'

'After my sister's wedding, you told me that it wasn't gender that mattered to you. That what you cared about was the person underneath. You told me that you didn't think anyone had ever understood you as well as I do.'

Leon rolled his eyes. 'I do think that, Kez. But the gender thing . . . Well, I was probably only saying that to justify being gay to you, not to make you think that I could swing the other way for true love. Here,' he handed her another tissue. 'Dry your eyes. You'd had better put some clothes on, too.'

Kerry dragged her T-shirt back on.

'And you asked me to marry you,' she continued.

'You know why I did that,' Leon protested.

'Yes, but I thought . . . I thought that maybe if we spent enough time together you might start to feel differently about me . . .'

'This is unbelievable. Look, do you want a cup of tea?' Leon asked quickly. He had to get away. Kerry nodded and sniffed away another tear. 'Do you want sugar in it?' She nodded again. Leon headed off into the kitchen, put the kettle on and leaned on the breakfast bar with his head in his hands.

Kerry fell back on to his pillows and began to cry again immediately. She buried her face in the place where his head had lain. It smelled of the wax that he used on his hair. Now she was embarrassed as well as sad. How could she have been so stupid as to think that he was just being shy when all along every time she had got near him physically, he had so obviously tried to get away. She remembered the nervous kiss in his car after her sister's wedding. He hadn't been trying to make it something more, he had been trying to make it something less. She had been absolutely stupid and now everything was ruined. She had tried to turn a friend into a lover and lost him on the way.

The kettle whistled. She could hear him pouring the water into mugs. He was probably desperate to get rid of her now. Kerry sat up and caught a glimpse of her face in the dressing-table mirror. Her mascara had marked out the tracks of her tears in muddy black lines. She would drink this tea, then call a cab. The key to her house was, after all, still in the bottom of her bag.

She would have to call him tomorrow and apologise in the cold light of day. She could blame it on the ecstasy she had taken at

Pride. She hoped she hadn't been wrong about him being the kind of person who found it easy to forgive mistakes.

Then the front door to the flat opened and suddenly they were no longer alone. Someone crossed the living-room floor in rubber-soled shoes that squeaked across the wood.

'Mmm. I don't recognise this jacket. Have we got visitors?' the intruder asked. 'I hope you didn't pick up some old slapper at Pride, Leon Landesman.'

'No, I did not.' Leon replied seriously. But then Kerry could hear Leon giggling. Someone was tickling him. Someone was kissing the back of his neck. 'It's just Kerry from work,' she heard Leon whispering. 'She's lost her keys and she can't get home. that's all.'

'Oh, buggeration,' said the intruder. 'Where is she?'

'In the bed.'

'In our bed? That's just great. And all I wanted to do was come home and roger you senseless all night. I guess I'm going to have to be on my best behaviour now. Quick, give me a kiss.' This was followed by more giggling.

'No, sweetness. Don't! Can't you wait until tomorrow morning?'

'Wait until tomorrow? But I've been wanting you all day. Do you know how hard it was for me to get through my shift thinking about you enjoying yourself at Pride? I cannot wait a moment longer.'

'But Kerry . . .'

'Jesus Christ. So what if Kerry's here? She knows you're gay, doesn't she?'

'She's a bit upset tonight. I don't want to rub her face in it.'

'Oh, Leon,' the intruder whined. 'I'm not going to have to put up with this on a regular basis until you get your divorce am I?'

'I don't want to upset her. I need her to marry me, don't I?'

'Yes, but it's not like a real marriage, Leon. You don't have to worry about sleeping around. There are no emotions involved here.'

'Just act a bit restrained for half an hour or so, can't you? I'll get rid of her. It's just that I think she might have got the wrong idea. I didn't realise she was so emotionally dependent on me.'

'Jesus, Leon! Sort it out. I don't want to have to share my

home with some pathetic little fag hag! She's already tried to keep us apart before. She didn't tell you that I called by the office that day because she hates me. She's a vicious little cow and if she thinks she's going to have some kind of hold over you just because of some dumb pretend wedding, you're going to have to call it off and find another bride.'

Kerry scrambled out of the bed and pulled on the rest of her clothes.

'Leon, forget the tea, I've found my keys,' she called as she fled through the sitting room. She tried to slip past the kitchen without looking, but she already knew the other man was Sam. He was back.

Gaetano opened the sports bag and shook its contents out on to his bed. They counted the money. Just two hundred and fifty-seven pounds. Not even three hundred as the Professor had said. Between the three of them, it was nothing. They could have done better taking the money they had spent on preparing the whole thing and betting it on a three-legged greyhound at the dogs. Gaetano scanned the boxes he had whipped off the shelves in the pharmacy with a critical eye.

'Are we going to be able to sell these?' Linzi asked.

'Fuck knows,' Gaetano was not at all happy. 'The Professor went completely pathetic on me and wouldn't tell me what to take. I just grabbed whatever I could reach.'

He picked up a packet of capsules and flipped it over to read the label.

'What do you think of this, Linz? You've got a psychology degree. See any names you recognise? Anything good?'

'Not straight off. No, hang on. I recognise this.'

Linzi picked up a slender package printed with turquoise-blue writing. Turning it over, she laughed a little ironically. Gaetano looked up eagerly, hoping to hear he had done well.

'What are they?' he asked.

'Well,' said Linzi, trying not to smile. 'This is the morning after pill, and these,' she added, picking up a tub of one thousand little capsules, 'are what you take for constipation.'

Gaetano didn't see the joke.

'What do you mean?'

'I mean, this is something you take to stop yourself getting

pregnant after unprotected sex and these are laxatives. They give
you the shits if you can't go.'

'Oh, fuck off, you stupid bitch. Stop messing around. What
are they?'

'Whooah, partner. Calm down. That's really what these things
are, I'm afraid. How much money did we get again?'

'Practically nothing. Absolutely fucking nothing.'

'Three-way split, remember?'

'You and the Professor didn't do a third of the job,' Gaetano
snarled.

'I drove the car.'

'Yeah, but I got the car for you to drive in the first place. You
could hardly keep it on the road. You were fucking useless, both
of you. I risked my neck for you two and now I find out that
the Professor's palmed me off with a pile of fucking laxatives.
I'm gonna fucking kill him tomorrow morning.' As he spoke,
Gaetano's lips bared clenched teeth. He didn't look as though
he was joking.

'He was probably just trying to make it look convincing, G. If
he'd been too helpful it might have been obvious that he was
in on the whole thing.'

'He nearly bottled out completely. When he comes round here
looking for his share of the money I'm going to make him eat all
this shit.'

Gaetano picked up the tub of laxatives and hurled them
against the wall. The impact made the tub pop open, scattering
thousands of tiny brown capsules, which rolled off into the far
corners of the room to be found jamming the Hoover from
then until eternity. Then Gaetano scrunched up a fistful of the
contraceptive boxes and threw them in the same direction.

'You gotta go,' he hissed. 'My parents are opening the café late
tonight for all those fucking homos on their march. You gotta go
before they get back.'

'OK,' said Linzi, sensing that a swift exit was probably for the
best in this instance anyway. 'I'll see you tomorrow morning.
It'll seem better by then. Really it will.'

Gaetano didn't even look at her.

She picked a fiver out of the haul for her taxi-ride home.

CHAPTER THIRTY-FIVE

Kerry sprinted down the stairs from Leon's flat but by the time she got to the bottom, she could barely see for tears. She wrenched at the door to the block so hard that her arms nearly left their sockets until the doorman pointed out a night door-release button with a faintly amused smile.

Outside, Kerry collapsed onto the pavement, not caring what her knees landed in. She clutched at her head as she tried to catch her breath again. Then it occurred to her that Sam might be watching her from the window and laughing, so she crawled into an alleyway that was lined with overflowing bins but away from critical eyes.

How could it be that in one day she had hit both the highest high and the lowest low of her life, she wondered as she sat upon a vaguely hygienic looking cardboard box. She had no money left in her tattered purse and though she had her tube pass, she couldn't remember the number of the Nightbus home or even how to get to Trafalgar Square to catch it. Alone and cold in the alleyway, Kerry headed in the direction of traffic noise. Maybe she could find a cabby who was prepared to wait for her while she went to a cashpoint. If only she had some transport of her own.

It was then that she saw Leon's bike. Parked at the top of the alleyway where it was light enough to be reasonably safe. She had grown to like that bike, but now, even that inanimate object looked smug. It was as if every cog and valve knew what she had done. She would never be able to sit behind Leon on that bike again. Kerry cleared her throat and spat at it. But then that didn't seen enough.

She delivered a smallish kick to the back wheel. Then the front wheel. Then she punched at the springy leather seat. Then she karate-chopped the number plate with her heel. Then another punch to the soft parts. A swing with her bag. And a kick and a kick and a kick.

Until a two-footed kick that could have won her points in a karate competition knocked the bike off its stand and crashing down on to Kerry where she lay in the gutter, toppled by her own clever move.

The bike's alarm started screaming.

Kerry scrambled out from beneath it and started to run.

CHAPTER THIRTY-SIX

Pretty soon, Kerry's bruised shins were hurting too much to run anymore. It took almost an hour to get back to Artesia Road at a limp. From time to time, Kerry was sure that she heard the warming up warbles of an early dawn chorus as she trudged the empty streets of South London.

Number 67 was perfectly silent. Kerry flicked on the light switch and tried to ascertain who was in by counting the shoes behind the front door. Linzi's favourite Doc Martens were missing. Fiona's rather more delicate ankleboots were there. The answerphone was disappointingly empty of messages and when she dialled 1471 to see if perhaps someone had called but not left a message, the number that the stilted woman gave was not a number that she recognised. Kerry poured herself a glass of water. She felt completely sober now, with that horrible clearheadedness that comes from having sat your hangover out and thought for far too long about something embarrassing. She wished it was earlier. She wished that Fiona was still awake to listen to her tale of woe and sympathise. The only glimmer of consolation was that it was Sunday and Kerry had twenty-four hours of potential sleep before she had to see Leon again at work.

She climbed wearily up the stairs and decided to skip cleaning her teeth. She eased herself beneath her duvet without bothering to undress but soon found that she was desperate for a wee. Kerry padded back across the landing. The bathroom door was blocked.

Kerry pushed the door and felt it give a little, so it obviously wasn't locked from inside. What had probably happened, she

decided, was that someone had hung too many towels on the
back of the door and one of them had fallen down to jam it.
It had happened before. The only thing to do was shove like
crazy until it gave way and have a word about the towel crisis
tomorrow.

But it wasn't as easy as shifting a towel. When Kerry had given
the door seven hard pushes to no avail she had to switch on the
landing light and investigate further. A triangle of fabric poked
out from beneath the door. It was silky, not towelling. Like
Fiona's dressing gown. Kerry got down on her hands and knees
to see just what was getting stuck here. She peered through the
tiny gap between door and frame.

'Oh, God! No!' There was a body on the floor.

Fiona had been expecting to see Tim that night. As she waited
for him to arrive after a week of agonising silence, she had
dressed herself in the outfit she knew he liked the best. She
had piled her hair up on top of her head and outlined her
eyes with mascara, though the finished result was pretty ineffective compared with the shadows that hung beneath her
eyes.

She was ready an hour before he was due to arrive. The
others had gone out. She sat alone in the sitting room with
the television turned up extra loud to block out the sound of
people walking past in the street outside. Every time she heard
a car door slam, she thought that she might be sick with the
pain of seeing him again.

Half an hour after he was supposed to have turned up, she
called him.

'You're meant to be here,' she said.

'I know,' he replied. 'I was going to give you a call in a moment.
I'm not coming over.'

'Why not?' she asked him.

'I don't think it's such a good idea, that's all. How are you?'

'You called off our engagement, how do you think I am?'

'Look, if you're just going to scream at me, I'm going to put
the phone back down straight away. OK?'

'I don't want to argue,' Fiona pleaded. 'I just need to talk to
you, Tim. We still need to sort some things out.'

'I don't think there is anything to sort out any more. We

couldn't have gone on as we were, Fiona. You know that as well as I do. I was going up the wall.'

'Then why did you ask me to marry you?'

'I thought it might make things different . . .'

Fiona didn't quite know what to say in reply to that.

'You're seeing Minky now, aren't you?'

She heard Tim sigh. He didn't answer her question.

'You're seeing her aren't you? I knew what was going on even before we split up.' She sobbed tragically. 'When I came round and found her at your flat that day.'

'Look, Fiona. Minky isn't the reason why I called off the engagement.'

'But you are seeing her?'

'She's been round a couple of times, that's all. It's nothing serious.'

'Nothing serious? Then why did you throw what we had away for her?'

'It had nothing to do with Minky.'

'I don't believe that. I think it has everything to do with her. She got dumped by her boyfriend and so she decided that she would split us up and have you instead. You know what she's like. She was sleeping with Wooders less than a month ago. Well, if you want his sloppy seconds, Tim. If you want to go to bed with a slag who'll sleep with her boyfriend's best friends.'

'Fiona. Shut up. You don't know what she's really like at all.'

'I don't know if I want to know. She's there now, isn't she?' Fiona spat. 'Isn't she, Tim? Isn't she?'

Tim put the phone down.

Fiona had stared at the silent receiver for a long, long time.

When Linzi got home, half an hour later than Kerry, she went straight to the kitchen to get herself a drink. And she was hungry too. The anticipation of that night's work had made her feel like throwing up whenever she passed a kitchen, but now that she had regained her composure, she thought she might fry up the whole of a packet of bacon she had bought the week before. Even if it was a little out of date.

She didn't notice the note that Kerry had left on the refrigerator door until she was closing it again. She pulled it off and read it while she waited for the kettle to boil.

'Linz, Fiona's been taken very ill. Gone to Casualty. Please come and meet me there as soon as you get in. Kez.'

Casualty? What had that mad cow Fiona done to herself now? Linzi took her time with her sandwiches. Let the bacon crisp up really nicely. Then it struck her that perhaps it wasn't just for altruistic reasons that she should go along to the hospital. A housemate emergency might be just the kind of alibi she needed at a later date.

CHAPTER THIRTY-SEVEN

Linzi didn't feel quite so pleased with her clever plan when she actually got to the hospital. Kerry sat alone in the waiting room on one of the hideous red plastic chairs – designed to hide the mess, Linzi guessed. Kerry looked awful. Her face was completely white apart from the black rings around her eyes. She didn't notice that Linzi had arrived until she sat down right next to her and put a cold hand over Kerry's tightly clenched fists.

'What happened?'

Kerry looked at Linzi with wet eyes.

'I don't know exactly,' she sniffed. 'I came home from Pride and found her collapsed on the floor of the bathroom. There was an empty bottle of vodka downstairs and she had a packet of sleeping tablets in her hand. I think she might have taken an overdose.'

'Jeez.' Linzi rolled her eyes. 'You're kidding. What a bloody idiot!! I bet it was over Tim. But she told me that she was getting over him. An overdose? That's such a loser's way to do things.'

Kerry's expression silenced Linzi at once. 'There's no point sitting here calling her a loser now. We don't even know if she's going to survive.' She gave out a strange, strangled sob. 'Her face was completely blue, Linz. The ambulancemen had to give her oxygen.'

Linzi's brows tipped towards the middle of her face in an approximation of concern. 'She'll be OK, Kez. She's pretty fit with all that training for the race. Where did they take her?'

Kerry indicated the corridor with her thumb. 'In there. But I think they might have had to take her up to intensive care since.' She wiped her nose across her sleeve and sniffed loudly.

'Have you called her folks yet?'

'I tried, but they're on holiday in Gran Canaria according to the housekeeper. Oh God, Linzi, what are we going to do?'

Kerry buried her face in Linzi's shoulder. Her tears soaked through the thin fabric of Linzi's shirt and on to her skin. Linzi patted her friend's back comfortingly and looked towards the door through which they had taken Fiona. She would be all right, of course. Linzi had never heard of an attempted overdose case dying once they had been found. As a nurse passed by, Linzi feebly called out 'excuse me'. The nurse waved a hand dismissively. She didn't have time to comfort weeping hangers-on that night. 'Why do you think she decided to do it tonight?' Linzi asked.

Kerry tried to rearrange herself comfortably on the hard plastic chair. 'I don't know. When I set off for Pride, she seemed to be happy enough. She told me that Tim had agreed to see her. He was supposed to be coming round to talk about things. Perhaps it didn't work out.'

'You're probably right. I don't think she's got a hope of getting him back.'

'He doesn't believe that she didn't do anything with Gaetano.'

'That's just an excuse, Kez. Tim was waiting for a concrete reason to call the engagement off. Nothing happened between Fi and Gaetano. Tim knows that as well as I do.'

Kerry raised an eyebrow.

'What do you mean by pulling that face?' Linzi had noticed.

'Oh, nothing. Look. There's the doctor that took her through. You try and get his attention.'

But he had already gone. Then, as Linzi looked towards the door in hope of news, it opened slowly and a tall man was brought through in a wheelchair. He held a wad of bandaging to his nose but it was soaked through with blood already. The nurse pushing his wheelchair leaned over to explain that someone would appear to take him to X-ray in a few minutes. He nodded painfully, then put his hand up to the side of his face and winced in agony.

Linzi was sure that she recognised him even through the mask of wadding and blood.

She did.

'Professor!!'

Kerry struggled upright in her seat when she heard Linzi call out. Linzi was already on her feet, dashing across the waiting room to the side of the man in the wheelchair. He reached out and took hold of her hand. Linzi marvelled at the deep purple setting he had gained around his eye.

'Christ!! What on earth happened to you, Prof?' She knew it was to do with the robbery of course. 'What are you doing in a wheelchair?' Gaetano had promised that no one would get hurt.

The Professor tried to take the bandage away from his nose so that he could speak but thought better of it. Instead he kept the bulk of it pressed to his nose and lifted the corner away from his mouth.

'The chemist's shop I was working in got robbed,' he began to explain in a barely audible mumble.

'Oh, God. And they beat you up?'

The Professor nodded slowly. 'And my assistant.'

'Your assistant?'

'Kicked her head in. She's had to go up to a ward, I think.'

Linzi's eyes glittered with panic but as Kerry was standing right behind her now she had to pretend that this was all news to her. 'Was she unconscious?' Linzi asked.

'Yes,' the Professor sniffed. 'Completely out of it. They think that he might have fractured her skull. Ow. Sorry, Linzi, it's really difficult to talk. My mouth's all swollen up. I've got to have an X-ray. Might have cracked my jaw.'

Linzi sank slowly into the red plastic chair nearest to his wheelchair. Kerry wondered momentarily why she seemed so upset by what had happened to this curious guy but she was too interested in finding out the gory details of his injuries to dwell on it for long.

'Have they got any idea who did this?' Kerry probed.

The Professor shook his head. 'The bloke had his face covered with some kind of mask. A balaclava thingy. I couldn't even tell if he was black or white and after he put Manjri out, I was too scared to start noting details. It's like my mind went out of focus.'

'They will find him eventually,' Kerry reassured the poor man. 'Somebody in the area must have seen him leave the shop. Perhaps he had a car. Did you hear anything? Did you recognise the sound of a particular engine? A car description can narrow things right down.'

'Kerry,' Linzi broke in. 'He'll have to put up with a load of questions from the police. Give him a break.'

'I'm sorry,' Kerry told the Professor. 'I didn't mean to pry. Honestly,' she sighed. 'What a night this has been. When I got home tonight I found our housemate Fiona passed out on the bathroom floor. Suspected overdose. We're waiting to see if she's OK.'

'I think I met her once. Wish her my love,' the Professor murmured. At that moment a porter appeared with a clip-board. 'Andrew Montgomery?' he asked.

'That's me,' the Professor said feebly. It suddenly struck Linzi that this was the first time she had ever heard his real name. Andrew. It suited him. A big, gentle name. 'I've gotta go for my X-ray now. Guess I'll see you at the gig on Tuesday, Linzi, if I can make it.'

'Yeah. Tuesday,' Linzi replied distantly.

'Who was that?' Kerry asked as the porter carted the Professor off, keeping up a running commentary on football that Linzi knew would be boring the musician in him rigid.

'Friend of Gaetano's,' Linzi explained. 'Plays in the band. Works in a chemist's shop. Says they're always getting robbed for drugs and that.'

'God, some people are real scum, aren't they?' Kerry spat. 'What kind of guy beats someone up like that? And God only knows what kind of state the girl is in. She's probably going to be scarred for life and not just physically. He must have been an animal.'

Linzi nodded in agreement.

'Friends of Fiona Davenport?' The doctor who had supervised Fiona's care had finally reappeared. Kerry waved her hand to attract his attention. He strolled across, flicking through his notes, smiling a little sadly.

'How is she?' Kerry asked desperately.

'Oh, she'll be OK,' the doctor told them. Kerry felt all the muscles of her body give out a collective sigh. 'She's gone into the recovery room now. We'll keep her in overnight, just in case. Did you manage to talk to her parents?'

'No. They're in Gran Canaria.'

'Bit of a nuisance, that. Still, if you could leave their details with the receptionist we'll try to get hold of them first thing. You may as well go now. She won't be able to see you until tomorrow. Good job you got home when you did.'

The doctor was called away by a nurse to deal with a drunk who had been getting out of hand while she tried to apply a bandage to his nasty glass wound. Linzi began to button up her coat.

'You're not going now?' Kerry asked.

'You heard him. He said that she's all right.' Kerry looked betrayed. 'Look, I've got to go, Kez. I need to catch Gaetano at home before his mother comes back. I left my wallet there. I won't see him until Tuesday otherwise.'

'Will you come back here afterwards?' Kerry asked.

'Yeah, of course. Or I'll see you at home.'

Linzi made a break for the automatic doors, almost having a fatal collision with an incoming RTA victim's trolley as she dashed to the nearest phone.

CHAPTER THIRTY-EIGHT

Linzi punched Gaetano's telephone number into the key pad. He had promised her that nobody would get hurt if they did over the chemist's shop. Now the Professor was sporting a broken jaw and some poor girl was lying unconscious in hospital.

The telephone in the Carlotti household rang and rang and rang. Just as Linzi was about to give up and put the receiver down, Gaetano picked it up.

'I need to talk to you,' she said, her voice shaking.

'It's the middle of the night, for fuck's sake,' said Gaetano. 'I want to go to bed. I'll see you tomorrow.'

'No way, Gaetano,' Linzi insisted. 'I need to talk to you now. I've just walked out of the accident unit. And guess who I saw there?'

'Who?' he asked petulantly. 'I don't know, do I?'

'I saw the Professor. He's got a broken bloody jaw and he says that the girl who was with him is in a fucking coma, Gaetano. I thought you said that nobody was going to get hurt? Just how unhurt is that?'

'Sssh, *cara mia*. We can't talk about this on the phone. I'll talk to you tomorrow morning. I'll come round to your place first thing. Yes?'

'No way. I need to talk to you about this tonight. You realise what you've done. You realise how much more serious this whole thing is now. We're not just talking about robbery any more . . . If she doesn't come round we could be talking about . . .'

'Linzi,' Gaetano cut her short, sensing that she was getting dangerously hysterical. 'I told you, we can't talk about this on the phone. Come over to me quickly. My parents won't be back for another hour. Get a taxi over and don't talk to anyone else about this on your way.'

'As if I could . . .' But he had already put down the phone. Linzi climbed into the next taxi almost before it had disgorged its woeful man with his hand wrapped in a tea-towel, followed by a whey-faced girlfriend who thought he was losing a fatal amount of blood from his pinky.

When she got to his house, Gaetano was already waiting downstairs but he ushered her quickly up to his room. 'If my mother comes home now you will have to climb out the window,' he told her.

'What? Why?'

'Because if she finds you here she will throw me out of the house again, that's why. And I don't want to have to go through all that shit. I've told her that we're not seeing each other any more.'

'You what?'

'It's the way it's got to be, Linzi. I had to. I can't live with you can I?'

'Christ, Gaetano. You're almost thirty years old. You're old enough to rob a chemist's shop with violence but you can't stand up to your own mother?'

'Don't push it, Linzi,' Gaetano warned her. 'You knew that what we were going to do tonight wasn't going to be a tea-party.'

'I know. But I'm really scared now, Gaetano. I don't understand why you had to hit the girl. She's really badly beaten up.'

'The Professor said that she would be soft but she wasn't. She kept trying to get in my way. The Professor couldn't stop her. I had to put her out of it.'

'You hit him as well.'

'It makes it look more convincing, doesn't it? Besides, he's had it coming for a long time.'

'What do you mean by that?'

'I mean he's always acting like he's the only one of all of us that's got any brains. He doesn't like it when someone else comes up with a good idea. That's why he was against my plan for the robbery.'

'Don't you think it might just have been that he didn't want to end up in jail?'

'No one was going to end up in jail. It would have been so simple, so perfect if he had just done everything exactly like we planned. But oh no, he had to get cold feet. He was acting like he wasn't part of it so well that he forgot that he was.'

Suddenly, they heard the sound of a key turning in the front door. High-heeled footsteps on the tiled floor of the hallway. A woman called up the stairs to Gaetano. Linzi instantly recognised the voice.

'Shit, they're back. I'll have to go down,' Gaetano said. 'She's seen my light on from the street. I've got to go and show an interest in how opening the shop tonight went. Since it was my idea to get her out of our way. Another great idea by Gaetano Carlotti. Besides, I need to create an alibi. She thinks I've been in bed sick all evening.'

'Gaetano, you can't go downstairs and leave me here now . . .'

He kissed Linzi on the top of the head. 'Look, the fire escape is right below the window. I'll come and see you at your place first thing in the morning, OK? And don't worry. The girl will be fine and no one will ever know the whole story of what happened tonight except you, me and the Professor. Providing you can both keep your mouths shut.'

With that, Gaetano left the room.

'OK, Mama. Don't come up. I'm coming down now.'

Linzi got up and walked towards the window. It was already half-opened so that she wouldn't have to make a sound forcing it. She looked out at the narrow black metal ladder which descended to the street. This was bloody ridiculous. She hadn't had to avoid someone's parents since she was bunking off school with Kerry. She was reaching one leg out through the window when she saw the corner of the black box peeking out from beneath Gaetano's bed clothes. Linzi pulled her leg back in.

Gaetano must have put the money from the robbery in that box. All the money. Including her share. She flicked back the duvet. The key was in the lock. Laughter and animated chatter floated up the stairs. Gaetano was busy with his folks. Acting as though nothing had happened.

Without bothering to open it first, Linzi silently picked up the safe box and tucked it inside her jacket. Then she climbed out of the window for real this time and let herself down into the quiet street below. Less than three weeks after promising that he would never lay his fist on a female again Gaetano had put one in hospital. There was no way that mother-worshipping jerk was keeping her share of the money for his stupid band now.

CHAPTER THIRTY-NINE

K erry had fallen asleep in the hospital waiting room. When she woke the next morning, she discovered that somebody had covered her with a blanket and for some reason the tenderness of the gesture made her burst into the tears that she had been fighting to hold back all night.

'You all right, love?' the woman who was cleaning the waiting room asked. 'You been here all night, have you?'

Kerry nodded.

'Who you waiting for? Your boyfriend?'

Kerry shook her head. 'My friend. A girl I live with. Fiona Davenport. She got taken ill suddenly last night. Do you know if she's OK?'

'Not me, love. I don't know anything about the patients. Ask the girl on the desk. She's the one will be able to tell you.'

While Kerry was standing at the desk with the blanket draped around her shoulders, Fiona's doctor walked up behind her. His eyes were sunken deep in his face. He hadn't slept at all that night but he still managed a smile for a concerned friend.

'You still here? Your friend's OK, you know,' he assured Kerry once more. 'But she's asleep now. Go home and get some rest.'

'Are you sure?' Kerry asked.

'Trust me, I'm a doctor.' The girl on reception shared the joke.

'OK. If you're really sure she's safe.'

'I'm sure.'

Kerry wandered out into the early morning car park with the hospital blanket still wrapped around her shoulders. As she passed the phone box, she considered calling Linzi to see if she would come out to meet her in Fiona's car. But then she thought better of it. She needed a walk and some time to think. She needed to be alone.

The sky was grey. The clouds had moved in while she slept. How quickly the weather changes at this time of year, Kerry found herself thinking. Yesterday the sun had been shining with intent to burn, now it couldn't be seen at all. How quickly everything can change, she continued to muse. Her watch told her that it was almost nine. She wondered if Leon was up and about yet. She wondered if she would get home to find a message on the answerphone asking why she had left his apartment so suddenly when Sam arrived.

She had a feeling that she wouldn't. It was completely clear to her now that Leon had wanted nothing more from her than her passport. If she had been a good friend to him, she told herself, she would have helped him out willingly and not asked for anything more than the opportunity for a good party in return. How could she have thought that things could be different? He had even offered her money for her trouble.

As Kerry neared the Underground station, she fished in the top pocket of her jacket for her Travelcard. Feeling the smooth round edge of an unfamiliar object, she pulled it out to remember with disgust that she was still carrying her sister's engagement and wedding rings. Not to mention the tiny emerald cluster which was taking up space on her own finger. Michelle had been right. It was all rubbish, this marriage thing. Even if your fiancé was heterosexual. As relationship sticky-tape, a wedding ring was as useful as the fluffy side of Velcro without the hooks to catch against. Kerry took her ring off and wrapped it in a tissue with the other two then she thanked whoever it was that hung out in the sky that she hadn't ever got around to announcing her fantasy engagement. At least it meant that she wasn't going to have to face the embarrassment of announcing that it was off again. She was, however, going to have to face Leon on Monday morning. If they had been like Tim and Fiona, she could have banished him from her sight for ever. As it was, she could only do a sicky. But that would be too obvious and it would only prolong the agony . . . She could also hand her notice in. But then what?

As Kerry turned into Artesia Road, she tried to comfort herself with the thought that things could only get better. After all, bad things happen in threes and she'd definitely had her three that week. First her sister's marriage going wrong, then the disaster with Leon, then Fiona's overdose.

But when Kerry saw the fire-engine parked outside number 67, she realised that as far as bad things were concerned, one of the above obviously didn't really count.

CHAPTER FORTY

Number 67 Artesia Road had been gutted by a mysterious fire in the small hours of that Sunday morning while Fiona recovered, Kerry dozed in a hospital waiting room and Linzi was God only knows where. The firemen decided that it had been deliberate. On Linzi's bedroom mirror, someone had scrawled 'SLAG' in lipstick as red as blood. And they had lost a lot of things as well: the television, the video, two CD stereos, the remains of which could not be found amongst the charred offering that had become of the sitting room.

The arsonist had robbed them of fingerprints to catch him by, of course, so they had no idea of his identity or mótive, but the strangest thing was that Linzi had disappeared. Her room had not just been stripped of electrical goods but of her clothes and most of her toiletries as well. Linzi's mother and father, briefly reunited by the trauma, were trying to obtain funding to make a television programme about sudden disappearances. Unkind people suggested that Linzi's departure was maybe a case of spontaneous combustion.

Fiona came out of hospital the day after the fire. Her parents had flown home from Gran Canaria early and whisked her straight back to Bristol without stopping to pick up what remained of her belongings at Artesia Road. Kerry followed the exodus west a couple of days later. Leon had offered to let her have sick-leave but she told him that she didn't think she was suited to the job any more. Leon didn't push it, which made Kerry sad. Neither did he mention the ring or the motorbike.

Back in Bristol, Mrs Keble seemed to be in her element. Kerry was the second of her little chicks to have flown back to the nest that week. Big sister Miranda had finally ditched Steve the plumber and left him with the house and the kids. Kerry took up residence in her old room and went into a deep sulk. She didn't bother to call back any of the people from school who kept telephoning to find out the truth about the night of disaster on the pretence of being concerned. When Fiona felt well enough, Kerry trawled round to the Davenport residence to visit her on her sick-bed but that was as far as the Keble's once-wandering daughter could be bothered to go. It seemed that anywhere else she went she was dogged by whispers that Linzi had started the fire herself and fled.

Living at home again was like being in a time warp. When Kerry got in one evening from a visit to Fiona, it suddenly struck her that she could be witnessing a tableau from her sixteenth year. Her father had just come home from work. He was sitting at the kitchen table, wearing his shirt and tie to which still clung the oily smell of heavy engineering. Her mother was cooking dinner. Tuesday night: burgers, chips and beans. Miranda was on the telephone arguing with her estranged husband about custody of their children using words of not more than four letters in length. Even Michelle's absence from this family scene was usual. She would have been out snogging in the car park behind the all-night newsagents.

'How was Fiona?' her mother asked.

'Looking better,' Kerry replied.

'Oh, that's good. I spoke to her mother in the post office this afternoon. It's been a terrible time for that family. One minute they're planning a wedding and the next minute their daughter is an invalid. It's like they've got a baby in the house again,' her mother said.'

'I don't think it's that bad, Mum.'

Mrs Keble turned the burgers over and smiled patronisingly. 'Your father's got some good news for you, sweetheart. Tell her your good news, Nigel.'

Mr Keble pushed a photocopied piece of paper across the table-cloth to his daughter. 'Bloke at work gave me this today. Says they're looking for secretaries at the place where his wife works. Says if you want it, you're as good as in. What with your exams and all.'

Kerry skipped through the details. The job was for a VDU operator at a big joinery place just down the road. Kerry remembered walking to and from school, seeing the women who worked there hanging out on the fire escape having a quick fag since smoking was strictly prohibited inside because of the sawdust. Kerry hated the noise and the smell of the place. Even walking past it for those few brief moments each day had been enough to make her want to run away into the hills.

'You see, love. All that gallivanting off to London when there's perfectly decent jobs just down the road from your Mum and Dad. You didn't really want to be dealing with that media business. No job security there. Work at Mitchell's, you got a job for life and the chance to get yourself a decent boyfriend. Bunch of hunks at Mitchell's, your sister says. I still can't believe it though,' Mrs Keble's eyes took on a distant look. 'That lovely Leon being one of those "homer-sexuals" . . .'

Kerry felt her eyes begin to glaze over. Miranda came back to the kitchen in tears. Steve was still refusing to let her see the girls. Mrs Keble slopped beans on to four plates while cursing both her sons-in-law. Kerry's father asked her whether she wanted him to tell his mate that she would have the job? Kerry nodded. Her mother put the hot plates on the table. Kerry took a forkful of the beans and they tasted like sawdust in her mouth.

A week later, Kerry was just about to leave for her first day of work at Mitchell's Joinery when the postman arrived. She opened the front door to him and took the bundle of envelopes straight from his hand. Brown, brown, brown. A pile of serious bills. And a postcard. A post-card of deep blue sea and soft white sand. They didn't know anyone who was away on holiday, did they? Kerry turned the postcard over and read the scribbled message with a quickening heart.

It was from her sister Michelle. Writing to the Bristol-bound Keble family from her new apartment overlooking the Sydney bloody Opera House.

'You're going to be late if you don't get a move on,' Mrs Keble called from the kitchen. 'Don't want to be late on your first flippin' day.'

'Yes, Mum!'

Kerry put the brown envelopes on the table beneath the telephone and stepped out of the house and into the drizzle, still clutching the postcard in her hand. She started in the direction of Mitchell's Joinery, her feet getting faster and faster as she neared the noisy, smelly warehouse, faster and faster as she reached the rusty gate and walked straight on past.

She walked to Fiona's. By the time she reached Fiona's street, Kerry was almost running. She hammered on the front door. Mr Davenport had already left for the office. Mrs Davenport for her class in t'ai chi. Fiona staggered down the stairs, her legs barely in working order after three long weeks in bed.

'You're not going to believe this!!' Kerry thrust the postcard into Fiona's hands. Fiona scanned the scrawled handwriting quickly. As she read her face cracked simultaneously into the widest of wide smiles.

'It's from my sister, to let us know her new address in Australia. But read the bottom bit. Read it. She says that she bumped into Linzi in Cairns.'

'I can see it. Linzi's in Cairns? What on earth is she doing there?'

'Well, I don't know, do I? But I think it's about time we found out.'

They scuttled into the Davenport's bijoux 'telephone room'. A converted cupboard beneath the stairs. Kerry began to dial the number scrawled along the side of the postcard. Frantically. Stumbling over the digits.

'What time will it be over there?' Fiona was concerned. 'You're probably calling her in the middle of the night.'

'Michelle won't mind if we wake her up. I don't know about you, but I think that this is a bit of an emergency.'

The phone was picked up at the other end. The person answering told Kerry, in an accent that was pure Birmingham, that Michelle did indeed live in the flat but that she had gone out to work and he didn't expect her back before midnight.

'Where's she working?' Kerry asked.

'At a bar in town. She only started last week. She got the job through one of her sister's old friends.'

'I am her sister. Which friend?'

'Linzi, I think her name is.'

Kerry made a fist of triumph.

'Thanks . . .'

'Benj.'

'Benj. This is Kerry. Will you tell Michelle that I called? And if you see that bloody Linzi girl on your travels, tell her it's about time she got in touch with her old mates from Artesia Road!'

CHAPTER FORTY-ONE

Three weeks later, Linzi met them at the airport in Sydney. With her newly tanned skin she looked more beautiful than ever, the shadow of London life long since vanished from beneath her eyes. She greeted her former housemates as if they had been apart for a thousand years. She glanced at their new suitcases a little guiltily though. Fiona had lost her Louis Vuitton in the fire.

On the drive back from the airport, she explained in an unbelievable half-hour what had happened on the night they last saw her in London. As she told them about the robbery, Kerry remembered the man in the accident unit and was aghast. Linzi told them that Gaetano had made her do it. Fiona found that quite easy to believe. They wanted to know why she hadn't gone to the police. Linzi said that she had been too scared. And rightly so, she had figured, when Michelle told her about the burglary and the fire. Linzi had guessed that Gaetano might be capable of that. Which was why she had to leave so suddenly once she had taken the money from his room. He would have had her head off. Killed her, probably. So Linzi had gone straight to Paris on the first Eurostar of that Sunday morning and from there to Thailand and from Thailand to where they were now.

'How much money did you get from the robbery?' Fiona was desperate to know. It was such a crazy story that she asked about the cash as though she were asking about the proceeds of some company merger.

The shadow of a guilty smile passed across Linzi's lips. 'Not enough,' she admitted. 'But there was other stuff in the box as well. I sold that.'

'Like what?'

Linzi squirmed. 'You promise you won't hit me?' Fiona nodded. 'Swear? I am driving after all.'

'Of course. Like what, Linzi? What did you find?'

'Like your engagement ring.'

Kerry clapped her hand to her open mouth in shock. Linzi visibly shrank at the wheel as though she still expected a blow. For a moment there was an extremely uneasy silence in the little hire-car. Fiona broke it. She broke it with the biggest and longest laugh she had ever laughed in her life.

'That ring had two thousand pounds' worth of bloody diamonds set in it!' she screeched.

'You're kidding!' said Linzi. 'I only got three hundred pounds. But I'll pay you back, I promise.'

'No problem, Linzi.' Fiona had laughed so much that tears were streaming down her cheeks. 'Tim filed an insurance claim after it got lost. When the money came through a couple of weeks ago, he felt so guilty about breaking off the engagement that he sent me the bloody cheque. That helped to pay for our flights here.'

'You didn't cash it?'

'Of course I did. After all he did to me, the very least I deserve is a sun-tan. I'm glad you sold that ring. If you hadn't I would have thrown it straight over there!!'

They were driving past the glittering expanse of Sydney Harbour. They wound down their windows and leaned out to get a better view of the sparkling blue and white.

That first night together in the Southern Hemisphere was spent at the beach bar and café where Linzi sometimes worked during the day and Michelle did a night shift three times a week. Linzi had already fallen head over heels for a fellow waiter who brought them free beers with such regularity that even she was soon under the table.

When the bar was officially closed and all the punters but the three girls had been pushed out on to the street, Linzi ordered a final round of beers for a last toast. She raised her bottle. 'To my very best friends.' Fiona and Kerry clinked glass upon glass. 'I'm so glad you're both here. I didn't think you'd ever want to see me again.'

'I didn't think we'd ever be able to see you again,' joked Kerry. 'We were terrified that something unspeakable had happened to you.'

'Well, I guess it has,' Linzi sighed. 'I've made myself an exile now. I suppose I'm going to have to stay out here for a while, then keep on travelling until I'm sure that it's safe to come home.'

'I can't believe you're on the run from the police,' Kerry laughed. 'My mum always said you'd end up either on the stage or in prison.'

'Mmmm,' Linzi snorted. 'I think a term in Holloway would beat temping in an advertising agency but I'm not quite ready to find out for sure. Anyway, what's the weather like at home? Having the usual sort of June?'

'Snow and hailstorms?' Kerry nodded. 'Pretty much.'

'You know what day it is today?' Fiona had been very quiet since the hilarity about the ring, but now she piped up again. 'Today is the fifteenth of June. Today is the day I was supposed to get married to Tim.'

Both Linzi and Kerry put their glasses down on the table. It didn't seem appropriate to raise a toast to that.

'Today is the day I would have walked down the aisle and promised myself to that dunderhead for ever. I would have been Mrs Tim Harper. The original Stepford wife.' She leaned on her elbow, looking at the pale amber beer swirling around in the bottom of her glass. Then she raised it, unexpectedly. 'Well, girls, here's to lucky escapes!'

The other girls cheered.

'And here's to not wearing jade!!' said Kerry.

'Did I say jade for the bridesmaids?' Fiona looked horrified. 'I couldn't have done. That would have been terrible with your hair.'

'Anything's terrible with my hair,' sighed Kerry.

'So,' Linzi continued. 'If things had gone according to plan, you would have been starting your married life tomorrow but now you're not. What are you going to do instead, Fi?'

'A week ago I would have said that was a pretty hard question,' Fiona said quietly. 'But I think I've got it sorted out now. I'm going straight to New York.' The other girls smiled. 'Peter, the idiot that they offered the placement to when I turned it down, managed to disgrace himself by getting drunk at a graduate recruitment seminar in Aberdeen. When it came for the moment for him to get up on stage and extol the virtues of First Orient's graduate training scheme, he just dropped his trousers and did a moonie. Hara called me the very next morning and begged me to take the placement up. Didn't seem to be an awful lot of point in refusing this time. It's not as though I'm going to be leaving a great deal behind.'

'You'll have a fantastic time, Fiona,' Linzi assured her. 'But don't forget who your best friends are when you're trekking around Bloomingdales.'

'Sure, I'll bring you back a pretzel.'

'Thanks. It's probably more than I deserve.'

'Your turn now,' Fiona moved the spotlight. All eyes turned towards Kerry, who was peeling the label off her beer bottle with a look of deep concentration upon her face.

'What are you going to do, Kerry Keble? Now that you've come this far.'

'Back to England, I suppose,' Kerry muttered.

'No way. Stay with me,' Linzi suggested.

'I can't, Linz. I've got things to go back for.'

'Such as.'

'My family.'

'But they live in Bristol. Please tell me that you won't end up back there.'

'I've got to get a job sometime soon.'

'You can get a job anywhere. I'll get you one here.'

'I don't know,' Kerry squirmed.

'You're not going back because of a man?' Fiona asked.

'Get real,' said Kerry. 'I'm going to be staying off men for a long while. It's just that . . . I don't know. It's just that I'm not sure that I'm ready for all this.'

'All this what?'

'All this . . . well, for the rest of my life, really. I mean, I'm fresh from my biggest balls-up to date. Falling in love with my homosexual boss. How stupid was that? I've had my heart broken and I've lost my job. I don't think I can handle anything more exciting than a stint at Mitchell's Joinery yet.'

'Well, you blew that one by coming out here,' Fiona observed.

'You're right. I guess I have.'

'Come away with me.'

The girls looked up to see who was addressing them. Michelle had finished her late shift in the kitchen and now stood by their table, drying her hands on a filthy beer-mat. 'You could come on a trip with me, Kez. We could go to the States and to Canada. See the Grand Canyon and Niagara Falls.'

'They're smaller than you think they are,' Linzi said wisely. 'If I were you, I would go to Zimbabwe. Victoria Falls are much bigger.'

'Yeah? Well, we'll still have a great time however big they are. What do you think, Kez?'

Kerry looked sceptical.

'We could go in two weeks.'

'That doesn't really give me enough time to get ready.'

'How long do you need to get ready?' her sister protested. 'What on earth do you need to bring except a toothbrush and a credit card? We'll travel light.' Michelle was sitting on the edge of the wonky table now. She slung a brown arm around her big sister's neck. 'You could use the insurance money from the fire.'

'I might need that money for an emergency.'

'Listen,' Michelle was having none of that. 'What kind of emergency are you going to have in Bristol? A nasty run in your tights?'

'Anything could happen,' Kerry said feebly, knowing even as she said so that it was hardly likely to be true in Bristol.

'Until I married Richard, Kez,' Michelle continued, 'I thought that adventures were for other people. I thought that I wasn't meant to do anything other than live out my days in the place where I was born. I realised that was wrong on the plane to Majorca. I wasn't being held back by lack of money. I wasn't being held back by a baby I'd dropped before leaving school like our Miranda. I wasn't being held back by anything but me. You said that I shouldn't do anything you wouldn't do, Kez. If I'd taken that advice, I would hardly have left Heathrow.'

Kerry blushed.

'You know I'm right.'

Fiona nodded.

'So which is it to be? Logging the planks at Mitchell's Join-ery or a taste of life on the open road? It's the saw mills or

Niagara Falls, Kez. We can sell my wedding ring to help raise more cash.'

'Sounds like a great deal to me,' Linzi chipped in. 'I can give you the number of a man in Bangkok. Come on, Kerry. You've got this far already. Now it's your turn to propose a toast.'

Fiona poured the last of her beer from the bottle. Michelle pinched some of Kerry's. There was silence while they waited for her to take up the challenge. Kerry stared at her own half-empty glass. They were right. They were all right. The only thing holding her back now was fear. She had no man to go back to and no decent job. In a week's time her friends would be all over the place and as for her family, well, in her heart she knew that no matter where she went and how long she went for, there would always be room for her when she got home.

The insurance money would be through before the end of the month.

'Ahem,' Kerry cleared her throat. 'I think I'd like to propose my toast now.'

'What's it to be?' asked Michelle.

'Of course, after way too much hesitation, she said that it had to be to the open road. And as soon as the insurance money came through we booked our tickets out of there and headed for the States. If you'd told me this time last year that I would be spending my first wedding anniversary in Canada with my sister, I wouldn't have believed you, but I don't have any regrets about letting my marriage go now. In fact I can't believe I chose the opportunity to wear a stupid dress for a day over the chance to do this.'

The French girl standing next to Michelle on the *Maid of the Mist* nodded. Then Kerry reappeared, having taken a photo of the Falls from the front of the boat. Her fringe was plastered to her forehead and her clothes were soaked through, despite her regulation blue plastic cape.

'You know what?' she said, pushing back the sweaty plastic hood, and shouting over the roar of the water. 'Linzi was right. They're not really that big.'

Michelle turned to her new friend again. 'Men, marriage and Niagara Falls,' she told her puzzled companion. 'When it comes down to it, very few things are the big deal you think they are.'